The sword and the scimitar

"Crowded with events that both forecast and mirror the conflicts of today . . . Thirteen-year-old Maria and nine-year-old Nico run away for a day . . . Caught up in events that will change history, before the day is out a calamity will befall them that separate the sister and brother and set them on unimaginable and radically different courses. David Ball's wealth of realistic detail and depth of characterization bring to vivid life this exciting 16th century historical adventure. I couldn't put it down, and thought about it for days later" Jean Auel, author of the bestselling *Earth's Children* series

"A weeping historical epic that encompasses diverse cultures and decades in a part of the world still scoured by the crosswinds of conflict. [Ball's] history is concrete, but a novel is not merely a history textbook. It must engage the reader with characters, literally individual humans with dreams, losses, flaws, quests, regrets, fears, faith and misgivings. Boris Pasternak did it. So did James Clavell, James Michener and Jean Auel. Like them, Ball has built an action-packed, often erotic and always sensual epic-adventure around a handful of well-developed characters swept up in the maelstrom of 16th century holy wars" *Chicago Sun-Times*

"Merely developing three-dimensional characters in modern commercial publishing is a rare notion; sustaining a reader's interest in them over nearly 700 pages is the literary equivalent of finding weapons of mass destruction in Baghdad . . . resonates with masterful and real details exceeding imagination. And infusing every action is the pungency of smoldering religious fires, not just Islam and Christianity, but Judaism, too. In that combustible mix of passions alone, Ball captures the essence of a modern catastrophe" *Denver Post*

"Ball proves himself a master storyteller, his richly detailed literary canvas bringing to life an age of religious fanaticism and conflict . . . A sweeping novel of adventure, war, treachery and love set against the backdrop of the conflict between Christian Europe and the encroaching Islamic Ottoman Empire . . . an intimate tangle of cruelty, love and revenge" *Cleveland Plain Dealer*

"An epic adventure with action, suspense, and romance. David Ball brings alive sultan's palaces, the world of corsairs and knights and the realities of 16th century medicine and combat" Phillip M. Margolin, author of *Wild Justice*

the sword and the scimitar

David Ball

arrow books

For Jean Naggar and Beverly Lewis,
who opened the door,
and for Greg Pearson, who turned on the light

Principal Characters

PARIS

Christien de Vries, a surgeon-knight of the Order of St. John of
   Jerusalem
Arnaud, the Count de Vries
Simone, Arnaud's wife
Bertrand Cuvier, a Knight of St. John
Philippe Guignard, a physician
Marcel Foucault, a barber–surgeon

MALTA

Maria Borg, a Maltese peasant
Nico Borg, Maria's younger brother
Luca Borg, their father
Isolda Borg, Luca's wife
Elena, a courtesan
Fençu, headman of the cave of M'kor Hakhayyim
Elli, Fençu's wife
Father Giulio Salvago, the *kappillan,* or parish priest, of St. Agatha's
Jacobus Pavino, the birdman of Gozo
Angela Buqa, a baroness
Antonio Buqa, her husband, the baron

ISTANBUL

Asha, a page in the Sultan's service in the seraglio of Topkapi
Alisa, a slave girl

Iskander, tutor in the school for pages
Shabooh, a page
Nasrid, a page

ALGIERS

El Hadji Farouk, a wealthy merchant and shipbuilder
Yusuf, his son
Ameerah, Farouk's wife
Mehmet, servant in the Farouk household
Leonardus, a master shipwright
Ibi, a gardener

HISTORICAL FIGURES

Dragut Raïs, a corsair
Suleiman, Sultan of the Ottomans
Jean Parisot de La Valette, Grand Master of the Knights of St. John
Romegas, commander of galleys, the Knights of St. John
Sir Oliver Starkey, the Grand Master's English secretary
Jehangir, a prince, Suleiman's youngest son
Joseph Callus, physician of Mdina
Domenico Cubelles, Bishop and Inquisitor of Malta
Don García, Viceroy of Sicily, Duke of Mdina Coeli
Ambroise Paré, a surgeon
Mustapha Pasha, Ottoman general
Piali Pasha, Ottoman admiral
Father Jesuald, heretic priest

Author's Note

Most of the dates included in extracts from *The Histories of the Middle Sea* by the Ottoman historian Darius were originally expressed using the Muslim calendar. For clarity they have been converted to the western, Gregorian calendar.

the sword and the scimitar

Book One

NICO

from The Histories of the Middle Sea

Begun at Istanbul in the year 1011 of the Hijrah of the Prophet (A.D. 1604)
by Darius, called the Preserver
Court Historian to the Lion of the East and West, the Sultan Achmet

Malta!

Never was there a more unlikely place upon which the fate of empires would hinge.

There are but five little islands in the Maltese archipelago. Of those there are only two of note, called Malta and Gozo. Both are largely barren, with little fresh water and a thin cover of poor earth in which only the most stubborn figs and melons will grow, and upon which only the most tenacious people survive.

In the time before history, well before the age of bronze, the islands were occupied by ancients who left crumbling temples and deep rutted tracks in the stone to mark their passage. Phoenicians followed in those tracks, and after them the Carthaginians, and the Romans. On his way to a martyr's death, the Christian apostle Paul was shipwrecked in a northern bay. During his sojourn he planted deeply the seeds of his faith, which grew far better in Malta than the figs and melons.

Vandal raids ravaged the island while the Roman Empire was being sundered into eastern and western parts. Malta fell to the eastern realm, Byzantium, in whose hands it lay until the year A.D. 870, when it was taken by the Arabs, the Islamic desert nomads whose conquests were sweeping much of the world, reaching in the west all the way to the Iberian peninsula.

There was a brief and bright moment then in Malta, when Muslims lived peaceably alongside Christians and Jews. It would not last.

Count Roger the Norman conquered the islands in A.D. 1090. A dispute in royal bloodlines gave Malta to the German Frederick, the Holy Roman Emperor. He used it as a penal colony and expelled the Muslims forever from the land. In their turn the Germans were expelled by the French under Charles of Anjou, and the French by the Aragonese. After the union of Ferdinand of Aragon and Isabella of Castile, the Spanish banned all religions in their realm save Roman Catholicism, giving rise to the Inquisition. Meanwhile the Moors, who had occupied the Iberian peninsula for nearly seven centuries, had steadily been pushed back by the Christian kingdoms. The last Muslim outpost, Grenada, fell in A.D 1492, a year that saw a great exodus of Moors and Jews alike from all the Spanish lands—including Malta, where St. Paul's seeds had finally borne full fruit.

Who in Malta survived such upheaval? Men of one religion, but of mixed blood and sundry allegiances. Their language was a jumble of Arabic, Semitic, and Italian, their dress and culture a muddle of East and West, their rulers an Aragonese-installed oligarchy of noble families on whose fiefs the peasants, the one constant of Malta, labored without end.

Through its history Malta suffered pestilence and plague and pillaging monarchs, droughts and corsairs and broiling summers. Though scorned for the poverty of its culture, arable land, and people, Malta was yet coveted for its perfect harbors and strategic location, which commanded the sea lanes between Africa and Sicily. It was this location, coupled with the rise of Ottoman power in the eastern sea, that granted the island an importance out of all proportion to its size.

Malta was placed squarely into history's destiny in the early years of the sixteenth century A.D. by a self-serving act of another Holy Roman Emperor, Charles V of Spain, who installed the island's most recent rulers, the Knights of St. John of Jerusalem.

Malta.

A tiny and coarse island, a mere six leagues long by three wide, no bigger in that great sea than a grain of sand upon a beach, yet O—what a grain!

What fortunes turned upon it!

—From Volume VII
The Great Campaigns: Malta

Chapter 1

MALTA
1552

O n the morning the slavers came, the children were looking
for treasure.

Swept up in their purpose, they didn't see the mast of the
corsair galley, all but obscured by the high rocks surrounding the
cove where the ship had anchored in the night.

They didn't see the dead sentry hanging upside down on the
watchtower. It was Bartholomeo, an older boy who lived on their
own street, his throat cut deep as he slept, cut from ear to ear. His
blood had already baked dry on the platform from which he was to
have sounded the alarm, a platform from which his killers had stolen
several planks of wood. The children didn't see Bartholomeo
because they were hiding from him, keeping to the deep gullies or
crouching behind the low stone walls that separated fields so dry and
barren that even the crows didn't bother to scavenge there anymore.
As long as they stayed behind those walls they knew Bartholomeo
couldn't glimpse them and spoil their plans. He would do that, and
just for spite: Bartholomeo was plain mean.

They couldn't see or hear the stream of galley slaves snaking along
the ravine a hundred paces to the east, men laboring in silence as
they hauled water beneath the watchful eyes of their guards.

And they couldn't smell the galley, because the wind was at their
backs, a *majjistral* blowing from the northwest. With the right winds
the smell of a galley preceded the sight, the stench an unmistakable
herald of danger. Had they smelled it, they would have known the
scent of doom. There would have been time to fear, time to flee.

Today, however, they smelled nothing but Maria's dreams.

"Father's going to whip us," Nico said solemnly. He was

breathing heavily, struggling to keep up with his sister as she led him toward the southern coast of Malta. The limestone over which they ran baked under a sun that was already scorching despite the early hour. "We're supposed to be cleaning out the dung pit."

"He'll never know," Maria said. She moved like quicksilver over the rocks, threading her way barefooted between stands of prickly pear. She was thirteen but small for her age, athletic and lean, her figure as yet betraying no sign that she was a girl. Her clothes were worn through in spots, and she carried a knife in her belt. Her hair was cut short and ragged, like a boy's. Her face was smeared with grime, her skin deeply browned by the sun, her green eyes lit with determination and adventure. "He's busy today, seeing the *capumastru* for a job building one of the knights' new forts. Besides, I'm not giving up until we've found it. If you'd rather slop shit than dig treasure, suit yourself. I don't care."

They'd been two long days at the dung pit beneath their house, hauling out pail after pail of human and animal excrement to be spread over a rocky field outside the village where their family tried to grow vegetables. They emptied the pit twice a year, when the flies in the kitchen got too thick. Except for the flies, Maria saw no point to it. Nothing had grown in that field for two years. It was the same all over Malta. The rains hadn't come, and there had been no grain from Sicily. Her own baby sister and brother, twins, had starved to death, like half the babies in the village of Birgu that year. "Nothing grows in Malta but rocks and misery," her mother often said. "Nothing but dung, that is. If only there were a market for it, we would be rich beyond dreams." It was perhaps the only matter in which Maria agreed with her mother. Spreading the dung was pointless, just another of Father's nasty chores. It was better to be here, doing something that mattered.

"We've been looking forever and we haven't found it," Nico grumped.

"We'll find it today. But you can go back if you want."

He would never go back, of course. He idolized his sister, who was the sunrise in his life. She protected him from the anger of their father and the despair of their mother and all the troubles of a hostile world. She wasn't like the other girls her age, not at all. Most of them covered their faces with *barnużi* and stayed indoors. "A woman should be seen but twice in public," Maria's mother said. "The day she is married and the day she is buried." Maria never listened. She was a tomboy with a hot temper, and she vowed never to hide behind a *barnuži*. The other girls shunned her. She shunned them back. That suited Nico because it left him someone to run with, someone who knew things and told stories and climbed rocks and hunted treasure. If she asked, he would follow her over the edge of the cliffs, even though such devotion often meant trouble for him with their father.

"I just don't want to get whipped."

"There are worse things."

"Like what?" Nico could feel the leather of his father's belt on his backside. There wasn't much worse than that.

"Like spending your life hauling shit. Like letting someone else find the treasure. Here we are," she said.

They'd arrived at their private place, a series of ruins situated on a plateau overlooking the sea. They'd never seen another soul there. Dust carried on the winds of eons had buried most of it, but there remained great megaliths of stone, marking a temple built by some ancient and forgotten race. A few stone columns still rose to the sky, while others had toppled into a confused jumble. There remained subterranean chambers and innumerable places to hide. They'd explored much of it, crawling through openings and burrowing beneath slabs, sometimes discovering new passageways and rooms merely by moving rubble and digging a little.

Somewhere in that labyrinth, carefully concealed in a box or a pot or behind a stone panel, Maria was certain there was treasure. Half a century earlier the Jews had been expelled from Spain and her domains, including Malta. During their flight from persecution, they were believed by many to have buried their uncountable riches, intending to return for them later. So far all Maria had found were seashells and some old bones, but even without the hope of treasure she'd have come anyway. She loved the ruins. There was a purity to them, from their smell to their glorious view of the sea to their telltale hints of glories past. She felt the presence and spirit of the people who built them, people who had money and enough food and wore clothes even more magnificent than the Knights of St. John, who strutted like peacocks through the streets of Birgu. These people had lived well, dancing and laughing and holding great feasts. She told Nico all about them as they dug at the bases of the columns and turned over stones.

"If they were so great," Nico said, pawing through the rubble, "why is this all they left?"

"They went to Franza. It's greener there. Everyone is rich."

"Who says they left treasure here, anyway?"

"*I* say they did. Dr. Callus told me. He spends all his time looking for it, too. Some Jews left it about a thousand years ago, after the king made them leave."

"Jews wouldn't leave money. Mother says Jews would leave their children before they'd leave their money."

"Well, *these* did," Maria huffed. "It was gold and silver. They couldn't carry it all. And I'm going to find it. I'll hide it until I'm old enough, and then I'm going to buy a castle in Franza." At the wharf she'd heard talk about France, about its mountains and rich fields of lupine. That sounded grand: she'd buy a castle and put slaves in her fields, growing lupine.

"What's lupine?" Nico asked.

"I don't know exactly, but I'll have lots of it. And servants, and all my clothes will be spun from silk, and my spoons will be made of silver. You can live with me if you like."

"Girls can't have castles."

She snorted at that. "Queens can. *I* will. You'll see."

They dug for a while without uncovering anything but more dirt and rock. She was almost ready to suggest they go look in the caves that dotted the cliffs overlooking the sea. Some were occupied, but not all. She knew the Jews would have had many clever hiding places, and caves would make good ones. She was digging with the tip of her knife when she heard a clink. She cleared away the earth with her fingers and found a small object. It was oval in shape, crusted with age.

"Look!" She held it up.

"What is it?"

"*Munita!* A coin!"

"It looks like a rock to me."

"Your head is a rock! It's old, stupid, but it's still treasure." She scraped it with her knife. In the sunlight she could see the dull glint of corroded metal. "There, look, don't you see? A man's head. He's wearing a helmet!"

Nico didn't see, but his eyes went wide anyway.

"You can keep it," she said magnanimously, passing it to him. "There's more here. What did I tell you? Now put it in your pocket. Whatever you do, don't show it to a grown-up. They'll just take it away."

"*Grazzi*," Nico breathed, scarcely believing his good fortune. He slipped the coin into his pocket and labored feverishly beside her, his enthusiasm renewed. They dug for more than an hour, sweat mingling with thick dust on their brows as they grunted and heaved and dug for her dreams. She unearthed a bowl, well preserved but broken in two. Buried beneath that they found a perfect white femur. "You see? It's a Jew bone," Maria said confidently. "A marker. They always leave them near treasure. We're getting close."

Nico gave a low whistle. They dug ever more furiously.

Maria stopped abruptly. She tugged his sleeve for quiet. "What was that?" she whispered.

"What?"

She cocked her head, listening intently. A blue thrush hopped among the rocks, looking for insects. A tiny lizard clung to the side of a rock. The wind blew steadily, dry and hot. "I thought I heard voices."

A moment later she shook her head. "Never mind. It was nothing."

❖

The timbers on the Algerian galliot creaked softly as the ship rode the gentle swells at anchor. Seawater lapped quietly at the freeboard. Soldiers stood in the poop with their arquebuses at the ready, nervously awaiting the return of the slaves fetching water from an inland spring. The ship had been brought about in the cove until her prow faced the open sea, ready for a quick departure.

She was a sea hunter, swift and lean, a galliot of the same type that had carried the legions of Rome and the trade of Carthage. Long and sleek, she was a fair-weather craft, shallow draughted so she could lurk in rivers and lagoons from which she might prey on rich shipping. Although her mast bore a single goose-winged lateen sail, it was not generally the wind that drove her through the sea, but the force of slave labor. She was primarily a rowing ship. Three men were chained naked to each of the twenty-four benches ranged along each side, pulling at their oars. During the long months of the sailing season they never left their stations. They ate, slept, and relieved themselves where they sat, in fair weather and foul.

Raïs Ali Agha, master of the Algerian vessel, wouldn't have come to Malta alone except in an emergency. The island was home to the Knights of St. John, the infidels whose base lay just two leagues distant, at Birgu.

He'd come to make fast repairs and to take on urgently needed water. He had nearly been a victim of his own success. A daring shore raid in Sicily netted him a hundred and thirty slaves. As he was making for Algiers, he encountered an unescorted French merchant-man. He took the ship without firing a shot, tying her crew belowdecks and offloading bales of silk and boxes of spices until his galliot rode dangerously low in the water. When he dared take no more cargo, he cut the merchantman adrift and made haste for home.

He would have made it easily but for a freak spring storm. The shallow draught of his keel was designed for speed, not for fighting an angry sea. The waves tossed the vessel like cork. A small cannon, a Portuguese-made verso taken from the French ship, broke free of the heavy timber balks to which it had been lashed. The gun careened wildly on the deck, smashing through water casks like tinder, then splintering wood and the helmsman's legs as it slid the other way. Finally it broke through the wood railing and toppled into the hold.

Only the beneficent hand of Allah guided the cannon onto a group of slaves rather than through the hull itself. The wretches were huddled together in fear of the storm. Their bodies cushioned the cannon's impact, preserving the hull, but the mouth of the gun penetrated the planking at the waterline, which, owing to the heavy load, was even higher than usual. The sea poured in with every swell. The boat was in mortal peril.

Only the quick reactions of Ali Agha kept them all from the bottom. Seventy captives were thrown overboard to lighten the vessel, their weight being greater than that of the silk and their value less than that of the spices. Most of them were children, kept in the rear hold, separated from their parents by a bulkhead. Ali Agha always divided his captives that way, finding it kept them more docile. He would have preferred jettisoning the adults, as the children were worth more, but it was the ship's stern that needed lightening, and there was no time to shift bodies or ballast. The children's screams were swallowed by heavy winds. The bosun's whistle shrilled and the overseer's whip cracked repeatedly as all aboard struggled to keep the craft from foundering. Soldier and slave alike bailed madly to keep up with the flooding in the bilge, half the men sick from the sea as they worked, their vomit mixing with the seawater that swirled about their knees in the keel.

Then, almost as suddenly as it began, the squall abated and the sea calmed.

Ali Agha surveyed the damage. The mast had held, but an improperly secured hatch had failed. Nearly all the food stores were lost, and much of the water. The three hundred souls remaining aboard his vessel could do without food for a few days, *insha'llah,* but not without water, and besides, he still needed to make repairs to the hull. The closest landfall was Malta. Reluctantly Ali Agha set course for the island. Despite his proximity to the knights' base, he imagined they would be otherwise occupied chasing his great-uncle, the legendary corsair Dragut Raïs. A few days earlier Dragut had captured the knights' galley *Caterinetta,* sailing from Marseilles with a fortune in scudi to be spent on the knights' new fortifications at Birgu. Storm or not, the humiliated knights would be swarming after the corsair like angry hornets.

Still, Ali Agha took no chances. His carpenters made short work of the repairs, using wood from a watchtower that stood above the southern shore. They troweled thick stopping into the seams around the patch to make it watertight, and then regreased a portion of the hull to restore the ship to its fighting trim. Now it remained only to await the new stores of water. The galley slaves rested idly at oars, baking beneath the white sun that had risen above the ridge of protective rocks overlooking the cove.

Guards stood on the gangway above the hold to ensure silence. No sound could be permitted until the ship was safely quit of the knights' lair. Just after dawn two of the captive Sicilians began fighting over a scrap of food. Their throats were quickly cut, their bodies thrown overboard. The wife of one of the men cried out, and her lifeless body followed her husband's into the water. After that the other captives were as silent as if their own throats had been cut. Raïs Ali Agha liked an obedient crew and company.

The captain glanced impatiently at the open sea and back at the ravine. The slaves were taking too long with the water. If he was seen while anchored in the cove, he would be easily trapped, escape all but impossible. The danger increased with each passing moment. The cove's towering rocks protected his ship from enemy eyes but blinded him to their presence as well. He was familiar with the God-cursed land of Malta, as desolate as it was dangerous. He'd raided the archipelago a dozen times. Generally he landed on the northern island of Gozo, always poorly defended. But he also knew this southern coast, choosing it now because of its isolation and for a little-known freshwater spring, difficult of access but in a sparsely populated area. The watchtower guard had been the first to die, before dawn, and men were dispatched to kill what cave dwellers they could find. Two lookouts stood on the headlands facing the seaward approaches, but Ali Agha decided to send more men up the cliffs. Ruins stood there, from which they could observe the approach of land patrols or enemy galleys.

At his order two men scaled the cliffs, carrying pistols and knives. The climb was treacherous, the going slow. At length they reached the top, then turned and scanned the sea. One of them signaled that all was clear. Then he turned and with his companion strode inland, toward the ruins.

❖

Nico saw them first.

He was no longer looking for treasure. He was using one rock to chip at another, trying to fashion a cannonball. As he wiped grit from his eyes he glanced out toward the cliffs. The blood left his face. His stomach soured with shock and fear. Maria was still bent over her work. He tugged at her shirt. She saw the sickness in his eyes, and followed his gaze.

A man was climbing onto the top of the cliffs. He was stocky and full-bearded, wearing pantaloons with a low crotch, and no blouse. He got to his feet, then turned to help a companion clamber up. The second man was a scrawny and dark-skinned Moor wearing a leather jerkin far too big for his slight frame. Both men wore sandals. Their turbans marked them as North African corsairs, the slavers who inhabited the nightmares of every Maltese, claiming more victims than disease and famine combined. From the time of the Carthaginians, slavers had wreaked havoc in these islands, but never with such devastating effectiveness as the corsairs from Africa's Barbary Coast. The previous year the most terrible of them all, Dragut Raïs, had carried away nearly the entire population of Gozo. His men passed over the islands like a shadow of death. Trees were cut, wells poisoned, houses torched, churches destroyed, livestock butchered. When the smoke cleared, more than five thousand souls had disappeared into the holds of Dragut's ships.

Even children, Maria and Nico had heard a thousand times.

Especially children.

Maria had never heard of their coming to this part of the island, where so few people lived and the cliffs were so high.

It didn't matter. The corsairs *were* here, now. One of them waved to the ship below. The two men started for the ruins.

"It's all right," she said quietly to her little brother, for his sake feigning a calm she did not feel. Nico's guts were not as sturdy as hers, and her own insides were twisted in terror. She knew he might begin wailing at any moment. She had to be strong for them both.

They were in a large courtyard overgrown with weeds and surrounded by a stone wall. On the seaward side the wall had three openings, two for windows and one for a door. If they could work their way around the clearing to the landward side, they could hide behind rubble there and then disappear through the inner wall into the ruins, where there were countless places to hide. They might even break and run for the watchtower, where Bartholomeo could help. She wondered why he hadn't already sounded the alarm. Surely he'd seen them, too. The fool was probably asleep, she thought angrily.

"Scoot back to that wall," she said. "Hurry, but don't make any noise. If we're quiet, they'll never know we're here."

They scrambled backward, bloodying their hands and knees on sharp rocks. Nico backed straight through a thistle patch, too sick with fear to notice the pain. As he crawled he mumbled and prayed, wishing he'd stayed home to work the dung pit, as his father had ordered. "*Ahfirli*, God," he whimpered.

"God doesn't want you to be sorry," Maria hissed. "He wants you to hurry!"

They were almost to the rubble of stones that promised their first shelter when a turbaned head appeared at the seaward door. Maria clutched Nico by the shirt and pressed him toward the ground. They froze still as death itself, trying to melt into the earth. To her horror she saw their passage had stirred up dust motes that now drifted in the air of the courtyard, lit by diagonal shafts of sunlight. They couldn't have left a better trail.

The corsair surveyed the big square. He knew *something* was there. He motioned his companion to silence. The walls cast dark shadows among the weeds and stones, making it difficult for him to see. His turban moved slightly as his gaze shifted between shadow and suspicion. He cocked his head to one side, listening. There was only the sound of distant surf pounding against the rocks below. He drew a knife from his sash and held it at the ready, absently passing it back and forth between big hands as he waited, its blade gleaming in the sun. He squeezed the hilt, then let go, then squeezed again: patient, wary, waiting. For long moments hunters and hunted remained motionless on opposite sides of the courtyard, the only noise the distant whisper of the sea.

Maria felt certain the pounding of her heart must give them away. She had one hand on Nico's elbow. He was trembling like a frightened rabbit. She dared not look at him, even to reassure him. She dared not move her head. She dared not breathe.

The movement of the turban stopped. Dark eyes bored directly into their hiding place. The corsair's eyes narrowed. He squinted, as if not certain what he was seeing. Maria felt his eyes like hot coals, burning inside her. It took all her courage not to flinch.

"*Shoof, walahi!*" The corsair roared a warning to his companion, then burst through the opening.

"Run!" Maria shrieked.

The children scrambled to their feet and darted through a doorway that opened into a narrow passageway running between ancient walls of limestone. Maria gripped Nico's hand tightly, ᴉnking him along behind her, catching him when he stumbled.

They turned left, then right, then left again, working their way deeper and deeper into the maze.

Behind them they heard the heavy thudding of the corsairs' footfalls. Maria came to a narrow opening cut in the stone. Roughly she shoved Nico through and plunged in after him. They both fell heavily, then scurried on hands and knees to another doorway. Over the ages the floors had filled with silt and rubble and dirt, so that doorways that were once full-sized were now only low passages. They had to crouch to get through. Maria cracked her head against a stone lintel. She cried out in pain and fell to her knees. Nico stopped to help her. He looked back and saw the flash of a turban as the first corsair pressed through the opening. The sight made him erupt in a fountain of tears. He sank to his seat, gasping for air between great ragged sobs. He couldn't move. The corsair got his shoulders through the opening, grunting loudly, and struggled to pull his lower half through.

Maria recovered first. "Come *on!*" Once again she wrenched Nico into flight. She knew their only hope now was to reach one of the subterranean rooms, where they might hide in silence. They crawled on their bellies, slithering through gaps and doors and breaches in the walls, pushing their way through dusty cobwebs. Sometimes they saw patches of open sky above them, while at other times they were cloaked in pitch-darkness beneath stone slabs. In one such place, feeling secure and invisible, they waited. For a moment there was only the sound of their own ragged breath, and they felt a glimmer of hope. But then through the blackness they heard muffled grunting and wheezing. There was no safety in darkness. Their hunters were not going to give up.

They scooted and burrowed and shinnied ever deeper into the maze, bloodying hands and knees in their headlong flight, no longer caring whether they made noise. They found a trench and scooted along it. They rolled beneath a massive slab and tumbled down a half-buried stairwell, from which they ducked into yet another passage. The ruins were without end.

Finally, coming to a place neither of them had ever been, they slipped through an opening into another room. Well above them a part of the ceiling had collapsed. A tiny shaft of sunlight dimly illuminated the space. It was a large burial crypt. Niches were sculpted in tiers into the walls, in which skeletal remains could be seen. The skulls of the dead leered at them through dark empty eye sockets, above mouths that seemed to grin at their predicament.

Maria looked up at the source of the light, wondering whether it might offer a way out. She stood and tried to climb, but the opening was above a smooth section of wall. There was no place to put her feet.

There was no way out. They were trapped.

She dropped to the floor and scooted into one of the niches, pushing aside the bones of its previous occupant to make room. She pressed against the wall, drawing Nico in close behind her. His body still convulsed with sobs that he was trying valiantly to muffle. He buried his face in her shoulder.

They heard the corsairs just outside the chamber. They were conferring in low voices, evidently uncertain as to where their quarry had gone. There was silence, and then a head appeared in the opening through which they'd just come. The man was breathing heavily from his exertions. Nico opened an eye to peek. At the sight of the man, his eyes bulged and his chest heaved. Despite Maria's efforts, his wrenching sob filled the crypt. Maria hugged him tightly as they heard the man's hiss.

"*Ta-eh-la!*"

Maria pressed harder to the wall. Nico's sobs grew louder.

"*Ta-eh-la!*" he said again. He slid in after them. It was the smaller of the two, the Moor, and they trembled as they watched his approach. They could see the whites of his eyes beneath the folds of his turban, gleaming, mocking, inevitable. They squeezed even closer together. The Moor reached out, and Maria lashed at him with her foot. He brushed it aside deftly and caught hold of Nico's ankle. Screaming, Nico was ripped from her grasp. Then he had her ankle, too, in a grip she thought would crush her bones.

Grunting from his efforts, the corsair laboriously dragged his two captives back across the dirt toward the entrance, on the other side of which his companion waited to help. Nico went limp with fear, but Maria kicked and flailed. She caught hold of a length of old bone and began hitting the Moor with it. Unable to swing freely in the tight space, she did little harm. The Moor pinned Nico with his body and tried to hit her. The first blow missed. He lunged and struck again, this time connecting with her mouth. She felt a tooth break. Shocked for only a moment and now enraged, she fought back with rabid fury. She let go of the bone. She raked his cheek with her nails and tried to scratch out his eyes. When he lashed out again she caught his arm in her teeth and bit through meaty flesh, tasting his blood in her mouth. He bellowed in rage and caught her by the muscle at her neck and shoulder. His fingers found a nerve that sent her limp with pain. She yelped and ceased struggling. With jerky motions, he dragged her the rest of the way by the neck.

A few moments later they stood in the sunshine in an alcove, all of them panting and streaked with grime, sweat, and blood. The Moor examined his forearm where Maria had bitten him, a ragged half-moon mess of teeth marks and muscle laid bare. In anger he cuffed her again. At that Nico tried to get away, but the other corsair, the big one, caught him by the collar. The two men hauled their young captives toward the edge of the ruins, pleased at their catch, however troublesome it had been. Such spirited youngsters would fetch a handsome price in the slave market.

As they neared the cliffs Nico yelled and began squirming, but his captor had him too tightly. He lifted Nico easily and draped him over his shoulder like a sack. The corsair moved carefully down a short embankment at the top of the cliffs. Maria saw them begin their descent. She knew that each second diminished her chances of helping herself or Nico. She struggled to reach the knife she carried in her belt, but the Moor tightened his grip. He lifted her onto his shoulders, her head on his left, her feet on his right. He laughed now at the spirit of the wildcat on his back. Thinking it was a boy he carried, he reached between the child's legs to squeeze his balls and silence his protests. The shock he felt upon discovering he carried a girl made him slacken his grip just a little. Maria felt it, and then she had her knife. The blade flashed as she stabbed mightily downward. She meant to gut him, like she'd seen the fishmongers gut tunny. She wasn't strong enough for that, but she managed to lay open the skin of his breast. Blood drenched his shirt. He shrieked in rage and pain, his left hand letting loose of her as he instinctively reached for his wound. Clenching her teeth, she stabbed again, this time aiming for his neck. He raised his forearm just in time. The point of the knife stuck hard in the bone. She lost hold of the knife, but it was enough. He screamed again and let go. She rolled off his back, landing on her hands and knees. She scrambled to her feet and ran for her life.

The corsair yanked the knife from his arm and flung it aside. He lunged for her, but she was too quick. He clambered up the rocky embankment. By the time he reached the top she was already in the open field, halfway to the ruins. He knew he could catch her. With long, sure strides, he closed the gap between them. Just as he nearly had her, she darted through the door, back inside the ruins.

At that moment he heard the bosun's whistle, the signal that the water was aboard and the galliot was making ready to leave. He cursed; he knew Ali Agha would not wait for him. If he didn't return to the ship immediately, he would find himself stranded on this dung-infested island. The boy—the *girl*—was not worth risking that. Nursing his two knife wounds and the more painful bite, he turned and hurried back. Where the ravine cut the cliffs on the opposite side of the cove he could see the end of the line of slaves, carrying water. They would be aboard quickly. He started down.

As soon as he disappeared over the edge Maria emerged from hiding and raced back to the ledge. The Moor was just beneath her, making his way down the steep rocks. Below him, almost halfway to the bottom, she saw Nico, still draped over his captor's back. She screamed in despair, "*Nico!*"

"*Mariaaaaa!*" Nico wailed back. The corsairs glanced up at her, then turned their attention back to their descent. Nico wailed again. "Maria, help me!"

Desperately she looked around. She picked up a rock, carried it to the edge, and hurled it. She knew she might hit Nico, but she was never indecisive, and it was better to kill Nico trying to save him than to kill him by doing nothing. Her throw was short. The rock shattered near the head of the Moor, the one who'd been carrying her. He scowled but kept descending. She jumped back and found another rock. It was almost too heavy to pick up, but she lugged it at knee level and returned to the edge. With a mighty grunt she heaved again. The Moor looked up at the noise, and the rock caught him square in the face. He tumbled silently backward, spinning in the air, then landing in a heap on the rocks at the water's edge. Maria cried out in rage. She hadn't meant to waste a rock on that one. She had to help *Nico*.

Nico bawled again, his desperate wail echoing against the cliffs on the far side of the cove. His arms flailed ineffectively as he vainly sought to throw himself from the corsair's back. The corsair himself struggled to keep his own hold on the rocks without falling. Maria hurled another rock, a lighter one. It fractured near the corsair's head, showering him with fragments. He slipped and nearly lost his footing. He let go of Nico, who slipped around, now clinging to the man for dear life with both arms around the corsair's waist, his legs dangling free. For an awful moment it looked as if they would both topple backward to their deaths. Slowly, with deliberate movements, the corsair consolidated his hold. He shifted Nico higher up onto his back and started down again.

The instant Maria saw she'd missed, she let fly with yet another stone, and another. One of the soldiers on the poop deck of the galliot looked up and realized what was happening. He raised his arquebus and fired up at the small figure. The ball slammed into the cliff just below Maria's feet. Despite the danger, she didn't stop. She was fearless, blind to all but her purpose.

At last one of the stones struck Nico's captor a glancing blow on the head. He nearly lost his grip again, and with his sudden movement, Nico slid down his back again, holding on with one arm, pawing for something to hold onto with the other. He slid all the way down the corsair's leg and then dropped to a ledge. Maria heard him yelp, but then he got up. He looked left and right. He quickly chose a path and started climbing sideways, away from the corsair, who had all but forgotten him in his effort to save himself. Maria willed Nico to speed. He was a good climber, at home on the rocks, certainly more nimble than the Algerian. "*Isa,* Nico!" she shouted, willing him to speed. "*Haffef! Haffef!*" She picked up more stones and kept throwing.

Freed of his burden, the corsair made his way the last fifteen feet to the bottom. He looked up at Nico, and back at his ship, to make sure he had time. Calculating, he scrambled over the rocks and took a position below Nico. He drew his pistol and aimed up at the boy, who clung like a fly to the rocks. The corsair said something to Nico. He would not miss at that distance.

Nico clung to the wall, crying. He couldn't move. His fingers were cramping, and he couldn't hold on. "Maria!" he yelled. "What should I do?"

Maria sank to her knees. She was exhausted; she could barely lift the rocks anymore. Her face was bleeding, and one arm was numb. She threw another rock, and another. They fell short. The corsair ignored her.

"Maria!" Nico called again, sobbing. "Maria! Help me, Maria!"

"Run, Nico!"

"Where? Where should I run?"

She got to her feet and flew east again along the cliff, to find a better spot from which to throw rocks. It was all she could do. She heard the roar of gunfire. She screamed. She flung herself to her belly and looked over the edge. Nico was still alive. Smoke drifted from the barrel of the corsair's firearm. He had aimed wide, intending to frighten the boy. It had worked. Nico was descending.

"Nico, don't give up!" she yelled, but if he heard, he gave no sign. A moment later he was down. The corsair snatched him up, tucking him under one arm. Nico didn't struggle. He stopped wailing and seemed to go limp. The corsair made his way toward the galliot, stopping at the inert form of his fallen companion. Still holding Nico, he cleaned out the dead man's pockets. Then he picked his way across the rocks toward the galliot. A few moments later he carried his prize aboard.

Maria began crying, enraged by her helplessness. She despised her tears. She kept throwing rocks long after they could do any good. They clattered down the cliff and splashed into the sea.

A whistle shrilled. Forty-eight oars lifted and flashed in the sun, poised like wings alongside the ship.

Thrum. The bosun's tambour sounded its sonorous call. As one, the oars dipped into the waters of the cove. She saw Nico tossed like a bale of cloth into the hold, and lost sight of him.

Thrum. The galley began moving to the pull of the oars, slowly at first. Sailors scaled the mast and extended the sail. It flapped limply, and then, as the ship cleared the cove, it snapped back and forth, as if undecided. Then it billowed in a quartering wind that caught the ship as if in a sling.

Thrum. The bosun's rhythm picked up, his two wooden hammers alternating on the leathern drum as the ship gathered speed. The oars dipped and pulled in unison to its call, then swept forward, to dip and pull again.

Thrum. The captain's voice carried over the water as he shouted orders. The helmsman heaved at the tiller. The graceful craft turned hard starboard, to the west.

Thrum. The sound grew fainter as the ship found its pace. From the cliffs the galliot looked like a water strider, an insect gliding across the sea, walking on long spindly legs of white oak. Maria blinked away hot tears and watched until the hated insect was but a speck on the horizon, carrying her little brother away.

"Nicolo," she whispered. "Nico, Nico."

Thrum. And then he was gone.

Chapter 2

"Bartholomeo! Bartholomeo!" Maria yelled as she ran toward the tower. She was halfway up the ladder before she saw him, her face almost level with his. His forehead and face were mottled purple and swollen, where the blood had pooled as he hung upside down. The rest had run out onto the lower platform.

Her scream caught in her throat, and she made no sound. For a moment she couldn't breathe. She backed down the ladder, fell on the last step, picked herself up, and started running again. She ranged over open fields, frantically picking her way through the rocks. She jumped hedgerows and the low stone walls that separated peasants' plots. She first thought to go to Mdina, to the civil authorities of the Università, but she knew they wouldn't listen to a girl. Her mother would have no practical ideas. She would dissolve in tears and recrimination, and then want to go to church.

Church. Maybe Dun Salvago, the priest. No, not him either. The Church wouldn't help Nico. She had to find her father. He would be working at the new fort. There would be knights nearby, strong, brave men who could do something to save her brother.

She dreaded her father's wrath, but there was nothing else to be done.

The island of Malta was small, twenty miles by twelve, and nearly flat, with a gentle slope that ran from sea cliffs in the south and west to the bays and harbors of the north and east. In the center of the island stood Mdina, the walled fortress city that had been the medieval capital. The nobles of Malta lived there now, shut away from the rest of the island.

Maria was a strong runner, but over the rocky terrain, scored with deep gullies, it still took her nearly an hour to cover the distance. As she tired she stumbled more often, picking herself up to run again, propelled by terror and adrenaline and sheer determination. She ran up onto the rocky peninsula dominated by Mount Sciberras, which was more hill than mountain. Goats ranged over its slopes, nibbling at prickly pear. She ran eastward along the peninsula, which divided two harbors. At its tip, where a lighthouse had stood since Phoenician times, the knights were building a new fort called St. Elmo.

She glanced across the harbor toward St. Angelo, an old Norman fortress that served as the headquarters of the Order of St. John. Behind the fort was the fishing village of Birgu, where she lived. There was a deep creek next to the village where the Order's magazines, arsenals, and docks serviced the knights' fleet of galleys. Her spirits surged when she saw one galley there, being provisioned by slaves. *They'll get Nico back!*

Both land and water near the new fort teemed with activity. Boats of all sizes crossed from Birgu carrying supplies and men. Burros made their way along rocky trails around the harbor, hauling panniers loaded with materials. Slaves and convicts toiled alongside laborers and craftsmen imported from Sicily, digging great ditches, breaking and clearing rocks, cutting stones, erecting walls and scaffolding, and hauling rubble to fill the voids between the inner and outer walls. Windlasses creaked and hammers rang against chisels. Men shouted orders in a dozen tongues.

Maria raced into the tumult. "My father! Luca Borg! *Taf fejn qieghed?*" She called out in Maltese, and then again in Italian—a dozen languages were heard in Malta. She met with blank stares and shrugs from the workmen. Racing from site to site, it took her nearly half an hour to find him. "Father! Father!"

Luca Borg had a bull neck and a ruddy face beaten by weather and a life of hardship. All his life he had been a big man, quick to anger. The famine had melted away much of his sinew and spirit, leaving the skin loose on his bones and a gaunt, haunted look in his eyes. During the famine he had sold his tools to buy food. It wasn't enough. Without work he stayed home and watched his two youngest children die. Since then he had worked off and on as a laborer, until the knights began the construction of Fort St. Elmo. Luca had borrowed money for new tools and had just found work once again as a mason.

He was dressing the side of a block of limestone with a broad axe and looked up sharply at his daughter's approach. "Maria? What are you doing here? Why aren't you home?"

She wiped the grime from her bloody face and tried to catch her breath. "They've taken him, Father! They've taken Nico!"

"Taken him? Who? Taken him where?"

"Corsairs, Father! Slavers, from Africa!"

"Now? At our house?" He stood straight up at that and started to move.

"No, Father. At the ruins. We were looking for treasure."

"Ruins? What ruins?"

Maria took a deep breath, and her words poured out in a rush. "On the south coast. Near the tower. They nearly caught me, too. I tried to help Nico, but I couldn't. They threw him in a boat and went away. I tried, Father, really I did, but I couldn't help him, I couldn't stop them. I saw Bartholomeo. They killed him. There was blood everywhere."

Luca's eyes clouded and his voice thundered. "Mother of God! What were you doing on the south coast? You were to be cleaning—" He didn't finish the sentence. He dropped the stone on which he was working and struck her with the backside of his hand. The blow sent her reeling into the dirt. Tears welled in her eyes. She picked herself up, her hand to her cheek, determined not to let the pain make her cry. "I'm sorry, Father, I know it was wrong, but we've got to help him. We've got to stop them!"

Luca gathered his tools and hurried up the hill. The *capumastru*, a master builder from Rhodes, was bent over a table made of thin stone slabs, reviewing plans and making careful notes in a book, and giving directions to foremen. Intent on his work, he ignored Luca's approach. Luca fidgeted with his hammer, turning it over and over in his big hands. He cleared his throat. Presently the man looked up, irritated at the intrusion. "*X'Gara? Xi trid?* What is it?"

Luca removed his hat and hurriedly explained. Despite the fact that he towered over the master builder, Luca was clearly intimidated by the man, seeming almost apologetic as he spoke. The *capumastru* didn't even wait for Luca to finish. "They took him, then? He's gone?" he asked, interrupting.

"*Sì, mastru,*" Luca said.

"Then it is finished. No one can save him now. There is nothing to be done. You're wasting your time and mine. Your first day on the job and already you are a problem. I have a fort to build. Get back to work."

Luca hesitated. "*Mastru,* please. I must make a report," he said.

"Very well, make a report. There is a brother at the dock. Be quick about it or don't come back. As it is, you'll forfeit a day's pay. Now leave me in peace. I have important work to do."

At the dock a serving brother of the Order of St. John stood near a boat that was being unloaded. He was not a full knight, but a half cross, a soldier. Yet along with his black habit he was cloaked in all the Order's arrogance, as if he were the Grand Master himself. He was conferring with the boat's captain. He ignored Luca and Maria.

"*Scuzi, illustrissimo,*" Luca said timidly, but the knight waved him imperiously away. Maria fidgeted. She did not understand the difference that came over her father when he was dealing with someone in authority. With his family, he was a lion. Now he was a lamb. Maria herself was all lion, and she had no time to wait on a conversation about cargo. "*Signore,*" she said sharply in Italian. "*Dovete ascoltare!* You are wasting time! There is something you must do!"

"*Iskot!*" Luca said, raising his hand to silence her.

Her father was the only man Maria feared, but she feared only his whippings, not his tongue, and she knew he would not strike her now, in front of the knight. Undaunted, she pressed on. "You must talk with us immediately," she said.

To the surprise of both Luca Borg and the boat captain, the knight turned with an amused look to see what the imperious child wanted. "*Devo?* Must I, young master?"

"*Sì,*" Maria said. She had to do the talking. The knight, like most of his brethren, spoke no Maltese. Maria knew Italian because her mother spoke it at home, but her father had never learned more than a few words. The knight listened to the story with more interest than the *capumastru*. He asked a flurry of questions. What had the vessel's standard looked like? How many oars? One mast or two? What was the shape of the sails? Then he sent his page to alert the castle. "Go with him," he said to Maria and Luca. "They will have more questions."

Maria fell in behind the page, but her father hesitated. She turned. "Father? Aren't you coming?"

Luca Borg knew it was too late to save his son. It was not too late to save his job, to provide for what remained of his family. "For what? Nicolo is gone. I cannot swim after him. I cannot even speak with these men. You were there. You tell them. Then come and tell me what they say is to be done." And with that, bent under the weight of his tools, he trudged back up the hill.

The page took her to Fort St. Angelo, the medieval castle. At the gate he turned her over to a different page, who led her inside to a courtyard, where he bade her wait while he hurried into the recesses of the castle. She was soon repeating her story to another knight, this one an intense Spaniard dressed in half armor. Moments later a mounted patrol thundered out of Birgu. To Maria they were glorious, fearsome angels who were going to find a way to save her brother. She waited on a bench, her legs dangling, too short to reach the ground. An hour passed, and then another. Knights came and went, ignoring her. They always ignored the Maltese, she knew, of whom they were often openly contemptuous. She waited and watched and bit her lip. Two hours later the patrol returned. Rigid in death, the corsair's body was draped over the hindquarters of one horse, Bartholomeo's over another.

After the men disappeared inside, there seemed to be no further activity. She thought they ought to be leaving for the galley, but no one came to tell her anything. They had forgotten her. She waited almost another hour before making a nuisance of herself with the page. Finally the Spanish knight reappeared. "There is nothing more to be done," he said. "Go home, child."

Maria was stunned. "You aren't going to send a ship to catch them?"

"It would take a galley mounted on wings to catch them now. And even if I had such a galley, where would I send it? Where have they gone? Did they tell you, perhaps?"

"You've got to try!"

"The Grand Master has more pressing business, child, than to waste a galley on such nonsense."

"This is not nonsense! This is my *brother!*" Maria fought back her tears. Everyone from the *capumastru* to the knight at the docks to this infuriating, arrogant man seemed not to understand the importance of it all. They seemed not to care. "I must talk to the Grand Master!" she said.

"Go home," the knight repeated, his patience at an end. "Giscard," he said, "take this boy away." The page escorted her roughly to the gate. She found herself in the street as the gate clanged shut. She turned and yelled, banging the gate with her fists, "You must send a ship! Do you hear me?" She knocked and pounded until Giscard returned. "Go away," he said hotly, "or I'll cut off your nose."

"The devil you will!" Maria said. "I'm not leaving until I see the Grand Master." She picked up a rock and started banging on the gate. The page flung it open and shoved her backward. She tried to push back but ended once again in the dirt.

"I don't want to hurt you," Giscard said, "but next time I will." The gate shut once more. In vain she looked for another way inside. The castle was impenetrable.

She trudged back toward the docks, her head down, her shoulders stooped. She asked a fisherman to help. She offered to work for him for the rest of her life without wages if only he would try to find Nico. He laughed at her and spat in the harbor. She was bewildered by all the indifference she'd met that day. No one was going to do a thing. No one even seemed to care. They were all cowards.

She didn't want to face her father. Giving him the news would serve no purpose. She wandered aimlessly through Birgu's streets, a tight maze that had changed little since the Middle Ages. The streets were narrow and crossed at odd angles, each turn never more than a bowshot from the next, an ancient defensive precaution. Most of the major streets emptied into the town square, where invaders could be trapped. The walls rose above her like the sides of a sheer canyon, cut only by Norman windows and balconies. In some places the sun penetrated for only moments a day, in others not at all. She found herself in the square, dominated on one end by a clock tower. The afternoon shadows were lengthening, the long awful day nearing an end. She went inside a church and stood in the nave. She lit a candle and knelt before the altar to pray. *Make them listen to me, God. Make them help Nico. Tell me what to do.*

Ten minutes later, as she was emerging from the church, she saw a procession across the square. There were two knights in the middle, surrounded by a retinue of pages, squires, serving brothers, and men-at-arms, perhaps twenty in all. It was a procession of the Order, making its way to the conventual Church of St. Lawrence for vespers, the afternoon prayer. She knew both knights by sight. One was the Spaniard d'Homedes, the one-eyed Grand Master of the Sovereign Order of the Knights of St. John. On this earth, only the Pope was his master. She generally saw him only on feast days, when he rode through the town on a splendid horse. On those occasions he wore a plumed casque and silver armor covered by a scarlet *sobraveste* with the cross of the Order emblazoned on the front. Now he was dressed plainly in a simple black habit, his exalted office marked only by a chain he wore round his neck, bearing an eight-pointed cross of gold.

The other knight was a Frenchman called La Valette. Regal and quite handsome, he was tall, proud, and aloof, a hard man who carried himself with dignity, and with the physical presence that came from a lifetime spent at war. It was he who had ordered the demolition of Maria's first home in Birgu. She had been only nine at the time, but she would never forget how he had walked into the house that had been in the Borg family for generations, just walked in like a king. He was then in charge of fortifications. He told her father the house was needed to make way for a ditch, to improve the defenses of Fort St. Angelo. The knights compensated Luca Borg for his property, but at a value less than it cost to replace. He bought a much smaller house, the one in which they now lived, in one of the poorest sections of the village. It had been built in several stages, the first room literally hewn from rock—a cave dwelling, with other rooms added later. The walls were crumbling and out of plumb, and the roof was a sieve. Maria's mother grumbled that Luca hadn't complained sufficiently about his treatment, but Luca hadn't wanted to make trouble.

Now the procession moved toward her, led by a boy carrying a standard. With a momentary pang she realized it was Giscard, the page who'd pushed her earlier. He saw her and his face went black. "You again!"

"I must talk to the Grand Master," she said imperiously. She drew herself up to her full height, which was still two heads less than his.

"Get back!" She was pushed again, and the procession crowded by her, indifferent boots clattering on cobblestone. "Grand Master!" she yelled. "Grand Master!" She ran down the hill toward the church. She scooped up a handful of stones and climbed up onto the back of a bench. The square was noisy, crowded, and dusty. Dogs chased chickens, and vegetable carts rattled and bounced along. Groups of peasants stood gossiping, grudgingly making way for the procession. When the knights were just abreast of her, Maria threw a rock. Two more flew in quick succession before the page saw her. The first two went wide, but the third found a mark: not the Grand Master, as she intended, but the other one, La Valette. It struck him on the cheek, drawing blood.

"Cowards!" she shrieked. "The Knights of St. John are cowards!" The first time she said it in Italian, the second time in Maltese, to be certain everyone understood. Gossip died in the square. The peasants fell silent, aghast at her impertinence. The page leapt forward, knocked Maria from the bench, and held a knife to her throat as she struggled to get free.

"Giscard!" Grand Master d'Homedes called sternly. "Leave him be. Bring the lad to me."

"I know him, Excellency," Giscard said. "He was at St. Angelo earlier. His brother was the boy taken by the Algerian galliot this morning. He's mad-brained and could use a whittling."

"I am not a *him*," Maria said, struggling to free herself from Giscard's grip. He let loose of her. She straightened herself and stood fearlessly, a dirty wisp of a girl all but lost in the midst of the knights, a reed among mighty oaks. "I am Maria Borg." She said it hotly and proudly, with great nobility. She glared at Giscard. "And I am not mad-brained, either."

D'Homedes regarded her sternly but not unkindly. "Evidently you are mad, child, as you have drawn the blood of my companion. Not many have lived to boast of that."

"It's easy to draw the blood of men who won't fight! Your Order is worthless!"

There were gasps from curious onlookers, who pressed closer to gape at the brazen child. No one, not the highest civil authorities, ever addressed the knights in such a manner. Hatred of their Order was widespread but always kept in check. The Knights of St. John had been granted the islands of Malta and Gozo over twenty years earlier, in the year 1530, by Charles V, the Holy Roman Emperor and King of Spain. In return, the Order paid him the annual rent of a falcon. The Maltese had long had their own government, the Università, but now it was the knights, the flower of European nobility, who truly ruled the islands. They could imprison citizens for petty crimes, hang them for insurrection, or flog them for displaying an intemperance like Maria's.

"I am aware of your brother's plight at the hands of the infidel," the Grand Master said sadly. "Would that I could help him."

"Then do so! You have ships and men! He is a Christian! Are you not a soldier of Christ, sworn to defend him? There were others, too. I saw them in the hold! It is your duty to free them!"

"I need no lesson in duty from you," he said icily. "Give thanks for your own safety. Your brother is in the hands of God. And now I have had quite enough of your impudence." He strode on, followed by most of his retinue.

Only La Valette remained behind. He was a practical man. The loss of the boy was regrettable, but slaves were the coin of the realm. One child was of no particular import, even though, given the chance, La Valette would avenge that child a hundredfold. But not this day. There were more urgent matters to attend to, and in any event, the boy's case was hopeless. Still, he felt sympathy for the girl, and above all he admired her courage. He would not punish her for having her say.

"You must learn to mind your tongue," La Valette said. "One of the less temperate young men in our service might remove it for you."

"I am not afraid of your men," Maria huffed. "There is little to fear; they run from a fight. And you! I know who you are. You destroyed our house. You said it was for defense, but you defend nothing. Now I think you strengthen St. Angelo and build St. Elmo only to have more places to cower."

Her words wounded La Valette more deeply than she knew. He was the embodiment of the Order, his life spent in its service. He was a cold man with a hot temper, the son of a noble family from Provence whose ancestors had fought with St. Louis in the Crusades. An intellectual as well as a warrior, he spoke seven languages, read poetry, and killed Muslims.

La Valette's life, his entire being, was dedicated to the single-minded struggle against Islam. As a galley commander, he made war against the enemy ships of the Ottomans and their North African allies, the corsairs. His raids were daring, his bravery undisputed. Captured and enslaved himself, he had spent a year chained to a Turkish oar until the Order paid his ransom. For a time he had been the Order's governor in Tripoli, a Christian outpost on a Muslim shore that Charles V had ordered the knights to defend when he gave them a home in Malta.

Though La Valette had seen many glorious victories, in the past few years the fortunes of the Order had declined. The humiliating loss of Gozo's population to Dragut Raïs the previous year had been followed by the fall of Tripoli. Then the Order's forces were routed in an ambush at Zuara, when the knights had tried and failed to capture that coastal outpost, hoping to use it as a base to retake Tripoli. The seemingly invincible Suleiman, Sultan of the Ottomans, was rapidly claiming the Mediterranean as his own. The courts of Europe, entangled in wars and religious strife, were all but helpless in the struggle against the Sultan, and by itself the Order seemed powerless to stop him. Morale was low, and even now, dedicated as they were to the fight, the knights were having to fortify their own island against further Turkish invasion. This defensive move proved the enemy had carried the battle to them, not the other way around. And now this commoner—this *girl*—was calling him a coward, accusing him of hiding behind his forts. It was ludicrous, of course, yet she made him feel small. "I would not expect you to understand," La Valette said.

"What is there to understand? If you don't try to find my brother, he will be lost forever. If you are too faint of heart, give a galley to me. I'll do it."

"I believe you would," La Valette said, "but for the moment you must rely upon your faith. God will protect him."

"Meaning you will not," Maria said, her eyes flashing.

"Meaning I cannot. And now I must go. God be with you, child," he said, and left her.

Defeated at last, Maria slumped on the bench. That night she didn't go home. She couldn't bear facing her mother, and she didn't want another beating. She walked all the way back to the south coast.

She spent the night on the cliffs, staring at the sea and whispering promises to Nico.

from **The Histories of the Middle Sea**

by Darius, called the Preserver
Court Historian to the Shadow of the Almighty, the Sultan Achmet

The people of the Barbary Coast of North Africa are a volatile mix of Moors and Jews, Berbers and Arabs, and renegades from all the Christian lands. To this day, the corsairs among them sally forth in galleys from ports, bays, and inlets scattered along the coast, in search of profit. Their voyages are financed either by their local rulers or by private investors, who expect a fair return for their risk. Naturally enough, these Muslim corsairs prey upon the ships and people of the Christian world, while, naturally enough, they themselves are preyed upon in turn by Christian corsairs. It is a timeless ritual in which fortunes turn quickly: a man might be master one day and slave the next. It is a harsh sea they sail, a sea in which neither side holds a monopoly on cruelty, or asks for quarter, or grants it.

These corsairs of Barbary were natural allies of the Ottoman Sultan and his navy-friends, if not subjects: for all his power, even a Sultan found it difficult to control such men as Kheir-el-din, known in the West as Barbarossa, and Dragut, the man who succeeded him and about whom much is written in these pages. Yet control was not necessary, so long as the corsair's sword naturally followed the Sultan's path. When it came to Catholic Spain, no path was more natural.

Using ships provided by the Sultan and propelled by Moors expelled from Spain, Barbarossa captured Algiers and all of Tunisia. He became admiral of the Sultan's fleet and found Tunisia the perfect base for his raids against Italy and Sicily. The Holy Roman Emperor and King of Spain, Charles V, recaptured Tunis, only to see his fleet—and that of the Venetians, the greatest sea power of the region—defeated at the Battle of Preveza in 1538, leaving much of the eastern sea in Ottoman control.

During these years Algiers was ruled by a bey, acting as the Sultan's regent. The Sultan trusted his bey but was prudent enough to install a legion of his elite Janissaries in the city, lest the Bey forget himself. Both bey and Sultan grew wealthy from the efforts of the corsairs, who paid them tribute. While silks and spices comprised a great portion of the wealth thus gained, no cargo was more prized than that most spendable of all currencies, slaves. Chosen not by their race or nation but by their faith, thousands might be taken at once, from other ships or in shore raids that carried away whole populations. Men, women, and children were harvested like crops: traded, sold, slain at will. No nation on the rim of the Middle Sea could long survive without them. Now, as then, they build the moles that protect Christian and Muslim harbors. They harvest the crops that feed hungry cities, and launder the fine robes of their masters. The galleys of the Middle Sea have an insatiable hunger for new bodies to power them, consuming them like brushwood on a great fire. The most beautiful slaves of all grace the harems of Topkapi, the Sultan's seraglio in Istanbul, while even the harems of Algiers are filled with the fetching daughters of European nobility. The prisons of Malta overflow with strapping Muslims who build the knights' defensive works, and the ships of the Vatican are filled with those who have followed the Prophet and not the Pope.

There are nameless tens of thousands of slaves, on every shore and in every ship, praying for deliverance.

Deliverance is the one thing they shall not have, unless they are lucky enough to find it through death, or ransom.

—From Volume III
The Corsairs and Beys of Barbary

Chapter 3

It was the smell that awakened him.

It washed over him in waves. His eyes were closed as it assaulted him, each wave a crushing odor of decay and death, of shit and sweat, of piss and blood and salt, and then of shit again. The air was viscous with it, and there was no breeze to carry it away.

At first he didn't know where he was. He listened to the creaking of oars and the rattle of chains and the flapping of the ship's sail, and the slow, steady tempo of the bosun's drum as the galliot rose and fell on gentle swells. And then he remembered.

He realized he was lying in water. He was on his back on a slight incline. He felt the water lapping at his belly, washing back and forth with the rhythmic motion of the boat. He opened his eyes and saw a patch of blue. A lone gull soared above the hold, playing with the wind against a cloudless indigo sky. He could see the legs and arms and shoulders of the slave rowers working on the level above him. He sat up. He was in the bilge, the lowest part of the galliot's hold. There were other captives nearby, crowded tightly amidst bales of cargo. He heard the murmur of different tongues. Arabic, he thought, and Spanish. He'd heard them on the wharves of Birgu, although he didn't know what they were saying.

He wiped his mouth. His hand came away red. The blood he'd

smelled was his own. His lip felt swollen. He dipped his hand into the water and wiped his mouth with it. Sickened, he spat. The water was mostly raw sewage and urine, produced by the naked slaves where they sat chained to the oars above him, and by his companions in the hold. He turned over on his hands and knees and retched. There was nothing in his stomach to throw up. He coughed and gagged and heaved. He crawled forward to get out of it, but there was nowhere to go. He pushed against a thicket of unyielding legs.

He rested. He tried to draw a full breath, to catch any hint of fresh air, but to no avail. It was far worse than the dung pit beneath his house, which at least was occasionally tempered with lime. For the first time in his life he wished he were in that dung pit now, hauling shit as his father had told him. He'd roll in it, he'd eat it, if only he could be there again. He tried to swallow, but his tongue was swollen and dry and caught at the back of his throat. He gagged again.

The person nearest him was a woman. She wore no veil and seemed about the same age as his mother. He caught her eye, but she looked away. He tugged at her sleeve.

"*Jekk joghgbok,*" he said. "Is there water?"

She recoiled from his touch and turned away, silent.

"Please," he said again, louder, to no one in particular. "Can someone give me water?"

No one answered. He thought maybe they hadn't understood.

"*Prego,*" he said in Italian, the tongue his mother used at home. "*Qualcuno mi darà l'acqua?*"

"Wait until I piss and you'll have your fill, like the rest of us," someone said.

There was bitter laughter, without mirth.

Nico had a thousand questions. He looked from face to face, trying to find a friendly one. Dark eyes brooded back at him from the shadows, returning his gaze with indifference, or hostility.

He drew up his knees and put his arms around his legs. He thought he could stand not having water if the smell would just go away, but as the sun rose in the sky, the hold baked and the stench rose like a living tide. The smell was palpable, enveloping everything, an extra presence like another captive. It invaded the pores of his skin and burned at his eyes and lungs. He could taste it. He knew that after a time some odors, no matter how unpleasant, seemed to go away. These never would. The entire ship reeked, every plank saturated with years of filth and misery and hopelessness. He buried his face between his knees. Outside the galliot he could hear the oars slapping the water, dipping and pulling and dipping again, and the soothing hiss of the sea against the hull. Each stroke took him farther from Maria, farther from home. Despite the heat he began to shiver. Then, quietly, so that no one might hear, he began to cry.

❖

In the late afternoon Ali Agha ordered his overseer to water and feed the ship's company. Despite their stop in Malta, there hadn't been enough storage containers to hold what they needed. What little they had would have to be rationed carefully. The rowing slaves drank first, because in either flight or fight, the lives of everyone aboard the ship depended upon their strength. Their water was flavored with vinegar, which they sipped from sponges applied to their lips as they rowed. Hard biscuits were distributed, sodden now from the storm. The soldiers and sailors of the crew were served next, their rations half that of the rowing slaves. Finally it was the turn of the captives in the hold. A short wooden ladder was lowered, and an overseer descended. He stepped on Nico's leg, then kicked at the boy to make way. Nico scrambled back, his eyes locked on the treasure being lowered in a bucket on a rope.

Water!

There wasn't nearly enough for everyone. Nico pressed forward, crowding with the others toward the bucket. A dozen rough hands manhandled him toward the rear of the hold. Desperate people sucked at the rim of the bucket, only to be immediately shoved away and replaced by others. Some of the larger men had two turns, but even they came away still thirsty. Whenever someone pressed too hard the overseer lashed out with the leather butt of his whip, momentarily easing the pressure. The slaves seemed so many animals, standing in the filth swirling at their ankles as they battled for survival in a chaotic maelstrom of elbows and anger.

Nico pushed furiously. "Please! Let me through! Please!" It was in vain. Except for two infants he was the smallest person in the hold, and he had no chance. As his desperation grew he pushed harder against unyielding flesh. An elbow found the bridge of his nose and brought lights to his eyes. He sank to his knees, where he was nearly trampled underfoot in the crush. Someone stepped on his hand, and then on the back of his knee. Nico fell to his face. Suddenly more fearful than thirsty, he struggled to get up. Once on his knees, he scurried away from the center of the hold instead of toward it. He nursed his hand; his fingers throbbed. His nose poured blood.

After the fourth bucket was emptied, the overseer called up and the bucket rose on its rope. Then the overseer himself was gone, too, deaf to the cries for more water, deaf to the pleas for food. The ladder followed him up.

Dejection and resignation settled once again over the hold as the captives scrapped for the best places to sit or lie down. Nico was near the port hull. He couldn't stand because the ceiling was too low, and there was no place to stretch out. He sat hunched over, pinned uncomfortably between a big man and a wooden post. He liked it better than lying in the slop of the bilge but wondered how he'd ever have a chance for water now.

He watched the big man, who was one of those who'd taken two drinks at the bucket. His neck was thick, his arms rippling with muscle. His hands were huge and heavily callused, and from the many burn scars on them Nico could tell he was a blacksmith. He was tending his wife and infant, who lay beside him. Now Nico saw the smith had not swallowed his second mouthful of water. The man leaned over and put his mouth to the child's. Carefully he tried to make it drink, but most of the precious liquid dribbled down the baby's cheek. The child was ill and didn't move or open its eyes. The man turned his attention to his wife, who appeared to be injured. Each movement made her gasp with pain. With great tenderness the smith took her head in his lap and seemed to kiss her. She moaned and coughed, losing what little water there was.

Near dusk the bosun's steady drumbeat slowed, and the oars slowed with it. The tambour fell silent, and the oars were shipped. The galliot anchored for the night on a dead-calm sea. The oar slaves settled themselves, their ankle chains rattling as they stretched out to sleep. From the decks there were murmured prayers in Arabic, and later low conversation and laughter.

In the hold the murmur of conversation fell away to other prayers, Christian prayers, and then silence. Time dragged. Someone coughed and someone cried. Nico heard a lowing sound, haunting in the gloom. He'd heard the noise before, from cattle. He only knew it was human now because he knew there were no cows aboard. Finally that sound stopped, too. Nico felt more alone than ever in his life. As dusk became night and blackness filled the hold, his only companions were stench and silent despair.

Later Nico needed to relieve himself. He held it for two long hours, until he was squirming painfully from the pressure. Finally he let himself acknowledge the futility of holding it. There was nowhere to go, and there wasn't going to be. Not even a slop bucket had been passed around. When he could wait no longer, Nico did what they all had to do. He went where he lay.

And then he tried to sleep.

❖

Half an hour before dawn the galliot was under way again, her oars pulling steadily against the sea. If there was a breeze to fill the sail, there was no feel of it belowdecks, where the oppressive heat baked the captives like crockery in a kiln.

During the morning watering Nico tried again to reach the bucket. He came away bruised and parched. He watched as the smith returned with cheeks bulging with water for his family. But this time he didn't lean over the child. Instead he put his mouth to his wife's, trying to coax her to drink. She moaned and wouldn't take it. With what little strength she had left, she thrust the child at her husband. He laid back the cloth that covered the baby's face. The child was dead. He stared for a long moment, then replaced the cloth. He leaned over his wife again, dribbling water onto her lips, but she took nothing. Finally, beaten, the smith sat up. He saw Nico staring at him. The big man looked away and swallowed what water was left.

There was no food, and Nico's stomach cramped with a familiar pain. Once, during the famine, he'd gone without eating for five days. He knew he could do so again, but he'd never been without water. Each hour made the vile crust in his mouth stiffer, more impenetrable to a tongue that seemed to grow larger and increasingly uncooperative. He knew he had to fight harder for the bucket. That evening he battled furiously, punching and kicking and biting. He clawed his way forward, worming his way between bodies and down the sloping deck that was slippery with filth. He bumped into a woman who slipped and fell heavily. His knee accidentally struck her in the face. She was clutching a scrap of bread, and the blow loosened her grip. He saw it and snatched it away and stuffed it in his mouth. The bread was even dryer than his tongue. He crunched at it but couldn't swallow it. He spit it out into his hand and put it into his pocket. He kept moving, but then stopped. He had never stolen anything. Guiltily he turned back, to help her up, but she stopped him with malevolent blue eyes of ice. Nico's mother warned him constantly of the perils of the evil eye, and immediately he feared this woman's gaze would cripple him with illness or strike him dead. He was afraid to touch her. He made the sign of the cross and kept crawling.

He saw the ladder through a forest of legs, but that was as far as he got. As he tried to get to his feet he himself was brutally knocked down. Someone kicked him. He wailed in pain, but in the melee no one heard. Afraid, defeated, he scrambled back toward the hull. He saw the woman again, more clearly this time. She was ill. Her face had a ghastly pallor. She opened her eyes. At the sight of him she smiled, but it was a mocking smile that chilled his heart. He turned away.

That night sleep wouldn't come. His head ached terribly. He couldn't make spit, and his tongue stuck to his teeth. Despite the heat he felt himself shivering. He raised his head to see if the woman was watching. Though her head was down, her face covered, he felt her evil eye boring into his soul.

He fished her bread from his pocket. He nibbled at it, choking down the tiny pieces, trying to make enough spit to soften them. It was no use. The bread raked his throat until it was raw. He swallowed it a crumb at a time.

He'd felt something else in his pocket and took it out. It was the coin Maria had given him the morning he was captured. It still felt like only a stone, but he began to rub it, watching the woman as he chewed. He knew his mother would have thrown laurel leaves onto a fire, or boiled a cat's tail, or hung a cowrie shell around his neck to protect him from the hag's evil gaze. It still felt like only a stone, but he kept working at it anyway, thinking that perhaps it was a talisman that might protect him. His nails chipped at the corrosion. "God protect me from the devil's eye," he murmured as he rubbed it between his fingers. "God take the devil away." He said the words over and over. As he did, he couldn't decide which he feared more, God or the evil eye, so he mixed in a few prayers asking God's forgiveness for stealing the bread. Then he heard his mother's voice, telling him that God could read his thoughts, especially the deceitful ones. God would know he was praying out of expediency, as an afterthought at that. He didn't know how to mend that, and he knew he wasn't going to give the bread back, either. He decided he was thinking about it too much. He went to sleep despising himself, certain that if he woke up at all, it would be to the flames of hellfire.

Instead, he awoke the next morning to the sight of bodies being lifted from the hold, their lifeless forms hoisted by the same rope that lowered water. He counted seven in all. As the first rose he realized with guilty relief it was the woman with the evil eye. He felt the coin in his pocket, convinced he had caused her death. He rubbed the coin as she ascended, and prayed fervently that his own evil had died with her.

The smith's wife was next, her body wrapped in the night by her husband. After her shrouded figure disappeared, the smith tied his baby to the rope. The bundle floated upward easily, like a feather. Nico heard splashes. Someone said a prayer. Others joined in, murmuring their devotions.

The smith returned from the rope and settled into his place. Nico saw the dreadful look on his face. "I'm sorry," he said. His words made barely a sound; his vocal cords weren't working properly. The smith looked at him dully. Almost imperceptibly he nodded. Then he lay on one side, using his massive hands for a pillow. His eyes remained open. He stared at Nico but didn't see him.

The afternoon brought a brief action at sea and a burst of hope. Anxious shouts rose from the deck. The bosun's whistle shrilled, and the beat of the tambour rose to dash speed, the oars keeping pace, twenty-six beats a minute, the slaves standing at their benches and heaving mightily against their oars, propelling the ship to fevered speed. Chains clanked, and the ship fairly flew through the water. Those in the hold heard a mighty splash nearby, followed a moment later by the distant boom of a gun. The captives stirred from their torpor. They sat up, cocking their heads, trying to make sense of it.

"Praise God, the Emperor's fleet!" a man cried.

"The Order!" someone said.

Nico's spirits soared. Of course! That was it! A galley of the Knights of St. John giving chase, come at last in answer to his prayers. He'd watched a hundred times as their great galleys set sail from the docks below the *castello,* their captains clad in glorious colors, strutting like gods on their decks, men of steel and honor commanding a thousand swords ready to shred the infidel. Since he was a child he'd heard of their legendary exploits at sea, tales of great battles fought by magnificent Crusaders who ran the corsairs down like rats and cut their godless hearts from their thieving, murderous bodies. Yes, Nico could close his eyes and see them even now through the hull, see their ship closing on this one as they raced to his rescue, the crosses on their red and white pennons fluttering in the breeze.

There was a brief rattle of arquebus fire over the noise of the tambour. They felt the ship change course sharply, and for a moment it seemed as if they would engage the unseen vessel. Nico's thoughts momentarily turned to dread as he imagined the other ship's ram piercing their hull, letting in the sea as captor and captive alike plunged to the bottom. A hundred pairs of eyes looked up at the opening to the hold, as if they might see something there, or force something to happen with hope and prayer.

The cannon boomed again, but Nico thought it was more distant now, and there was no splash. There was no more arquebus fire.

After twenty minutes the killing pace of the tambour flagged a little, settling into a still-frenetic stroke that the oarsmen maintained unabated for an hour afterward. Nico listened for more gunfire but heard only the lash of the overseer's whip as it tore at the flesh of the oarsmen, and an occasional command from the *raïs*. At length the tambour slowed again. A while later the whistle sounded, and half the slaves fell to rest while the others continued at a more leisurely pace.

From the deck there was laughter. There was no ship on earth swift enough to overtake an Algerian galliot in full flight. She was an eagle, the rest all hawks. In the hold the captives could only imagine what savior the ship might have outrun, what salvation had been lost forever. The hope that flickered briefly in the hold dimmed once again into the familiar gloom of despair.

At the evening's watering the smith made no move to help himself to drink. He was still on his side, in the same position he'd held all day. He opened his eyes at the tumult surrounding the buckets, then closed them again. Nico felt too weak to even try. The two of them lay side by side while the rush for water went on without them.

Nico awakened to his fourth day of captivity. He blinked and winced in pain. His eyelids were gritty, each blink like sackcloth being drawn across his tender eyes. He knew if he didn't have water soon, he would die. With difficulty he rolled over and found himself face-to-face with the smith, whose eyes were open. They stared at each other.

There began the familiar commotion that preceded each watering, the clanking of buckets and the posturing of thirsty captives as they jockeyed for position. Nico looked beseechingly at the smith. "Please," he croaked, his voice a whisper. "Help me drink."

The full water bucket was lowered into the hold behind the overseer, who stood on the second step of the ladder, his feet just above the slop in the bilge. The bucket was quickly emptied and just as quickly disappeared upward. The smith didn't stir.

The second bucket came and went. Still there was no movement from the man. Glumly Nico thought maybe he wasn't going to get up at all, not even to help himself.

"Please," Nico begged again. He wondered whether the man was even awake. His eyes were open but clouded, his stare vacant. His expression never flickered.

A third bucket descended into a thicket of upraised hands. Some of it spilled, to angry shouts. And then it, too, was gone. Weakly Nico got to his knees. He would have to attempt it alone.

The smith stirred. He raised himself on one elbow, then got to his knees. "Ple—" Nico started to plead again, but the man had made a decision. He took a small cloth packet from his trousers.

Without a word he pressed it into Nico's hands. Nico opened it. Inside were six gold Venetian ducats. Nico gasped. It was more money than he'd ever seen. He looked up at the man, puzzled. The smith quickly took the packet, wrapped the coins again, and stuffed it into Nico's pocket. Then he caught Nico's arm in a steel grip and moved quickly toward the ladder, towing Nico behind. The smith was the biggest and strongest man in the hold; those blocking his way parted like the sea before his prow.

Before Nico knew it they were in front, at the ladder, his mouth at the bucket. He swallowed as quickly as he could, choking and coughing at first, but then he held a mouthful, and another, and a third, the water brackish but glorious. It seemed to disappear into the tissues of his mouth before it had a chance to go down his throat. The overseer started to push him away, but the smith's arm blocked both him and the slaves fighting for a share. Nico drank still more, gulping greedily. But then the bucket was gone.

Nico looked gratefully at his benefactor. *"Grazzi,"* he said, waiting for the man to take his own turn. But the smith didn't respond, his gaze now fixed on the overseer. With stunning speed the smith lunged forward and caught the overseer by the throat, pushing Nico back out of the way with his other arm, into the bilgewater. The overseer's eyes lit with surprise and rage. He moved to break the hold, but the smith's grip was iron, long-tempered in the forges of his shop. Eyes cold with deadly purpose, his fingers slowly crushed the overseer's windpipe. He lifted the man from the ladder and held him in the air, suspended by his neck. The victim's eyes bulged, his arms waving wildly as he strangled. His whip fell into the muck. Someone snatched it up and shook it in the air. A chorus of defiant shouts rose from the hold.

The next moment a swarm of guards descended the ladder from the gangway, preceded by the long shafts of their halberds, their axelike blades hacking at upturned faces, the barbed steel spikes at their ends plunging into soft flesh. When a way had been cleared, six guards dropped into the chaos. Two of them took on the smith while the others hacked at the frenzied throng.

Nico scooted further back, his eyes riveted on the deadly struggle near the ladder. The overseer's face had mottled and then gone blue. Even then, after he stopped struggling, the smith's grip never slackened. In the cramped space the guards couldn't use their halberds. Nico saw the glint of a blade as a short knife found the smith's side. He never flinched, but instead seemed impelled to greater effort. He used the lifeless body of the overseer as a battering ram. He slammed it against his attacker, who fell on his back into the bilge. Instantly two slaves swarmed atop the man, pinning his arms as he drowned in the filth. The man let go of his knife, which dropped at Nico's feet. The boy stared at it, too afraid to move.

The smith still surged against the Algerians, using the overseer's body as a shield, letting it take the repeated assaults of the guards' blades. For a moment it looked as if the smith, incredibly, might prevail. He seemed beyond pain, far too much for the smaller men to stop; one after another they fell as the smith swung the body against them. But as strong as he was, he couldn't move fast enough. One blade found its mark, and then another. A shower of blood sprayed Nico as more men poured into the crowded hold, their practiced blades working efficiently and savagely against the remaining resistance. A moment later the brief uprising was over.

This time Nico counted twelve bodies lifted from the hold: four guards and eight slaves, two of them not yet dead. The smith's body was the last to go. They lifted him out by the ankles, with ropes. Nico watched quietly as the man's legs rose, and then his torso as he dangled upside down, his eyes open, as expressionless in death as they had been in life. Then he was gone. A moment later Nico heard the familiar splashes.

He sat dumbly, unmoving. He realized he was shaking. He knew death only too well, but always from disease or famine. He had never seen a man killed by other men.

Within moments, however, all he could think about was how he was going to get his next drink of water.

Some of the captives whispered about the retribution that was sure to befall all of them. Yet up on the poop, the captain was quite unconcerned with the morning's events. As always, he was serene in the hands of Allah. His fate, and that of his ship and everyone aboard, had been written long before the voyage ever began. It was the will of Allah that brought the storm, and His will that so many survived. And now, in their moment of need, if Allah wished them to drink, He would provide. If not, *malish, mektoub*. Never mind; it is written.

And indeed, that afternoon the galliot entered a small bay on the island of Lampedusa, in the strait between Sicily and North Africa. The ship's boat was dispatched, and it soon returned with casks of fresh water, food, and supplies to replace those lost in the storm. The captain saw that all aboard had their fill of water. For food he provided stale ship's biscuits, rock-hard but filling. Nico greedily devoured all that he could. To his surprise, it wasn't very much at all.

The decks were rinsed with seawater, while bucket after bucket of bilgewater flowed out of the hold up a human bailing chain, carrying away the sewage. The stench didn't ease much, but the place seemed vastly more bearable.

At dawn the next day the tambour sounded. A new overseer strode the gangway between the rows of oarsmen, whose long wooden arms pulled at the sea, beginning the next leg of their voyage. It was too early in the season for the easterlies to fill their sail, so their progress depended upon the power of oars, and upon the overseer's whip to drive them. They were twelve more days in all. Once they rounded Cape Bon, they held a westerly course that never lost sight of the African coast. Six more times during the journey they stopped for water and food.

Nico had water twice a day, without having to fight for it, and something to eat every dusk, though never enough to fill his belly. His nights remained largely sleepless, filled with daydreams of home, and sweet visions of Maria. His days were an endless nightmare of guilt and anger and self-recrimination. Over and over he told himself how much trouble he was going to be in when his father caught up with him. He never doubted he would see his home again. If no one came looking for him, he would escape. He felt the bulging cloth packet in his pocket. The smith had given him a fortune—enough, he was certain, to buy his freedom.

Still having no idea where he was bound or what lay in store for him, Nico munched his hard biscuit and rubbed Maria's coin. Suddenly he stopped. He counted days in his mind. He did it a second time, working backward. He couldn't be certain, for one day ran into another. But somewhere in the past three days he knew it had been May 24.

His tenth birthday.

from The Histories of the Middle Sea

by Darius, called the Preserver
Court Historian to the Emperor of the Two Seas, the Sultan Achmet

It was a time of great religious strain, not only in Malta but in all the world around the Middle Sea. Martin Luther had nailed his theses not to the door of a castle chapel but directly through the heart of the Church itself, whose corrupt officials watched his heresy spread from Germany until it threatened to engulf the whole of their world. Perhaps only the conflict between the heretic Shi'ite Muslims of Persia and the orthodox Sunnis rivaled that between Catholic and Protestant for breadth, passion, and fire. There was a key distinction. In Islam, conversions by force are prohibited, while in the Catholic world orthodoxy was still invited through coercion and fear at least as much as through conviction, utilizing the uniquely Christian tool of the Inquisition—which had no equal in the world.

The Inquisition had been established in the thirteenth century A.D., to combat sorcery and heresy. From its root grew the abomination of the Spanish Inquisition, calculated to help the monarchy eradicate Jews and Muslims who had feigned conversion and risen to the highest levels of civil authority. Organized under the Grand Inquisitor, the Dominican Torquemada, whose hatred of Jews knew no bounds, it found use both as a religious tool and as a political one, and its fires quickly burned out of control. Even the Pope who unleashed it was unable to restrain its excesses.

Half a century later, in A.D. 1542, desperate to combat the new Protestant threat, Pope Paul III put new clothing on an old wolf, christening it the Holy Roman and Universal Inquisition, and placing authority over its offices in the hands of a congregation of cardinals. While the suppression of false doctrine was still the core of its existence, the extremes of the Spanish Inquisition were not to be tolerated. Denunciations were to be approached with the greatest of care, for the Church had learned how easily a man might fall prey to the temptation to betray his neighbor over some dispute unrelated to faith. The *preferred punishments were to be less radical than before, involving acts of penance, fines, or perhaps even exile.*

Yet when he needed them, the old tools lay within the Inquisitor's grasp: his stake still burned hot, from time to time.

—From Volume I
The Religious Conflicts: The Inquisition

Chapter 4

Father Giulio Salvago had arrived in Malta in 1546, on the same day they burned his predecessor at the stake.

Salvago stepped off his ship and made his way from the wharf up the steps that led to Birgu, the ancient fishing village that nestled on a small peninsula behind St. Angelo, the castle that served as headquarters for the Order of St. John. There was no one to greet him, but he realized he had arrived in the midst of some momentous event. At the top of the steps he was quickly swept along in a large and boisterous throng making its way toward the village square. Dogs barked, and children perched on the shoulders of their fathers, straining for a better view. Men cried and beat their breasts, and women tore their hair and swooned with religious fervor. Monks moved through the crowd, their voices raised in prayer. There was brisk business in standing-room places, sold by those who had waited since before dawn to those eager to feel the heat of holy fire on their faces. Every window and rooftop overlooking the square was crammed with people.

Salvago caught bits of conversation and prayer. "*Eresia . . . Luther . . . Jesuald . . .*" His heart began pounding. He knew his predecessor was named Jesuald.

In the center of the square a stake had been driven into the ground. Wood and brambles were piled high against its base. To a slow beat of drums, a man was brought to the square. He rode in the back of a cart, drawn by a mule that pulled him down the main street from the prison beneath the bishop's palace. He wore a tattered shirt. Salvago was jolted by the realization that the shirt was a chasuble turned inside out, on which a diagonal cross of St. Andrew had been painted to signal his doom. Beneath his chasuble could be seen scars and bruises from his long confinement. "*It serves the swine right. He has not repented. . . .*"

Salvago crossed himself and pushed forward, straining with everyone else to see.

Jesuald struggled against his chains, trying to shriek something from beneath his gag, which had been cinched tightly across his mouth to prevent his unrelenting blasphemies from infecting the flock of penitents, now mesmerized by the rhythmic procession of death. His eyes were wide and bulging, not from terror but from rage.

He was dragged from the cart, his hands bound behind him. His gag slipped.

"Only faith can save you all," he cried. "Not the Church, which is man's temple, not God's. Only faith, and hope, and love—" He was knocked to the ground by a guard, who roughly tied his gag again.

Friars moved slowly through the crowd, holding shimmering candles aloft as they chanted, "*Pray for the lost soul of Jesuald, who today faces his Maker. . . .*"

Jesuald tried to stand but stumbled. Guards caught him by the arms and pulled him upright. No member of the Church participated in this portion of the proceedings. Jesuald had been tried in an ecclesiastical court, but his sentence and his executioners were secular. The Church would not have his death on her hands.

"*Pray for the lost soul of Jesuald. . . .*"

The prisoner was led to the stake, where he was tied with thick ropes that had been soaked in water, to slow their burn. There was no iron collar of a garrote on the stake. Because Jesuald refused to recant, he would not have the mercy of death by strangulation before the flames began, as was the common practice.

Instead he was to be burned alive.

As the knots were drawn tight Jesuald managed to spit out his gag once again. "Priests must be allowed to marry," he cried. "Celibacy is not the word of a perfect God, but of imperfect men! The Church seeks its own ends in these—"

"Sacrilege!" roared a monk, who hurled a rock. It struck Jesuald in the temple. His head lolled toward his shoulder. He blinked, trying to recover his senses.

The bishop of Malta sat atop a dais, in violet robes lit by the midday sun. He was flanked by priests, priors, the Archdeacon of Mdina, and assorted nobles gathered for the occasion. He tried to ignore the distraction at the stake and with a gesture to the crowd commanded silence. There was a hush as the Captain of the Rod, reading from a parchment, rapidly pronounced sentence.

The captain stepped back, bowed to the bishop, crossed himself, and nodded to the executioner. A reed torch was touched to the kindling at Jesuald's feet. Riveted, the crowd held its collective breath. The flames flickered and swirled, and died. There were disappointed cries. The executioner stepped forward. His torch flared once more. Again the flames licked briefly at the fuel, probing at the feet of the condemned. Again they went out, producing tendrils of smoke that curled toward the sky. Now there were whispers: was it an omen? People crossed themselves and pressed closer, straining for a better view. The executioner produced a fresh torch, lit it with the old, and knelt again to his work. The flames at Jesuald's feet remained tentative, creating more smoke than heat, choking those spectators closest to the stake.

Jesuald opened his eyes and gazed toward heaven. "Look to the Bible," he croaked, "and not to man. Not to bishop or Pope, but to the word of God." Another rock flew, and another.

"I came to watch a burning, not a stoning," a peasant roared. "Let him rant!" The crowd was with him, and the stones stopped.

Jesuald did his best to oblige them. His blasphemies continued, though his voice was weaker, and few could hear. The bishop cast a blistering look at the executioner, as if the heat of his gaze might help the hapless man make a fire.

Then, as it was clear the flames were going to die yet again, a wind arose. It began in the harbor off San Lorenzo wharf, where ripples on the water marked its path. It moved up the steep street toward the square, gathering itself into a small whirlwind that scattered dust and stung the eyes of those it touched. It passed through the crowd and kissed the flames, which gathered intensity at last.

The bishop saw the debris and felt the wind, and he rose to his full height. "The breath of God," he proclaimed, and there were murmurs of awed assent. The bishop read from his scriptures, and in stentorian voice all but drowned out the tortured sounds now escaping from Jesuald's throat. The flames caught hold and licked hungrily at the wood, which popped and hissed and grew quickly to a roar. The heat drove back those nearest the pyre, who shielded their faces with their hands, but could not look away.

"Lord's mercy! Lord's justice! Pray for the lost soul of Jesuald. . . ."

Salvago finally reached the center of the crowd, his way made easier by onlookers who saw his dress and parted to give him room. He saw Jesuald's face contorting through waves of heat, his features twisting in agony. Blistered lips mouthed a final heresy as the flames licked at his flesh and his clothing caught fire. There was a last guttural scream. The crowd was hushed, the square silent but for the crackle of flames. Salvago turned his back to the wall of fire, his nostrils filled with the stench of burning fat and flesh, his eyes closed in prayer for his fellow cleric's soul.

❖

The next morning, with the smell of death still clinging to his clothing, Salvago was summoned by Bishop Cubelles to an audience in his palace. Cubelles had sharp features, a trim black beard, arched eyebrows, and a prominent nose. Before discussing parish affairs, he wished to satisfy himself that his new priest carried none of the taint of the one just departed.

"So you have been with the bishop in Palermo," Cubelles said. "He writes your praise in glowing terms."

"He is too kind, Your Grace," Salvago said as he knelt and kissed the ring.

"We trust you understand that ideas favored in Sicily are not always those we hold dear in Malta," Cubelles said. "There are dangerous currents in the air."

"I have brought none with me, Your Grace," Salvago said with an easy smile.

"We understand the bishop has a concubine."

"It is true, Your Grace. In Sicily it is still not an uncommon practice," Salvago said. "Even in Rome—"

"*Cujus regio, ejus religio*," Cubelles interrupted frostily. "The bishop is a devout and good man, and no doubt well loved among his flock, but in this diocese it is not his lead you must follow but our own. You must commit yourself totally to the service of God, which permits no mistress but Christ, no Church but the true Church, and no bishop but the one before you." His sharp eyes pierced Salvago with the question.

"Of course, Excellency," Salvago said. "I am committed to such teachings. It saddened my heart to see my predecessor so fallen from God's grace."

"You have no quarrel with our judgment?"

"Neither with the judgment, Eminence"—Salvago looked his bishop in the eye—"nor with the punishment."

"We understand each other, then," Cubelles said.

"Perfectly, Your Grace."

❖

Salvago had followed a long and tortured path to his new parish. He was the second son of the Baron Amatore Salvago, a respected patrician with vast estates in Sicily. The young Salvago attended the best schools. He was quick with numbers, and his mind showed an easy fluency with Latin and Greek and with the great philosophers. There seemed to be no limit to his future. Though his oldest brother would be the next baron, Salvago seemed destined for a distinguished career in banking or commerce.

It was the baron, however, and not Salvago, who entertained such notions. There was a wild streak in him that no one, neither his father nor the local authorities, could tame. He was bone thin, with a long, gaunt face, sharp nose, and dark, brooding eyes. Despite the severity of his features, he was quite handsome. He attracted beautiful women, bedding them with ease. His friends were an assortment of vagabonds and artisans who were glad to carouse with him, at his father's expense.

The baron assumed his son would mature with age, but Salvago reached his eighteenth birthday without showing signs of tempering. He spent more than ever, running up huge debts for drinking and gambling. Sometimes when he woke up in the morning between an empty bottle and a strange woman, with only blackness where his memory ought to be, he was tormented by shame, but the sensation never seemed to outlast the hangover. In the confessional he was both prolific and insincere. *"Bless me, Father, for I have sinned. . . ."* He would rise and do penance. Thus cleansed, he was free to sin again.

An orgy at the family's country estate in which tapestries were trampled and furniture destroyed brought Salvago's father to the end of his patience. "I will continue to provide your allowance," he said, "but only on condition that you leave Messina and never return."

The arrangement delighted Salvago. He visited Syracuse, Naples, and Rome. Befitting his character, he managed to ascend the cultural heights of each city before exploring its depths of depravity. In Florence he dined with the Medicis, with whom his father did much business. They attended a concert at the Boboli Gardens, where he became drunk and, on a bet, swam the Arno River from city wall to city wall, without his clothes.

Venice captivated him. He spent long days in the library of the doge, reading Plutarch and Livy. With the doge's niece, he toured the Basilica of San Marco. No more splendid building existed outside Constantinople. Salvago was overcome by it all: by the sweeping views of the piazza from the balcony; by the mosaics that graced every surface with scenes from the Bible; by the *quadriga,* the magnificent team of four bronze Grecian horses that had once stood over the Hippodrome in Byzantium, pulling the chariot of Lysippus; and, most of all, by the beauty of the woman beside him. Just as dusk was falling and the basilica emptied of supplicants, he led her behind the Pala d'Oro, the Screen of Gold that shimmered with countless sapphires, rubies, emeralds, and pearls. There, behind a cabinet near the tomb of St. Mark and beneath the gaze of Tintoretto's angels, Salvago ravished her.

It was in Rome that his path to redemption began. He visited the Vatican, cynically intending to purchase an indulgence to wipe away his sins. Such bribes were a long-standing practice of a corrupt Church, but a bishop frostily informed him that indulgences were now forbidden.

Salvago wandered the Holy See. He had heard of the Sistine Chapel and wanted to visit, but was told it was closed so that the artist Michelangelo might finish a commission for the Pope. A guard accepted a piece of silver and Salvago's promise to remain mute, and the Sistine door was opened. Salvago descended the steps, then looked upward in awe at magnificent frescoes unlike anything he had seen before. He lay on his back on the cold marble floor, transfixed: the clouds had parted and he was looking directly into heaven. There was the Creation, and God separating the light from the dark, and Jonah, and their perfect brilliance was beyond his comprehension.

For brief periods over two days he watched Michelangelo. The old man had completed the ceiling many years earlier, and now he was working on a massive painting on the west wall above the altar, on the far side of the chancel screen. He worked alone on a scaffolding, his labor illuminated by a candle in his cap, his brush moving in strokes so bold and sure the hand of God Himself seemed at work. The fresco was dark and deeply disturbing. It was the Last Judgment, a grim vision of the torment awaiting unrepentant sinners. Salvago stared for hours, his soul stirring with longing for something beyond the life he knew. He saw himself in the painting, standing at the gates of hell. He knelt on the cold floor and prayed.

He arose with a feeling of rectitude, but it was typically fleeting. Once outside the Vatican, he breathed the glorious air of Rome, spotted a friend, and quickly reverted to form. By that night he was wenching his way through the city. In the alcohol-hazed days that followed he gambled heavily on cockfights and horse races, losing progressively larger sums of money. One night he lost a bet he couldn't cover. He tried to cheat, and a terrible brawl ensued. He was beaten savagely, left for dead beneath a bridge. It was three days before someone found him.

In his delirium, near death, images of the Sistine swirled through his darkness. Satan danced with Christ to Salvago's tune. Then Christ, beneath His crown of thorns, beckoned to Salvago to help Him lift His cross. Salvago reached for it but instead found his hand on the hem of the Virgin Mary's lilac robe, and he was trying to kiss her, trying to feel beneath the robe, trying to pull the robe away. Demons battled angels while hellfire licked at the gates of heaven, and Salvago was caught between. He saw God and Adam, their fingertips almost touching, and Noah, in a stupor of wine, vomiting gargoyles. Salvago saw his own face and flayed skin in the hands of St. Bartholomew, whose knife ran bloody with Salvago's sins; and there was Charon, the image of death with his horns and grotesque, protruding eyes; and Minos, the judge in Hades, and yes, it was he, Salvago, rowing their boat of the damned on the river Acheron, and the currents of hell were winning, pulling him down, down into a whirlpool of fire . . .

He awakened screaming for a priest. "*Bless me, Father, for I have sinned,*" only now there was nothing self-serving in it, nothing but the haunted cry of a man who genuinely repented his sins. He spent three weeks recuperating and praying. He emerged from the experience filled with purpose, his eyes on the glorious road to redemption.

Giulio Salvago, the profligate son of nobility, had decided to become a priest.

He entered the Seminary of St. Mark, in the foothills near Messina. It was the first truly passionate experience of his life. For the first time he found himself without guile, as sincere in his devotions as he had once been in debauchery. He applied himself with zeal, impressing his tutors with his quick grasp of theology.

He found pleasure in the simple life of St. Mark's. His room contained nothing but a cot, a washbasin, and a crucifix. He became shepherd to the seminary's herd of goats, a job no one else wanted. Carrying only a breviary and a flask of water, wearing nothing but sandals and a woolen cassock, he wandered the Peloritani Mountains with his animals for days on end, fasting and meditating. He felt the numbing cold of night and the searing heat of day, and reveled in his closeness to his Maker. He camped on a bluff near a spring, where by night he could watch the great bowl of the heavens and by day gaze across vineyards that stretched away across the hills to the sea. Sunrises and sunsets ran together. He watched his goats graze and prayed and marveled that his former life had so completely missed the true beauty of God's world.

Salvago was ordained in his twenty-sixth year. He spent a year in Palermo as a lowly assistant to the bishop, a post regarded as temporary while he awaited his first real assignment. He was hard-working and obedient, and was regarded by all who knew him as a model priest. Well born and well connected, he appeared destined for greatness within the Church. The combination of his personality, his rectitude, and his lineage made him perfectly suited for it, the bishop told him. Though Salvago knew it made him guilty of the sin of pride, he secretly agreed. Yes, he was ambitious. Yes, he coveted a position within the hierarchy. In this way, he thought, he might best serve his Lord. He believed God had begun the miracle of his conversion in the Sistine Chapel for a reason, and that it was God's will that he return to the Vatican, where great reforms were sweeping the Church. As he himself had been transformed, so would the Church. Salvago wanted to be part of it. The bishop promised to say a word in his favor upon his next visit to Rome.

When his assignment finally came it was a blow to his dreams, a sharp descent from the Vatican.

Malta!

Though he had never been there, he knew of the island. It was, in every sense, a place in the opposite direction of Rome. Disappointed, he nevertheless resigned himself to it, believing that God would reveal His purpose in due time. He found solace in knowing that at least he would be close to his sister, Angela, who had married a Maltese nobleman. They lived in Mdina, a short distance from Salvago's new parish.

As he was preparing to embark for Malta, word arrived that the priest he was to have assisted had been relieved of his position. There were no details, but it meant Salvago would be *kappillan,* master of his own parish. It was a wonderful opportunity, to have so much responsibility so soon.

❖

Salvago found the island a grim and gray place, dirt-poor and barren. Although it was but a short distance to Venice or Florence, Malta was mired in another age, Gothic sackcloth to their Renaissance silk. Ideas that flowered in Rome withered in Birgu.

Nevertheless, he set himself with single-minded purpose to his work. His parish was three hundred strong, and without doubt Christ's work needed to be done among them. Truly, he saw, they lived in a valley of tears. Yet though they were backward and illiterate, diseased of body and impoverished of mind, given to superstition and swayed by magic, their souls were as solid and devout as any in Christendom.

His church was dilapidated. The eaves sagged and the walls were crumbling. The altar was broken and without ornament. He wrote his father for money and beseeched his brother-in-law, the Baron Antonio Buqa, to contribute something as a boon to his soul. Buqa protested that St. Agatha's was neither his own parish nor a great cathedral, but his wife, Angela, Salvago's sister, hounded him until he grudgingly relented. Before long the church had a new face. Rafters were replaced and a tile roof installed. The walls received a fresh coat of lime whitewash. An Italian knight with whom Salvago had once caroused in Venice contributed a tapestry that had been in his family for years. It depicted the Last Supper, and now adorned the wall above the altar. A small but elegant Virgin, carved from the pristine white marble of Carrara, graced the altar. Salvago ordered a new bell from a brass works in Milano. Without anywhere to hang, it was stored in the sacristy. He bided his time, waiting until he had enough money to build a proper belfry.

Years passed. Salvago worked hard and lived simply and found great fulfillment. His home was the one-room rectory behind the church. His worldly possessions were few. He owned two cassocks, a white cotton alb with a sash, and a chasuble, richly embroidered with golden fleur-de-lis. Beyond that he had one pair of sandals, a rosary, a leather-bound Breviary, and the one extravagance of his new life, presented to him by his proud father on the occasion of his ordination: a silver crucifix inlaid with perfect rubies. He wanted nothing more. Whenever he had extra money, he used it to help the neediest families of his parish, or to make modest improvements to the church.

Despite the time he spent on the church itself, he never lost sight of his first order of business, that of tending the needs of his parishioners. He suffered with them through drought and famine and plague. He shared their joy in weddings and on feast days. He baptized their babies, confirmed their young, and buried their dead.

It was on behalf of one such family that he'd spent most of this day. Upon hearing the news of the Borg boy's kidnapping, he'd hurried straight to the Order's headquarters in Fort St. Angelo. As Salvago was himself noble, he moved easily in their circles, even as a priest. The bishop often used him as a liaison with the Order, or occasionally to patch relations between the families who made up the island's nobility. He was admitted to see the Grand Master without delay, but he had no better luck with the one-eyed Spaniard than had Maria the day before. The Grand Master grew a pained expression as Salvago beseeched him for help. "Not that foolishness again," d'Homedes said. "I have no ships to spare. Not for one captive—not for a hundred."

Salvago next went to the Università. Before the knights were granted the Maltese islands by the Emperor Charles V, the Università had been the governing body. Over the years it had seen the steady erosion of its authority as the knights took over defense and then slowly usurped other powers. Salvago's reception there was sympathetic but proved fruitless. "As much as I would like to help, Dun Salvago," said the official, "we have no galleys to mount a pursuit. You must beseech the Order."

Salvago visited the docks. A Greek privateer was moored there, taking on supplies. It was one of the many private Christian galleys that under Sicilian license preyed upon Muslim ships. The master was polite but blunt. "I'd guess he was Algerine," he said. "They've been active in these parts the last few weeks. I'd never catch him anyway, and if he's on his way to Algiers, well, I'd sooner follow a lion into his own lair."

Salvago offered to pay, having little idea how he might raise such a sum as he promised, but the Greek wasn't interested. He spat into the harbor. "I don't understand why you would bother troubling yourself over the natural order of things, Father—especially over a mere slave."

Salvago had thought about that himself. There was the loss of a soul to consider, of course, but it was more than that—it was the need to make his parishioners feel as if someone cared, as if they did not need to forever be victimized by corsairs, as if there was a flicker of light in their universe of darkness. An effort that produced nothing was better than no effort at all, he reasoned. A few years earlier, a rare tornado had battered the island. Salvago had been visiting a family in Birgu. As the storm reached the heights of its passion, he stood with them inside their flimsy house, trying to hold shutters and doors and walls against nature's onslaught. When the storm abated, the house lay in ruins despite their efforts. Yet they had tried, against overwhelming odds. Was this any different? Could he ever fail to try?

Now, defeated once again and with nowhere else earthly to turn, he went to the Borgs' house to offer them the comfort of the Lord. It was near dusk, and just as he was about to knock the door opened. Maria Borg was leaving, and appeared to be doing so stealthily. She glanced behind her and stepped out into the street, nearly bumping into Salvago.

"Oh!" she said in surprise. "Dun Salvago! I didn't see you."

"Maria!" Even in the fading afternoon light the bruises on her face and neck were clear to Salvago. There was a fleck of blood at the corner of her mouth. "I heard about yesterday. Were you hurt badly?"

"It wasn't them, Dun—"

"*Maria!*"

A voice boomed from inside the house behind her. "Maria? Is that you? Where are you going?"

"Out, Father. I have to . . . to get thistle for the fire."

"We have enough. Go back upstairs."

She hesitated only an instant. Salvago saw her set her chin and make her decision. "I'm sorry, Father," she whispered to him, her eyes beseeching him to be quiet. She slipped past him and ran down the street.

Luca Borg got to the door and pulled it the rest of the way open. He was startled to see Father Salvago. He stepped out into the street and looked after Maria, her figure just disappearing around the corner. His eyes smoldered, but he checked himself. "I told her to go inside."

"She must not have heard you, Luca," Salvago said. "Perhaps I distracted her."

Luca seemed unconvinced, but for the moment there was nothing to be done.

"I am sorry about Nico," Salvago said. Luca only nodded. "I

brought bread." Salvago held out a freshly wrapped loaf, donated by the baker. It was still warm from the oven. Luca hadn't seen such fresh bread in a month. His eyes devoured the loaf.

"Thank you, Father. Come in." Luca ushered him into the house. "Isolda!"

"If this is not a convenient time, I can come back."

"Not at all. Isolda! Bring warm milk! We have a guest!"

Salvago's eyes adjusted to the gloomy interior of the house. Only one small window faced onto the street. The pane was made of linen soaked in oil to make it translucent, and normally it was kept covered. There was a rough wooden bench, a single chair, and a table in the room that served as kitchen, living room, and dining room. Two sheep lay beneath the table. Behind them was the dung pit. Standing against the rear wall was a ladder that disappeared up into the rafters, where platforms beneath the eaves would serve as bedrooms for the children.

"Sit there, Father." Luca indicated the chair, and Salvago sat. "Isolda!" Luca called again. "Come, woman, will you!"

On one wall was a small shrine that Luca had built for Isolda, devoted to the symbols and relics of her faith. A crucifix hung in the center of the wall, holding a bloody Christ twisting in agony beneath His crown of thorns. A shelf held the relics: a candle made of beeswax from a hive in Bethlehem, a piece of wood from the rudder of the wrecked ship of St. Paul, a fragment of cloth from the hem of St. Peter's robe. Each had been purchased at great expense from sources who swore to their authenticity. Isolda prayed to them all.

The opposite wall was for whenever the first wall failed. More shelves there held amulets, creams, and potions, each endowed—so the village sorcerers promised—with mystical or medicinal properties. There were tins of bitterroot and horehound and neatly tied piles of tamarind bark. There was senna for demons of the bowels, a pig's eye bound in a dried rabbit's ear to keep loathsome vapors at bay, and dried tortoise blood wrapped in olive leaves to thwart the evil eye. No one, least of all Isolda, could tell where prayer ended and spell began. She embraced Christ with one arm, the sorcerers' tools with the other, uncertain which to trust more completely. Luca put up with it grudgingly. As far as he could tell, none of it had much effect, except for emptying his already lean pockets.

Isolda Borg emerged from behind the bed curtain. She had been cleaning, muttering her Paternosters and her Aves as she wielded her straw brush, working the floor, stirring and reorganizing the dirt, shuffling it into new piles, sifting out bits of sheep dung to be tossed in the pit. Dust motes floated in the air, caught by pale beams of sunlight that seeped through cracks around the door.

She breathed deeply, as if she were exhausted, each breath like a sigh. Dark circles surrounded her eyes. She was wrapping a scarf over jet-black hair that was pulled straight back into a severe bun. Her dress never varied. Her short form was draped forever in black. At the sight of Salvago she hurried to loosen a string that held a cloth that fell over the back wall, cloaking the items that now embarrassed her. "Father Salvago," she said. "I'm sorry—I did not expect you." She glared at Luca for bringing the priest inside their house so thoughtlessly. Luca seemed not to comprehend her anger. He went to church only for funerals.

Though appalled at superstitions that ran dangerously close to witchcraft, Salvago chose not to make an issue of it just then. Isolda Borg was not the only parishioner who tried to cover her bets in such ways. Besides, today was not a day to raise such questions.

Isolda was one of St. Agatha's most regular communicants, and her habits mirrored most of Salvago's female parishioners. Six days a week she rarely left the house. She was reluctant to go outdoors, where there was plague, and sin, and men who looked at women. She sent Maria to the market and to do all the errands. Every night before supper she would open the window that faced onto the street, and exchange gossip with Agnete, the harridan next door. Neither woman could see the other. Separated by a wall, they would watch the narrow street and the stone walls on the houses opposite, noting every shadow and bit of garbage, every rat that scurried on four legs and every scoundrel that scurried on two. Whenever someone passed in the street, the two women would quickly draw their veils over their faces and melt into the shadows of their homes. They traded delicious gossip about scandals and petty sins and the sure damnation awaiting the various lost souls of Birgu.

Only on Sunday would she leave the house, to attend Mass at St. Agatha's, which she would not miss were it hailing fire from the sky.

"Will you have some onion soup with us, Dun Salvago?" she

asked now. She turned to an iron pot that hung over the fire, and stirred the thin soup with a wooden ladle.

"Thank you, no," he said. "I came by to express my sorrow at your loss."

Isolda stirred the soup harder and made no reply. Salvago knew her history. It was filled with the harsh realities of Malta. She had come to the island with her first husband in the same year as the Knights of St. John. A carpenter looking for work, he found death from a fever instead. She married Luca Borg, a Maltese, the next year. She bore him six children. Four had died of famine or disease. Each loss, Salvago supposed, had sucked a bit more warmth from her, and now her son Nico was gone, too. It would be little surprise if the latest blow turned Isolda as hard and unforgiving as the island itself, her spirit desiccated by hard life and the hot sciroccos that blew from Africa. Salvago knew that for years she had beseeched her husband to leave the island, to return to her own home in Italy. It was in vain. Luca knew nothing but Malta and would never consent to leave, no matter how difficult the circumstances.

Salvago also knew that Isolda prayed to God to deliver her from her hell on earth. In the confessional he had recognized her sigh and sorrowful plaint: "When I am dead, only the worms will be as happy as me."

Her husband seemed to Salvago like many of his other parishioners—burdened by the harshness of his life. Famine and poverty and the loss of his children had sucked the essence from him. He was a private man who rarely went to church. He worked when there was work, and slept when there was none, and each day simply tried to make it through to night.

"I only wanted to tell you that I had visited the Order." Isolda looked at him expectantly. Luca looked at the floor.

"They . . . they promised to do everything they could." Salvago realized it sounded even emptier saying it than it had hearing it. Isolda turned silently back to her soup.

Luca grunted. "It would never have happened if Maria . . ." His voice trailed off. His big fists clenched and relaxed and clenched again.

"I heard she talked to the Grand Master yesterday," Salvago said. "That took great courage. She is a spirited child."

"Talked! She confronted him, is what they say. Threw a rock! She'll get us arrested. If it weren't for her foolish dreams of treasure, Nico would be here today, and she wouldn't have needed to talk to anyone at all."

Salvago thought of the bruises he'd seen on the girl. Luca had done no more than any father would have under the circumstances. Indeed, another man might have beaten her to death, and no one would have questioned it. "I would not presume to interfere in your affairs, Luca, but don't be too hard on Maria. She is but a child caught in an adult's world. She made a mistake, but after all, it is the corsairs who are to blame."

"She should have been in the dung pit, where I told her to be. There are no corsairs in *there,* Dun Salvago."

"She has suffered greatly, Luca. You have only to look in her eyes to see it."

Luca shook his head vehemently. "It is *Nico* who suffers," he said. "It is his *mother* who suffers. Maria brought it all upon us with her disobedience. She is an empty-headed dreamer. Her will is stronger than an ox. I have tried to break her of it. Life will, soon enough."

"We must pray to God for Nico's soul," Salvago said. "God will preserve him."

"God has abandoned him," Luca said bitterly.

"*Luca!*" Isolda was horrified, but Salvago ignored the comment. He bowed his head and led them in prayer.

Chapter 5

The great guns boomed from the hills above the harbor, telling the city that a ship laden with riches was making her way to port. Tavern keepers and prostitutes readied themselves for the influx of sailors and soldiers, while eager merchants hurried down to the dock, seeking to profit from booty and slaves.

A barge bearing the *limam-raïs,* the harbormaster, rowed out to meet the galliot of Raïs Ali Agha. The two men drank coffee on the poop deck while the copious inventory of bounty was taken by a scribe for the purpose of calculating the tax due the Bey. As the galliot nudged the wharf, her slaves began dropping their oars into the water, where a light boat picked them up. The ship's rudder and sail would be removed as well until the next voyage, so that slaves might not commandeer her in an escape attempt.

In the hold Nico realized that the commotion signaled this was not an ordinary stop. A ladder was lowered, and the captives were ordered out. As unpleasant as their quarters had been, no one desired to be the first. It took an overseer's whip to begin the exodus.

Nico rose from the stinking darkness of the hold as if from the grave. As his head emerged he savored the precious breeze, breathing deeply of the sea wind, the first he'd enjoyed in nearly three weeks. He got to his knees and then stood unsteadily on the upper deck of the vessel as he took in his surroundings. The ship and the wharf were crawling with activity. Released from their chains, the bench slaves were hoisting bales of cargo onto their backs as they were led away to their terrestrial prison. Nico blinked in the brightness as he took in the harbor and the magnificent city that lay beyond.

Unlike the plain stone structures of Birgu, the buildings here were whitewashed, achingly brilliant in the midday sun. A huge kasbah stood sentry over the city, commanding the harbor from atop a steep hill. Nico imagined the fortress must belong to a king or a bishop. He saw minarets and domes, and a rampart that ran near the water's edge and then up the hill, surrounding and protecting the city, broken only by bastions and a few heavy gates. Beyond the city walls there were lush gardens, green orchards, and tall windmills that turned gracefully in the breeze.

Bisecting the harbor was a mole, a massive stone breakwater laid in the sea that ran to an islet upon which stood the ruins of old Spanish fortifications. Slaves labored atop the mole, struggling with heavy blocks of masonry with which to make repairs to a wall that was forever being devoured by a hungry sea. A gate separated the mole from the city. Another gate with an iron portcullis led to a long shoreline where war galleys lay beached like gray whales, careened on their sides for scraping and greasing. From the same shore, a small fleet of fishing boats put to sea, their sails nodding and bobbing as they rounded the mole and passed into the open sea.

Nico stared at the place in awe. It made his own port of Birgu seem puny and insignificant by comparison. He knew it must be somewhere important.

"*Hawn* Constantinople?" he asked a sailor.

The man laughed at his stupidity. "*El Djezair,*" he said.

Nico's eyes widened.

Algiers.

He'd heard tales of the city on the docks at home. The Jewel of Sin, they called this place in the ports of Europe. The Theater of All Cruelty. Despite Nico's wonderment, it was a mere colony of Constantinople, a backwater bauble in the glittering Ottoman realm. Yet still it was a thriving place, founded by the Phoenicians, sacked by the Vandals, conquered by the Spaniards, then finally seized for the Ottomans by the corsair Kheir-el-din, known to all the Christian world as Barbarossa, who in turn expelled the Spaniards.

Algiers.

A great African hopper into which Berber and Moorish blood were stirred into a brew that was lethal to Christians, costly to traders, and endlessly irritating to kings and popes. Almost unopposed, her corsairs fed upon the fat traffic of the sea. Her streets teemed with life, her markets with bounty, her prisons with uncounted thousands of slaves. Once captured, none escaped her embrace except through the sweet release of ransom or death.

Now her newest acquisitions streamed off the ship, Nico in their midst. Instinctively he tried to hide between adults, peering out at new and bizarre sights. They were led down a ramp to the dock, then through a great wooden gate and into the city proper. At the gate Nico looked up. Iron spikes were set in the masonry along the tops of the walls. Almost all of them bore sun-baked human heads, parboiled and then dried in sacks of salt before being mounted to remind all who entered Algiers of the penalty for disobedience. Nico stopped to gawk at them, moving again only when someone behind him pushed.

They climbed through a maze of streets that rose from the harbor, every path and lane choked with dust and swirling with unfamiliar sights, sounds, and smells. The city was a great bazaar. Crowds of people thronged the narrow streets, with goats, sheep, and children everywhere underfoot. Cripples slept in darkened doorways, alms cups at their feet, while pickpockets worked the crowds. Water sellers carrying bulging bearskins sold cool drinks from brass cups. There were fine horses, proud and high-strung, and monkeys on leashes, and great lizards, gutted and hung to dry. There were nomads hailing from the great desert, soldiers from Istanbul, and tradesmen from the ports of France and the Venetian Republic, a hodgepodge of mankind wearing costumes of every sort—fezzes and turbans, silk caftans and heron plumes, burnooses and bells. There was a cacophony of noise, from the groans of camels to the bleating of sheep; the discordant sound of horns and flutes pierced the endless babble of commerce. Vendors hawked cloth and cheap jewelry from shadowy stalls, sipping strong coffee and watching the procession of new slaves with trifling interest.

Nico's awe was overshadowed only by his need to eat. The ship's biscuits had kept him from starvation but left him with a deep hunger that clawed at his belly. Almost everything he saw reminded him of it. Asses hauled panniers loaded with fresh vegetables. Plump chickens ran free in the streets. Camels knelt in the shade, chewing languidly on grasses that looked rich and sweet to Nico's ravenous eyes. Live quails were cooped in reed cages. He smelled spices and roast mutton and hot bread, odors that made him ill with longing. Hunks of blood-red meat hung in butcher stalls, and brochettes roasted on open braziers. Clouds of flies swarmed everywhere; to Nico even they looked edible.

The markets and streets were a powerful mélange of odors. There was storax, a fragrant balsam; strong kif and pungent thyme; and the awful reek of rotting vegetables and flesh. Among the worst of the smells, Nico realized, was his own. The stench of the hold had followed him inland. He noticed for the first time that he was caked with layers of filth. He wiped at it as he walked, without effect. He thought how nice it would be to take a swim just then, to rinse it off, and he was seized with a terrible longing as he realized that he couldn't. He glanced over his shoulder, back toward the glittering sea, searching the horizon for any sign of the galleys of the Order of St. John, still certain they were coming. The horizon was empty and the sea beyond reach. He turned away from the bittersweet sight, filled with self-pity.

A vendor carrying a tray of sweetmeats stood to one side as the procession passed. Impulsively Nico snatched one from the tray. The vendor, a young boy, shrieked in rage, shouting to the guards for help. Nico had just bitten down on the heavenly treat when an unseen hand knocked him off his feet. He hit the ground with his chin, biting his tongue. Bits of candied plum mixed with blood dribbled onto the ground. Dazed, he struggled to his knees, grabbing at the bits. He stuffed them into his mouth again as a boot found his side, knocking his breath away. Once again morsels of sweetmeat spewed from his mouth onto the ground. He blinked the dust from his eyes and reached again, his mind fixed only on the food. The next thing he knew he was on his back, staring at the colorless sky. He heard the snap of a whip and felt an awful fire at his belly. He cried out and raised his hands to protect himself. Twice more he felt the lash, and then he was dragged to his feet and propelled roughly back into the procession. He stumbled. One of the other captives caught him by the arm. "You fool," the man hissed. "You risk your life for a sweet?"

Nico was not defiant by nature, not like his sister Maria. He felt himself shaking from his brush with disaster, disaster foolishly courted for a fleeting taste of sugar. His ribs ached. His belly stung and his tongue hurt. With all that, he guessed that if they hadn't killed him already, they weren't going to. They didn't seem shy about such things. He could still taste the sugary plum, mixed though it was with grit and blood. It would be a long time before that sweet taste left him.

And he knew that Maria would be proud.

❖

The men spent the night in the spacious courtyard of Ali Agha's home. Those who could not fit inside the bagnio, a private prison occupying a vaulted bathhouse, slept beneath the stars. Lacking blankets, they huddled together to ward off the cold. After the hold, it seemed like heaven.

Shortly after dawn the next morning, the courtyard filled with visitors. There were traders and money changers, and even many slaves, some wearing rags and leg irons, others well dressed and walking free. The slaves looked for friends or relatives among the newly arrived captives. Despite the muddle of tongues, Nico understood much of what was said. He had a quick ear, and the language seemed something of a pidgin blend of Spanish, Italian, and Moorish, all of which he often heard in Malta. Eagerly he asked questions, but he was of an age that no one took him seriously or bothered with a reply. He wandered unnoticed among the adults, listening to their exchanges.

You will suffer horribly if they know your family has money. You'll be tortured to make your appeals for ransom more urgent.

Ransom is your only way out.

There is no way out.

If you are taken as a beylik slave, make your peace with God and pray for a speedy death. If you have money, buy poison.

Swallow what money you have, or they'll take it from you.

If they know you swallowed money, they'll cut it from your living belly.

"I am Baba," a boy said in Italian, appearing through the crowd. His liquid brown eyes brimmed with friendship. He was a few years older than Nico. He seemed but a waif, his clothing poor, his feet bare, yet the boy moved freely, almost authoritatively through the compound, even greeting the guards. "You are Sicilian?"

"Maltese," Nico answered eagerly, delighted for someone to talk to. "What is to become of me? How can I go home?"

"All in good time," Baba said. "I can tell you anything you like. I used to be a slave, like yourself."

"I am not a slave," Nico retorted hotly.

"Ha!" Baba waved at the others. "You are keeping poor company for a freeman."

"I am not a slave," Nico repeated.

Baba shrugged. "It is not I you need convince," he said. "I wish only to be your friend. As I have said, I was a slave once, myself. From Brindisi, in the Kingdom of Naples. But I worked my way to freedom. As you can see, I make my own way now."

Nico's face lit at that. "Such a thing is possible?"

"In Algiers all things are possible with the help of the Compassionate."

"Who is the Compassionate? Is he here now?"

"He is Allah, of course. He is here always." Baba appraised him carefully. "You are the son of a noble family?"

"No."

"You are very sly, I think. And far too beautiful for a commoner. You are the son of a count? An emperor?"

"A builder," Nico said importantly. "In Birgu. By today he will be raising fortresses for the Knights of St. John."

"Not a thing I would admit in this place if I were you." Baba eyed Nico suspiciously. "I still think you toy with me. So you have a trade, then? You know building? You are a mason, or a carpenter?"

"Not yet. Papa says I'm still too young. Next year he's going to teach me."

"Next year he is not," Baba said. "Not unless—"

"Unless?"

Baba lowered his voice conspiratorially. "You have no skill, so you must feign one, or buy your way to a good position. Have you something for baksheesh?"

"For—?"

Baba rubbed his fingers together. "Money, to make business."

"I have nothing," Nico lied.

"A pity. Without it you will be sold at auction in the Bedestan. All cattle and slaves are sold there, except those fortunate enough to find a proper master beforehand. Without help you will become a *beylik* slave, and you will die in the quarries. Or you'll be sent to the galleys, chained to a bench from which you will beg for death. With baksheesh I can get you work in the orchards, or even the *palmerie*. It is the best life here. You will have enough to eat, and the work is not difficult. Dates are shipped all the way to Venice, in crates. I can help you hide in one, from which it will be a simple matter to escape."

Venice! The ducats burned like hot coals in Nico's pockets. The money shouted freedom while his head answered caution. He squirmed with indecision.

Baba saw his uncertainty. "And I thought you a nobleman," he said, pity in his voice. He gave an indifferent shrug. "Perhaps you were not born a slave, but it is clearly your destiny to die one." He turned and walked away.

Nico felt hope slipping away on Baba's heels. His caution melted. He might never get another chance. "Wait!" He fumbled in his pocket and withdrew a precious coin. He held it out carefully, so that no one else could see. "Is this enough?"

Baba eyed the coin. "Hardly," he said indifferently. "Others will pay more. Positions in the *palmerie* are not easy to come by. There is shade and cool water. Fruit drops from the trees." He handed the coin back. "Better to save your money. You can use it to buy food, in the quarries."

"No!" Nico fished in his pocket once again. "Here's another. It's all I have, I swear."

The money vanished into Baba's pocket. "You are wise to trust me. And now I must attend to your business." Nico's heart pounded as Baba melted into the crowd. Never before had he made a bargain with money. Now he'd done it with a fortune, for his future.

The slaves were stripped naked, then sorted by a group of men that included the captain, Ali Agha. By some mysterious selection process, some were chosen for the endless living death of the galleys, others for the slow, crushing death of the quarries. Some were led away in chains, some without. One raised his voice in spirited anger. Nico strained on tiptoes to see. With stunning speed, the man's head was stricken from his shoulders by a guard wielding a great scimitar. The man's body dropped to the sand, where it twitched a moment, and then lay still. The guard meticulously cleaned and resheathed his blade. Ali Agha brushed at a troublesome fly and continued as if nothing had happened. The line of slaves moved forward.

Nico debated what to do with the ducats he'd taken from his pockets before stripping. He saw others surreptitiously swallowing what they had. One man's money was discovered and confiscated, and that made up Nico's mind. He casually raised his hand to his mouth and put a coin on his tongue. He tried to swallow. The coin was too big and caught in his throat. It wouldn't go down, and it wouldn't come up. He gagged and finally coughed it up. His throat ached and his eyes watered. A scrawny man in the next line stared at him, larceny in his eyes. Nico clutched the money tightly, Maria's coin with the others, and tried to cover his nakedness with his fists.

As he neared the front of the line, he saw Baba with an important-looking merchant, who conversed with the captain as each slave came to the front. At the sight of Nico, Baba hurried over. "You see that man?" Baba whispered. "He is very powerful. A trader, a Jew who acts as a middleman. It is his whim that sends a man to the galleys or to the *palmerie*. Allah has truly smiled upon you, my good friend Nico. The Jew has agreed to help you, but only if you have more money."

"He has agreed? Truly?"

"May the devil himself devour me if I lie. But you must hurry, before it is too late."

Nico pressed the last of his ducats into Baba's hand, relieved to be done with them. "You are kind to me, Baba," he said, his face shining with gratitude. "I will not forget you."

At last Nico stood in the front, mortified at his nakedness. Before today he had never taken his clothes off in front of another person. Now a thousand eyes seemed to be focused on him, and he reddened with embarrassment. "This is the one of whom I told you, master," Baba said to the dealer. "His family is poor. There will be no ransom. He has no skills, no money. He is too slight to become a warrior, too young for the oar. His appeal, I think, is obvious."

"Yes, he is quite beautiful." The dealer looked first at Nico's teeth, forcing open his mouth, pulling on a molar to see if it was firm. Nico tasted salt and onion. Next the dealer pried open Nico's hands, looking for calluses. He saw Maria's coin. "So? What is this?"

"Just a stone," Nico whispered. The dealer threw it to the ground.

He took Nico's genitals in his hands. Nico recoiled. The dealer squeezed sharply, to stop him. Nico gasped and froze as his budding manhood was roughly assessed. "The scrotum is yet unwrinkled. There is no hair. He has not yet descended." He turned Nico's face one way, then the other. He inspected his hair for lice and looked in his ears. He grunted with satisfaction. "Beneath the filth, there is but one destiny for this one. He will make a fine *garzóne*. Private auction, tomorrow." The dealer moved on.

Nico looked beseechingly at Baba, who wasn't saying the right things—he hadn't even mentioned the *palmerie*. But Nico couldn't catch his eye. Knowing his chance was passing, Nico called out to the dealer. "Sir! I can work in the orchards! I know how to pick dates!"

The dealer laughed. "That trick again, Baba!" Baba tossed the dealer a coin and flashed Nico a wicked grin.

"Baba!" Nico cried, only now realizing the deception. "Please! Tell him!"

Baba laughed.

Nico just managed to scoop up Maria's coin as he was taken away.

❖

The next morning Nico and two other boys were brought into the Bedestan, into a private area isolated from the rest of the slave market by rich hanging silks. Three bidders reclined on plush cushions beneath a purple canopy, where the auctioneer fawned over them, pouring coffee and snapping his fingers for silver plates heaped with food. Behind the cushions were arrayed household servants and retainers of the bidders, and servants of the auctioneer. To one side stood a bare-chested guard wearing white pantaloons and a red sash around his waist, into which was tucked a massive scimitar.

Once again all three boys were ordered to strip naked, then to parade back and forth in front of the canopy. They were ordered to jump as high as they could, and then to turn their backs and touch their toes. Nico turned and strutted with the others, listening to the men beneath the canopy laughing and joking with each other. Nico's cheeks flushed in anger at their levity. He wanted to defy them, to refuse to do as they ordered, but his eyes kept coming to rest on the scimitar. He felt the hair at the nape of his neck tingling and thought better of it.

The other two boys were auctioned first. They approached the canopy one at a time, to be prodded and probed by the men inside, after which there was spirited bidding. Finally the auctioneer called Nico forward. The man twirled his finger, indicating that Nico should turn around. Nico obliged, still trying to cover his nakedness. The auctioneer flicked at his modesty with a crop, and Nico dropped his hand.

The bidding for Nico took longer than the others, and the price went higher. In the end he fetched the princely sum of four hundred and forty Algerian doblas, only ten less than a healthy camel would bring. "Stand before your master!" barked the auctioneer. "He is El Hadji Farouk, prince of merchants, shipbuilder, and trader. He has twice made the pilgrimage to Mecca and counts the Sultan, bless his name, among his friends. His ships are the finest in all the seas. He trades silks and carpets in ports from Marseilles to Istanbul. Serve him well, boy, or he'll return you to me and I'll play draughts with your balls."

Nico stood timorously before Farouk, trying to study him without staring. Farouk seemed old to him, wrinkled and a bit fat. He was dressed in money. He wore a velvet red fez, and his vestments were of the finest silk, his slippers encrusted with jewels. His fingernails were lacquered and he smelled faintly of perfume.

Sucking on a date, Farouk regarded his acquisition carefully. Farouk bade him drop to his knees. He took Nico's chin in his hand and turned his head from side to side, trying to peer past the grime and the bruises. Nico chanced a look into his new master's eyes, hoping at least to find no malice there. Farouk's eyes told him nothing.

"What is your name, child?" Farouk spoke in Italian.

"Nicolo Borg. I am called Nico."

"If you wish to keep your tongue, Neekoh, you will address me as master," Farouk said, smiling thinly.

"Yes, master."

"Are you educated, child?"

"My sister taught me numbers, master."

"Your sister! A girl who knows numbers! Is she here?"

"She is . . . home, master. In Malta."

"A pity. Can you write, then?"

"No, master. I have no need of writing. I can remember."

El Hadji Farouk seemed amused. "What can you remember better than writing?"

"Everything, master."

"Is this so? Numbers? Names?"

"Yes, master."

El Hadji Farouk's eyes flickered with interest. "An idle boast can be a very dangerous thing." He had a whispered but animated conversation with the auctioneer, who chuckled and turned to pass instructions to Farouk's scribe, who sat behind them.

"Tell me, Nicolo Borg," Farouk said. "Do you fear your God?"

"Yes, master."

"Do you fear me?"

Nico took a deep breath, wondering which way to answer. "No, master," he said at length.

"Then perhaps you are not so bright as I judged." Farouk leaned forward, intent. "What can you remember better than writing?" he asked again.

"Everything, master," Nico repeated.

"You speak Italian. What other languages?"

"Only Maltese, master, and a little Spanish."

"Arabic?"

"No, master."

"Then you had better listen carefully." He rattled off a series of numbers in Arabic, completely at random. "*Ashara, talehta, sifr, khamsa, sittaashar, ishreen, talateen, itnaashar . . .*" There were more than twenty numbers in all, spoken clearly but quickly. The scribe copied them down as he spoke.

El Hadji Farouk regarded Nico carefully. "Did you hear me well?"

"Yes, master."

"Can you repeat them back to me?"

"Yes, master."

"In the order I gave them?"

"Yes, master."

Farouk had another murmured discussion with the auctioneer. They chuckled together and seemed to conclude some agreement. The auctioneer snapped his fingers, and the guard standing beside the canopy stepped forward. He drew a great scimitar from his sash, the blade flashing in the sun, and stood ready.

Farouk spoke again. "Now, Nico, I want you to repeat the numbers as I said them. But before you begin, let me heighten your interest by telling you of the little wager I have made with my good friend, the esteemed thief who serves as auctioneer. If you fail, as he seems certain you must, I will pay double for you. In exchange for the expense and my natural disappointment, your body will be quartered. Your head will be hung just there, until the crows have finished with your eyes." He waved toward the masonry arch above the gate. Embedded in the keystone there, casting a long shadow down the wall, was a sharpened iron hook. The iron was caked with corrosion, the color of old blood.

Nico stared at the hook and absorbed the words, and the color left his face. He found it difficult to breathe, and fought back a wave of dizziness and nausea. His temples throbbed, and his heart drummed like thunder. He couldn't think of a single word El Hadji Farouk had just uttered. All the words ran together into a stream of nonsense that evaporated in the hot desert of his fear.

"A regrettable waste of such a fine boy, I think we all agree," Farouk continued. "But if you succeed, as I believe you will, then you will remain in one exquisite piece, and I will pay nothing." His eyes gleamed. "A good sport, don't you think, Nico?"

The courtyard buzzed as merchants and money changers overheard the stakes. A pile of money soon grew on a cloth thrown at Nico's feet as others joined the wager. From all over the Bedestan people came to watch. An elderly man scolded them for gambling, which, he reminded them in a shrill voice, was strictly forbidden by the holy book. El Hadji Farouk gravely pondered that. The others awaited his verdict, as he was the only one among them who had made the pilgrimage to Mecca. Finally he proposed that a tenth of all bets be delivered to the mosque as *zakat,* a purification payment that would render the rest of the wager religiously pure. A satisfied murmur arose at the ingenious solution. The betting resumed unabated.

The object of their game knelt naked and terrified, appalled by his own casual boastfulness. He tried to calm himself, to think. He took deep breaths. His heart slowed a little, and his head cleared.

El Hadji Farouk settled on his cushion and sipped his drink. When the last bet was placed, he nodded at Nico to begin.

Nico closed his eyes, concentrating. He stumbled a little over the pronunciation. *"Ashara, talehta, sifr . . ."* The scribe scribbled on his paper at each word, ticking off his answers.

Nico stopped once, and the courtyard fell deathly silent. The auctioneer smiled confidently, prepared to collect his modest winnings. The guard took the handle of his scimitar in both hands and rose on the balls of his feet, awaiting the order.

Slowly, carefully, Nico resumed his recitation. *"Talateen, itnaashar, khamseen, 'al feyn . . ."*

The last few words were drawn out, as if Nico seemed to fear stumbling. And then he was finished.

Holding his breath, he opened his eyes.

Farouk looked at his scribe, whose face bore an astonished look. The auctioneer's expression fell to blackness. Farouk beamed; Nico's knees went weak with relief. There were shouts and laughter as the observers in the courtyard pondered the minor miracle they had just witnessed. Bets were settled and men shook their heads in wonder.

"Tell me, Nico . . . ," Farouk said with a mischievous look.

Once again the courtyard became hushed.

Nico looked up, dreading what might be next. "Master?"

"Can you do it backward?"

Nico felt the blood rush at his temples. He didn't know what to say.

"I await your answer," Farouk said levelly.

"I think so, master," Nico replied hesitantly. "But I would rather you not bet on it."

Farouk roared with laughter. "Well said. No wager, then. Try anyway."

Nico closed his eyes. He summoned up the words in his head and said them backward. He reversed two. A few of the spectators hooted when the scribe announced his lapse, and they shouted grisly suggestions for punishment. But El Hadji Farouk was finished with his sport and well satisfied with his acquisition. He passed a purse to the auctioneer. Despite the outcome of the bet, Farouk still had to cover tribute to the Bey, who, if he wished, could match any bid and keep the boy for himself. Farouk had no intention of letting that happen.

As Farouk rose to leave, the auctioneer kissed his hand and uttered a stream of blessings upon his person and his house. Farouk addressed Nico once again. "This is my son, Yusuf," he said, indicating a dour man with a pockmarked face. Yusuf was the largest, hairiest person Nico had ever seen. He wore a sleeveless vest, beneath which dark patches of hair sprouted from his massive arms, back, and chest. "In my absence he is master of my shipyard and majordomo of my house. Obey him in all things as you would obey me. I depart now for Tunis and will be gone some months. In the meanwhile learn well what Yusuf has to teach you."

"Yes, master." Nico didn't know whether to bow, but Farouk turned away from him and had a quiet conversation with his son. Nico felt their attention on him as they talked, and he saw Yusuf nod repeatedly at his father's instructions. After Farouk departed, Yusuf brusquely ordered Nico to get dressed. They walked quickly through the streets, Yusuf with long, sure strides, Nico half running to keep up. Nico had seen other slaves in chains, but evidently this was not to be his lot with El Hadji Farouk. He felt almost free, hiking unfettered behind a man who paid him no mind. He thought about running away, something that seemed not even a remote possibility to Yusuf. Just then Nico saw a man who might have been a guard or a soldier. He stood near the souk, imperious and proud, a white felt bonnet on his head, a long sword at his side. He glanced at Nico with the same cold indifference he might reserve for a bit of dirt on his red leather boots. Nico thought of the heads impaled above the city gate and of his own narrow escape from the same fate. He decided to run away later, when he knew more. He hurried to catch up.

"What am I to do?" he asked Yusuf.

"Obey," said Yusuf over his shoulder.

"Yes, but what else? What are my duties?"

"It is my father's wish that you learn the skills of the household and something of the shipyard. If you prove adept, you may accompany him on his many travels as his *garzóne*."

"What is a *garzóne?*"

"You will pour his coffee and tend his needs. Keep his sheets warm and his blood hot. Do it well and you will serve him many years. He may even free you. Fail and—enough questions. We have arrived. No one enters the house of Farouk who smells as you do."

They entered a domed building. Yusuf gave instructions to an attendant, who led Nico down a corridor, past rooms that billowed steam. He heard the splash of water and the echo of voices. He had no idea what purpose the building might serve. But when he was stripped naked and plunged into a steaming pool, he was certain Yusuf's orders had been to boil him alive. The water was scalding on his delicate skin, a matter made worse by a surly attendant who scrubbed him with an abrasive cloth, apparently determined to remove his hide altogether. Afterward he was rinsed in ice-cold water. He was relieved to be done with the ordeal. He'd heard of the dangers of washing, well known to cause sickness. Surely a cleansing this thorough would strike him dead with the pox.

He found a pile of fresh clothing next to his own. In a panic he felt in his old pants and retrieved Maria's coin, relieved to find it was still there. Next time he'd remember to put it in his mouth. He donned the baggy white pants and a collarless blue shirt that signified his status as a Christian slave in an important household. It was the most elegant clothing he had ever worn. The attendant wrinkled his nose as he picked up Nico's old rags, handling them as he might a pile of dung, and pitched them into a box.

The house of El Hadji Farouk was magnificent. It was larger and more sumptuous than the severe stone mansions of Malta's nobles in Mdina. It was situated close to the harbor, just up the hill from Farouk's shipyard. They entered through a wrought-iron gate guarded by an immense, muscular blackamoor, across whose massive shoulders there rested a great sword. "He is Abbas," Yusuf said. "A mute. Fail in your duties and it is his sword that will cleave your head from your shoulders." Nico smiled at Abbas, whose face remained cold, as if chiseled from stone.

They passed through the vestibule, and Nico's eyes went wide at the splendor. Colorful Turkish carpets hung on whitewashed walls. The floors were cool marble, strewn with fat cushions. Charcoal braziers stood at regular intervals. The house was arranged around a large courtyard. A fountain bubbled in the center, almost hidden by lush, fragrant gardens. Brightly plumed birds swooped between tall palms. Various rooms fed off the colonnaded walkway that ran around the perimeter of the courtyard. The kitchen was in the rear, brass and copper vessels stacked high on either side of the door. The rich aroma of roast mutton filled the air.

Nico couldn't suppress a smile. Baba might have betrayed him, but perhaps the betrayed would have the last laugh. He had fallen directly into the lap of luxury.

It was a busy household. A dozen servants bustled about, greeting Yusuf deferentially and looking at Nico with friendly curiosity. A young man emerged from the kitchen. He was good-looking, perhaps sixteen or seventeen, and a full head taller than Nico. He was lean but muscular, his skin dark, his features Roman. His features darkened as he listened to Yusuf's whispered instructions, until he was looking with undisguised hostility at Nico.

"This is Mehmet," Yusuf said to Nico. "In this household his word is mine. You will obey him as you obey me." That was the second time in an hour Nico had heard those words; with a staff this large he guessed he'd soon be reporting to the cook's dog. Before long he learned that the dog would have been a happier choice than Mehmet.

"Come with me," Mehmet said coldly. "There is work to be done."

"Are you a slave, too?" Nico asked.

"I am your master," Mehmet said. "That is all you need know."

For the rest of the afternoon Nico scrubbed walkways, hauled slop from the latrine, and lugged heavy rugs outdoors, where he beat them with a heavy board. Mehmet scolded him at every turn, complaining he was too slow, too weak, or too stupid to do the work properly. Nico worked even harder, his face streaked with dust and sweat. It was past dark when he finished the last of the rugs. His arms ached and he was weak from hunger.

"It is time to clear away the dinner plates," Mehmet said. "The mistress has finished her meal." He led Nico across the courtyard and into the family quarters. Soft strains of music sounded from behind a doorway draped with a Persian carpet. Mehmet lifted the drape and called quietly within, to announce his presence. He stepped inside, Nico just behind. They stood in a dining room lit by tallow lamps hung in wall sconces. The floor was thick with carpets. The room smelled of myrrh, burning in cones in the corners, and of rich food, still heaped in bowls on low trays.

El Hadji Farouk's principal wife, Ameerah, sat on a cushion, listening to a girl play the lute. Ameerah wore a jeweled scarf and a veil of white silk, but now the veil hung at her shoulder. She was bare-faced. Three other women, Farouk's younger wives, sat in order of their age at Ameerah's side. They, too, were unveiled. They looked at Nico fleetingly, then cast their eyes down and giggled amongst themselves. The youngest was thirteen.

"Allah's blessings, madam," Mehmet said, bowing.

"Who is this with you, Mehmet?" Ameerah asked, looking with interest at Nico.

"A Maltese, madam. He is called Nico. The master purchased him today at market."

"Ah, the boy who remembers. Already I have heard of it from no fewer than four eyewitnesses. Your feat, Nico, began the day as a whisper and ended as a whirlwind. At the first telling there were twenty numbers. By the last there were a hundred, and three suras of the Koran. Certainly the stuff of legend. Come here, child." She spoke in the pidgin tongue Nico had heard earlier, and he had no difficulty understanding her.

He approached her shyly, blushing and hoping desperately she wasn't going to ask him to remove his clothing, as everyone else in Algiers seemed to do. She did not raise herself from her pillow but touched his pant leg and bade him kneel. She studied his face and touched his hair. He tried not to look at her, but she moved his head until he had no choice. She was not pretty, but she fascinated him. She was a bit plump and looked very soft. She seemed about the same age as his mother, but she certainly didn't look at him with his mother's eyes. Her manner was friendly, but there was something more in her expression, something Nico couldn't read. Her eyelids were darkened with kohl, her hair reddened with henna and tied with scarlet ribbons. Rubies adorned her ears. Her clothing, like her husband's, was luxurious.

Ameerah sighed. "Such a pretty thing! I can see he did not buy you for your memory, but rather as more fruit for his loins. Would that my husband showed the smallest measure of passion for me that he devotes to scripture and his boys." Her complaint seemed good-natured, and the other wives all laughed. "Perhaps one day soon, Nico, you can give me a demonstration of your skills," she said.

"*Sì,* master," he replied in Spanish.

There were more giggles. Ameerah smiled. "Some may think me master in this house," she said, "but you may address me as madam."

"Yes, madam." At Mehmet's prodding, Nico stood and began clearing the trays. The plates and bowls were still heaped with leftover food: couscous and mutton, bread, onions, and fruit. Nico's stomach rumbled with anticipation as his eyes devoured the feast. There had been plenty to drink all day, the water even freshened with herbs, but nothing at all to eat. It seemed forever since he'd had a solid meal. He bent to pick up the first tray. As he straightened up he tripped over Mehmet's foot. He fell to the ground, spilling food everywhere. Nico reddened with shame. He was certain Mehmet had tripped him on purpose, but he dared give no sign of it. He busied himself cleaning up the mess.

"My apologies, madam," Mehmet said. "Despite his prowess with numbers, this one is quite clumsy. It is all he can do to worry the dirt from a carpet with a paddle. Without doubt he'll be gone within a fortnight. I'll transfer him to the stables, where he can do less harm."

"You'll do no such thing. Tomorrow I would like him to fetch my morning bread. Surely he can handle that."

Mehmet's eyes flashed, but he nodded and gave a light bow. "Of course, madam."

They carried the trays to the rear of the house, Nico's nose deliciously close to the bowls. He expected they would go to the kitchen, but Mehmet led him to an alley behind the house. To Nico's horror Mehmet began dumping the food into the street, one bowl at a time. Goats and beggars stood ready to joust in what was apparently a nightly ritual, and between them they made short work of the banquet.

"I am very hungry," Nico said, looking wistfully at the disappearing bounty. "Is there something for me to eat?"

"You are a slave in the household of El Hadji Farouk," Mehmet said. "Until you are here two years, that time in which you are most likely to die of disease or be put to death for displeasing the master, you are not worth feeding. Your work is done for the day. You may go into the town, where you will find food."

"How will I do that?"

"That is up to you. Surely a boy so clever with numbers can find himself something to eat. Here. This is where you sleep. Be ready for work at the cock's first crow." With that, Mehmet left him.

The room dashed Nico's illusions about luxurious surroundings. His quarters consisted of a flat-roofed shed behind the compound. It was too low to stand in. In Birgu, such a dank and smelly dwelling would have been the donkey's. There were eight other occupants in the shed, living in filthy straw: seven chickens, and a gardener Nico had seen earlier in the day. He was a Sudanese, and despite his russet skin and perfect teeth, he was the ugliest man Nico had ever seen.

One ear stood straight out from his head, while the other appeared to have been hacked off with a rough blade some years earlier. His hair was prickly and grew in patches, like brambles. His eyes were too large, his nose too small. His smile lit the room like a lamp. He greeted Nico enthusiastically. "Welcome," he said, touching his forehead, then his heart. "You can make your bed over there. We could turn out the chickens, except the cock chases the rats away. You can change the straw for new if you like, but you must walk to the market outside Bab el-Oued to do so, and then you must pay for it yourself. Have you any money?"

"No."

"A pity. It is hard to come by."

"Not as hard as food, I think. Please, master, do you have something to eat?"

The gardener grinned. "You must call me Ibi. I am not your master, but it is your good fortune that I *am* master of the evening meal. We'll go to the souk together."

"They don't feed you, either?"

"No. They keep me because the soil I touch sprouts roses, where only weeds grew before," he said. "Beauty spawned by ugliness. I count my blessings they don't kill me."

Nico found Ibi to be a wellspring of useful information. Nico brimmed with questions, but one in particular. "Does Mehmet hate everyone?" he asked.

"Nearly so," Ibi said, "but he is particularly jealous of you. Word of your trick with numbers in the Bedestan preceded you to the household. Already there is talk that you will replace him."

"Replace him? How can that be? I mean him no harm."

"It is not your intent he fears," Ibi said, "but your beauty. He has long been the master's *garzóne*. Now Mehmet grows long in the tooth. He is no longer a boy, and he must see his charms fading. Neither is he clever in the head, like you. You make him tremble for his position. Is this so difficult to understand? You must be very careful. You'll need to be very clever—and very lucky—to become *garzóne*."

Nico looked at him quizzically. "I have heard that word several times now but still don't know its meaning," he said.

Ibi laughed not unkindly at his innocence, and in terms that Nico could understand graphically explained a *garzóne*'s primary duty.

Nico's eyes grew wide and his blood ran cold. His experience in such matters ran only to watching dogs in the street, locked together in what seemed a lengthy and uncomfortable union. "Does it hurt?" he finally asked, his voice a whisper.

Ibi tilted his head. "I confess I don't know," he admitted ruefully. "My face is not pleasing to the eye, and neither man nor woman can but turn away at the sight of me. But surely not, I think, for so many do it."

"Well, *I* won't need to," Nico said confidently. "Before the master returns, the Knights of St. John will come for me, and they'll take me home. My sister will make them."

Ibi smiled. "I am certain of it," he said gently, "but until then you would be wise to do everything in your power to please your master. You are lucky to be bought by such a powerful man, if cursed to be bought by such a cruel one. If you please him in his bed, he will guard you more jealously than his own wives. On feast days he will parade you through the city in clothing fit for a bey, so that other men may see his good fortune, and be jealous. If you also manage to please him by learning the affairs of his shipyard, you will have importance in his house. You will travel where he travels, eat what he eats. There is no better life for a slave. And then, in Marseilles or Venice, if by chance your knights have not yet managed to free you, perhaps you will have the opportunity to make your own way home."

"And if I fail?" Nico asked.

"Our master has many moods. He may flay the front half of a slave while setting the back half free. You are beautiful, so perhaps your end will be better than the others. Still, an end it will be. If he is angry, he may have you tied behind an ass and dragged through the streets for sport, until what's left of you sickens even the dogs. He is endlessly creative when it comes to punishment. When I first arrived and began cultivating the gardens, a Greek mason displeased him while constructing a garden wall. The man was buried alive, face up, with only his nose showing for the six days he lived. The master had me plant an olive seed in each nostril before I laid down the last portion of soil, so that one day he might enjoy Greek olives. He laughed at his cleverness for a week. The rest of us laughed with him, out of fear we might inspire another planting.

"You must be very careful, Nico. This house is full of jealousy and intrigue. The master sleeps with everything, it is said, even a sheep, while the mistress cuckolds him under his very nose. She carries more influence than is fitting for a woman. It is said she has the passions of a rabbit and the cunning of a cobra. Everyone fears her anger, which is almost as dangerous as her husband's. Slaves are sold or put to death at her whim. I am often thankful I have the face of a beast and a gift with flowers, for everyone leaves me in peace. I do not envy you your looks, which I fear will be more a burden to you than a blessing. Mehmet will try to betray you, while the mistress will try to seduce you. If Mehmet succeeds, you could end in ruin. If the mistress succeeds and you are caught, you'll lose your head."

"Caught doing what? And what is 'seduce'?"

Ibi laughed and shook his head. "For a child with such a mind as you are said to possess," he said, "I believe you are as ignorant as the soil that holds my roses."

❖

Their evening meal came in two courses. The first was provided by an emaciated beggar who slouched in a doorway, holding an alms cup in a bony hand. His eyes were closed, infected, and swarming with flies. "Allah's blessings," he intoned in a low singsong, "to those who remember charity." His cup was empty, but someone had left half a loaf of bread. Ibi snatched it up so deftly the beggar never noticed. He broke it in two as they walked, and handed half to Nico.

Despite his hunger, Nico accepted his share reluctantly. "But he was a beggar," he said. "And he was blind."

"All the better that he cannot see his loss," Ibi said earnestly. "Besides, his bread eats as well as a rich man's." That claim, Nico decided, was something of an exaggeration. In the dim light he saw the decayed loaf was swarming with maggots. He picked a few of them out, then gave it up as hopeless and wolfed it down.

Although it was dark, the streets were nearly as crowded as in the daytime, lit by cook fires that flickered in braziers and by a full moon that hung like a great golden pendant above the walls of the city. Despite Islamic injunctions against alcohol, the taverns were doing a brisk business, while houses of prostitution flourished beside them. "Algiers thrives equally on pain and pleasure," Ibi told him. "Even though you are a slave and a Christian, if you have money you'll be as welcome inside as the most prosperous and devout Muslim."

They stopped across an alley from one of the taverns. Ibi motioned to Nico. They melted into a darkened doorway and waited. Soldiers wandered by, singing and laughing. Slaves hurried past on their masters' business. After a time an old man emerged from the tavern. He stood unsteadily. He leaned against a wall for support and then relieved himself. He staggered across the alley and passed directly by their door. Ibi sprang from the darkness and tripped him, propelling him into the shadows of the doorway. By the time he hit the ground, Ibi had his purse and was sprinting down the street. Startled by the suddenness of it all, Nico hesitated. The man rolled over and caught the leg of Nico's trouser. Nico tore free of his grip and jumped over him, racing after Ibi, leaving the victim shaking his fist and hurling the imprecations of a vengeful God upon his assailants. The two slaves darted through the crowd, rounding a corner where they paused to catch their breath. Ibi was laughing, but Nico's stomach was beginning to ache with shame. Since leaving Malta he had stolen from a woman, a boy, a blind beggar, and now a drunken old man. Nico's thoughts ranged from the gallows in Birgu, where thieves were hanged, to the heads adorning the wall by the gate of Algiers, whose crimes he could only imagine. And there was the matter of his immortal soul. In his head he could hear the damnation of Father Salvago. "It's a sin to steal, Ibi," Nico said. "And a crime! What if someone had seen us?"

Ibi scoffed. "Did you not see the yellow band he wore? He was only a Jew, so there is no crime. By day he will steal from you in the marketplace. By night you will steal from him in the street. It is an arrangement honored by all. No one will protect him. Besides, you are in no position to be particular. Some nights your dinner will come from a wealthy merchant. Other nights it will come from a child. Some nights you will go hungry, while others you will feast like the sultan. Last week I had a whole chicken. I stole it from a whore, who stole it from a sailor, who stole it from the souk. You have a choice, my young friend. Either you will grow up quickly in the ways of the world, or you will grow up not at all."

Nico was too hungry to argue the point, and besides, he wasn't sure of himself anymore. Perhaps Ibi was right: unless he wanted to simply give up and die, the rules he'd learned at home would not work here. He'd learned that on the ship, and from Baba, and now in the streets of Algiers. The only thing he owned were his wits. If he was going to survive, he needed to start using them—damnation or no.

The Jew's purse had only a few aspers in it, but it was enough to buy two brochettes of lamb and a handful of olives. The juicy meat slid easily from the cedar skewer into Nico's mouth. He nearly cried from the pleasure. After he was done he licked the skewer, then chewed and sucked it until it splintered. He wanted to take more time with the olives, to savor each one, but hunger prevailed and he swallowed them in one gulp.

That night, nestled in his straw bed, Nico thought of Ibi's graphic descriptions of a *garzóne*'s functions. He slipped his hand beneath his trousers and touched himself. It was not much more than a bean. It served well enough for pissing, but nothing more. He couldn't fathom the interest in it. His hand slipped around to his backside, and he touched himself there. He'd never even put a finger inside.

He was a long time going to sleep.

Chapter 6

Nico was awakened by blows to his feet. He leapt from his nest of straw, yelping in pain. Mehmet stood in the darkness, holding a cudgel. "The cocks have crowed and Allah has received His morning adulation, and still you sleep like the dead," he said. "Now fetch bread for the mistress, and be quick about it." He gave Nico some coins, a cloth in which to carry the loaves, and directions to the bakery. "Return before the light of the rising sun strikes the minaret, or you'll bemoan the day you were born. The madam has no taste for cold bread."

Nico followed Mehmet's instructions precisely, but they led him nowhere near a bakery. He was at the city wall near the Bab el-Oued by the time he realized Mehmet's treachery. Timidly he asked directions of a shopkeeper, who brusquely waved him down a narrow lane. There was no bakery. Nico consulted a water seller, who sent him back the way he'd come. The quarter was a bewildering maze, and all the streets looked alike. He became hopelessly lost. Above the city he saw the sun lighting the battlements of the kasbah and knew it would not be long before the mosque near his house felt its rays. He didn't know what to do. He was still looking up at the hillside when he inadvertently walked on a merchant's spices, arrayed in neat piles on a blanket. The man jumped to his feet and began pummeling the stupid boy. Nico ran away, only to be nearly trampled by a pack of camels emerging from an alley on their way to the meat market. He flattened himself against the wall as they brushed against him. His stomach knotted, and he felt his eyes welling with tears. Angrily he pushed them away. *I am not a child!* He pestered everyone he saw until finally a fellow slave showed him the way.

He was so late the dawn loaves were already cool. There was nothing he could do about that. He hurried up the hill, the aroma overpowering. He opened the cloth and turned a loaf over, thinking he might peel back a bit of crust and nip a piece of the soft bread from within. He knew it would have to be done carefully. Because he was already so late, he dared not take the time. It was the only good luck he had that day.

Mehmet was waiting next to Abbas at the gate. He cuffed Nico on the ears and berated him for laziness and stupidity. He examined the loaves carefully, seeming disappointed that they were untouched, and incensed that they were no longer hot. "The mistress has already demanded your whereabouts. You'll have five lashes for tardiness," he said, making a sign to Abbas. Before Nico knew it his shirt had been yanked down around his arms and he was forced against the wall. The blackamoor was mercifully swift. His blows fell like lightning, raising bloody welts. Nico whimpered. His father's belt never carried such fire as this.

"Such is Allah's wage for sloth," said Mehmet. "Now quit your whining before your wages increase, *walahi*. Get dressed and take the bread to the mistress. Stop in the kitchen for honey and milk. Quickly!"

If Ameerah was the least concerned about his tardiness, she gave no sign of it. She was still in her bedchamber, reclining on her pillows. Smiling, she beckoned him enter. Stiffly he crossed the room and set the tray near her pillow. His shirt rubbed against his back, making every movement painful. "What is the matter?" she asked. "Are you ill?"

"It is nothing, madam," Nico said. "I hurt my back, that's all."

"Turn around." She noticed the flecks of blood on his shirt. "Remove your shirt."

His fingers worked nervously at the buttons. He heard the soft rustle of robes and felt her presence behind him as she stood. The touch of her fingers on his back startled him. "Mehmet is treating you harshly, I think?"

Nico was unsure how to respond. He thought it possible Mehmet was listening at the door, and in any event knew that he had no standing in the household. "It is my fault, madam," was all he could think to say. "He is impatient with me because I am stupid and coarse and slow to learn the ways of this house."

"Such an answer proves you are far more clever than you make out," she replied. "Still, you need fear Mehmet no more today. I asked him to leave us alone. Perhaps I can help bring you along in ways that are pleasing to our master. But first I must tend your skin." She dipped a piece of gossamer silk into a bowl of water and dabbed at his scarlet weals. He winced, but her touch was soothing. "Turn around," she said when she finished.

She was standing quite close. He looked up at her. "You've been crying, too, I see," she said. Once again her concern reminded him of his mother. Once again she tended him in a very different way. She wiped at the traces of his dried tears. "You have the eyes of a doe," she said. "Your lashes are long, almost like a girl's." He stiffened at that, and she laughed brightly. "You should not take offense at well-meant words. Those eyes will serve you well if you learn how to use them." She ran her fingers down his cheek and raised his chin so that her lips were close to his own. He could smell her scent and feel her breath and the pounding of his own heart. He was exquisitely uncomfortable in her presence. Ibi's warnings were fresh in his mind about the dangers of being alone in a room with the wife of El Hadji Farouk. He had no choice, however, but to take her lead.

"I am hungry," Ameerah said. With relief Nico moved to serve her. At her bidding he cut a thick slice from the bread, then used a wooden ladle to apply the honey. As he handed her the bread she got honey on her fingers. She licked it off slowly, then took him by the hand. She dipped his fingers into the honey, and then, to his utter surprise, she licked his fingers one at a time, drawing her tongue over his hand slowly, delicately, holding his eyes with her own. Though it tickled him, something told him laughter was not the response she sought to her extraordinary behavior. He wasn't sure what to do to please her. He took her hand and put her fingers in his own mouth. It seemed to be exactly what she wanted. For a long moment her eyes closed, and he thought she moaned. He withdrew his hand quickly. "Did I hurt you, madam?"

She saw his concern and smiled. "Only with pleasure," she said. "The master will be well pleased." She let go of his hand, and the moment passed. She settled herself on her cushions and bade him sit. "Show me a remembering trick." She told him the names of her uncles, aunts, and cousins, and clapped when he recited them back flawlessly. Though she could not read, Ameerah had learned several complete suras of the Koran. It had taken her years of practice. She recited a few verses to Nico, who repeated them instantly. "If you were not such an innocent boy and these verses were not holy," she said, "I would think you a sorcerer and have your tongue removed from your head." Nico couldn't tell if she was joking. He thought not.

They played such games for an hour, until she said it was time for him to leave. She saw his look of longing at what remained of the bread, and gave him a fat chunk, dipped in honey.

Mehmet was waiting outside the door and snatched the bread from Nico's hands. "You know you are forbidden to eat this."

"But the mistress gave it to me!"

"And I have taken it away. For your disobedience you will not leave the house to find food tonight. If you complain to anyone, you will earn another beating."

❖

One morning Yusuf told Nico that in accordance with El Hadji Farouk's instructions, it was time that Nico learn about the building of ships. Farouk's shipyard, the largest on the Barbary Coast, built galleys for any corsairs or merchants who could afford them.

"What must I do there, master?" asked Nico.

"Observe," said Yusuf, without further explanation. Nico could scarcely believe his luck at having such an easy task. Glad of any excuse to be away from Mehmet, he intended to learn whatever he could, and perhaps find some means of escape.

Yusuf ran the shipyards from a shed situated near the city gate, where he spent most days with papers and records. The true master of the yards, however, was Leonardus, the shipwright. Yusuf had him brought to the shed and explained in the pidgin Moorish dialect what he wanted. "The boy is to learn about galley construction," he said. "He is not to leave your side."

Leonardus was a robust, energetic man with a full gray beard, jet-black hair, and eyes that, despite being reddened by alcohol, carried a hint of violence. He flashed an engaging smile, bowed lightly at Yusuf, and to Nico's astonishment launched into Maltese, not a word of which Yusuf understood. "I'm hung over and need a whore, and you, you fat worm, you thieving asshole of a swine, you bring me a snot-nosed child and want him to learn how to build *ships?* Why not bring me a dog, too, and let me teach it to sail? You think this is as simple as dipping your wick in another man's behind, eh?"

And then, his mien ever polite, Leonardus switched smoothly into the pidgin, giving a slight bow to Yusuf. "It shall be my very great honor and pleasure, effendi," he said. Yusuf's expression had darkened as Leonardus spoke in Maltese. It was clear he suspected the insult, but he only nodded dismissively, and waved them out of the shed.

"*Jien miniex mahmug!*" Nico said indignantly in Maltese after they left. "I am not snot-nosed!"

Leonardus regarded him with surprise and delight. "But you *are* a child, no? I had that part of it right. By the blessed teats of the Holy Virgin, you are from Malta?"

"Birgu, sir."

"Sweet balls of Christ, there's two of us now!" He gestured at the workers milling about the yard. "The rest of these swine are Spanish and French, more stupid than the wood they work. And that one"— he gestured toward Yusuf—"his mother delivered him from the wrong hole. I'll cut his throat one day."

"Excuse me, sir, but isn't it dangerous to say those things you did to his face? What if he understood?"

"That poxy bastard is a sadistic one, but he's got bilgewater for brains. He hurt me once, true enough, but his God-cursed heathen father will not let him touch another hair on my pretty head," he said. "They need me too much. They can't build their own ships the way I can. They've never learned my secrets, and they never will, by God." He pulled a flask from his belt and opened it. "Anyway, it's good to have a fellow slave from our poor little rock in the sea, even if he does lack whiskers." He took a long drink and passed it to Nico. Nico hesitated but was determined to prove himself. The fire burned all the way down his throat. He coughed and his face turned bright red. Leonardus laughed and slapped him on the back. "Well done, lad. You'll do fine at my side. We'll have hair on those balls in no time."

For the rest of the day Nico trailed the big man like a puppy, delighted to have someone from home to talk with, and Leonardus didn't seem to mind his endless questions. Leonardus was a slave himself. He had been a sailor on a Maltese merchant vessel, but in Venice he found work with Vettor Fausto, a renowned master shipwright. He worked in the carpenter's guild and eventually became a master himself. In time he returned to Malta to begin building his own ships. His future seemed secure. One week before he was to be married he had taken a galley, the first built in his own yard, out for brief sea trials. His ship was captured off Sicily by the corsair Barbarossa. "It was my own blunder," he said, "an error of design. I had the gearing wrong. The outriggers were a hair too close to the hull and the thole pins too far aft. She couldn't turn as neatly as that crafty red-bearded son of a whore, and he took me without a shot. It served me right; I was hoist on my own petard. It wouldn't happen today, I'll tell you that. My ships turn second to none."

Leonardus spent the next two years chained to the oar, an experience that nearly drove him mad. He once tried to kill himself during a fierce sea battle, when his vessel was locked in mortal combat with a Spanish galley. He stood at his oar, thrusting himself between a Spaniard with an arquebus and the captain of his own galley, intending to eat the shot and end his misery. To his everlasting regret, Leonardus ended up saving the captain's life, while himself being only wounded in the shoulder. That winter, recuperating in Algiers, he leapt at the chance to escape the oar for good by demonstrating his shipbuilding skills. Barbarossa had been named *kapudan-i-deryâ*, admiral of the sea, by Suleiman, the Ottoman Sultan who was determined to wrest control of the Mediterranean from the Christians. The new admiral was only too glad to place Leonardus in the service of Farouk, from whom he bought his ships.

Leonardus learned that his skills were a mixed blessing. Master shipwrights were priceless, their tricks as mysterious and closely guarded as any sorcerer's. Though he would never be killed, neither would he ever be ransomed or freed. He would die a slave, building ships for his blood enemies for use against his own Christian brothers. "I wish I'd died at the oar," Leonardus said.

After many attempts to escape, he now spent each night chained inside a shed in the shipyard. He always had plenty of alcohol, and four or five times a month his guards brought him a whore from the city. It was an extraordinary acknowledgment of the shipwright's value.

"Well," Nico said, "I'm going to escape. And when I do, you can come with me."

Leonardus laughed. "I'll be there, captain," he said. "But don't fail. You'll see why tonight. For now, we have work to do."

Leonardus supervised an army of workmen, and despite the amount of alcohol he consumed, he moved quickly from one end of the shipyard to the other, worrying over every detail. The shipyard was vast and busy, its crews engaged in a score of different tasks. There were five galleys in various stages of construction, laid out next to each other on slipways that rose gently from the harbor. Three of the galleys were new. The first one's ribs were in place, so that the ship looked like the rotting skeleton of a beached fish. Another already had its planking, and men swarmed over the hull, working on the superstructure. Carpenters drove bronze nails and fitted dowels, while caulkers filled seams with oakum, a loose hemp that was impregnated with tar. Other workers greased the hull with a mixture of tar and heated wax that would help the vessel glide through the water and also resist the teredo worm, which otherwise would turn an unprotected hull into a weak honeycomb. "On the first two ships I built here, I saw to it that a place was left unprotected on the hull. I hid it from these thick-headed bastards by using colored wax but no tar. The worms did their work and the galleys were ruined," Leonardus said. "But then Dragut Raïs caught me. He was the only one of the lot cunning enough to understand what I'd done."

"What did they do?"

Leonardus removed a boot. He had only two toes: the big one and the little one. "The other foot is the same," Leonardus said. "Yusuf, that hairy toad who brought you to me, cut them from me one joint at a time. He took two days with a dull blade for each toe. He told me that from then on, I would continue to be able to walk only as well as my ships continued to float. Now my ships float perfectly. I haven't lost a toe since."

There were two other ships in the yard, large galleys that had been captured from the Spanish. They were not being refitted or repaired, but completely dismantled, and then the materials were reassembled into new ships that were smaller, lighter, and much faster than before, the way the corsairs preferred. "In that, God curse them, they are right," Leonardus said. "Only the Spaniards would make ships as fat as their women. They're both too broad at the beam, but sailing one will only make her husband unhappy, while sailing the other will get you killed." Every piece of the ship was carefully marked and set aside, then trimmed to the desired shape. With care and a few extra loads of timber, three ships could be made from two.

Foremen came to him with questions about oars, masts, framework, and rigging. Leonardus seemed to know everything. His authority was absolute, his eye for perfection unwavering. He was voluble and quick-tempered, and he cursed his men in four languages. He stopped at a saw pit, over which a great log was supported on crossbeams. One man stood below ground, working one end of the saw, while another stood above, both men laboring to keep the blade true on a line that had been snapped on each side with chalk cord. To Nico the cut looked perfect, the heavy sharp teeth taking great bites from the log, the sweet-smelling dust billowing into the pit. To Leonardus, however, something looked amiss. He leapt into the saw pit and knocked the sawyer out of the way. "*Hijo de puta,*" he roared, "are you blind of the French pox, or just dim-witted? You've got it cocked!" With the sawyer on top he backed the blade off, then got it started again, working just to one side of the previous cut. When he climbed from the pit he ordered the pit foreman whipped for failing to notice what had been happening.

Nico was troubled. "You're a slave yourself," he said. "How could you have another slave punished?"

"Because they're working on my ships, by God. Go careless on me yourself, and I'll order your nose clipped."

"But they're not your ships. They belong to the enemy!"

"*Veru,*" he acknowledged with a nod, "but they're *made* by me. I don't expect you to understand, lad. There comes a time in a man's life when he has to choose between what is right and what might keep him alive. They are not always the same. The truth is, I am a coward. I don't mind if they kill me, but I loathe losing little pieces of myself. So I choose to build fine ships, keep my toes, and sail my whores." And he had another drink.

❖

That evening Nico found out what Leonardus meant about not failing in escape. All the workers were forced to assemble at one end of the shipyard, beneath a hill overlooking the harbor. Leonardus stood at the front, Nico at his side. On the hill stood a lone cypress tree to which two lengths of wood had been nailed, crossed in the shape of an X. Yusuf and three guards appeared, leading a prisoner whose ankle chains were so short he had to hop to keep up. At the clearing the prisoner was forced to his knees.

"What are they going to do?" Nico whispered.

"Not they," Leonardus said in a low voice. "Yusuf. He enjoys this too much to let someone else do it."

An eerie silence fell over the yard as Yusuf beat the man methodically, never breaking a sweat. The only sound was that of leather crop against flesh and bone, punctuated by the anguished cries of the victim. Yusuf worked carefully, gauging just how far he could go without killing the man or rendering him unconscious. When he judged he could go no further, the guards dragged the prisoner to the cross, hoisted him by the legs, and crucified him upside down. Nico stared at the man's face, barely recognizable as human. His lips were moving in prayer.

"He tried to escape last night," Leonardus said. "But he's a Frenchman—like all his countrymen, blessed by the Almighty with balls but no brains. He tied himself to a piece of planking and tried to float out of the harbor, pretty as you please. Only the planking he chose wasn't big enough to hold him. He flailed around just long enough to alert every guard in the city. He didn't even have the luck to drown. They fished him out, and now he'll hang there as a reminder. If he lives long enough, he'll escape all right, just as soon as I launch the next galley. He'll be lashed to the cutwater of the keel, beneath the ram, where he'll hang like an ornament until his bones fall into the sea. Yusuf makes me knot the ropes in front of everyone in the yard."

Leonardus took a drink from his flask and looked at Nico. "I've done it thirty-one times since I've been here. Mind yourself, lad. I don't relish doing it to you."

from ***The Histories of the Middle Sea***

by Darius, called the Preserver
Court Historian to the Master of the Abode of Felicity, the
Sultan Achmet

One cannot understand the history of the Middle Sea without under-standing something of the religious currents that swirled through that sea, currents that began as ripples on the shores of the Levant and rose from time to time into waves that threatened to engulf whole civilizations, setting man against man in the name of God.

It was not always so. In Damascus, the Church of St. John the Baptist was built on the ruins of a Roman temple. There was a reliquary inside that contained the head of the Baptist, venerated by Christian and Muslim alike. In the early days of Muslim rule, Christians prayed in that church on Sundays, Muslims on Fridays. The children of Abraham showed the world that they could live side by side, in peace.

It was not Damascus, however, but Jerusalem that was to show the way men would live—a way lit with darkness. Where was the common thread binding Muslim and Jew, Jew and Christian, woven more beautifully than in Jerusalem, the very city of God? Wherever did that thread unravel so well?

For Muslims, Jerusalem is the third holiest place, after Mecca and Medina. The pilgrimage to the Dome of the Rock and the al-Aqsa mosque completes the fifth pillar of Islam, the hajj. For Jews, the city is the ancient capital of Israel, in which rose the sacred Temple of Solomon. For Christians, it is the site of the crucifixion of their prophet Jesus, blessed be his name. In the last days of his life he entered the city from the Mount of Olives, delivered his prophesy of the fall of Jerusalem, and spent his last night praying in a garden, called Gethsemane. Near this place was built the Dome of the Rock, on the rock that supported Solomon's temple; the rock where Mohammed, blessed be his name, rose to heaven; the rock that marked the spot where Abraham—patriarch of the Hebrews, revered by Christian, Muslim, and Jew—nearly sacrificed his son Isaac.

David, the great king of the tribes of Israel, established his capital in this holy place, bringing with him the Ark of the Covenant, the chest containing the tablets of God's law given to Moses on Mount Sinai. It was to house the Ark that David's son Solomon built his temple, a temple destroyed by the Babylonians, rebuilt, and destroyed yet again by the Romans, who left only a wall. Not simply a wall, say the rabbis, but a sacred wall, from which the shekhinah, the Divine Presence, never departs. The destruction of the temple foreshadowed relations between Jews and Christians, the latter's priests declaring that it was not the Romans who killed Jesus but that line of vipers, the Jews, who, for their repudiation of Christ, were forever condemned to wander homeless.

In A.D. 336 the Emperor Constantine built the Church of the Holy Sepulchre, to mark the site where Jesus was crucified and buried. Three centuries later the church was destroyed by the Persians but was restored in time for the Muslim conquest of Jerusalem in A.D. 638—a conquest accomplished without the loss of blood. Umar, second Khalif of Islam, was taken to the church to pray but declined, fearing such use would desecrate a Christian holy site. Instead he built a great mosque of wood nearby, called al-Aqsa, to mark the spot where Mohammed (peace and blessings upon him), riding al-Buraq, a white winged steed, was brought by the angel Gabriel to pray. With Abraham, Moses, Jesus, and other prophets (peace upon them all) praying behind him, Mohammed ascended through the heavens to receive the word of Allah.

These, then, were the Rock, the Wall, and the Church that were to so divide the world.

During the first holy war, armed Christians swarmed upon Jerusalem, putting to the sword Jews in their synagogues and Muslims in their mosques. By the tens of thousands, women and children were massacred alongside husbands and fathers by the warriors of Christ, who, standing victorious in streets awash in blood, declared the Kingdom of Jerusalem.

The Christian pilgrims making the journey to the Holy Land were protected by two orders of knights, Christian monks sworn to poverty and celibacy. One, the Poor Fellow Soldiers of Jesus Christ, made their quarters in al-Aqsa, in the Temple of the Lord on the Temple Mount, and so called themselves Templars. The second order, the Hospitaller Knights of St. John of Jerusalem, ministered to the sick from a large hospice in the Patriarch's Quarter of the city, very near the Church of the Holy Sepulchre.

Jerusalem later fell to Saladin, the great Kurdish Sultan of Egypt and Syria. He took the city without slaughter and struck down the golden cross above the Dome of the Rock, raising in its place a crescent, the symbol of Islam. The two orders of knights left the city, but Saladin did not expel those Christians and Jews who wished to remain in peace, in keeping with the principle that the conquered of Islam be allowed to retain their religious laws and practices. Muslims consider Jews and Christians to be ahl al-kitab, the People of the Book, whose scriptures are based on divine revelations, and therefore sacred. Indeed, in later years the Sultan Suleiman issued a firman formally permitting the Jews to make and keep a place of prayer at their sacred wall. He was said to have purified the site himself with rosewater, and was hailed as a benefactor of Israel.

Yet there were few Jews left in Jerusalem to accept Saladin's offer to remain. Those not expelled by the Babylonians or slain in the holy wars had fled, settling in any corner of the earth that would have them. Many of those lived in Spain, remaining there until the dark years of Ferdinand and Isabella, when they were forced to leave their homes once again. Some returned to the Levant, while others fled to Holland, Morocco, and even Istanbul, where they found a favorable climate in which to practice their trades. Those who remained behind in Iberia were encouraged to convert to Catholicism. Those who refused were put to the torch, or forced to don slavery's chains.

Never in those years was the hatred between Jew and Muslim the equal of the hatred between Christian and Jew, or Christian and Muslim. But who can know the way to best measure hatred? Who can know its bounds?

—From Volume I
The Religious Conflicts

Chapter 7

M aria's life began to change forever the day the storyteller came to Birgu.

She awakened just before dawn. She was nestled on a bed of straw atop a tiny wooden platform beneath the rafters, which were so close she couldn't stand up. She drifted in and out of sleep, watching the night sky turn to morning through a hole in the roof. In the blackness she saw the Seven Sisters, the Pleiades. It was her favorite constellation, for it reminded her of a kite. She closed her eyes, dreaming that she might scamper up a string to that kite and let it carry her away. When she opened her eyes again, the stars had been swallowed by the pink dawn sky. A cloud drifted by, lit coral by the first rays of the sun. As always, her first thought was of Nico. She said a prayer for him.

She heard the familiar sounds of a Birgu morning. The brass bell of the clock tower in the square tolled seven. Cocks crowed and mules brayed. The wheels of the baker's wagon clattered along the cobblestone as the cart carried fresh bread up the hill to Fort St. Angelo. The water seller's lilting song competed with the clamor of pots and pans. Hogs snuffled and snorted as they rooted through mounds of garbage in the street. A child cried. She could hear the creaking windmills on Senglea, Birgu's small sister peninsula that cut into the Grand Harbor. There was the steely voice of Agnete, the petty old tyrant next door, yelling at either her husband or the dog. A growl sounded in return, from either her husband or the dog.

She heard her father rising, making sounds that never varied except on Sunday: the hiss of piss in the chamber pot, the scuff of leather sandals as he carried the pot over the dirt floor, and the creak of window hinges and the splash as he pitched its contents into the street. Then a dry cough and a spit, and the rattle of his tools as he hefted the leather pouch to his shoulder. The cupboard opening: he'd take a clove of garlic or an onion for breakfast, and a hunk of day-old bread for lunch. The door closed heavily behind him as he left for work.

Reluctantly she stirred from her comfort. She sat up and shook off the straw. She wanted to leave before her mother got up. Lately she tried to time it that way, to slip out of the house without seeing anyone. Once gone, she would stay away as long as possible. Life was more tolerable that way. In the weeks since Nico's kidnapping her father's beatings had eased, but his looks were still venomous. Her mother's eyes were dark pools of sorrow. The knot of guilt in Maria's belly was bad enough, but she couldn't bear being in the house with those haunted eyes a moment longer than necessary—even if the alternative was doing her chores.

There would be no chores today, however. Today she would skip them.

Today the storyteller was coming.

She crept down the ladder, carefully avoiding those crosspieces that she knew would creak. Halfway down she let go and dropped lightly to the dirt floor. She was hungry, but she passed the kitchen without stopping, fearful she'd make too much noise. She slipped out the front door, closing it softly behind her.

It was still quite early, so for a while she wandered aimlessly through the crooked streets of Birgu, already bustling with gritty commerce. Some of the passages were so narrow she had to stand sideways to make way for old men riding donkeys or vendors pushing their overloaded, creaking carts. She stepped around the puddles of night water thrown from windows. Veiled women balanced heavy loads on their heads, wicker baskets bulging with cloth and fruits and breads. In darkened doorways she could see knots of old men, gossiping together and playing draughts. She wandered along the docks, watching sailors tend rigging and sails.

At midmorning she went to the square. It would be an hour or two before he came, but she wanted to get a good seat. As she sat on the cobblestones she noticed a young woman taking a place nearby. She was the prettiest girl Maria had ever seen. Her eyes were soft and luminous. Her skin was perfect. She threw off her woolen cloak and shook her brown hair. It was shiny and hung in thick braids that fell to the small of her back. She saw Maria studying her. "Hello," she said, smiling. "You're staring. I'm Elena."

Maria blushed. "I am Maria. Maria Borg. It's just that I haven't seen you before."

"I rarely visit Birgu. More often I go to Mdina, but I would not have missed this." She waved at the growing crowd.

"Neither would I," Maria said. "I can't wait for the stories."

Elena smiled. "I can't wait for the storyteller."

"What do you mean? Is he a friend?"

"Of sorts. I've known him before. He's from Italy, you know. From Florence."

"*Florence!* Have you been there?"

"No, but someday I'll go. Someday I'll leave Malta forever. I believe I'll see Italy first. After that, I suppose I'll go to one of the north countries—England, or Brandenburg, or Bohemia. A woman there can make her own way in the world, you know." Maria listened with astonishment. Such notions were preposterous in Malta, which still had deep roots in the Dark Ages. "In Cologne there are women tailors and silk makers," Elena added. "And in Munich I could own a brewery!"

"A what?"

"A brewery. For making beer."

"What is beer?"

"A drink. A person can get very rich making it. We haven't any in Malta. There isn't *any*thing in Malta, of course. In the north countries they drink a lot of it. Why, in those countries, anything is possible. In the Netherlands even the poor have too much to eat. Breakfast of bread and butter and cheese, brought by a servant dressed in silks. Dinner of vegetables and meat pie. They pick fruit right off the streets, and there is wine in all the fountains. They eat their meals off pewter and drink from crystal goblets."

Elena acknowledged she'd never left Malta, yet she detailed the delights of Flanders and Strasbourg and Genoa and Toulon as if she'd lived in each place. Maria listened raptly. Elena said she was only fifteen, but she was already quite the most sophisticated person Maria had ever met.

Though Maria had no knowledge of exotic places to share, she was not to be outdone, revealing her dream of going to France and marrying a king. Elena accepted the pronouncement without hesitation. "What a wonderful plan," she said. "Invite me, if you please, to your wedding."

They lost track of time with such chatter, until an expectant hush fell over the crowd and someone had to lean over and quiet them.

The storyteller had arrived.

There were storytellers in Malta, of course, mostly the old men and women who repeated the folktales they'd heard themselves as children. But none held the mystique of this man, who had been all over the world, following the winds and telling his tales wherever men would pay to hear them. He would stay in one place for a few days or a week, until the next ship departed for some friendly port, and return again whenever the currents were favorable. He held court on a stool beneath the clock tower that dominated the square. His audience gathered around him in a semicircle, pressing forward intently so as not to miss a word. He captivated them from the first instant. He sang songs and told proverbs. He juggled and turned somersaults. He teased and told riddles as he strutted back and forth. Eyes twinkling, he stopped before Elena. Bowing deeply, he showed the audience that his hands were empty, then reached behind her ear and produced a flower, to cheers and thunderous applause.

He recited a long poem from memory. He told stories about horses that rode through fire, and dogs that saved the lives of their masters. Children shrieked at the tale of a dragon in the Grand

Harbor. Women tittered at the scandalous account of the man who sold his soul to the Muslim devil. Men sat spellbound by the legend of the four winds, the magician, and the magic lamp. Maria and Elena sat close together, lightly holding hands. They reacted as one to most passages, clapping and giggling and whispering to each other throughout the performance. The storyteller worked for nearly two hours. As he finished Elena leaned over to Maria. "I have to leave now. I will be here again tomorrow. Will you come?"

"Oh, yes," Maria said eagerly.

The Italian collected the meager pile of coins his audience tossed onto a cloth at his feet. As the crowd began to dissipate, Elena made her way down a side street and disappeared from view. A moment later the storyteller followed. Maria watched them leave. She assumed Elena was going to hear more stories, in private. She wished she'd been invited.

✛

The girls met again the next day and instantly carried on as if they were old friends, chattering until the storyteller arrived. This time he did something new, something remarkable. After performing his magic tricks, he opened a knapsack and withdrew a thick book, its burnt-orange covers made of leather. He opened it on his lap. Though he handled it carefully, its pages were well worn, creased and smudged from constant use. A silence fell over the square. In a soothing, deep voice, he read a knight's tale, and poetry, and stories of a land called Arabia. Not everyone understood, for the words were Italian, but no one left: people scarcely breathed. It was the first time anyone had ever read a story from a book in front of Maria, except Dun Salvago in church, who read words she didn't understand. She had no such trouble now. She understood every enthralling word.

He read eight stories in all, and he even read some on demand. "Find a story about serpents," a peasant called out. The storyteller thought a bit, turned to a certain page, and soon snakes were slithering from the book and into the crowd. "Tell us a story of love," Elena called then. The storyteller caught her gaze in a way Maria didn't understand. He thumbed to a different place, and soon a beautiful young princess stood among them in that square, and they were witness as she spurned one noble suitor after another until one day a simple peasant turned her head and they ran away together, to the terrible wrath of her father, the king. It was titillating and shocking, and for Maria an exquisite expression of her own fantasies. There were other tales of distant lands, enchanted lands, lands where rivers ran cold and blood ran hot; and tales within tales within tales. The girls hardly dared breathe as they listened. But then, when the Italian took a brief rest, they talked excitedly about what they'd heard. The stories inspired both of them to grand flights of fancy, and it became difficult to tell where their dreams ended and the tales began.

As she had the previous day, Elena whispered goodbye and slipped away just as the storyteller was finishing the afternoon's performance. Maria had her own idea and boldly approached the storyteller before he could get away. He barely glanced at her, for his eyes were on Elena, who was once again awaiting him beyond the press of the crowd.

"Are there more stories in that book?" Maria asked.

He laughed at her ignorance. "Of course. A hundred—a thousand! More than even I can remember." He opened it for her and turned it so she could see. He even let her touch a page. She did so gingerly, reverently, in much the same way as her mother handled the holy relics in their home. The touch of parchment was jarring, and she spoke impulsively. "I want to learn to do what you do," she said.

He looked at her with an air of amused condescension. "To juggle, or tell stories?"

"To read." The instant Maria said it out loud, she knew it sounded preposterous.

"Read!" He snorted, laughed, and slapped the book shut.

Maria flushed. "Yes. I could, you know."

His face was red with merriment. "I've heard of a pig could do that, but never such a one as you!" He opened the knapsack and put the book inside. "I'll use that in one of my stories! I will, I say!"

He rose to leave, still shaking his head in amusement. Despite his reaction Maria could still feel her heart racing from her brush with magic. She wanted to talk with Elena, but already her new friend had disappeared, the storyteller not far behind.

That night in her sleep Maria heard the stories again and again, heard the inflections in his voice, saw the characters in her mind. What other tales might that one book hold? What mysteries, what secrets of the world, were contained in those pages? She knew the notion was foolish and bold. It didn't really matter. By dawn there was no uncertainty left in her mind.

Later that morning she and Elena met again for the final performance, only this time when it was finished, the storyteller made quick farewells and hastened to board a Spanish ship that was bound for Sicily. The two girls watched from the quay as the ship departed the harbor. Even before it was lost to view, Maria had revealed her grand plan.

At first Elena thought it was a joke, but she quickly realized Maria was serious. "Read! Whatever for?"

"Because . . . well, *because,* that's all. Because I could open a book whenever I liked and the stories would take me away. Because I want to, I guess. Don't you want to know how?"

"Of course not! What a mad notion! Don't be silly. You're just a girl. There are better ways to spend your time. Don't waste it on idle dreams."

"Like yours, of owning a brewery?"

"But I'm going to *do* it."

"Well, so am I."

Elena smiled. "All right, then," she said. "I believe you. You can visit my brewery, and read to me. And now I must go home."

Maria realized that while she'd told Elena nearly everything there was to know about herself, she still knew very little about Elena. "Where do you live?"

"South and east of here."

"In Zejtun?" Maria asked, naming a village.

"No. Farther."

Maria frowned. "There's nothing farther than that but the sea!"

"I'll see you again," Elena promised, and she waved goodbye.

❖

A week passed with no sign of Elena. Maria went to Mdina to look for her, remembering that Elena had said she went there more often than Birgu. She quickly realized it was futile: the streets of the old walled city were crowded, most of the women veiled. One morning on her way to gather fireplace fuel, Maria asked questions in Zejtun, but to no avail. No one knew of her friend. She left the village and began walking eastward, gathering brambles. It was a chore she ordinarily performed seven days a week, sometimes twice in a day. Often she had to travel several miles to gather enough for a fire. The thorny bushes were one of the few things that grew in profusion in Malta, although in years when the droughts were bad even the brambles didn't grow. Then the Borg household had to pay to use the communal ovens. If there was no money for that, whatever food they ate was cold.

Some bushes she hacked free with a knife, while others broke by themselves at the base and tumbled along in the wind, and she had to run to catch them. It took a deft touch to avoid shredding her skin on the savage thorns. She used flat chunks of limestone, the island's other abundant resource, to crush the bushes, hurling the rocks down again and again until they were flattened. Then she'd add them to a pile that she fastened with twine and carried on her back, the bundle floating above her like a great prickly cloud, bobbing and bouncing as she trudged along.

She made her way nearly to the coast, to an area she'd never worked before. Ever mindful of corsairs, she was careful to venture only where she could see a sufficient distance to avoid being surprised by anyone. The air smelled of rain, and immense gray and black clouds were gathering over the sea. Such early summer storms were often intense but fast-moving, so she decided to keep working.

The storm was stronger than she thought. The wind picked up and she leaned against it, balancing her load carefully, her eyes stinging with grit. A gust whipped at her furiously, tugging at her load so hard she staggered. She'd made her last knot poorly, and the twine parted. The wind ripped again, and the entire load wrenched free. Maria gave a little cry: hours of work were being scattered, the brambles tumbling away faster than she could catch them. She trapped one, then another, and anchored them with stones near a carob tree. Some of the brambles were rolling and bouncing over the edge of the cliff, into the sea. She ran after them and tripped, gasping with pain as she fell. She'd gashed her knee on a rock. Big drops of rain began to pelt her, stinging her skin and mixing with her blood, and running down her leg in rivulets. The rain came in torrents, driven by wind that had grown suddenly cold and lacerating.

She made her way down a steep slope toward some rock outcroppings that faced the sea and promised shelter. She saw the mouth of a cave, one of scores that riddled the cliffs along the coast, and ducked just inside the entrance. Shivering, she dried her face on her sleeve and shook her hair. As she bent to tend to her knee she heard a noise and froze. She knew it wasn't corsairs, for she had kept a careful eye out for ships. She cocked her head and listened intently. At first the sound wasn't clear over the storm, but then she made out voices. They were speaking Maltese, not Arabic, and she heard children. She crept forward on a narrow path and peered into the cavern.

It was a huge cave. In the middle of the floor, thirty feet below her, people were gathered near a large candelabrum, their heads bowed, their voices chanting in unison, almost as if in prayer. But these were not the words of service she knew, not words like Father Salvago used at St. Agatha's. They were different words, unfamiliar words: *Baruch ata Adonai*, and *Eloheinu*, and others she could not make out. Behind them she could just make out a wall hanging that bore an image of some sort.

Her mother had spoken of devil worshipers, who were said to dwell in places such as this. The odd murmuring made her nervous, and when the people began to sing she knew she didn't want to hear any more of their secret words and evil songs. Barely breathing, she began to back away, up the slope toward the rain.

From a nook she had overlooked in the darkness, a massive arm reached out to stop her. The big man blocked the passage before she could react. She went for her knife, but her assailant saw the movement and was quicker than she. Her knife clattered away into the rocks. He caught her by her jerkin and with one arm easily lifted her from the ground, her legs kicking furiously but connecting with nothing but air. He carried her quickly inside, making his way down a steep slope. As soon as there was room he set her down and pushed her along in front of him.

The singing stopped abruptly. Maria saw anxious faces turned toward her—men, women, and even children, staring with a mixture of surprise, fear, and suspicion. Maria stopped, but the man behind her pushed again. "Look what I found," he said. "A wet pup, spying."

"How did she get in?" asked one of the men, stepping forward. He glared past Maria to her captor, who did not meet his gaze. From his manner and tone, Maria judged him to be the leader. "Why didn't you stop her outside? You were asleep, weren't you, Villano?"

"What does it matter? I caught her, didn't I?"

"Too late, it seems."

"I was not spying," Maria said. She was afraid, but she was furious, too. "I was only taking shelter from the storm. Let me go. I've done nothing." She took a step backward, as if to leave, but Villano put his big hand on her shoulder.

"Are you Christian?" the leader asked.

"Of course I am," she said indignantly. "Everyone with a soul is." She squirmed again, but Villano's grip was unbreakable.

"I'll kill her," Villano said, as matter-of-factly as he might have announced the hour. "I'll throw her off the cliff, so they'll find her with a broken neck, drowned. They'll think she fell—*if* they find her."

Maria gasped. "Why would you hurt me? I've done nothing to you! Leave me alone!"

"You saw us. That is enough."

"I don't know what you were doing, and I don't know who you are. I don't care, either. Let me out of here and I'll never come back."

The headman regarded Maria thoughtfully. A large woman stood at his side, also staring at Maria. "Do not act hastily, Fençu," she said in a low voice.

"What would you have me do, Elli?" he asked.

She fidgeted. "I don't know."

"We have no choice," said Villano. "We *must* kill her or we are all lost."

"Stop it. I know her."

Maria stared in shock as a girl stepped forward into the light. "*Elena!*"

"I met her in Birgu," Elena said to Fençu. "Her name is Maria Borg. She is the daughter of a mason."

"That may be who she is to you," Villano said, "but she is death to us. Let me kill her, I say!" His face danced in long shadows from the candles.

Elena flashed in anger. "Kill her because you fell asleep at your post? If you'd been outside doing your job, you could have chased her away or warned us. What if she'd been the *gendarmi?* We'd all be in the dungeons, or worse, because you're too lazy to stay awake."

Villano scowled. "It was raining. . . . It doesn't matter! She's seen us. She has to die."

Maria was watching Fençu. His expression made it clear that he was weighing that very possibility.

"Does she?" Elli said. "She is only a child. Are we become murderers now?"

"It would not be murder, Elli, but self-defense," Fençu said to the big woman. The calm way he said it made Maria's blood chill.

One of the other men spoke up. "We can chain her here. We need a slave."

"She would escape," said Villano. "Who here will take that chance?"

"None of this is necessary," Elena said. "*I* will vouch for her. She will say nothing against us."

Villano snorted his disgust. "How can you know that?"

"Because she is not like the others. And Elli is right. We cannot harm her. We are not killers."

Fençu paced back and forth. Finally he drew his knife from his belt and stood before Maria. He was thin, just bone and sinew and muscle—a wiry, tight coil of a man. She sensed that he would be good at his business, that he would eviscerate her so quickly she wouldn't even feel it. "I don't like any of my choices," he said to her. "But I like killing you least of all."

"It is you who holds the knife," Maria said with a bravery she did not feel.

"Yes, but it is you who directs its course," he replied. He seemed to come to a decision. "If I let you live, do I have your word you will never speak of what you've seen here today?"

"You fool!" Villano hissed. "You would accept the oath of a *Christian?*" He drew his knife and stepped forward.

Fençu turned to face him. "If you wish to use that, it must be against me first." He opened his arms as if to welcome a blow. Villano was by far the larger of the two, but he stopped, unwilling to strike his leader.

"It is not the oath of a Christian that moves me," Fençu said to him, "so much as the word of Elena, who has more sense than you will ever have." He turned back to Maria. "You have a power over us, Maria Borg. If you say a word to the *gendarmi,* your *kappillan,* or anyone at all, it is true they will take us away. They will put us in prison, and then they will chain us to the stake and warm their backsides on our stinking flesh. But they will not catch all of us. There are hiding places they will never find, and at least one of us will survive. I am willing to wager it will be me—or Villano here."

Fençu leaned closer. "You have my oath: the one who lives will hunt you down and cut your throat, and the throats of your mother and father, and all your brothers and sisters." He saw tears shimmering in her eyes and a drop of blood at her lip. "Do you believe me?"

She nodded.

"I must have your pledge of secrecy."

She tried to speak, but her voice produced only a squeak.

"You are a fool!" Villano hissed at Fençu.

"Say it!" Fençu commanded, ignoring him.

Maria saw Elena's look. *Speak now or die,* her eyes said.

"I—I swear it," Maria stammered. "I will tell no one about you or this place."

Fençu held her gaze for a long moment. Slowly he straightened up. Finally he took a deep breath. It seemed to transform him. "It is finished, then," he said, nodding. He glanced at Villano. "Finished, I say. Do you hear me?"

"If you are wrong," Villano said, "our lives are upon your head."

"As always they are." Fençu sheathed his knife. He addressed the others in the cave. "I say again: it is done." He turned to Elli. "I am hungry, wife. Where is the *lechem mishneh?*" She hurried to a primitive stone oven and withdrew a hot loaf. Fençu bowed his head and muttered a rapid blessing, which the others repeated. After that, the tension in the cave disappeared as quickly as the steaming loaf, which was passed from hand to hand. Fençu tore off a piece and offered it to Maria. Surprised, she shook her head. "I will understand if you want only to leave," Fençu said. "But as a friend of Elena's, you are welcome to stay and eat and make a dance with us."

Maria shook her head. She did want only to leave.

"As you wish," Fençu said. "Music!" he commanded. One of the men produced a fiddle, and Fençu and Elli began to dance, and soon most of the others joined in. Elli was a cheerful woman who was twice as wide as her husband and nearly half again as tall. They made a comical couple, teasing each other and laughing together.

Maria watched them with a sense of unreality: it was as if the knife to her throat had never happened. Only Villano seemed still upset. He glared at her and took a share of bread before ascending the path to his guard post. "Sleep again and I'll sew your pant legs together," Fençu called after him. "And then I'll steal your boots." Villano made an obscene gesture and grumbled something. The others laughed. Fençu twirled his wife, who moved with a step that belied her size.

Elena put an arm around Maria's shoulder. "You're still shaking," she said sympathetically. "I'm sorry for all this."

"As am I," Maria said. "I owe you my life."

"I'll walk you home," Elena said. "But you're bleeding!" She'd noticed Maria's knee and knelt to examine the injury. She ripped off a bit of her sash and bound the wound. "What were you doing here, anyway?" she asked.

"Gathering brambles. I've never come this way before."

"I know where to find guano," Elena said. "It burns better and it's easier to carry."

"Guano?" Maria said. "I don't want a flogging. The piles all belong to someone."

"Not all of them. You only have to know where to look. The nobles don't own everything, and the birds don't always let on where they're going to drop things. Come back tomorrow and I'll show you."

"I . . . I don't want to come back."

"You needn't worry about them," Elena said, indicating the others. "Fençu has made a decision. They will all abide by it. It is the way of this place. They are good for their word. So long as you keep yours, they will leave you alone. I would put my life on it." She saw the doubt that remained in Maria's eyes. "This cave is called M'kor Hakhayyim. It means 'the source of life.' It is the best place to live on the island. Tomorrow, or a week from now, if you return and allow it, the people who live here will make you think you were born in this cave—or at least make you wish you had been."

"I saw his eyes," Maria said. "Villano, I mean. He would have killed me."

"Yes. He has a quick temper. Fençu would have as well if there were really no choice. I'll admit I was worried for you. It could have gone either way. You must understand. If our secret is discovered, it would mean imprisonment or death."

Maria gathered her courage to say what she was thinking. "I never would have thought you were a . . . a *devil* worshiper," she said.

"Devil—?" Elena laughed. "Is that what you think we are?"

"Well, aren't you?"

"Of course not! We're Jews!"

The revelation struck Maria dumb with shock. She didn't know whether that was better than devil worship or not, and it was a few moments before she could respond. "My mother says it is a sin to be a Jew," she said finally. "They killed Jesus."

"I don't know about that," Elena said. "All I know is that I was born a Jew and have to hide it."

"I know most Jews left Malta a long time ago," Maria said. "I heard they had to leave so fast that they left behind all their gold and silver. My brother Nico and I used to hunt for it. Lots of people do."

"Ah, the treasure stories! How I wish it were so."

"Well, you should look. There's probably a fortune in this very cave. Anyway, I thought all the Jews who didn't leave had to become Christian."

"Some did, but some only pretend. They call us *marranos*. It means 'pig.' Fençu was born a slave because his parents refused to convert. His real name was Naphtuhim, but his master couldn't pronounce it and gave him the nickname Fençu, which means 'rabbit.' He loves that name, because for a Jew rabbit is no more proper—no more *kasher*—than pig. When he was old enough he converted, and by law he was freed. Fençu says from that moment he was a good non-*kasher* Christian. He knows some of the prayers, and he keeps all the Christian relics. You see—already the *shiviti* is being replaced." She pointed. Maria saw one of the young boys removing the wall hanging she'd seen earlier, replacing it with a brightly polished crucifix. Except during prayer, anyone entering the cave would think it was filled with devout *conversos*.

"What about you?" Maria asked. "Is this your family?"

"Yes, but not by blood. My real family lived in Gozo. When I was ten the plague came to our village. Everyone died but me. I never even got sick. There was no one left, and no one outside the village would come to help. I knew about Fençu, because before his conversion he had been a friend of my father's, a slave beside him. I knew he lived in Malta, but for more than a year I couldn't find him. After I did, I came to live with him, and that's when I found out he was a *marrano*. We have no rabbi and no Torah, but he does his best to observe the traditions. To keep us safe, he teaches us short verses from the New Testament."

"Father Salvago says it's a sin to abandon your religion."

"He wouldn't say that about *Jews* who do." Elena shrugged. "We don't think about it much. Fençu is very practical-minded. He says he likes being a Jew well enough, but not enough to die for it, or to spend his life in slavery for it, as my father did. My father was proud of his refusal to convert, but Fençu once asked me if I ever saw him light a menorah with his hands in wall chains. I didn't. 'I light one every week,' Fençu says. And he does. The first thing he told me when I came to live here was that because I didn't look Jewish, it was better not to admit it. He didn't need to tell me that. I had already learned it, because a pig has a better life on Malta than a Jew. I used to worry that I was doing wrong, but Fençu says God understands. He says God likes a wily Jew."

❖

Maria spent a sleepless night, her nerves still taut after her brush with death, and her conscience on fire.

They are Jews.

She was not religious by nature. She went to church because her mother made her. Much of the time she couldn't understand what was being said in St. Agatha's, and the rest of the time she wasn't listening. But she knew enough to realize that whatever she did, her soul was in jeopardy. While it would be sinful to break her oath to Fençu, it would be sinful not to break it, not to tell Father Salvago about the forbidden rites taking place almost in the shadow of St. Agatha's.

Her dilemma was compounded by her opinion of Elena. She certainly did not seem like a sinner or lost soul. She was not cold or dull-eyed like the other girls Maria knew. She dreamed things, the way Maria dreamed things. She was warm and wise and funny, and she was the first person Maria had ever met who treated her like a friend. And today Elena had saved her life. Though Maria did not know what to make of the others in the cave, how could she tell on such a person as that?

But they are Jews!

How could she ignore a lifetime of stories? Quite apart from killing Jesus, her mother had told her, the Jews sometimes boiled Christian children alive, or dismembered small animals and ate the twitching remainders raw. All of this was written, Isolda had said, somewhere in the New Testament. Maria thought of all the dark places in that cave where such things might easily happen.

Maria had heard lurid tales of what happened to devil worshipers and Protestants and Jews, and as a young girl she'd seen it herself: a bonfire in the village square, where her parish priest, Father Jesuald, had been burned at the stake. She couldn't imagine that happening to anyone else, at least not on her account. Still, she knew God would not have devised such a punishment if some people didn't deserve it. And if she knew of a sin and did not tell of it, wouldn't she be in as much trouble as the sinners themselves? Wouldn't the dark-robed Inquisitors who worked the dungeons beneath the bishop's palace burn her as quickly as they would the others? But how could they find out? So far as anyone knew, there had been no real Jews on Malta for more than sixty years, except for slaves. No one she knew ever even spoke of *marranos*. So their secret was safe, it seemed.

Unless *she* told. And if she did that, Fençu would surely do as he promised. Her mother and father would be sacrificed over her need to tell a secret she wished she didn't know in the first place.

She prayed, asking God to tell her what to do. Hours passed and dawn came, and God did not speak to her or give her a sign. In her practical way, Maria took that for an answer: surely His silence on the matter meant that she did not have to decide just yet. She was free to see Elena again, and the others in her cave. After a week or a month, if they seemed truly evil, she could act then.

Satisfied with her solution, she spent that morning with Elena, scouring other caves along the coast in a hunt for bat guano. Though they had to crawl into some tight places, there were indeed great mounds of it, hardened and blackened by the centuries. They dug some free with an iron scoop that Elena had brought. When they had enough, Elena invited her to explore M'kor Hakhayyim. Maria declined, but Elena took her by the hand. "You needn't worry. Villano is a water seller in Mdina. He'll be away all day today. So will the other men. The only ones there are the women and children. If you aren't comfortable, I'll walk you home myself." Her expression persuaded Maria.

They returned to the lone carob tree that marked the place, a tree that had somehow survived drought and man. The cave was much like hundreds of others that riddled the limestone of Malta. Some could be reached only by sea, others by climbing down sheer cliffs. As they descended the difficult slope to the entrance twenty feet above the water, Maria realized just how well hidden it was.

M'kor Hakhayyim was sculpted by the eons and embellished by the people who had dwelled in it for countless generations. A communal kitchen occupied the center of the main cavern, a vast room that Elena called the grand ballroom. The room had a high, arched ceiling that soared into the darkness, creating a vault, like a great cathedral. Stalactites hung like chandeliers, as did clusters of bats. The limestone walls were blackened by the soot of cook fires and engraved with letters and symbols whose meaning had long been forgotten. The seaward wall was punctuated with openings, some natural, others man-made. They provided fresh air and, in the morning, allowed the sun to stream into the cave in parallel beams that lit the walls and floor below. At night tallow fires danced in wall sconces, so the grand ballroom was never gloomy. A freshwater spring bubbled year-round, feeding a small pool.

Short ladders around the perimeter of the main room gave access to the ledges and recesses that served as bedrooms. Some were no more than niches, large enough only for one nest of straw, while others were more spacious, holding entire families. Elena's niche was decorated with candles that she had made, filling the space with warmth and light.

In all, Elena said, nearly twenty people lived there. Besides Fençu and Villano, there were a silversmith, a blacksmith, and a boot maker, along with assorted wives and young children, whose delighted squeals rang off the walls as they played hide and seek or tag in the endless labyrinth of the cave's upper passages. For food the residents gathered hazelnuts, tended sparse plots of vegetables, and hunted small game. They pooled their money to buy grain.

As Elena had promised, all the men were in Mdina or Birgu, working. The women were tending to the chores of the great household and greeted Maria warmly. Elli stirred a bed of coals beneath the stone oven, while Leonora, the blacksmith's wife, put Elena and Maria to work slicing eels for a pot of stew. After that Violante, the boot maker's wife, enlisted Maria's help making soap, while Imperia didn't seem to do anything but chatter and gossip and ask questions about Birgu.

What struck Maria most about the women was their lack of reserve. They were open and frank and quick to laugh. Elli joked about things. She joked about the noises her husband made while sleeping. She joked about a stray gray hair growing out of Imperia's nose. She even joked about her own large frame. Maria knew her own mother would condemn such behavior as brazen and somehow profane. Yet Elena was right, and it left her dazed: already she felt almost at home. She even tried a joke of her own, about the unsavory appearance of something in the cook pot, and felt an extraordinary warmth inside when it made the others laugh.

They shared a meal together, a delicious vegetable stew into which they dipped great chunks of hot bread. As they relaxed around the cook fire Elena brought out a dulcimer, a beautiful instrument of dark cherry wood that had belonged to her father's master in Gozo. She played beautifully, the worn felt-covered hammers moving delicately over the strings, producing a lovely lyrical melody that she said was Persian. Even the littlest children stopped their games to listen.

In the afternoon Elena walked Maria back to Birgu. On the way they lingered on the heights above the village, near the monastery of Santa Margherita. There was a small clump of trees, and they sat in the shade and shared cheese and spring water. There was a grand view of the harbor area—the peninsulas of Birgu and Senglea, and Mount Sciberras, the hill that dominated the peninsula on the far side. "It's pretty today," Maria said, looking at the prominent fortress of St. Angelo, and the partially completed forts of St. Elmo and St. Michael, and all the huts growing up around them.

"Not so pretty as Barcelona or Marseille, I think."

"You've talked that way before. How do you know of such places?"

"People tell me."

"What people? No one I know knows any such thing. Most people I know never even leave Birgu."

"Men. Sailors."

"My father would beat me if he saw me talking to a sailor."

"Then you mustn't let him see."

Maria giggled at the scandalous thought. "No. I suppose not." She looked appreciatively at Elena. "You say the things I'm thinking sometimes," she said. "I like that."

"Well, you're the first person I ever met except Fençu who didn't laugh at me when I said I'm going to the north, where a person can do whatever they like." They watched a galley leaving the harbor. "I can't look at that ship without wondering where it's going," Elena said. "I wonder what it would be like just to go along to the second—no, the third place it stopped, and to step off, just to see what was there. I'm going to find out one day."

"I would like that, too," Maria said wistfully. "I could look for Nico. He's out there somewhere."

"The whole *world* is out there. Maybe one day we'll find a way to explore it together." They drank a toast to that, of spring water.

Maria was reluctant to part with Elena. She couldn't remember a finer day.

She returned home with a heavy basket of guano. Elena was right: it burned hotter and longer than the brambles. Her father warily eyed the prize but did not ask where she'd gotten it. "You'd better not encounter the *gendarmi*," was all Luca said as he leaned forward to enjoy the fire.

❖

Mining guano took less time than gathering brambles. Maria was able to use her spare time to visit Elena, although she could never stay more than a few hours without raising questions at home. She grew more comfortable with each visit, though she was wary of encountering Villano. There was little chance she would meet him on the road, as Mdina was to the west and she lived to the north, but she was always careful to leave well before he might return. Yet no one but she seemed to even remember the incident that had introduced her to M'kor Hakhayyim. It was as if she had imagined it.

Elli and Fençu were childless and welcomed her as if she were their own. Fençu presented her with a gift, a leather sheath he'd made for the knife she carried in her belt. Leatherwork was only one of his many talents. He was a carpenter by trade but could do anything with his hands. He could work iron and shoe a horse, set a trap for a weasel, mend his own clothing, or make wooden tops for the children. Sometimes he worked on galley repairs for the knights or did odd jobs around Mdina for the nobles. On those days he had to wear a yellow headband to signify he was born a Jew. Most times there was no work at all, or if there was, there was none for Jews, even converted ones.

He built crab traps and hung them from ropes that dangled from the rocks outside the cave. Twice a week he lifted them dripping from the water, red claws flashing between slats. He took the crabs to Birgu, where he traded them for pilchard or cod. When Maria asked why he would trade a delicacy like crab for common fish, he explained that much of what he caught—crabs, hedgehogs, and rabbits—was forbidden by the Bible. But as with his religion itself, in matters of food he was ever pragmatic. Faced with starvation, he said, the biblical restrictions would go the way of the wall hanging when the *gendarmi* got too near. "I would feed my family a pig from snout to tail before I'd let them starve," he told her. "God would understand. He likes his Jews alive." Maria thought it was a wonderfully practical, if somewhat scandalous, way to think.

The cave was ideally suited for defense from corsairs, and Fençu had seen to various improvements. From the hillside above the entrance was concealed by a steep slope, and from the sea by the rock formations that she'd seen the first day. The opening was barely large enough for a grown man to pass. Two exits had been carved from the rock at the rear of the cave, providing well-concealed escape routes that led into a ravine cutting through the hillside above. Every few weeks Fençu held drills in which the cave's residents practiced loading and firing the ancient guns and crossbows that comprised the arsenal. One could only pretend with the guns, as there wasn't powder enough to spare. Women and children were taught to throw rocks and knives, and everyone took turns acting as lookouts. They had no cannons and no knights, but the people who lived in M'kor Hakhayyim felt quite safe. "In Birgu there are only weak walls," Fençu boasted. "We have the rock of the island itself."

Maria came one day during drills, and Fençu brightened when he saw her. "Perfect!" he said. "The younger children were about to practice, and they need a target." He handed her a wooden sword. "Invade the island, please," he said gravely.

Beginning in the low surf, she waded ashore, gamely swinging the sword. She was shot thirty-eight times by small children using every weapon in the imaginary arsenal, but even then she wouldn't surrender. With Fençu and Elli cheering her stubborn bravery, Maria did not yield until Elena and the children picked her up and tossed her back into the sea. They plucked her out and spent the rest of the afternoon eating fish they pulled fresh from the water and cooked in a bed of coals on the gravelly beach. After the meal there was more practice with the guns, and finally the fiddle and dulcimer that meant dancing until nightfall.

❖

Though Elena had told her the name M'kor Hakhayyim meant "source of life," Maria decided what it really meant was "source of endless secrets." No sooner was one revealed to her than another would follow. While hiding from some of the children during a game, Maria found a burlap sack stowed behind a pile of loose rock in one of the upper passages. "It is a shofar," Elena told her. "Fençu made it from a ram's horn. He blows it at Rosh ha-Shanah and Yom Kippur." Elena tried it, but only a weak moan resulted. Maria fared a little better, producing a noise they both thought was quite like a flatulent sheep. They dissolved in laughter.

They went deeper into one of the upper passages, where Elena pulled something from a narrow crevice. Elena carefully drew it out and removed the covering. Maria gasped at its beauty. Doves flew above galleys, all moving toward a distant land with gentle green hills and a wide river. "It's called a *mizrach*," Elena said. "Elli painted it. We hang it on the wall in the direction of Jerusalem, so we know which way to pray."

Their most prized possession was a megillah, a parchment that had been in Elli's family for generations. It was covered with handwritten Hebrew text. No one in the cave could read it, she said, but Elli's mother had once told her it contained passages from the Book of Ruth. The balance of the parchment had been lost in a fire from which the megillah, but not Elli's mother and father, had been saved. Now it was carefully rolled in an oilcloth and kept in a niche above the menorah.

Another sack held an ornate silver container, a vessel carved with an elaborate filigree of myrtle and willow branches. "It's an *etrog*," Elena said. Before she could explain further, Fençu appeared behind them. "That used to be an ugly candlestick that belonged to the Inguanez." Maria knew the name—a noble family of Mdina, one of the most powerful on the island.

"They gave it to you?" she asked.

Fençu laughed. "They didn't even know they owned it," he said. "It was forgotten in a storeroom behind their stable, along with a hundred other pieces. I only borrowed it from that darkness and made it into something to glorify God." He grinned at her expression as she realized what he was saying. Convinced that the nobles of Mdina were overburdened with wealth, Fençu occasionally helped himself to whatever trifles of silver or crystal or brass he could purloin while working on their splendid homes. With the help of Cawl, the silversmith, Fençu would recast the metal into more practical, less recognizable forms. The *etrog* container was but one piece. A collection of small brass serving dishes had made an exquisite menorah, while the crystal was resold or kept for use in the cave. "We have the only crystal chamber pot on the island," Fençu bragged. He used the money he earned to purchase necessities, but never failed to give something to needy families—"even to authentic Gentiles," he told her.

Maria thrashed and squirmed through another restless night.

They are Jews and thieves.

She trembled. *Do the fires of hell burn twice as hot for twice the sins?*

Despite her prayers, God remained mute regarding His will in the matter. By dawn, working alone, she had reduced the crime in her mind until it was all but insignificant. While she was awed by the noble families of Mdina, she did not much care for them. She knew of a mason who had worked for her father who'd been run over by one of the Inguanez sons driving a cart. It cut him nearly in two, and her father said the driver paid the victim no more heed than he might have to a rat. Compared to that, could one condemn Fençu? There even seemed to be a sort of odd justice to it all that appealed to her, as Fençu rearranged the island's lopsided wealth just a tiny bit.

Maria was neither stupid nor completely naive, and she knew she was looking for reasons to make things all right. While she was willing to do that, she would *never,* she told herself, turn her back on something *truly* evil. So that day, when she returned to M'kor Hakhayyim, and the day after, and the day after that, she did not forget to watch for anything that had the unmistakable look of Lucifer about it. And each day that she did, Elena and Fençu and the others lulled her with their normalcy. They enticed her with their high spirits and with their warm bread, with their games and with their laughter. She wasn't certain what it was about the two places where she spent her time, but it appeared sometimes as if things were backward: it was the residents of the sun-washed village of Birgu who seemed to live in the darkness, and the cave dwellers of M'kor Hakhayyim who seemed to live in the light—Elena above all.

One night Luca noticed the leather sheath Fençu had given Maria. "Where did you get that?"

"I traded some guano for it," she lied easily.

"The guano is not yours to trade for anything. Bring it all home from now on," he said gruffly. He took the sheath and kept it for himself.

Elena was right, Maria thought. *I mustn't let him see.*

❖

Though she hoped to, she was not able to avoid Villano forever. One day as she was leaving the cave she encountered him just outside the very passage where he'd surprised her. She saw his big form looming above her, and she jumped back. Villano scowled at her, displaying a mouthful of dark teeth. Maria saw there was no place to flee unless she wanted to jump in the sea. She stooped and snatched up a rock, prepared to hold her ground. Villano stared at her for a moment. Then a great grin blossomed on his face, and he burst out laughing. "A worthy polecat you are," he said. He rummaged in a packet he was carrying and tossed her something. Maria had to drop the rock to catch it. Her eyes went wide as she realized what it was. "*Api!*" she breathed.

"Don't papists eat *api,* or is it only Jews and devil worshipers?"

The precious honeyed sweet disappeared into her mouth. Villano laughed again. He stepped by her and disappeared into the cave.

❖

Some weeks later Maria spent a terrible night, certain she was dying.

She'd felt odd for two days, and then all night she had cramps, painful spasms that twisted her insides and left her gasping. Her breasts, buds that they still were, felt tender. She felt around them and in her armpits, certain she would find one of the dreaded buboes that meant the plague was at hand. She found none, but that didn't mean they might not appear by morning.

Whenever the plague came everyone knew it was God's retribution for the sins of man. She ran her mind over her recent transgressions. In the past week alone she had coveted a silk scarf, lied to her father, and taken a piece of bread from a stall near the market. All the children did it, and the vendor didn't mind, but she hadn't paid for it. And then, of course, there was her great sin: she was helping to conceal the Jews and thieves of M'kor Hakhayyim.

Mortal sins, venial sins—any one of them might have led to this punishment.

She turned restlessly. She curled into a ball, trying to fight the invisible hand that was squeezing her insides so painfully. Near dawn she felt wetness between her legs. When it was light enough she saw with horror she'd been bleeding. Even the straw was dark red beneath her, where the blood soaked through her pants. Now she was absolutely terrified. She couldn't possibly tell her father or mother, and she couldn't just lie there and bleed to death. Elena would help. She'd spoken of a doctor in Mdina. Maria cleaned herself with the straw and fastened her pants. She sneaked down the ladder and raced from the house.

She collided with the butcher, just emerging from his shop. In one hand he held a cleaver, in the other the head of a sheep. His apron was splattered with blood. As she recovered her composure she saw him looking at her, looking down *there*. She saw his eyes take in her own blood, saw his expression cloud with anger—or was it disgust? It distressed her that he appeared to know what was happening to her, while she didn't.

Her run to the cave had never taken so long. She arrived in tears and out of breath. To her surprise, Elena's eyes betrayed no fear when she heard. "You're not dying," she said, laughing as she hugged her, "you're a woman!" She explained what she knew of the monthly flow, provided Maria with some clean rags, showed her how to use them, and gave her a special tea to ease the cramps.

Maria was not altogether pleased. She was proud to be a woman, she supposed, but the idea of cramping and bleeding every month seemed more like a punishment than a blessing. She found it hard to believe that all women did that. No woman she knew had even hinted at such a thing. Then she had a fresh worry about Elena's revelation. "I'm not ready to have a baby," she said.

"You only have to worry about that if you've been with a man and the blood *doesn't* come," Elena said. "But never lie with a man during your bleeding, or else your baby will be a leper and the man will become simple-minded."

"Lie with a man?" Maria's stare was blank.

Maria listened, stunned, to Elena's descriptions of the act itself, and that it somehow led to conception. Maria had great difficulty believing that she herself could have been conceived that way. Never once had she seen her father and mother kissing or even being particularly kind to one another. She could not imagine Luca Borg without his pants on, or Isolda with her skirts hitched up, or the two of them together in an embrace sufficiently passionate to have produced offspring.

"Affection and *scopare* have little to do with each other," Elena explained. *Scopare,* she called it. *Fucking.* The word was delicious. Maria repeated it over and over until they both began giggling, and then their knees went weak and Maria practically peed in her pants. "But how do you know these things?" Maria asked.

"Because I'm a courtesan."

"A—?"

"It's something like the storyteller. Men pay me to pleasure themselves, to take them where they want to go. I make them believe what they want to believe, that's all." Elena smiled at the look of puzzlement that remained on Maria's face. "I'm a *whore,* Maria," she said.

Maria had heard *that* word before, in church. When she'd asked her mother about it, Isolda hit her on the ear with a stick and told her to pray for forgiveness. "But you could be arrested," she said, worried. "Whoring is against the law!"

"Starving should be against the law," Elena replied. When she left Gozo for Malta, she told Maria, she couldn't immediately find Fençu. She had no food and no money. She was too old for the orphanage at the hospital in Rabat. The few jobs that existed were only for men. She went to Mdina, the walled inland city where the nobles of Malta lived in their grand mansions, shutting themselves away from knights, commoners, and corsairs. She stole a loaf of bread, and was caught. The merchant was dragging her to the courts, to have her flogged and placed in the stocks. A nobleman saw the commotion and intervened. He paid the merchant for the loaf and bade Elena take a seat in his carriage. He listened to her story and instantly offered her a job as a scullery maid. That night he took her into the pantry and showed her what he really wanted. Elena hated his hands on her, but her hunger pangs were fresh, and she was afraid to protest. The man was gentle. He gave her jewelry and spending money. For the first time in her life she had enough to eat. Then his wife discovered them in the pantry. She put a carving knife in her husband's buttocks, and Elena in the street.

Elena soon found another patron, one of the *jurati* on the Università, the same civil authority that deemed whoring illegal. One night in the throes of passion he slapped Elena, and the act seemed to raise him to new heights of excitement. He slapped her again, harder. She ran from the house and never returned. Next was a Knight of St. John, a dashing young Aragonese who kept her as a mistress until the Grand Master ordered all his knights to renew their vows of chastity. After that came a priest. "There's no one like a knight for sanctimony," Elena told Maria, "unless it's a priest. By night he bedded me, and by day reminded me I was a hell-bound harlot. In the end he kept what he owed me and said he'd pay it to the service of Christ on behalf of my lost soul."

From then on, Elena found it was better to do it with different men for a fixed price paid in advance: no entanglements, no sermons, no outraged wives. She slept with educated men who had traveled the world, filling her head with dreams of a better life than she could find in Malta. She had continued the work even after locating Fençu. No one at M'kor Hakhayyim knew what she did to make extra money, she said, and no one cared. M'kor Hakhayyim was a place where no one inquired too deeply into another's business.

❖

Maria floated home on the soft, lovely cloud of knowledge that she had avoided the plague, become a woman, and learned the secrets of men and women, all in the same day. Nevertheless, she spent another restless night.

She was carrying three stupendous secrets, secrets that were somewhere between delicious and depraved.

Jews and thieves, and now a whore.

Three sins, worth thrice the hellfire.

She did not pray for guidance. It didn't matter. None of it.

As for the Jews, her only caution to herself was that she must never join them during a Sabbath meal or some other religious occasion. She would always depart before such observances, to preserve her soul. Just in case.

As for the thieves, she knew she did not care.

As for the whore, their bond was forever sealed. Elena was perfect. Maria knew that if she were a man, she would be in love with her.

❖

The only place where Maria and Elena did not see the world in precisely the same way was in the matter of Maria's newfound dream of reading.

"More likely you can catch a ride on the back of a hawk and fly to the moon than learn that," Elena said. "No one would teach you. The only schools are for high-born boys. You're not only just a girl, you're poor at that. Even if someone would teach you, what do you have to read? Are you going to steal a book?"

"Maybe I could buy one."

"With what money?"

"I could become a whore, like you."

Elena regarded Maria wryly. "You're too young."

"I'm thirteen! And you're only fifteen!"

"It isn't the years, it's the breasts. You'll need some first. You're still a stick. Maybe another year or two."

"Well, then. I could learn to read your *megillah*."

Elena laughed. "You really are foolish. That's *Hebrew*. They'd put you to the stake just for asking!"

Maria flushed at her own ignorance: she didn't even know the difference between Hebrew and Italian. Her idea was preposterous. No one she knew had any books. No one she knew could even read except some of the master builders, and of course Father Salvago— and she didn't know if he could read *real* languages, languages that people actually *talked*. He only read words from the great Bible. She knew those were Latin words and that no one she was acquainted with understood them—not even her mother, who could repeat whole bits of the gibberish and explain not more than three or four words. The knights had books, of course, but they kept to themselves and never mixed with the low people. Some nobles of Mdina could read, even the women, but they were nearly as arrogant as the knights, and quite as remote to a girl like

Maria. Among people she knew, books were even scarcer than money.

Maria brooded about it. She wasn't certain why it seemed so important. Even a man who knew how to read could do little with it, although her father, she realized, could be an exception if he chose. Despite his natural skill with stone, he would never be more than a simple mason, for he couldn't read a plan. He was not a stupid man; he simply refused to try. When he looked at the lettered sheets the engineers made, his eyes got round in fear, as if the words held some secret too terrible to bear. So the Rhodiots and the Greeks who could read the words would always run the work sites, and the Luca Borgs of the world would always be their labor or do small jobs, like simple walls that required no plans.

Yet if a man might advance with reading, certainly a woman could not, at least not on the island of Malta. Still, she didn't care if the idea was foolish. She closed her eyes and saw the mysterious scribblings in the Italian's book. If she could count to a hundred— and she could—there was no reason she couldn't learn to read those scribblings.

She decided to ask Father Salvago. She approached him after services, as he was walking to the little rectory behind the church. She fell in beside him. He exchanged pleasantries with her, then realized she had something on her mind.

"Is there something I can help you with, Maria? Are your parents all right?"

"I . . . yes, thank you, Dun Salvago, they're fine." She took a deep breath. "I want your help, that's all. I want you to teach me to read."

The priest cocked his head as if he hadn't heard. "*Read?*"

Her face worked at a brave smile. She nodded. "Read."

He waited, expecting her to reveal the prank. But her gaze was earnest, her eyes beseeching. "You're serious, aren't you?"

"Yes, Father. *Please* teach me."

He stopped walking and turned to her. "You're silly and brash," he said dismissively. "I am not a teacher, Maria. I am a priest. Now go home." Shaking his head, he disappeared inside the rectory.

As she was leaving St. Agatha's Maria walked past the auberge of France, the dormitory where many of the French-speaking knights lived. She peered through one of the windows and saw long shelves that held row upon row of leather-bound volumes. She'd never thought much about them, but suddenly they seemed like the ships leaving Grand Harbor, ready to carry her away to unknown destinations, to places girls were forbidden to venture.

And perhaps that was the real reason she wanted to learn, because she wasn't supposed to. She didn't really know why it mattered. She knew only that it did.

Chapter 8

Nico rose every day before dawn and did not retire until well after dark. He settled into a routine in which the majority of his time was spent in the shipyard with Leonardus. Each morning he spent an hour or two with Ameerah, from whom he learned the arts and graces of the household. His greatest torment came once every two weeks, when he was subjected to a bath. His protests fell on deaf ears; two weeks was the minimal standard for the household staff.

He learned to change linens and wash clothing. "Are not such jobs better suited for a woman, madam?" he asked Ameerah as he scrubbed a gown.

"The master never travels with a woman," she said. "You will have to satisfy his every need."

He was taught to judge spices in the market, and the plumpness of a dinner chicken, and the quality of storax, used in perfumes that Farouk presented as gifts to his wives. He learned to salt fish and count money. Ameerah sent him to a storyteller in the souk and had him repeat the tales to her. She listened raptly, assuring him that his master enjoyed such diversions and would be well pleased. He served her refreshments and nervously withstood her attentions, which grew ever more familiar. She taught him to feed her with his fingers, in the manner she said the master would wish to be served. She had him brush her hair using a jeweled Venetian comb. She sometimes changed her clothes while he was present, only partly concealing herself behind a Persian silk screen. He saw her bare back as she changed from bathing robe to prayer gown. She seemed not to notice his presence, but he turned away to protect her modesty. He saw the other wives only at dinner. One day he realized that no one ever entered Ameerah's chambers while he was with her, because Abbas stood guard at the door. When he left he noticed that Mehmet was always lurking somewhere nearby, his expression dark.

At night Nico's education in the arts of thievery and cunning continued with Ibi as the two foraged in the city for food. They broke into shopkeepers' stalls, and once they raided a storehouse where they found so much fruit that they gorged and were ill for two days. Nico scaled trellises to reach terraced roofs, where meals were often served in the heat of summer. On one such occasion he stole a complete dinner, crockery and all. Private houses were the most dangerous, belonging as they did mostly to Arabs and Turks—some of them even to Janissaries, the elite soldier corps. While they almost always found something, there was rarely enough. The greater their hunger, the bolder and more desperate their efforts became. Nico did not need Ibi to tell him what would happen if they were caught.

One evening in the souk Nico stopped to watch a magician performing. The man did tricks with fire, and with a snake and a rope. A few in the crowd tossed coins to him. Nearby another man played a game with shells and pebbles, fooling everyone who looked on, and taking their money when they were foolish enough to bet that they knew where the pebbles were. That gave Nico an idea.

The next evening Ibi was at one end of the busy square, taking bets that the boy in the bright red turban, a boy who had performed before the Beylerbey in Cairo and the Sultan himself in Constantinople (may his name be blessed), could remember a verse, or a difficult series of names or numbers, or anything else proposed by the disbelieving.

A crowd of dubious onlookers gathered, one of whom placed a bet of two hundred maravedis that Nico could not recite the names of twenty-seven uncles and great-uncles of the bettor's family. The bet was taken. The man rattled off the names, and the crowd's skepticism grew with each name. No mortal could remember such a litany. Nico whispered to Ibi, who announced haughtily that the list was insufficiently difficult. Nico would accept only if the man added the names of his brothers, brothers-in-law, and nephews as well, and the names of his horses, if he had any.

The bets grew to four hundred maravedis, and then to six hundred, enough for Nico and Ibi to eat like royalty for a month. When the last coin was thrown down, Nico rattled the names back flawlessly. As the crowd applauded his fantastic display he smiled modestly in triumph. However, he had overlooked an important detail: there had been no one to write down the names. As Ibi reached to scoop up the maravedis, the bettor trapped his hand in the dirt beneath his leather sandal. "He made a mistake," the man growled.

"Never," Nico said. "I'll do it again. Backward, if you like."

"Too late. It's my family and you failed, I say! That's my money on the ground, and you owe me two hundred!"

"You owe me fifty!" another thundered. A long sword was drawn. Knives appeared from belts, and the crowd smelled blood. Nico and Ibi barely escaped with their lives.

"I think we'd better forget sorcery," Ibi said that night. "Stealing is easier."

❖

Whenever the cannon sounded the approach of a ship—there were different numbers of blasts, depending upon the type—Nico hurried to the docks to study the faces of newly captured slaves. He asked questions of anyone who would talk with him, and answered theirs. It was always the same. There was no word of home, and the mighty galleys of the Order of St. John were nowhere to be seen. Nico was undaunted. It was simply a matter of time. His mind never left escape, and his faith in God's soldiers never wavered.

The knights grew large in his mind, consuming much of his idle thought. Their armor was bright with God's blessings, and their swords dripped with infidel blood. He promised himself he would join their ranks one day and clean out the corsair nests of North

Africa with the tip of his blade. Nico had dreamed of joining the knights ever since he could remember, but his father always told him such ideas were foolish. He was both a commoner and Maltese, and the knights would never permit either kind of vermin among their noble European ranks. Nico swore he would find a way.

One afternoon in the Bedestan, flush with the bravery that came from such dreams, he saw Baba, the boy who had stolen his money when he first arrived. Boldly Nico strode toward him. Baba turned and saw him. Nico launched himself at the hated thief, fists churning. They tumbled to the ground, rolling over and over, and Nico's fury seemed to overwhelm the larger boy. Baba managed to pummel Nico's nose and cheeks, but then he got to his feet and ran away, unscathed. Nico left the encounter bloodied but giddy with victory.

Each night as he drifted off to sleep, Nico held Maria's coin like a rosary and said his prayers out loud. He asked God to remember his rescue and to help guide his hand in smiting his other enemies: Mehmet the tormentor, and Yusuf the executioner, and for good measure Ali Agha, the galliot captain who had delivered him to the godless hell of Algiers.

"If you try to avenge every wrong done you in this world," Ibi said from the darkness when Nico finished, "your life will be spent in vengeance."

"Yes," Nico said thoughtfully. "I guess it will." There was no regret in his voice.

"Then you are better to change gods," Ibi said. "If you convert to Islam, you will never be enslaved on the galleys or work the quarries. Don the turban and you may even be set free."

Nico was aghast. "My soul would burn in hell! And if you think this is so true, why haven't you converted?"

"God has long forgotten me, as I have long forgotten Him. When I was a child I prayed for a solid month. It went no better than the next month, when I prayed not at all."

"Your faith is weak!"

"Not weak, my young friend. It is gone. And if retribution is your goal, you should not trouble yourself unduly over the identity of the one you worship. Since I was a child I have been a slave in both Sicily and Algiers—one a Christian country, the other Muslim. I have seen that the Allah of Barbary practices vengeance as well as the God of your fathers. And here Allah will be of far more use to you. Mehmet himself is a renegade. He converted, and now look at the power he holds."

"Mehmet practices no religion at all! He ignores the muezzin! I've seen him drink wine!"

Ibi chuckled. "Everyone is devout inside a mosque. It is when they leave that they become forgetful, and their devotions suffer. In the house of Farouk only Yusuf is without blemish in his faith. The master himself drinks much wine, except during the holy month of Ramadan, when he drinks twice as much. Yet he has made the pilgrimage to Mecca. It is so with all men, as they walk the path to paradise: while one foot treads in vice, they are careful to keep the other in virtue. You must choose the path that offers you the best chance to escape the life you otherwise face. Convert, my friend."

"Never!" Nico turned away from the blasphemy and tried to sleep.

Later he asked Leonardus about it. The shipwright told him that he'd wanted to do so himself, but his skills were too valuable. "You'd be better to convert before you know too much, if they'll let you," the shipwright said. "Nearly all the corsairs are renegades, kidnapped from their parents and converted, or raised as Muslim from childhood. Even Dragut, the best of them all."

"But I want to be a knight," Nico said.

Leonardus spat on the floor. "They're nothing but corsairs themselves, wearing crosses! What does it matter in whose name you plunder or kill?"

"It matters to God," Nico said hotly. "Everyone knows that."

Leonardus only laughed and drank from his flask.

❖

No matter what Nico did, no matter how hard he tried, he could not please Mehmet. The older slave continued to sabotage him at every turn, never missing an opportunity to make him look bad in the eyes of Yusuf, who received regular reports of his incompetence. Nico was blamed for broken crockery, for sugar missing from the pantry, for grain that spoiled after a rare storm. The cook taught

Nico to prepare *macolique,* a specialty favored by the master. Proudly Nico served it to the women, who gagged at the bitter taste. Mehmet had spoiled the dish with alum, but it was Nico who looked the fool. Every day there was something new, some minor scandal in which Mehmet always ensured he seemed suspect. The injustices burned at him, but it was pointless to protest. Against Mehmet he had no voice.

Naturally, Nico far preferred the freedom of the shipyard to the intrigues of the household. He never had to do any real work, and there was always something interesting to watch. The blacksmith sweated at his forge making bolts and brackets or sharpening and repairing tools. The sail makers stitched together the goose-winged lateen sails, while the rope makers twisted hemp fibers first one direction into yarn, then back the opposite direction into larger strands, then again the other way into rope. Mast makers used bulky wooden planes and long draw knives to ply their craft, while carpenters and joiners cut frames and trimmed planking, into which trenail mooters fitted wooden pins. Riggers prepared nets to keep boarders at bay and to prevent fallen masts from crushing the crew in battle. Nico was everywhere, climbing over spools of rope, sitting atop the shed roofs. He watched gulls wheeling overhead against the deep blue sky, listened to the pounding of the surf, and felt the sea air ruffling his hair.

Most of all he enjoyed being with Leonardus. He felt safe with the man, and at home because they shared a language and the same lost homeland. Though Leonardus had a sharp tongue, there were times when he complimented Nico on performing an errand well. Sometimes he even smiled at the boy, a favor he rarely bestowed on anyone.

Leonardus held forth about every subject, filling each moment with his recollections of the sea and tales of the corsairs who sailed it. He knew currents and winds, landmarks and harbors, and he seemed to have a story about them all. Nico couldn't tell where fact ended and fiction began, but it didn't matter; he was endlessly entertained. He learned of the tribe who used a mysterious and dream-inducing plant to entice the scouts traveling with Odysseus. "They were called lotus-eaters," Leonardus said. "They lived on Djerba. That's Dragut's island now. He's one clever bastard, that Dragut. They call him the

Drawn Sword of Islam. There was a Genoese admiral, Andrea Doria, who had Dragut's little fleet outnumbered, outgunned, and blockaded in the harbor at Djerba. Any mortal man would have been defeated, but not Dragut. He built a road all the way across the island and put his galleys on rollers. The islanders worked as his mules and hauled them overland to the opposite shore. He sailed away, safe as a nun's teat. It took the great Doria two days to even realize he was guarding an empty harbor. He was a laughingstock from the Pillars of Hercules to the Golden Horn. I'll wager he ate lotus himself after that."

Leonardus rattled on, mixing lessons about the qualities of a good mast with legends of the Sirens, pointing out the flaws in the stitching of a lateen sail while reminiscing about the guilds of Venice. He taught Nico to tie knots, to count to a hundred in Turkish, and to judge from the color of water in the harbor what its currents were doing. Though Nico sensed that he himself was smart, he was in awe of Leonardus, whose knowledge seemed without end. Nico absorbed everything, enraptured.

Best of all, without Mehmet around he was able to eat. Shipyard workers were generally the best-fed slaves in Algiers, and Leonardus was the best-fed of them all. At midday the workers sat in the shade and ate their loaves, while a slave served Leonardus—and his new assistant, Nico—roast chicken, eggs cooked in saffron, and nectarines. Leonardus paid him no mind whenever he wrapped fruit or chicken for Ibi in a cloth and stuffed it in his shirt.

❖

One day Leonardus began laying a new keel. This, he told Nico, was the most complicated part of building a ship, the part that separated a master shipwright from an amateur. This was where the dimensions and proportions of the ship would be determined, and the structure of the hull defined. "Everything flows from this step," he said. "Do it wrong, and at best the galley will be second-rate, if she floats at all. Do it right, and she'll glide through the water like a young cock through an old whore."

From the lumberyard he selected long pieces of cedar and laid them out in the slipway. These would become the false keel, which could be replaced as repeated beachings wore it through. Atop these he laid lengths of fir, which were joined to form one piece. All of that was quite simple, but there followed a bewildering series of steps, to which Nico paid rapt if uncomprehending attention.

Leonardus worked quickly. Nico did his best to keep up, carrying rods, string, papers, and scribing tools. Darting here and there, Leonardus placed stakes, snapped chalk lines, and directed cuts. Laborers held strings, moving them as he directed. "This is the baseline," he told Nico. "You! Hold that over there!" He clambered over a brace and marked a point with a nail.

His hand swooped along lines only he could see. "This marks the longitudinal curve of the hull . . . the string on the batten boards will guide the placement of the structural frame pieces . . . we must divide this length precisely into thirds, and use the result to make a new mark . . ."

Nico nodded dumbly as a tangle of strings and boards rose over the keel, marking where permanent members would take their place. Three carpenters helped measure critical points along the beam. Two worked the rod, while the third called results to Leonardus, who copied the numbers onto a paper.

Leonardus scratched himself and squinted down a line. "This is the trickiest part," he said. "The frames have to become progressively trimmer, narrowing at the stem—just so, do you see? Take it too sharply and she'll yaw like she's drunk. Take it too slowly and she'll lurch at sea like a floating pig. Now come along while we practice our witchcraft." He turned and strode into the mold loft, the shed where the curved futtocks that formed the lower ribs of the frame would be laid out, cut, and joined. During this process Leonardus allowed no one inside except his new apprentice, Nico. "On this," Leonardus said, "I work alone. They've never seen it done, by Christ, and they never will. You're here only because Yusuf insisted, but it doesn't really matter. You'll have to see me do it a hundred times before you make any sense of it, and I'll be dead long before I've done this another hundred times."

As Nico peered over his shoulder, Leonardus drew a *mezzaluna* on a sheet of paper. "I make as the radius the extent by which the stem frame is narrower at the base than the midship frame." The compass moved with practiced ease across the paper. "Then I make eight parallel lines inside, like so. Each line will represent every fifth frame, and when I'm finished, I will have calculated the dimensions of each frame."

After a few moments he leaned back, satisfied. "By God, look at that line, will you? She looks like the curve of a woman's thigh, just inside where it joins——" He looked at Nico and smiled. "You wouldn't know that now, would you? It looks right when it's that way, that's all you need to know. Just the sight of it makes me hard. I'll have a whore tonight, by the holy deprived loins of Jesus."

He began transferring the measurements that the carpenters had called off in the yard, reading and copying. "Fifteen, fourteen and three, thirteen and eight, thirteen and two——"

"Excuse me," Nico said suddenly. "You said thirteen and eight."

"That I did."

"It was thirteen and six. I heard him tell you when he called it off from the measuring rod."

Leonardus scowled. "Nonsense, lad, I wrote it myself. You see?" He showed the paper to Nico, who stared without comprehension. "What in the devil am I showing you for? You can't even read."

"No, sir," Nico said. "But it doesn't matter. It was thirteen and six. You just wrote it wrong, that's all."

"By the blood of Christ, lad . . ." He was about to turn back to his work when he straightened up. "Very well, we'll check." They went outside, and Leonardus himself remeasured the dimension. "Thirteen and six it is," he said, shaking his head.

Back inside, Leonardus bent over his paper once more and made the correction. As he worked, a curious expression came over his face. Slowly he straightened up.

"How did you do that?" he asked.

"What?"

"Remember one number out of a hundred, so you knew there was an error. How did you do it?"

Nico shrugged. "I don't know exactly. It's just something I can do."

Leonardus didn't speak for a while. His gaze made Nico uncomfortable, for it seemed suddenly cold. "What did I say about the measurement of the second frame?" Leonardus asked quietly. "Do you remember that?"

"Yes, sir. That it would be determined by the amount of the two smallest of your calculations from the midpoint of the floor, to the second mark." Nico said the words without having any idea what they meant.

Leonardus stared at him, comprehension dawning slowly in his eyes.

"Does El Hadji Farouk know you can do that?" His voice was full of menace now, his body tense.

Nico squirmed. "Yes, sir. But what does it matter? He said it was a good market trick, that's all. That someday I might perform with monkeys."

Leonardus sprang like a tiger. He caught Nico by the neck and shoulder and slammed him against the wall. Stunned, choking, Nico dangled in his grip. Leonardus's face was flushed with rage. "You filthy child whore! You vile, stinking—Christ's blood, you've been spying on me!"

Nico was crying. "No!" he gasped. "Never! I don't know what you mean! I'm not spying. I'm just watching!"

Leonardus cuffed him viciously. "He would kill for these secrets! He's never been able to get them any other way, and now, by Christ, he's got them through you! What have you told him?" He slapped Nico, his eyes frenzied and red, the veins pulsing at his temples. "What did you tell him?"

Nico fell to the floor, coughing. "Nothing! He's not even here! No one has asked me anything!"

Leonardus grabbed an adze from the table and stepped forward. "And they never will, by God, because a dead boy can tell them nothing!"

Nico held up one arm, to ward off the blow from the razor-sharp tool that would take off his head in one swipe. "Please, Leonardus! I swear! I hate them! I would never tell them anything!"

The blade pressed at Nico's neck until it drew blood. "They would force you! They would take your toes, as they took mine! They would pull your intestines out through your belly and let the dogs gnaw at them! How long will you keep secrets when they slow-roast you? You would scream the secrets to them if it meant you could live!"

"Then I would lie! I'm going to be a knight! I would never help them, not even to keep my toes! I am not a coward, like you!"

Leonardus flinched as if he'd been stricken. He sank to the floor, breathing heavily. The adze quivered in his hand. The clever bastard Farouk! Algerian shipwrights practiced the art of shipbuilding, while Leonardus knew the science. The Algerians managed well enough, but they all knew his ships had a minute advantage at flank speed, which could mean the difference between returning home with a hold of bounty and returning home with nothing—or not returning at all.

Corsairs clamored for his ships. Farouk could sell five times as many as Leonardus could make. Perhaps it was only a matter of time before Farouk knew all the secrets anyway—every shipyard sought them, many had them, every master protected them—but Leonardus was damned if he was going to make it easy. His knowledge preserved his neck. He knew he should kill Nico, kill him right then and there, and be done with it. But he had grown to like the boy, who in any case had not seen the entire process. Partial knowledge would do Farouk little good. And incorrect knowledge, Leonardus realized, could do him great harm.

"*Tajjeb wisq,* lad," he said, nodding. "Man to man, I will trust the word of a fellow Maltese. When they finally ask you, you'll tell them you don't know, because if you seem to give up information too easily, they'll know something is amiss. That will cost you a beating. And then this is what you will tell them." And he spent the remainder of the afternoon teaching Nico the secret mathematical formulas to build a ship that, if ever launched, would make straight for the bottom.

❖

Ameerah was the first wife of El Hadji Farouk, but she was barren. Though many men would have divorced her, Farouk did not. It was his second wife who had borne him his son Yusuf. She died in childbirth, leaving Ameerah the principal wife.

Ameerah did her best to please him sexually. There had been a time when his passions ran hot, but his desire for her had long since faded, and it had been years since he had favored her with a visit to her bed. Whenever he wished a woman, he took one of his younger wives or one of the concubines he kept in the cities to which he traveled. But most often, El Hadji Farouk preferred a boy.

Ameerah had never minded sharing her husband, particularly since she could bear him no heirs, but when he no longer desired her at all, it was more than she could endure. She took lovers—dozens of them, freeman and slave, Moor and Berber, sometimes even Abbas, the massive blackamoor—while her husband slept in a drunken stupor under the same roof. The danger excited her as much as his boys excited him.

As Mehmet's own star with the master had dimmed, she had taken him to her bed. He had climbed in eagerly, a sycophant seeking to curry her favor. Between caresses Mehmet told her everything about the master and about everyone else in the household. She despised him. Yet he was an adept lover and pretended to enjoy his evenings with her, and he guarded her privacy carefully. She slept with him because he knew her secrets and could now betray her only at the cost of his own neck.

She saw how he tried to harm Nico's interests. Mehmet's lies and manipulations were obvious as he sought to maintain his position in the household. The alum in the *macolique* had been typically coarse and transparent; Mehmet had used far too much.

But subtle or not in his desperation, Mehmet was becoming dangerous. She considered ordering Abbas to use the silk cord, but she had no wish to displease her husband, who continued to show passing interest in Mehmet's skills. Even that was diminishing. She supposed it would not be long before El Hadji Farouk would strangle Mehmet in a fit of rage, or sell him to the Bey, whose tastes were less discerning. She would not regret his loss.

It was little wonder that Mehmet plotted against Nico. Nico's beauty was unmatched, his skin soft and unblemished. His long eyelashes curled sensually. The eyes beneath them were still innocent. The boy was without guile, and his mind was a treasure. When he repeated the stories he heard in the market, he remembered everything perfectly, down to the inflections used by the seasoned storytellers, so that even when he didn't understand a meaning, he was able to tell the story as though he'd crafted it himself. She enjoyed watching him grow before her very eyes. The child would become a formidable man indeed.

Slaves rarely interested her any more than the roosters who strutted in the alleys, and ordinarily she did not understand her husband's fascination with boys. Yet she understood it with Nico, whose appeal was evident. She wanted to mother him, to protect and nurture him. After the incident with the alum Ameerah had told Nico not to let himself be victimized. "Though you are more intelligent than anyone I have known," Ameerah told him, "it is Mehmet who is the more cunning. You must seek ways to outwit men like him, or they will forever gain the advantage."

But aside from protecting him, from the moment she first saw him a different idea took root, an idea as tantalizing as it was dangerous. She wanted to have this boy before her husband could. She teased him endlessly, her own fascination rising each time he blushed or turned demurely away. She had never taken a lover younger than fifteen or sixteen, she supposed. She wondered whether Nico's skills of the flesh might be trained to equal those of his mind. She decided to find out.

On the morning of *jum'ah,* when the wives paid their weekly visit to the mosque, Ameerah feigned illness and sent them without her. She told Mehmet to see that she was left undisturbed except for her morning meal.

She was in her private bagnio, drying herself with a thick towel, when she heard the soft rustle of carpets followed by the aroma of fresh bread and honey that meant Nico had arrived in her bedchamber. He would be sitting near the door, dutifully waiting. She applied powder and perfume, and dressed in a diaphanous gown, over which she wore a thicker dressing robe of silk. She tied her hair with ribbons, pushed back the hanging carpet, and stepped into the room.

Nico stood instantly, greeting her with a polite smile. Her outer robe was partially open in front. Beneath the sheer material, she knew he could see the swell of her breasts. She made no effort to hide herself. Embarrassed, he diverted his eyes and moved up and down on the balls of his feet.

"I am hungry, Nico," she said. She sank into her cushions, supporting herself on one elbow. He approached timidly, holding the tray stiffly, clearly sensing that something was very different. "Sit down," she said, beckoning to a cushion.

As was his custom, he cut a piece of bread that he carefully layered with honey, and then poured her some heated goat's milk. He held the cup out to her with both hands. She took it from him with one hand and set it down beside her without drinking. Slowly, holding his eyes with her own, she guided his other hand to her cheek. He stiffened and drew in his breath. She smiled at his innocence. He held his hand perfectly still, in order that an incorrect movement might not offend her. His hand was still warm from the milk and felt wonderful against her flesh. She closed her eyes and slowly, sensually, kissed his fingers.

She opened her eyes and saw that his eyes were not closed, and not even upon her, but wide open, staring at the ceiling. He was deep in thought.

"What are you thinking about, Nico?" she said softly.

"A model of a ship, madam," he said eagerly. "Master Leonardus told me that's what they do in Venice, make a model before they build the ship. Also, I was thinking that your bread is getting cold. Would you like some now?"

The little-boy way he said it ruined the moment for her. Her eyes suddenly welled with tears. She dropped his hand and wiped at her eyes. *He's only a slave. Why should he affect me so?*

"Have I made you angry, madam? I didn't mean to. What should I do?"

She pulled her robe closed at her neck. "Leave me," she whispered.

Nico lay awake all that night, worried that a test had come and gone, and that he had failed even to begin it. He knew it had to do with sex. He wanted to awaken Ibi, to tell him what had happened and ask his opinion. But he was ashamed of his own stupidity. What worried him most was that his own ignorance of such matters would not serve him well with the master, with whom he knew he was destined to have a similar encounter. Ignorance with the master, he knew, would lead to displeasure, and from the displeasure of El Hadji Farouk, everyone told him, there was but a short path to death.

There was no way to know how long it might be before he faced that test. Word had come that El Hadji Farouk had gone unexpectedly from Tunis to Venice. Such changes in plans were not unusual, and in this case meant Nico might have a reprieve of several months.

He wondered if he might find a way to escape before then. Surely Leonardus was ready to try again. Nico broached the subject the next day, when the two were alone. "We should be making plans to leave, don't you think?" he asked.

"Mmm, I suppose," was the only reply. Nico had learned enough about Leonardus to be suspicious. It was the fourth or fifth time he'd brought up the subject. Leonardus, he realized, always got quiet and noncommittal whenever it came up—and Leonardus was never quiet or noncommittal about anything. This convinced Nico that the shipwright was planning something. Yet as he poked around the shipyard and watched everything and kept his ears open, there was no sign Leonardus intended to do anything about his captivity in Algiers except die in it.

Chapter 9

The boy worked the cliffs of Gozo alone, dangling from a rope nearly two hundred feet above surf that pounded and foamed on the jagged rocks below. At its upper end the rope was fastened around a tree, while at its lower end the boy hung in a makeshift sling that he could raise and lower with an ingenious series of knots.

The boy knew every secret of the limestone cliffs. During the day he searched for pigeon nests, always well hidden. He would watch for the adults to fly in and out, noting their locations. While they were gone he would fix a rolled net above the opening, and then find a ledge nearby in which to sleep, and tie himself in. After dark, when the birds were inside, he would unroll the net. The next morning he would reach into the cleft to gather his prize of eggs and meat. It was dangerous work that killed many who tried it, but the boy had been scaling the cliffs since he was six, and he was nimble and fearless on the rope.

There was a time when the cliffs gave him enough to eat and even plumage to sell, but the birds had suffered his attentions for too long and were becoming scarce. He knew of other hunting cliffs, at Imgarr ix-Xini and Ta' Cenc, but had been afraid to try them, fearing he might encounter someone. He had lived alone for a long while now, and the longer he had no contact with people, the more he feared them. The time was coming, he knew, when his growing hunger would overcome fear and force him to try.

In recent weeks he'd spent more of his time hunting for berries, but the hot weather had done something to the bushes, and a whole day of foraging wouldn't fill his belly. Fishing was no better. He had lost the last of his hooks trying to take a big haddock, and he had no way to replace it. Even his knife, the precious heavy hunting knife of Damascus steel that had belonged to his father, had shattered that morning when he dropped it from the rope. He'd recovered the hilt, but most of the blade was lost in the water. He could sharpen the stub of blade that was left, but it wouldn't be much of a knife anymore.

Life was getting difficult. He was going to have to do something soon, something new. He didn't know what, but for now he ignored his hunger and played his game. He loved the feel of hanging so far above the rocks, where, at the end of the rope, he could kick himself away from the cliffs and soar like a bird out over the water, until the arc brought him gently back again, and he could push away once more. Sometimes he passed hours that way. Now he did a series of arcs, leaning back in his sling, arms and head loose. He touched off with his bare feet, not even having to see the cliff, just knowing where it was, then swooping and soaring in long lazy arcs, until he touched to do it again. He looked up at the sky, at the clouds and the sun swirling round and round, blinking on and off behind the cliff . . .

He sat bolt upright.

A man stood atop the cliffs, staring down at him. No one ever came to this part of Gozo, the island that lay just to the north of Malta. He hadn't seen anyone in nearly a year, except from a great distance.

He was hopelessly exposed. The sun was behind the man's head, so the boy couldn't see his face. He couldn't tell if the man was armed. "Leave me alone," he called up.

The man didn't move.

The boy took what was left of his knife and held it out, trying to conceal the fact that the blade was missing. "I can kill you with this," he said.

"I suppose you could if you clubbed me with it," the man said, eyeing the broken weapon. "Do you kill everyone who comes to fish here?"

"Go away. These are my cliffs."

"A thousand pardons, Your Lordship," the man said with a polite little bow. "I didn't know." He sauntered off along the cliffs. The boy heard him whistling softly. As soon as the whistle faded, the boy shinnied up the rope. From the top of the cliffs he watched. The man disappeared from view and then reappeared a while later, at the base of the cliffs near the water. Deftly jumping from rock to rock, he made his way onto a short gravel spit. He never looked up, but settled himself in to fish.

❖

Fençu put cheese on the hook and tossed the line into the water. He felt the boy's eyes on his back but did not turn around. After an hour he took some bread and a bag of hazelnuts from his wicker basket and absently began to eat. It wasn't long before he sensed the boy's presence, much closer now, and then he saw his shadow stretching over his shoulder, onto the rocks and into the water. He turned and looked up. The boy's face was gaunt and dirty, his cheeks thin, his clothing ragged. The boy didn't meet his gaze. His eyes were on the bread. Fençu tore off a chunk and held it up. The boy snatched it away and wolfed it down in two gulps.

"My name is Fençu." He held out a handful of hazelnuts.

"I am Jacobus," the boy said between mouthfuls. "I didn't see your boat."

"I hid it in the bay at Xlendi."

"You know Gozo?"

"I used to live here. I haven't been back in some time. I thought I'd see how the fishing was."

"You're not very good at it," the boy said, eyeing Fençu's line. "You'll never catch anything that way."

"I usually do all right." Fençu smiled. "I'm not as hungry as you, anyway."

"I wouldn't be hungry if I had hooks."

Fençu rummaged through his wicker bag. "Take one of these. Mind you don't lose it. Go on and show me."

Jacobus checked the hook. The tip glinted in the sun. "You keep it sharp." He quickly fastened the hook to the line. Fençu handed him a chunk of moldy cheese for bait, then winced as Jacobus instantly devoured it. The boy got on hands and knees and turned rocks over until he found what he wanted, a shiny black beetle. He skewered it with the hook, the beetle's legs thrashing furiously. He moved down the spit and put his line in the water in a place Fençu had dismissed as too shallow. Five minutes later Jacobus caught a fish. He brought it flapping onto the spit and knocked it senseless with a rock. Working rapidly, he used the stub of his knife blade to scrape the scales and hack off the tail against a stone. Then he ate it raw, entrails and all, ripping the flesh from the bones with his teeth.

Fençu watched with distaste. "I'll grant you know how to fish," he said, "but you could learn something about cooking."

Jacobus wiped blood from his mouth and licked his fingers. "My father taught me to fish. He taught me the cliffs, too."

"Is he a birdman?"

"He was the best, except for me. Until he fell. They had to cut off his leg. After that he only kept sheep."

"Where is he?"

"Dead."

"What of your mother? Your family?"

"The corsairs took them. They took everyone."

Fençu knew the story well. Two years earlier, the Knights of St. John had mounted an attack against the corsair Dragut in Tunis. The attack failed. The Turks sent a fleet commanded by the admiral Sinan Pasha, accompanied by Dragut and his corsair galleys, to mount a raid of reprisal on Malta and Tripoli. Their fleet had arrived the previous summer. Deterred by the defenses of the Knights of St. John on the main island, Sinan and Dragut turned their attentions to Gozo. Dragut had a score to settle. Some years earlier his brother had been slain there, his body burned by the governor, one of the knights. As the fleet approached, the people of Gozo fled their homes and retreated inside the walls of the island's citadel. It was a poorly fortified stronghold, and resistance collapsed quickly. The Turks took everyone into slavery. In all, five thousand souls were carried off—nearly every man, woman, and child. Only twelve old men were left behind, to tell the others on Malta what would happen to those who defied the Turks.

Twelve old men, Fençu reflected—and a boy.

"Why didn't they take you?"

"I was working the cliffs. I never came home until the baskets were full. Sometimes I would stay three or four days at a time. There must have been guns fired, but I couldn't hear over the noise of the sea. I was bringing the baskets home when I saw. By then most of them were on the ships. The island was on fire." He paused, and swallowed. His eyes watered. Ashamed, he wiped them. "I hid. I got closer to try to see my family, but then I had to run. The Turks had patrols out, to poison the wells and burn everything. They chased me. I got back to the cliffs and hid three days in a cave, until I couldn't stand it anymore. When I came out everyone was gone. I went back when it was dark. Even the dogs were gone. I couldn't find our hut. It was near the *castello*. Everything was burned. I got what I could out of the ashes— some netting, some hooks, and this knife. Mostly the Turks took everything, though."

"So you've lived alone all this time?"

"There's no one else. No one comes to Gozo who means anything good. When anyone comes I hide." He stared at Fençu. "Until you. I've done all right, but there haven't been any berries lately, and the hunting hasn't been too good. I need fishhooks, and a new knife. I had some good rope, but it's wearing out, too. I'll be all right. I just need to figure out how to make things."

Fençu had three knives that he used for different tasks. He took the smallest of them and handed it to the boy. "You can have this one. I don't need it."

Jacobus looked at the treasure but didn't take it. "I don't have anything to give you in payment," he said.

"Catch me some more fish. It's why I came."

Jacobus grinned. Soon he was working three lines in the water.

While he fished he finished off Fençu's hazelnuts and the last of his bread, and still he looked famished.

Jacobus tended his lines and hooks and between catches pointed out birds. He knew them all: thrushes and doves, warblers and blackcaps, golden orioles and nightjars, quails and snipes. Some he trapped, and some he only watched. "I caught a falcon on the cliffs once," "My father sold it to one of the licensed falcon trappers, who sold it to the Knights of St. John. I heard they used it to pay the Emperor rent for the islands," he added proudly. "My father made more from that one bird I caught than he did for a whole season of shepherding. He said our falcons are the most famous in the world. There are kings who have them, did you know that? They use them for hunting." The whole time that Jacobus chattered, he caught fish.

It was late afternoon when Fençu rose, his basket bulging. "I'd better be going," he said. "My boat is small. I want to cross the channel before dark."

Jacobus looked wistful. "You could stay here tonight," he said in a small voice. "I have room. We could make a fire."

"My wife expects me."

"Oh." Jacobus pitched a rock into the water.

Fençu shouldered his basket. "Why don't you come with me?"

"What for?"

"You could stay with us. We live in a cave, too."

"I'm *eleven*," Jacobus huffed. "Or even twelve, maybe. I can take care of myself."

"I'm certain of it. It's just that I could use another hand at fishing. And I thought you might be lonely."

Jacobus shook his head. "I like living alone."

Fençu shrugged. "As you like," he said. "Maybe I'll see you again. Good fishing, Jacobus. Beware the corsairs."

He strode back up the spit, stopping to gather some grass. He dipped it in seawater and spread it over the catch to keep it fresh. He turned and waved. Jacobus waved back.

By the time Fençu reached his little boat in Xlendi, the boy had caught up with him and taken his hand, and they rowed the channel together.

❖

Jacobus took a niche high in the cave and made himself a comfortable bed of straw. Fençu was glad of another hand to provide food, freeing himself to work more often as a carpenter, which, like his thieving, brought in hard cash. In the first few days they fished and trapped small game together. "Keep a sharp eye out for the village captains," Fençu warned him. "They'll turn you in to the Order for illegal hunting." By edict of the Grand Master, the penalty for that was three lashes and a year chained to a galley bench. A second offense carried a life sentence at the oar.

"I'm not afraid of the Order," Jacobus said. "But they'll never catch me anyway." Even Fençu didn't have the boy's talent for hunting. The cook pot soon brimmed with delicacies he caught. He brought home eels from springs near Mdina, and turtles from St. Paul's Bay—all of which was fortunate, because Jacobus ate enough for three.

He learned of Fençu's Jewishness with complete indifference. He had no religion, and no ambition other than to keep a full belly and to kill the men who had taken his family.

Except when he was alone with Fençu he was painfully shy, still afraid of people. He descended from his perch in the cave only long enough to get something to eat. He never ate with the others, but carried his bowl and spoon back up to his nest. From the shadows there he watched the odd religious ceremonies, the dances and the games. He was invited to join in but never did.

In the end—only a fortnight after he came to live in the cave—it was a wildly entertaining Jewish ceremony that coaxed him from his perch, along with the presence of a girl from Birgu named Maria Borg.

❖

Maria's remaining reserve about the Jewish celebrations at M'kor Hakhayyim melted at Purim, a festival that celebrated the triumph of good over evil. It was a story of Jews living among non-Jews. Fençu had spent all afternoon making preparations. As the hour grew late Maria made her goodbyes, still reluctant to be present during religious ceremonies. She saw that the afternoon storm that had drenched the island had not yet lifted, but it appeared as if the clouds were beginning to lighten. Rather than try to run home through the rain, she decided to wait a little longer, until it passed. She sat near the entrance, well out of the way, and watched what was going on. Fençu was standing near the spring, his audience ranged around him on the floor, near the fire. He had just finished a round of magic tricks, causing lumps of clay to disappear behind the ears of the children, finding eggs in places where eggs weren't supposed to be, and making one break over the head of Cawl, the silversmith.

With his audience sufficiently boisterous, he began the story of Purim. "Blessed are you, O Elohim, source of the universe, who has sanctified our lives through your laws," he recited from memory, "and commanded us to read the scroll of Esther." He looked at his audience and shrugged. "Alas, as I have no scroll of Esther—and could not read it if I did—you shall have to trust me for the rest." The children screamed and clapped excitedly, for they had been through this with Fençu before.

As she watched, Maria noticed Jacobus watching from his own isolated perch, high up on the opposite wall. She'd seen him there before, and realized he was watching her. She gave him a little wave. She couldn't tell if he waved back; she could see only the top of his head and the whites of his eyes as he peered down into the firelit cavern.

Fençu began the story from the Old Testament, of Esther, a demure Jewish girl; a Persian king named Ahasueros; and the evil Grand Vizier, Haman, who intended to slaughter all the Jews in the kingdom, as he thought them rebellious and disrespectful.

Fençu didn't simply relate the story. He played each of the parts, changing his voice, dress, and posture for every character. When he became Esther his voice rose an octave. His eyes fluttered and he fainted dead away. The children whooped with laughter. Maria, shivering from a draft, drew closer and sat down near the fire, next to Elena.

Fençu turned into King Ahasueros, strutting and puffing beneath a crown of osprey feathers, his voice booming through the cave. He became the king's wife, Vashti, with falsetto voice and dizzying swoon as the king banished her for defying him. Maria was suddenly aware of another presence next to her. It was Jacobus. He was ignoring Fençu and staring unabashedly at her, his doe eyes wide in wonder. She smiled. Gravely he touched her hair and did not take his eyes from her face.

Fençu was transformed into the hero, Esther's uncle Mordechai. He ducked behind a pillar of rock and emerged wearing a long cape and a stern expression, and delivered an impassioned speech warning Ahasueros about evil in his kingdom.

"You look like my sister Romana," Jacobus whispered.

Maria took his hand in hers. "You look a little like my brother Nico." This time he returned her smile. She turned back to the performance. She felt his gaze still upon her, but as Fençu performed, Jacobus gradually seemed to relax until finally his attention was riveted on the one-man play.

Whenever Fençu became the villainous Grand Vizier Haman or even uttered his name, the children twirled their groggers, the noisemakers that Fençu had made for them, and tried to shout down the evil man, for Haman intended to kill all the Jews in the kingdom. The first time it happened, Maria only watched what the others did, giggling at the raucous display. The second time, she grabbed a grogger and twirled it, shouting along with everyone else.

Brave Esther, at grave peril to her own life, revealed to the king that she herself was Jewish. She condemned the Grand Vizier, and the king ordered him executed. By the time Fençu—or Haman—was hanged, eyeballs bulging, cheeks puffed, body writhing at the end of the king's noose, even Jacobus was cheering and stomping his feet, though his hand remained firmly locked in Maria's.

There was a modest feast afterward, and Maria stayed for that, too. Elli handed her a cup of warm honeyed goat's milk. Maria demurred, thinking it had some religious significance. Fençu grinned at her reluctance. "Don't worry," he said, reading her mind. "Even drinking it at Purim won't make you a Jew."

It was a marvelous evening, at the end of which Esther's Jews had been saved, Maria had decided once and for all that the Jews of M'kor Hakhayyim couldn't be the Jews of the stories she'd heard, and Jacobus had decided that when he grew up he was going to marry Maria Borg.

❖

After that Maria rarely missed a celebration. She was still uneasy about participating too directly herself, lest she inadvertently be committing a sin, and she was careful to hide her activities from her father, who would bloody her backside for consorting with Jews, converted or not, and from Dun Salvago, whose Church would do much worse. She reasoned that it was all right if she just watched and listened, and occasionally touched or tasted, so long as she kept her silent promise that at the very first sign of the devil she'd run like the wind and never come back.

At Hanukkah she saw the celebration of the miracle of the oil, when one of the menorah candles was lit each night for eight nights. At Sukkot, the fall harvest holiday, they all built a *sukkah* over-looking the sea. It was a hut made of stones and brambles and branches, decorated with dried weeds and candles. There had been no harvest that year, but Fençu hated to miss any occasion to celebrate, or to give thanks. "Though we live in a mansion," he said, indicating the cave, "we may someday have to live in a hut"—at which he pointed to the *sukkah*—"and we must rejoice in either house that Elohim might provide." And rejoice they did, with onion soup and hot honeyed water. They lit a bonfire and danced beneath the stars to the music of Elena's dulcimer. On every visit Maria brought Jacobus small candies. He hovered near her until Elena shooed him away for being a pest.

Though she had moments of happiness in the cave, Elena persisted in dreaming of leaving Malta, where the future for a whore, Jewish or not, was so much less than she wanted for herself. She had slept with men who put visions into her head that she could not shake, visions of riches and happiness and love, all easily found elsewhere. She and Maria told and retold stories that the Italian storyteller had read, most often the dreamy stories about love. Maria liked those best, despite their far-fetched images of men and women who adored one another. She had never seen two such people on earth. The closest were Fençu and Elli, who seemed at least good friends and laughed easily together. But of romantic love, the love of their fantasies, there seemed no trace in all her universe. "That's because there isn't love like that in Malta," Elena explained. "Only *scopare*. For love we must go to Franza. And do you know, you could even find someone there who would teach you to read."

Franza. Again it was France, fueling Maria's dreams. France, with its ethereal fields of lupine and its silver spoons and grand castles, and love, and books that girls could read. Everything of importance and beauty in the world seemed to exist only in France, while everything that was drab and dreary seemed to exist only in Malta. At first they talked idly of escape to that world, as they might talk of floating away on a cloud. But constant discussion made the idea grow in their minds. Little by little it consumed them, until finally it was real and they began earnestly saving money to buy passage.

At first Maria sold guano and harvested reeds, to sell for use in making torches or as thatch for the roofs of Birgu. As hard as she worked, she was discouraged to realize how little she earned. It would take a pile of guano the size of Sciberras to buy passage.

She sought odd jobs, though she had to be very careful about it. Luca would thrash her if he knew, for it would make him seem as if he couldn't support his family, even though there were many times when he couldn't. She was sure she could keep it from him. He worked from sunrise to sundown and was not there to challenge her, and so long as she took care of her chores he tended to ignore her. Maria had long since learned to manage her mother, who behind her gossipy and scolding tongue was quite timid, weepy, and weak.

Jobs were not easy to come by. Most people shooed her away, their faces creased in disapproval at her immodesty. But not everyone. A weaver hired her to spin yarn. She worked a few hours at a time. Weeks passed with promises of pay but no money. She pressed him gently at first, then more forcefully as one, then two months passed. When she threatened to quit he put her out. "I know your father," he said. "If I see you here again, I'll tell him." The money was lost, but she was determined he would not get the better of her. The weaver's wife kept a stall at the market, where she sold his yarn from thick spindles. Fençu gave Maria some soft tar from the docks where he sometimes worked, and while Elena distracted the weaver's wife, Maria gooped three spindles of yarn with the stuff.

She found a job gutting fish. The labor was backbreaking and smelly. The first evening she worked until dark, her hands freezing in cold silvery mountains of tunny. As she worked the fishmonger came up behind her. She felt his hands on her shoulders, and before she knew it they were groping at her front. She whacked him with a fistful of entrails and never came back.

Elena continued her evening work, while during the days she and Maria began making candles, a craft at which Elena excelled. She and Maria sweated over a great iron vat, stoking the fire and stirring a bubbling broth of animal fat, then skimming waxy white tallow from the surface. They gathered rushes along the coast and stripped out the pith for candlewicks. Using a long blade that Fençu made specially for the purpose, Elena sculpted the candles into elaborate shapes. Sometimes she added color, for which the nobles of Mdina paid extra. Maria had the idea to make a model of St. Agatha's, her parish church. There was nowhere to place the wick, so Elena added a bell tower and put it there. Father Salvago beamed when Maria brought it to him. "A masterpiece—and that is exactly the belfry the church shall have one day." He bought it to display on the altar, but he could afford to give her only a few maravedis for it.

The girls used the poorer tallow to make soap. Though the candles were beautiful and the soap strong, neither earned them much money.

One night a man paid Elena with a goat instead of money after a tumble in his hayloft. The animal had pendulous ears and great luminous eyes but was scrawny and sick. They had to carry her back to the cave. Fençu took one look at the emaciated creature and shook his head at their folly. "She'll be in tonight's stew," he predicted. They ignored him. They dipped a cloth in honeyed water. The goat downed it eagerly, cloth and all, and they took turns nursing her. Day after day they filled baskets with tender green shoots of marram grass, which grew along the shore, and she devoured it. Elena took to stealing flowers from the gardens of the noble mansions of Mdina, allowing the goat to nibble her way back to health on primroses and violets. She fattened rapidly. They named her Esther, after the Jewish girl in Fençu's Purim story.

One day Jacobus appeared with another goat, a buck that he'd found in the wild. "You can have him," he told Maria proudly. The gift was gaunt and his horns were thin, yet somehow he was quite as noble in bearing as Esther. His hair was short and red, except for his beard, which was long and white and gave him a sagacious air. They called him the King, for Ahasueros.

Maria's father, like most of his neighbors, kept sheep in his house and had always made disparaging comments about goats and their keepers. So Maria added goat keeping to her long list of deceptions. She found that on the whole, she liked the goats much better than sheep. They were nimble and intelligent, almost crafty. They were curious about everything, were terribly independent, and had a restless streak that matched her own. The King was high-strung and fastidious, Esther affectionate and sensitive, and it wasn't long before Elena spotted the King straddling Esther's back, humping wildly. "Look!" she called to Maria. "They're fucking! We're going to get a herd!"

Five months later Esther delivered three healthy kids, two females and a male. After Esther's colostrum ran she obliged Maria and Elena with abundant milk. She was a colossal producer, and they milked her fat teats three times a day. They traded two of the kids, the male and one of the females, for a mature milk goat, giving them two producers. Not long after that they picked up another wild goat, and before long the girls were leading a small herd over the stony fields in search of forage, usually with Jacobus tagging along behind them.

They experimented with making cheese. The first few batches were inedible, but they improved with practice. Fençu built a press and showed them how to make hard cheese by squeezing out most of the moisture. The climate in the cave was perfect for storage, and the cheese ripened slowly. Elena kept some for the cave stores, while Maria tried to sell the rest in Birgu. It was difficult, as people either already had their own source for cheese or couldn't afford it. They sent her away, though she kept trying.

Then one morning Maria saw the knight La Valette in the street outside the castle, on his way down to the quay. He had been named General of the Galleys, becoming one of the most powerful knights of them all. Though she hated him and all his Order for failing to chase after Nico, she would gladly take his money. As usual, he was surrounded by a dozen pages and servants-at-arms, a phalanx of arrogance that cleared a path for the mighty knight. As usual, Maria was undeterred. She stood in their way and blurted out her request.

"She's been pestering the quartermaster for weeks," one of the brothers told La Valette. "He says we have no need of her goods."

La Valette stopped and looked at her. She thought he looked like one of the kings on coins she'd seen at the market. His hair was gray, his face lean, his bearing proud. Though it had been little more than a year since she'd met him last, she doubted he would remember her. She was wrong. "I see you've lost none of your bravado, Maria Borg," he said. "Your manners are rash, and you've forgotten your station."

It stung her that he delivered the rebuke with dignity rather than scorn, as she would have expected. She did her best to betray no sign the reproach even registered. "I seek only to sell cheese, Your Excellency," she said. "I had not realized one needed a station to do so."

A page moved to strike the insolent girl, but La Valette stayed his hand. He appraised her coldly. "I'll take all you can give me," he said at last. "Wrap half in cloth, for my auberge. Take the rest to the cellars, for my galley slaves. Mind that your price is fair." He nodded slightly and moved down the hill. Maria smiled brightly at his scowling page. The next morning she delivered half her heavy load to the auberge, the dormitory in Birgu where the knights from Provence and Auvergne lived while in Malta. A surly steward opened the door. She glimpsed ornate woodwork and tapestries, but it was the rows of lovely books that held her eye. She offered to carry the cheese inside, hoping to have a closer look. "You'll soil the floor," the steward grumbled, and took her packets from her.

She walked through Birgu to the end of the peninsula, where the castle of St. Angelo stood above the harbor. She passed over a wooden drawbridge and presented herself at the castle gate. A page led her through the grounds of the fort. She'd never been so far inside, and she gawked at everything. Great cavaliers soared above her, with thick walls that looked as though they could withstand the very hellfire of Lucifer's own cannons. She climbed upward, following the page across a rampart that overlooked Birgu, then up again through a series of ramps and doors toward the magisterial palace that dominated the promontory and served as quarters for the Grand Master. The bailey in front of the barracks was crawling with knights and men-at-arms, tradesmen and their carts, and craftsmen who worked on the fortifications.

Then the page led her down several flights of stairs, hewn from the rock that plunged to Kalkara Creek. They halted at a wide doorway cut from the stone. The opening was barred by a heavy door secured with metal bars. On the other side were caverns that honeycombed the rocks beneath Fort St. Angelo, caverns in which the Order's galley slaves were imprisoned when not at sea. She glimpsed gaunt faces and dark eyes. A chill ran up her spine.

"Swill for Mohammedan swine," the page called out in Arabic, and at once a thicket of lean, muscled arms appeared through the grillwork, weaving and grasping like so many brown serpents. Straining with the heavy load, and more than a little nervous, she lifted the basket toward the door. It was ripped from her hands and yanked to the bars. The slaves inside fought over the cheese, howling and snarling like hungry dogs. Frightened, she stepped back. The page smirked at her discomfiture. The basket fell to the ground. She snatched it up but fought her impulse to race up the stairs, determined not to give the page the satisfaction.

True to his word, La Valette bought everything Maria and Elena could produce, and they thought their fortunes were made. Every Friday they counted their money. Their savings grew steadily, but painfully slowly. Then five of their newer goats, including three milk producers, caught a fever. They staggered and stumbled and ran in circles for two days, never slowing even to sleep. Fençu force-fed them a potion and bled them. They died anyway.

Maria, who handled all the money, did the calculations. "If we buy new goats, it will be another three years before we'll have enough for passage. If we don't buy new goats, it will be five." She looked at Elena, discouraged. "I'm going to be *eighteen* before I can leave here," she said in despair. "*Ancient.*"

Waiting so long was more than they could bear. They visited the wharf below Birgu where merchant vessels docked, carrying grain and timber from northern ports. They met an old mariner who ran a big galley to Sardinia, and offered to work on his ship for passage. He laughed. "There's nothing the two of you can do on my ship but lift your skirts," he said, "and there's plenty of that in every port. There's no good luck to be had carrying women on a working ship. I'll not tempt Poseidon with the likes of you." They received variations on the same answer from other captains, giving up only when the harbormaster ran them off the quay.

Dejected, they sat on the low seawall, dangling bare feet above the water. Fishing boats bobbed in the creek, making their way out to sea. *Dghajjes* ferried men and animals across the harbor, their pilots standing, pushing long oars back and forth to propel the boats through the water. Ships were being loaded and unloaded, some at the quay, others by lighters in the harbor. Across the creek on Senglea, a peasant pushed a cart loaded with grain up the incline toward the windmill atop Molino hill. His wife struggled beside him, the two of them slipping and sliding as they strained against the load. Except for Fort St. Michael, which stood above them, it was a scene that had changed little in generations.

"We'll never get out," Elena said, "unless we hide on a ship." She said it almost casually. A moment later they looked at each other, their blood racing at the outrageous idea.

"We could find one that's going just as far as Sicily," Maria said, "so the passage wouldn't be so long. But there's no way to sneak on."

"I know a way." Elena talked rapidly, explaining her idea.

"How would we make him fall asleep?"

"I know a soothsayer," Elena said. "She helped me once when I was pregnant."

Maria looked up sharply. "You were *pregnant?*"

Elena ignored the question. "She can do anything with roots and spells. She can make a bird fall from the sky just by rubbing a beating rabbit's heart on a pile of guano."

"Why would anyone want to make a bird fall from the sky?" Maria did not share Elena's unwavering confidence in such things.

"It's just something she can *do*," Elena said. "And she can get us on a ship, too."

Lucrezia was ancient, her skin like yellowed parchment, the lines on her face as deep as the gullies that scarred the island. Her apothecary was a clutter of bat wings, rodent skulls, and other tools of her trade. There was a musty smell about the place, a smell of dried blood and old dreams, a smell of insect parts and animal skins and limitless curses and cures. She made their potion. "The devil's own nectar," she proclaimed. "Just one drop and even the hardiest sailor will sleep for a week."

❖

They found their ship, a large three-masted galleass from Barcelona. She had three holds, gun ports on two decks, scores of hiding places—and she was leaving for Palermo in two days. The girls hugged and danced. The gentle breeze off the harbor had never felt so fresh, so lovely, so full of hope.

Though the scheme was Elena's, it was Maria who shored up their courage. As they made their preparations Elena felt her courage flagging: the doing was not as easy as the talking. "What do you think they do to stowaways?" she asked Maria. "To women, I mean, if they catch them?"

"Don't worry! They'll just put us off at the next port—and the next port is where we're going. What can they possibly do besides that?"

They told Fençu of their plans. He agreed to care for their goats and to sell them when the price was right. Once he received word of their whereabouts he would send their money. "You are fools, you know," he told them, but he gave them three golden florins for their journey. "Even fools must eat," he said.

Jacobus dissolved in tears at the news. He climbed to his nest and hid, refusing to come down. Maria climbed up and sat with him. He threw his arms around her waist and buried his head on her shoulder. She stroked his hair. "You can help Fençu care for the goats, and you can keep some of the money when he sells them," she said.

He looked at her with red eyes. "I don't want money. I don't want goats. I want you. Don't leave, Maria." A great tear rolled down his cheek, and he hid his face in shame.

She swallowed hard. "It's all right," she said. "I'll be back." She didn't know whether it was true or not. It didn't matter to Jacobus. She had to pry his fingers from her jerkin before she could leave, and her own lip was quivering. By the time she'd said goodbye to Elli and Imperia and the others, she was in tears.

She left her house for the last time without saying goodbye to her parents. She felt a tightness in her throat, but there was nothing she knew to say, and she couldn't tell them what she planned. She carried nothing but the clothing on her back, her blanket, and all the money she and Elena had saved. She slipped outside and didn't look back.

Just after eleven they squatted behind the stone wall of the

Carmelite convent that overlooked the creek. They had bread and cheese but were far too nervous to eat. The galleass was to sail just after dawn. By midnight all was quiet aboard the ship. They could see the dim figure of the watch officer moving about. He smoked a pipe on the quarterdeck and pissed over the bow. They waited.

At three o'clock the watch officer relaxed on the gunwale, his legs draped on either side, his back propped against a halyard. He pulled his cap low over his eyes and rested his chin on his chest.

Elena took a deep breath and walked bravely onto the wharf. Oil lamps flickered on their posts, causing her shadow to dance eerily along the hull of the ship. She tossed a pebble. It plinked against the hull and fell into the water. The watch officer sat upright. Confused, he looked around, and then he saw her. She drew a bottle from the sack and made an obscene gesture.

A moment later she was aboard. Maria watched them in the shadows. The sailor immediately pressed Elena's back to the rail and tried for a kiss. Coyly Elena slipped away, her low giggle just audible. He reached for the bottle and took a long swig of the wine, laced heavily with Lucrezia's potion. He caught her by the waist and drew her to him. This time he got a kiss. She broke away and bade him take another drink. He obliged gladly, drinking deeply. He wiped his chin on his sleeve. He said something and laughed, then led her into the darkness.

The two had hardly settled themselves before Maria was scampering up the gangplank, cringing as it sagged and creaked under her weight. She stepped aboard and ran lightly across the deck to a spot between the ship's wheel and the binnacle box.

The harbor was calm. The ship barely moved in the water, yet she could feel the sea beneath the keel. She heard ropes groan and timbers creak softly, and the whisper of a night breeze through the ship's rigging. Above that she heard something else quite nearby: the heavy sighs of passion as Elena kept the watch officer occupied. Maria realized they'd climbed into a longboat, suspended on ropes from posts near the starboard rail.

She tiptoed across the deck and climbed a companion ladder. On the upper deck she banged her head on a brass lantern hanging from a gimbal. She tripped on something and fell into a thick coil of rope. She made little noise, though her temple throbbed. A moment later she lifted the wicker grating that covered the rear hold, and slipped inside.

The hold was pitch-black, the hull clammy to the touch. The air was stale and smelled of rotted wood, salt, and urine. She found a narrow perch on a crate and settled in to wait. The motion of the ship seemed amplified in the cramped space. She forced back her nausea, wondering what vermin and vile creatures lurked in the darkness. Even so, her smile was nearly bright enough to light the hold.

We're going to Sicily. To Franza.

She counted slow rolls of the ship, stopping when she got to a hundred. She did it twice more. Time stretched interminably. Through the grating overhead she saw the first glimmer of dawn. Another hundred, and another.

She knew something was wrong. It would soon be daylight, and still there was no sign of Elena.

❖

Elena expected the sailor to pass out, intending to leave him in the longboat and slip away to the hold, to hide with Maria until the ship sailed. But something was wrong with the potion. The sailor quickly drank half the bottle, which should have finished off the entire ship's company. The only effect she could detect was that his poker went soft. An hour after he began, he finished the last of the bottle, his pants down around his knees. She played with him expertly, trying to arouse him, but the only thing growing was his frustration.

She leaned over and took him in her mouth, trying everything she knew. He leaned back and moaned, taking her head in his hands and working her the way he wanted. Five minutes passed that way, then ten. A man's failure in such matters can make time seem to stop. They were each acutely aware of it, each trying ever harder, but no matter their efforts, still there was nothing: only the night grew longer.

Elena cursed the old woman and her brew. All by itself, she thought, the wine should have made the sailor pass out—the potion must be keeping him *awake*. She considered whacking him over the head with the bottle, but that needed more courage than she had.

Just as dawn was beginning to light the eastern sky, she heard crew members begin straggling aboard. The ship was still deep in shadows. There was still enough time to hide, but only if she moved quickly. "I'm going," she whispered.

The officer's eyelids were heavy. "Be off with you, then," he snarled. "Never had a woman so plain she couldn't get me up."

She slipped over the edge of the longboat and dropped lightly to the deck. She started toward the rear hold and ran squarely into a crewman. She yelped, and he grunted in surprise.

The ship came alive quickly. A knot of sailors crowded around Elena. The watch officer tumbled from the longboat to the deck with a thump and a curse. Groggily he got to his feet, fastening his trousers. The men roared with laughter. One of them held Elena as another tore at her clothing. A third clutched her by the hair and tried to kiss her. Elena struggled mightily, but she was overpowered.

Maria sprang from the darkness and launched herself into their midst, punching and biting and flailing. With a lucky swipe she gouged one sailor across his eyeball with her fingernail. The shriek he produced made the others hesitate. The first officer arrived, and behind him the captain, who stormed into the fray and restored order with his lungs and a truncheon. He locked the two stowaways in his cabin and sent a sailor for the harbormaster.

In the cabin Elena sobbed bitterly. Her cheek was bruised and her dress was torn, but that wasn't why she wept. "Why didn't you stay hidden?" she wailed at Maria.

"I wouldn't leave without you!"

"I would have been all right! You should have gone! It was all for nothing! Now we're both stuck here forever!"

Later that day Maria stood before her seething father. "So you want to leave Malta," he said scornfully. "You think yourself too good for your family. Yet you run with . . . with a *whore*."

"Don't call her that, father. She's my friend."

"Your *friend!* You choose such a one for a friend!" He was going through Maria's things as he spoke. He dumped the contents of her money sack onto the table. Maria bit her lip. Elena's money was in there, too. She'd been carrying it all. Luca stared at it for a time. When he looked up his gaze was withering. "Or are you a whore now, too?"

Maria's eyes welled with tears of rage. She glared at him and said nothing.

"What is it that poisons your mind? Why would you want to leave your family, your home?"

She fought to keep the despair from her voice but, despite her effort, couldn't help weeping. "Because there's nothing here," she said finally.

Luca Borg took up his cane and whipped her. He kept all the money and forbade her to leave the house.

"There's nothing anywhere," he said.

Chapter 10

Every four months Leonardus made a trip with a slave crew to the small port of Shershell, four days by oxcart to the west of Algiers. The men were escorted by a guard of Janissaries, who prevented escape and provided protection against the Berber tribes who lived in the mountains and stole slaves whenever they could. The crew worked in the forests above the port, marking, cutting, and hauling wood.

Leonardus inspected the trees, selecting pine for the keels and cypress or cedar for other parts of the ships. Before a tree was cut he could visualize what it would yield. The shapes danced in his head until they were hewn from the tree, as a sculptor saw form inside a block of marble. "What do you see in that cedar?" he asked Nico, pointing at a gnarled old tree.

"Wood. Bark. Just a tree," Nico said.

"Just a *tree?* Lord's balls, boy! It's like a woman wearing skirts! You have to imagine the shape beneath! There, do you see, where the branch parts from the trunk, like a woman parting her legs, waiting for a plugging? If that's not the rudder of a warship waiting to be freed from its prison of wood, I'm the son of a whore myself!" He looked at Nico and laughed. "You can't see it, can you, lad? You're not even playing with yourself yet, much less sailing a woman's straits. I'll fix you up with one of my doxies. She'll have your rudder up in no time."

Nico blushed at the gentle mocking. He squinted at the tree, trying to see what Leonardus saw, but only after the tree had been felled, the bark stripped, and the excess wood cut away did Nico see the rudder Leonardus had seen all along. And nowhere in any of it did he see the faintest hint of a woman. For that, he guessed, he'd need some wine.

Leonardus was everywhere in the cutting operation, directing the woodchoppers who felled the logs, the sawyers who trimmed them, and the laborers who loaded them on carts for the journey down the mountains to the port, there to be stowed aboard the galleys for the trip home. Leonardus marked each piece, some to be softened in the soaking pits, others to be seasoned, and he kept a detailed record in a book.

They camped in an olive grove near the water. Shershell had been an important Roman port called Caesarea. There were ruins to explore, old stadium walls and columns and baths, and marble statues that lay on their sides between the olive trees, their faces hacked away by the Arabs, for whom graven images were considered an affront to Allah.

Nico swam naked in the warm water of the bay and waded in the rocks along the shore. Leonardus showed him where to find mussels in the tide pools. That night they boiled them over their campfire, drenching them with lemon juice that ran down their chins. Leonardus insisted Nico drink with him, but Nico had discovered that alcohol disagreed not only with his head but with his stomach, and so he only pretended. Leonardus got roaring drunk. He sang to the saints and danced in the sea. He fell facefirst into shallow water. The Janissaries dragged him onto the shore and into the olive groves, where slaves were chained for the night. They clamped him into an ankle iron between Nico and the marble remnants of Aphrodite.

Leonardus slept in a stupor for an hour, but then he grew restless. He rolled over on Nico, who pushed him away. Leonardus mumbled and laughed and babbled, in Spanish and Italian and in the bastard dialect of Barbary. Nico covered his ears with his hands, trying to sleep. He was just drifting off when he heard a few words in Maltese.

"*Melita, Melita . . . dgħajsa . . . Melita . . . bicca . . .*" There were other words, all disjointed and rambling, but those words registered.

Malta. A boat. Pieces.

Nico sat up. He shook Leonardus, hoping the man would say more in his stupor. "What is it? What do you mean?" Leonardus drooled and turned over.

Nico didn't sleep the rest of the night. He turned it over and over in his mind, trying to turn the words into sense. Of course, Leonardus was planning something; he'd been sure of it all along. But what? *Pieces?* What pieces? The shipyard was full of pieces. Then he was just as sure that he was wrong. It meant nothing, just drunken babble.

Or was it? He fell asleep to the words. *Dgħajsa. Melita.*

The day they returned to Algiers, while Leonardus was occupied in the store yard, Nico sneaked into the mold loft. It was the only place that was secret at all, generally off-limits to all but Leonardus, the master carpenters, and himself. It was a working shed, a single mammoth room filled with the sweet aroma of freshly cut wood. The floor was a soft carpet of sawdust and curled shavings. Tools hung from hooks on wooden posts, everything in its place. Leonardus kept an orderly shop. The walls were lined with neat stacks of seasoned lumber, while shelves held pieces that had been marked for cutting and joining. Boards were propped against walls or supported on sawhorses, then laid out on the floor, where they took shape according to the patterns calculated and drawn by the shipwright.

Nico searched everywhere. He lifted pieces of wood away from the rear wall, thinking he'd find false boards concealing a room. He stomped on the floor behind the stacks, expecting a trapdoor beneath the sawdust. There had to be a place big enough to hold a small boat. He climbed atop bunks of lumber and looked above the beams that supported the roof.

Nothing.

Discouraged, he sat down. Perhaps in Leonardus's own shed. It was too small. Perhaps the oar house, or . . .

He rested his head in his hands.

Pieces.

He opened his eyes and looked again at the bits of wood, the half-worked pieces that had been cast aside, as if they'd been cut wrong. Some of them had, but others . . . He rummaged through them. *Yes!* There was the port side of the aft section of a small craft. Taken alone it seemed nothing more than another piece of waste, until he saw its opposite number, leaning against a different wall, behind a pile of cedar. When he realized what he was seeing, he pawed through the stacks again until he'd found four sections. It was just the ribbing of the frame, but it all fit.

He couldn't find them all, but he knew they were there somewhere, visible to anyone yet invisible to all. Pieces of wood among pieces of wood. He dragged two of them out into the middle of the floor and placed together. They fit perfectly, awaiting only planking, dowels, and caulking. There was even a half-round mount cut in each side of the keel. When fitted together, he knew they'd hold the base of a small mast, for a sail. A group of carpenters who knew what they were doing would have it seaworthy in an hour.

Nico could barely suppress a whoop. Leonardus had built a miniature caique under the very noses of his captors! It was a small boat, big enough for perhaps only four men. He crossed himself and whispered, "Please, God, make it fit four men and a *boy*." He carefully put everything back again and left the mold loft.

The next day, while he and Leonardus were eating, Nico could hold it no more. "Take me with you," he said.

"I'm not going anywhere."

"When you escape. I want to go with you."

"You talk nonsense."

"I found the boat."

"Clever lad, to find a boat in a boatyard."

"I'm not an idiot, Leonardus. You're building a caique. I found the pieces."

Leonardus didn't reply at first. He sucked an orange and watched some laborers struggling with a cart loaded high with muslin for making sails. The load was about to tip. "You there!" he bellowed to an overseer. "See they mind that rut! Dump that cloth in the mud and I'll have your balls for ballast and your foreskin for a sail!"

Still watching the cart, he spoke to Nico in a low voice. "You seem to be a boy from whom secrets are ill kept. This is the second time my instinct has told me to kill you. My instincts are not often wrong." He ate the last of his orange, wiped the juice from his beard, and belched.

"I can keep a secret. Take me with you."

Leonardus considered it. He and three carpenters had built the boat over a period of months, a piece here, a bit there. If the other men knew Nico was aware of their secret, they would cut the boy's throat whether or not Leonardus approved. They all knew the risks and the penalty for failure. The boat would hold four men and the food and water they would need for the journey north to the Balearics. There was no room for another, not even one so small as Nico, whose weight would jeopardize them all.

As fond as Leonardus had grown of the boy, he couldn't risk it. He couldn't stand another failed attempt. He would make the Balearics or die trying. He considered telling Nico the truth. The boy was young and bright and would have plenty of time to engineer his own escape. But a dejected Nico might be more dangerous to this secret than a hopeful Nico who thought his own skin depended upon keeping it. Leonardus didn't want to harm him to silence him. There was only one way to handle it.

The shipwright sighed, and nodded. "*Kollox sew,*" he lied. "You can come. There is more work to be done before we're ready, and it's dangerous. It'll want a few more weeks, or even months."

A broad smile lit Nico's face. He launched himself at the man, wrapping his arms around his waist. "You won't regret it," he said. "I'll make you glad! You'll see!"

Leonardus pushed him away, his expression hard. "Mind yourself, lad. We need no scenes. If you so much as raise an eyebrow out of place, you won't live long enough to be keelhauled. I'll cut your throat myself." He drained his flask and strode off.

Nico fairly floated through the next few weeks on his new wings of hope, as he carefully sought to preserve the secret. Whenever he found himself near the mold loft, he sauntered past as casually as he could. He fought the impulse to examine the progress of work on the caique, fearing that he might be observed. He stared at the sea, and when he felt the breeze on his face, it was all he could do not to yell out loud—it was the breeze of freedom he felt.

He tended quietly to his household chores. Though the idea troubled him, he thought he ought to avoid Ibi, so as not to inadvertently give away the secret. He continued to bring meals to the gardener but spent as little time as possible in their shed. Yet one night Ibi was awake when Nico came in, waiting with news. "I was in the market last night," he said. Nico had not gone along. "I saw Mehmet."

"Oh? I didn't know he went to the place."

"Nor did I. It was most curious. I observed from a distance. He was at the scribe's. I saw Mehmet pay the scribe and put a letter in his sash."

Nico yawned. "Why would he do that? There is a scribe in this household." In fact, El Hadji Farouk had three scribes, who attended to his various businesses. They worked from a small room near the front gate.

"That is the question I myself have puzzled over. I have no answer, except that he wishes to conceal something."

Nico shrugged. "Perhaps he has written the devil and wants no one to know. It is nothing to me."

"I would not be so certain. The only reason Mehmet does anything is for some unsavory purpose. I fear his intentions where you are concerned, my young friend. It is clear his hostility for you knows no bounds."

"Yes, but how can he hurt me with writing?"

"How should a simple gardener know the answer to that? I only tell you so you might be wary. While a man sleeps, are not the seeds of his destruction easily sown?"

"What should I do?"

"Worry."

❖

Unlike a man intent upon escape, Leonardus worked furiously to complete the latest galley, upon which the live work—the construction of the keel and hull—had been completed. Nico stood in the prow as the partially finished boat was launched down the slipway into the harbor, where workmen would begin the dead work, that of fitting it with benches, cabins, and partitions for the hold. "Any horse's ass can do this part," Leonardus said, "and fortunately I'm blessed with a score of Spaniards who fit the bill."

First there was a slight list to starboard to be corrected. "Fresh off the slipway and less than two degrees of list," Leonardus said proudly. "By the short hairs of the saints, they'll not match that in Venice!" He filled a cup with wine, for use as a level. He set the cup on the poop deck and called out instructions to the laborers toiling in the bilge, who shifted ballast between movable planks. Each time he bellowed his orders, he drained the cup while they complied, then filled it again to check their progress. In his zeal for precision, he went through five cups, after which he was listing only slightly, and the ship not at all.

After that the mast was hoisted, and seamen rigged the brails that would control the amount of sail catching the wind. The central gangway was laid in, and the pontapieds, the stand-and-sit boards used by the rowers at ramming speed. A light bronze half cannon was fitted to the bow beneath a half deck, while two Turkish *darbezens,* swivel cannons that threw scatter shot, were fixed to the gunwales. Under the watchful eyes of armed guards, newly milled oars were balanced with lead weights until they swung perfectly on their pins. Afterward, as with all oars in Algiers, they were stored under lock and key, to keep them out of the hands of slaves.

As the ship was transformed from an empty hull to a corsair's dream, a sleek and efficient killer, Nico felt a taste of the pride that drove Leonardus. Nico had been transformed along with the ship. On his first day at the shipyard, he had refused to descend the few steps into the hold of a new galley and couldn't even bring himself to watch the laborers at work there. Even without the stench, his memory of it was too fresh. Now he thought better of it. *I am not a child. I am going to escape, and someday I will be captain of a ship like this.* When he stepped at last into the hold, he found it smelled of cedar and held no ghosts. As he walked the vessel, he both hated and admired Leonardus for using his skill to produce such a dreadful weapon, and yet he longed to be her captain, his sailors and knights ranged behind him, ready to do battle. The vision brought thoughts of his reunion with Maria, and the sight of Birgu, and home. Even the thought of the whipping his father would give him seemed something to look forward to.

His impatience had another edge. Everyone expected that El Hadji Farouk would return any day. If he and Leonardus departed soon enough, it meant his long-dreaded day of reckoning with Farouk might never come to pass. Nico kept looking to Leonardus for a wink or a nod or some signal that all was ready, but the shipwright was forever impassive. When the two of them were alone Nico didn't mention the topic, determined to show he could be trusted to keep silent.

A new fear seized him. He thought of Ibi's revelation, that Mehmet had visited a scribe. If Ibi was right and Mehmet meant him ill, whatever he was planning might ruin everything. The thought gnawed at him. Were Mehmet's looks more venomous of late than usual, or less? Were his tricks more subtle? And that itself began to worry him: there had been no tricks for more than a week. Mehmet must be up to something.

He had to find the paper. Whatever trouble it held, he knew that he would find it either in Mehmet's quarters or not at all. Mehmet lived in a small room near the vestibule, off the interior courtyard of the house. As with the other rooms, it was visible from most places in the courtyard. A curtain served as door to the room. Nico watched the comings and goings of the staff. There was usually someone around, and Mehmet himself was unpredictable as he tended to affairs of the household. He might appear anywhere, unannounced. The only time he was away was every other Wednesday morning, when he went to the baths.

Of course.

Tuesday night Nico told Ibi what he intended. "Be vigilant," the gardener said. "If you are seen, I will be planting pieces of you in the garden for a week."

The next morning as Nico returned from the bakery, he saw Mehmet leaving through the iron gate, a roll of fresh clothing under his arm. Nico hurried to the kitchen, where the cook gave him warm milk, which he took with the bread on a tray to Ameerah's quarters. Though she was still friendly toward him, their morning ritual had changed. She no longer wished him to feed her, and her instructions were more practical than sensual.

This morning she wished to have Nico rearrange her furnishings. Inwardly he groaned as he hurried through the chores, pushing mats and stools and cushions where she directed, then pushing them elsewhere when she changed her mind.

"You seem preoccupied, Nico," she said.

"I am sorry, madam. There is much to do, that's all." When at last her changes were completed he lingered in the courtyard, doing his best not to arouse suspicion. One of the houseboys swept the marble floors. The cook seemed to have nothing better to do than to lounge near the kitchen, smoking a pipe. Finally a moment came when Nico thought all was clear, and he slipped into Mehmet's room. His palms were wet with sweat and his mouth was dry. The room was plain, windowless, and shadowy. The only furnishings were a low table, a wooden case, a sleeping mat, and a light woolen blanket. He searched beneath the bedding, his heart racing every time he heard a sound outside. He opened the case, in which Mehmet's clothing was neatly folded. He riffled through the garments, then lifted them out and scoured the box for secret compartments. There was nothing.

There was virtually nothing else in the room, save an oil lamp in its niche on the wall. He lifted the lamp and saw that it sat upon a piece of tin. He lifted that and smiled: one page, filled with flowing writing. He tucked it in his pants and replaced the lamp.

He tiptoed to the doorway, stopping behind the curtain to make certain the way was clear. The cook had gone inside the kitchen. A houseboy hurried by with a chamber pot. Ibi was on the far side of the central garden near the fountain, bent over his shovel. Just as Nico was ready to dart out, Mehmet strode through the vestibule, only steps away.

There was nowhere to hide. Nico knew he was caught. He pressed himself against the wall. It was too late even to replace the letter. He took a deep breath and closed his eyes, as if that might help conceal him and his crime.

There was a loud crash in the courtyard. Mehmet cursed loudly. "You clumsy fool! You'll pay for that!" Nico peered through the curtain and saw Mehmet striding toward Ibi, where the gardener was scurrying to pick up the pieces of a decorative urn he'd over-turned. Flowers and dirt were strewn on the marble floor, mixed with shards from the urn.

"A thousand pardons, master," Ibi said, trying unsuccessfully to avoid Mehmet's pummeling. Mehmet cuffed him on the side of the head as he issued a torrent of abuse.

Nico saw the cook emerging from the kitchen, but his eyes were on the commotion. Nico slipped through the curtain, crept partway around the gallery, and then turned through the colonnades into the courtyard, hurrying forward to help clean up the mess. Mehmet glared at him. "I should have known you were nearby," he said. "You'll pay for this, too." He turned and walked to his room.

Nico knelt next to Ibi and picked up bits of urn. He saw blood on Ibi's cheek. "Thank you," he whispered.

"Did you find it?"

"Yes. I'll go to the scribe's tonight."

All day Nico felt the letter burning next to his skin, worried that surely Mehmet would discover it missing before he could return it, and that he would guess from the commotion in the courtyard who'd taken it. The day dragged interminably. He felt the hot scirocco blowing from the great desert that lay beyond the mountains, and watched the dust that it carried turn the sun blood red. When the sun was shimmering near the horizon and it was time to leave, Nico stopped to say good night to Leonardus, who had not yet been chained in his shed for the night.

The shipwright was in his chair, watching the spectacular sight. He took a long drink from his flask and looked up at Nico. "We're leaving Friday night, lad. It's *jum'ah,* the Muslim sabbath. The yard will be closed. They won't miss us until we're long gone. With a kind wind and the grace of the saints, we'll be in Mallorca in a week."

❖

The scribes worked in small stalls in a covered section of the market. They sat on creaking wicker chairs and leaned over rickety wooden tables, their quill pens scratching on thick parchment. For a few aspers they wrote letters, drew up papers of indenture, and prepared contracts. If a client knew what to say, the scribes would take dictation, or they could make up something to fit the circumstances. Some were renowned for their flowery prose, others for their calligraphy. Ibi had told Nico which scribe he'd seen working for Mehmet, and Nico was careful to approach a different one.

"I wish you to read this for me," Nico said.

The scribe furrowed his brow and leaned over the document. "It is from your lover," he said, smiling. He looked at Nico again. "For your father, perhaps?"

"My brother."

"He is most fortunate."

"Just tell me what is in it."

It was written to a trader in Tunis:

I miss thee and cannot abide the days until thy next visit. Pray make haste, my love, for the hours pass with wretched slowness in thy absence. There were flowery declarations of passion, followed by a playful piece that made him blush: *. . . or else I shall be forced to take my entertainments from the slave boy about whose memory I wrote thee, as he finds the full flower of his manhood. Already he pleases me greatly, but I do not need a boy, my love. I need thee.*

A.

Nico's hand shook as he took the letter back from the scribe and gave him a coin. He understood why the madam did not have Mehmet use the scribe in the house. Ibi had told Nico of her dalliances, and such a letter would get her sewn up in a sack and thrown into the harbor. He should never have touched the letter; it was none of his affair. He wished Ibi had never mentioned it. Now it was going to be devilishly difficult to get the letter back to where he found it.

He was almost back to the house when an awful possibility dawned on him. Why would Ameerah trust Mehmet with such a letter? It was a very dangerous business. Why wouldn't she use one of her maids? He realized he didn't know very much about her affairs, but he knew she felt no great affection for Mehmet. And then it occurred to him: she had not done it at all. The words in the letter were of Mehmet's devising, or the scribe's, not hers. *He is jealous of you,* Ibi had told him. *He grows long in the tooth. Already there is talk that you will replace him.* Ameerah herself had warned him to be wary.

Yes—Mehmet intended to use it against Nico, to poison the master against him.

Nico thought he ought to simply destroy the letter. He and Leonardus would be long departed before it could do him harm. But there was more than that. If he was right, it was clear that Mehmet meant Ameerah harm as well. She had been kind to Nico. Leaving Mehmet free to plot against her, leaving her blind to his ill will, would be unpardonable.

But he was assuming a great deal. What if the letter was genuine? Ibi warned him the mistress could be cruel and vindictive. If he was wrong, he was placing his own neck in jeopardy. He despaired of ever being cunning, as Ameerah herself had told him he must be.

Cunning or not, he knew he must take the risk and visit her.

❖

Ameerah smiled grimly as Nico finished repeating the words in the letter to her. "You have done the right thing," she said. Mehmet, sensing his own doom, intended to present the letter to Farouk. Mehmet would claim that he had uncovered her infidelity, removing both Ameerah and Nico. Even though his own days in Farouk's bedchamber might be numbered, Farouk would reward him handsomely for such information.

"What must we do, madam?" Nico asked. "Could you order Abbas . . ." Shocked by his own thought, he left it unsaid.

"The silk cord would be pleasing, it is true," she said. "But it would be more rewarding still to use Mehmet's own methods against him. It is my husband who should devise a suitable end for him. My husband's tastes in such matters are exquisite."

She decided what to do. "You must return to the scribe and have him make a new letter." She thought carefully and dictated wording that showed Mehmet plotting to rob his master of funds. They counted the number of words in the first letter, and tried to make the second letter the same. "Tell the scribe to make it look precisely like this letter," she said.

"Will Mehmet not know the difference?"

"He is a fool. He cannot read a word, and anyway will have no cause to examine the letter before he presents it to my husband. I would love to see the look on his face when he realizes he's handed my husband the instrument of his own death. Now you must hurry. Tell me when you have returned, and I will divert Mehmet so you can safely replace it in his room."

❖

The new letter did indeed look like the old, even to the flourish at the end. Nico was slipping out of Mehmet's room, greatly pleased with his newfound cleverness, and relieved for the mistress, when three blasts of the cannon shattered the afternoon stillness along with his euphoria.

Three blasts: an important vessel. He felt the rumble in his feet and dread in his soul. He had allowed himself to believe they wouldn't sound at all before he was gone.

Praying it was a fleet of corsairs, he climbed a trellis and scampered up a tile roof onto a terrace from which he could see the harbor. There it was, a great merchant galley, her oars propelling her inexorably forward. He couldn't make out the pennant, but it wasn't necessary.

Three blasts: the master had returned.

Farouk would not come home immediately, for he would pay the obligatory courtesy visit to the Bey, bearing the gifts of a prosperous voyage, so there would be a few hours to prepare. The household crackled with activity. A sheep was slaughtered, the oven fires stoked. Fresh flowers were arranged, and sticks of incense placed in silver holders. Linens were changed, the carpets beaten three times. Ibi bent over his gardens, the cook over his pot, Mehmet over Nico, and Yusuf over them all, until everything was ready.

Knowing what his father would wish, Yusuf sent Nico to the bathhouse, where he was steamed, massaged, kneaded, dried, and dressed in fresh clothing. Mehmet gave him a scent to wear, which made Nico suspicious. In fact, he realized that Mehmet was being unnaturally helpful, almost kind. Nico guessed it to be only the natural mercy of the shepherd leading the lamb to slaughter, as Mehmet presumed his letter was about to do its work.

The evening arrived, and so, quite late, did El Hadji Farouk. He saw no one at first except Yusuf, with whom he dined. The entire household heard Farouk's voice raised in anger. Evidently some aspect of the trip had gone badly, and Farouk's mood was black. It was not a good omen, Nico knew, his nerves strung more tightly than ever. Together he and Mehmet served the two men their feast. Farouk ignored them, lecturing Yusuf as he drank heavily from a silver carafe of wine. As the slaves were clearing away the dishes, Farouk glanced at Nico. "Come to me when I have finished with Yusuf."

"Yes, master." Mehmet heard the exchange.

Nico and Mehmet carried serving dishes away from the room. By now Nico knew enough Arabic to understand most of the rapid conversation. He asked Mehmet about what he thought he had overheard. "Is the master leaving tomorrow morning?"

"Yes," Mehmet said, deep in thought. "Yusuf has displeased him, allowing an important matter to lapse, and now he must journey to Bone. It seems you will have but one night to make a favorable impression, after which he will undoubtedly take you with him."

The news shook Nico, who saw himself in trouble no matter how the night went. If he pleased the master, Farouk would take him to Bone, and Leonardus would sail without him. If he displeased the master, Ibi would have new compost for his gardens.

Mehmet walked around Nico, inspecting him for his debut. "The master's tastes vary as much as his moods. Follow as he leads. Anticipate his needs. See that he never wants for refreshment." He stepped behind Nico, straightening his collar and smoothing a stray hair. "Turn around for me and raise your arms," Mehmet said. "Your tunic requires adjustment."

Nico didn't sense the menace, never suspected what was about to happen. Obligingly he turned and raised his arms. Mehmet swung the cudgel in an arc, aiming his blow with the same care with which he gauged its force. It landed squarely between Nico's legs. Nico yelped and collapsed in agony, clutching his groin.

Mehmet leaned over the writhing boy. "Do you think you are so clever?" he hissed. Through a haze of tears and pain Nico saw the letter in his hands. "Do you think I have no friends among the scribes? And now you've fallen, you clumsy fool." Mehmet took Nico by the collar and drew closer to him. "Even now you keep the master waiting—you seem to have no sense of duty. Your first night as *garzóne,* and already you disappoint. As Allah is my witness, you are a pathetic creature indeed." He concealed the cudgel beneath his garments and left the room.

Nausea swept Nico in waves. He hunched up on his hands and knees and threw up repeatedly, each spasm increasing his agony. He wiped his mouth with the sleeve of his blouse, staining it with blood. He realized he'd bitten his tongue.

Gingerly he reached beneath his trousers, trying to feel what had happened, but even his own gentle touch added to the fire. He groaned. Sweat poured from his brow. He scooted into a sitting position against a cushion, and pulled down his trousers. One testicle had swollen to the size of a plum. The skin of his scrotum was stretched and shiny, colored a deep bluish-red. It looked fearful, as if it must surely explode. The shaft of his penis had taken part of the blow and was swollen in the middle where the vessels had ruptured. He whimpered and wanted to die.

"*Nico!*" It was the voice of El Hadji Farouk.

He struggled slowly to his feet, each movement producing some new agony. Gasping, he steadied himself against the wall.

"*Nico!*"

Hands shaking, ears ringing with pain, he wiped the tears from his eyes. With a supreme effort, he pushed back the carpet hanging over the door.

Farouk sat in one corner of his dining room. "Where have you been? I've been calling." Nico realized he was quite drunk. Perhaps that would save him.

"I am sorry, master."

He held out his cup. "Pour for me."

Knees quivering, Nico waddled to the carafe. His stomach was sour, his skin clammy. He poured the wine and tried not to whimper. He forced a smile. Farouk's nose wrinkled in distaste. "You smell like vomit."

"I had an . . . an accident, master. There was no time to change. I can do so now if you like."

"According to Yusuf, your accidents seem as numberless as your excuses."

"I will do better, master. I wish only to please you."

"You will have your chance when you explain what you have seen in the shipyard. Tomorrow you will travel with me and my scribe, who will record everything."

"Record, master? What is it you would like to record?"

"Details of the hull construction. How the devil shipwright makes his frames."

Nico remembered what Leonardus had said. *When they finally ask you, you'll tell them you don't know, because if you seem to give up information too easily, they'll know something is amiss.* Nico's mind raced. Tonight, of all nights, he did not wish to displease Farouk and have his beating—or did he?

"Well? I am waiting."

"I am ignorant of such things, master, but I have learned to use a plane and a carpenter's adze. I can make a—"

"Do you think me a fool? You were told to observe every detail. Yusuf tells me you have been in the mold loft while the frame was being designed. You held the measuring rod and worked numbers with the shipwright. You are a boy who forgets nothing."

"I . . . I held the rod, master, that is true, but I paid no attention to the numbers. I did not know they were important. I have no schooling. I cannot—"

"Enough!" thundered Farouk, his face red with rage. "We shall see tomorrow what you remember. A carpenter's plane, you say? Very well. We'll see what such a tool can do to loosen your tongue." To Nico's relief he let the matter drop, and yet the evening went from bad to worse.

Nico had always been made by Mehmet to appear clumsy or inept, but now between nerves and pain he accomplished it all by himself. He could do nothing right. He spilled the wine, and in his haste to recover he knocked over a candle that nearly set fire to a cushion. He dropped a honeyed apricot onto the floor. Each task seemed impossibly difficult, each error magnifying itself in the smoldering furnace of Farouk's displeasure.

The hadji took long swallows from his cup. Nico poured more, praying that the drink would quickly carry the master away, but Farouk drank like Leonardus, without an end. Kind one moment, harsh the next, he rattled about the Sultan and the Sublime Porte, about commerce and carpets, about an unsavory trader in Oran. He laughed at a joke he couldn't remember precisely enough to retell. He talked to himself, and at other times asked Nico questions for which Nico could not conceivably have answers. Nico tried to tell a story, but Farouk waved him to silence, bored. Nico's ordeal dragged endlessly, and he knew it was going badly. Twice he begged to excuse himself. Twice Farouk refused.

The candles were burning low when Farouk's mood suddenly turned. He gazed at Nico. "You may have the grace of a cripple," Farouk mumbled, "but as the Prophet is my witness, your features are fair." He reached for Nico and pulled him close. Nico whimpered in pain. Farouk didn't notice. "Undress me."

Farouk was nearing torpor. Nico struggled with his clothing, gasping from the effort. Farouk grumbled. He turned onto his stomach and told Nico to rub his back. Nico complied, hoping it would put Farouk to sleep, but a moment later Farouk turned over, grabbed Nico by the shoulders, and pulled his shirt down, running his fingers over the skin on Nico's back. Had Nico not been in such agony the touch might have tickled. As it was, it just hurt. Nico bit his lip and said a silent prayer.

Farouk groped Nico's thigh and then his buttocks. There was nothing gentle in his touch. Nico clenched his teeth and braced himself, trying to think of what to say, what to do, how to pull away, but now Farouk's hand moved slowly to his groin and found the swelling there beneath the cloth. Misunderstanding, Farouk grunted with satisfaction and squeezed.

Nico couldn't help himself. He screamed. He rolled away, desperate in his pain. Farouk's eyes fluttered open in surprise. He glared at the boy. "*Eyh*—?" He sat up and struck him with the back of his hand. He pulled at Nico's clothing and dragged him near again. Each movement intensified Nico's pain. Each protest served to further enrage Farouk, whose expression burned with fury. He struggled to his knees, intending to take the unwilling boy by force. But something in the boy's eyes, something in the tone of his shrieks, made it impossible. With each attempt, Nico yelped and moved further away, his eyes shining in terror.

"Bastard!" Farouk swore. "Maltese swine!"

"Please," Nico whispered, raising his hand to ward off the blows. "You don't understand. I'm ill." Farouk's blows rained on Nico's head and shoulders.

"Yusuf!" Farouk roared. "Yusuf! Mehmet! *Someone!*"

A moment later Yusuf burst in, blinking back sleep. "Father?"

"What devil lives in this boy? He is of no use! I want him beaten." Farouk stood, reeling. He steadied himself on the wall and spat on the cringing boy. "He is . . . no, not just beaten. I want him bastinadoed. Yes, that's it. Two hundred strokes, do you hear me?"

"Of course, Father . . . but two hundred? Surely that will kill him. At the very least he will never walk—"

"*Obey me!* Do it over two days. Draw it out, slowly! I want to know the secrets he carries. After that he is to be sold. Give him away if you must. I don't care. I want him to work the quarries. I want him at the oars! I just want him out, do you hear? *Get him out!*" He tried to kick Nico but stumbled and fell backward onto a pillow. "And send me Mehmet," he said. "I must . . ." He closed his eyes and lay back on his pillow. "Mehmet, Mehmet . . ."

"At once, Father." Yusuf bowed. He hauled Nico to his feet and hurried him out of the room. He shouted for Abbas, who emerged from the darkness and led Nico down the corridor. They passed the dimly lit figure of Mehmet. Only vaguely aware of the other's passage, Nico glanced up at him. Mehmet smirked and disappeared into Farouk's chamber.

Abbas took Nico to one of the bagnios attached to the rear of the compound, an abandoned bathhouse. A rusty iron bar fell into place behind Nico as the blackamoor secured the door.

Nico curled up on the tile floor. A while later he moved, trying to find a comfortable position. In one corner he turned onto his back and propped his legs up against the wall, so that his feet were in the air, one on each wall. He felt blessed relief as the blood ran from his groin. In the silence he heard the rustle of rats. Wild-eyed, he turned his head to see them, but they were lost in the gloom. He wondered if they could smell his fear and his helplessness. He knew rats had an instinct for weakness. He worried they'd eat his balls, attracted by the blood. Once he'd seen what they'd done to a baby goat that had gotten caught in a trap and was bleeding from its hindquarters. The rats had come in the night, and he could still remember the awful mess the next morning. He cupped his hands over his crotch and said his prayers, and to the long litany of his enemies he prayed God to smite, he added the rats, too. He tried not to think of the morning. He knew of the bastinado.

But what ate at him even worse than pain or fear was knowing that Leonardus was leaving in two days and Nico wasn't going with him. Nico knew he couldn't spend his life as a slave, fighting the Mehmets and the rats. If he couldn't go, he wanted to die.

In the middle of the night his eyes opened to a noise. Jolting from sleep, he waved his arms wildly, afraid the rats had come.

"*Nico!*" It was barely a whisper. "Nico! Are you alive?"

It took a moment to register. *Ibi!* "Yes!" Nico lowered his legs. They'd gone numb. He turned over and got to his knees, trying to make things work right. There was throbbing in his groin, but it was better than before, and he could move. He struggled to his feet, and stood at the window. The top of his head came only to the bottom of the opening. He stood on tiptoe until he could just see the bramble patch of hair, highlighted beneath a glorious moon, and the one ear prominently extended. Ibi reached through the window and took Nico's hand.

"Are you all right?"

"I think so. They . . . Mehmet . . . hurt me." Quickly he explained what Mehmet had done.

Ibi gave a low whistle. "I am sorry for you, my friend."

"It is my own fault. I have let him outwit me. I seem to be cursed."

"I brought something for you." Ibi passed a packet through the window. "It is from the cook. He says you will like it better than your *macolique*."

"Food? I can't eat anything. My stomach . . ."

"It is a medicine called opium. You must eat the cake in the morning, at first light, before they come for you. You must consume it all. It will make your head float before they . . . before they take you." In fact, the cook had said Nico should eat it over the period of ten days. If he took it all at once, the dose would kill him. But Ibi had seen what two hundred strokes of the bastinado would do to a full-grown man. Opium was the better way for his young friend to depart from this life. "Do you understand? You must trust me. You must eat every bit."

"I will," Nico promised. He dropped the packet onto the floor. "Ibi?"

"Yes."

"Do you think the knights will ever come for me?"

"I am certain of it."

"I am, too, most of the time. Leonardus says they'll never come."

"Master Leonardus has been unlucky in life. Do not listen to him."

"I hope they come tonight."

"If I were a believer, I would pray it so."

Nico squeezed his hand. "I'm afraid for tomorrow."

Ibi squeezed back. "It is not as bad as they say," he lied. "But eat everything all the same, do you hear? It will ease your ordeal. You will feel nothing. And now I must go. I will see you again. May your God be with you this day, my friend."

And then he was gone.

Nico spent the long night lost in a nightmarish delirium of visions. He couldn't shut out the eyes of his troubles, the eyes of the devil: corsairs at the cliffs, eyes gleaming in the catacombs as they reached for him; the witch in the galliot's hold, who cursed him with her evil eye. Sightless eyes in shriveled skulls, impaled on city walls. Farouk's eyes, malignant embers glowing with drink and rage. And, much closer now, the red eyes of the rats, patient eyes, waiting for him to sleep. He thrashed and moaned and wondered at what point God had taken him from the living and left him among the dead.

Chapter 11

La illaha illa Allah! There is no God but Allah!

The melodic cry wafted through the darkness before dawn as the muezzin called the faithful to prayer. Nico lost himself in its soothing rhythms. As he came slowly awake, he realized what he was listening to, and guiltily launched into his own morning ritual.

Holy Mary, Mother of God . . . He stirred and felt the awful ache between his legs, and the perfunctory words of prayer died in his mind.

He didn't feel much like praying. He needed to piss.

He got up slowly and relieved himself. There was a lump inside his penis, as if an apricot pit had lodged there. For a long moment he couldn't go. He pushed, and nothing would come. Then, when it finally began, he felt as if he were pissing a stream of fire. He yelped in pain at the weak dribble. His urine was bloody. He groaned; there seemed to be no end to his agonies. And that brought his mind to the morning's dread business. He remembered Ibi's visit and the cook's packet. It was time to eat it. He returned to the corner where he'd slept, and looked around on the floor.

The packet was not there.

Confused, he felt his pockets. They were empty save for Maria's coin. The bagnio was not large. He explored every other corner, thinking he'd become confused. There was no mistake. The cake was gone. Had Ibi's visit been only a dream?

And then he remembered the rats. Of course. They must have taken his medicine away. Stricken with a sudden thought, he touched himself, worried they'd bitten him, but the only wounds he had were those made by humans.

He lay back down, listening to the muffled sounds of the household. Each time he heard footsteps he thought they were for him. But an hour passed, and another, and no one came. There was no pleasure in delay, no relief. Waiting only made the terror burgeon in his brain. He closed his eyes and saw the board from which he would be hanged, upside down, his neck and shoulders on the ground. He saw the truncheon they would use, and heard the sound of bones being crushed.

He wanted them to come. He wanted it to be over. He wanted to die.

New footsteps. He sat up. With a clank the door bar was thrown back. Heart pounding wildly, he struggled to his feet. The door creaked open on old hinges. Abbas entered, carrying a truncheon. He made no move toward Nico but instead stepped aside. To Nico's astonishment, Ameerah entered. He smelled her perfume, and her warmth filled the room. He wanted to run to her, to hide in her arms. Then, with a start, he realized her presence could mean only one thing. It was she who had come to deliver him to his punishment.

"He's making *you* do it?" Nico asked.

Ameerah shook her head. "My husband departed early this morning. If he knew I was here, he would kill me. It is possible he has no memory of last night, but there is no way to be certain. I could not let this horrible thing happen to you. Yusuf has accompanied the master part of the way and will return this evening. Yusuf has ordered Abbas to administer forty blows this morning, to loosen your tongue. Tonight it is Yusuf's intent to question you about some matter of shipbuilding, and then he himself will complete your punishment. Abbas obeys Yusuf, as do all here, but he is . . . he is in my debt. He will do as I ask. His blows will fall on this." She held a pillow. "You must scream as if the devil Iblis has possessed you, or the deception will be known. Tonight I will try to think of a way to drug Yusuf before he can do you more harm."

"But what of Mehmet? Surely he will tell."

"Ibi came to me last night. He told me what Mehmet had done to you." Her eyes glimmered. "Alas, Abbas found Mehmet this morning before I could punish him, in the street outside the walls. I fear the dogs were already working on him. It appears from what was left that his throat had been cut."

Nico gulped. "Cut, madam?"

"It is a great tragedy, of course, as all who knew him revered him so. Perhaps he fell on his own knife. Whatever the case, his day of judgment is at hand."

❖

It was easy to scream. Abbas swung the truncheon so hard it jarred Nico's bones, even though the blows fell on the pillow. Nico screamed from depths he never knew he had. When it was over Abbas wrapped his feet and lower legs with bandages that had been smeared with lamb's blood, and left him in a spare room near the kitchen, without chains. Victims of the bastinado had no need of fetters.

Ameerah brought him broth. "It smells like gunpowder," Nico said, grimacing.

"It is saltpeter and sulfur," Ameerah said. "A mixture known to the cook. It will make you sweat like you have a death fever. If you have no fever, Yusuf will be suspicious."

Nico drank it all. Within moments his stomach was sour. Half an hour after that he began vomiting. His skin developed a gray pallor that seemed the very shadow of death. Beads of sweat streaked his forehead. He didn't need to pretend; between his groin and the broth he stood on the very threshold of hell. Near dusk he sensed the presence of Yusuf, who nudged him with his boot. Nico groaned. Yusuf grunted and left, intending to return after his evening prayers.

Darkness fell and a full moon lit the sky. Nico awakened from a deep sleep, and felt much better. His stomach had settled and he could move. More importantly, he felt braver. During the day, waiting for whatever fate was about to befall him, he had come to an important realization. *I don't have to wait for something to happen to me. I can make something happen.* If he waited passively for Yusuf's return, he would be at the man's mercy, and he had no doubt Yusuf would be endlessly inventive in adding to his pains. Besides, a new hope had seized him. It was only Thursday, and he wasn't dead after all. Leonardus wasn't leaving until the following night. The shipyard would be closed all day Friday, for the sabbath. He decided to find a hiding place and wait.

He was going home.

He slipped out of the room, past the kitchen. The cook didn't look up. He moved silently, carefully, through the shadows of the garden, toward the rear wall. His groin still ached, but the swelling had gone down and his excitement was far greater than his pain. He got to the top of the wall by climbing a trellis, then dropped to the other side. He nearly landed on a mangy dog that was scrounging in the alley for scraps. They both yelped in fright.

When he was well away from the house, he removed the heavy bandages Abbas had wrapped on his feet. At the shipyard there was yet another wall to scale. He walked its perimeter, looking for a way up. He saw the two night guards just inside the gate, hunched over their fire. Near the water's edge he found a broken-down cart that had been left next to the wall. A moment later he was inside, in the soft dirt behind the rotted hull of a boat. He crouched for a few moments, listening. The guards never stirred. The yard was quiet.

❖

Yusuf performed his ablutions, knelt on a silk mat, and said his prayers. The cook brought him a light meal of couscous and fruit. Yusuf wasn't hungry and left the bowl untouched. Instead he pocketed Spanish pincers and a paring knife and went to question Nico. He had no doubt the boy would be talkative. He preferred to torture the shipwright himself, but his father had always adamantly refused that course, certain it would fail, content to leave things as they were so long as Leonardus continued building his ships. The boy had presented an unusual opportunity, but now Yusuf knew that his father's passions might well destroy both the boy and the opportunity. But whatever Yusuf's opinions, he knew better than to disobey.

He entered the room next to the kitchen and lit a lamp. The nest of straw was empty. Irritated Nico had been moved without his being informed, Yusuf called for the cook, who professed ignorance. Abbas appeared, his eyes impassive, his face unreadable. Yusuf questioned the mute. Yes, Abbas nodded, he had been at his post at the gate the entire evening. No, he shook his head, he had not seen the boy.

The wives and servants were awakened, every room searched. Nico was nowhere to be found. Yusuf went out the gate and around the house to the alley, to Nico's quarters. Ibi was asleep, alone except for the chickens. He swore he hadn't seen the boy. Yusuf knew someone was lying. After the bastinado, Nico would have needed help to escape over the wall, since the gate was still guarded. Unless the boy had learned to fly, there was no other way out. A fast and savage whipping did nothing to alter the gardener's story.

A search was conducted of the streets in the immediate neighborhood. The boy couldn't have gone far. As he and Abbas searched doorways and alleys, Yusuf asked himself where Nico would go. He might know someone in the city, someone who would offer him shelter. Possible, but unlikely. Or he might head for one of the city gates, yet they would be closed and locked for the night. That left the shipyard, filled with places to hide. Yes, Yusuf decided. A wounded animal would hole up in familiar surroundings. Leaving Abbas with orders to complete the search near the house, and to search the house itself once again, Yusuf hurried down the dark streets toward the harbor. At the gate he saw the guards fast asleep beside the dying embers of their fire, wrapped in burnooses to ward off the night chill. At his roar they leapt to their feet and flung open the gate.

"The boy, Nico," Yusuf growled. "Have you seen him?"

"But of course not, master," one guard said, terrified.

"He would not likely have appeared in your dreams," Yusuf said, brushing past him. "I'll deal with you tomorrow."

Though angry, Yusuf felt little sense of urgency. He was not concerned that Nico would escape; the boy couldn't steal a galley. He was concerned only that Nico would embarrass him. He sent the guards in different directions. "Keep your eyes on the ground," Yusuf told them. "He'll be crawling."

❖

Nico crept into the mold loft. He lit one of the tallow lamps and turned it low. He worried about the guards seeing it, but he had no choice. He needed light to work, and there weren't enough windows in the loft to let the moon illuminate the room. He'd wanted to see Leonardus, who would be locked in his shed for the night, but first he needed to prepare a hiding place. He didn't know how long he'd have before someone came looking.

He crossed to the rear wall, where a tall bunk of fir was stacked. He was going to remove some of the long boards on top, replacing five or six rows with much shorter pieces, which he would stack at either end of the bunk. This would leave a hollow just big enough for him to lie flat in, while the ends of the lumber would seem undisturbed. In the unlikely event someone actually looked on top, he intended to cover himself with more wood. It wasn't terribly clever, he knew, but he didn't have a better idea. If he kept quiet, it should work for a day.

He slid a long piece of fir off the top of the stack and set it along the wall. He moved a second piece, and realized he'd have to shift some scrap before he could do any more. It was the same wall where one of the pieces of the caique had been stored, among this very scrap. He looked for it. The piece wasn't there. He picked up the lamp and searched everywhere. He assumed Leonardus had already moved them, and searched for the assembled frame.

He searched in vain. The pieces were gone.

He went back to work on his hiding place, but then his nerves got the better of him. Where was the caique? He put out the lamp, opened the door, and listened. Silence. He moved quickly across the open space between sheds, feeling naked and exposed in the light of the moon. Each time he came to a cart or a platform or a shed, he hid for a moment, watching, listening. He heard voices, but they seemed distant. They must be outside the shipyard, which remained dead quiet except for the sounds of the sea.

He came to Leonardus's quarters. The shed was made of wood, just large enough for a mat and a table, where the shipwright sometimes worked on his drawings. The guards let Leonardus have lamps, but there was no light from within. "Leonardus!" he whispered loudly, tapping with his fingers on the door. "Leonardus! Are you awake?"

Nothing. Leonardus was probably dead drunk.

He went around to the opposite side, where there was a window. It was too high to look in, and there was nothing on which to stand. He returned to the door and rattled it gently. To his surprise it opened. The lock was broken. "Leonardus?" The shed was empty. Leonardus's leg chains lay on the mat.

Nico stood quietly, his eyes scanning the shipyard as he tried to understand what was going on. He saw a movement near the water. Even in the silvery moonlight it was difficult to make out what he was seeing. There were three or four men, he thought, at that distance nothing more than indistinct shadows. They appeared to be dragging something down the gentle slope between the slipways on which the galleys were beached. Nico crouched and watched, refusing at first to believe his own eyes. But then the awful shock of betrayal hit him.

You lied to me! You're leaving tonight!

Outraged, he stood to run. A strong hand gripped his shoulder and spun him around. He found himself staring into the cold, murderous eyes of Yusuf. The man hadn't yet seen the others. His gaze was riveted on Nico's feet, which, he had just realized, were quite undamaged. "What in Allah's—"

Nico tried to break away, but Yusuf's grip was too strong. Nico yelled, "Leonardus! Help me!" Startled, Yusuf looked up, and saw the men nearing the water. He bellowed for the guards.

Leonardus and his companions heard Nico's call. The shipwright turned and saw the two figures struggling. "Hellfire!" he muttered. He thought briefly of running to Nico's aid, but it would be insanity. He turned and with his three companions furiously dragged the boat toward the water.

Nico ducked, twirling out of Yusuf's grip. He started down the long slope. He couldn't run at full speed for the pain, but he was still quicker than Yusuf, who was huge and out of shape. He heard Yusuf panting, his footfalls heavy as he lumbered along behind. Nico ran around the soaking pit, through a forest of pitch barrels, and between two storage sheds. He thought he smelled smoke, but never slowed, dared not turn to look. Yusuf was not going to give up.

Nico saw a pile of scrap oak, pieces of varying lengths left over from the milling of ships' oars. Barely breaking stride, he snatched one up and kept running. He rounded the corner of a workshop and pulled up sharply, holding the board in his hands, too out of breath to be afraid at what he was about to do. A second later Yusuf appeared. Nico swung the oak with all his might. He wanted to hit

Yusuf in the face, but the board was too heavy and it caught Yusuf full in the chest. Yusuf howled and staggered to his knees, clutching his chest and coughing. Shocked at his own violence, Nico backed away, and for an instant stood dumb and immobile. Yusuf glared at him, breathing heavily. He began to get up. Nico sprang to action. He hit the big man again, this time on the side of the head, swinging the board with a mighty grunt. Nico heard something crack and knew it wasn't the oak. Yusuf crumpled to the ground in a heap. Nico was about to throw down the board and run, but then he stopped. *He saw my feet.* If Yusuf somehow survived, Abbas and Ameerah would pay with their lives for helping Nico escape. He took a deep breath, raised the board, and brought it down again on Yusuf's skull. This time there was no doubt of the outcome. He dropped the oak and ran.

Leonardus and the others had reached the water. He and another man jumped into the boat while the other two pushed the boat into deeper water. "Leonardus!" Nico yelled. "Leonardus, wait! I'm coming!" He saw Leonardus looking in his direction, but there was no reply.

The two men in the water pushed until they were up to their waists, and then they were hauled by their britches over the gunwales and into the boat. At once four oars appeared, and the men began rowing. The caique was on its way. Nico hit the water and plunged in, splashing through the shallows just a few feet behind them. He fell and got up, sputtering, and surged ahead, yelling at the top of his voice. "You said I could come! Wait! Leonardus!" The oars worked furiously and the boat kept moving. The fugitives never paused, never turned. They raced across the harbor toward the mole, the narrow breakwater that separated the inner harbor from the open sea. They'd beach the boat and drag it over the mole, and then they'd be gone. Nico pushed through the water, flailing and struggling until he was up to his waist. It became too difficult to run, so he started swimming.

The gate guards converged on the body of Yusuf. One of them carried only a sword, but the other had a Spanish musket. They heard Nico yelling and saw him swimming toward the fleeing boat. The guard with the gun primed the match, raised the weapon, sighted down the long barrel, and fired. The ball struck one of the carpenters, who toppled forward into the boat. The others stopped rowing and heaved him over the side, the boat rocking violently. The delay was all Nico needed. He pushed himself over the floating body and grabbed hold of the gunwale. Leonardus was on the opposite side, his oar already in the water. The man closest to Nico was a Genoese, a carpenter Nico recognized from the yard. He brought his oar down on Nico's fingers. "*Vada via!*" Nico yelped, and let go. Once again the boat began to pull away.

"Leonardus! Leonardus! You lying son of a whore, you said I could go!" At that the shipwright finally turned. He glanced up at the shore, where he knew the night guards had only one gun, and then at Nico, treading water. He sighed. "God's balls, boy! Am I to have no peace from your wailing? Hold oars!" he commanded. "Take him in!"

"Are you mad?" cried the other man, a sail maker from Barcelona. "We leave him behind, I say! Less weight! More water for us!"

"Do as I say!" Leonardus thundered, and the little craft swung about. Strong hands grasped Nico by the arms and shoulders and pulled him into the boat, raking his groin over the gunwale. He fell heavily into the bottom, racked once again with pain. Yet, propelled by his rage, he struggled up and began pummeling Leonardus. "You bastard! You were going to leave—" A bell sounded from the shipyard, the loud alarm that meant fire. In a moment every man on the waterfront would be racing to Farouk's yard.

"Shut up and row!" Leonardus ordered, shoving Nico backward onto his bench. Shocked into silence, Nico took up his oar and plunged it into the water. The four rowed as if they had the very devil at their backs. Another gunshot sounded. The ball went wide. They reached the mole and scrambled out of the boat. They dared not drag it over the jagged rocks, so they unloaded food, water, mast, and sail and hustled everything up and over the mole to its seaward side. They returned for the boat, which, emptied of its supplies, they managed quite easily. It was much lighter than Nico expected, and then he realized its hull was nothing more than sailcloth heavily soaked with pitch, nailed to the wood frame. Nico stumbled along, struggling to carry his share, but the three men did most of the work. They lowered the boat into the water, loaded the stores, clambered aboard, and began rowing again. "By Christ," Leonardus huffed at last as they sliced through the water, "if that isn't the Mediterranean parting like a woman's thighs to our loving prick. We'll be home in a fortnight."

"Won't the galleys be after us?" Nico said, gasping as he strained at his oar.

"Not for a while," Leonardus said. "We drilled holes in a few hulls before we left, but if Iblis is working with us tonight, that will be the least of their problems. Look."

The hills of Algiers were beautiful, the domes and whitewashed houses bathed in serene moonlight. Cook fires and lanterns flickered throughout the city. The kasbah loomed over all, its tower lit around the top like a beacon. It seemed a peaceful, pleasant place. In the shipyard, near the water, there was a bright glow. Flames were just visible, licking at the sides of a building. Nico remembered smelling smoke, and by the location of the fire guessed what had happened. "You set a slow fuse in the oar shed!"

Leonardus grinned. "That I did, lad. Without oars their galleys are as worthless as a whore without a hole. It'll be a day before they can fit a ship to give chase. The heathen bastards will never find us."

"They would have found *me*," Nico said angrily. "You were going to leave me. You lied about leaving Friday. You never meant to take me at all."

"True enough," Leonardus admitted cheerfully. "Yet here you are anyway, *le?* You are as hard to shake as the French disease. Your own actions are what saved you. You took care of yourself, and you learned there's only one person in the world you can trust. Someday you'll thank me for the lesson."

They stopped rowing and raised the mast, the shaft of which slid neatly through a hole in the forward bench and into the fitting bored in the keel. Leonardus ran the sail up. It snapped and then billowed in the strong southerly breeze. In the moonlight the scirocco was clearly visible. Tendrils of dust stretched across the sky in tentacles that curled and danced eerily on the wind, licking at the heavens. Every so often there were glimpses of brightly glittering stars. They rowed toward the north star, and under both wind and oar the boat fairly flew through the water.

The hours passed and dawn came, and still they rowed without pause. They scanned the horizon anxiously but saw no trace of another sail. The wind stayed fresh and following all day, their course steady. They had food to eat, mostly dates, and plenty to drink—a large goatskin of wine, for Leonardus, and one of water, for everyone else.

In the afternoon they began rowing in shifts. Nico's arms ached, and his hands were a field of blisters. The Genoese carpenter sitting opposite had to ease his efforts to match Nico's, so that the boat wouldn't turn in circles. Leonardus kept them on course with a crude compass he'd made using an iron needle magnetized with a lodestone. He put the needle inside a piece of straw and floated it in a cup of seawater. Every so often he called out course corrections. Giddy with freedom, he sang and told stories and drank wine and rowed. He talked of finding a vessel bound from Mallorca to Malta. "I'll wait for a three-masted galleon," he said, "with four decks, a hundred guns, and a thousand men to man her. I'll not be captured at sea again." Their spirits rose with each passing hour.

Just after dawn of the third morning, Nico noticed beads of seawater appearing all over the tarred muslin hull just beneath his bench. He showed Leonardus. "Bloody Christ!" the shipwright said. "That's French material. I should have known better!" The fabric was failing under the strain. No one needed Leonardus to tell them what it meant.

They were still two full days from land, and their little boat was coming apart.

They tried one repair after another, but they had no tools and no pitch. They kept rowing, with greater urgency than ever. As the day wore on, the beads spread between ribs of the hull, and the size of the beads grew larger. The leaks were getting worse. Once the fabric ripped, the boat would sink.

"There's too much weight in the boat!" said the Genoese. "We've got to pitch the boy."

"We'll do nothing of the sort," Leonardus said, but the carpenter had given him an idea. "Get out, the both of you," he said to the men. The carpenter raised his oar, ready to use it as a weapon. "I'm damned if I will," he said.

"We'll all die if you don't," Leonardus said. "You can hold on to the gunwale. With less weight she should float."

"Send the boy."

"I would, but he doesn't weigh as much as you do. There's less benefit to it. He and I will row, and pull you in the water."

"For two days?"

"For a hundred, if need be! Now over you go, before we lose her altogether!"

Grumbling, the two men slipped over the side into the water. For long hours they hung on while Leonardus and Nico rowed. They had to lower the sail because Leonardus thought the wind, though helping to propel the boat, would place too much strain on the hull. Their progress was further hindered by the drag of the two men in the water. The pair rowed all night, unable to tell whether they'd made one league or twenty.

Disaster struck at dawn.

The wind rose and the sea began to pitch the little boat. Nico watched the beads growing. Without warning the fabric gave way, ripping abaft from the center rib clear to the stern. There was no time for panic. The boat went under in seconds. Neither the Genoese nor the Spaniard could swim. They flailed in the water and coughed, and sank from sight. Leonardus could swim, although not well. As the boat went down the mast struck him a glancing blow on his head. Stunned but still conscious, he kicked and stayed just afloat. Nico, a strong swimmer, caught hold of the goatskin that had contained wine. Treading water, he removed the stopper and squeezed out what remained of the wine—precious little by then. Between kicks, he blew into the skin, clamping off the neck as he took each new breath. He got the stopper back in, tied it off and swam to Leonardus, who grabbed hold of it.

Nico swam around, looking for the other goatskin. He couldn't find it. He was exhausted from rowing. He found the wood and canvas hull, floating just below the surface. It gave him a little buoyancy, but if he tried to put his full weight on it, it sank toward the depths. So he would kick once or twice, rest a few seconds on the rising hull, then kick again as it went down. It gave him some relief, and so long as the waves didn't get too bad, he knew he could do it for a long time.

They floated that way for a day and a night, and into the next day. Nico stayed awake all night, but Leonardus drifted off once, taking .

a lungful of water before he caught hold of the skin again, sputtering and cursing. They didn't talk much. The sun rose and scorched their heads. Thirst tore at them. Nico kept scanning the horizon, certain he'd see land or ships at any moment. He never lost hope, and felt less afraid with Leonardus at his side.

Leonardus was exhausted. He'd found the food crate and put the goatskin inside it. It was easier to hold on, but even so, he kept slipping into the water, constantly having to right himself. His arms were shaking with the strain. "Are you all right?" Nico asked.

"I would be if you hadn't poured out my wine, you brainless turd of Maltese flotsam." Leonardus cursed and trembled and his brain baked, and as the hours passed he mumbled about Circe, the sorceress daughter of Helios and the ocean nymph Perse, and about knots and sails and what he'd like to do to Perse, and to Circe for good measure. Nico worried for his sanity.

In the late afternoon Nico squinted at something on the horizon. At first it was only a tiny patch of gray against the blue sky, but he grew excited. "Leonardus! A sail!" Half an hour later he could see others as well. They were approaching not from the south, as pursuers might have, but from the northwest. "There's more than one," Nico said eagerly. He described what he saw.

"By the sainted hole of the Virgin," Leonardus said. "Let it be the Emperor's fleet!"

They floated and waited. The little patches grew bigger, until Nico could see the goose-wings raised before the wind. "They're lateen," Nico reported. "Galleys. Maybe it's the Knights of St. John!"

"You and your cursed knights," Leonardus said. "If it is, I'll cork my cock and never touch another drop of wine."

The lead ship's oars swept steadily as she cut through the water. Whitewater curled at the prow. Finally Nico was able to make out the flag at the mast. He'd been praying for a white cross on a red field. His heart sank. "The pennon is green on red," he said. "And I see turbans on deck."

"Green on red? Are you certain?"

"Yes."

"Better a shark's fin, then. If it isn't the spawn of Satan, Dragut."

At the word Nico almost forgot to tread water. Everyone in the

Mediterranean trembled at the very name, knew the stories about the legendary corsair. "If ever God made a place below hell," Leonardus had often told him, "Dragut would be lord of that realm, and even the devil would dread him."

Leonardus squinted at the oncoming fleet. His vision was blurred, but finally he saw the lead galley clearly, from the cut of her planking to the brass ram at the prow. "God's bloody balls," he grumbled, "if he hasn't come for me in one of my own ships." He knew Dragut would return him to El Hadji Farouk, whose wrath in light of his son's death would surely be troublesome. The only thing worse would be if Dragut kept him as a rowing slave, or took him to Djerba, his island near Tunis, and imprisoned him there. No wine, no whores: the old fox was as pious as he was ruthless.

Leonardus had spent enough years as a slave and had no desire to face such a future. He waited to see if by chance or luck the fleet might miss them, that as bleak as their prospects seemed, they might continue floating north, and by some miracle find themselves beached in Mallorca. But with each sweep of the oars, it became clear that luck had abandoned them that day. He heard Arabic from the decks, and the call of the ship's lookout, who had spotted something in the water.

Leonardus made his decision, regretting only that he had no wine with which to toast it. Nico's back was to him. The boy was watching the devil draw near. "If you are to survive your encounter with him, you must be strong, Nico. Fearless. A man, not a boy. Tell him you are Venetian. The son of a shipwright. The son of a master."

"Why?"

"Venetians are the best shipbuilders. You'll be someone of value to him. It will serve you well."

"I understand," Nico said. "But what will he do with you? He knows who you are."

There was no answer to his question.

Leonardus had let go of his box, and gone to meet Perse.

from **The Histories of the Middle Sea**

by Darius, called the Preserver
Court Historian to the Refuge of All People, the Sultan
Achmet

*Three giants towered above much of humanity in the eventful years before
the great battle of Malta. One was lord of the Ottomans, the Sultan
Suleiman. One was lord of the Knights of St. John of Jerusalem, Jean Parisot
de La Valette. And the last was lord of the Middle Sea, Dragut Raïs. I can
do no better to impart knowledge of the third man than to quote from the
correspondence of the second:*

The devil has set a fox to sea, treacherous and cunning and
quick, and called it Dragut Raïs. It remains for the hounds of
Christ to destroy that evil creation, lest they themselves be
destroyed.

I met him twice in my life. Once it was he in chains, and
once it was I. His manner was kindly, even playful; yet at sea
and in battle he has shown that there is no act too despicable,
no depredation too base for his taste.

He is a man of contrasts. He lives austerely, a man of simple
faith. Yet he is a bloodthirsty killer, an evil genius for that false
faith. There is no greater tactician at sea than he, nor any man
more rapacious.

What a pity Dragut has wasted his life as an infidel. How I
would love to make such a man my own!

—*From the captured letters of La Valette,
taken in battle fourteen years after his death from the frigate*
San Giovanni

Known as the Drawn Sword of Islam, Dragut was the greatest of all the corsairs—even greater, this historian submits, than his mentor Kheir-el-din (known in Frankish lands as Barbarossa, or Redbeard), who lacked his pupil's sheer brilliance for battle. There was no seaman on earth who was his match, save perhaps the knight Fra Mathurin d'Aux de Lescout, called Romegas. As the two men never faced each other directly in battle, one may never know for certain.

A gifted commander, Dragut was as ruthless in battle as he was lucky. He knew every shoal and current of the sea he called his own. He knew her breezes and her moods, knew her every cove and inlet, knew when to pounce and where to hide. No other man dared defy orders from the Sublime Porte in Istanbul, but Dragut was as headstrong as he was daring. "The sea is big and the Sultan is far away," he was often heard to say. So long as his successes were many and manifest, even the Sultan Suleiman—may his name be blessed—turned a blind eye.

Dragut was the son of an Anatolian peasant and a Greek Christian woman. At the age of eight he was rescued from a peasant's life by a Turkish governor passing through his village. The official saw something special in the child and took him to Egypt to be educated. This was not unusual: in this manner was the entire Ottoman Empire built. Save for the Sultan himself, all civil and military leaders were selected and advanced on the basis of merit rather than birth, while birth rather than merit was the European standard. Almost all of these leaders, occupying the very pinnacle of society, were taken as children from Christian families and raised in the Muslim faith. Thus did the Osman Sultans cleverly avoid the establishment of a Turkish aristocracy that might seek to usurp their authority. In the process they also created a gifted stable of servants whose only loyalty was to the Sultan. It was a system of enlightened genius, though recent years have seen its slow erosion by jealous and influential Turkish families who seek to advance their own sons.

The young Dragut excelled in school, became a gunner on a Moorish galley, acquired a brigantine, and soon fell in with Barbarossa. Dragut quickly came to command several galleys of his own, which he used to mount daring raids on Christian shipping and ports. He was captured and spent time at the oar as a slave before being ransomed for three thousand gold pieces by Barbarossa, who in his life surely never made a better bargain. Dragut's successes were legion in the years that followed. He took seven thousand captives from Bastia in Corsica and five thousand from Gozo in Malta, and enslaved the entire city of Reggio. He captured Tripoli from the Knights of

St. John, later serving as its governor, and made a daring escape from under the very nose of Andrea Doria. As Barbarossa tormented the Holy Roman Emperor, Charles V, Dragut tormented the Emperor's son, the Spanish king Philip, whose entire Christian fleet he captured at Djerba. It was thus he built his legend: he humiliated his enemies and showered kindness upon his friends.

After Barbarossa's death Dragut became leader of all the Barbary corsairs, those loose allies of the Sultan who operated freely from their North African outposts. The corsairs paid tribute to the Sultan or to the Beys who ruled his domains. Their ships often joined the Ottoman fleet in battle against the common Christian enemy. At the height of his powers he was appointed commander of the fleet by Suleiman, and he journeyed to Istanbul to pay tribute to the Sultan. It was during that voyage that he rescued the young boy named Nicolo Borg.

Of all the odd turns of fate in those singular years before the great battle of Malta, none was more singular than Dragut's presentiment of his own death. During a raid on the Maltese island of Gozo, Dragut's brother was slain. His corpse was burned by the governor, depriving him of entrance to paradise. Even as Dragut swore vengeance, he had a premonition. "I have felt the shadow of the wing of death in this island," he told his commanders. "It is written that I, too, shall die in the territory of the knights." His intuition was oft repeated throughout the Maltese islands, as indeed it was in every Christian corner of the Middle Sea, where, predictably, the fervent wish was that the premonition would come true sooner rather than later.

From Volume III
The Corsairs and Beys of Barbary: Dragut Raïs

Chapter 12

For the spawn of Satan, Dragut Raïs reminded Nico more of his own grandfather. Lean and sea-weathered, he was in his late sixties, but only the whiteness of his beard suggested his age. He was in superb condition. His body was battle-scarred but displayed no infirmities of flesh or spirit. His eyes were alight with intelligence, and his expression seemed kind, almost impish. Amidst Janissaries who were dressed ostentatiously, Dragut wore a simple white robe and tan turban. He sat on a mat beneath a leather awning that arched over the poop deck, reading the Koran. He looked up as one of his sailors presented Nico, dripping and shivering, for inspection.

"And who might you be, floating in the sea?" He spoke in Arabic.

"I am Nicolo Borg," Nico answered in Italian. He was out of breath. He forced himself to think not of the death of Leonardus but of his words. He knew his life depended upon his wits. "I am a shipwright. From Venice."

"A shipwright! *Ya sa-lehm!* And so young!" Dragut laughed, switching to Italian. "Not a very good one if swimming is how you choose to travel."

"Our galley went down two nights ago, swamped in a rough sea. My father drowned."

"A pity. No ransom, then. Still, I may find use for a shipwright's apprentice—even a wrinkled and skinny one." Dragut waved at the sailor. "Chain him in the hold." He returned to his reading.

If Nico had learned nothing else of late, he had learned not to go passively. He thrashed madly against his captor, dragging his heels, his eyes on the stinking black hole that yawned below the deck. "I'm the son of a shipwright!" he cried. "I'll not be chained in that pit by the son of an Anatolian peasant! I'll die first!" He broke away from the sailor, ran for the side, and leapt over the gunwale into the sea. He started swimming. There was great laughter from soldiers on the deck, and a few of the Christian oarsmen cheered at Nico's pluck.

Eight other galleys in Dragut's fleet were ranged in a V shape astern of the flagship. Several of the archers stationed on the fighting foc's'le of the first of these galleys raised their bows. All were expert marksmen. None would miss at that range, so they placed quick wagers on which joint of which limb of the swimming boy they would strike.

To their chagrin, Dragut ruined their sport. "Fetch him aboard," he ordered. A whistle shrilled. All oars were shipped, and the archers unstrung their arrows. A light boat was lowered into the water. Three men jumped in, and quickly caught up with Nico. There followed a loud bout of thrashing and yelling as their prey fought wildly. A short while later Nico stood on deck once again, coughing and sputtering. Dragut gave a signal, and the fleet resumed its eastward journey.

"You fight well," Dragut commented. "More like the whelp of a sea monster than a shipwright. I may yet grant your wish and let you drown yourself, and no doubt save us all a great deal of trouble. But first I must satisfy my curiosity. How does it happen that such a budding Leviathan pulled from the sea should know of me, the simple son of an Anatolian peasant?"

Even without Leonardus's tales, Nico knew a great deal about Dragut, one of the most famous and feared men in all the world. He had raided Malta no fewer than five times, most recently when he had all but emptied the island of Gozo of people. Ordinarily Nico would have trembled in his presence, but the last words of Leonardus had registered well. *If you are to survive your encounter with him, you must be strong. Fearless. A man, not a boy.*

"As the hare knows the hawk," Nico replied hotly. "Who does not know of the corsair who made a fool of Doria in the lagoon of Djerba, but let himself be caught and chained by Doria's nephew in Sardinia? Who does not know of the thief who steals women and children from their homes? Who does not know of the son of Satan, who kills Christians without cause? Just as I know your own brother was slain in Malta, I know of your premonition. One day you'll face a ship of the Order of St. John, and I'll be standing on her prow. I'll gladly fulfill your premonition, and hang your head from the ram!"

The sailors heard Nico's rash words with varying measures of disbelief, watching for Dragut's reaction. Had Nico encountered any other corsair, he might well have lost his life then and there. But the outburst served only to heighten Dragut's interest. Perhaps remembering his own youthful encounter with a Turkish governor who plucked him from a field of peasants, Dragut of all men knew that Allah moved in mysterious ways. He was intrigued by Nico, whose face was as well formed as it was rich in character. Certainly his spirit had not been softened by his time in the water. Perhaps this was nothing more than an impudent child whose destiny was to survive the sea only to spend the rest of his days in chains. Or perhaps something more had been written in the book of his life. Whatever the case, Dragut decided to learn what he could during the long voyage ahead.

"Such grand passion from such a small lad! I kill only Christians who need killing, and spare the rest for slavery," he said. "That is more than I can say for the soldiers of Christ, who kill the women and children of Islam without mercy! You boast of commanding one of their galleys. The son of a shipwright is not likely to find welcome in their Order—or is it noble blood that so boils in your veins?"

"My blood is good enough."

"Not for the Order, I suspect. In any event, you are not likely to be hanging my head from anything just yet, though I look forward to the day you try. For now, however, you will cool your hot blood in my hold. I have nowhere else to put you. Behave yourself, and you may sit with me on my deck at times. Otherwise I'll feed you piecemeal to the crabs. The choice is yours."

Gravely Nico thought it over. "I agree," he said. "But I'll not wear chains."

Dragut grinned. "Now the hare dictates terms to the hawk. Do I have your word you'll not raise your hand against any man on this vessel or interfere in its operation?"

Nico looked at the Janissaries ranged around the deck, the fierce and heavily armed soldiers who fought for a share of the ship's prizes and who were now watching him with amused contempt. "You do."

"Very well, then," Dragut said amiably. "No chains."

Both pleased and surprised at his success, Nico went without struggle to the hold. There were no other prisoners. The stench was powerful, but he was able to stand on a crate, his head just above deck level—not free, but not chained, either. He watched the Christian rowing slaves, the overseers, and the Janissaries. Compared to Ali Agha's ship, the crew seemed disciplined, patient, and even more dangerous.

Despite his exhaustion, Nico passed his first night in the hold without sleeping. He wept for Leonardus, his tears evaporating in the warm night air. "Why did you do that, you son of a wh—" He could not bring himself to say it of the dead man, though he knew Leonardus would say it of him. "Why did you leave me? Why did you give up?" He talked at length to the shipwright, as if the man were standing next to him. Nico realized that he had not missed even his own father so much. In his dreams he had seen the two of them returning triumphantly home. He had seen himself with Maria again. But in the pictures in his head he never saw himself with Luca. He was always with Leonardus. In his months in Algiers he had come to think of himself differently than before. *Tell them you're the son of a shipwright,* Leonardus had said.

He had, and it was true. In his heart, he was just that. *I am the son of Luca and the son of Leonardus.*

Nico had all but stopped wondering why his life had been shattered so unfairly. Losing Leonardus brought it all back. He had been so very close to home, to freedom. He had tasted it, and felt it in the breeze on his face. And now not only freedom but Leonardus had been sucked from him: a whole world stolen, and the night seemed black indeed.

In the days that followed they kept their eastward course, making landfall at an island off Sardinia called San Pietro. They slipped in after dark and away again before dawn. There was a long crossing over open water to Marettimo, an island off the west coast of Sicily. After that they hugged the Sicilian coast, stopping each night for shelter in coves that were all but invisible from the sea.

True to his word, Dragut invited Nico to sit with him at mealtimes. The corsair never ate until after his crew, and he always shared the same frugal fare. He quizzed Nico every chance he had, about an endless variety of subjects. Nico displayed a prodigious knowledge of ships and the sea, repeating what he had learned from Leonardus. He answered questions about Venice, about her ship-yards and guilds and the revolutionary building methods of Vettor Fausto, to whom Nico said his father had been apprenticed. When Nico didn't know an answer he made one up, and when he did know an answer he embellished it, using the tricks he had learned from the storytellers in Algiers. He could never tell what Dragut thought of his answers, or how much the man knew himself of what he asked, but every so often the corsair's eyes twinkled at one detail or another, and he seemed amused.

The miles whispered by. Nico searched in vain for any sign of the forces of the Emperor Charles, but the entire Holy Roman Empire seemed oblivious to Dragut's passage, while Dragut acted as if the coast were his own. At one point Nico knew he was tantalizingly close to home. He thought long about how to broach the subject with Dragut. "You would sail so near Malta so quietly?" he finally asked. "I thought you could not pass the place without taking a prize or two."

Dragut smiled. "I'll test the premonition another time," he said. "For now, Allah's business leads me elsewhere."

"To Djerba?"

"Istanbul."

The word stabbed Nico with despair. In all the world, no place seemed farther from his home. He peered over the starboard rail, rubbing Maria's coin and saying a prayer. Had he seen any hint of land at that moment, or the sail of a ship, he would have jumped overboard—or at least, he thought he would—but there was nothing save empty sea. With each stroke of the oars, he felt his chances slipping away, until he knew it was too late, at least for this voyage.

The days slipped by as easily as the sea. The fleet cruised northeast, along the sole of the boot of Italy, and across the Gulf of Taranto to the heel, and then across the channel of Otranto in the Adriatic to the Peloponnesian peninsula, which, like so much of the world, was part of the Ottoman Empire.

The old man and the boy continued to talk at every mealtime. Nico realized that Dragut was taking his measure, although he didn't know for what purpose. He found himself liking the man, despite his reputation. Surely the devout grandfather sitting at ease on his deck, sipping water and chatting amiably, was not the bloodthirsty corsair of legend.

But then, off the coast of Corfu, Nico saw the corsair at work. They had laid in for the night in one of several coves that shared a common channel to the sea. Perhaps Dragut saw something, or heard or smelled it, or perhaps he only sensed it. He commanded battle silence. Oarsmen took their feet off their chain rests as a precaution against noise, and the cook fires in the deck braziers were extinguished. Near midnight Dragut and two of his captains, along with the agha, or commander, of Janissaries, set off in the ship's caique. An hour later Nico heard the soft splash of their oars as they returned. Orders passed quietly from ship to ship.

Just at dawn Dragut led his fleet around a woody spit and surprised three Dalmatian war galleys protecting a merchant ship laden with riches for the Vatican. They, too, had sought shelter for the night, but their ships were poorly situated and ill prepared, and Dragut had caught them napping. The Dalmatians were heavily armed mercenaries, but their commander had anchored them in a spot that, though well concealed, prevented them from seeing an approaching threat until it was too late, rendering their half cannons and bow chasers all but useless.

Dragut attacked swiftly and silently, with only the rattle of ankle chains and the creak of oars upon their thole pins giving hint of his approach. He had the additional advantage of the sun rising at his back, blinding the enemy. Nico watched from his perch in the hold, transfixed as the galleys raced forward, gathering momentum until they reached ram speed. The oars caught the sea and the sun caught their spray, casting pretty rainbows over the low Dalmatian galleys whose sleeping crews were about to die.

When silence was no longer necessary, Dragut shouted commands to his bosun, whose whistle passed the orders to the overseers, whose whips passed the orders to the brown, bloodied backs of the oarsmen. Nico didn't understand Dragut's tactics, but it was clear the man was a master. His oarsmen obeyed as one, all rowing at once, at the full tempo of war, then shifting suddenly, one bank resting while another bank rowed, then turning sharply as one side back-rowed while the other held steady. The slaves on both sides of battle—the Christian slaves on Muslim ships, and the Muslim slaves on Christian ships—faced an unhappy dilemma. Their obedience and skill could bring defeat to the opposing fleet, for whose victory they most ardently prayed—even though that victory might plunge them, still chained, to their deaths with their ship. Yet if they did not obey commands instantly, if every sinew did not strain to its limits, the overseer would swing sword instead of whip, and their headless bodies would tumble into the sea.

Far too late the Dalmatians stirred to action. Trumpets thundered as pikes and halberds bristled. Marksmen propped arquebuses on notches, and sporadic fire erupted from the sleeping ships. Dragut took them swiftly. A demi-culverin was fired from the prow, loaded with two iron balls joined by a chain. The shot dismasted the merchant galley. The mast crashed down onto the luckless slaves who rowed her, crippling the ship. More shots followed in quick succession from Dragut's consorts, spraying the heavily manned war galleys in a crossfire of deadly grapeshot. Dragut had a variety of weapons at his disposal, some old, some new, and he employed each with patience, discipline, and great skill. Wave after wave of arrows soared through the air, wreaking horrible damage on unhelmeted men. The bolts of steel crossbows penetrated wood and armor, while a steady hail of arquebus balls hissed through the air.

One of the war galleys began to move, but too slowly. Dragut's grapnels flew over the gunwales, and, wearing a leather jerkin and no armor, he led his men as they swarmed over the enemy decks. Men cried, oars cracked, and steel clashed against steel. There was no wind, and smoke hung over the battle like mists of fog rising from a swamp. The salt air was heavy with the smell of blood and powder.

Nico glimpsed a blessed sight: the scarlet tunic of a Knight of St. John, emerging from a cabin while struggling to don his cuirass, a piece of armor that would protect his chest and back. Normally he would have been captured and ransomed, but he was in no mood for surrender and he fought like a man possessed. Mightily wielding a two-handed sword, he cut down a half dozen attackers before falling to the blow of a battle axe. Nico's heart fell with the man's body. His knights were mortal after all.

Within ten minutes the engagement was over, the rout

complete. On all the Dalmatian ships, Muslim oarsmen were quickly freed of their chains. A great cry arose from their throats in praise of their savior Dragut, who ordered that the surviving soldiers, now disarmed, take their places at the bench. In a timeless ritual of the sea, a quick rattling of chains signaled the changing of the order: men once free were now slaves, while men once enslaved were now free.

A number of apostates, former Muslims who had abandoned their faith and joined the ranks of the Christians, were pointed out by the oarsmen. Dragut ordered his swordsmen to work, and their scimitars swung easily through stretched necks like scythes through stalks of wheat. Nico tried to shrink to nothingness in the hold, fearing the bloodlust might reach his own neck. But there was no bloodlust. It was merely the orderly business of the sea, done as neatly as such a thing could be done.

Dragut dispatched men from his own command to take charge of each of the other vessels. Ropes were thrown to the two disabled galleys, which would be towed by their own consorts. Weapons, powder, and other provisions from the Dalmatian galleys were brought aboard Dragut's ships, along with three cases of silver bullion that were found hidden aboard the merchantman. Dragut ordered them placed in the hold where Nico waited. "The Pope's tithe for Allah," he called happily, and after that Nico's feet rested upon a fortune.

Dragut reboarded his ship in high spirits, amused because it was the fourth time he had found enemy shipping in that very cove. "It is as easy as finding goldfish in my own fountains at my palace in Djerba," he chuckled, "only the goldfish know how to hide." He was anxious to be under way, but first, in garments freshly stained with powder and blood, he led the faithful in morning prayer. Then his fleet, now thirteen vessels strong, continued south along the Peloponnesian coast.

Nico was a long time calming down, and he did not emerge that day from the hold. His heart raced at all the death and the speed with which it was delivered. Since leaving Malta he had learned how easy it was to kill, and how little it seemed to matter. It was impossible to imagine that any force on earth could have beaten Dragut that morning. The corsair had returned immediately to his reading. His countenance was serene, the encounter already forgotten. Nico regarded him with new fear and respect.

I will beat you, son of Satan, he swore. *Not today, but one day.*

❖

What unsettled Nico most was that despite what had happened, he still liked Dragut and enjoyed his company. Dragut was not highly educated, but he showed keen interest in the world around him. History fascinated him, especially tales of the great generals and conquerors of other ages. He carried two books, wrapped in oilcloth. One was the Koran. The other, Herodotus's *The Histories,* was written in Greek. Dragut consulted both books often. In addition, he knew mythology, cosmology, and navigation. He knew of European court politics, and details of the life of the Florentine da Vinci, and the names of every bird and fish he saw. He was particularly interested in the works of Copernicus, the Pole whose odd theory that the earth revolved around the sun Dragut had heard from a priest. Dragut was disappointed when Nico said he knew nothing of the man. "A pity," he said with genuine sadness. "The priest lost his head for his God before I could question him further."

They passed rocky bays and heavily wooded peninsulas, and Dragut had a story about each one. He talked of other times, of battles and kings; of Alexander the Great, and Darius the Persian, and Agamemnon and Genghis Khan, all of whom had walked these shores and sailed these waters.

Occasionally when Dragut mentioned a place, Nico would know something of its history—only bits and pieces, of course, whatever he'd learned from Leonardus—but enough, for a mere boy, to impress Dragut. "Over that horizon you will find Bodrum," Dragut said, indicating a place out of sight. "It was a Greek city-state, the birthplace of Herodotus. It was also the site of the Mausoleum of Halicarnassus, one of the great wonders of the ancients."

"I know of Bodrum," Nico boasted. "The Knights of St. John built a castle there, and called it after St. Peter."

"So they did. And Suleiman drove them from that castle, washing them from the shores of Anatolia like the sea washes sand from a beach."

"He was only lucky," Nico said.

Dragut laughed. "Yes, indeed. He is a man who is often lucky. He had similar luck, I believe, just—" He calculated by the sun, and pointed more to the southeast. "Just there, at Rhodes." He looked at Nico and saw from the boy's unhappy expression that he knew its history as well. "A lovely island. One of my favorite in all the world. There are butterflies there, you know, an entire valley filled with them. There was also a colossus there, a statue of the sun god Helios that stood over Mandrákion harbor. A sculptor named Chares built it of bronze, in memory of the lifting of a long siege. Your beloved knights lived there for two hundred years until another siege—not such a long one, this time—when Suleiman drove them out. That was thirty years ago. They wandered for ten years. No one would give the brave knights of Christ a home, for the Christian kings all feared them."

"Not all," Nico said. "The Emperor Charles gave them a home."

"He gave them a *rock,*" said Dragut, chuckling. "It was a gift of expediency, given only because they agreed to guard it for him. It is no matter. One day soon Suleiman will drive them out once again—even from that barren place."

"He will not," Nico said hotly.

"He will. They trouble his shipping and the peace of his realm."

"As you trouble theirs."

"Ah, but I never gave my word not to do so. At Rhodes Suleiman spared the knights in exchange for their solemn vow to leave him in peace. They traded their honor for their lives, making a promise they did not keep. Such men can have no future in Suleiman's world."

"It is not his world, and I grow tired of history," Nico said. He rose and walked to the prow. Dragut smiled and opened his Koran.

They sailed northeast through the Aegean—"the Sultan's bay," Dragut called it—with the Greek peninsula off the port side and Asia Minor to starboard. All of it, with the exception of a few islands that belonged to the Genoese, was Ottoman. They sailed past enchanted islands, past Andros and Chios and Lesbos, and past the site of another ancient wonder, the Temple of Artemis in Ephesus, built by Croesus and destroyed by the Goths.

They spent a night at the neck of the narrow strait of the

Dardanelles, near the ruins of Troy. Dragut indicated an expanse of water and the hilly land beyond. "This is the Hellespont. It was here that Xerxes, king of the Persians, mounted an invasion of Greece. He laid two boat bridges across the strait and marched his armies across them, all the way to Thermopylae. A storm destroyed the boats, and Xerxes had the sea whipped as punishment."

Dragut stood with his hands behind his back, looking wistfully out over the strait. "Imagine it! How often I wish I had his strength, to whip the sea!"

❖

Dragut was the *imam* aboard his own ship. Five times a day he led the fleet in prayer. It was an inspiring sight, as all oars held steady and ships grew hushed and a deep peace settled over the fleet. Captains and crews prostrated themselves wherever they could find the space, and their prayers floated as one over the sea, toward Mecca.

Dragut was not a proselytizer, but he spoke to Nico in simple if glowing terms of the paradise that awaited believers. "You would know many of the names in the Koran," he told Nico. "Noah and Abraham, Adam and Moses. Even Jesus is known as a blessed man, a prophet." He held the Koran in both hands. "You should listen to the words in this book," he said. "Every word is God's, delivered to Mohammed by the angel Gabriel."

"There is nothing but blasphemy in that book. Father Salvago said so."

"There is grace in it," Dragut replied patiently. "Grace, and the infinite beauty of God, who teaches us that all humans are equal under Him. His very voice is heard in the perfect poetry of these pages, a voice that utters universal laws in a way even the simplest Bedouin can understand."

Nico scoffed. "All humans equal? Who, then, are the slaves that propel this ship?"

"A man might live as slave or master, depending upon how Allah has penned the book of his life," Dragut said. "Yet it is not a man's chains or the lack of them that sets him above or below his fellows, but rather the strength and purity of his faith. There are no differences in rank among men who follow the teachings of Mohammed. Even the Sultan bows before God."

"As does the Emperor Charles, before Christ."

"Ah, but Charles leads a world where blood rather than faith sets a man's table in life. At Allah's table there is only one banquet, shared equally by all who believe."

They sparred back and forth that way throughout their voyage. Nico listened, sometimes responding with words he'd heard Father Salvago use, sometimes remaining silent. He was polite, if distant to a discussion in which he could not hold his own. He simply wasn't very interested, and he was always wary of Dragut's tricks.

One evening as they entered the Sea of Marmara, nearing Constantinople, Dragut made his intentions about Nico clear. They had finished a simple but delicious meal of bread and roast chicken. Dragut sliced an apple for dessert and handed a piece to Nico. He often did this, never displaying ostentation or rank.

"I have given much thought to your disposition, Nico Borg, and I have prayed long on the matter. It was no accident that you were left drifting at sea. It was the will of Allah that I find you there. I believe it is also the will of Allah that you be given the chance to see the light of the one true religion. And so when we arrive in Istanbul I will present you for service to the Sultan, who may or may not choose to accept. His phrenologists must first pass judgment, although I have no doubt of the outcome. Yet for this to be possible, you must first don the turban and say the words 'There is no God but Allah, and Mohammed is his Prophet.' You must do it freely, willingly—for no one may be forcibly converted to the one true path. The light on that path must shine from within your heart and must be truly meant."

"The Sultan's service? What do you mean?"

Dragut explained the system of the children of tribute, called the *devshirme,* the levy of Christian boys taken every few years by the Sultan's agents from various reaches of the empire. One boy was selected from every forty households. Only the most fit and sharp-witted were chosen, and only those who first freely converted to Islam. The majority would become Janissaries, the Sultan's elite troops. A very few, the most gifted of all, became palace pages.

Trained in the illustrious royal schools, they were groomed to rule the empire on the Sultan's behalf.

"The *devshirme* is not the only way such children are found. Sometimes they are discovered in a field, or"—he smiled—"drifting at sea. However it happens, one such child is a greater treasure to the Sultan than a hold full of bullion."

Nico swallowed. He struggled to understand the implications. "You say don the turban," he said, "and repeat . . . those words. Would that make me a Muslim?"

"Yes. This troubles you greatly, I know. Yet in this you must trust an old man such as myself. Once you have given yourself to the service of Allah, you will come to embrace Islam with your heart and soul. You are too intelligent to do otherwise."

Nico trembled, and watched the sea. "If I do not do this, what will become of me?"

"I have no need of a Christian slave, even one so bright as you. Even if I did, it would be sinful to squander your talents in my household, whose needs are so sparing. You are the son of a shipwright, and I have no doubt you may one day be a gifted one yourself. Allah's soldiers on earth need ships, but alas, I have no shipyard of my own in which to employ you. I buy my galleys or take them from the infidel at sea. Therefore, you will remain with me until I return to Barbary. There is a shipyard in Algiers from which I purchase my best galleys. I will sell you to its owner, a man named Farouk. If you serve him well, he will treat you well. He is a poor Muslim but an excellent shipbuilder, and he will provide a future for you that is better in many ways than an unbeliever deserves."

Nico did his best not to betray his shock, replacing it with bravado. "I would rather die than be a slave to any man," he said.

Dragut nodded respectfully. "A noble sentiment, but your death is a matter for Allah to decide. Only unswerving faith in Him can set you free. And as for slavery, you will come to learn that in this world all men are enslaved, by their birth or their love of wealth or position. It is only what you make of your slavery that matters. And a slave in the service of the Sultan, a slave who has been trained in the palace schools, can become anything on this earth, except Sultan: a general, or an admiral, or a judge of men. The governor of a province, or even Grand Vizier. It is the way of enlightenment, Nico. It is the way of the Ottomans."

"I saw what happened to the men on the Dalmatian ships who abandoned their faith," Nico said.

"They abandoned the wrong one."

Nico's head pounded with the pain of his choice.

Abandon God!

It was true, God seemed awfully far away. For a long time Nico had thought sure He was deaf to his endless prayers.

Hellfire awaits those who commit mortal sin, Father Salvago said. Even Nico knew there was no greater sin than turning one's back on the one true Lord.

His wrath is terrible indeed. Salvago's caution was delivered weekly, in clear-cut terms. Eternity was probably not long enough, Nico thought, to contain all the torment and damnation God would devise for him, if he did as Dragut suggested.

It was impossible to imagine himself as a Muslim. There were no Muslims in Malta except for the Order's slaves. Until he met Dragut, all that he had seen of Islam he had seen in Algiers, a world of intolerance and cruelty. He had found Muslims altogether a rough lot, although he didn't know if that came from religion or the Arab nature. Besides, Islam seemed to him a lot of work: prayers five times daily and, during Ramadan, fasting every day for a whole month. Nico had fasted during famines, and cared little for the practice.

No. Despite the peace he felt in the presence of Dragut's simple faith, Nico was a Christian. Even if he knew precious little about it, his God was his God—even if sometimes He seemed to have forgotten one of his own children.

But then Nico's mind turned to what troubled him even more. As much as he wanted to serve God, he could not do so if he were dead. And as much as he feared God in the next life, he feared El Hadji Farouk in this life more. The only real question was which was the most effective path to escape. From Algiers, and its devil Farouk, there would be none. From Constantinople, and its devil Sultan, he might find a way.

His only chance for a future lay in accepting what had been offered.

He thought of what Leonardus had said. *There comes a time in a man's life when he has to choose between what is right and what might keep him alive.* And he realized that the choice might not be quite so limited. There might, indeed, be a way out.

It was in Algiers that he had first understood he was smarter than a lot of other people, even adults. He didn't know how this could be true. He only knew that it was.

He would pretend.

He would make a secret pact with God. He would do as he must do to preserve his skin. He would don the turban of Islam and say the words but not mean them. By day he would grovel on a mat and move his lips for Allah. By night, in bed, he would pray to God. Not to the impostor, but to *God*.

Only men would be fooled; he and God alone would know the truth of the matter. And there would come a day when he would escape. He would return to Malta and join the Knights in their holy crusade against the unholy infidel.

Yes, it was a good plan. It would work.

Dragut was watching Nico carefully. While he knew nothing of Nico's history with El Hadji Farouk, he was not foolish enough to believe he was offering the boy a real choice. With one so young, he reasoned, it didn't matter. Nico knew many things, it was true, but he knew them without benefit of wisdom, in the same way a parrot might repeat a curse without cursing. The boy had learned the false words of his priests, but he did not yet comprehend: they were mere words, which had not yet tainted his being. His soul was still malleable.

Nico would come to the light of Allah; Dragut knew this without doubt. For now, the boy would pretend: this he also knew without doubt.

For Dragut, that was enough.

"I await your answer," he said, feigning impatience.

Nico looked into the warm, likable eyes of Allah's assassin, the eyes that were appraising him so carefully. Nico held his gaze, unflinching. *You think that somehow time will deliver me to your way,* he thought. *You are wrong in that, son of Satan. I can fool you. I can fool all of your kind, and I can do it until the day of your death, which will come at my hand.*

"As much as it hurts me to admit, it is clear to me that my own

God has abandoned me on my journey. I cannot deny that Allah must have led you to my rescue. I am eager to accept Allah into my life, because He has remembered me. I will convert, and I will do it freely."

Each delighted with his deception, the old man and the boy shared a cup of strong, sweet coffee.

The next morning before sunrise, Dragut sent one of his crew up the mast, to serve as muezzin. He faced east, then west, north, and south, his voice floating over the water as it carried the poetry of Islam: "Allah is most great. There is no God but Allah, and Mohammed is his prophet. Come to prayer. Come to salvation. Allah is most great. There is no God but Allah."

Dragut wrapped a turban around Nico's head and then washed his hands, feet, and face, using seawater dipped from a bucket. "This is the prayer of dawn, the *salat al-fajr*. In each of the five daily prayers you must surrender your soul to Allah, and all else to the Sultan, His deputy on earth. Forget your past, for it does not exist. Serve your new masters well, and paradise will be your reward. Serve them falsely, or ill, and even death will not release you from your torments."

Dragut knelt on his prayer mat. Nico, his heart pounding, followed suit. Dragut carried a *saif,* a small scimitar with a hilt of silver and brass, overlaid with tortoiseshell and coral. The blade was inscribed with verses from the Koran. Its edge had slain countless enemies of Allah, and now its tip pointed toward Mecca.

"*Bis'mallah. Ar-Rahman. Ar-Rahim.*" The corsair's voice was deep and mellifluous. "In the name of God, the Merciful, the Compassionate." Then he nodded at Nico, indicating the moment had arrived.

Nico said the words: "There is no God but Allah, and Mohammed is his prophet." Dragut, holding his right wrist with his left hand, put his forehead to the mat and began reciting *al-fatihah,* the opening and essence of the Koran.

"*Praise be to Allah, Lord of the Worlds, the Beneficent, the Merciful.*

"*Owner of the day of judgment.*"

Nico put his own forehead to the mat, and repeated the words. In his fist he clutched Maria's coin. Silently, he added his own prayer.

"My Father, who art in heaven, hallowed be thy name."

"Thee alone we worship, Thee alone we ask for help."

"Please, Father, forgive me, for I must do this thing."

"Show us the straight path, the path of those whom Thou hast favored."

"They can make me bow, O Lord my God, but they cannot make me believe."

"Not the path of those who earn Thine anger nor of those who go astray."

"I will have no other God but thee. As I will always carry this coin on my body, I will carry thee in my heart. Please make and keep me strong. Amen."

Nico touched his forehead again to the deck and stood. Dragut regarded him warmly. "You have acted wisely," he said. "You are ready to walk the path Allah has chosen for you." Dragut paused for a moment, thinking. "Henceforth you shall be called Asha, Protector of Fire."

"Fire?"

"The fire is Suleiman, your Sultan—the man who shall set your heart aglow with the light of God."

Nico nodded without believing a word. "I am Muslim now?" he asked. It had been awfully easy, he thought. Surely not enough had transpired to make a sin.

"Not fully. Not until you have learned to read the Koran, and not until you have been circumcised. All of that will come in Allah's time."

"Circumcised?" Nico gave him a blank look. And when Dragut had explained, Nico no longer thought it was quite so easy after all.

❖

Constantinople.

Istanbul.

Suleiman.

The words rang in Nico's head as the fleet neared the end of its voyage and he began seeing signs of the Ottomans on both shores, and each dip and sigh of the oars brought him closer to his destiny. He stood on the deck next to Dragut, who had traded his simple seaman's attire for a light purple turban, wound high on his head and secured by a ruby that flashed bloodred in the morning sun, and ceremonial silk robes embroidered with gold and silver thread. He carried a splendid jeweled sword and stood erect, the proud lord of the sea taking in the heady sights of empire.

Constantinople. The Rome of the East, it joined the three waters of Marmara, the Bosphorus, and the Golden Horn, and it spread, like Rome, across seven hills. He saw it for the first time just after dawn. The sun rose over Asia, on his right, and lit Europe, on his left, igniting the domes on the mosques with golden fire. Minarets soared toward heaven like white lances, behind billowing stands of soft cypress and cool willow. It was overwhelmingly beautiful, a city of silk and satin, of belvederes and pavilions, of gardens and grace. Truly, he knew as he looked in awe, this must be the center of the universe, the most magnificent city on earth. He almost laughed out loud at its splendor, and he couldn't imagine he'd ever mistaken the gritty trinket of Algiers for this, the very pearl of God.

Constantinople. Founded by a Greek named Byzas on the site of a fishing village, and called Byzantium. The Emperor Constantine made the city his capital, calling it New Rome, but it soon was known as Constantinople, capital of all Eurasia for a millennium. Her harbors thronged with merchantmen hailing from Egypt to the Black Sea, from Marseilles to Beirut, their sterns elaborately carved, their holds filled with caviar and timber, casks of olive oil, and bolts of rich cloth. In the quarters of Pera and Galata across the Golden Horn, her streets thronged with Franks and Florentines, with blue-eyed Circassians and hard-eyed Tartars, with Jews and Christians and Muslims from every corner of the world. Her walls withstood earthquakes and Attila the Hun, but not Mehmet II, the Ottoman Sultan who, a hundred years earlier, had successfully conquered the city, now known to Turks and Muslims as Istanbul, or Dar-es-Saada: the Abode of Felicity.

Istanbul. The seat of government of the largest empire on earth, an empire that spanned half the civilized world, stretching across three continents. While the rest of the world was mired in the Middle Ages, Ottoman culture had flowered like a garden of Eden. Not since Rome had a civilization so dominated mankind. All of it was ruled from Topkapi, the seraglio that stood atop the first of the seven hills. Topkapi, where peacocks strutted, gazelles nibbled at tulips behind turreted walls, and exotic birds made nests in sparkling fountains. Topkapi, the seat of government, administration, and learning, the palace of the sultan that included his harem.

The Sultan, Suleiman. Possessor of Men's Necks, the Shadow of God on Earth, Lord of Lords of this world, King of Kings, King of Believers and Unbelievers, Emperor of the East and West; Padishah of the Mediterranean, the Black Sea, Rumelia, Anatolia, Karaman, Zulkadir, Azerbaijan, Iran, Syria, Egypt, Mecca, Mdina, and All the Arab Lands.

The Sultan, Suleiman. Called the Magnificent by Europeans, who stood in awe of him, but known to his own people as Kanuni, the Lawgiver, for he had written down the Koranic and Ottoman laws by which enlightened men lived. He was patron of the arts and sciences. His armies flowed like rivers over the earth.

Suleiman. Admired and feared. He wrote poetry, and killed his enemies without mercy. Though he was the first son of Islam, in his own city of Istanbul neither Christians nor Jews feared him. By the Sultan's grace all men worshiped freely in their mosques and churches and synagogues. *Suleiman*: he prayed during the battle of Mohács, while outside his tent his Janissaries built an avenue of pyramids from the heads of ten thousand enemy knights, to stand in the shade of the two thousand heads already mounted there on poles. After prayer he finished a letter to his mother, imparting the day's important news. "It rained," he wrote.

All of this Dragut explained as they sailed. He pointed out the great edifice of the Hagia Sophia, the cathedral built by the Emperor Justinian. Its golden dome was so large that even now men feared to walk inside, believing that surely it must collapse. Beneath that dome the sun had set on an empire: with the Ottomans at the gates, the residents of Constantinople gathered there to make their peace with God. A day later, a new empire dawned beneath that dome, as the Sultan declared the cathedral a mosque, and his followers gathered there to pray to Allah. Now four minarets flanked the Hagia Sophia, like golden stalks waving in the breeze of heaven.

And there, said Dragut, pointing, was the unfinished Suleimaniye mosque, the jewel of Sinan, the Sultan's architect who had so transformed the city. Above every dome and minaret and cupola was a gilt crescent. "The crescent resembles the moon in its first quarter," said Dragut, "but it is the two claws of the Ottomans, joined at the base."

They rounded Seraglio Point. Dragut ordered his deck cannon fired in salute to the simple gray granite tomb of Kheir-el-din, the corsair who had captured Leonardus at sea and whose fiery torch had passed to Dragut. No military venture ever departed from Istanbul in which the Sultan's commander did not first stop at that tomb to pray.

They passed the Sultan's marble quay and sailed into the Golden Horn, a wide, deep creek that served as a natural harbor for the Sultan's fleets. It boasted a shipyard that rivaled the great arsenal at Venice. From the city above them, guns and trumpets sounded greetings to the Drawn Sword of Islam, a welcome of thunder so grand it seemed to roll from heaven itself. Cheering men stood atop crenellated walls, waving banners.

"Do they always give such a welcome?" asked Nico in wonder.

"Never to me, but always to the commander of the Sultan's fleet."

"Is he coming to meet us?"

Dragut laughed. "The Sultan appointed me three months ago. I received word of it only a week before I found you at sea, and set a course to come here. It was why I found you at all, the reason I knew Allah had intervened." He pointed. "Look, they have set the doves to flight. It is a great honor."

A thousand doves rose from the palace in a pristine white cloud. Their shadow passed over the galley, blotting out the sun. The birds swirled and fluttered and found their bearings, and set out as one toward the heavens, the Sultan's announcement to Allah that his commander had arrived.

Dragut's ship neared the quay below the iron sea gate of Topkapi, where a delegation waited to greet them: the grand chamberlain and the chief usher, and behind them the agha of Janissaries, with an honor guard forty strong, all in full splendor, standing still as statues in their blue robes and white feathered bonnets, on carpets strewn with pearls.

The oars were shipped, and the galley nudged the dock.

And thus it was, on the twenty-second day of the month of Dhu'l-Hijjah, in the year 959 of the Hijrah of the Prophet, that

Nicolo Borg, late the son of a builder from the fishing village of Birgu on the island of Malta—a boy newly christened as Asha, Protector of Fire—followed the corsair Dragut Raïs, newly appointed commander of the Sultan's fleets, onto the shores of Istanbul.

Book Two

CHRISTIEN

from *The Histories of the Middle Sea*

by Darius, called the Preserver
Court Historian to the Prince of Allah, the Sultan Achmet

Driven from Jerusalem by Saladin, the two Catholic orders of professed monks, the Hospitaller Knights of St. John and their rivals, the Knights Templar, moved to Acre, the last capital of the Christian warriors in the Holy Land. In A.D. 1291 Acre itself fell to Muslim siege, and the two orders were driven from the Levant into the sea. They found temporary refuge in Cyprus. There the Templars were persecuted by Pope Clement and Philip IV of France for suspicion of heresy and immorality, while the Order of St. John gathered strength and numbers for twenty years. Not long after the Grand Master of the Templars was burned at the stake, his order in ruins and most of its wealth having passed to the Hospitallers, the latter captured Rhodes, a lush and beautiful island in the Dodecanese, and established its new convent there.

Now with an island for their base, the Knights of St. John became a seafaring order of corsairs in the service of Christ, protecting Christian merchant ships at sea. They preyed upon Muslim shipping from the protected harbors of Rhodes. Though their numbers were small, they were tough men who fought with legendary skill, hard men to whom pillage came as easily as prayer. The Order's traditions were unwavering, the ranks of professed monks filled with noblemen hailing from the greatest houses of Europe, men who served their Grand Master under vows of poverty, chastity, and obedience.

The sun was just beginning to rise over the Ottoman Empire. Rhodes lay athwart the empire's shipping routes, and the increasingly militaristic knights interrupted trade between Istanbul, the Levant, and Egypt. Muslims making their pilgrimage to Mecca were captured and enslaved. For many years the knights gnawed thus at the Sultan's belly—never strong enough to present a military threat to the empire, but ever an irritation. Determined to drive out the infidel, Mehmet, the Sultan who conquered Constantinople, mounted a fierce siege of Rhodes. The Order had heavily fortified the island, and Mehmet was unsuccessful.

Such was not the case with Mehmet's son, Suleiman. In the first major military campaign of his reign, he took the city of Belgrade, striking at the door to central Europe. The next year, only his third as Sultan, he turned his attention to Rhodes. The knights fought bravely but stood no chance against the four hundred ships and five army corps of Suleiman. In victory, the Sultan showed magnanimity toward his enemies out of respect for their valor. He allowed the knights to leave Rhodes with their banners and their honor, their arms and their relics, their camp followers and even their animals, in exchange for their solemn oath that they would leave his minions in peace.

It was an oath the knights would not keep.

For seven years the Order had no home, taking only transitory residence in Sicily and Italy. Finally, in exchange for the annual payment of a falcon, they were granted the islands of the Maltese archipelago by the Hapsburg Charles V, the Holy Roman Emperor and king of Spain, who saw the wisdom in having such a military force to protect his southern flanks from Suleiman and his allies, the corsairs of the Barbary Coast.

The expulsion of the knights from Rhodes left the Ottomans as the dominant power in the eastern Middle Sea. Suleiman's armies and their artillery were the envy of the world, and his navy was growing in power. The Christian kingdoms of Europe were at each other's throats, unable to unite against their common enemy.

In the same year that Charles granted Malta to the Order, a future knight was born to a noble family in Paris, born to the same timeless traditions that had bound generations of his ancestors.

—From Volume V
The Order of St. John of Jerusalem

Chapter 13

PARIS
1530

The infant lay naked in his cradle, nestled in blankets. His eyes were attempting to focus on his own tiny hand, outstretched before him, his fingers bathed in bright colors streaming from the massive stained glass window above the altar. The window's panels depicted John, his own hand outstretched, baptizing Jesus. A frigid autumn wind howled outside the chapel, stirring copper leaves that had tumbled from the magnificent old beech trees that lined the priory grounds. The ivy-covered chapel had changed little since medieval times. Gray-robed Benedictine monks from a nearby abbey raised their voices in plainchant, as thick candles flickered in stone sconces along the walls.

Next to the baby's cradle knelt Arnaud, the eighteenth Count de Vries. He was a big, quick-tempered warrior, his face scarred from a hundred battles. Behind him the oak benches were filled with those who had journeyed to the priory to witness the solemn rites. In the pew behind Arnaud was his firstborn son, Yves, who was six. The heir to the de Vries mantle and fortune had been born with a deformed spine. He was sickly and pale, and had barely survived infancy. Next to him sat his mother, the countess Simone, a flaxen-haired beauty from Provence. She was as slight and perfectly formed as her husband was big and blemished. She wore a modest shawl to cover her golden hair. In the opposite pew sat her father, the Duke of Toulon, his hair snow white, his eyes beginning to cloud with cataracts. His eyes brimmed with tears of pride as, with what dim vision remained to him, he looked upon the form of his grandson, who was to so honor his line. Behind the old duke sat a congregation of lesser nobles and distinguished guests.

Seated on a high-backed velvet chair in front of the altar was the prior of the French *langue* of the Order of St. John of Jerusalem. He wore the simple black habit of the Hospitallers, representing the camel skin worn by John the Baptist, patron saint of the Order. The prior sat behind a heavy oak table, upon which rested his ceremonial armor: silver breastplate, plumed casque, polished mail gauntlets, and a heavy double-edged sword in its lavish scabbard. The table also held rolled parchments and piles of paper and heavy ledgers. At either end of the table sat two Grand Crosses, knights who were to bear official witness to the ceremony. They, too, wore black habits, with simple white crosses adorning their breasts.

The chapel bell tolled, and the chanting monks fell silent. At a signal from the prior, Arnaud de Vries lifted his newborn son from the cradle. Proudly he held him up before the knights. The child screamed lustily. It was a good sign. He was strong and tough: a future general of the galleys, perhaps, or even Grand Master. Three doctors had sworn to the child's robust constitution and his fitness for the Order. Now the boy himself ratified their opinion with his strident cry: he was worthy; he would stand tall and fight the enemies of Christendom; and, if God so favored him, he would die in the glory of His service.

"My lords," said Arnaud, "I present you my son, Christien Luc de Vries. I pledge his being to God, and his life to His glorious and sovereign Order of St. John. I pledge his fealty, that he may serve thee well and gallantly and faithfully." Though the knights were hospitallers, all men knew their true renown sprang from their courage, tenacity, and ferocity in battle. Their galleys sailed the Mediterranean with almost mythical prowess, carrying the holy battle of the Cross to the Crescent.

"I pledge his heart and his soul, that he may distinguish himself among the distinguished, as a humble servant of our Lord." Every noble house in Europe competed to place a son in one of the Order's eight *langues,* or tongues: Provence, Auvergne, and France, the French *langues;* Castile and Aragon, the Spanish; and one each from Germany, Italy, and England.

"I pledge his purity of line, that through his noble blood he may bring grace and honor to the Order. I pledge his very life, that he may carry the banner of the holy religion, and that he may die for the glory of Christ." From each of the *langues* came three classes of knights. The infant Christien was being pledged for the highest of those, that of military knight, or Knight of Justice.

"All this do I solemnly pledge, with the full faith and honor of the house de Vries."

The prior nodded. "Have the proofs been completed?" he asked.

"They have, my lord," replied one of the knights. He stood and presented the report of the commissioners of proof, the officials who had examined the applicant's lineage. Even such a venerated family as the de Vrieses was not exempt from the formal proofs required to ensure that no bastards or half-breeds, no men of common strain or recent nobility, no men with any taint of plebeian blood might blemish their Order. In this, the French *langue,* perfection of nobility was required for at least four generations, on both paternal and maternal sides.

For this candidate, the proofs were piled high upon the oak table. There were written testaments, deeds, and census lists. There were birth and marriage registers, baptismal records, and sworn statements of notaries and peers. Atop the other documents a rolled parchment bore the seal of Francis, the king of France. It attested that the current count, Arnaud, pure of heart and blood, had faithfully served His Majesty for fifteen years in his wars against the Holy Roman Empire, just as Arnaud's ancestors had served other Valois kings, and the Capetian kings before them. The royal testament carried no greater weight with the prior than that of any other. After all, the king's own line had existed a mere two hundred years.

The child's pedigree was summarized on a large piece of cream vellum that bore names and titles and crests. A notary stood and read the genealogy, his voice ringing off the ancient stone walls of the chapel: "*Christien Luc de Vries, fils de Arnaud, le Comte de Vries; fils de Simone, fille du Duc de Toulon; petit-fils de Guy, le Comte de Vries . . .*" The roll of nobility stretched back not mere generations but centuries, back to the man who rode at the side of the king now known as St. Louis, in Tunisia, and even further back than that. There had been noble de Vrieses longer than there had been an Order of St. John.

"I accept this evidence on behalf of the Order," the prior said solemnly. "I accept your pledges, and welcome this Christian soul as it begins its journey along the sacred path to the Lord's grace." He set bread and water next to the child on the floor, to signify the life of poverty that awaited him as a man. A heavy purse of gold florins was presented by the count to the prior. The count leaned over the table and with a flourish signed the document sealing their agreement, which was then countersigned by the two knights.

Thus was it done: when the child Christien reached his majority, he would journey to the Order's new convent in Malta, which that very year had been given to the knights by the king of Spain, Charles V. There Christien would swear fealty to the Grand Master, take the vows, and be formally admitted to the Order to which he would devote his blood, his honor, and his very existence.

❖

While there was no doubt as to the lineage of the candidate, no question as to his suitability for the Order, and no doubt as to the intent of the count regarding his second son, there was, nevertheless, a problem: as he grew toward the age of reason, the candidate had other ideas.

The problem was that Christien Luc de Vries wanted not to lop off heads in the name of the Order, but to study them, in the name of science.

His formal education began at the age of five. The finest tutors schooled him in reading and writing, while the best warriors introduced him to wrestling, the first of the many arts of war his father required him to master. He did well enough at both, but what really captured his interest were crickets and butterflies, cockroaches and centipedes, worms and spiders—anything that wriggled or fluttered or crawled. He kept his treasures in jars until long after they'd turned to powder.

The count was gone for long periods, sometimes years at a time, fighting in the never-ending wars in which France was then engaged. Whenever he was home he preferred that the family stay in its city house, near the Place St. Michel. Simone thought Paris was too smelly and crowded, so whenever the count was away she took her sons to the family's ancient château, located in the wild forest of Boulogne not far from the city walls. She considered its air better for Yves's frailties, and the game-rich forests better both for Christien, who loved to explore them, and for herself, as she could indulge her passion for riding, honed and perfected during her childhood in Toulon, where she'd learned to ride along the coast. After Christien's birth Arnaud had presented her with an Arabian—a sleek, swift mount that was as spirited as the countess herself, and whose hair, also like her own, was the color of wheat. Mother and sons would take long rides through the forest, Simone and Christien on horseback, with Yves following along in a carriage driven by the equerry.

It was on those rides that Christien's interest in nature blossomed. He asked endless questions about the world around him, wondering how God made an apple taste like an apple, or a flower bloom in the spring, or a king scratch himself like a commoner. Simone rarely knew the answers, but she encouraged his curiosity. Christien chased frogs and turtles, then poked and prodded and studied them. Yves shrank from such creatures, while Simone bravely tolerated them. Despite her loathing for things that slithered and crept, she even spotted specimens for him on her own. Once she spied a lizard sunning itself. She pointed it out to Christien, who managed to chase it beneath a rock. He couldn't get it to come out and couldn't move the rock by himself, so gamely she slipped from her horse to help. As they struggled to move the rock, the lizard darted from its shelter. Simone astonished herself by trapping it beneath her cloak. She shuddered at the repulsive creature wriggling beneath the material, but it was the look of delight in Christien's eyes as they got it into her bag that she always remembered most.

Christien's specimens soon filled boxes and shelves, and then even drawers in his wardrobe, until the maid was afraid to touch anything unless she'd looked first. The cook found snakeskins in her crockery and fish skeletons in the crystal. She complained to the countess, who lectured her son to be more careful where he stored his treasures.

When Christien was eight, his schooling broadened to Latin and Greek, history and the classics, mathematics and astrology, and of course archery and swordsmanship. He often took lessons with Bertrand Cuvier, son of the Marquis de Meaux. Like Christien,

Bertrand had also been pledged as an infant into the Order of St. John. Unlike Christien, Bertrand adored swords and war games. He decorated melons as human heads, painting on faces and beards and wrapping them with turbans. He spiked them atop posts, then gleefully struck them down with his short sword, whooping and cursing their infidel blood.

Bertrand helped Christien catch mice and trap rats. Together they smoked out groundhogs and snared squirrels. Christien wanted only to study them, but Bertrand's interest was perhaps more typical for a boy his age: he delighted in plucking the wings from a moth, or devising some torment for a particularly gruesome spider. Occasionally he would spear a specimen rather than capture it alive, or coax it from a tree with an arrow, swearing to Christien that it had refused his offer of honorable surrender. He never visited the Château de Vries without bringing a trophy or two for his friend to study. Their prize catch was a two-headed garter snake. Christien kept it in a box in the barn.

Christien spent a few hours each week in the château's library, where his tutors lectured him in the art and history of war. Among the history books there, he found a volume of illustrations of the human body, by Galen. It had been purchased not by his father, who cared little for books, but by his great-great-grandfather, whose appetite for the written word knew no bounds. The old man had spent without care, filling whole rooms with rich volumes. Some were elaborate handwritten copies, while others were newly printed on the presses then spreading through the continent. He had purchased an original *Astronomic Calendar* of Gutenberg's, a score of different Bibles, and academic texts of every sort. Christien spent hours poring over illustrations and reading about medicine. Even in the history books, his attention was diverted from his father's course. He read how the body of Alexander the Great had been carried home to Macedonia in honey. That set him to thinking about methods of preservation. He tried various concoctions for preserving his own collection of specimens—sugar water, vinegar, horse piss, vegetable juice—and he kept meticulous notes on the merits of each. He began a sketchbook, filling it with detailed notes and diagrams.

❖

One spring morning the Valois king, Francis I, brought his royal party to hunt on the grounds of the de Vries estate. Francis was renowned as a patron of the arts, a lover of scholarship, a man with a memory as prodigious as his curiosity. When one of his huntsmen disturbed a large rat snake, the king commented on its size. Christien ran to the château and returned, out of breath, proudly presenting his two-headed snake for royal inspection. While the mortified Count de Vries stood livid behind his lord, the king openly admired the marvel and accepted the serpent as a gift from the boy. The king's reaction did not save Christien from a scalding lecture that evening about his despicable hobby.

"It isn't a hobby," Christien bravely countered. "I've been reading, Father. I want to study medicine."

The idea was so preposterous that Arnaud thought his son was joking. "Nonsense, lad. You are to join the Order of St. John."

Christien drew a breath, stood as tall as he could, and stared up into his father's fiery eyes. "But I don't want to."

Arnaud snorted. "Your preference is of no import! Imagine if everyone did as he pleased, without regard to God or country or duty! Imagine the chaos! A man must follow the path his father has set for him. Yours was ordained on the day of your birth. That is the end of it."

"I won't be a knight, Father," Christien insisted. "I'll be a doctor."

"A *doctor!*" The count's tone was withering. "You are the son of a count! Not a cutler. Not a farrier or a cooper. Not a butcher, by God, or a . . . a *snake* keeper. You are a *de Vries!* Why would you wish a commoner's post? There is no honor in doctoring! Doctors *clean* a battlefield! A de Vries is born to litter it!"

Christien's eyes still flashed defiantly, so Arnaud abandoned words and gave his son a thorough caning. A while later the fire crackled with Christien's sketchbooks. Specimen jars flew from Christien's window, shattering one after another on the gravel in the drive.

Christien learned nothing from the encounter but to be more discreet. There was an attic in the château, a series of passageways that connected the upstairs rooms. Every boy who ever lived in the château had played there. Christien brought in a table and sawed off the legs so it would fit. It was cramped but private, and he studied by candlelight. Within a week there were a dozen new jars and fresh piles of paper. His father did not suspect and had little opportunity to look, for he still traveled incessantly in the service of his king. So long as there was no shortage of wars for the count, there was never a shortage of specimens for his son.

When Christien was eleven, his formal military training began in earnest. Some of the finest swordsmen in France, men who served his father in war, worked long hours honing his reflexes, which were quick, and his warrior instincts, which were sound if not inspired. Christien was swift and strong, naturally gifted with the sword, but the blade he preferred was much smaller. Cutting things open fascinated him. His jars now held cat brains, cow tongues, rabbit kidneys, and other more unsavory parts.

One day he and Bertrand heard a wailing in the barn. They found a dog, its ear half ripped off and its belly bloodied, by either tusk or claw. The dog had dragged itself into the barn to die, and was nipping at its own exposed intestines, tearing them further. "Probably a boar," Bertrand said. He drew his knife, intending to put the animal out of its misery.

"*Attendez,*" Christien said, his mind on a surgical drawing he'd seen. "Perhaps I can help it." Warily the two got a blanket over the animal and soon had its feet bound and a rope cinched around its jaws as a muzzle. While Bertrand held the struggling animal still, Christien used needle and thread from the château to sew up the wound.

"You're wasting your time," Bertrand said as Christien wrapped a dressing around the dog's belly. "The cur will chew it off and eat his own guts."

Christien thought about that problem. From the storeroom he took a bit of the tanum bark and urine mixture the equerry used to tan leather. It was a foul, bitter-smelling concoction, and he and Bertrand each added a bit of their own piss to finish it off. Christien smeared it on the bandage, wrinkling his nose at the odor while the dog growled at him. When he finished he gently unbound its legs and deftly removed the muzzle. The dog nipped at him, then limped off to a corner where it curled up to nurse itself. It nosed at the dressing but didn't rip it.

Christien brought food and water twice a day and did his best to keep the rats away. The dog lived for two days—two days Christien was certain it wouldn't have survived without his treatment. He was proud of the effort, and later opened up the dead animal to see what he might learn.

A few days later, inspired by the dog, he caught a frog, cut off its leg, and meticulously sewed it back on. Neither frog nor leg survived the operation, but Christien knew he'd sewn muscle to muscle and skin to skin, and his stitches were neat as those of a seamstress. He hadn't even had to wonder very much about how to go about it—somehow he'd done it by instinct.

He was captivated.

He started a new book, on the cover of which he carefully lettered:

Remedies and Cures, by Doctor Christien de Vries

He filled it with his own observations, and with preparations recommended by the cook, decoctions devised by the equerry's wife, and the accumulated medical wisdom of the château's maids and washerwomen.

"*For the fever of ague,*" he wrote, "*wrap a live spider in the skin of a plum, and swallow it down without water.*"

"*A pregnant woman should not look at an ugly or deformed person, lest her baby be born the same.*"

"*To stop a nosebleed, place an iron key on the neck.*"

"*To cure a fright, boil a puppy in water and feed the broth to the victim.*"

He begged money from his mother to buy new books. Though Simone loved the richness she saw in the mind of her son, marveled at the curiosity he displayed, and cherished his gentleness of manner and his independence, she knew that his continued resistance to his father's wishes would only bring them all pain. When the count was home she tried to insert herself between them, doing her best to soften the count's passions as he tried to bend his son to his will, at the same time trying to convince Christien that he should do his best to honor his father's wishes.

And then, of course, she gave Christien money for more books.

❖

Christien was sixteen when the countess summoned a noted physician to attend to Yves, who was suffering chills. Trained at the great medical center of Montpellier, Dr. Philippe Guignard had recently accepted a teaching post on the Faculté de Médecine in Paris. His preeminence was verified beyond question when the king's own premier physician consulted him on a matter relating to the royal person himself. Guignard wore a long red robe and a mortarboard, the symbols of his profession, and covered his delicate hands with velvet gloves. His brown hair fell in thick curls to his shoulders. His eyes were piercing, intelligent, and arrogant.

Guignard finished detailing instructions for Yves's care with the countess and was preparing to leave when Christien boldly drew him aside. "Begging your pardon, sire, I would like to observe your work. Would you mind if I accompanied you for a few days? I could . . . I could help you. I am interested in what you do."

Guignard was immediately wary, searching for any hint of mockery in the surprising request. The son of a count was not likely to have any real interest in medicine, and of course he would never stoop to becoming a physician, as lofty as that position might be for a commoner. But the boy seemed genuinely interested, even producing his own book of remedies and cures, filled with notes and drawings of surprising sophistication.

"Your father would approve of this?"

"Of course," Christien lied, "so long as it does not interfere with my other studies."

Glad of any opportunity to impress an heir of the count, the doctor consented. Christien devoted every spare moment to following the doctor on his rounds in Paris, lugging his books and instruments. A few days became a few weeks, and a few months.

Of course Guignard was current in the most modern medical practices. He spent much of each day examining excreta, and put Christien to work preparing specimens. Patients brought in bags of feces, which Christien spooned onto a silver platter for Guignard's perusal. The doctor carefully probed the piles, checking consistency, odor, and shade, then rendering his diagnosis and prescribing treatment.

The urine flask was equally vital to his work. After patients filled it he swirled it, sniffed it, and held it up to the light. Guignard could identify more than a score of different colors and densities, and describe the significance of each. There were infinite subtleties of smell, and variations due to sex, age, and mental state. Even the sediment could be broken into ten distinct types. To the seasoned observer, such nuances might indicate dispersion of vitality, the presence of an atrabilious humor, deficient digestive power, or— when white or slightly reddish—the advent of dropsy.

"I can diagnose most problems without ever seeing the patient," Guignard noted proudly, "so long as I see their leavings." And it must have been true: Christien rarely saw the good doctor so much as touch a patient, except to take a pulse or check a fever, while yet diagnosing and treating a host of illnesses: catarrh and ringworm, migraines and gout, ailments of the liver and fevers of the brain.

Guignard refused to accept a great many cases, avoiding those with a poor prognosis, which was most of them. For those he did accept, he consulted not only medical texts but also books on astrology and numbers, and, having been a priest before taking up medicine, a Bible. Guignard's treatments involved medication, diet, or surgery. Every effort was dedicated to striking the proper balance between the all-important humors—hot and dry, cold and moist— that, when out of balance, made the body ill.

Guignard was a good teacher with a keen pupil. He taught Christien commonsense remedies: patients must not eat fruit after salad, the mixture of which could overload one's humors, and they must avoid strenuous sex, which might induce seizures.

He taught remedies of the pharmacy: when to call upon the apothecary to prepare purgatives for syphilis, emetics for poison, and tinctures of lead and mercury to cure the vapors, those exhalations of the liver and stomach that produced hysteria and depression. He prescribed ground boar penis for pleurisy, pigeon dung for eye irritations, grease for burns, and verbena to induce menstruation.

He taught remedies of the knife: when to call upon a barber-surgeon to perform bloodletting, essential in releasing malignant humors. For pleurisy, blood was drawn from the elbow of the arm opposite the affected side. The basilic vein was bled for woes of the liver or spleen, the temporal vein for melancholy or migraine. Every malady had its vein, and every vein its malady.

In all areas, Guignard's knowledge was as prodigious as his ego.

From memory he quoted Avicenna, the Persian doctor whose *Canon of Medicine* had stood unchallenged for four hundred years, and Galen, whose works had been the standard for more than a thousand. Christien proudly showed him a new textbook of anatomy by Vesalius, a Flemish physician. "Throw it into the bonfire," Guignard said vehemently. "He is a fool to challenge the old masters." In awe of his teacher, Christien very nearly did just that.

Christien's tenure with the physician only heightened his passion for the healing arts, although there was something vaguely dissatisfying to him about Guignard's practice, which seemed remote from its very subjects, the patients. Christien yearned to touch, to probe, to explore—activities Guignard disdained. Yet the man was the epitome of his profession, and Christien was too busy learning at his side to worry about such things. He soaked up information and each night related the day's events to Bertrand, who had little faith in any healer but God and considered all physicians quacks. "We'll see just how good a doctor he is after your father finds out what you've been up to," Bertrand said.

There was an occasion when Guignard did something that profoundly troubled Christien. The doctor was treating what he diagnosed as bilious fever in the young daughter of a shopkeeper. He prescribed vervain, made from a common plant. The very same day he diagnosed the identical fever in the daughter of a duke. Instead of vervain, he prescribed mumia, which he told the duke was a distillation of the spices secreted by corpses embalmed by the ancients. "This drug has been gathered at great expense from mummies found in the catacombs and tombs of Egypt," he said. While the use of mumia was common among the wealthy, Christien had in fact seen the doctor fill the vial with vervain, the same drug that he used for the shopkeeper's daughter. He brooded for a few days, then summoned the courage to ask about it.

"You are mistaken," Guignard retorted, bristling. Christien agreed that he must be, but then asked about the use of different drugs for the same fever in two girls the same age.

"Same fever, different physical condition," Guignard said frostily, his tone signaling an end to the discussion.

"Same fever, different purse," Bertrand said later, with a smirk.

Both fevers abated; both patients were happy. Christien remained unsettled, while Guignard remained cool.

Guignard left the hands-on portion of his work to a barber-surgeon named Marcel Foucault. Marcel kept a shop near the Porte de Montmartre and was as rough and ragged as the neighborhood in which he worked. His clothing was plain, his apron generally spattered with bits of blood and hair. His fingernails were cracked and dirty, his hands scarred. Though he and Guignard might work together on a case, their status was not equal. Guignard was a respected member of the Faculté de Médecine. By the grace of the king, he and his fellow physicians were the elite of the medical establishment, with monopolistic control over the practice of medicine, in which learning was always more highly regarded than skill. A physician's ability to heal was less important than his knowledge of illness. Surgeons such as Marcel were generally of low birth and had little or no education save that of experience, most often gained in battle. In Paris they treated patients only by leave of the physicians, comparative patricians who did not themselves touch a medical instrument—or a patient, if it could be avoided.

One afternoon Guignard, Marcel, and Christien were leaving the home of a patient they had bled. Two stories up, at the house next door, a brace holding a supply of roofing tile suddenly gave way. Workmen shouted warnings as a shower of heavy tiles cascaded to the street. One of the tiles struck the head of a mason who was hauling a cartload of brick. He lay moribund, bleeding profusely from a deep fracture on the right side of his skull. Guignard and Marcel knelt to examine him.

Guignard's evaluation took but a second. "He is a dead man," he said, rising to his feet. "The wound is mortal. There is nothing to be done."

Marcel stanched the bleeding with the corner of his apron. "It is probably so, Magnificus," he agreed, "but if you have no objection, I shall do what I can."

"*D'accord*," Guignard said with a shrug. "I have a lecture to prepare." Brushing the filth of the street from his robe, he strode off.

Christien helped Marcel carry the injured man inside the house being repaired. They laid him out on a table. Marcel's hands were still bloody from the previous patient and he wiped them absently on his apron as he bent over his patient. Christien opened the lid of Marcel's instrument box to expose a jumble of stained and rusting knives, pincers, tongs, saws and scissors, a small brazier, and fourteen different cautery irons. There were tangled sutures, and needles of every description: curved, straight, and barbed. Marcel also kept his fishhooks in the box, which in his spare time he loved to bait and toss in the Seine.

Marcel neatly snipped away the mason's hair, his skill as a barber evident. Then, with a razor, he deftly laid back a flap of skin on either side of the injury. He mumbled and fretted as he worked. "*C'n'est pas bon*," he said. "The cover of the brain is broken. Perhaps Monsieur Guignard was right. Perhaps I should have left him in God's hands." Still, he did not give up.

Despite an initial bout of queasiness, Christien watched intently, surprised to see the patient's left arm jerking and twitching as Marcel carefully probed the wound. "You have done this before?" he asked. "I have not read of it."

Marcel snorted, intent on his work. "Never even in my dreams."

"Then how do you know what to do?"

"Sometimes I pray God to guide my hand." Marcel smiled. "Sometimes it is the wine I consumed the night before. Sometimes I do nothing. Sometimes, as now, I simply do what seems necessary." He extracted a clump of hair, fragments of bone, and sharp bits of tile, tossing everything onto the floor. When he could find nothing more, he used snips to smooth the edges of the broken skull, and pincers to lift its depressed edges away from the brain. He washed the wound with wine, to flush out any pieces of debris he'd missed, then sewed the dura together and sutured the scalp. He rinsed the area once more, and then with Christien's help fashioned a protective cover out of a stiff length of cowhide. They bound it over the man's skull, using cloth strips to hold it in place.

Marcel wiped his hands as Christien cleaned and packed up his instruments. The mason's wife and brothers, who had been summoned and were waiting outside, came in to take him home. "If he lives, which I doubt," Marcel said to Christien in a low voice as they carried him away, "his mind might never again rise to the level of that of a chicken. I fear he will never walk or talk again."

The mason regained consciousness the next day, complaining

only of a mild headache. His left hand displayed a tremor that had not been there before. But tremor and all, he was back on his scaffold a week after the accident. Marcel and Christien visited him every day, monitoring his astonishing recovery. "That was God's work, not mine," Marcel said.

The experience was an epiphany for Christien. Philippe Guignard represented authority and learning and the greatest traditions of his profession. Classically educated, he knew entire texts by heart. He wore the long robe of his calling with great dignity, and his hands, even when they were not sheathed in velvet gloves, were clean. Marcel Foucault was rough and crude and quite illiterate. All that he knew came from direct experience. He wore the short robe of his calling with great humility, and his hands were dirty. The contrast between the two men could not have been greater, and seeing it removed all doubt from Christien's mind. He no longer wanted to be a physician. He wanted to be a surgeon.

Guignard took the shocking news as a personal affront. He seethed at the thought Christien would ever consider surgery over medicine. The very idea turned all the standards on end; it was against the proper order of things. Because the Count de Vries had been away when Guignard met Christien, the doctor had never spoken to him about his son's ambitions, and he was therefore unaware of the count's implacable opposition. Guignard had been considering offering to sponsor the lad, who was gifted and bright and would be a credit to the profession.

Instead Guignard now mocked him for his ambition. "You would learn to cut hair then?" he asked scornfully. "Your father will be very proud."

Christien, now certain of his course, smiled at the question. His father had already pointed out that the post of physician was beneath Christien's station in life, beneath contempt itself. Now a physician had told him that the post of surgeon was even lower. "It seems, sir," he said, "that I must forever strive for that which is beneath me. I thank you for your help and your instruction. When I have learned—properly, of course—I will be honored to cut your hair."

Christien had always been careful to keep up the daily duties laid out for him by his father, who despite his long absences received regular reports by mail from the tutors. Christien knew if he was caught his dreams would be dashed forever, but so long as he kept up the side of his life ordained by the count, at least he had a chance to pursue his other goal. He could only hope he could achieve it before the day came when his father would expect him to report to the Grand Master in Malta. The best and quickest education for a surgeon was to attend the College of Surgery at St. Côme, but without the count's blessing that would be impossible. That left only apprenticeship under a barber-surgeon, after which he might sit for examinations. It was, by far, the longest road to the lowest level of the medical profession.

Bertrand still thought he was daft for his dream, and tended to echo the count. "If you want to cut things," he said, "you'll do better with the sword of St. John than the knife of Marcel Foucault." But Christien was determined to press on. He went to work for Marcel.

Like Guignard before him, Marcel was initially skeptical of Christien, suspecting trickery or some hidden motive. The children of nobility did not dirty their hands on the guts of the rabble. But Christien was as eager an apprentice as any Marcel had ever trained, and would do anything asked of him. Furthermore, he had medical books that were of interest to Marcel, although the older man could neither afford nor read them. Such texts were always written in Greek or Latin, never in the vernacular, as the Faculté disapproved of spreading such information to uneducated eyes. Christien had a copy of the *Chirurgia Magna*, by the eminent fourteenth-century surgeon Guy de Chauliac, and even a copy of Galen's *Surgery,* written by the second-century Greek whose works on anatomy were still widely used, though they were based primarily upon observations of pigs and apes. To most physicians and surgeons of the modern world, Galen was still God; to Marcel, who knew no better, his drawings did not much resemble the insides of any men *he'd* cut open. Still, he sat raptly with Christien as they examined the pictures together and Christien translated the Greek.

Marcel, for his part, was a good and patient teacher. His instruction was immediate and practical. On his very first day at Marcel's side, Christien sewed up a gaping hand wound, where a butcher's cleaver had missed the mark. He set a fracture, removed a spike from a carpenter's foot, and trimmed a client's beard. "You have a talent for cutting, sire," Marcel said, directing his pupil's hand. "But pay as close attention to the barbering as you do to the surgery," he was to repeat often. "It's where the money is."

Christien accompanied Marcel on his rounds, following him from the slums to the homes of the wealthy to the Hôtel-Dieu, the only public hospital in Paris. In every respect Marcel's practice was vastly different from Guignard's. It was gritty and bloody work, noisy and chaotic. For Christien it was also exhilarating and important. Little could be done by physicians for the great killers, fevers and plague. But much could be done by surgeons for a host of maladies. The work was urgent and often dramatic: he watched Marcel cut a live baby out of a dead mother, repair a leg broken in seven places, and put a dangling eyeball back into its socket, after which the patient swore he saw better than before.

Events did not always go so well, of course. They treated an ulcerated arm, untended for too long by a patient who did not relish a visit to the surgeon. They drained the pus and cleaned out the maggots, irrigated the wound with vinegar, and dressed it with hemp soaked in turpentine. For a few days, the treatment seemed to be working. But then the maggots returned, and the patient developed red streaks all the way up his arm. Two days later, he was dead of the gangrene.

Amputations were the most trying. Christien almost didn't make it through the first one because he had to hold down the patient, who was wide awake. It was not the blood and sinew, but the shrieking and crying that made it near unbearable. The patient chewed clean through the bit of wood Marcel had jammed between his teeth, and then took off a chunk of his own tongue. He broke an arm restraint and hit Marcel in the face, knocking him down. Christien got the strap reattached while Marcel fitted a helmet-like device around the furiously struggling patient's head. Marcel picked up a wooden mallet and delivered a solid blow, the force of which was directed to the proper spot by the helmet. The patient fell still at last. "I don't use it often," Marcel said in answer to Christien's look. "Sometimes they don't wake up again, and sometimes when they do, they aren't right in the head anymore."

Marcel constantly emphasized the need for haste in surgery, and in this case the brief delay proved fatal. By the time he finished with the cautery iron, the patient was in shock. By the time Christien got the helmet off, he was dead. Marcel angrily slammed the mallet into the wall. "It was just a damned *leg*," he said. "He killed himself with his carrying on."

Though Christien was both shaken and discouraged, the next few procedures went perfectly. The recovery of those patients made the failures sting a little less, and when they actually paid for Marcel's services, with a chicken or a sack of grain or even a coin or two, Marcel positively beamed with success.

Under Marcel's guidance Christien practiced the art of phlebotomy, using a lancet to purge blood from the veins. It was done only when a physician was present to direct the work. Except in an emergency, Marcel would never bleed a patient without the advice of a physician. Christien, having worked with Guignard, found this reluctance hard to accept. "A doctor doesn't know nearly as much as you about a body," he said. "He never even touches one. I would rather have you work on me anytime."

Marcel smiled. "He knows about it from reading," he said, and it was in this manner that the medical establishment practiced: the men who read the books rarely touched the patients, while the men who touched the patients rarely read the books. Christien was one of the few who did both. Even with the best of both worlds, he was left with endless unanswered questions. There often seemed little relation between treatment and outcome. Some patients died from apparently trivial wounds, while others recovered from assuredly fatal ones, and he rarely felt that he knew why.

He pressed Marcel for a cadaver to dissect, so that he might compare it to the drawings and descriptions in the anatomies, but Marcel could do nothing. Dissection was quite rare and under the rigid control of physicians at the Faculté. Many opposed it on religious grounds, or because they believed nothing worthwhile could come out of anything but books, or because they wanted to jealously guard their prerogatives, fearing the influence of the surgeons. "If I should drop dead one of these days," Marcel told him, "you may open me up and have a look around. Otherwise, I fear you'll be waiting a long while."

Christien worked like a dervish to keep up his double life. He awakened before dawn and never retired before midnight. In the mornings, for his father's tutors, he endured lectures about artillery, or the science of fortifications, or the intricacies of fire hoops and the latest flamethrowers, called trumps. In the afternoons he practiced swordsmanship, marksmanship, and close combat with a knife. He studied the tactics of sea warfare, and memorized the stores list for a war galley. He knew the key events in the tenure of every Grand Master since the founding of the Order in Jerusalem.

In the evenings he worked at Marcel's shop, barbering lice-infested heads, pulling abscessed teeth, or cleaning tools and sharpening blades. After that he trailed Marcel through the slums, where his practice seemed to run twenty-four hours a day. Late at night he read or preserved specimens, until exhaustion overtook him and he slumped over his work. He loved the grueling schedule and tried not to think about the day of reckoning he knew must surely come.

It was nearly two years later that Bertrand inadvertently delivered the means to that reckoning, in the form of Christien's long-coveted cadaver.

Chapter 14

It was growing dark as the horse-drawn cart emerged from the forest, parting the mists that rose from the Seine. Bertrand whistled gaily as he drove. He stopped next to the house, hopped from the seat, and began banging on the door as if the house were on fire. "De Vries, you surgeon's apprentice whore! Come out!"

Christien leaned out an upper window and grinned at the sight of his friend. "What is it? I'm studying!"

"Of course you are! Precisely! But enough of toad parts and lizard tongues! I brought something truly worthy of your efforts!"

"What is it?"

"A Huguenot! Now quit your chatter and come open the door. I need your help to get him inside. He's getting stiff."

"A Huguenot? What do you mean?"

"What do you think I mean? And after all that money your father has wasted on tutors! A *Protestant* is what I mean, diverted in his journey to hell for a brief sojourn at the Château de Vries!"

Christien flew down the stairs, out the door, and into the drive. There was a tight white cocoon of cotton in the back of the cart, a shroud of the sort used for pauper burials. Christien saw the swell of a belly, the broad curve of big shoulders, and the unmistakable outline of a head. A bare foot extended out the end, its toes hairy on top.

He gave Bertrand a wary look. Bertrand smiled brightly, his teeth flashing in the dusk. He had filled out in manhood. He was tough and clever and hard-drinking and still thoughtful. "Consider it a token of my regard for your mad pursuits," he said modestly, bowing lightly. "I nipped him from the undertaker. Actually, I nipped the undertaker's horse, too, and his cart. I saw him by chance as I was passing the Boar's Head tavern. He stopped there just after he took this one down from the gibbet. He was on his way to the cemetery. I've listened to you complaining about the lack of such . . . er . . . meat for your table and was only too happy to seize the moment."

"You stole the cart?"

"I could hardly steal the body without stealing the cart, could I? Never mind, the undertaker is still in the tavern, probably face down by now and nearly as stiff as his charge here. I'll wager he isn't even aware anything is missing. By the way, his name is Beaufort."

"The undertaker?"

"No, the corpse. Now let's get him inside before he catches cold." They pulled on the dead man's ankles, sliding him to the edge of the cart. Beaufort's waist folded and he slipped to the ground with a thud. "He must weigh twenty stone!" Christien said, gasping.

"*Oui*, though I suppose he'll weigh less when you're finished with him," Bertrand said. "Then we can carry him out in pieces." They heaved again and got him up, his body stiffened from rigor mortis. Holding him under the arms, they dragged him on his heels to the château. They struggled up two steps, through the door, and down a corridor toward the kitchen. Christien pushed open the door to the pantry.

"In here?" Bertrand said, with a hint of distaste. "Do you intend to season him with saffron? Protestants are better served with bile."

"There isn't a table in the cellar," Christien replied, huffing with effort. He swept aside bottles on the table where the cook prepared preserves. "Let's get him up on this." With a final heave they got the corpse onto the table.

Bertrand wiped his hands on his pants. "When will your father be home?"

"In the morning, if he comes at all," Christien said. "He and Mother are at the city house. He may not arrive for another day."

"*Bon*. I suppose he might object, even if this is a Protestant."

"Object? My father would do to me what I'm about to do to this body."

"Well, then, you must work quickly, and tonight we'll dump him in the river." The Seine, which made a gentle loop around the edge of the estate, carried away the flotsam of Paris, among which could often be seen rotting corpses.

"Do me another service," Christien said. "Go fetch Marcel. He'll want to see this. He may bring a few students. You'd better hurry. I haven't much time."

Christien gathered lamps and candles from around the house. He set them on the pantry shelves, bathing the room in flickering light. From the attic he retrieved his sketchbooks, his scales, and the box that held his surgeon's tools. He laid back the shroud and gazed upon the occupant, his excitement growing. He walked around the body. The man was naked, his clothes forfeited with his life. He stared up at the ceiling through lifeless eyes. He was a perfect specimen except for his broken neck, snapped by the noose. That in itself, thought Christien, would make for an interesting examination.

Picking up a lancet, he began quite gently, almost as if his patient were alive. He'd never opened a chest before and found the first cut difficult, both from his own hesitation and because the skin was tougher than he thought. Quickly abandoning delicacy, he was soon hacking and cutting more like a butcher. He cracked back the chest and laid open the abdomen to the pubic bone, staring in awe at what he'd exposed.

Perching on a stool, he munched on a peach and considered where to begin. He located Galen's humors: yellow and black bile, blood, and phlegm. He laid back nerves, exposed muscles, and dissected arteries and veins. He prodded eyeballs and probed ears. He made careful measurements and recorded the weights of organs. He gauged and groped, pondered and poked. He took copious notes, comparing what he observed to what was in the books that were propped open on the table, and sketched every specimen with a practiced hand. He found something that puzzled him: the right kidney was no higher than the left. Vesalius and Galen were both quite specific on that point. Certainly Christien was not prepared to dispute their word. He considered the possibility that Beaufort, being a Huguenot, was somehow malformed. He made a note of the discrepancy and moved on.

Nearly three hours had passed when Bertrand reappeared with two nervously giggling prostitutes, a flagon of wine, and no Marcel.

"Where is he?"

"Out barbering, I suppose," Bertrand said, shrugging. "His wife didn't know. I found these two instead. They aren't students, but they're willing to learn." The girls strained to look into the pantry to see what Christien was doing, but he blocked the way. One of them kissed him boldly instead and offered him a drink. Christien grinned but drew back. "Entertain our guests," he said to Bertrand. "I must work."

"It shall be my great pleasure," Bertrand said, bowing deeply. He took one woman on each elbow. "Ladies, at the order of the Lord Surgeon de Vries, we shall commence our own anatomy lessons, in the library." He led them away in a rustle of petticoats and laughter.

Christien lost himself once more in his work, trying to match his reading with his observations, and his observations with his questions. Where in all this flesh was the soul? Did the heart and lungs dissipate the humors? How did the liver form blood, or the brain form thought, or the eye form sight? He worked until his eyes glazed and he had trouble focusing. Twice Bertrand came for him, and twice Christien sent him away.

It was nearly four when Bertrand appeared again, now more

insistent. "Frankly, *mon ami,* I am beginning to worry about you," he said.

"I'm fine," said Christien, not looking up.

"Perhaps so, but I am apprehensive about any Parisian who prefers the body of a dead man to that of a live woman. Here, have a bit of this. It will bring you to your senses." He held out a glass.

Christien's muscles were aching with fatigue. He set down his lancet and took the drink. He returned Bertrand's toast and swallowed gratefully, feeling the sweet burn of brandy.

Bertrand regarded the array of books, paper, tissue, and organs piled around Beaufort, whose arms and legs were spread wide. The top of his skull and his brain were missing. Various organs were stored in jars: a liver floated in honey, a heart in vinegar, three fingers in wine. Bertrand wrinkled his nose at the unpleasant odor. "I think your friend is beginning to ripen," he said.

"I suppose you're right. I've done what I can for one night. We'd better dispose of him."

"In a little while," Bertrand said. "First it is time you refreshed your memory about the insides of a *woman.*"

Two hours later, as the sun was rising, the four of them were still in the library, half drunk and all undressed. Christien heard a frightful sound and sat bolt upright. "Horses! *Merde!* What is he doing home so early?"

In a frenzy of panicked whispers they struggled into their clothes. Christien hurried the women to the garden door, and then he and Bertrand raced to collect Beaufort. There was no time to hide the jars, so Christien pushed them back among the preserves while Bertrand threw the shroud over the corpse. They lifted Beaufort from the table and made for the door. Beaufort's legs were askew, his arms dangling from the shroud. Something dropped to the floor, something viscous and glistening and dark.

"What is *that?*" Bertrand hissed, trying not to step on it.

"It's a—" Christien didn't finish. The front door opened and they heard voices.

"We're too late," Christien whispered. "We'll never get him to the river. We'll have to hide him in here until tonight." They set Beaufort on the floor behind the shelves, and Christien started to clean up the table. As Bertrand moved to help him, his elbow struck a jar from the shelf. It crashed to table and then to the floor, spattering grape jelly everywhere.

A moment later, eyes smoldering, the Count de Vries stood in the doorway of the pantry, sword in hand as he readied to confront the blackguards he'd heard pillaging his house.

✤

What had seemed to the count to be Christien's fanciful remarks about medicine had suddenly become real. In a cold fury he sent Bertrand to the city with the women, and disposed of Beaufort in the Seine. He paced and fumed and pounded his fists as he drew out Christien's story. He crawled into the attic and emerged with an armful of specimen jars that followed Beaufort into the river. He went to the barn and, one by one, smashed the surgeon's tools between hammer and anvil, rendering them into useless shards of scrap. He crushed the scales with a stone. He ripped the pages from the medical books, tossing them one handful at a time into the raging fire.

Simone tried to calm him, but even she could not temper his rage. It was late afternoon before he could manage to speak in a level tone. "You are a humiliation to me," he said to Christien. "I have no idea how such poison has seeped into your blood. You will cease this nonsense immediately. I shall write the Grand Master and request that he admit you to the Order without delay."

"I will not take the vows of the Order, Father. I will not go to Malta."

"We shall see about that," the count replied icily.

✤

A few days later Christien went to Marcel's shop, determined to do his stint at barbering despite his father's prohibition. He found the door barred from the outside. Even when Marcel was away, his shop was never closed. There was always an apprentice or helper around. Puzzled, Christien went around the back. He found Marcel sitting on the stairs that led up to his room, above the shop. His eyes were red, a half-drunk bottle of cheap Bordeaux at his side. He raised the bottle to Christien. "You've come to the wrong place, sir, if you seek to have your beard trimmed or your leg shortened," he said. "The guild has taken my license. I am neither barber nor surgeon. Should you need a cook's helper, however, I am handy with a knife."

"On what grounds can they do such a thing?" Christien asked, outraged.

"A matter of the annual fees. They say I failed to pay them."

"Did you fail?"

"Of course not. I have the cachet to prove it. They said it didn't matter: their records show nothing of the sort."

"Piss on their fees! We shall pay them again!"

Marcel took a long drink from the bottle. "I may be nothing more than a surgeon, Christien, but I am not dim-witted. I have already tried to do just that. It is not so simple. Their rules are clear. I am not eligible until next spring."

Christien snorted. Rules were made for commoners, not the nobility. The bureaucrats could not possibly reject Marcel with Christien at his side. "Come," he said impatiently. "We shall fix this together. They will not dare refuse a de Vries."

"That is just the problem, my young friend. They *have* not dared refuse a de Vries. I have friends in the guild. This has nothing to do with rules or money. It has only to do with your father, who seems to wish me ill."

A short while later Christien stormed up the drive to the château. A group of soldiers and horses congregated near the entry, signaling the presence of a visitor. It was not an unusual sight. The count always had one guest or another, on military business. Christien paid them no heed as he dismounted and raced inside.

He burst into the library. His father sat in a great leather chair talking to his guest, whose face Christien couldn't see. The count glowered at the intrusion and waved his son away. Christien ignored him and strode forward.

"You have always taught me to face an adversary directly, Father, to look a man in the eye before you strike. If you wish to sabotage my desire to be a surgeon, it is one thing. But it is cowardly to injure those who would help me. Look *me* in the eye, Father, and tell me how you dare."

"By God, you tread on dangerous ground," said Arnaud, his eyes narrowing. "I will discuss this with you later."

"We will discuss it now! I will not be silent! I will have my—" At that moment the man in the chair turned around. Christien stiffened and his words died in his throat. He immediately recognized the long scar that distinguished the face of Le Balafré: it was François de Lorraine, Prince of Joinville, the Duke of Guise. In all the realm there was no more powerful man save the king himself.

"I have not seen you in some years, Christien," Guise said amiably. "I see both you and your anger have grown well."

"Forgive me, sire," Christien said, flushing. "I did not know—"

"No matter." Guise waved him silent. "Your father and I were discussing Metz."

The talk of war was everywhere in Paris. The Holy Roman Emperor, Charles V of Spain, forever at odds with France, was again mustering his armies, this time for a march on the city of Metz, the defense of which Guise had been named to lead.

"The king has graciously made me his lieutenant," Guise said, "as I am busily making your father my own, so that we may answer the Emperor's impudence with a worthy response. But now, what is this of surgery? I had long thought the Order of St. John was to receive the honor of another de Vries."

Recovering from his surprise, Christien realized it was to his advantage to have Guise in the room. It was a gross breach of etiquette to raise such a dispute in front of the duke, but Christien didn't care. He knew his father would not be able to walk out or resort to physical means of persuasion. So he plunged forward. As he unburdened himself Guise rubbed his scar and listened, a faint glimmer of amusement in his eyes.

The count sat quietly at first, seething under Christien's onslaught, but then, duke or no duke, he could contain himself no more. In a fury he jumped up, his hand on his sword. "Enough!" he thundered. "You will hold your tongue or I will cut it from your head!"

The duke raised a calming hand. "By your leave, Arnaud, perhaps I may suggest a solution. A temporary arrangement, if you will. A truce."

Arnaud could barely conceal his disapproval of the duke's

intrusion into a matter that by rights was his alone. "Of course, my lord," he said without enthusiasm. "I would be honored for your thoughts."

"Let the boy come to Metz in my service," Guise suggested. "He wishes to be a surgeon? I will introduce him to the subject as he has not imagined it before. Perhaps it will cool his ardor for the trade. In the meanwhile, he will have provided a valuable service to His Majesty, who is always short of surgeons in a fight. Afterward I shall speak with the Grand Master, with whom I am not without influence. The knights are an order of hospitallers, are they not, Christien? Why, the Grand Hospitaller himself—the officer who tends to their medical facilities—is traditionally of the French *langue,* if I am not mistaken. Perhaps, Arnaud, it is your son's destiny to be Hospitaller, and you are quarreling with him over nothing. I will do what I can to pave his way, and to convince him of the wisdom of that choice."

"If the Grand Hospitaller had any medical training at all, it would be as a physician, sire," Christien said hotly. "There are no surgeons in the Order. They are beneath the contempt of all save those who need them. I have no wish to be a physician, or a knight for that matter."

The duke's face went red while his scar went white. "Your *wishes,* Monsieur de Vries, are of no concern to the king." His rebuke was cold.

Father and son stared at each other, at an impasse. Neither of them liked the idea. Christien regretted his impulsiveness, knowing he had trapped himself. Now he had no choice: a suggestion from the king's lieutenant in the matter of Metz was the same as a suggestion from the king himself.

Three weeks later, riding with a massive train of soldiers and mules and wagons, Christien de Vries set off for war.

Chapter 15

from The Histories of the Middle Sea

by Darius, called the Preserver
Court Historian to the Lord of the Two Horizons, the Sultan Achmet

No rivalries on earth were more bitter than those that raged in 1552 between the Christian kings of Europe. The French monarch, Henry II, had no passion greater than the persecution of Protestants. Charles V, the king of Spain, was a Hapsburg, one of the royal family that comprised the principal dynasty of European nations. He was also Holy Roman Emperor, the successor to Charlemagne, king of the Franks, who some centuries earlier had established the empire as heir to Rome. At varying times the empire spanned much of Germany, Austria, the Netherlands, Switzerland, Bohemia, northern Italy, Spain, Sicily, and Malta. Elected from within the House of the Hapsburgs, the Emperor modestly considered himself God's secular deputy on earth, just as the Pope was His spiritual vicar. While it was the Pope who crowned the Emperor, the conflicts between the two were both endless and predictable. The hope of empire was to create a realm much like that enjoyed by the Ottomans, in which disparate temporal states would ally themselves into a cohesive spiritual whole. As was the case between the Sunnis and Shi'ites, however, God's various earthly deputies and vicars enjoyed little in common but hatred for one another. Only in the relentless assault of the Protestants did Pope and Emperor suffer alike. Ten years before the great events of Malta, a peace agreement reached in Augsburg allowed the Germanic states to choose between Catholicism and Protestantism. Most of the German princes chose the latter.

A harsh winter seized the continent, a fact that did not deter Charles from his desire to increase his domains. Already master of central Europe, he wished to add the cities of Metz, Strasbourg, and Verdun to his stable, cities infected by the Protestant plague. He led a massive army in a siege of Metz, where six thousand of the French king's faithful, under the command of the Duke of Guise, huddled against cold and cannon. It was a remarkable moment: an anti-Protestant Catholic king defending a Protestant city against the persecution of a Catholic emperor. Did ever Suleiman fight so hard against his Islamic rivals, the heretic Shi'ites of Persia?

—From Volume VI
The European Powers

Christien saw his father only once at Metz.

It was a raw November morning. A light snow was falling. The stone walls reverberated under the unceasing thunder of the emperor's guns. The throaty roar of the city's defenders had fallen silent after a lightning dawn sortie. The wounded were dragged back inside the city walls, heaped in carts or piled on litters, and brought to one of the operating theaters.

Christien was awash in a steaming sea of blood and bones. The air in the great stone chamber where he worked as apprentice was heavy with smoke and chaos. The surgeons at that station were Celts, battle-tested veterans who made even Marcel seem slow. They spoke Walloon, a dialect he had trouble understanding. When he didn't know what to do they showed him with sign language.

"*Vite! Vite!*" one snapped, words he understood perfectly.

Faster.

He worked without pause as the porters kept the relentless assembly line moving. The instant he finished one casualty, another appeared before him. He set a fractured femur, sutured a ripped belly, dressed the shredded and charred face of an artilleryman caught in the flash of his own powder. He sewed up what was left of a hand after a battle axe had done its gruesome work. There was no anesthesia of any sort, save unconsciousness. Speed was the only ally in the race against shock.

Christien hadn't been warm in a month: not while he worked, not while he slept. He warmed his hands over the coals of the braziers that heated the cautery irons, or in the steam that rose from the viscera of his patients. Sometimes he could hardly see what he was doing through the vapor clouds of his own breath. That morning his toes were numb and his teeth chattered. Worst of all for his work, his fingers were stiff. The blood had frozen on them again and made them slippery, so he couldn't hold his instruments properly. He fumbled, trying to tie off a vessel, his own shivering aggravated by the vibrations from the rumbling artillery. As he sutured a flap of skin over a bony stump the muscles in his hand cramped, followed by a painful spasm in his back. He straightened up to stretch. He wiped his brow with his bloody sleeve and looked across the room.

Arnaud de Vries sat at one of the surgical stations, the flesh of his left arm shredded by grapeshot. Christien realized the count had been watching him work, and couldn't tell whether his expression came from having his own ragged skin and muscle cut away, or from his opinion of what he was watching his son do. Arnaud never flinched as his surgeon worked; his eyes remained locked on his son. The only sign that he felt anything at all was when his jaw muscles tightened. When the surgeon finished, Arnaud stood, stiffly donned his breastplate, took up his sword, and strode out without a word.

Christien watched until he was gone, and bent once more to his work.

❖

There was nothing formal about his apprenticeship at Metz. Christien was given a table, instruments, and an endless supply of patients on which to learn his craft. He worked a lot on instinct. Mostly his instincts were sound. When they weren't, men died. There was little time for reflection about those who perished under his hand, or even because of it. He heard the men who moved quietly at night among the carts of wounded, using a knife or a hammer to mercifully dispatch those who had no hope. At least the ones who got to his table had a chance. Whenever he could he watched the others work, but there was rarely time for the luxury of study.

So many of the wounded died that it was believed there was something wrong with the medications being used by the surgeons. The duke sent an appeal to the king for medical supplies. Some weeks later, in the middle of the night, the king's envoy managed to smuggle fresh stores into the city.

Christien was working on a soldier whose shoulder had been hit with a shot from an arquebus. The lead ball had flattened on impact and left a gaping wound, shattering both flesh and bone. Christien probed for the ball with his fingers. He couldn't feel it, though he thought that might be due to the cold. He enlarged the wound with a razor and was probing again when he saw a man approaching his station, lugging a wooden chest. Already the visitor had caused something of a stir among the other surgeons as he passed through the room, and Christien was his last stop.

"Good day, *monsieur*," the man said, setting the box down. "I have brought you aloe and scammony, earth of Limnos and zinc oxide, and a host of other medicines. I trust you can make use of them."

Christien nodded at him. "So you are the one? I have heard talk of it—the man who sneaked *into* this city, when others of sanity would seek a way out?"

The visitor smiled. "I confess—I am the foolish one."

"I am Christien de Vries, sir. Merely an apprentice, but you have my thanks."

"I am called Paré. I, too, am but an apprentice, as I have been all my life."

Christien glanced up. "You are Monsieur Ambroise Paré? The surgeon?"

"Some use that epithet. Others are not so kind." Paré was intent upon Christien's procedure. "You had better pick up the pace, sir, if you don't mind my saying. That wound will not await your leisure."

Christien returned to his work, his fingers trembling. Paré! Surgeon to the king! He had written works on surgery and anatomy, works reviled by the medical establishment because they were written in French instead of Latin or Greek, but treasured by the students who used them. "I have some of your books," he said.

"In such a place as this I can only hope you have not used the pages to make dressings or kindling."

Christien grinned and shook his head. He extracted the flattened lead ball and tossed it on the floor. He took the forceps from the table, picked up a strip of cloth, and dipped it in boiling oil of sambac that bubbled in a cauldron on the brazier. He would plunge the scalding strip deep into the wound before it cooled.

"Why are you doing that?" Of course Paré already knew the answer and was merely testing the depth of Christien's knowledge.

"Because gunpowder is poisonous," Christien answered. "The oil will kill the poison before it can kill the patient. Everyone uses it."

"Since you have been here, how many such wounds have you treated this way?"

"Just over a hundred and twenty, sir. My notes are not complete. Sometimes there is not time to finish them. More, perhaps."

"And how many have died?"

"More from infection than from the gunshots themselves, I fear. I don't always know, because they're taken away before their prospects are clear to me."

"I think our treatments are sometimes worse than the wounds we seek to heal. I, for one, am not so certain that gunpowder itself is poisonous."

"Then what causes the suppuration?"

Paré shrugged. "Something else. The air itself, perhaps. When there are flies about, I've suspected them of conveying pus. But of course there are no flies in winter at Metz. It is a question that occupies me greatly. Yet whatever the cause, I have found a remedy that works better than boiling oil. It is a cool mixture—egg yolks, oil of roses, and turpentine. I discovered it quite by accident, when I ran out of sambac. Though I thought surely it would kill the patient, I had nothing else to use. But my patient suffered less than those who received the oil, and he healed better as well. I've used it ever since, with promising results. Perhaps you would care to try it?"

Christien looked uncertainly at his unconscious patient. "It goes against all that has been written on the subject."

"So it does. But if the ancients write that the sun passes overhead from west to east, and your eyes observe otherwise, which will you believe? Will you trust my eyes, that have seen so much? And besides, what are your patient's chances now? That wound is particularly grievous. Questions of infection aside, you know your boiling oil will surely rouse him, and the shock will likely kill him."

"It is true," Christien said thoughtfully. "Very well, I'll try it."

Paré had a supply of the mixture in the chest and showed him how to apply it. He worked quickly, his touch gentle, his fingers nimble. He deftly stitched the wound, then washed it with an astringent of red wine and vinegar. He closed it with a gummed bandage. "In two days you must cut away the dead tissue and cleanse it again," Paré told him.

"But that would certainly kill him." Even Marcel was clear on that point. After initial treatment a wound was better left untouched until it resolved itself.

Paré smiled. "Of course—that, too, is much written of. But now that you've dared depart from ancient wisdom, perhaps you should try it and judge the results for yourself." Christien did just that, and the results were striking. Four days later his patient was sitting up and complaining about the cold and the food.

But it was the reaction of the other surgeons that surprised Christien the most. Paré was a tireless teacher. He had approached them as well and been rebuffed. Yet one by one they all wandered by Christien's station over the next few days to see for themselves what such radical methods accomplished. While the results were nothing short of miraculous, the Celts heaped abuse on Christien. Though their condemnation was delivered in Walloon, he needed no translation: he had abandoned tradition and ignored the truths of history. Though his hands were needed and welcome at Metz, surely he had no future as a surgeon.

Despite the evidence of their own eyes, the Celts' cauldrons kept bubbling.

Paré was unconcerned with their censure. "It has been thus since Roman times," he said. "They say my patients are cured by chance, by coincidence, or by God. What does it matter, so long as they are cured?"

Paré also departed radically from convention in performing amputations. The accepted practice was similar to the treatment for gunshot wounds. Spurting arteries were seared with a red-hot iron, or sometimes the entire stump was plunged into a boiling mix of treacle and oil. Paré favored the use of ligature, tying off vessels one by one before cutting the bone, and he avoided iron and oil altogether. This brought him more ridicule, although never by the patients he treated.

Christien realized that Paré was an extraordinary healer, whose advice—to question and test everything he'd been taught—resonated profoundly within him. He worked near Paré as often as he could, but their time together was short. Time, luck, and the winter had not been with the Emperor Charles. Guise had prepared Metz well, while the Emperor Charles was ill with gout, and his troops died of exposure, starvation, and wild epidemics of disease that raced through their encampments outside the city walls. The day after Christmas the siege was lifted, and the decimated Spaniards began their retreat. Christien remained in the city for several more months, caring for the wounded.

❖

Though he had lost the confidence of the Celtic surgeons, and thus their endorsements, Christien returned to Paris with glowing letters from the duke himself and from Paré, and with all the cocky self-assurance of a surgeon tested on the battlefield. With such testaments in his pocket, he knew two things for certain: he would find a way to take his examinations, and the Order of St. John would have to find itself another knight.

His father's stance, however, had not softened. "I forbid you to take the examinations. I have received the Grand Master's reply to my letter. You will report to Malta in the autumn."

Christien argued heatedly, but the count was unmoved. For two days the house crackled with hot tempers and fiery words.

Simone rarely interfered in such matters, but now she felt she must. She did not fully understand Christien's ambition, ill suited as it was to his station. War frightened her, but surgery did as well, perhaps even more so: if one was savagery, the other was sorcery. Part of her wished Christien would simply content himself with doing his duty and remove the anguish between himself and his father, yet she knew he would never be content with that. Besides, she allowed herself to want something more for him than to repeat the endless battles of his father. She suffered terribly each time Arnaud went away, wondering if this was the occasion when she would finally become a widow. She had no wish to suffer that way over her son.

She argued with Arnaud, who listened briefly and then cut her off, delivering a discourse about politics and war and duty.

"I detest it when you resort to political arguments, Arnaud," she said. "You do it only to aggrieve me, for you know I find them tiresome. Retreat from that world for a moment, into this one."

He was not to be put off, however. The Ottomans, he reminded her, were a growing threat. Killing Muslims was an honorable and sacred undertaking, and despite the alliance between France and the Ottomans against Charles, one day the whole of the civilized Christian world would have to band together to stop Suleiman and his heathen hordes. Until that day it would fall to the Knights of St. John to worry the Sultan and carry the banner of Christ. The opportunity for glory lay squarely in Christien's path.

"The 'whole of the Christian world,' as you put it, Arnaud, has not done anything in my memory but turn its weapons upon itself," she retorted. "Is there no other way to serve God and king than by killing? Why can you not allow Christien his own mind in this?"

"Because it is not his mind that matters! Every noble house wants a son in the Order. I shall not be denied."

"Ah, so it is merely your vanity you seek to serve, Arnaud, with the life of your son?"

Arnaud glowered at the remark. He rose from his chair and threw on his cloak. "I permit you great latitude, Simone," he said. "More than any man I know would permit his woman. But you are quite out of bounds with your tongue. This is not your place, and I shall not listen to more." He stormed from the house.

The count left Paris again only two days later, this time to join the king in Picardy, where the Emperor Charles, refusing to accept defeat, was carrying his war to the Flemish town of Hesdin. As Simone waved goodbye to Arnaud, she already knew her course. The count was being typically pigheaded. As she did whenever that was the case, she set about righting things in her own way.

She decided to visit the Faculté de Médicine and persuade them to allow Christien to take his examinations. With his certificate a fait accompli, his father would have to soften his stance. Even if he didn't, at least Christien would have won his license before joining the Order, giving both of them a measure of what they wanted.

When the count discovered her interference he would be furious, but his fury would pass, as it always did.

She sent a note to the school of medicine near the Place Maubert, requesting the honor of a meeting with Dr. Philippe Guignard and his peers on the Faculté. She had no illusion, of course, that they would respond as well to a mother's reason as they would to bribery, so she went to her meeting prepared with a heavy purse.

She was received cordially enough by Guignard and the others, dressed formally in their caps and long red velvet-trimmed robes. They gathered around a long table and invited the countess to sit at its head. They listened politely as she made her request. Their attention intensified as she sweetened it with her generous gift and a promise of much more to come.

Guignard cleared his throat uncomfortably. "As much as it would please us to grant your request, Countess," he said, "it is a question of order. Your son has not served the appropriate length of time under a licensed barber-surgeon."

"That is nonsense," Simone snapped. "He has been apprenticed to Marcel Foucault for nearly three years. He has served his king at Metz."

"Regrettably, Monsieur Foucault's license is not valid," Guignard said, shrugging. "The time your son spent with him will not count in his favor, and by itself his time at Metz is not sufficient. Perhaps he can find another sponsor. Perhaps in another year or two . . ." He raised his hands, a gesture of helplessness.

The problem, Simone knew, was that Arnaud had done his work first. She wondered what he'd given them. It didn't matter: her florins sat untouched. She emerged from the meeting deep in thought. Her maid, waiting in the courtyard, handed her the reins of her Arabian and helped her up, and then mounted her own horse. They rode because there was but one passenger carriage permitted in the narrow streets of the city, and it belonged to their majesties, King Henri and his queen, Catherine de Médicis. If the queen needed the carriage, even the king rode a horse.

They crossed the Petit Pont to the Île-de-la-Cité, where Simone stopped at Notre Dame to light a candle and say a prayer for Arnaud's safe return. Then she resumed her journey, crossing the wooden Grand Pont to the right bank, past the shops of the jewelers and the bookbinders where she and Christien had purchased so many of his books. She turned onto the quay toward the Louvre, intending to leave the city through the Porte Saint-Honoré. The river teemed with boats and barges, some bringing fresh fish from the sea, casks of wine from nearby vineyards, or stacks of wood from nearby forests. As usual, the quay was a tumult of commerce.

Simone threaded her way among carts and wagons, dodging stevedores and water carriers, longshoremen, and washerwomen lugging wicker baskets of laundry to be cleaned in the river. She fumed and plotted as she rode. There was still the Board of Barber-Surgeons, which actually gave the examination, but she knew they were somehow under control of the Faculté, and of course Arnaud would already have done his work there. She would have to think of something else. There were other schools, at Montpellier and in Geneva. Perhaps she could find a way to enlist her father's help.

A heavy cart stood outside the door of a warehouse on the rue Magdalen, being loaded with lime. A porter emerged from the doorway and heaved a heavy sack onto the cart. The load jarred the cart, and the wheel chock suddenly gave way. The cart moved slowly at first, its yoke dragging behind as the porter dashed to catch it. The cart bounced and bounded down the incline toward the river, gathering speed. The porter yelled a warning that no one heard. The cart shot out of the side street onto the quay, barely missed a mule, and collided broadside with Simone's mount.

Simone never saw it coming. Her horse was bowled over as if by a direct blast of cannon fire, and indeed there was a roar like cannon as the air was driven from its lungs.

The countess lay on the quay, unmoving. The horse lay next to her, breathing deeply, gutturally, the sound in its lungs like the roar of fire in a broken bellows, all of it mixing with the screams of Simone's maid and the shouts of men running to help. Flecks of red froth appeared at the Arabian's mouth. Wild-eyed, it struggled to its feet, staggered, and then fell again. Until it stopped, no one dared go near the countess, for fear of being crushed themselves.

Finally the horse lay still.

Two men got Simone into the cart and took her to her city house.

❖

His nerves nearly deserted him at the sight of her. After treating so many wounded, it was as if he didn't know what to do.

Not you! Mon Dieu, *not you!*

He shook it off and raced for his room, retrieving his bag from its hiding place. He nearly knocked Yves over in his rush as his brother hobbled down the hall on his cane.

Christien knelt by her bed. Her pulse was fast but strong, her breathing regular. He felt no fractures of her skull, and when he looked in her eyes he did not see the dilation that meant death was near. He began cutting off her clothing.

"*Attendez,*" said Yves from the doorway. He fidgeted. "I have sent for the doctors."

"I *am* a doctor," Christien said icily, not looking up.

"Not yet," said Yves, without malice, but firmly. "Wait until there is someone with more—" He fidgeted with the head of his cane, not knowing exactly how to say it. "Just wait, Christien," he said. "*Please.*"

Christien ignored him and carefully examined Simone. Her head was intact. He saw no sign of broken bones or crushing injuries in her chest, abdomen, or pelvis. Relieved, he finally got to her leg, which he already knew had been broken just above the knee. It was not a compound fracture, although there was a great deal of swelling and blackness where she had hemorrhaged beneath the skin. Beginning at midthigh, well above the injury, he probed gingerly with his fingers, trying to understand the extent of the break. Where he should have felt bone, he felt softness.

"*Ahhh!*" He blanched as his mother cried out. She did not awaken fully, but thrashed and then stiffened. He comforted her, then bit his lip. He was still well above where he thought the pain ought to be sharpest. The bone was not simply broken, he realized. It was crushed and could not be set.

Christien felt a pit in his stomach. He suddenly hoped the other doctors would arrive soon.

She stirred again, and then awakened. The countess was a stoic with pain, but now she cried out loud, cried though Christien stroked her forehead and whispered comfort to her. "You're going to be all right, Mother," he said. She seemed not to hear him.

He looked at Yves. "You'd better send a messenger for Father."

❖

Philippe Guignard arrived with three other physicians, the very same men with whom Simone had met just an hour earlier. Despite the fact that Guignard was cold to him, and despite the misgivings he'd had while working beside him, Christien was relieved she would be in his hands: he knew there were none better in Paris.

Christien tried to remain in the room while they examined Simone, but firmly they asked him to leave. It was not the time for argument. They closed the door behind him. He stood in the corridor with Yves, feeling sheepish. He lost himself in thought; the brothers said nothing to each other.

Twenty minutes later Guignard and two of his fellows emerged from the room, their faces grim. Guignard addressed Yves. "Your mother's situation is grave. The first four inches of her femur are crushed above the knee. Evidently the rail of the cart struck her there."

Whenever Yves was nervous, his left hand displayed a slight tremor. Now Christien saw the hand fluttering like a leaf, even as Yves sought to still it on his cane. "Will she walk again?" Yves asked.

"Walk!" exclaimed Guignard. "It is enough to ask if she will live. An injury like this can easily kill—even a woman as strong as the countess. She has already developed a slight chill, and it is the coming fever we must fight. You need have no fear, sire. I shall make the necessary arrangements. Everything that can be done shall be done."

"We must take her leg," said Christien abruptly.

Yves nearly jumped at the words. Guignard looked at him as if he were mad. "Take her leg below the knee and it will do no good. Take it above the knee and it will kill her," he said. "Even a *surgeon* would know as much."

Christien let the insult pass. "To leave the bone crushed inside her leg will kill her."

"On occasion, yes. Other times, not. Our treatment must be scrupulous. However, should I deign to discuss such a matter at all, sir, it shall not be with you."

"I have seen it done, at Metz. Paré did it."

"*Paré!*" Guignard passed the name like gas, to the vast amusement of his fellow doctors. Paré was notorious, the subject of some ridicule among the Faculté. "Indeed? The little cutter took a leg, did he, and above the knee?"

Christien shifted uncomfortably. "It was an arm, actually, but the injury was similar, caused by grapeshot. He took it between the elbow and shoulder."

"An arm and a leg, similar! I see you learned well in your month away at war. Or—*pardon*—was it *two* months?" Guignard's companions snickered as he fixed a disdainful gaze upon Christien. "The vessels that high in her leg would pump out her life's blood before the cautery iron could seal them. A team of surgeons with a dozen irons could not do it quickly enough."

"We would not use cautery. We would use ligature."

"Ligature, indeed." The radical practice was not well accepted in the Paris medical community, which stood resolutely behind the time-honored iron. "Frankly, sir, I will not dignify such an insult upon the sanctity and honor of medicine with a response." He turned to Yves. "The count is away?"

"He is with the king at Hesdin, Magnificus," said Yves. "I have already sent for him."

"Then until he arrives it is you, of course, with whom I must deal. By your leave, sire, I will prepare a list of necessities for your mother's care."

"You shall have everything you require."

"The first thing," said Guignard with a thin smile, "is that you kindly keep your well-intentioned but ill-informed brother out of my way."

❖

Acutely aware of the importance of his patient, Philippe Guignard left nothing to chance. Simone was given enemas and poultices, pills and potions. Hot stones were soaked in white wine, then wrapped in sheepskin and placed on either side of her leg. An earthenware jar was filled with decoctions of vinegar, wine, and nerval herbs, and placed at her foot.

Specialists were summoned—an occultist, a botanist, and an alchemist. Simone was probed, prodded, and massaged. She endured it all gracefully through a white haze of pain, for which she was given brandy.

Christien wanted desperately to help but was unwelcome in her room during the day. While Yves would never attempt to force exile upon him—he was not that strong—Christien remained away voluntarily during the day, for fear of upsetting his mother. His chance to see her, and care for her himself, came at night.

In the evening Guignard left an assistant with the countess, with orders that he be summoned immediately should her condition warrant. The assistant was a poor medical student whose silence Christien easily bought with a few coins.

Christien monitored his mother's progress and checked every order given by Guignard against his own texts. And he prayed.

❖

The fever came, as they knew it would. Guignard brought mumia.

"Is that truly mumia," Christien asked him, "or the vervain I saw you mix for the shopkeeper's daughter?" If there had been any civility left in their relations, that comment ended it.

The mumia had no effect. Christien used cool compresses on her overnight. The next morning, a furious Guignard ordered them removed. "Do you know nothing? The cold will congeal the humors and block the channels of her body. Her tissues will receive no nutrients."

"Her fever is better."

"Perhaps it seems so, to a *novice*. I will have her bled. Stay out of my way."

Christien tried to persuade Yves to order Guignard to change his treatment, which was too conservative. Such a severe injury required an aggressive response. "The wound will suppurate," he told Yves. "It will spread from her leg to the rest of her body. She will die if we don't take it."

Yves trembled at the thought. "But she isn't even *bleeding!* How can you suggest we take her leg?"

Christien patiently led his brother through his thinking. When he finished talking, Yves seemed persuaded, and promised to address the matter the next morning. But Yves was a man swayed by the last argument he heard. Guignard rebutted Christien's arguments, and Yves changed direction once again.

Yves was desperate for his father's return. He did not want the responsibility for his mother's life on his hands, but he was trapped. He could certainly not give control to Christien, and he could not entirely give it away to Guignard, either. *He* had to be in charge. As cowed as he was by Guignard, he was more afraid of his father, who would have him flayed if he thought any possibility had been overlooked during his absence.

"Can you summon another physician, perhaps?" Yves stammered and shook as he asked it. Guignard seethed but bowed lightly. "Of course, sire, if it is your wish."

Dr. Jean Fernel came to the house, accompanied by a bonesetter from the Faculté. Fernel's reputation was legendary, as even Christien had to admit. This was the king's own physician, and as if to press home the point, two of the king's Swiss guards accompanied him. Fernel examined the countess, reviewed the course of treatment prescribed by Guignard, and even listened to the doctor's discourse on Christien's opinions. Fernel found no fault with Guignard's treatments, although he did not share his regard for what he termed the "Arabic garbage" of Avicenna, the Persian whose methods had been widely accepted for four hundred years. Fernel preferred the wisdom of the ancients, Hippocrates and Galen. He traded a few good-natured and learned barbs with Guignard, even including Christien in the discussion to demonstrate his open mind. And then he delivered his opinion about amputation, a matter on which both he and the bonesetter agreed.

"As it is, we believe the countess may well not survive. However, any attempt to take her leg," Fernel said, "will remove any doubt whatever. It will surely kill her."

Christien was outnumbered by men who knew more than he. And his own opinions, he knew, were on the edge. The truth was that in Metz, even Paré never took a leg above the knee.

Amputations were done only on the distal extremities. But that meant nothing, Christien thought, if it was the only chance. "But sir—" Christien began to argue again.

"If it *is* your wish to kill her quickly," Fernel said, bristling at Christien's insolence, "a pistol would be more humane."

❖

The injury swelled and seemed to localize, stretching and tightening the skin until it burst. Guignard examined the discharge with satisfaction, taking pains to explain its significance to Yves. "You see it is thick and white," Guignard said. "It is known as laudable pus. If your brother were correct, it would be watery and fetid. Fortunately more seasoned minds have prevailed. We are still not out of danger, but this is a good sign indeed." Yves looked at his brother with growing scorn as the opinions mounted against him. Christien himself was racked with doubt: the very finest physicians of the day were tending his mother, and all he could do was argue.

The archbishop of Paris came, a train of attendants in tow. Guignard was deferential; the bishop was physician of the countess's soul, and his ministrations had precedence. The bishop heard her confession. "Trust in God," he told her. "Divine grace is your salvation. The power of God towers over that of man."

The abscess grew, revealing fragments of bone. Guignard brought in a surgeon. The wound was seeping at the edges and the surgeon recommended cautery. Guignard tried leeches first, for two days. They did not correct the problem. Reluctantly he approved cautery but did not give her a narcotic sponge or alcohol, for fear it would weaken her needlessly. "Better the quick pain," he said.

Christien helped hold his mother down. He knew what to expect, and tried to close his ears to the horror and his nose to the smell, but to no avail. Blessedly, she passed out quickly. Christien could only watch, his cheeks streaked with tears. He stroked his mother's hair. He thought this new insult to her flesh would only fester again. There was no end to that path, he argued with Guignard. The doctor disagreed.

Simone was clearly weakening. She tried to eat, but could not hold her hand still, and she had to be spoon-fed. She had always been slight; now she grew thinner. Guignard worried over her urine. Christien worried more over her eyes, which were dimming. He sat with her for hours, looking for ways to distract her. They talked of everything. She couldn't sleep, so he read to her from one of the comic novels of Rabelais, a writer and priest of Simone's acquaintance who had died that spring in Paris. She laughed weakly at the farces and wept copiously at the romances, but her tears were from pain. She bit her lip until it bled. She had trouble concentrating, and dropped thoughts midsentence.

Christien had sent for Paré immediately, but the surgeon, like the Count de Vries, was in Hesdin, under siege with the king's army. Now Christien visited Marcel, who had found work as a stevedore on the quay. He agreed to come that night, but only after Guignard was gone. Marcel examined the leg and shook his head. "I would not attempt it," he said. "It is beyond my skill. Guignard is right. You must let God's will work itself."

More doctors came. They congregated in the halls and on the stairway and talked in low voices. Whenever Christien approached they fell quiet, refusing to discuss the case with him. Guignard was increasingly exasperated by Christien's growing boldness in challenging his course of treatment. He could not throw Christien out of his own home, and yet Yves was unwilling to do it for him.

Simone was constantly thirsty, yet often could not keep even water down. She was swept by waves of nausea. Christien thought it was from the oxycrate, a mixture of vinegar and saffron that Guignard ordered for her. So he made her a broth, of chicken and pork. She could not keep that down, either. He changed it to veal and partridge, and she managed better.

He heard her crying at night, after he'd left her to sleep. It was not a sound he associated with his mother. Other women might cry, but never the countess.

Chapter 16

Simone heard them arguing. She ached for her son, who it seemed was losing all his battles of late. What made it more difficult was that in the matter of her own treatment, she herself did not agree with what Christien proposed. She had no desire to lose her leg, any more than she wanted to see Christien suffer over it. Convinced she would never have the opportunity to persuade the count to allow Christien the free rein of his dreams, she called her son to her side. "You know I have always admired your independence of mind," she said. "I must confess I have never understood your interest in the . . . the innards of others."

He smiled. "Nor have I, exactly."

"I think it is in many ways an admirable sentiment, a noble calling. But it was the sentiment of a commoner, the calling of another. You are a man now. There are realities to confront, Christien. I think it is time for you to follow the path your father has set. You bring him great distress with your stubbornness."

Her words stunned him. "But I have heard you argue with him on my behalf!"

"So I have tried, and so I have failed. There is a time to fight and a time to yield. In my own battle, I feel the time coming when I must yield. In yours, I have no wish to leave the two of you at odds. He is the count, and you are his son. He has chosen the best path for you. It is the way of things."

"Please don't say that, Mother. You are not leaving, and I want nothing to do with the Order of St. John."

"It is your duty. Above all things, a man must do his duty."

"My duty is to help you through this."

"You must trust Dr. Guignard as I do," she said. "And the archbishop. I am in their good hands. I want for nothing more now but peace and salvation."

Her words wounded him anew. He knew she hadn't meant to insult him, but she had clearly removed her own blessing of confidence from him. It was little surprise, he thought bitterly. He had done nothing to justify her faith in his ability as a surgeon, in a case where surgery, he still believed, was perhaps her only hope. But she was so weak now that he suspected he'd waited too long anyway. There seemed to be nothing to do but wait and pray.

❖

The slightest movement brought her agony, and her servants tried to avoid doing anything that upset her. Guignard ordered absolute quiet. Late one afternoon Christien went to find herbs for her broth. He returned to find her bedding wet with urine. "How could you let her lie in this?" he demanded of the assistant, by then alone.

"The doctor ordered it," the assistant replied nervously. "Moving her is too painful and will do her more harm than good. From now on she is only to be cleaned in the mornings."

"She will not lie in her own piss, by God," Christien said. He rigged a sling and bullied the assistant into helping him. Despite the tenderness with which they lifted her, the countess was in excruciating pain throughout, and she was clearly weaker afterward. Christien berated himself. Even in this little thing, perhaps Guignard was right. He held her hand until her tremors stopped.

"I am weary of the pain," she whispered. "I want to let go."

❖

Suddenly, remarkably, the countess rallied. She took nourishment and kept it down. She sat up; she smiled. The pain was not as great. Guignard was guardedly optimistic. Yves was ecstatic. The bishop called it a miracle.

Only Christien was left to brood: he thought this was surely the blossom before it withered. He had seen it in Metz, when a gravely ill patient briefly flourished only to sink again. It was only one case, of course. As in all things medical, his knowledge was incomplete, his wisdom only partly formed. But he looked at her leg, and it seemed no better. The pus was darkening. He was certain her death still lurked within that festering hell.

He felt the terrible pit in his stomach once again, for he knew one thing for certain. The moment of truth was at hand.

If he was to act, he had a day, two at most, in which to do so.

He read incessantly through the night, looking for anything he had missed, any evidence that would bring him peace or sway Guignard or Yves.

Trust your eyes, said Paré. How was this possible when his eyes had seen so little?

Trust the ancients, Hippocrates and Galen and Avicenna, said Guignard. How was this possible when the ancients penned eleven different treatments in six separate books?

Burn Avicenna, wrote Paracelsus.

Hang Paracelsus, thundered Fernel.

The fact was not lost on Christien that despite their differences of opinion, not one of them—*not one*—supported his point of view.

I am a fool, he thought. *If their great minds are at odds, who am I to dare something different?*

Trust God, said the bishop. *It was His will that summoned the cart. It is His will alone that will decide her fate.*

He agonized on the whipsaw of faith and knowledge. The learned world was telling him he was wrong. The spiritual world was telling him he was wrong. How dare he challenge their wisdom, the wisdom of the ages? How dare he put his mother at risk? She herself said to leave this in the hands of Guignard. The king's physician agreed. Even Marcel, to whom he would entrust his own life.

Quit pissing upwind, Bertrand said.

I trust no one. Least of all myself.

He cursed God, and fate, and medicine, and his own indecision.

He returned to her room. For the first time in ten days she was sleeping peacefully.

Leave her be! She is better.

He lit a candle. He laid back the bandages and looked at her thigh. There were faint streaks of red. Guignard and the others had seen them, too, and pronounced them irritation. He didn't care what they said. He knew what they meant.

He *knew*.

It would never become any clearer. He would never get more comfortable.

He could wait no longer.

He lightly kissed her forehead. "Forgive me, Mother," he whispered. "I must do this thing."

He couldn't do it without help. He went out to find Bertrand. It was nearly three in the morning, and he feared his friend would be off with a whore. But Bertrand was home, and came fully awake as Christien explained. He knew his friend's tone well enough not to argue, even with a course he thought foolish. "Of course I'll help," he said. "Your father can only kill me once."

Guignard's assistant slept on a floor mat, near the countess. Christien woke him with a whisper. "Go home," he said. The assistant saw Bertrand and knew something was amiss. Christien pressed a golden florin into his hand, expecting the money to have its usual magical effect. It didn't work.

"What are you doing, sire?" the assistant asked suspiciously. "I cannot leave now. The doctor would have me caned." A few moments later Bertrand had him sitting in a corner, next to a wardrobe. His arms and legs were tightly bound to a heavy chair, his mouth gagged, his face creased in terror.

Bertrand smiled wickedly at him and wiped off the scalpel he'd used to cut the strips of cloth to bind him. "If you make trouble," he whispered, holding the tip of the blade close to the assistant's bulging eyeball, "I'll use this to remove your liver."

Bertrand prowled the house quietly gathering up supplies, while Christien prepared his instruments. He sharpened them with a snakestone, then wiped them clean and rinsed them with turpentine. He prepared a narcotic sponge with a mix of mandrake, belladonna, opium, and brandy. He touched a bit to his tongue, which tingled at the pungent brew. He wasn't certain how to gauge the strength of it. Such drugs were rarely used. He could only hope it was strong enough to put her out without killing her. He didn't know if he could do this if she put up a struggle.

Christien sat gently on her bed and lifted her head off the pillow, holding the cup to her lips. Simone stirred and winced. "Here, Mother, you must drink this," he said. She nodded and swallowed, grimacing at the taste. He quickly tipped the cup, delicately trying to force another long drink before she could protest.

"I don't care for brandy," she said. "Why must I drink this?"

"Dr. Guignard ordered it."

"Where is his assistant?" The drapes of the bed canopy hid the bound man from her sight.

"He fell ill, Mother. He had to leave. He asked me to stay with you."

"Very well." She drank more. He felt low and miserable at her trust.

"What else is in this? It is vile beyond words."

"Medicine, Mother. Drink it all. As quickly as you can, and it will be over. You can sleep then." She finished the cup and lay back on her pillow. Ten minutes passed, then fifteen. She seemed to be asleep. He felt her breath on his cheek. It was regular, strong. Bertrand entered the room, carrying a pile of linen and a pail of water. He set it down and began lighting candles and lamps. Simone's eyes opened. She had a dreamy look on her face. She saw Bertrand and noticed the candles and lamps burning around the room. "What is it?" she asked. "What . . . my tongue . . . Christien. My head . . . put . . ." She closed her eyes again and sighed deeply. Ten minutes later he thought it was safe. They propped a chair against the door. Yves was still in the house, and it wouldn't do to have him barging in.

Christien tied her down with leather straps, knotting them carefully so they wouldn't cut into her skin. He wrapped a piece of wood in a cloth and put it in her mouth, making certain her tongue was clear. Then he bound it tightly so she couldn't spit it out. It was cool in the room, but Christien was sweating, his mind on the procedure. He had worked and reworked every step, every movement in his mind, so that he could do it swiftly. If he faltered, if he slowed, she would die. If he fumbled, if he doubted, she would die. He whispered instructions to Bertrand, who arranged everything neatly on a table, on one of the linens. There were the needles and the catgut, the scalpels and forceps and probes.

The teeth of the saw shimmered in the candlelight.

Christien took up a scalpel.

"Your hand is shaking," Bertrand said. His voice sounded loud in the room.

Christien nodded. He had never felt this way in Metz, or any other time. He closed his eyes and tried to still his nerves. He pictured the veins he needed to cut, the arteries, the muscles. Speed was everything. He looked at his mother. Her eyes were closed, her features serene. He took a deep breath.

The first cut was deep, straight, and sure. It brought her instantly awake. Her eyes bulged and went wide. The muscles in her jaw worked furiously as her teeth clamped on the wood in her mouth. She stiffened and arched her back. Bertrand leaned over her, placing his body weight over hers to dampen her struggles. Her scream was muffled, and it nearly shook Christien's resolve. He closed his mind to it.

Speed, he thought. *Speed.* His blade worked furiously at her flesh.

Blessedly, as with the cautery, Simone passed out. Her struggles ceased.

Christien did not get the femoral artery tied off cleanly. The suture slipped. A great quantity of blood spurted from the vessel before he could stop it. Her warmth drenched his face and his clothing. He knew it wasn't as much as it seemed, but any amount was too much. He cursed his clumsiness and wiped the blood from his eyes. He heard Bertrand getting sick in the corner. Guignard's assistant struggled furiously against his bonds, his eyes wide in horror as he watched, his protests muffled by his gag.

A cock crowed outside. It was just getting light.

It took much longer to employ ligature than cautery, but Christien was still fast. Three minutes and thirty seconds after he began, he reached for the saw.

❖

Count Arnaud de Vries rode like the wind on the long road from Hesdin, rode until his horses wore out. He traded one in Abbeville, bought one in Poix, and stole one in Beauvais as he thundered toward Paris. The messenger sent to alert him about his wife hadn't been able to get word into Hesdin for nearly ten days. There was only one thing in the world that would have drawn Arnaud away from the king's service at that moment, and he prayed he wasn't too late to see her. He slipped out of Hesdin in the middle of the night during a rainstorm, which left the roads muddy and treacherous. Still, he made remarkable time. It took him two days, two nights, and eight horses to make the journey, during which he stopped only long enough to change mounts.

He rode through St. Denis and at last saw the city walls looming in the dawn. The guard at the gate stopped him. "The gate will open in half an hour," he said. Arnaud clubbed him with the hilt of his sword, opened the gate himself, and rode on.

He arrived at the townhouse at the same instant as Guignard. The doctor didn't even take time to greet him, and explained Simone's injuries as they hurried together into the foyer and up the stair. "I am pleased to say your wife is much improved. She has been very near death, but just yesterday took a turn for the better. She is not out of danger, but—"

Arnaud shook the handle of the bedroom door, which was blocked from the inside. Puzzled, Guignard called out for his assistant to open the door. A moment later, Bertrand did so.

The count and the doctor entered the room and stopped dead still. It was a moment before the enormity of the scene registered on their brains: the bloody linens and bedcovers. The tools, now washed but still arrayed on a table. The leg, wrapped reverently by Christien in preparation for burial, beside the bed. The countess, pale and unconscious. Guignard's assistant, bound and gagged, his face red as he struggled anew in his chair.

Christien was sitting on the bed. He looked up at his father. He stood. His eyes were bloodshot, his face lined with fatigue. He swallowed. "I took her leg, Father," he said.

"You fool!" hissed Guignard. He raced to her side and felt her pulse. "She was getting better! How could you?"

"She would have died," Christien said defiantly. "I am certain of it. Her leg would have—"

"You did *this,* on your own account?" Arnaud said it slowly: the immensity of it was slow to dawn on him. "You did *this,* without the approval of the doctors? You did *this,* without experience or license or authority. . . . *You* are certain? How *dare* you!" He stepped forward and struck Christien with a backhand that knocked him to the floor. He knelt at Simone's side, consumed with grief. He stroked her hair. On the opposite side of the bed, Guignard put back the covers. The sight of the shortened limb, the stump and the tightly wrapped bloody bandage, nearly drove Arnaud to despair. "How *dare* you do such a thing?" he said again. "By the love of Christ, I ought to kill you as you've tried to kill her. She is not one of your filthy experiments. *She is my wife!*"

Christien got up, his hand wiping the blood from the corner of his mouth. "And she is my mother. She is not dead. She came through it well."

"Not so well, I fear," Guignard said, replacing the covers. "Her pulse is weak. The pain has dissipated her strength. All our previous gains have been undone. I cannot possibly continue to serve as her physician, Count. It is clear I must leave this in . . . in *his* hands."

"You do not have my leave to depart!" thundered Arnaud.

"He's right, Father. *I* will care for her," Christien said defiantly.

"By Christ, you will do nothing of the sort." Arnaud turned to Guignard, his voice thick. "Sir, I implore you. If it takes a command from the king himself, I shall place it in your hands before this day is out. Do not leave her side."

"Her condition is grave, sire. All we have worked for—" He shrugged. "Nothing but the grace of God will save her now."

"Then you will remain, and be His instrument. My son will interfere with you no further."

Guignard sighed. "I fear it is too late for such an assurance," he said. "However, I shall do what I can."

❖

Guignard pushed Christien aside completely, relying upon his own counsel and knowledge as to her treatment. With the count at his wife's side every moment, there were not even any late-night opportunities for Christien to observe her. He was shut out of her room entirely.

He spent the first night in the library. Once he heard a long wail of agony from her, as she awakened to her pain. The sound pierced every corner of the quiet house. It tormented him long after it had ceased. He crept through the upstairs hall and listened at the door. He heard his father talking to her. He heard his father weeping like a child.

After a long and difficult night, the count emerged from his wife's chamber. His eyes were red-rimmed, his beard ragged, his hair wild. Christien heard his footsteps and went to meet him. Arnaud's features darkened at the sight of his son. "She yet lives, but not for long. They say she will die."

"She *isn't* dead, Father. And she isn't going to die."

"Then only by the grace of God and Guignard," the count retorted. "*Your* arrogance is *her* undoing. Had she died of the accident it would have been God's work. I could have lived with that. Now, if she dies, the work is yours. Her blood is on your hands."

"Father, I—"

Arnaud looked at him through tormented eyes, his voice barely above a whisper. "If you hated me so, if you wanted to hurt me, I would rather you put a knife in my throat."

Christien blanched. "Please, Father. I don't hate you. I didn't want—"

"I don't care what you wanted." He turned to go.

"Father. Her . . . her leg. If you will let me do nothing else, I would like to . . . to bury it."

Arnaud stopped, his back to his son. He stiffened and did not turn around. His fists slowly opened and closed again. "I will not bury my wife in pieces. It will have to wait for the rest of her. When it must be done . . . *I* will do it."

The queen ordered her physicians to render every possible assistance to Guignard, and now new doctors filled the halls. There were no new treatments, nothing radical or magical to be done—simply the practice of sound medicine. Christien, banished from the second floor, heard them talking. The countess was losing ground. It was a death watch. Christien felt more miserable with each report.

Later, the count's comments brought an unbidden thought to Christien. Whether Simone lived or died now, he would never know whether it was he who was responsible for the outcome, or Guignard, or God. Angrily he pushed the thought away, surprised at his own vanity. It mattered only that she live. But simply having had the thought made him feel petty, and his misery worse.

Bertrand tried and failed to comfort him with words, and switched to brandy. They sat in the kitchen and drank until the cook threw them out, and then sat in the courtyard, just inside the wall. Christien drank until he could barely stand. His father was right. He had been arrogant and self-assured, and if she died now, it was by his own hand. The hand of a boy who was not yet a surgeon, who had never finished his apprenticeship.

His mother was no more than one of his experiments.

Yves had been excoriated by his father for not having prevented Christien's butchery. Now Yves took pains to punish his brother by delivering devastating reports about their mother's condition. "Father is beside himself," Yves said. "He is nearly helpless. He will not eat or drink. He prowls the halls and cries out loud, and he curses your name."

Christien aimlessly walked the streets of Paris. He began near dusk, passing in the shadow of the Grand Châtelet, the grim prison. Near midnight he found himself on the rue St. Denis, where prostitutes tried to lure him into the darkened alleys where they plied their trade. He sat outside the Church of St. Sepulchre, where the barber-surgeons of Paris took their vows and paid their annual devotions. He had lived and worked for the invitation to go inside and don the short red robe, and now bitterly castigated himself for the arrogance of that dream.

He stood outside the Cimetière des Innocents. The year after he was born, the plague filled the cemetery until the grounds could not hold another body. Even now, so many years later, the stench still seeped from the ground and hung in the air. The neighborhood stank of death. He passed the Cimetière de la Trinité, its hallowed grounds now supplied with fresh bodies by the doctors at the Hôtel-Dieu, the public hospital.

Places of death, places of failure.

And now when the Angel of Death comes for my mother, it is I who hand her over.

He walked through the city gate at the Porte Saint Honoré and down to the banks of the Seine, where he sat until dawn. He tossed stones into the river, and watched the day's barge traffic beginning. He wandered through the Bois de Boulogne, near his home. He watched deer drinking from a pond, and saw a fox chasing a rabbit. Finally he found himself near the loop in the river where the Seine flowed around St. Paul's.

He went inside the cathedral and stood in the vestibule, looking up into the great nave. He inevitably found comfort here, where he felt the presence of God. He knew now as he looked up that he had at last found the bounds of his confidence.

He walked down the aisle toward the altar, the sound of his boots echoing against the stone walls, along which the carved heads of saints stared down upon him: Matthew and Thomas, John and James, Mark and Luke. He felt their pity, and their scorn, and their love. He crossed himself and knelt before the Virgin.

He bowed his head in prayer. The afternoon sun streamed through the stained glass windows, falling into soft colored pools of light that warmed his head, just as the light had fallen upon him as an infant, when in the priory chapel his father had pledged him to the Order of St. John.

Bless me, Father, for I have sinned. I ask Thy pardon for those sins, as I ask for Thy grace.

Forgive my arrogance, my vanity, and my pride. Forgive my disobedience of my mother and father.

O Lord, there is so much to forgive.

I beseech Thee: take me and not her.

He drew a deep breath.

If Thou wilt save her, I will join the Order of St. John in Thy service.

❖

The bishop said God had spoken in the matter of the Countess de Vries.

The good doctor Guignard modestly said it was the sound advice of Galen that had lit the path to a cure, despite the ill-advised interventions of Christien.

Marcel, in private, said it was all Christien's doing that she lived.

To Christien, who honestly didn't know, it no longer mattered.

On his twenty-third birthday, in the year 1553, he mounted his horse outside the Château de Vries. His father rode on one side, Bertrand on the other. They started down the drive, beginning the long journey to Marseilles. There the two young men would board a ship bound for Malta, where, at the Order's convent in Birgu, they would swear the solemn oaths.

Christien turned and looked toward the château, somehow certain he would never see it again. The sun was in his eyes, and he had to squint to see her. From the balcony, where she was seated in a soft leather chair, Simone waved goodbye.

Book Three

MARIA

Chapter 17

MALTA

I'm leaving now, Mother." Maria opened the door.

"You go half naked?" Isolda said. "Why will you not wear a dress? And a *barnuża*? Must you be so immodest? Only witches and loose women refuse to cover themselves."

It was an old argument. On the rare occasions when they were seen in public, most girls Maria's age dressed like her mother did, in long formless clothing, with a hood that covered their heads and could be drawn over their faces. But Maria still dressed much as she had as a young girl. She wore a jerkin, a sleeveless tunic made of goatskin that extended to her hips and was cinched with a belt. Beneath that she wore a long-sleeved blouse. Her pants, their hems ragged, extended only to midcalf. As always, she was barefoot. Her mother never ceased to be scandalized by so much bare skin, convinced that a woman seen was a woman seduced. Yet Maria never relented. "I am not a whore, Mother, or a witch. But I'm going for guano, not to church, and I won't wear a hood. I have nothing to hide."

"*Maria!* For shame!" Isolda crossed herself. "It is no wonder you are an old maid. No one comes to call for you anymore. No one will, when you drive them away with such vulgar talk."

"I'm not an old maid yet, Mother. I'm sixteen. You have to be seventeen to be an old maid."

"Mind your tongue! And you should have been married a year ago!"

On Maria's fifteenth birthday, Luca had arranged a union with the son of the blacksmith. Maria had never spoken to him, but she had seen him near his father's shop. He was nearly thirty. His face was fleshy and ran with sweat. He treated his mule with contempt, and Maria knew she would fare no better. As was the custom, the eager groom sent her a fish decorated with garlands of ribbon, and with a ring in its mouth. While the couple's parents were negotiating the dowry, she left the fish in the sun until it ripened so fully the smell drove even the dogs away. Then she sent it back, the ring untouched. Her father was outraged, but Maria stood her ground. "I don't love him," she announced.

"*Love!*" her father thundered at the preposterous notion. "What has love to do with it? Love will not fill your belly in famine or keep you warm on a winter night! You need to rid yourself of such ideas. This is a good match."

"It *will* keep me warm on a winter night," she said, "or I would rather sleep alone. I can't stand him. I'd sooner marry his mule."

No man on Malta would allow such anarchy in his own household. Luca whipped her, but Maria never cried out and refused to yield. When it was over she straightened her clothing, struggling not to let her face betray how much he had hurt her. Later she was saved from Luca's plans for her only because the blacksmith's son became engaged to another girl. Luca beat her again, furious she'd lost a husband at a time when husbands—even bad ones—were painfully hard to come by. So far there had been no other candidates.

Now her mother busied herself at the fire pit, sweeping and stirring the ash. What little light seeped into the room from the window seemed to disappear there, swallowed by the dust. "It is always so with you," Isolda grumbled as she worked. "Everything for yourself, for your silly dreams. First you take my Nico, and now you take my pride." Maria flinched. There was nothing she could say to that. In the three years since Nico had gone, no day passed without pain, without longing and regret. "You should—" Isolda began to say.

"Goodbye, Mother," Maria said, cutting her off. She pulled the door closed behind her. The morning sun on her face felt glorious. She was glad to be outdoors. After her abortive attempt to stow away with Elena, Maria had spent two years under almost constant confinement in her house. The first time she disobeyed her father and left, he found her and dragged her home. He chained her to a post. After two weeks of it she agreed not to defy him. He released her. At first she was allowed to leave only to go to church with her mother. It was on those occasions that she had no choice but to wrap herself modestly, the way her mother insisted. Gradually she was permitted the freedom to leave for three hours—never a moment longer—to gather guano or brambles for the fire. Luca had no time for that chore and no money to pay for it, and Isolda was too frail. When Maria did that, she dressed more practically.

She hurried past St. Agatha's, the parish church. Her father was working on the new bell tower. Father Salvago had at last raised enough money to get it started and had hired Luca to build it. It looked, Maria thought, exactly like the bell tower on the candle she and Elena had sold to him as they tried to make money. Two laborers hoisted cream-colored limestone with a block and tackle attached to a wooden beam, while Luca leaned through an arch, fitting a stone. He marked it, trimmed it, then set it again, sometimes making five or six adjustments before he was satisfied. He was a painstaking craftsman. He seemed more comfortable with his stone than with people, Maria often thought. Certainly he touched it with more gentleness, more care. Intent on his task, he didn't see her.

The guard at the gate regarded her lustfully, and beckoned for her to join him inside his post. She ignored him and hurried away from the village. The island looked pleasant, almost dreamy. The autumn rains had cooled the land and washed it clean of summer dust. Here and there patches of wildflowers sprouted among the rocks and weeds, beneath a flawless sky. She waved at Roccu, a burly peasant toiling behind his donkey. He worked his fields every day, good weather or bad, trying to coax onions from the stingy soil. Both his arms were locked in struggle with his plow, so he tossed his head in greeting, a broad smile on his face.

There was little traffic on the footpath. She ran through quiet villages and past abandoned farmhouses, always keeping an eye on her surroundings. The coastal defenses had been improved by the Knights of St. John in the past few years, and there were more watchtowers than before, manned by soldiers now instead of civilians. Still, she was invariably aware of the closest cave or *wied* in which she might find shelter. She would never again be surprised by corsairs.

She saw the carob tree that marked the cave. Jacobus sat in its shade, waiting for her. Though younger than Maria, he was taller than she was. His chin already bore the modest beginnings of a beard. He waved at her approach. "I collected a whole sack today," he said, proudly hoisting the heavy load.

"You're wonderful," she said, squeezing his hands in gratitude. He often collected the guano for her, so she wouldn't have to spend what little freedom she had on that chore. Most often she spent the extra time with Elena, but not always. Sometimes he accompanied her as she walked the fields with the goats, or sat on the cliffs and watched the sea, pitching pebbles into the water, or playing games with the children of M'kor Hakhayyim.

"I can get more if you want," he said eagerly.

"It's more than enough for one day, and more than you need have done, really. You're sweet to do it, Jacobus." A shy grin blossomed on his face. He would collect a mountain of guano for such a compliment.

"Where's Elena?"

"Two of the goats are missing. She went to hunt for them. I waited here for you."

"We can wait for her down at the water. Let's—"

"*Maria*," he said, touching her sleeve, interrupting, pointing out to sea. "Look—isn't that Grima's ship?"

Jacobus had eyes as sharp as the falcons he caught. The galley was barely a speck on the horizon. She peered at it, trying to be sure. It was a few moments before she knew he was right. Her heart leapt. "He's a week early! I've got to go!"

She started to run, then stopped. She came back for the guano sack, but Jacobus waved her off. "I can bring it," he said. "You'd better hurry. He might give it to someone else."

He picked up the bag and started to run behind her, hoping to keep up, but she was far too swift and he lagged behind. He wasn't even jealous. He didn't understand her interest in it, but he knew that nothing on earth was more important to Maria than the cargo Antonellus Grima was bringing to Malta, just for her.

❖

Though her dream of escaping the island had been shattered, Maria's dream of learning to read had never died. Being locked away in her house had only fueled her desire. For a long while she had no idea what to do about it, but then one day it dawned on her. The reason no one would take her seriously was that she didn't own a book. She needed to get hold of a real book, one that was actually hers. Only then would anyone realize she wasn't simply an empty-headed dreamer.

But how to get a book?

First she needed money. She and Elena still had their goats, and though Elena protested it wasn't necessary, Maria had delayed fulfilling her dream until every maravedi was paid back that Luca had taken from her the day they were caught trying to leave. Maria also paid Jacobus a small sum for helping tend the herd, as she could not be around as often as before. He cared nothing for her money, but she insisted. It had taken a long time, but finally Elena was paid back, and there was a little to spare.

Elena solved the next problem. She'd met a widower who bought her services once a month. "He doesn't even make me lift my skirts," she said. "He only wants me to come and talk. Can you imagine?" The widower was Antonellus Grima, a merchant who traveled twice a year to Sicily to trade cumin for grain. Though he couldn't read, he knew of booksellers in Messina. Maria called on him, and asked him to buy her a book on his next voyage. "It doesn't matter which one," she told him eagerly. "Just be sure it has lots of words. And it would be nice if it had kings or queens in it."

Grima laughed at her foolishness. "A girl, with a book! You might as well save your maravedis for an extra head, for all the good it will do you. You're chasing vapors, child, and wasting good money doing it. And all to read about lords and ladies! I've not met a king or a queen, but of all the lesser nobles I've met— and I've traded with a few—not one is worth a pile of horse leavings. You should forget your high notions and get married. Have babies."

"Thank you, Sur Grima, but for now I prefer the book, if you please."

He had agreed to make the purchase, and now his ship was sweeping down the coast on its return from Sicily. She ran the three miles to Birgu without stopping and was waiting for him when he trudged up the street from the docks. He saw her anxious look. "Yes, yes, I have it. A moment, please. You'll wear an old man out."

Once inside the shop he rummaged through his things and found the precious packet.

Carefully she unwrapped the cloth. For a moment she couldn't touch it. It was bound in red leather, its pages fresh and pristine, the color of cream. She opened it. The print was clear and black and fine. She held it close to her face and drew a deep breath, luxuriating in the rich smell of leather and ink. "It's beautiful," she whispered. "What is it called?"

"*The Courtier.*" He could not read and said it from memory. "By a man named Baldassare . . . something. The bookseller said it'll teach you to be a proper princess. All the nobles read it, in every court from Madrid to Vienna."

"It's perfect." Her eyes watered, and she clutched the book to her breast. "How much do I owe you?"

"Eighty maravedis, but if you don't have it now—"

"But I told you I would, and I do!" She surprised him by extracting a sizable sum of money from her pocket and carefully counting out what she owed. Then she stunned him with a quick hug. "*Grazzi,*" she said, and she was off like the wind. She flew out the door and up the narrow street to the square, dodging carts and pigs. She thought perhaps she ought to wait until later, after her father had gone home, but she couldn't. He would not object if he knew she were going to church, and that was exactly her plan.

She was going to St. Agatha's to see the *kappillan,* Dun Salvago. She would ask him—no, she would *tell* him this time: he was going to teach her to read.

❖

Father Salvago was seated at the table in the sacristy. The parish register lay open before him. He was writing in it with his quill pen, recording the list of parishioners who had attended the last Mass. On a separate sheet he was making note of those who had not made confession during the past year, in order that he might pay them a visit and give them a friendly reminder, lest their souls be imperiled.

His attention kept returning to a letter next to the register. It was from his mentor in Sicily, the archbishop of Palermo. The letter was chatty, filled with news and gossip. The last few sentences in particular caught his attention.

> *I read your last letter with interest. Though you seem absorbed in your work, I sensed in every line your impatience for the opportunity to serve your Lord in Rome. I understand your desire, as I share it myself. I know Malta is not Eden, but Bishop Cubelles writes me that you have transformed St. Agatha's into the Lord's garden nevertheless. I can only counsel you to remain serene and to continue your good works. Surely the Lord will smile upon you—perhaps sooner than you expect.*
>
> *I have recently returned from a brief visit to the Holy See. Though (mercifully) he is dead, Lucifer's understudy Martin Luther continues to force great change upon our house. I fear we have only begun to comprehend the effect of his evil. The Church will need good sons to serve her. A man of your abilities and background will not toil in Birgu forever. Perhaps it is not too soon to share my own glad tidings. I have been told to expect a summons to Rome, where through the Lord's grace I have always been fortunate in my friends, who favor me. If this should come to pass, your own summons cannot be far behind.*
>
> *Be patient, Giulio. The Lord smiles upon His disciples. Your day shall come.*

He set the letter aside.

The Vatican.

How well the archbishop knew him! And how true it was—after all these years, it was not a heart but the rock of St. Peter that beat inside his chest. What man could fail to be attracted to the very center of power, where such momentous events were taking place? What man would not wish to have some influence, however small, in the ecumenical councils in which men of stature, men of consequence, men of God were deciding issues that would forever affect the faithful? What man would not wish to make his stand there, against heresy? The new order of Jesuits were already making their mark, and needed to be watched and countered at every turn. And what splendor! Pope Julius had made Michelangelo the Vatican architect, the very man whose art had shaken Salvago's soul to its quick, and it was said his vision for the rest of the church was as grand as heaven itself.

Rome! Great issues, great beauty, great opportunity. Robes of purple, robes of red, a robe of white. He could close his eyes and see the majesty of it all, remember perfectly the glories of the Sistine, where he had begun his journey—

"Father?"

He opened his eyes, his reverie interrupted. Maria Borg stood at the door to the sacristy. She was holding something. "I have a *book,*" she said, her eyes glowing.

"So I see. Come, bring it to me."

She moved forward. "It's mine. You must teach me to read it, Dun Salvago."

He smiled. "I *must?*" He looked at her carefully. This was not the same stick of a girl who a few years earlier had asked him to teach her to read. In the years since, he had seen her occasionally in the streets, and more often in church, when she was always with her mother, and cloaked behind a *barnuza*. Maria appeared now without the cloak, and her dirty face and unkempt hair could not disguise the fact that her features had softened and she had filled out. For perhaps the first time, he truly focused: she was beautiful and radiant. She was a woman.

Blushing from her own boldness, she thrust her book at him. "Yes. Must . . . *please must,* I mean. I bought it myself, Father. I earned the money with my goats, and sent a man to get it, all the way to Sicily, and he said it has princes and kings, and now God is going to help me learn to read it." Her words tumbled out breathlessly, quickly, her eyes shining with hope.

"Did He tell you that?"

"I prayed it. I know you are the answer to my prayer."

"As I told you once before, I am not a teacher, Maria. And I have little time."

"Just an hour or two a week, that's all I want. I will pay you a goat, Father." She had thought long about that and discussed it with Elena.

"A goat! The Lord's work is never done for a fee."

She flashed a triumphant smile. "Then you agree this is His work!"

"I didn't say that. I only meant—"

"Of course you shall keep it for a gift, not a fee," she said. "Not for yourself, but for the parish. Please, Dun Salvago. To read is all I want, and a goat is all I can give."

Salvago had countless reasons he shouldn't bother with such a fool's errand, but her enthusiasm was irresistible. He regarded her appreciatively until she blushed again. He smiled indulgently. "Very well," he said with a sigh, "we'll begin next Monday. Be here at three." He stood.

In her exuberance she forgot herself and bounded forward to hug him. "Thank you, Father, and God bless you!" Awkward at her girlish and unexpected move, he gave her a pat on the back.

"Three? What for?" Luca Borg stood at the sacristy door, holding a trowel. He had come to ask a question of Father Salvago, and heard the last of their exchange. He looked disapprovingly at his daughter, who straightened herself, her radiance fading at his sudden appearance.

"Well, Maria? I asked you a question. What for?"

She looked at him defiantly, as if daring him to deny her. "I am—"

"I have agreed to teach her to read," Father Salvago said quickly, trying to avoid an argument. "My apologies, Luca. I should have asked you first."

"*Read!*" Luca spat the word. "That foolishness again! Reading is useless. You're wasting your time. You should be home!"

Maria almost said, "To do what?" but she knew now was not the time for belligerence. If her father forbade it, Salvago would respect his wishes, and her dream would be forever crushed. "But Father," she said, pleading, "I could help you read notices in the square, and even plans, for your work."

"There are criers in the square," he said, "and there is no plan I need for my work."

"It is my pleasure to teach her," Salvago said, realizing with some surprise as he spoke that he had moved quite rapidly to her cause, and that he meant it. "I would enjoy trying—if you will allow me, of course."

Luca's big hands worked nervously around the edges of his trowel as he struggled with the idea. There were a hundred reasons to deny her wish, not least of which was his own distaste for the idea that his daughter might do what he could not. But now she'd enlisted the priest, and the priest was his client, and Luca had no wish to seem an ignorant ox. And perhaps it wasn't such a bad thing, anyway. Maybe she would have less time to spend with her whore friend in her cave.

"Very well, Dun Salvago," he said. "Waste your time if you will."

❖

They worked in the sacristy. It was a simple room, lit by two small leaded-glass windows. One wall held a wardrobe, in which Salvago's vestments were kept, and an ambry, a cupboard that held the consecrated oils. On another there was a single bookshelf, holding a candlestick, a crucifix, a Bible, and an hourglass. Beneath the shelf there was a sturdy table of rough-hewn yellowed oak that had gone hard as iron, where Salvago worked on his sermons and read. Three quill pens rested on an inkwell. There was only one chair, so he borrowed two blocks of stone from Luca's rubble at the base of the belfry and made another.

She was early for her first lesson. She walked into the sacristy carrying her new book under one arm and leading a goat on a tether. The goat immediately made for a tidy pile of parchment on the edge of the table.

"I didn't think you were serious about the goat," Salvago said. "It isn't necessary."

"We made a deal, Father," Maria said. "The goat is yours."

He smiled and asked her to tie it outside. She handed him her book, but he set it aside. "The word of God before the word of man," he said. "And the alphabet, before either may become clear." In fact, he had never taught anyone to read before, and he wasn't altogether certain of the best way to go about it. He had asked Don Andrea Axiaq, the irascible master of the tiny grammar school in Mdina. Salvago was nervous even speaking to the man, who had been tried with Salvago's predecessor Father Jesuald, the priest executed for heresy the day Salvago arrived in Malta. Axiaq had recanted and was pardoned, but he was still suspected of radical thought. Yet Axiaq was the only person on the island who had what Salvago needed. Axiaq scoffed when he heard the purpose. "The best way to teach a female to read, Father," he said, "is to not bother in the first place. She'll have forgotten the first lesson before you've finished the second, and she'll have no use for it all, anyway. Erasmus and Virgil will find no home in the mind of a girl. Plautus will have penned his plays for an empty house."

"If that is God's will, then so it shall be," Salvago agreed. "But this child's mind and spirit are livelier than most. She is determined, and I will try. Now if you don't mind, I will be happy to borrow that slate board from you, and some scraps of chalk."

"God's will is lost on you," Axiaq said gruffly. "You should worry after her soul, not her mind." He gave up the board and chalk, but that was as far as he would go: he was not going to teach a priest how to teach a girl. "My time would be wasted twice over," he said.

Undaunted, Salvago pressed ahead. He began by making letters on the slate, which he propped on a table and leaned against the wall. He cleaned the board with a wet cloth and carefully drew the letter *A*. He held out the chalk to her. With a thrill of anticipation she wiped her hands on her pants and took it from him, holding it as if it were a sacred relic. Her hand shook a little at first. She looked at his letter, and then inched the chalk along, clenching her teeth as it screaked on the slate. Dissatisfied, she rubbed out her first mark with her finger and began again. As she finished the trailing curlicue she sat back and let out her breath. The letter was cramped, but it was, quite clearly, an *A*.

"A good beginning," he said approvingly. "If you don't throttle the chalk like the neck of a hen, the next one will come easier."

She laughed, and her nerves settled. They went through the alphabet, first upper case, then lower. After each letter he had her say its name, and then repeat it. "*Bellissimo*," he said approvingly after an *M*. "Your letters have grace, as do you."

She blushed. "Thank you, Father."

"*Brava*," he said, clapping, after the *Z*. "I'm certain even Dante never wrote with such flourish." She had no idea who Dante was, but took it as a compliment.

After that they made numbers, which she found easier than the letters. Although she had never seen the finished numbers written down before, they seemed to lodge quite comfortably in her mind. There was an elegance to them, a neat order that intrigued her. She had always been able to do minor sums, but only in her head or with her fingers. Now, to see them taking solid form on slate, made her shiver with pleasure.

They worked for hours, lost in study. She did well, but she grew tired, and the numbers and letters began running together in her mind. They heard the creak of the wood ladder as Luca descended from the belfry, finished for the day. "Enough for now," Salvago said, and he stood at the door and waved as she ran down the street. The last of the sun's rays caught Maria's hair. She moved lightly, a wisp of a girl lit with enthusiasm. She looked back at him, smiled, and waved. Watching her, he felt a surge of pride. He would delight in lecturing Axiaq on the will of God, even though it was delivered by an inexperienced teacher, and to a girl at that. Plautus might have an audience after all.

She had to wait a week for the next lesson. In the meantime she practiced drawing the letters she could remember in the dirt, with a stick. At night she traced them on the beam above her bed, with her finger. She thought wistfully of Nico as she tried to remember which was an *m* and which was an *n*, and then she worried that what she'd traced was an *s* after all. Nico would have known immediately. He was always quick that way, much quicker than she.

❖

The next Monday she drew her letters on the board again. She wanted to try it alone first, as Salvago watched. Her cheeks were flushed, her eagerness evident as she wrote out the letters, one after the other. She glowed from inside; he'd never seen such enthusiasm. "That's an *a*," she said, her hand sure, "and a *b,* and—"

"*D*," he interrupted, glancing at the board. "The loop on the *b* goes the other way." He showed her, then corrected her patiently as she worked through the rest. She remembered how to make nearly half the letters perfectly. "I am proud of you," he said when she finished. "Only one lesson, and no exercise book with which to practice." He'd been unable to obtain one from the schoolmaster.

"I had *Il Cortegiano* to look at," Maria reminded him, referring to the book she owned. "It has all the letters, I think."

"So it does," he said. "And now we shall read together." He moved his chair next to her limestone seat, and pulled the Bible from its place on the shelf. The heavy book smelled of leather and parchment and the ages. He opened it to the Book of Matthew. It was in Latin, of course. The print was dense and difficult to read, each verse beginning with elaborate calligraphy that seemed to dance off the page. Salvago's finger traced the words as he spoke them. He read from the Beatitudes, so she knew some of the words as he spoke them. "*Beati pauperes spiritu, quoniam ipsorum est regnum caelorum. . . .*" He glanced at her. Her eyes were lit, and she seemed enraptured. Her lips moved silently as she watched his finger moving over the jumble of letters. She was, he realized, quite stunning. The thought shocked him, and he quickly turned his attention back to the words.

"*Blessed are those who hunger and thirst for righteousness. . . .*" He felt her nearness now, her presence next to him, sensed her breathing. He was unsettled, yet unwilling to break the spell, and he read without pause for nearly half an hour. When he stopped at last, he realized she was shaking her head. "What is the matter?" he asked.

"I see no connection between the letters and the words, Father," she said. "I don't know how you're doing what you're doing. I don't know how you are *reading*. It seems . . . enchanted. I don't mean *magic,*" she said quickly, "or anything dark like that. And I know this is God's word, but it is just . . . too much." She blinked back tears of frustration. "I don't think I'll ever be able to learn."

Salvago pondered the problem. He didn't remember how he'd been taught, didn't recall the tricks his teachers had used or the order in which they had done things. Reading was something that just happened. He did remember that his instructors never mixed reading and writing. These were two different skills, taught separately, years apart. Perhaps he was making a mistake by attempting too much too quickly. But he doubted that. The pupil was bright; it was the teacher who was lacking.

After much thought he realized he'd simply skipped an obvious step.

He picked up the chalk and wrote on the slate. "D . . . e . . . i," he said, pronouncing each of the letters separately, then running them together. "These are the letters that spell out the word for God. There, do you see? *Dei.* Here, then, another. H . . . i . . . e . . ." He spelled out *Hierosolymam.* "Jerusalem."

It was such a simple thing, and yet it made all the difference.

"Yes," she said, pleased. "I do see." He followed the same process with her name, and his own. With each example the flower of understanding seemed to blossom in her mind.

He gave her a present before she left that day. It was a portfolio of vellum he'd gotten from Bishop Cubelles, telling the prelate he needed it for his studies. It was true in a way, he thought, and the bishop had more than enough of the parchment. Salvago wrote all the letters in his best hand, running them down the left side of each page, followed by whole words. "Practice copying at home," he told her. Her eyes shone with gratitude. In two days she filled both sides of eleven sheets, writing in a tiny scrawl in order that she might practice thousands of letters without wasting space. Her work lacked polish, of course, but she regarded the finished sheets as if they were the work of God. And truly, she thought, they were.

❖

She lost her nervousness but none of her eagerness. Once uncorked, her enthusiasm spewed forth. Her pen looped and swirled, crafting letters that each day showed more skill. Her laughter sparkled like her letters, her face was fresh, her skin perfect, and he found himself losing himself in her presence, as if he had the attention span of a schoolboy. Once, when she saw he wasn't paying attention, she wrote ten letters backward, each perfect but reversed, and she giggled at the look on his face when the letters finally registered. "You think always of God," she said. "I think you must step in every puddle in the street that way."

He averted his eyes. "You are learning very well," he said.

"Thank you, Father. You are a good teacher."

"I think we should change the lessons to three times a week. Assuming your father approves, of course."

She drew a sharp breath. "Do you really think you can? Will you have the time?"

"I will find the time," he said. And he knew he would find the time five days a week, or seven.

❖

He begged an Italian grammar from Axiaq, and began working with her on that. She learned more quickly than before, because she knew most of the words. She wrote lists of conjugations and columns of vocabulary. He thought she was brilliant.

"I have something for you," he said one afternoon. He produced an exercise book, the very same one used in the boys' school in Mdina.

"You are a gift from God, Father," she said. She clutched it to her breast and pecked him on the cheek. It was quick and innocent, but sent a shock through Salvago that resonated to his spine. He cleared his throat. He showed her how to use the book and gave her an assignment.

She practiced her letters at night, copying words and repeating them aloud, working until Elena's candles burned to a nub. She felt a thrill every time she did it, every time she felt the miracle flowing from her own hand or heard the magic coming from her own lips.

"You are the picture of pretentiousness," Luca said, watching her. He ate an onion and went to bed.

"The only words you read should be those of the Bible," Isolda said. She prayed to the Virgin and joined him.

The next morning she saw Jacobus, on his way to take care of the goats. "Maria! You must come with me. The goats found a new patch of marram, partway down the cliffs. I followed them and found some old carvings in the rocks there. I'll bet they're treasure markers or something! Come on and I'll show you. We can throw some rocks, too."

"I'd like to, but I have to meet Dun Salvago."

He eyed her book and looked down. "All you want to do anymore is *that*," he said. "I didn't know it would take so much time to learn." He kicked at a pebble and sent it rolling. "You've forgotten your goats."

She heard the real tone in his voice: You've forgotten me. She smiled at him. "I'll come tonight, after lessons. I promise."

❖

Salvago invited Maria to accompany him on his regular visit to see his sister Angela Buqa in Mdina. "Bring your book," he told her. "My sister will read it with you."

Maria worried for days over the impending visit. "She's *nobility,*" she said to Elena. Elena helped her brush her hair, and gave her a touch of scented water for her neck and cheeks. "You look noble yourself," she told her. "Baroness or not, she'll be jealous of you."

Maria and Salvago rode together in his cart. Its great wooden wheels jolted over the miserable path, pitching them back and forth each time a wheel bounced over a stone. They braced themselves against the sides, but twice she fell against him. Her touch and scent unnerved him, but she recovered quickly, chattering and laughing, oblivious to the physical contact. She talked of her goats.

Mdina was situated on a hill, with a splendid view of the island. They passed through the city gate and made their way through narrow streets, turning through another gate into the inner court-yard of the Buqa mansion.

Maria felt herself transformed. She no longer inhabited the gritty world of Malta, but instead had arrived at the fairy castle of her dreams, a gaily colored world of privilege and luxury. A footman greeted Father Salvago politely and helped them down from the cart. A manservant showed them inside. Maria took in every sight with wide, disbelieving eyes: she had not known such opulence existed anywhere else but in her dreams. The reception room was larger than her house. There were real windows, made of glass. The floor was tile. Heavy tapestries lined the walls. She breathed deeply, for the house even smelled rich. Her eyes rested on the bookshelves, sagging beneath scores of leather-bound volumes. She clutched her own book and smiled.

Maria stared at a portrait mounted over a large fireplace. The man was clearly noble, dressed formally in kilt, long gray stockings, and red-soled shoes. He had bushy gray hair and a full beard, and frowned down at her with striking gray eyes. "My sister's husband, the baron," Salvago said.

With a rustle of skirts, the baroness entered the room. Maria turned and was smitten. Angela moved with grace and good breeding, the perfect noblewoman. She presented a striking contrast to the large and aging man in the portrait. She had delicate features, a small mouth, and a long neck. Strands of pearls were plaited into her auburn hair, which was coiled in the back and fell into ringlets at her ears. She wore a dress of brocaded velvet with threads of silver and gold woven throughout, along with pearls that matched those in her hair. Her dress was open at the sides, revealing a patterned underdress beneath silk laces. Maria memorized every exquisite detail, to repeat to Elena.

Angela greeted her brother warmly, and Father Salvago introduced her to Maria. Angela regarded her with a forced smile. Her brother was forever bringing unsavory guests from his parish, and it took all her strength to cope. Angela beckoned them toward a low table. Maria was about to sit on an elegantly embroidered chair when Angela held out a handkerchief. "Perhaps you would be so kind?" she said, eyeing Maria's pants.

It took Maria a moment to understand: Angela wanted her to put the handkerchief on the chair. She felt her cheeks burning a little, but she complied, sitting with all the grace she could muster.

"You look as if you might be more at home on a rock than on a chair," Angela said.

Maria nodded happily, deaf to the mockery. "Yes, *Barunessa,* but this is very comfortable on my . . . bottom." Father Salvago chuckled but shot a disapproving glance at his sister, who wore a perfect if humorless smile.

They were served bread and preserves, and a hot drink that Angela called coffee, recently imported from the Arabian peninsula. "It is the very finest in the world," she said. Maria tasted the drink and nearly choked, wincing at the bitter taste that even honey didn't mellow. "It's very good," she lied. She eyed the preserves. She'd never seen them, either. She wasn't certain she wanted to try them, especially not if they were as fine as the coffee. Salvago and his sister were engaged in small talk. Trying to be unobtrusive, she picked up a piece of bread, and with her tongue delicately sampled the sticky red mess. She thought she would die from the pleasure, and licked the bread clean, then ate it. She did the same to four of the six pieces on the tray before Angela noticed. "Perhaps you would rather have the jar," she said. Maria nodded brightly.

Later Angela invited her upstairs, while she changed clothes for lunch. Maria counted eight wardrobes in the room, and she could see more in another. "How many dresses do you have?" she asked.

"More than I know, I suppose. Fewer than I wish."

Maria stood in front of the mirror. She'd seen a tin mirror once, but this one was full-length, Venetian glass with a gilt frame. She turned around, staring at herself. She was pleased with her face, which she'd never seen in such sharp detail. She tugged at her ears, opened her mouth, and wiggled her tongue. She giggled, forgetting herself. She stood sideways and noticed the swell of her breasts beneath her jerkin. She'd never thought much about them before, but she stared at them now, and at her hips. Her shape was as surprising to her as it was agreeable. She touched her hair, which she'd braided before coming. She saw she'd done a poor job of it. Wisps of hair strayed onto her cheeks. She tried to hide the strays, but they fell again.

"You should dye it," Angela told her. "And whiten your skin. It's unfashionably brown."

"From the sun. I spend a lot of time outside, with my goats."

"Ah, with your goats. I should have guessed. I thought it was just the dirt. There are herbs, of course."

"For goats?"

"For your skin." Angela stood next to her, straightening her dress.

Now Maria could see both their images, side by side. Suddenly her own reflection looked plain, rough clay next to perfect porcelain. "Really? Do you think I should?"

"Probably not." Angela sat at her dresser. She worked on her hair in another mirror, watching Maria out of the corner of her eye. Maria's attention had turned to a set of tortoiseshell brushes. She touched them as if they were made of silk. "Do you like it here?" Angela asked.

"Oh, yes! It's so beautiful!" Maria gushed about her dreams, about living in a house like that someday, a house as big as a castle. Then, feeling bold and important, she even shared her dream of having servants and fields of lupine. She caught herself, blushing. "I'm sorry," she said. "I didn't mean to go on so."

"*Lupine!*" said Angela brightly. "How very original that you should wish to raise a pretty little weed. And a whole field of it, you say! Whatever will you do with it?"

"I . . . I don't know, really. It's just silly." Maria smiled, and dropped her gaze. She couldn't tell whether Angela was trying to be nice or mean. Her face said one thing, her mouth another. And now Maria was mortified about lupine. Was it really a weed? She said nothing more.

Lunch was a sumptuous banquet, with baskets of fruit, steaming bowls of vegetables, and slices of meat that Maria didn't recognize, all of it served by two attentive footmen. Salvago and Angela were talking about Angela's husband, Antonio, who was away on business. Maria picked up a piece of meat with her fingers. She had the food to her mouth when she saw the baroness pick up a fork and gaze in her direction. Angela stopped talking in midsentence and stared at Maria with arched brows, a look somewhere between horror and delight in her eyes.

Blushing, Maria put her food back down on the plate. She wiped her hands on her jerkin. She picked up her own fork but held it by clasping her fingers around the handle, rather than nestling it gracefully in her hand as did the others. It was awkward, but she managed to eat nevertheless. Trying to make her more comfortable, Father Salvago made a small joke about the inefficiency of a fork compared to the fingers God gave His children. It did little to settle Maria's growing embarrassment. The rest of lunch went the same way. At every turn Maria felt on the brink of some disaster, ready to tumble into the social abyss in which everything about the *Barunessa* Buqa reminded her she belonged.

"Well," Angela said when they finished. "To the great business of the day. My brother tells me you own a book."

"Yes. *The Courtier.*" Maria said it well; she'd said the title a hundred times to herself.

"I know it well. I have a copy. Shall we read?"

"Oh, yes, please." Maria proudly produced the red leather volume. Without taking it, Angela walked to the bookshelf. She pulled down a different edition, this one richly bound, its leather dyed deep purple, its pages gilded, pressed, and filigreed.

The book rang with the lively wordplay of courtiers in the ducal palace of Urbino as they debated the merits of individualism and the nature of man. Angela selected certain passages and read them out loud as Maria followed along in her own text. The experience began in exhilarating fashion. It was not simply that Angela read so well, but the fact that the book had *ideas* in it: about love and honor, and about the *uomo universale,* the many-sided man. Even Salvago laughed at passages that were anticlerical, passages his sister seemed to find with uncanny ease. She found other passages with equal ease, passages that seemed clearly directed at Maria, about dress and wealth and bearing and station, passages in which there were many words whose precise definition Maria didn't know, although she understood their meaning well enough the way Angela said them. " 'Thus those who are most distinguished are of noble birth,' " the baroness read, and it was clear she took pleasure from Maria's discomfort.

Salvago intervened then, for he, too, knew the work. He pointed out another section, about those of humble birth whose virtues had brought glory to themselves and their descendants. But despite his effort, the breeze in Maria's sails had already died. As brother and sister sparred, she finally closed her book. "I'm tired," she said. "I think I'd like to go."

"It is a shame when ideas are so troubling, dear. It is the price of the words, one must suppose. Still, it *was* your book," Angela said.

"I'm tired, that's all," Maria said.

"Of course you are."

Maria rose to leave. Acting on an impulse, she tried to curtsy. Elena told her it was common among the nobility. She didn't pull it off well. This time she didn't need to see the expression on Angela's face to know she looked silly. Embarrassed, she excused herself and went into the foyer while Father Salvago said goodbye to his sister.

"Really, Giulio," Angela said. "I wish you weren't so distracted by this . . . girl. This island is more desolate than even I supposed. Tell me, is it her mind that interests you, or her breeding?"

"Don't mock her," Salvago said severely. "I admire her desire to improve herself, to learn to read."

"Really! And to think for a moment I imagined your interest carnal rather than literary. How peevish of me."

"*Angela!*" His color rose.

She smiled sweetly. "It's only that you are easier to read than *The Courtier.* If I hadn't seen that look so often during your wilder days, I might not recognize it now. I haven't seen such obvious lust in your eyes since the orgy at Messina, when Father nearly disowned you. Even then I never knew you to pluck your fruit so long before it ripened, brother dear—at least not since you were a boy and would eat anything green."

"I will not listen to this! How dare you!"

"Forgive my impertinence, Father Salvago, dear. It's only that I worry for you, for your ambitions in the Church. Whatever would the bishop say? He burns his disappointments, you know. This isn't Sicily. Take care you don't become his kindling before you can fulfill your Vatican dreams."

"That is enough, Angela."

"Quite," she agreed. She took his hands. "Until next Sunday, then. Antonio will be here. Don't be late." She smiled grandly and offered her cheek.

On the return trip to Birgu Maria fought the impulse to cry. The world of Angela Buqa glittered less brightly than it had that morning, and Maria knew it was only because of her own low birth. Her mirrors would always be tin. "Your sister is very nice," Maria said lamely.

"My sister is a prig," Salvago said. "Please forgive her vanities." His mind was a turmoil of denial and guilt and confusion. Nothing in the world so infuriated him as his sister when she got that way.

They rode the rest of the way to Birgu in silence.

Chapter 18

I brought you this." Jacobus handed her a tightly wrapped cloth packet.

She was sitting on the beach, her nose in her book. She set the book down, opened the packet, and smiled at the delicate sweet nougat inside. "*Qubbajt!*" she said. "I love it!"

"I traded some feathers for it," he said.

"You're sweet," she said. "Wildflowers last week, and now this!"

He sat down next to her. She'd been making letters in the sand with a stick. He stared at the book and then at the sand, his eyes wide with curiosity. "What is that?" he said, pointing.

"An *L.* Here," she said, picking up the stick. "Let me show you. You see? *J-a-c-o-b-i-s.* That is your name." She looked at it and knew it wasn't right. She smoothed out the *i* and replaced it with a *u.* "There, *that's* your name," she said with certainty.

He tried it and made an indecipherable scratch. "I'm not very good at it," he said.

"It takes practice."

He rubbed it out and tried again. Frustrated, he stood. "It's not for me. It's magic," he said. "Something for nobles." He tossed the stick aside and walked down to the water. He picked up a rock and skipped it. A galley slipped by offshore, and beyond it, farther to sea, they could see boats bobbing on low waves as fishermen cast long nets for tunny, mullet, and hake. "Let's find some mussels," he said.

She waded in after him. They peered into the rock pools, calling out whenever they found something. They collected the shells in a cloth. Jacobus watched her working, but only when she wasn't looking. All day he'd been working up his courage. He'd never felt a pit like this in his stomach, not even the first time he'd swung out from the cliffs on a rope a hundred feet above the sea. He swallowed and plunged ahead. "Do you think you would ever want to be with me? I mean, that you could care for me?"

She looked up with that smile that so melted him. "Jacobus! What a foolish thing to say! I care for you more than you know."

He leaned over and plucked a mussel from the water, hiding his own smile.

"You remind me of my brother Nico, you know."

His smile died. His cheeks felt hot. "Oh," he said. He took a deep breath. "I don't want to remind you of your brother."

"No? You would have liked him, I know you would. I can't say anything better about a person."

He didn't know exactly what he wanted to say, and was too shy to try. "Never mind," he said, trying to keep the misery from his voice.

❖

Salvago paced the room behind her as she sat at the table and read out loud. Some words she read quickly and easily, others with more difficulty, still others not at all, when she would ask for help. He watched her from a position where she could not see his gaze. She stumbled over a word. He leaned over her shoulder, and she pointed. His cheek brushed her hair, and it sent a shock down his spine. He smelled her fragrance. Normally she wore no perfume, but her friend Elena did, and it was that he smelled, that coupled with the odor of her straw and her goats, and it was fresh on her. And his eyes took in the swell of her breast beneath her shift. He felt himself growing hard beneath his robes, and it was all he could do to keep from pressing against her. Instead he pressed against the back of her chair. He felt an overwhelming agony of desire in the brief touch, and nearly came inside his cassock. He was instantly awash in a flood of guilt. He straightened up.

"You must go now," he said quickly, his voice thick.

She turned and looked at him. "Is something wrong?" she asked, concerned. "Are you ill, Father? You look as if you have a fever!"

"No. It's only—there are pressing matters to which I must attend."

She stood to go. "Of course. I'm sorry. I'll see you in two days."

"No," he said. "Not—not so soon. I'll send word. Really, I'm very busy." She looked at him uncertainly. He looked away. Her face, her body, her hair—he couldn't look anymore.

After she left he fled to the rectory. He fell to his knees beside his cot and prayed to God to give him strength. Prayer brought no peace. His breathing remained heavy, his chest constricted, his loins on fire. He had not had such feelings since before he entered the seminary. No, that was not right—even before the seminary, he had never felt that way.

I will not call her back. I will end this madness.

Each time he closed his eyes that night, he saw Maria, saw her without her clothing, saw her beneath him, opening her legs to him, crying out for him. He sweated and prayed, but the fever she induced in him wouldn't leave.

❖

Days passed, and he regained control of himself through prayer, pushing his thoughts aside. He sent word she should come the next Monday.

Luca and his workers were making a racket in the bell tower, and after Maria came in Salvago closed the door behind her. He was businesslike, almost cold. He had just begun the lesson when Elena burst into the sacristy. "I am sorry—Maria, you must come. The goats. They're ill. They're going to die. Fençu and Jacobus are off fishing. Elli doesn't know what to do."

Salvago crossed himself. "What's the matter?" he asked.

"Grain, Father," Elena said. One of her customers had paid her with grain instead of cash. She'd brought it home on a wagon. She and Maria had stored it, intending to feed it gradually to their herd. "They broke through the fence and got into a whole pile of it. They're all sick, Maria. They're swelling up. Elli says they're going to burst!"

"I must go, Father," Maria said. "Pray for them, will you?"

"I'll do more than that," Salvago said. "I'll give you a ride in the cart. I had charge of the goats at the seminary. Perhaps I can help." He hitched the cart himself and drove the mule like a racehorse.

When they arrived the goats were in terrible shape. The strongest kicked and bawled, their bellies grotesquely distended. Others lay on their sides, their breathing fast and shallow. Two were already dead. The children were trying to keep the remainder of the herd away from the grain and rebuild the rock-and-wood barrier the goats had broken down. Elli rose, her hands bloody. She tried her best to hide her shock at the appearance of a priest. "I don't know what to do," she said to Maria. "I've bled three of them, but I don't believe it helped."

Maria knelt next to Esther, the goat who'd started their herd. She placed her hand on the goat's belly, but the touch made Esther thrash in pain. Maria drew back, afraid. "Father—?"

"I have heard of this," Salvago said, "but I have never seen it."

"What can be done?" Her voice was a whisper.

"I believe there is a way," he said. "I'm just not certain *I* can do it."

"If you don't try, they'll die."

"I'll need a sharp knife." Elli gave him the short blade she'd used to cut into the veins. Salvago knelt next the goat and gently probed her side. Eyes wild, she struggled against him, trying to rise. Maria held her down. Esther bleated reedily and sighed.

Salvago found a soft area behind the rib cage, high on the flank where the bulge seemed greatest. He held the knife in both hands. "Guide my hand, Father." He plunged the knife down. Esther jerked as the blade penetrated her flank. Salvago withdrew the knife to a whoosh of air, followed by a pink bloody froth that bubbled around his hands from the goat's rumen. With the pressure released, the goat's side returned to its normal shape. They made a poultice from seawater and soil, pressed it against the wound, and waited. Maria stroked her goat's head, whispering to her.

A few moments later Esther struggled to her feet, breathing heavily. She took a tentative step, and another. And then, as if nothing at all had happened, she headed straight for the pile of deadly grain. Elli clapped in delight and shooed her away, and she and Elena began helping the children to secure the mound.

Salvago and Maria moved from goat to goat, repeating the treatment. Each time the recovery was miraculous and swift. Salvago watched Maria's hands as she handled the goats, so tender and yet so strong, so slender and yet so sure, and there was a moment when she had to prod him, to bring him back from his reverie. Altogether they treated seventeen goats. When they finished they were exhausted, their faces and clothing caked with blood and grime. They washed themselves off in seawater.

Cawl, the silversmith, was the first of the men to return to the cave. His expression soured at the sight of the priest, and he responded in monosyllables to Salvago's greetings. Fençu and Jacobus returned soon after, carrying their catch. Fençu regarded the priest warily but thanked him politely when Maria told him what the priest had done.

"I must return to Birgu," Salvago said.

"Nonsense, Dun Salvago," Fençu said. "We are in your debt. You must join us for a meal." Jacobus's eyes widened, but Fençu knew what he was doing. "Go, Jacobus, and help Elli make the preparations," he ordered. Jacobus understood what he wanted, and raced to make certain all was ready. Although the Jewish artifacts inside the cave were never left out in the open, he would make sure.

They had had official visitors before: a census taker from the Order and a *ministrali* from the Università. Still, Cawl looked at Fençu as if he were mad, to invite the devil into their den.

They made their way down the steep slope to the cave, where Elli labored over the cook pot and fussed endlessly over their guest. They showed him only the front of the cave, the spring and the kitchen. Though Salvago was fascinated by the cave and impressed by its comforts, he sensed something of the subtleties swirling around him. There were furtive looks and hurried whispers, and blankets hastily arranged, as if to cover something. He misread the reason behind them, however. As bowls of stew were being passed around, his gaze fell upon the base of a candlestick that was all but lost to view. It was silver and had only oval bezels on the base where precious stones once rested. Salvago recognized it immediately, for it had belonged to his sister. He smiled inwardly. Surely these people needed its light more than Angela. At Fençu's request he delivered grace before the meal, standing before a crucifix in its niche on the south wall.

During the meal Salvago was acutely aware of Maria's presence. He watched her whenever he could, trying not to be too obvious. Her eyes shone in the glow of the fire, and her laughter rang easily and often. She was very much at home in this cave of *conversos*. He longed to make the others disappear, longed to rise and go to her, to take her to one of the dark places in the shadows behind the fire. Tormented, disgusted with himself, he turned his attention toward something Fençu was saying.

That afternoon when they returned to St. Agatha's, Maria thanked him for the hundredth time.

He waved off her thanks. "Some of the goats will still die," he said, "from the pus that will come."

"But not all." Her eyes glistened. "You are a gift to me, Father," she said. "A gift to all of us."

He said nothing, lost in an awkward mélange of pleasure and deceit.

❖

She was grateful, genuinely grateful, but nothing more.

Why should there be more, Salvago?

Still he tried for more, in another way. He had been ready to terminate Luca Borg's employment, as work on the bell tower had progressed as far as it could with the money he had. Already Luca had offered to work for half wages, knowing that otherwise there would be no work until spring, if then. Luca was desperate. Salvago approached Antonio Buqa, his brother-in-law, imploring him to provide the additional funds. Antonio grumbled but finally agreed.

Salvago told Maria of his success, even though he had not yet told Luca. Again she seemed pleased, but nothing more. He knew that she cared nothing for him as a man. He was a priest, a teacher. Yet that wounded his pride. He wanted her to look at him with different eyes. He wanted to be a man to her. It was ludicrous that his pride should be wounded. Vain, impossible, unholy. It was insanity.

And he couldn't help himself.

Alone on his cot, he closed his eyes and thrashed half the night. Her skin held him: its perfume, its perfection, its radiance. Unable to deny his flesh, he masturbated. Afterward he crawled from his bed, lay face down on the floor, and prayed. He scourged himself, shredding his back with a knotted leather thong. For days he couldn't sleep. His appetite left him.

Lord, help me. Near Thee I want to be a priest. Near her I want to be a man.

He moved through their next lesson as if through a dream, everything cloudy and vague and surreal. He corrected her letters and could not still the tremors in his hand, even when he rested it on the table. To hide it he stood and recited a list of words for her to write. Soon, softly, his hand touched her shoulder. For her it was nothing at all, only casual contact as he looked over her shoulder. For him it was like touching fire. Unaware of his desire, she concentrated on the work. It was all he could do not to gasp out loud.

Of course, nothing more.

Her very indifference began to make him angry. It was unreasoned anger, impossible anger, but still it ate at him.

❖

It was a bright Tuesday afternoon. The air was crisp with approaching winter. Maria ran through the streets carrying a parchment, her heart racing with excitement. The previous evening, by the light of a candle, she had finished her surprise. She'd read the result to Fençu and Elena and everyone else in the cave. It didn't matter that it was the New Testament, from St. Matthew. She'd written it from memory, a few passages at time, and finally—in her own hand— there were the Beatitudes. Her Jewish audience listened intently, awed by her magical powers if not by her choice of scripture. "Something from the *Nevi'im* would have been better," Fençu said good-naturedly.

And now she was going to give it to Father Salvago. She'd rolled it neatly and tied it with twine. She arrived at St. Agatha's, where she saw her father working in the belfry. He was giving his two helpers directions as they stood below, mixing a batch of mortar. In her exuberance she waved. He saw her and nodded, then turned back to his work.

It wasn't a lesson day, and Salvago was not expecting her. For days he had not been himself. He'd begged off their lessons the previous week, claiming illness. He was sitting in the sacristy, melancholy and alone. Customarily he drank very little, but now a bottle of wine sat nearly empty on the floor beside him. He was not happy to see her. He had finally and firmly decided to end the lessons, to put an end to his torment. It was the only hope for his sanity.

"I have something for you, Father." Her smile was radiant.

"I have no time today, Maria," he said gruffly. He stood, a little unsteadily.

In her excitement she didn't feel his mood. "I promise, I won't be a moment. You need only listen, and then I'll go." She unrolled the vellum.

"*Blessed are the poor in spirit. . . .*"

She read fluently, smoothly, never stumbling, and he was deeply touched by her thoughtfulness.

"*Blessed are the meek. . . .*"

He studied her as she read. Her tan jerkin was soft and supple. She wore a ribbon in her long hair. He watched her hands, poised over the page, delicate, slender hands that had produced the writing on the sheet, hands that, like the letters themselves, had grown more graceful, more poised, more lovely each week.

"*Blessed are you that hunger now. . . .*"

He watched her breathing, the rise and fall of her breasts, the lines of her throat, and the shape of her mouth as it formed the words he knew so well. He glossed over her little errors of omission or phrasing. He saw her cheeks alive with color, alive with life.

"*Blessed are the pure in heart. . . .*"

When she finished she looked up, knowing what pleasure she would see on his face. Hands trembling, he took the parchment from her. He examined it closely, with immense pleasure, and then he looked into her eyes. She smiled. He stepped forward, arms opening, intending to hug her. Startled but not alarmed, she drew back. "Father!" she said, her smile now uncertain. Her proximity was suddenly too much for him, and all of his passion welled up and he lost himself, and he was upon her. He swept her up in his arms. Stunned, she struggled, but he was too strong for her.

He laid her on the table, on her back, and his hands were on her, ripping at the cord that bound her jerkin, and when it fell away he pulled up her blouse, and his hands groped for her breasts. She cried out, but her cries went unheard behind the thick walls of the sacristy and the pounding from the belfry as Luca Borg split a stone. The silver crucifix that hung from Salvago's neck got into her mouth. She thrashed violently, trying to get it out, and she coughed and cried again, ripping it from his neck. He smothered her cries with his own mouth, trying to kiss her. She bit his lip hard, and tasted his blood. She pounded him with his own crucifix. It fed his madness. He pressed against her, fumbling at her pants. He got them down and felt himself throbbing, unable to stop, blind to her look, deaf to her cry, and he put his fingers in her. She was dry and tight, and she yelped in pain. He heard nothing but the frenzy of blood pounding in his ears, and then his cassock was up around his waist, and his pants dropped to his ankles, and with a violent shove he plunged inside her, thrusting, pounding, until his seed exploded from him and he cried in anguish and ecstasy and pain, terrible pain, his own cries now blending with hers. Yet still he did not hear her voice; he was blind and deaf and dazed. His hips bucked again, and he lay upon her, panting, his breath coming in great ragged gasps.

He lay there until the pounding in his ears subsided. He realized he could no longer hear sounds from the bell tower. There was only the sound of her sobbing. He lifted himself unsteadily, pushing up off the table. He bent to pull up his pants and felt a dizzying rush of blood at his temples. Dazed, he looked upon her. Her face was twisted in pain, her skin streaked with tears, her hair disheveled, the ribbon she'd worn lying on the table.

The parchment had fallen to the floor, along with the candlestick and the hourglass. The glass was broken. When his mind came back to him the horror of what he had done overcame him, and he reached to help her. "God help me," he whispered. "Maria, please forgive me. I don't know what came——"

"Get away!" Slowly, painfully, she pushed herself up and onto her elbows, and then she stood. He saw she was holding the quill pen, and only then realized she'd stabbed him with it. He felt his neck. The quill had nicked a small vessel. The wound was not serious but bled profusely. Between that and his lip, there was a great deal of blood, some of which had gotten on her face. Behind her, on the table, he saw more blood, and realized most of it was hers. It was on her pants, too. She clutched at her clothing, trying to fix it, brushing at it in a vain attempt to wipe away the stains and the horror. She only smeared it, and then she wiped her cheek, all the while her chest heaving with great sobs. As she got her pants up her eyes fell upon the heavy candlestick. She snatched it up and turned, ready to bash in his skull.

And at that moment Luca Borg tapped on the door of the sacristy and walked in. "Excuse me, Father, there is a problem with the——" He stopped, his mouth frozen before he could say whatever it was he came in to say. His eyes took in the blood, the candlestick in her hand, and the broken glass. He saw the terrified look on her face and the distraught one on Salvago's.

"*Father!*" Maria dropped the candlestick and flew to him, running right across the broken glass. Her feet trailed blood, but she felt nothing. "Father! He . . . he hurt me! He——" And she couldn't say it, and she buried her head in his chest. Luca made no move to comfort her. He stood rock still, unsure of himself. He pushed her away, gently but firmly. She saw the veins pulsating at his temples. His gaze clouded and fixed on Father Salvago. "Leave us, Maria," he said huskily. "Go home."

"But Father——"

"*Itlaq! Mur id-dar!*"

Maria bolted from the room, stumbling as she went. She ran through the sanctuary and half climbed, half fell over the rail, jarring two startled parishioners on their knees. Once in the street she just ran, ran with no thought of going home, no thought of anything at all but the terror. Birgu was a blur of faces and noises and places unrecognized. She ran through the haze, oblivious to it all, and finally, after what might have been one hour or three, not knowing how she'd even found it, she collapsed in M'kor Hakhayyim into Elena's arms, sobbing hysterically. It was half an hour more before she could get her story out. Her emotions veered wildly, from grief to rage. She paced and yelled and cried until her throat was raw. Realizing she was still holding his crucifix, now nothing but a ruby-encrusted sacrilege, she unwound the chain from her cramped fingers and threw the hated thing across the cave. It clattered off the wall and fell into some black place. She pounded bare fists against the rocks, until her hands were bloody. She tried to wash herself in the spring. The water was cold, and she began to shake uncontrollably. She needed to vomit. She hunched over, her insides twisted painfully, and heaved until there was nothing left but bile. Still it wasn't enough; still she wanted more to come, but it would not. All she could do was retch and cry.

Cawl came home, and later Villano, and each looked quizzically toward the noise. Elli shooed them away. Fençu stepped up onto the little ladder to Elena's perch and peered inside, his features etched with concern. "What can I do?" he whispered. Elena shook her head. He needed no second invitation to leave. He wanted no part of some woman trouble.

Finally, long after midnight, when the worst storms had passed and she was exhausted, Maria curled up in a ball and laid her head in Elena's lap. Elena stroked her hair, held her, and rocked her in the flickering candlelight.

"How could he . . . how? It hurt, Elena, it hurt so badly, and he wouldn't stop."

"Your father will kill him," Elena said.

"Yes. I pray for it."

"It will only make things worse."

"They could not be worse."

Elena didn't respond to that. Salvago was no commoner, and in

Malta only the knights were as powerful as his Church. *Oh, Maria, my dear Maria. What will become of you?*

Maria cried again, her soft wail filling the cave, her body racked by sobs. Elli brought a cup of honeyed goat's milk that she'd warmed on the fire. Maria drank it gratefully and a little later threw it up.

Finally, at dawn, she slept.

Chapter 19

Maria did not return to Birgu until late the next afternoon, Elena at her side. All the way home she worried to Elena that the *gendarmi* would already have arrested Luca Borg for the murder of the *kappillan* of St. Agatha's. Ordinarily a man's rights were absolute when it came to defending a daughter's honor, but against the Church, who knew which rights might prevail? Her father was a bull, and his wrath would have been awful. It would not surprise her to see him on the gibbet, and it would be because of her.

Isolda's eyes were red. At the sight of Maria she burst into tears, crossed herself, and disappeared behind the drape of her bedroom. Maria pushed it aside. Isolda was already face down on her bedding, sobbing. "Mother? What has happened? Where is Father?"

"He will be . . . here . . . ," Isolda began to say, but she couldn't finish for her tears. Maria had no wish to press it. Her mother was of no use in stressful situations. There was nothing to do but wait.

At least they had not taken Luca . . . yet. Relieved at that, Maria sat down next to Elena, whispering and weeping. She wrung Elena's handkerchief, twisting it until it was knotted, the waiting unbearable. No matter what Luca had done to Salvago, she didn't know how much of his anger might remain to flare at her.

Just at dark they heard footsteps on the cobblestone. One man. The door opened, and Luca Borg stepped inside. To Maria's astonishment he hung his bag of tools on its hook. Had he been at *work?* Surely that could not be.

He turned and saw them, his features highlighted by the tallow lamp. He stood quietly, staring.

"Father?" she said at last, her voice weak. "What did you do, Father?"

His gaze turned to Elena. "What is she doing in my home?"

"*Ahfirli,*" Elena said quickly, rising. "I'll leave."

Maria caught her by her sleeve. "She is here because I invited her."

"This is my house."

"Really, it's all right," Elena said softly. "I'll meet you later."

"If she must leave, so must I," Maria said.

"Suit yourself," Luca said.

It was going all wrong, before it had begun. Maria stood. "Father, please. I must know. What has happened with . . . with . . ." She couldn't finish.

He regarded her as he might a stranger. His expression had no softness to it. "What has *happened?*" he asked. "What has happened is what I warned you would happen. You brought this upon yourself. You have shamed yourself and dishonored me. You wallow in disobedience and revel in your pride. When will you learn your place in the world? When will you stop trying to be someone you are not?"

They heard Isolda weeping on her bed.

Maria shook her head in disbelief. "What has pride to do with this? He hurt me, Father! I did nothing!"

He shook with rage. "You wish me to say shameful things? Very well! He said you tried to have your way with him. You pawed him like a whore, and he stopped you before you could disgrace yourself! I saw you once before, hugging him! *Hugging* him!"

Maria remembered—it was the day Salvago had agreed to teach her, when she'd given him a quick hug of gratitude. She was dumb-founded. It was a moment before she knew what to say. "That was nothing! But you believe him before me? You believe that nothing happened? But you *saw!*"

"I saw nothing!"

"You saw blood!"

"*His* blood, where you stabbed him! I saw his wound!"

"Why would I do that unless he was hurting me?"

"Because he would not let you have your way!"

"And what will he say if I have his child? That the conception was immaculate? Of course! That is his profession, is it not?"

"*Blasphemy!*" Luca Borg roared. "You are a blasphemer and a whore! You will shut your mouth!"

Maria shook her head. "Do you want to *see?* Do you want to see how your own daughter has been violated?" Furiously she tore at the sash on her jerkin and fumbled at the button on her pants. "I'll show you where he ripped me!"

He caught her by the hands and lifted her almost off her feet, propelling her back against the wall. Her shoulder struck a shelf, sending bowls and cups to shatter on the floor. His face was close to hers, and she could feel his spittle and his contempt in every word. "You run with that whore and dress like one yourself, and expect me to believe you a *virgin?* What madness lurks in your mind? Show me you aren't a virgin, and I will ask only . . ." His face was so hot it went white. "*Which man was first?*"

She tried to slap him, but he caught her hand and shoved her to the floor. He towered over her, trying to control his rage. He did not hit her, because in such a rage as this his strength would get away from him, and he would probably kill her—yet he would be well within his rights. He would be judged by men who understood his shame, men who would share his grief at the loss of both his daughter and his honor.

"There have been no others, Father! How could you think that? And he isn't a man! He's an animal! I didn't tempt him!" She was furious with herself, because she was half sobbing while she tried to speak, and it made everything sound all wrong, sound weak. "I didn't do anything, except to read!"

"And in so doing you have summoned the devil to our door, Maria. Your soul is in immortal peril. But I would have known that even if he hadn't told me. I know your way!"

The light of understanding slowly dawned on her face. She struggled to her feet. "I see it now. You did nothing at all, did you, Father? He lied to you. You knew it was a lie, but he found some way to bully you."

He did hit her then, a fierce blow to her temple that brought lightning to her eyes and knocked her from her feet. She landed hard and hit her head on the floor. She blinked, trying to clear it. Her nose bled and her ears rang, shutting out her mother's lacerating wails. Elena ran to her side.

"Get out!" Luca Borg snarled at Elena. His chest was heaving, his big hands opening and closing. "Take the other whore with you, and leave my house."

❖

Maria had run from the sacristy, leaving Luca Borg standing dumbfounded, holding his heavy maul, a tool he used to cleave stone. His face was streaked with sweat.

"I—I have never seen the like of it, Luca," Salvago had stammered in panic. "She threw herself at me. I tried to push her away, but she was determined. You know how strong-willed she is. She wouldn't go." The priest shook his head. "I have no experience with this sort of thing. I was rough with her. Please forgive me. I grew angry. I told her she was risking her soul. She was furious, Luca. She stabbed me." He held up the quill pen she'd used, its tip black with ink and red with blood. He put his hand to his wound.

Unblinking, Luca took it in, his brain working to comprehend what his eyes were seeing. His eyes went to the blood at Salvago's collar. Even in his shock, Luca could make sense of that.

But his eyes went to the table, too, to the blood there, and that blood made no sense to him. There was more than there should be, and it was in the wrong place. Salvago followed his gaze, and saw the question in his eyes. "You see? I bled everywhere. It was all my fault, for agreeing to teach her to read. You were right in the first place. You know that, of course. You told me I was wasting my time. I had no idea. No idea."

Luca closed his eyes, his mind reeling. He was seeing things that no man wanted to see, things that were beyond his understanding. "But Father, I don't see how she could have—"

"It is as I told you, nothing more. *Luca!* Look at me." He dropped his hand and let the trickle of blood continue. "I will make no trouble over this. I will say nothing to anyone about it. It need go no farther than this room. There will be nothing to stain the honor of your family. You know how this would seem if anyone were to learn of it. I want only to spare you such humiliation."

Luca clenched the maul in both hands. The muscles rippled in his big arms as he squeezed and relaxed, squeezed and relaxed. Sweat poured from his brow.

"It will be all right, Luca. You'll see as we finish the bell tower. You want to do that work for the church, don't you? I have no wish to find another mason, but how can we work together if there is discord between us? Think of it, Luca. There will be work until spring. There will be time to help her, as we make this all right. You would be right to lock her away, but you mustn't be too hard on her. She was impulsive, that's all. She has always been that way, hasn't she?"

Luca nodded.

"Of course. That was what led to poor Nico's loss to the corsairs, wasn't it? It is her great weakness, but time and patience can change that. The important thing is that your honor is not lost, Luca."

Luca looked at him, his eyes blank, his brain still churning.

Salvago straightened his clothing. "Now we must get on as if nothing has happened, before the sexton returns from Mdina. We wouldn't want him to think anything was wrong, would we? I would hate for the bishop to learn of this. I fear he would make terrible trouble for you, though of course I would do everything in my power to help you. I'm afraid he would think first of the honor of the church, knowing it must be preserved at any cost. He would permit no stain on that." He knelt to pick up the papers and the bits of glass. "I think we should discuss the supports for the roof, don't you think?"

Slowly Luca set his maul on the table and knelt to help him.

❖

Having dealt with Luca Borg, Salvago spent two nights and two days on his knees, trying to deal with his conscience and with his God.

The bells rang for Lauds, and Prime. He did not hear. The sexton knocked timidly at the door. "Father? It is time for Mass."

"I am ill," Salvago said. "Leave me."

The bells rang for Vespers. He never rose from his knees.

Father, forgive me, for I have sinned. Deliver me from this sorrow. Help me to find purity of heart. Show me Thy will.

He could not eat or sleep. He lay all night on the stone floor, oblivious to the cold. At dawn he ripped off his clothes and scourged his manhood until the skin was shredded and bloody. He wept and beat his fists on the wall. He had never felt such loathing for any human being as he felt now for himself. His mind reeled at the evil that gripped his soul.

He prayed for the strength to quit the priesthood. He resolved to tell the bishop what he had done. No, he would not stop at the bishop. Stripped of his vestments, he would turn himself over to the civil authorities. More than once, he rose to do just that.

Each time he stopped, thinking of the lessons he had learned after the failings of his own youth, lessons he often recited to his congregation. *The sins of a man's past need not define his future. A life devoted to Christ is still within his power.*

I am a good priest!

He knew it to be true, and he could not ignore it. Yes, the sin of Maria was awful, a horrible wrong. But arrayed next to that were other deeds—done, it seemed now, by a different man.

No. Not a different man. They were done by me.

There was Santu Spiritu, the tiny hospital in a church at Rabat. It had blankets and medicine because Giulio Salvago had seen to it. There was Mariola Zammit, who had not bled to death of a compound fracture because he had found her alone in her field. *That* Giulio Salvago had applied splint and tourniquet and carried her on his own back three miles to help. Baptisms and births, weddings and funerals, souls helped because he had been there to help them. Countless deeds, big and small—unsung, unpraised, all but unnoticed. Works done with humility, without reward asked or expected. Good works, done for the grace of God.

I can do more, Father, if it is Thy will. I can turn this into some-thing beneficial by rededicating my soul to Christ. What more can any man do?

He would find some means of penance, some means of expiating his sins with good works. Salvation was still possible.

Father, if it is possible, let this cup pass from me. Let me find peace, though my faith be imperfect. I will forevermore deny my flesh and serve only Thee as a son of the Church.

Was that not worthy penance, a lifetime of service to his Church? Yet could there be true repentance if he didn't confess? Could there be forgiveness without repentance? If he confessed, his ability to serve his Church in little ways at St. Agatha's—or in bigger ways, God willing, at the Vatican—would be destroyed forever. His mind went round and round the argument, and if the logic was flawed, as of course he knew in his heart that it was, he would correct those flaws with good works, and overwhelm the bad with the good.

What was not flawed, he told himself, was his love of his Church.

What was not flawed, he told himself, was his desire to spread the word of Christ, and to enforce the will of His Church.

I must know Thy wish, Lord.

He knew a priest who had killed a man. That priest still served humbly and well. He knew priests who kept secret wives, and priests who occasionally used the collection plate for worldly ends. Good men with blemishes. Good men who continued to serve.

He was not prepared to abandon his Church. He could not allow good works to be snuffed out by a confession to the bishop, for if he did that all would be lost, and in the end, good souls, deserving and innocent souls, would suffer for his one sin of lust with Maria. *One sin must not destroy me. One sin must not destroy a good priest.*

He knew she would not make trouble. He could only pray that she was not with child. Somehow he would find a way to make things up to her.

Father, forgive me, for I have sinned. Help me to work Thy greater good. Help me to put the darkness behind me, and to see the light of Thy spirit.

He lifted his face from his hands and heard the bells of Vespers. This time he rose for them, knowing finally what he must do. It was time to tend to his flock.

Amen.

❖

Maria stayed with Elena for a week, then another, and another, without going near Birgu. Each week seemed to make the horror recede a little. She tended her goats and walked along the cliffs.

Jacobus knew something was horribly wrong but sensed it was a woman thing, and mostly he gave her a wide berth. She slept a great deal, and wept, and talked to Elena about what to do. "You must stop thinking about it," Elena told her. "There is nothing you can do now but find more trouble."

She awoke one morning feeling ill. Her stomach was sour and unsettled, as if she needed to throw up. She drank water, but it didn't help. The nausea took her to her knees, but nothing would come. She was retching when it struck her: *This must be the sickness that comes before a baby.* She asked Elena, hoping for reassurance that it was something else. "It's probably just a fever," Elena said lightly, but her real answer was in her eyes, and she knew it. Her shoulders sagged. "If it is . . . that," she said, "we can see Lucrezia. She can give you something."

Maria didn't know what she wanted, although she was certain she didn't want any remedies of Lucrezia's. She was restless. Her appetite deserted her, her hunger replaced by a sick feeling that gnawed at her belly and wouldn't leave her. At night she tossed and turned, unable to sleep. Dark circles lined her eyes.

I want to hurt him, she thought one moment.

I must listen to Elena, she thought the next, *and put this behind me.* She had always been sure of herself. Now she changed her mind a dozen times a day. She could not do little things, simple things. A mere word from Fençu or Jacobus about the weather or the sea could make her dissolve in tears.

One Sunday morning she went to Mass at St. Agatha's. The belfry was not yet complete. The rubble of stone and pallets of sand around the base told her that her father was still working there.

She went inside. No one sat, as there were no benches. She stood near the back, obscured by the crowd, and watched him. He read from the New Testament and smiled at his parishioners. Through benediction and blessings, he seemed maddeningly normal. And then he caught her eye. She saw all the color run from his face, as if a breeze had swept through the church and taken it from him. Head high, she stared at him. She couldn't read his expression, and then he looked away. She crossed herself and left. She walked the narrow streets of Birgu, wandering aimlessly. She stood near her house, watching. She saw her mother in the window, and then she saw it close.

That afternoon she waited near the church before Vespers, when she knew he would be returning from his sister's house. She heard the *clip-clop* of his donkey's hooves and heard the cart wheels rattling on the cobblestones. Then he pulled around the corner. He stopped the cart and sat rock still. The dust settled. An eternity of silence passed between them.

"What do you want?" he asked at last. The weeks of silence had convinced him he was right, that she would do nothing. Her presence now was unsettling, an affront to peace.

"I don't know," she said. "I want your apology for what you did."

"I have done nothing but pray for you." He put his hand to his neck. "What you have done is to steal my crucifix. I want it back."

"Your *crucifix?*" She shook her head. "You worry about a piece of silver? You should worry about its *meaning*."

"It is your good fortune that I have not pressed charges with the *gendarmi* for its loss. My patience is not without limits, Maria. Consider it a warning. And now, if you please, get out of my way."

A boot maker emerged from his shop, carrying a stiff leather hide. "Hello, *sur kappillan*," he said brightly to the priest. Salvago nodded politely.

Maria had not moved. "I think I'm pregnant," she said, loudly enough that the boot maker heard. The man turned as if he'd been stricken, and hurried back into his shop.

Salvago blanched and dropped the reins. She'd hurled at him what he feared most. He gathered his composure and the reins. "Then you must look to God," he said.

Her eyes flashed; his denial made her angrier than ever. "God has no prick, Father. I am looking to His priest, who does."

Now Salvago worked to control his own growing fury. "Get out of my way, Maria," he said. He whipped the mule and his cart lurched forward. She had to jump aside lest the heavy wooden wheels crush her feet. One of the wheels bounced through a puddle and splashed her with mud.

As she watched him disappearing through the narrow streets, she finally knew what she wanted to do. Elena was wrong, telling her to meekly accept her fate.

There was no meekness in Maria Borg. None at all.

❖

She went to the Università, the civil authority. Though the Knights of St. John were the true masters of the island, the Università still held sway in certain matters, including crimes committed against the king's law. A petty thief could be tried there and put to the stocks— and by Maltese, not the foreign knights, who cared nothing for the troubles of the common people. She knew nothing of its workings but hoped it was a place where she could make herself heard. She expected to be turned away at the door, but she walked right inside, where she stood among notaries and tax collectors and minor officials going about their business.

"I want to see the *Hakem*," she said to one who was passing by. The *Hakem* was the head of the civil and criminal court, with jurisdiction over all Malta, and head of the militia. She might as well have asked to see the Pope. The official's mouth turned up in the faintest trace of a smile. Without deigning to reply, he kept walking.

She found others, without knowing their rank or duties: the *falconiero,* who caught falcons, and a *baglio,* keeper of the prisons. They all shooed her away without listening.

Finally she was recognized by one of the *catapani,* a low-level official who tended weights and measures on the island and who knew her father. "Come in, Maria," he said, bidding her take a seat on a bench in an office where six other men were at work. He settled himself beside her. His manner was condescending; he was clearly amused at the boldness of this mere girl. "And now, tell me about this weighty matter that seems to so distress you."

His amusement did not last long. By the time she finished, his face had gone waxen. He looked around the room, to see whether the others had heard. If they had, they gave no sign. "You are a fool, child," he hissed. "Never repeat what you have said to me, not to anyone, do you hear? Do you wish to find yourself in prison? And your father as well? Such a tale can only end badly—"

"It is no tale," Maria said. "He . . . violated me. What are you going to do about it? I want to see the *Hakem*."

"That is quite impossible."

She raised her voice defiantly, so loudly, the others in the room looked up. "Very well. If you insist, I will tell everyone in this room my story. Perhaps one of them might—"

"Stay where you are," the *catapan* said. "Perhaps I can find a magistrate." Abruptly he left the room.

He returned half an hour later. He led her up a flight of stairs, then past a row of offices where various officials sat working. They entered a high-ceilinged room, much the same as the others. Two men sat at a heavy oak table beneath a great red and white shield. One of the men had severe features above a long jet-black goatee; he was writing in a journal. The man next to him was big, with a full gray beard and bright gray eyes. Maria's heart sank. She recognized him immediately, from the portrait hanging in his mansion. He was one of the most powerful nobles in Malta, one of the four *jurati*.

He was the Baron Antonio Buqa, husband of Angela Buqa.

Salvago's brother-in-law.

He looked at her indifferently. She took a deep breath, determined to press on. The man next to Buqa beckoned her to advance. She guessed him to be the magistrate, one of the highest officials. His expression was severe, but not unkind. Maria began to repeat her story to him. He waved her to stop before she could finish. "Be silent, child," he said. "How old are you?"

"Sixteen."

"Then this is a matter for your father, not for you. And most certainly a matter for the Church. Even if I wished to raise the point—which I do not, I might add—I would have no jurisdiction. Leave us now. And cover yourself. You are quite indecent."

"I will not be pushed away so easily," Maria said stubbornly. "I want to see the *Hakem*."

The voice was cold and final. "I *am* the *Hakem*," he said.

❖

Terrible cramps came, and then her flow. She was immensely relieved, yet she cried anyway, cried like a baby. Her tears confused her. They came often now, came for no reason, came when she saw a sunset, or ate a piece of cheese, or saw children playing. Tears for stupid things, for little things. Tears that never made her feel better, tears that left her drained.

Jacobus approached her timidly with a gift of seashells, trying to penetrate her black mood. "Leave me alone!" she said. "Go away!" He hung his head and she felt worse than ever, but she couldn't help it.

She went to the bishop's palace in Birgu. The entry door was imposing and heavy, and seemed as tall as her house. She found a groundsman in the courtyard and asked where she might find the bishop. He directed her to a low doorway on the far side of the yard, beyond a central garden.

A sacristan was at work inside, placing candles in a cabinet. She requested an audience with the bishop, but she wouldn't tell the sacristan what it was about. He told her to leave. "I will not. Tell him it is about one of his priests. I have a complaint."

"Yes, child? And that would be . . . ?"

"I will tell only the bishop."

"Then you will tell no one at all. His Grace is occupied."

She hid in the garden. In the early afternoon she saw him, walking with the sacristan. She stepped from her hiding place, and the bishop started in fright. Maria ignored the sacristan's glare. "I am Maria Borg," she said calmly to Cubelles. "Your priest Salvago violated me. I want to know what you will do about it."

The bishop's features hardened. "That is a serious charge, my child."

"Ask him about it, Your Grace. That is all I want."

"You may be certain of it."

She had fully expected him to waffle or to refuse outright. His straightforward reply caught her by surprise. "Th-Thank you, Your Grace." Feeling a trace of hope, she left.

Cubelles summoned Salvago immediately. The priest was gaunt, his features haggard. Dark circles rimmed his eyes. It was clear he hadn't slept in days. His hands displayed a slight tremor. "I have been ill, Your Grace," Salvago replied to the bishop's query. "A touch of ague, nothing more. It will pass."

Cubelles did not mince words as he repeated Maria's charge. Salvago looked his bishop square in the eye, his gaze never faltering.

"The child has gone light in the head," Salvago said. "I was teaching her to read."

"*Read!* A girl? Whatever for?"

"It was a foolish thing to do, Excellency. My fault entirely. I realize that now. I'm afraid she grew attached to me. She made advances. I rebuffed her. She is angry."

The bishop regarded him thoughtfully. Salvago was a reliable and obedient priest, a good shepherd to his flock. He worked tirelessly to improve the parish of St. Agatha's and the lives of his parishioners. The proofs were manifold. There were no whispered rumors about his behavior, and such rumors invariably made their way to the bishop's ears. There was no reason whatever to doubt his word.

"This is most distressing," Cubelles said. "I had been expecting to talk to you of another matter. I have received word from the archbishop. He said he had written you before about the possibility. There is need next spring for a priest fluent in French and German as well as Latin." Salvago read and wrote all three, in addition to Maltese, Sicilian, and two dialects of Italian. "A matter of research, I believe, at the Holy See, for the Council in Trent. It will last three years, perhaps more. A minor assignment, possibly, but one that carries great honor. He sent the request to me, knowing of course that while I would regret losing you, I would consent." The bishop gazed at him thoughtfully. "Frankly, that will be quite awkward should this matter not find its way to silence."

Stunned, Salvago lowered his eyes. "I am humbled by your consideration, Your Grace," he said. "I hope to prove myself worthy of your confidence. The girl will not long trouble us. I know her well. She will come to see the evil she is doing, and lay it aside for the good of her soul."

"See to it," Cubelles said.

❖

She was in the congregation the next morning, watching him, her face brazenly upturned in arrogant accusation. He concluded the service smoothly and afterward sent the sexton to intercept her. The man escorted her to the rear door, showed her inside, and excused himself. Salvago closed the door. She did her best to hide her fear.

He drew himself to his full height and stared unflinchingly into her eyes. "You have been very busy," he said.

"*Sì*," she said, staring back.

"You are meddling in things that are much larger than you, Maria. You have no idea what you are doing. You must stop this foolishness. I cannot fathom what you intend, but there is no possibility you will prevail. None at all, do you hear?"

"I did not start this, Father. I wish only to end it. I have heard you say that a sin must be confessed. That is all I want. Then I will let it stop."

"Very well. I confess. I am truly sorry for what happened."

"Not to me. To my father." She thought about that. "And the bishop."

"It is not your place to make demands of me."

"I thought confession was God's command."

"I will not debate you, child!" His face darkened; he was seething. "Stay out of my way, Maria. Do not push me further, lest you destroy yourself. You have no idea the trouble I can bring you."

"You have already given me all the trouble I can imagine."

"Then you have not imagined well enough."

❖

Maria returned to the bishop's palace. The gate was barred to her.

The next morning she waited until the prelate left in his carriage, making his weekly journey to Mdina. She caught it from behind and leapt inside.

"My dear Lord, child," Cubelles gasped, putting his hand to his chest in fright. "Can you not find a less disquieting way to announce yourself?"

"Your sacristan would not let me see you," she said. "There was no other way. I want to know what you are going to do." As before, she was calm, almost matter-of-fact, and that unsettled Cubelles considerably. He would have found it easier to deal with a ranting madwoman.

"I have interviewed Father Salvago. He assures me your charges are groundless. Apparently there are no witnesses to these claimed events, save your own father."

"He did not see it all."

"Yet Dun Salvago tells me your father will bear him out."

"He has twisted my father."

"So all the world conspires against you, child? I think you must pray forgiveness for your false witness."

"It is he who needs forgiveness, Your Grace."

"I have known Giulio Salvago for years. He is a good priest."

"He is a better liar."

"*Coachman!*"

The driver drew up the reins sharply and jumped from his seat.

"Now, if you please," Cubelles said firmly, "my patience is at an end. Leave me proceed."

"You must *do* something," Maria said, refusing to move.

"Unquestionably," Cubelles said. "I shall pray for you, of course." He nodded at the driver, who reached up and caught her roughly by the arm, pulling her toward the edge of the seat. He lifted her out onto the cobblestones and set her down. Off balance, she fell. The driver climbed back into his seat and whipped the mules.

Maria picked herself up and watched them go.

The Church had given her its answer.

❖

Jacobus didn't understand. Overnight Maria seemed to have lost all her sparkle and fire. She sat alone in the cave, staring at the fire, and the others avoided her, too. Sometimes at night he thought he heard her weeping. She showed no interest in the goats. He made her a blanket from rabbit skins. She accepted it politely but without warmth.

He thought it must be because he was ignorant, too simple for a woman who could read. But that made no sense, either: he hadn't become ignorant overnight. He tried to strike up small talk with her, but it quickly withered.

Using expensive bits of wood imported from Sicily by the Order and expropriated from the Order by Fençu, Jacobus made a lute, piecing the pear-shaped body together from much smaller pieces. It was a triumph of perseverance and quite handsome-looking, but an acoustic disaster. Everyone laughed at the sound except Maria.

In his misery he mentioned it to Fençu, who by now had learned the truth of the matter from Elli. "Don't fret, Jacobus. It is nothing to do with you. It's that someone . . . someone insulted her deeply."

"I'll kill them," Jacobus said hotly.

"You can't," Fençu lied smoothly. "They've left the island already and won't be back. The best thing you can do is give her time. She'll be all right, you'll see."

Still Jacobus brooded. He wanted to ask her about it, to show his concern, to let her know she could rely upon him to protect her. It was out of the question. Even if he felt bold enough, he knew he wouldn't know how to say all that. Such words were beyond him.

❖

Her father came to the cave. He stood outside and called down to her. For a long while she ignored him. But that was foolish, she told herself as he called again and again. *I have done nothing wrong.* She braced herself for his wrath as she climbed the steep path to where he waited by the carob tree. But he seemed subdued, and in that, somehow more dangerous. There was a desperate tone to his voice. "Please, Maria. You must let this pass. You must stop making trouble."

"I did not make the trouble."

"You make it now, then."

"Has he threatened you with your work?" She knew the answer from his eyes.

"For myself, I would not care. But your mother will suffer."

"*I* have suffered, Father."

"You brought that upon yourself. Now you visit it upon others." His eyes flashed their old anger. "I have raised a . . ." He could not finish. The power seemed gone from him. He knew it was no use. She would never see reason, not even if he beat it into her. "To the devil, then, for all of us, on the back of your pride. May our ruin be upon your conscience."

As she watched him walking away, a lump rose in her throat. She felt petty and small. Her life seemed to cause nothing but trouble for everyone she knew. Though she was furious at her father, the last thing she wanted was to hurt him or her mother. Yet she knew she was not finished. Her anger was stronger than her guilt. No matter what Luca Borg said, she could not give in.

Only one avenue remained to her, and it was obscured in mystery. Everyone knew the Knights of St. John were the true masters of Malta. If a man needed hanging, it was usually the Order that hanged him. If a peasant stole a rabbit, it was the Order that chained him in the galleys. Even the *Hakem* of the Università paid homage to the Grand Master. Maria knew vaguely that the Order was somehow tied to the Church, and that the Grand Master somehow had the ear of the Pope. It was said that not even the bishop wielded more influence in Rome.

However it worked, she was certain the Order could make Salvago pay.

She presented herself at the gate of the Castello St. Angelo and demanded to see the Grand Master. She fully expected the page's rejection. "He is not here," the boy said with disdain.

"Then I will wait," Maria said.

"Suit yourself, so long as it's out there." Day after day she waited, knowing he would have to emerge from the castle sooner or later. Only after three days did a knight finally notice her presence and inquire as to her business. "The Grand Master is in Spain," he said.

Maria glared at the page, who snickered. "What of La Valette?"

"He is away on caravan," the knight replied.

"Who, then, might I see with a serious charge about someone?"

"Regarding?"

"A priest."

"The bishop."

Dejected, she left the castle.

"You must forget this," Elena said gently. "You cannot fight him. No matter how you try, you'll never hurt him as he hurt you."

A part of Maria wanted to do just that. She despised standing in foyers and reception halls, trying to make herself heard to arrogant people who wouldn't listen or didn't care. She wasn't even certain what she was trying to do. Did she really only want his confession? Did she want revenge? Justice? Or something else? She only knew her pain hadn't stopped when he did. It seemed to go on, a nightmare with no end. She kept feeling him inside her, groping and tearing at her flesh. Sometimes the memory of it made her retch. Sometimes it made her weep.

She hated herself, for her weakness. She hated him for being stronger than she, and for making her afraid. In a way she envied her mother, who knew how to hide from the world, behind cloak and tears. She wished she could hide and knew she could not.

In the end, she supposed, Elena was right. It didn't really matter what she wanted. Against Salvago, pillar of the Church, she had no voice.

Chapter 20

That might have been the end of it, but for the Purification of the Virgin.

The icy winter winds blew from Europe. It was early February, time for the Feast of Candelmas, celebrated to commemorate the Blessed Mother's presentation of her child to the temple. There was a tradition that all the parish priests of Malta and Gozo met on that day with the Grand Master. He would address them on the problems of the day, after which they would present him a gift of a richly decorated candle. Every year the candle grew more elaborate, more magnificent, as local craftsmen vied for the honor of producing it.

In a land where relations were often strained between the Order, the nobility, and the Church—with the peasantry caught between— Candelmas was always greeted with great optimism and fanfare. Along with the priests, all of the most important dignitaries of the islands attended, and even those commoners who could crowd themselves in were invited to join. It was the occasion of this ceremony that gave Maria her idea. She told Elena immediately.

Elena thought it was funny until she realized Maria was in deadly earnest. This was beyond revenge; it was lunacy. "Don't do it," Elena warned. "You will visit more trouble upon yourself. You might as well piss on a hornets' nest."

"What more can he do to me now?"

"I don't know. But I don't think you should try to find out."

"Well, I'm doing it. Are you going to help me or not?"

"Of course," Elena said without enthusiasm.

In the middle of the night they sneaked into St. Agatha's to get what they needed, and carried it back to the cave in a sack. Elena expertly worked the waxen tallow until it was just the way Maria wanted. Then Maria picked up a knife and with a deliberate motion cut her palm, letting the blood drip onto a plate. With a goat-hair brush she finished the work.

She stood back and regarded it proudly. Despite Elena's fears, not a flicker of doubt shadowed Maria's mind. She needed only to think of *him* and all qualms vanished.

It was four in the morning when they slipped into St. Lawrence, the conventual church of the Order of St. John where the ceremony was to be held. The interior was dimly lit by votive candles and two oil lamps suspended from the ceiling on chains. Fine tapestries lined the walls of the church. Above the sacred altar hung an image of Our Lady of Damascus, which the knights had kept with them from the time of their origins in the Holy Land.

Already there were nearly two dozen candles standing on a trestle table in the vestibule, brought by villagers who wanted them blessed by a priest for Candelmas. In the center of them all, standing on a silver platter and draped with crimson damask, was the Grand Master's gift from the parish priests. Maria removed the cover, revealing the work of Mattheus Carnoch, a noted silversmith. His candle was magnificent, crafted in the shape of Fort St. Angelo. Around the base of the fort, bas-relief images in copper and tin depicted religious scenes—the Blessed Mother, the presentation of Jesus in the temple, the shipwrecked St. Paul. It was an exquisite work. They replaced it with their own, carefully covering it again.

"Ours is smaller," Elena said nervously.

"But better," Maria replied. "Anyway, no one will notice until it's too late. Everyone will be watching the Grand Master." They put Carnoch's work beneath the table, where it was concealed by the tablecloth that ran to the floor. An hour before dawn they left the church, stopping to rest on a low wall near the harbor. "We just have to wait now," Maria said.

"I . . . I don't think I can," Elena said. "I feel ill." Her face was ashen. Her nerves were not as strong as Maria's.

"You should go home and rest," Maria said. "I'll see you this afternoon."

"I don't want to leave you."

"Nonsense. I'll be fine. I'm only going to hide and watch. I'll tell you every detail."

Maria had one more item of business to complete before daylight. She needed the necessary clothing. She slipped in and out of her house easily, without disturbing her parents.

Three hours later the service began. The old Grand Master, the one-eyed Spaniard d'Homedes, had died. The new Grand Master, elected by vote of the knights, was a Frenchman, Claude de la Sengle, a grave and proper man. He wore a simple black habit, and around his neck the Cross of Profession, its eight golden points flashing. There were twenty knights in his train, including most of his Sacred Council, composed of the leaders of the langues of Auvergne, Provence, France, Aragon, Castile, England, Germany, and Italy, the eight national groupings of the Order of St. John. Behind them came some of the Knights Grand Cross, the most senior members of the Order. A score of Maltese aristocrats followed, and then priests and friars, who took their seats of honor flanking the nave. Mattheus Carnoch was there, to see his work unveiled. Only rarely on the island did such a confluence of noble and holy blood come together in one place.

At the rear of the church there was a little room left over, for commoners. Maria Borg stood among them, cloaked in black, her face concealed by the barnuża. Her robe was heavy and oppressively hot, and she found it difficult to breathe. She had to continually adjust her hood and veil but was grateful for the anonymity.

The conventual chaplain led the service. A monk sang the Nunc Dimittis, his deep voice resonating through the church. Prayers and more hymns followed. The Grand Master spoke grandly of reconciliation between the Order and the clergy of Malta. He announced plans to construct new fortifications and import more grain from Sicily. He spoke in French, so that Maria, along with three-quarters of the nobles, monks, and priests in attendance—and all of the commoners—did not understand what he said. She tried to see Salvago, but in the crowded church her vision was partially blocked. She saw with regret that Bishop Cubelles was not in attendance. He would have been sitting near the Grand Master. Instead his place of honor was occupied by the archdeacon of Mdina, a pompous and portly man.

When the Grand Master finished, four priests, including the archdeacon, rose from their seats and filed to the trestle table holding their gift. One priest at each corner, they lifted the large silver tray and carried it forward in solemn procession, singing a hymn. They set it on a stand in front of de la Sengle. "Your Excellency," said the archdeacon, "in the name of the Father, and the Son, and the Holy Spirit, accept this, symbol of the victory of light over darkness." The Grand Master nodded graciously.

Throughout the church, people strained to see Carnoch's elegant craftsmanship, artistry that would forevermore grace the chapel altar of St. Anne's, inside Fort St. Angelo. Such candles were for display, not for burning. Such candles were for the ages.

With a flourish, the archdeacon pulled away the linen.

It took a long moment before what now stood on the silver tray became clear, during which there was stunned silence. At last someone gasped; another muttered a prayer. Mattheus Carnoch crossed himself, and shrank in his seat.

What faced the congregation was a large model of St. Agatha's. Planted nearly upside down in the bell tower was the silver crucifix of Giulio Salvago, its rubies glistening blood red. Real blood ran from its end, staining the front of the church. For those few who might not recognize the crucifix, the initials *G.S.* were etched on the bell tower. Below that, printed in small bloody letters on the façade, the words were clear:

THE KAPPILLAN HAS SHAMED THIS HOUSE

The Grand Master glared at the archdeacon. The priest trembled, his jowls as crimson as the damask he held in his hands. His mouth worked, but no sound came out. Finally, gathering his wits, he threw the cloth back over the candle. A shock wave of murmurs rippled through the church. While not everyone had seen what now lay hidden beneath the linen, enough had. The service was brought to a speedy conclusion. Hymns were skipped, the sermon forgotten. The benediction was half its normal length, delivered by the archdeacon, who, having at last found his voice, spoke so quickly it seemed his tongue must be on fire.

Nobles, knights, and clerics began to leave, making their way through the crowd of commoners, who stood aside to open a path to the doorway. Well concealed in their midst, Maria held her *barnuža* firmly in place, leaving only a tiny slit for her eyes. She saw dignified faces, white in shock. Righteous faces, grim in fury. Impassive faces, secretly savoring scandal. And finally, the face she sought. She wasn't certain what she relished more on that face: the agony, the anger, or the fear. Certainly his step was unsure. Beads of sweat glistened on his forehead. His eyes were averted, his gaze locked on the floor. He did not see her.

Beneath her *barnuža* Maria smiled a joyless smile. She knew she had hurt him. She had struck a blow from which he would not soon recover. But the taste of it was more bitter than sweet. It wasn't enough. Only once before in her life had she known hatred, for the men who took Nico. She had never found the bounds to that hate, and she knew this would be the same. She honestly wanted *not* to care anymore. She wanted to be done with it now, to take Elena's advice and put it behind her. As long as he drew a breath, she doubted it was in her. Still, despite its limits, her little victory was sweet.

She took a long walk afterward, strolling along the south coast to the towering cliffs of Dingli. The sun was glorious, and she felt its warmth and life. For the first time in weeks she truly heard the gulls and watched them play on the air currents. Her stomach rumbled with the first real hunger she'd felt in a long while.

Perhaps, after all, there had been more light in that candle than she'd thought.

❖

It was late afternoon. Maria was still a distance from the cave when she saw smoke billowing from the escape tunnels near the carob tree. The smoke was dark, not like that the cook fire sometimes made. She began to run. "*Hemm xi hadd?* Elena? Fençu? Are you all right?" Near the tree she saw the ground was saturated with blood. She saw tufts of hair from a carcass.

The goats.

She raced down the path to the entrance but had to stop. The smoke was choking, too thick to go in. "*Min hemm?* Anybody?" There was no answer. She turned and saw Elli near the water, with four of the children. She scrambled down the hill, slipping and sliding and scraping arms and legs as she went. Elli was standing in the shallow water, picking out bits and pieces of things, trying to rescue them before the waves took them. She seemed confused.

"Elli? Elli? Are you all right?"

"We got here as they were leaving," Elli said. "They let me stay, because of the children. They have Fençu, and Elena, and Jacobus, and—"

"*Who,* Elli? Who has them? Where have they gone?"

Elli looked bewildered. "I don't know. My *mizrach.* Look what they've done." She clutched a bit of her wall painting. Sodden from the sea, it was coming apart in her hands. She struggled up from the water and tripped, gashing her knee on the sharp rocks. Her blood mixed with the sea foam around her dress, turning it crimson. The *mizrach* fell to the rocks, disintegrating further. She began to sob. She tried to pick at the painting, but the thick paper was dissolving, its colors smearing, the images no longer recognizable.

Maria helped her up. There was a pile of things Elli had already tried to rescue. Maria recognized Fençu's beloved *megillah,* the parchment with the Hebrew words. It had been shredded first, then thrown into the water. She saw the shattered remains of the iron cook pot, and shards of the shofar, the ram's horn that sounded *tekiah* at Rosh ha-Shanah. A cotton sabbath cloth had caught on a piece of the horn. It fluttered and whipped in the wind.

"Who, Elli? Was it Salvago? Was he here?" She caught Elli by the shoulders, trying to bring her out of her shock. "Was it the priest, Elli?"

Elli held a piece of the *mizrach* to her cheek. She shook her head. "The *gendarmi,* from Mdina. Other men, too. One of the *jurati,* I think. He said Fençu stole a candlestick. He seemed to know about it. They found it, too. Fençu never melted it. I told him he ought to, but he liked that one. They said we hunted game without permission. We did, it's true. Whose permission but God's must we have in order to eat? The magistrate took the pelts, to use in court. He took the *etrog* container, too." She looked up slowly when she said that, as a moment of clarity returned to her. At the same instant Maria's hand flew to her mouth as it hit her, too.

"They must know we're Jews."

Maria steadied herself, fighting off the dizziness that overwhelmed her as the world swirled out of control.

"They *must* know," Elli said. "But why wouldn't they say so? The *gendarmi* only said Elena was a whore." The confusion settled over her again. "Can you imagine? Elena would never . . . Jacobus hit him when he said that, and they took him, too. He's just a boy, he didn't know what he was doing, but . . . Please, Maria, help me find the rest of the *mizrach,* will you? Fençu loved it so. He will be so hurt to see it like this." She groped among the rocks. "They burned everything they couldn't break. The straw, our bedding. They'll burn us, too. I need to find a place for the children to stay. They said Fençu will spend three years on the galley bench for the hunting, if he ever gets out of prison for the candlestick. That couldn't be right. They can't send a man to prison if they've burned him first." She was rambling, babbling, her voice all but lost in the roar of the surf. "They slaughtered some of the goats, to roast at the Candelmas festival tonight. They took all the rest, Maria. Everything. They'll slaughter us, too. Slaughter us like the goats, don't you think?"

Maria's brain reeled. *I brought him here. This is all my doing.* "Stay with the children, Elli. Wait for Cawl and the other men to come home from Mdina, and then get away from here. Hide. I must go to them."

"No! They asked me where you were. They want to arrest you."

"For what?"

Elli wiped at her eyes. "What does it matter?"

❖

Maria was still in her clothing from the morning, the robe and *barnuża*. She hurried into Mdina, hiding her face and slouching a little, like the other women on the streets.

She found Elena in the square. She was hung in a *rituni,* a large net suspended from a beam. Generally, prostitutes were only ordered to move away. Occasionally they were lashed. For more serious offenders, however, the authorities hauled out the *rituni,* in which the offender might hang without food and water for days. People came to stare, to point and laugh and taunt. Some of the men, the ones she'd been with, recognized her, and hurried away, often with their families in tow. Maria drew her *barnuża* tight and approached the net. She heard Elena then, weeping softly.

"*Elena!*" she whispered.

Elena looked down in alarm and wiped her eyes. "You shouldn't be here! Go away! They'll catch you, too!" Her voice was hoarse.

"Are you all right?"

"Yes, but I'm thirsty. Do you have water?"

"I'll bring some." At that moment a guard came and shooed her away.

Maria hid until late that night. She sneaked through the deserted streets, back to the square, keeping an eye out for the guards who sometimes patrolled the streets, even after the gates were locked. "*Elena!* I brought a skin." She passed it up, but it wouldn't fit through the net, so Elena had to prop it up outside while she stuck the neck through the mesh. She drank deeply. "Thank you," she said, her voice low and hoarse. "It was the *jurat* Buqa who ordered this," she said bitterly. "I reminded him I'd slept with him once. He denied it, of course. He told me they are going to boil holy water and scald my thighs with it before they let me go."

"It wasn't Buqa," Maria said miserably. "This is Salvago's work. You were right, Elena, and I was wrong. I never thought . . . I should never have done this. It's *my* fault."

"You never did anything wrong, Maria. He did. Don't give him the satisfaction of thinking he won."

Maria felt the tears gathering at the corners of her eyes. She took the skin back and grasped Elena's hand. *He* has *won,* she thought. "Do you know where Fençu is? And Jacobus?"

"I only know they flogged them both. They might be in the *fossa* or the prison." The *fossa* was a deep ditch where prisoners were often confined after punishment.

They heard someone coming. Maria hid. Two men strolled at a leisurely pace through the square. They stopped and looked at the *rituni* and the whore inside. They laughed quietly and walked on.

"You'd better leave," Elena said. "You are not safe."

"I'll be back tomorrow," Maria promised. She went to the *fossa* and peered over the edge. It was empty. That left only the prison. She could never reach them there, not without money. The thought sent her back to Elena. "Do you have any money hidden at the cave? I'll need it for bribes."

"I did, but they found it. They took it all."

❖

Devastated, she tried to think of what to do. She knew Cawl and the others likely had no money. There was no one else to help. She found a perch in the rocks near Birgu Creek and huddled beneath her robe, listening to the water lapping against the sides of the boats. Sleep would not come, only guilt and self-recrimination, and fear for her friends. *How many lives will be destroyed because I wanted revenge?*

As the sun rose over Sciberras, she knew there was only one thing to be done.

She went early. She knew he would be there, waiting.

The door to the sacristy was partly open. It took all her courage to walk in. He was sitting at his desk, staring at the flame of a candle that had burned to a pool in its dish. He looked up at her. It was clear that he hadn't slept either.

"So your cowardice extends to my friends," she said. "I would have thought you would just rape me again and then kill me."

His expression did not change. Leaning forward, he pulled something from a canvas sack on his table. Maria's heart skipped when she saw it, but she kept a steady expression.

"Ah, yes, your friends," he said. "The fools who went to that cave didn't know what they'd found." He turned it around and around. "It is very well made. It's an *etrog* container, if I am not mistaken. It is most remarkable to find such a thing in a cave." He looked up at her. "I believe *Jews* use it, for one of their filthy rituals. They put fruit in it." He paused. "Do you know, Maria, what becomes of *Jews* in the kingdom of God?"

"I don't know what you mean," she said without hesitation. "My friends are *conversos*. Christians. I have prayed with them myself. If the thieves who went to the cave gave you everything they found, then they gave you a cross as well. That is what they pray to. They will tell you so, and I will swear to it."

"I'm certain you will. In fact, I have no doubt you are strong enough to die for that story, on a rack," Salvago said. "But I wonder—how will the children do near fire? Or your friend—Elli, isn't it? What will she say with a hot iron at her eye?" Her eyes told him it was all but over. "So much trouble over this," he said. "Ordinarily I would take great pains to extract the truth from your friends. But you have it in your power to see it all ended. Don't you understand? I need only tell the *gendarmi* it is all a mistake, and your . . . *conversos* can go back to their lives. I will leave you in peace, Maria Borg."

She knew he could see her fear. She could not hide it. "What is your price?"

"You must first agree that your lies will stop. I must never hear another whisper about these things."

"They are not lies."

"Very well," he said, shrugging. "Then we are finished already. I must go now. There is much work to be done, with whores and thieves and *marranos*."

With every shred of her being she wanted to defy him. But there was no decision left to be made now, none at all. Elena was hanging in a net, and Fençu and Jacobus were in cells. Every friend she had in the world was at risk, because of her.

Only because of her.

Her shoulders sagged. She was beaten. "*Kollox sew*," she said, nodding. "I will never speak of the rape again."

Salvago stood before her. "It is not enough, Maria. Get to your knees."

"Please. Do not make me do this. I will say nothing more to anyone. You have my word, and my word is good."

"*Get on your knees.*"

Slowly she sank to the cold stone floor.

"There was no rape," he said. "You must say it."

"There was no rape."

"You must swear it in the name of your Savior."

"You would add to your sins by making me commit another?" She said it dully, too numb now to feel the pain.

"Say it!"

"There was no rape. I swear it."

"In the name of the Lord Jesus."

"Please," she whispered.

"In the name of the Lord Jesus."

She closed her eyes and felt a hot tear searing her cheek. "I swear it in the name of the Lord Jesus." Barely audible, but she knew he heard.

"Next you must say it to the bishop himself and forever cleanse this stain from your soul."

There was no going back now, no argument left inside.

Of course she must go to the bishop and say it. Of course she must cleanse this stain from her soul.

She went to the palace in a fog. Everything ran together. The jolting ride in the cart, and the leering sacristan who admitted her, at Father Salvago's side, into the bishop's drawing room. Falling to her knees once again, tears pouring now down her cheeks. Domenico Cubelles, kindness and compassion on his face, listening to her confession as she admitted her lies. The feel of his fingers on her forehead, tracing the sign of a cross. His words, as he prayed for her salvation. *Lift up your heart, my child.* A cup of milk in a silver chalice, warmed, handed to her as they tried to calm her tears. *Lift it up to the Lord.*

Climbing back into the cart, assisted by Father Salvago, who touched her as gently as if she were a porcelain feather. His face, a minute or an hour or a year later, as he told her it was time to get down, that face twisted—perhaps in anguish, or was it anger? Were those tears in his eyes as he took his leave and the *gendarm* led her by the arm?

She didn't remember. It might have been a dream. It all ran together, lost in the creak of iron hinges as they closed the heavy stocks over her, and she said the words they told her to say, said them over and over, as loudly as she could with parched throat and cracked lips, said them for three days, so that everyone, knight and priest and commoner, could hear.

I lied about Dun Salvago. The sun beat down on her in the square, and she said it again and again, and all could see from her tears and anguish the remorse she truly felt.

I lied about Dun Salvago. May God have mercy on my soul.

❖

The priest was true to his word.

Elena and Fençu and Jacobus were released the same day she was. She was glad they hadn't seen her in the stocks, and that no one else from M'kor Hakhayyim had, either. Only her father saw. He was there one evening when she looked up, standing across the square. She couldn't see him clearly. She blinked and cleared her vision, and he was gone.

The *gendarmi* told them all their belongings were forfeit, including, of course, their goats. They returned to M'kor Hakhayyim and began putting the pieces back together.

Jacobus told defiant stories about his confinement, wincing as Elli tended the bloody weals on his back, but trying to remain brave in front of Maria. He thought more highly of her than ever. He had gone to jail for defending Elena's honor. Although there was no open talk of it, he knew Maria had been in trouble as well, and he thought it was for the same thing.

Elena sat near the spring. She held a bit of charred cloth, all that she could find of her possessions. Maria sat with her, desolate because she knew they'd taken everything Elena had. Her money, her candles, her goats—everything. Elena's eyes misted, but even so, she did her best to comfort Maria, knowing the guilt she felt. "You must remember it was the priest who brought this about, not you," she said. "He has taken only our things, not our dreams."

The cave had more hiding places than an army of *gendarmis* could find in a week, and Fençu found the menorah, still hidden in its customary place.

"You must destroy it," Maria told him when no one else could hear. "Dun Salvago found the *etrog* container. He *knows*."

At first Fençu was not inclined to do any such thing. "I have already done much to deny my faith," he said. "Perhaps it is time to be willing to die for it." But there was Elli to consider, and the children and all the others. In the end his pragmatism won the day. He and Cawl stoked the fire until it was roaring. They melted the menorah, to use its silver to buy things they desperately needed. "One day we will rebuild," he said simply, watching the fire. "Our home is M'kor Hakhayyim, the source of life. There will be another menorah."

Maria drew strength from their strength, but as the menorah melted she knew there was something else she had to do. She could not let his evil be. She could not let the threat of his retribution hang over their heads.

It took her a while to think it through, to be sure. She collected marram grass to use in place of straw for bedding, and helped clean the ashes from the cave, and picked debris out of the spring. Fençu bought new spoons, a cook pot, and other necessities. Maria and Elena and Jacobus went to the fields, looking for wild goats to start a new herd. Slowly life returned to normal.

One Sunday morning before dawn, she quietly climbed up near the throat of one of the cave's chimneys, to one of the weapons caches. She felt along a cleft in the rock until her fingers touched the cold steel of an arquebus, an old Spanish matchlock rifle. She felt again for a tin of powder and a sack of shot. She wrapped everything in her robe, climbed the rest of the way up the chimney, and crawled out one of the hidden exits. She concealed everything in a ravine and returned to the cave to wait.

No one noticed in the afternoon when as she stirred the fire she took a live coal and put it into an ember tin, a small metal box with air holes. A while later she excused herself to take a walk, retrieved her packet from the ravine, and walked to the road that connected Mdina and Birgu, her mind racing with her plans. She had not prayed about it, for fear her resolve might falter. When it was done she would bury his body beneath a mound of rocks, so that no one would ever know what had become of him.

Nothing mattered now, except to finish it.

She found a pile of huge quarry stones dumped amidst a wasteland of rock. There were countless places to conceal herself, from which she would have a commanding view of the approach from Mdina. He would come that way as he returned to Birgu from his sister's house.

She took the gun from the robe. Though she'd never actually fired the weapon, she had practiced with it many times during Fençu's drills, and knew what to do. It was heavy and awkward. She worked patiently. There was plenty of time.

She poured powder into the barrel, and tamped in a lead ball. She threaded and clamped a length of slow match into place. She shook priming powder into the flash pan. When all was ready she checked the ember tin, shielding it with her hand and peering through one of the holes.

The coal glowed red in the blackness.

Dark red, like the rubies on a crucifix.

Dark red, the red of old blood.

There was nothing to do now but wait.

Nearly an hour later, she saw dust rising from the road. Her heart began to pound. She crouched as close to the rocks as she could. She lit the slow match with the coal. It crackled and then burned more steadily, just above the flash pan, its tip glowing in the breeze, waiting for the release of the trigger.

He came into view. His face was placid, unsuspecting, his mind elsewhere. Maria tried not to let anything about him distract her, tried not to let her concentration waver. She hefted the weapon, the muscles in her arms quivering with the strain. She propped the butt of the gun against her shoulder and steadied the barrel against a rock.

You are about to die for what you did to Elena and Fençu and Jacobus. She took careful aim, just ahead of his position, working out exactly when she would have to pull the trigger.

You are about to die for what you did to me.

He was quite close now, his donkey's hooves clip-clopping on the rocky path, his cart bouncing along. The smoke from the match got into her eyes. She rubbed them quickly and blinked, trying to clear her vision, now clouded by tears. She aimed at the center of his chest, at the crucifix hanging on its chain. It struck her that he had a new one. The old one would have been an embarrassment, she supposed, no matter that she—*the whore*—had recanted.

Her hands sweated as her fingers worked the match. Her mouth was as dry as the powder. Her muscles ached as she sought to keep the heavy barrel from wavering. It seemed to have a life of its own, moving from the crucifix to his belly to the center of his nose. He bounced in the cart, which made it worse. Holding her breath, she pulled the trigger. The mechanism moved match to powder, and the weapon fired.

The heavy lead ball thundered from the barrel, striking Salvago in the head at almost the same instant as the roar from the gun sounded. There was no breeze to carry away the smoke, which hung heavily in the air. The kick of the gun threw Maria from the rocks to her back, where she lay stunned, gasping for breath. Her shoulder throbbed painfully. The gun lay at her side in the dirt. Gasping, she struggled to her feet and scrambled back up to look.

Salvago was still upright in his seat. He seemed dazed, his hand at his scalp where the ball had creased his skin. He took his hand away and stared at the blood. Slowly it dawned on him what had happened. He scanned the rocks.

And then he saw her.

She knew there was no time to reload. She had a knife in her jerkin. If he came for her, she would stab him with it. For now she picked up a rock and waited, gazing defiantly at him, daring him to come, dreading that he would.

He didn't move. She threw the rock. It struck him on the shoulder. She picked up another.

But Salvago still did not climb down. He stared at her. For a moment it appeared he wanted to say something to her. He swallowed and his lips began to move, but the words died somewhere inside him.

He flicked the reins and a moment later was gone.

❖

Once out of her sight, he stopped his cart and climbed out, overcome with nausea. Violence made him physically ill. He thought about whether he ought to send the *gendarmi*.

There was not much point, really. She had sought her measure of revenge and failed. And now it no longer mattered. That afternoon he had bid his sister and brother-in-law farewell. He was making his way now to the wharf, to board the grain ship bound for Syracuse. From there he would catch another, to Civitavecchia.

The port of Rome.

The port of the Vatican.

At long last, the mother Church had summoned her son to her bosom.

Book Four

ASHA

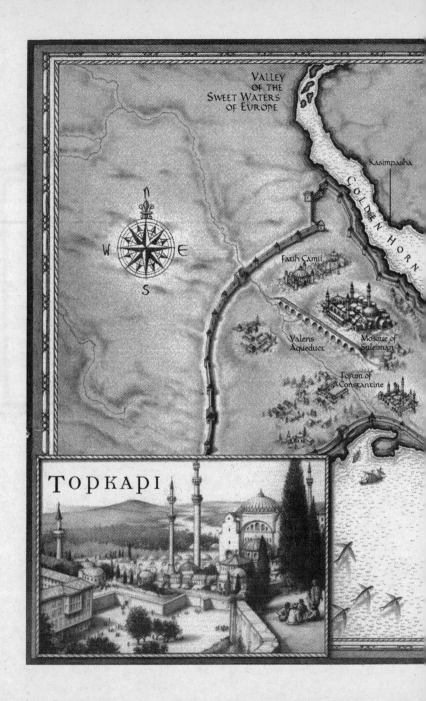

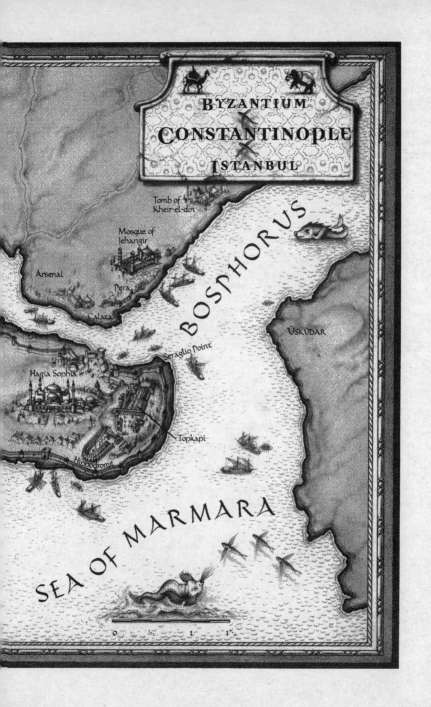

BYZANTIUM
CONSTANTINOPLE
ISTANBUL

Tomb of
Kheir-el-din

Mosque of
Jehangir

Arsenal

Pera

Galata

BOSPHORUS

Üsküdar

Seraglio Point

Hagia Sophia

Topkapi

Hippodrome

SEA OF MARMARA

0   ½   1   1½

from **The Histories of the Middle Sea**

by Darius, called the Preserver
Court Historian to the Lord of the Glorious Realm, the Sultan Achmet

Who are the Turks and the Ottomans? It is simple. To be Turk is a matter of birth. To be Ottoman is to be a citizen of empire. To be Ottoman is a state of mind.

That state of mind sprang from the loins of Ertoghrul, a minor tribal chieftain who helped the Anatolians fight the Mongols. It was his son, Osman, who was the first to gird on the Sultan's sword, the sword of the house that bears his name, the house of the dynasty of the Ottomans.

In a prophetic dream Osman saw his descendants ruling over a realm with its seat in Constantinople and its influence felt even more widely than that of the great empires that had come before: the Persians, the Romans, the Arabs. He saw it stretching from the Caucasus to the Balkans, saw its subjects taking the waters of the Nile, the Tigris and Euphrates, the Danube. He saw falling snow in the north of this empire and blowing sands in the south.

To achieve his dream Osman united loose clans of Turkmen, rugged nomads called ghazis who roamed the steppes of Eurasia on smart, tough ponies. Their tribes had been driven to the west by the Mongols. These Turks filtered into Anatolia and under their Sultan began nibbling away at the frontiers of the Byzantine Empire, the eastern half of the old Roman Empire, crumbling under the weight of its own decadence.

The third Sultan, Murad, established a base at Gallipoli, a peninsula on the European shore of the Dardanelles, from which his armies probed Europe and began to attract the attention of its fractious masters. One after another the towns of Byzantium fell as the Ottomans consolidated their hold over all of Anatolia, the Balkan peninsula, and the Crimea, finally claiming nearly all the Black Sea.

At last, their strength sufficient, they struck for the great prize of

Constantinople. Known from antiquity as Byzantium, this city was a cross-roads of seas and continents, of cultures and commerce. In A.D. 1453 the seventh Sultan, Mehmet, laid siege to the city with his artillery, in whose use his gunners had been instructed by Europeans. The students outshone their masters, and the city that had for centuries held at bay Hun and Slav, Arab and Avar, fell at last to Mehmet's guns.

The conquests did not stop there. The ninth Sultan, Selim, known as the Grim, defeated the Mamluk armies, drawing Damascus and Cairo into the Ottoman fold, followed by Palestine and its holy city of Jerusalem, and the Arabian peninsula, with its holy cities of Mdina and Mecca. These conquests made the Ottoman Sultan the caliph, the spiritual leader of Islam.

The empire did not flourish solely by force or by chance. The first Sultan, Osman, established principles that guided his successors and survive to this day: the pursuit of justice over power and wealth, and a tolerance for all the people of the earth. Under the broad Ottoman tent live men of diverse religions, races, and cultures. Though the empire is Muslim, its Sultan the premier defender of the faith, many of its subjects practice other religions, which the Ottomans tax but do not forbid. Only pagans and the Safavid dynasty of Persia, composed of heretic Shi'ite Muslims, draw the unwavering attentions of the Sunni sword of our Sultan.

It was Orkhan, second Sultan of the house of Osman, who began the practice of using Christian mercenaries rather than fighting nomads to defeat his enemies, a practice that later matured into the devshirme, a levy of the brightest and strongest Christian boys from the Balkans and other regions. The genius of this system was its creation of a caste of gifted, zealous men whose only loyalty on earth was to the Sultan, who could thus turn his attentions to matters of empire rather than the intrigues of court that so plagued other dynasties. The devshirme did more to put a bloom on the Ottoman rose than perhaps any other feature. In Europe a man of incompetence and low character could attain the highest levels of society so long as he was born well, while a man of great gifts might languish forever as a peasant. Among the Ottomans only merit and ability mattered.

By the tenth Sultan, Suleiman, Osman's dream had come full flower: the empire he ruled had no equal in all of written history.

—From Volume II
The House of Osman: The Sultans

Chapter 21

I am called Asha.

It is a Persian name, given me by Lord Dragut. It means Protector of Fire.

Fear not, Maria. I am still Nico.

I have never forgotten thee, as I pray each night thou hast not forgotten me. I trust good fortune has smiled upon thee, and upon our mother and father.

I reside in the seraglio, the Abode of Bliss, which is a jewel in the crown of Istanbul, the Abode of Felicity. Above the palace gate is written "May Allah make the glory of its master eternal." Its master is the Padishah, Suleiman, Lord of the Two Worlds, Shadow of God on Earth, Possessor of Men's Necks. I am told to say these things whenever I utter his name. There are other titles for him: I think the best is Kanuni, the Lawgiver, for truly that is his mark among men.

I write this by the light of a candle, shielded by my blanket. It is three in the morning. I know this from the hourglass that keeps the time for our prayers. There is no other time to write thee. We retire near midnight and rise at dawn, and our day is supervised at every moment. Even now the danger is great. I risk not simple punishment but death. The eunuchs watch us from raised platforms. Most are vigilant, but they cannot see all things at all moments. Of more danger to me is the Page of the Key, who prowls with guards through the dormitories. If I am caught writing during the hour appointed for sleep, I shall feel his lash on my belly. If he reads this letter, I shall lose my very head, for the thoughts I wish to write are forbidden, and would reveal a liar, the Nico beneath the Asha. No one knows I am from Malta. When I came here I lied so that I might find work in the shipyards and thus escape. Alas, fate has not smiled upon that wish, yet the lie remains: they think me Venetian. Still, I *must* write, must put words on paper to make them real, for fear I might otherwise lose thee forever. It is only the thought of thee, Maria, that has kept me sane in the years since I last saw thee.

Though I have written this letter in my head a thousand times, it has taken three years to begin. At first, of course, I could not write. The Sultan taught me through his tutors, as he teaches all his children. Besides music and poetry we are taught Greek and Persian and Turkish and Arabic, and, for those of us who can manage, even Italian and Spanish, so that one day, when we rule all the world, our subjects will understand us.

You see:

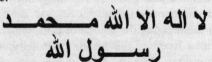

La illaha illa Allah! Mohammed rasoolu Allah! There is no God but Allah, and Mohammed is his Prophet!

I have chosen these words only because they show my finest calligraphy. I must admit I write them with pride. My hand, it is said, forms the best characters in the school, a talent that is much prized. I say the same words at prayer five times a day. I say them from my head, but never from my heart.

I am still Nico.

Learning to write was easy. Stealing pen, paper, and ink was not. Everything is watched. There is an official for each detail of life in the palace—a man to watch paper, another to watch pen, and a third to allot ink—and when all is not accounted for, heads roll. Until now there was no place to hide the letter once written. I was confined to the Küçük Oda, the Hall for Newcomers, where they watched me even as I relieved myself. But I have been promoted to the second school, which is in the dormitory called Büyük Oda. It is the Great Hall, a huge building constructed of stone. At times the earth shakes here, and so the walls have grown cracks that make hiding places. One is near my cot, where a loose stone permits me to conceal small things. So I will write a little whenever I may. It is my prayer that one day I will meet a trader in whom I may place my trust, that he may give thee this letter, and that it will find thee well.

I am a student in the Enderun Kolej, the royal school in the palace. It is said to be the finest school in all the earth. I was brought here by Dragut Raïs—yes, Dragut, scourge and pillager of our islands. "Forget your past," was the first thing he told me, "for it does not exist." Though he is my patron in the court of Suleiman, one day I shall kill him. This do I swear, for no matter his words, I am a page with a past: I am still Nico. This letter is my proof.

The year I came here there were six thousand boys my age, levied from among the Sultan's subjects throughout his domains, from Egypt to the Balkans. All wished entry into this school, which the Sultan himself once attended. The aghas felt our skulls, looking for bumps, and gave us tests. One hundred were selected. I am one of the chosen. My skull, it seems, is well shaped for the House of Osman, and it is said my face is pleasing to the eye. Thus I am now an *içoglan*, a page of the privy household.

The other boys, the ones not taken, were sent to schools outside the palace. The lowest is at Gallipoli, where students are trained for sea duty. I thought of trying to seem stupid, so that I might be assigned there and find a means to escape, but before he left, Dragut told me something else: "Though you seek to fool, do not fail to impress. On this will your future, your very life, depend."

I protested that I had not sought to fool anyone, but he only smiled. I am relieved that of all men, he alone seems able to look inside my head and know my thoughts, though I deny them. Iskander, my *lala*—my tutor—suspects me of not being who I say, but though he is the equal of any warrior on earth, his mind is not the equal of Dragut's. Iskander tries to draw me out, testing, probing, but it never leads anywhere. I could fool him all day, though the same is not true of Dragut. Yet for reasons I do not understand he did not betray me. His patronage has been of great value to me, and though he has long since departed to make war on the infidel—forgive me, I mean our own Christian navies, of course—I have come to trust his word. He was right: birth is of no consequence here, only ability. Even a boy of low origin such as myself can become Grand Vizier, second in rank only to the Sultan. Among the Ottomans failure in competition is not worn well. There is no gain in doing poorly. There is only gain in doing well. Do well and advance. Advance and find a way to escape. These are the words I say along with my prayers. My opportunity will come.

I want to be the *raïs* of a galley. Nothing is freer than the sea, no glory greater than to lead a ship into battle, no taste sweeter than that of victory over your enemies. With my own galley, God willing, I may go wherever I wish, whenever I wish. With my own galley I might turn my guns on Dragut or on a merchantman. With my own galley I am master. I swear to thee now that one day the Sultan himself will escort me through the Gate of Majesty and down to the Golden Horn, where I will step aboard that galley. He will think it is to further his interests, while in truth it will permit me to bring this letter to thee with my own hands. It is to this end I play the Ottoman game of phoenix, in which they seek to put an end to the Christian boy Nico, and from the ashes of his soul raise the Muslim man, Asha.

I am treated well, especially considered next to my life in Algiers. Someday I may tell thee of that time, which I would as soon forget. Most of the recruits are Slavs, from the Balkans, or from the conquered territories of the Turks. There are no Jews or Gypsies, but there are Bohemians and Hungarians, Poles and Russians, and Circassians and French—the last kidnapped or taken in war. I am the only Maltese.

Like me, all pages were born Christian before they were taken in the *devshirme,* the levy. Unlike me, they have embraced Islam. They must do so of their free will or face terrible consequences. The year I arrived, one page decided he could not in conscience follow the divine path. He was not yet big enough to serve as a slave on the Sultan's galleys—a fate worse than death—so his *lala* settled for the lesser punishment and lopped off his head. All the pages watched. His head rolled to my feet, where his sightless eyes beheld mine. I felt his accusation, even in death. I am shamed that I have not shown his strength of faith. I hope thou dost not think too ill of me, that I have not given all for my God and escaped this place through the Gate of the Dead.

Most taken in the levy will become Janissaries. If I cannot become *raïs* of a galley, it is what I myself wish, to become a master of Janissaries, an agha, but for now they laugh at me and tell me I am better suited for writing and study, and life at court. My teachers say I was born to write the history of the Ottomans, not to make it. They speak of Asha; Nico will do neither. The Janissaries are the Sultan's very best soldiers, the elite of the elite. They have no equal on earth save perhaps the Knights of St. John, though even in that I am not certain. They seem beyond human. They are expert with bow, musket, and scimitar, and most speak four languages. I have seen them massed together in the first court, standing for hours without movement or sound, their hands clasped in front of them in the fashion of holy men, looking in their white felt bonnets like so many marble statues. Statues they are not: they have warred for their Sultan from Trebizond to Damascus, from Budapest to Smyrna—places I never knew existed before the House of Osman taught me. When their training is complete and they leave their barracks and go out into the world, they walk on shoes that are spiked with iron, and carry torches that burn hot for Islam: thus they are said to be one part iron and one part fire. It is said they shall march on Rome one day and circumcise the Pope. I do not credit this blasphemy, but if anyone on earth could do it, I believe it would be the Janissaries.

We learn to ride and shoot, to cast the javelin and wrestle. At sport, it is true, I am not the equal of the Albanians, who are the fiercest of all the boys here, or even of the Serbs and Croats and Bosnians, whose very spirits seem bred for war. Though I try mightily to beat them, it is usually they who draw first blood. Very well, it is *always* they who draw first blood. For the moment the only games I can always win are those used by the tutors to refine our memories. They show twenty different colored stones in an order that is always changing, then mix them and ask us to replace them in order. I can do it without thinking. I am the only one. I sometimes think my memory is my curse. I remember everything—every word, every story I am told, every sura and verse. In this school I would rather be accomplished at sport, as it makes a man fit better with his friends than does a good memory. Yet in some ways my ability has been an advantage. I have advanced faster than the others, learning in one month what takes them six, and I believe that advantage will only increase with the years, when wisdom becomes more essential than physique. The coursework is no trouble. Apart from the languages, we are taught *isaret,* a sign language used in the court, along with history, geometry and geography, mathematics and law, and of course, the Shari'ah of Islam.

The Chief White Eunuch is the Kislar Agha. He is Keeper of the Gate and master of this school. He is fat, cruel, and unmerciful, and he has summoned me before him a score of times, to test me. It is my nerves that are most tested on such occasions, for his displeasure is terrible indeed. I gather I have done well enough, for he has not yet had me flogged or beheaded, Allah be praised. I write that last from habit.

Oh, Maria, already the hourglass is half emptied. The hour nears when the muezzin will call for prayer. There is so much to tell thee. My hand cannot write quickly enough.

Four times a year I am paid, as are all pages, and twice a year I am given new robes: two rich kaftans of scarlet, and light cotton robes for summer. I wear a cap, and my hair hangs long from each side, in the manner of Joseph, son of Jacob, who wore his hair this way during his long years of slavery. It is to remind us we are slaves of the Sultan. There is no shame in it; all men and women are slaves of the Sultan. As pages, we may not grow a beard, for a beard signals freedom. For me it is no matter: nothing grows on my face anyway.

I am required to use the *hamam,* the bath, once a week. That nonsense began in Algiers and just got worse here. I did not like it at first, but now I savor the smells of the bath—

sandalwood and musk—and I have grown accustomed to the cleanliness of life. You would not recognize me in my silks and without my dirt. I smell as sweet as a rose. Even my clothes are washed with scented soaps. The food is as plentiful as the other miracles of the place. The Ottomans know nothing of famine. There are figs and melons, plums and pears, and even red cherries from Saryar. There is swordfish served in grape leaves and roast lamb served on skewers. Although I have seen such things with my own eyes, I must admit my own fare runs more to rice and broth and sesame oil. Yet there is always plenty of it, and a sweetmeat when things go well.

On the face of the earth there surely can be no more beautiful place. It is a paradise of satin and silk, of white marble and pink jade and tooled leather. Gilt and mosaic tiles cover every surface, making even Allah's rainbow seem pale.

The seraglio straddles a finger of land, surrounded on three sides by water. Sometimes in the evening I am able to scale the ramparts, where I sit and watch the sun and moon, the numberless stars and the equally numberless ships that sail the Bosphorus. From there it seems I can see forever, yet I must remind myself I see only two continents and two seas of the Sultan's realm. There is more, of course. More beyond sight, beyond imagining.

Though I have seen but a fraction of the palace, it is easily larger than the whole of Birgu. It is greener, too, although you know that takes but little green. The gardens are an Eden of fountains and pools, planted with trees and flowers carried from every corner of the earth. There are tulips and roses, lilacs and hyacinths, boxwoods and narcissi—flowers whose names were once as unfamiliar to me as their sight and smell. By day the air is alive with their color, by night sweet with their perfume.

Peacocks and ostriches roam freely with gazelles and deer. The fountains shimmer with goldfish and silvery carp. I have drunk from a freshwater fountain, using a cup secured with only a silk string. The cup was made of gold!

Every day envoys arrive bearing gifts for the Sultan. Though they hail from the greatest courts of Europe, from France and

Venice and Russia, it is the Sultan and not their own sovereigns whom they call the Magnificent. Their gifts are presented to the Chief Present Keeper, and there are so many the Sultan rarely sees them. In the gifts can I see the awe of their givers. I have only heard of most, but with my own eyes I have seen an emerald the size of an egg. Diamonds are as sand beneath the feet of the Sultan, whose pockets are filled daily with aspers and gold coins to dispense among his subjects. The pages who undress him at night are allowed to keep whatever he has neglected to give away. It is a job I would not mind.

Life in the seraglio is organized to the finest detail, all of it centered, of course, on the Grand Seigneur, whose every need is tended, whose whims are anticipated and satisfied before he even has them. His water is carried fresh each day from a spring in the hills above Eyüp and guarded by the Janissaries. There is a Pickle Server, and a Bearer of the Royal Tray, whose sole mission on earth is to hand a silver to the Padishah. There is a Parer of Nails and a Keeper of Robes, a Chief Turban Winder and a Keeper of the Ornaments of the Imperial Turban. These pages, whose number I might join, will become ministers and viziers and *beylerbeys,* all of them lords of the realm. There are so many, too many to name: a Master of the Napkin, and pages who stand over the Sultan's bed with lighted candles to prevent assassination attempts. There are those who stand alert while he sleeps, ready to restore his bedcovers should they slip during the night. They, too, have no other occupation, content that through their efforts the most exalted being on earth shall never feel a night chill. Perhaps one day, if I write well and learn metaphysics and geometry, I shall with my own hand feed the Lord of the Age a pickle. For now I see him only from a distance, as one might see a cloud. Whenever he approaches a whistle is blown softly, permitting us to hide so that the eyes of the Padishah shall not be taxed looking at commonplace things.

There is a Master Cook, of course, and a Comptroller of Butter. The Chief Confectioner alone has four hundred assistants, and there are fifty tasters to make certain no poison reaches the Sultan's lips. Countless hundreds of cooks feed the endless thousands who live here, here in the center of government and learning and law and religion, here in Allah's garden, the center of all the world. With one hand (and the help of three thousand assistants) the *Bostanji Bashi,* the Head Gardener, sees to the cultivation of bulbs and bushes. With the other he holds the scimitar of state, with which he lops off the heads of traitors and troublemakers. The heads are parboiled and salted and hung over the gates, through which pass the flower of the empire. It is always thus in the seraglio of Suleiman: blood above, silk below.

Every manner of man may be found here, all working with great dignity to further the interests of empire: there are physicians and philosophers, astrologers and architects, carpenters and water carriers, timber cutters and grooms. Suleiman is father to us all.

Along with my other studies I am learning a trade. All here do so, from page to Janissary, following the Ottoman custom against the day of adversity. Even the Sultan: he is a goldsmith. I chose to be a woodcarver. I am given exotic woods from all corners of the earth. I have carved Koran stands from the satinwood of Ceylon, and miniature galleys from fragrant sandalwoods. My best work, I think, is the engraving of wall panels that bear the Sultan's *tugra,* his seal. I am pleased to say they are highly regarded. One hangs, I am told, in the palace of the Grand Vizier. Mostly I love the smell of the shavings and the feel of the sharp tools in my hands. The workshop has a glorious view of the sea. I can see the real galleys from there, plying the Marmara on the Sultan's business. They keep fresh my desire to be master of a ship one day. When that day comes, all men will call me captain: *Raïs.*

Asha Raïs: it has a pleasant ring.

The royal stables house the Padishah's forty favorite horses, plus mounts for his pages and viziers, with whom he takes exercise or makes the hunt. Some horses are bred for speed, and all for war. There are fast Arabians, sturdy Turkomans, cunning Karamanians, and noble Persians. The last are ridden by the Akinjis, the savage light cavalrymen who sow confusion and terror in the hearts of their enemies. The horses here have a better life than any man of Malta. Each mount is tended by several groomsmen, devours rich grain from a velvet bucket, and wears jeweled bridles, saddle blankets inlaid with sapphires, and stirrups made of solid gold. They want for nothing.

On feast days I have seen creatures called elephants. They are larger than our house, large enough to crush a man with one foot, yet docile as fawns. They have long gray noses as thick around as my chest, from which they spray water! There are giraffes, yellow-necked giants tall enough to peer over the battlements of St. Angelo. I swear it, Maria! And there are lions and other bizarre beasts that perform tricks—even pigeons that wear pearl anklets, and turn somersaults in the air for the Sultan's pleasure. Owls are used for hunting, along with falcons and hawks. They wear jesses of leather and silk. I have not examined their droppings but imagine them inlaid with amethysts and rubies.

I could write thee of such marvels for weeks without pause, though I have seen only the smallest portion of it all with my own eyes. It is as if Allah—I mean God, of course—built a paradise for Himself on earth and left His keys with the Sultan. I was near despair when I first left thee, and even now I yearn for thy comfort, but it is into Suleiman's lap I have landed. There are harder ones.

The dawn grows near. May the angel Gabriel protect thee. Be certain I shall write again, as life and the Chief White Eunuch permit.

Chapter 22

"The house of Osman is master of all life and death. The bringer of good, the adversary of evil. To it do you owe your breath, your sustenance, your life. The Sultan is your father, your protector."

The voice of Iskander rang out over the ranks of his pages. He was mounted on his massive Turkoman charger and dressed in magnificent silks and leather: a consummate warrior, the epitome of Ottoman ferocity, grace, and ingenuity. Olive-skinned and muscular, he had an aquiline nose and a striking black mustache waxed into elegant curves. There was iron in his high cheekbones and steel in his dark eyes. He held power of life and death over the twenty pages arrayed before him, their bright faces upturned. He was their *lala*—their mentor, their tutor, their terror.

Other *lalas* rode before their own charges, giving similar speeches, preparing their pages for the games that were about to begin. Iskander's words were as familiar to Nico as the first sura; he repeated them endlessly. Now Iskander's horse pawed at the ground and pranced nobly back and forth as he spoke, as if to emphasize the master's words.

"For your father the Sultan I will teach you to run like the wind, fight like the devil, and worship like the damned," he said. "Or I will teach you to die trying." Today, in these fast and perilous games, all knew that some of their number might do just that. Yes, Iskander would teach them how to die, just as he taught them how to live. He was schooled in all the graces of palace life. He could play the fiddle and the cane flute, mend the hem of a silk robe, and cook a seven-course meal. He instructed his students in the domestic arts of the palace and in the martial arts of the field—wrestling and archery, swordsmanship and marksmanship. For every discipline there were other instructors, of course, the very cream of the empire, but the *lala* was always there.

Iskander never bedded his own pages, only those of the other *lalas*. It was in his other vices that his unpredictability lay. His eyes often burned red from hashish, and it was said he would crawl through fire for opium. All Nico knew for certain was that Iskander could turn from gentle tutor to brutal inquisitor in the space of a breath. He was forever testing, challenging, seeking to rid the Enderun Kolej of the weak, the unfit, the infirm. Of every twenty boys who began with him, only five would last to the end.

Today, in the ruins of the Hippodrome, the colossal stadium built by Septimus Severus, a few more would be dismissed for failing to distinguish themselves on the field of honor—a field where the Emperor Constantine and sixty thousand of his subjects once watched chariot races and state executions, a field where sometimes the Sultan himself sat on a throne of lapis lazuli, watching the greatest warriors of the day engage in contests of skill and strength. Today it was two teams of pages from the Enderun Kolej who would compete—one team wearing sashes of red, the other green— and it was the Agha of Janissaries who would preside. He sat beneath a silk awning next to the Kislar Agha, the master of the Enderun Kolej. Though the two men held immense power, the contrast between them was striking—one, the warrior, hard and lean and brown; the other, the eunuch, soft and fat and white.

Eager crowds pressed in on either side of their pavilion. Warriors claimed the best vantage points. Besides the Janissaries there were Peyks, the foot guards; Sipahis, the cavalry; and Solaks, the Sultan's archers. They wore gold robes and gilt hats, satin bonnets and quilted turbans. These seasoned fighting men would coolly judge the ranks of pages and place discreet bets. Beside the soldiers were crowds of guildsmen and merchants, whose own betting cushions jingled with silver.

"War is brutal," Iskander said to his pages, the reds. "War destroys. Yet there is an ecstasy to it that the rest of life cannot match. When you die on the field of battle, when you hold your guts in your hands and know you are about to perish for the glory of Allah, you will dance in your own blood, secure in the knowledge that you shall sit in Paradise at the side of the Prophet. One day I expect each of you to die for Suleiman, son of Selim Khan, son of Bayezid Khan, son of

Mehmet Khan, conqueror of this unconquerable city. In the name of Suleiman, greatest of them all, you pages gathered here shall one day lay claim to all the world."

He raised his javelin over his head, its banner whipping in the breeze. "God is great!" he yelled. His charger rose on hind legs and pawed the air.

Stirred to frenzy, the pages of the red team roared back in unison, Nico among them: "*Allah Hu Akbar!*"

Near the other end of the Hippodrome, the greens raised their cry as well. "*Allah Hu Akbar! Allah Hu Akbar!*"

At that Iskander rode off, his green sash streaming behind him. In typical fashion he would fight against his own pages, probing for weakness.

The teams formed at opposite ends of the Hippodrome. The reds gathered beneath the porphyry obelisk of Theodosius, now three thousand years old, carried from Heliopolis in Egypt. The greens massed beneath a twisted column that was in fact three intertwined bronze serpents. Their great heads once supported the golden tripod that stood before the Temple of Apollo at Delphi, one of the treasures of the ancient world looted by Constantine as he sought to grace and glorify Constantinople, his new Rome.

In the field between them were the remains of the spina, a wall that had supported grand statues. The spina terminated in pylons that marked where the chariot racers were to turn. Now it all lay in ruins, a litter of toppled marble columns and shattered piers, remnants of glories past. Much of the stone had been stripped from the Hippodrome, used to build the even greater glories of Ottoman Istanbul. The games the Ottomans played—the important ones—were held not in a stadium but in the world. It was on this insignificant rubble of old glory that the pages would meet, vying for the honor of establishing a greater, new glory.

Nico stood with his friends, all nervously preparing. Each page had been issued a breastplate of stiff leather and brass, a helmet with a nosepiece, and a heavy oak javelin that was nearly twice his own height and as thick around as his wrist. The tips were blunted and wrapped with cloth to render them less deadly for the games, although this precaution was not always successful.

"I'm hungry," Shabooh grumbled. He was a skinny Bulgarian

whose lean frame looked as if a good stiff breeze might blow it away. "Cinch my breastplate, will you?"

"You're always hungry." Nico tightened the leather straps beneath Shabooh's arms, then turned to let Shabooh do his.

"True enough, but trust the agha to make the games during Ramadan, when we are too weak to piss, much less fight." It was the afternoon of the last day of the ninth month of the lunar calendar, a month during which no food or water could be taken between sunup and sundown. Everyone's strength was at low ebb. The Kislar Agha had chosen this day for that very reason, to test the mettle of his pages.

"You'd better not be too weak to piss on Titus," Nasrid said. Nasrid was a burly Macedonian whose neck was as big as Shabooh's waist. "He's riding with the greens today, and he's the very devil on a horse." Titus was an Albanian, the fiercest of all the pages. He was always the fastest runner, the best archer, the last wrestler standing. "He'll come after you, Shabooh, because you're smallest, and because first blood tastes best."

"*Last* blood tastes best," Shabooh said, "and if we ride together, we'll beat him together."

Nico felt the weakness of hunger, too, but the knot in his stomach stemmed from something other than fasting. He had played this game once before, the year after he came to the palace. He'd broken his leg that day, and it was not the pain he remembered but the humiliation. He was afraid now—not of injury but of failure. He was terrified he would fall in the first rush, or even in the first three.

"You are lucky to ride Mujahid," Nasrid said to Nico, looking approvingly at his mount. "Fit for an emperor, that one. Far more worthy than his rider today."

"I hope you're right," Nico said, grinning. He had never ridden Mujahid, a glorious chestnut Persian. There was always a new mount for the pages, in order that they learn the feel of different horseflesh and remain forever adaptable. Nico ran his hands down each leg, checking knees and cannons, ankles and hooves. Nasrid was right. Mujahid was superb.

Cooing, Nico slipped the horse a handful of sweet radishes he'd kept from the previous evening's meal. Nico had considered eating them himself. He could have done so secretly earlier in the day, but he chose not to violate the *sawm,* the fast of Ramadan. As Mujahid delicately emptied his palm, Nico wondered whether a horse could violate the fast by eating. But then he remembered the groomsman said the gelding was one of a dozen captured from a French galleon. "So you are a eunuch, Mujahid," he said. "But a good Christian one. Eat well, then, my friend." Mujahid nuzzled him, looking for more. Nico stroked his nose and saw the spirit in the eyes. "Fly for me," he whispered. Mujahid whinnied softly and stretched his neck against his reins. He was ready.

A trumpet sounded. The pages swung up into their saddles.

Nico sat in line with the other reds, anxiously watching the Agha of Janissaries. The agha held a *çevgen,* a staff bearing horsehair tassels and strings of small bells. Its ringing would signal the start of a fast and furious game. The object was simple: to throw the javelin at an opponent's head, face, back, or chest and knock him from his horse. The last team with a player in the saddle won the game. There were few rules save winning. Javelins could be used in any manner the combatants saw fit. Teams of litter bearers stood on the perimeter, waiting.

Silence settled gradually over the Hippodrome. "Go with God," Nico said to Nasrid and Shabooh. He leaned forward and gave Mujahid a pat.

Almost imperceptibly the agha wiggled the staff. The bells tinkled. The peaceful arena erupted.

From opposite ends of the Hippodrome the two lines of horsemen roared toward one another, bursting forth with bloodcurdling screams. Nico's heart was in his throat, and he bellowed with the best of them. Mujahid raced over the ground, nostrils flaring, mane streaming, his stride smooth and sure. Nico knew this horse had seen battle. The two lines closed at full gallop, weaving and leaping through ruined pillars and walls. The obstacles and the onrush of the greens made it impossible for Nico, Nasrid, and Shabooh to ride together as they had planned. They were quickly separated, each caught up in his own battle.

Nico selected his target, a husky Bosnian, and spurred Mujahid forward. Just before their horses came abreast of one another he let go his lance, hurling it at the other boy's chest. Instantly he knew it was a bad throw. The lance went wide, glancing harmlessly off the

Bosnian's shoulder. At the same instant Titus the Albanian loosed his own weapon, having chosen Nico, not Shabooh, as his first target. Nico saw the flash of wood and swung low in his saddle, hugging Mujahid's neck. The missile sailed harmlessly by, thudding into the soft earth as Mujahid galloped past their adversary. Nico pulled up sharply at the west end of the stadium, just short of the throng of spectators. Though he came within inches of the Janissaries, they stood rock still, unflinching.

Nico turned back toward the field, now all but obscured by thick dust. His heart pounded. It would go this way for perhaps a dozen rounds: brief bursts of terrifying speed, an instant of wild combat, and then a momentary respite while the field was cleared. As the dust settled he saw that six pages had been unsaddled in the first clash. Three got up by themselves and ran in shame from the field. Three lay unconscious and were hurriedly carried away by the bearers. Gamesmen rushed to pick up fallen lances and ran to hand them to those horsemen still mounted, for the next surge.

Nico looked down the ranks of the reds and saw Shabooh and Nasrid, still in their saddles. He raised his lance in happy salute. He tasted blood and realized he'd bitten his own lip. He smiled at the stupidity of a self-inflicted injury and at the exhilaration of surviving the first pass.

I am still mounted.

The agha waited for silence, for that utter Janissary stillness that so unnerved those who knew what murderous havoc they wreaked in battle, and to what thunderous noise. Horses snorted and whinnied and pawed, eager to rejoin the fight. At last the little bells of the *çevgen* tinkled, and like two great squalls at sea the ranks of horsemen surged toward one another once again, clashing in a maelstrom of hooves and dust and screams. Javelins soared through the air, flying into the chaos. Wood clashed on wood, lance parried lance. Pages cried and pages laughed and pages screamed, and their helmets rang like bells under the blows.

In the midst of battle a trotting horse suddenly stopped dead still, catapulting its rider head over heels onto the ground. After the initial rush of horses passed, bearers raced to fetch him, only to retreat in panic as several horsemen swung round for another go at lingering opponents, without first waiting for the bells. Their horses swarmed right over the bearers, one of whose robes got caught up in the feet of a fast-moving stallion. The man tumbled like a weed. He lay still for a moment, then rose unsteadily to his feet. His mouth poured blood. He shook off his dizziness, spat out a tooth, then roared in laughter along with the crowd. Gamely he ran to complete his duty, dragging the unconscious page from the field by the ankles.

Each run produced feats of strength, bravery, and cunning. Nasrid caught a javelin in midflight, twirled it around like a baton, and hurled it back at his attacker, catching him square in the face and knocking him cleanly from his mount. Both sides cheered him: this was the stuff of legend. Another page swung down below his saddle to avoid an attack, pitching his javelin between the front and rear legs of his own horse. The shaft entangled the legs of a horse going in the opposite direction. Horse and rider went down hard in a fall that might have killed them both. The crowd watched apprehensively, then cheered as the brave horse struggled to its feet and trotted off the field. The page got up more slowly and to less fanfare.

Several times Nico used his javelin as a parry, holding the weapon midshaft and deflecting slow bolts that came his way. One hit him in the thigh, glancing off his leg and whacking him on the cheek as it tumbled away. He yelped and nearly fell, but hung on and swept past his attacker, swinging his javelin like a club. He struck his opponent in the chest and knocked him to the ground. It was his first coup. He could scarcely believe his luck. At the end of the run he whirled round on Mujahid, who rose on hind legs and pawed at the air. Nico flashed a grin of giddy triumph.

I am still mounted.

Three more runs, and then five. The *çevgen* tinkled; the Hippodrome rumbled; the javelins flew. Bones broke and blood ran, and the litter-bearing business was brisk. The page Titus circled around behind Nasrid. His horse pirouetted, and the Albanian swung his lance, sending Nasrid tumbling to the ground. Too late Nico raced up to help. Nasrid was out cold, and Nico could only hurl his lance at the retreating figure of the Albanian. It fell short. "I'll have you, you son of a devil," he yelled. Titus never even looked around. He laughed.

With every wave of battle Nico appreciated his horse anew. Mujahid never wavered when steadfastness was required, anticipating events almost as well as Nico. He knew when to respond to the press of Nico's calves and when to take charge, leaving his rider to fight. He knew when to hesitate and when to surge, when to wheel and when to run. He was a crafty battle horse, as much a weapon beneath Nico as the javelin was above him. At each end of the field Nico felt Mujahid's energy as he prepared for the next run. He was magnificent, and, Nico knew, a very large part of the reason why he was still in the saddle.

On one rush Nico saw Iskander coming straight for him. Trying not to be too obvious, he sought to engage himself elsewhere, so that his tutor would not have a chance to unsaddle him and judge him weak. Iskander was having nothing to do with that diversion. He wanted to engage Nico head-on, and he would have no less. He matched Nico's progress through the field of broken marble, moving his own mount to intercept. Nico clenched his teeth and raised his javelin against Iskander, only to have another page strike first. The other javelin caught Iskander in his throwing arm. Iskander dropped his lance. For an instant Nico hesitated, not wishing unfair advantage over his unarmed *lala*. Too late he thought of his tutor's oft-repeated phrase: *Take advantage where you can.* Iskander flashed by, intact.

The next time they met Nico threw first, standing in his stirrups and heaving with all his strength. He missed. Iskander's javelin passed his in midair and struck Nico a glancing blow to the helmet. Stunned, Nico somehow hung on. He stopped at the east end, breathing heavily, tasting blood flavored with dirt and sweat. His ears rang from the blow. His mouth was hot and dry, his throat parched, his ribs and thigh aching. But he was euphoric.

I am still mounted.

After ten waves, there were fourteen greens and twelve reds still mounted, Nico and Shabooh among them. As they regrouped, Nico and Shabooh conferred. "It is time to avenge Nasrid, Asha," Shabooh said, grinning wickedly as he regarded Titus at the other end of the field. Shabooh's voice was thick. Nico realized his friend was drooling a river of blood. His lip was slack, his jawbone clearly broken. But the little Bulgarian was breathing fire, not blood, and seemed not to notice.

The agha's *çevgen* tinkled, and their two horses set off at full tilt, six paces apart, bearing down directly on Titus. Nico took the left flank, Shabooh the right. Titus saw their approach and chose Shabooh as his target. He hurled his lance, and it glanced off Shabooh's shoulder. Titus turned hard to the left, trying to cross in front of Shabooh. But they were ready for him, and turned at the same instant, their horses flanking him, one on either side. Nico swung his javelin up and Shabooh caught hold of the other end. They held it between them and hoisted it to chest level. Titus reacted too late. They caught him at midchest and bowled him over backward.

Shabooh whooped in triumph, his horse wheeling, his face bloody. He saluted Nico with a nod and fierce grin, and passed out. He toppled from his saddle.

As he awaited the next run Nico trembled from lack of food and water, and fought the nausea of a prolonged adrenaline surge. His head ached from Iskander's blow and from the heat. He desperately needed something to drink, but the red ball of the afternoon sun still hung above the Hippodrome, all but lost in the haze. Ramadan would not end until the sun went down, when one could no longer distinguish a white thread from a black one. He tried to spit, but nothing would come. Yet all the discomfort paled next to the giddy thought:

I am still mounted.

Eight combatants remained. At the agha's bell, Iskander raced toward Nico, clearly signaling that they were to meet. Their horses circled, Iskander thrusting and poking with his javelin. He landed one solid blow on Nico's chest, another to an arm. Nico lashed back viciously, catching his *lala* square in the cheek, just below his helmet. The blow laid away a great flap of Iskander's skin, but the *lala's* expression never flickered. Nico surged forward again, javelin flashing. Iskander parried, oak clashing against oak. They sensed but did not see the others fighting around them, sensed but did not hear the roar of the crowd, now wagering on their struggle; sensed only the dust and the grit in their teeth and each other. They controlled their horses with their legs, Mujahid maneuvering for position against Iskander's much larger Turkoman.

Nico whipped his weapon sideways, catching Iskander's hand against his javelin, breaking his fingers. Iskander's grip slackened.

Nico struck again, at the shaft of Iskander's javelin. It fell to the ground, leaving the *lala* exposed. For a split second Nico again hesitated, unwilling to press home the advantage. Reacting instantly, Iskander caught hold of Nico's weapon. They wrestled for it, hand to hand, muscle against muscle, fist against face, their horses flank to flank, circling while their riders struggled.

Despite Iskander's injuries, his strength and experience began to tell. He thrust the javelin at Nico, then yanked it back. Nico fought for balance. Iskander pushed again, driving the edge of the javelin into Nico's neck. Nico gagged. His hand flew to his throat. Iskander backed away and swung the lance, catching his pupil square in the ribs. Nico snapped backward to the sensation of his throat choking, his chest burning, his legs going to rubber, and day going to night. He was unconscious before he hit the ground.

At the end of the day the greens were triumphant, with three combatants still mounted. Their captain, Iskander, accepted the trophy from the Agha of Janissaries. It was a silk sack of dried ears, taken in combat at the battle of Mohacs more than thirty years earlier. All had been harvested from Hungarian heads by the agha himself. It was a singular honor for the greens. Iskander was deeply moved.

No one died of the games, although two pages lay in deep coma. Another lost an arm, mangled beneath sharp hooves. There were scores of milder injuries, including broken teeth, fractured bones, and flayed skin. In all, it was much milder than the game of mounted darts played by the half-mad Akinjis, but the crowd was well pleased.

When he awoke that evening in the page's hospital, Nico listened to Nasrid's narrative of his last encounter with Iskander, which Nico didn't remember. Nasrid had regained consciousness just in time to witness it. Now he embellished a bit, until it seemed that Nico had not fallen at all but instead had slain Alexander the Great himself and claimed the sack of ears for the reds. Nico was suffused with pride. Not only had he not fallen, he had very nearly defeated his own *lala*.

The three pages were in ruins. Nico's ribs were broken. Nasrid's face was a swollen mass of black and blue, his nose twisted, his lip split, his thumb smashed. A physician had bound Shabooh's jaw with a loop of brown cotton that Nasrid swore was a turban pulled from a camel's ass. Through broken bones and teeth, Shabooh gurgled in laughter. Clutching themselves in pain, the others joined him. None could remember a finer day.

At that moment Iskander appeared in the door, his face and hand bandaged. He betrayed no sign of his thoughts, and it was all Nico could do to suppress a grin at his near triumph. The feeling didn't last long. Iskander checked on his other injured pages, and then stood at the foot of his cot. "You have proven much today, Asha," he said.

Nico blushed. "Thank you, sire."

"Mainly you have proven that it is fortunate you are intelligent, as you will never become a warrior." Nico thought Iskander must be joking, but his *lala's* expression showed him to be in deadly earnest. "Twice you had the advantage, and twice you failed to press it," he said.

"But sire—" Nico started to protest.

"There is no 'but,'" Iskander said. "In battle you would have paid with your life for your hesitation. Worse, your men would have paid with *their* lives. The Sultan requires commanders of forthright courage to carry his banner, men who will seize every advantage on land or sea. You will never have the chance, Asha. You have proven today how perfectly suited you are to wield a pen for the Sultan, rather than a sword. I would not trust you on the field of battle."

"Sire, I assure you—"

"For your weakness you spent the last two hours unconscious, and for that you missed the evening prayer. For such inattention you shall miss *iftar* as well."

The *lala* strode off. As much as Nico regretted missing the feast, he was even more upset by Iskander's judgment. Without the approval of his *lala,* he had no prayer of ever going to sea.

His hunger if not his disappointment was eased somewhat when Nasrid stole half a flask of medicinal wine. They broke the fast by getting light-headed.

Later Nico lay on his belly, on a mat beside his bed. It was *Laylat ul-Qadr,* the night Mohammed received the first revelation of the Koran. The Night of Power. Nico mouthed the words of prayer, his body bruised, his mind on the games.

Bis'mallah. Ar-Rahman. Ar-Rahim.

Praise be to Allah, Lord of the Worlds

Master of the Day of Judgment . . .

Unbidden, a thought came to him, a sweet moment of silent satisfaction.

No matter what Iskander said, I did not fail. I almost beat him.

I am an içoglan—a page of the privy household. God is great.

His mind returned to the litany.

Thee alone we worship, Thee alone we ask for help.

Show us the straight path, the path of those whom Thou hast favored,

Not the path of those who earn Thine anger, nor of those who go astray . . .

Quite without meaning to, he forgot his other prayers.

❖

I must tell thee of the prince, Jehangir. He took a liking to me. I don't know why, really. He is older than I by several years. He was born with a deformity of the spine, near his neck, and it has made his shoulders hunch over. He stoops at the waist and one of his feet is clubbed, all of it making him a graceless vessel indeed. He is called Jehangir the Lame, or the Crooked, although never to his face, and certainly never in the presence of anyone of exalted rank. It is a whispered name, yes, but one given without malice to the Sultan's youngest son, whom everyone likes. Though his father made him governor of the province at Aleppo, it is well known that it is not Jehangir who governs, but the wise and gifted viziers sent by Suleiman to labor at his side and guide him gently in beneficial ways. He returns often to Istanbul to be near his father, who adores him above his other sons.

The prince has a pet monkey that gives him great amusement. The monkey was brought from Africa, from a forest where the trees are said to grow as closely together as the piles of a Persian carpet. The creature is quite striking. It has dense, speckled fur that sparkles in the sunlight, and blue rings around its eyes that render it as mischievous-looking as its white beard makes it seem wise. In all it is as graceful and agile as the prince is not.

Walking with Jehangir one morning, the monkey escaped its lead and bounded away. There was great consternation, for the monkey was beloved by the prince. The courtyard was filled with great and humble personages alike: ministers and eunuchs, chamberlains and pages. The monkey moved over the ground like the wind, making straight for the Gate of Felicity. A host of the Sultan's blue-robed Janissaries, the most fearsome of all the world's warriors, rose up as one to divert it from its path, their great scimitars useless. The monkey turned away from them and bounded toward a mosque, then turned again toward the entrance to the harem. It moved much more quickly than its pursuers, who could not tell from moment to moment if the creature was looking for prayer, companionship, or escape. Its last path was blocked by one of the eunuchs, looking huge in his high-coned turban. I would have expected the monkey to have leapt eagerly into his embrace, for with the barrel chest, elongated, dangling arms, and crabbed hands unique to his kind, the eunuch seemed almost more monkey than the monkey. Instead, the monkey darted up onto a fountain. Just when it seemed cornered, it jumped over the heads of its chasers, and back out into the open courtyard. Everyone present joined the chase, and as we were in the third court, the Sultan's inner sanctum, not a sound was uttered by anyone save the monkey, and it was screeching like a hundred *djenoums*.

Then, as luck or fate would have it, the monkey came straight toward me, perhaps because I happened to be hiding a pomegranate. It jumped into my arms. I am ashamed to admit I fell onto my backside from the shock of it. I dropped the fruit, which the monkey grasped. Somehow I had the presence of mind to catch hold of its harness. The prince soon hobbled up. Though he seemed friendly and well-mannered, he enjoyed a laugh at my loss of dignity. He took his monkey back, along with my pomegranate. Iskander, my *lala,* saw the forbidden fruit, which I had intended to eat that night after prayer. It was an infraction for which I later paid with ten lashes to my belly. Had I not caught the monkey, he told me, I would have paid twenty.

Jehangir invited me to eat with him. Though the art of conversation is one of the many tasks for which I am trained, I was quite nervous at the prospect of having to converse with such a noble personage. I needn't have worried. The prince quickly put me at ease. I think the malady that deformed his spine and foot also affected his mind in some small way. He was not simple, really, but he was not concerned with great matters of state, either, although he was governor of a province and a potential heir to the throne of Osman. He often spoke of his older half-brother Mustapha, the most likely heir, who at that moment was governor of Magnisiya. Jehangir idolized him and told stories of their days together in the seraglio, and actually it was he and not I who did all the talking. I confess I was at least somewhat diverted by the sumptuous banquet that lay before us. All of the wonderful odors of the kitchens, odors I had only smelled and guessed at for years, suddenly took form on the prince's table, brought by servers and pages such as myself, who fawned over me—the simple boy from Venice (forgive me, but the lie is easiest to say if it is said often)—almost as much as the prince. I sat on red leather, and my napkin had gold fringe! There were bowls heaped with grapes and peaches and sweet melons. I devoured a goodly share, along with steaming roast mutton and a whole pigeon cooked in sauce, plus three servings of sweet yams. For dessert there was water ice flavored with fruit juice. It is made from snows carried by camel from Mount Olympus and stored in great vaults beneath the palace. Although I lay awake all night on my bed, vomiting the rich food to which my stomach was not accustomed, I never enjoyed a meal more.

At table I had a chance to look at him, though always discreetly. His face was not well-formed or pleasing, yet it was sociable. His skin was ashen. He smiled often, at some simple thing I said, some tale or levity. That stood out because smiling is a pastime that does not find frequent exercise in the seraglio, where dignity is measured in sternness.

Afterward he produced a book that he asked me to read. It

was a collection of fables written in Turkish, a language he said he cared not for, though he liked the tales well enough. So as I read I translated for him into Persian, the language of poetry and culture, a trick with which he seemed well pleased. It was a small thing, just as my "capture" of the monkey had been. But fortunes have turned on smaller things. Better to have luck than skill, my *lala* always teaches, for luck is naught but the beneficent smile of the Almighty.

After that, whenever the prince was near he asked for me. He said he found my company easy and my voice pleasing. He would sit for hours in the courtyard, listening to me read while he played with his monkey or pitched pebbles into the fountain. If I would think him not listening and pause, he would stop his play and turn to me impatiently. "Read on, Asha," he would command. He could have had anyone do this—there are storytellers in the palace whose gifts at such things far exceed my own, performers who have spent a lifetime telling tales. Yet the prince wanted me.

Mostly he liked to play games, and pursue other distractions in which he found me a happy companion. It is well known that all princes of the house of Osman are poets, and Jehangir struggled to write his own, mostly *gazels* of five to fifteen lines. All Ottoman poetry concerns love, a subject about which both the crooked prince and his ignorant young companion know very little. That did not stop us. He would pen a few words to an imaginary lover:

> The sea of my heart is stormy, tormented with fire
> For thee
> A prince, helpless, tossed on the waves of thy love . . .

Or something equally dreadful. And then, if he seemed arrested in thought, I would suggest a word or two—gently, of course, for I would never presume to coach a prince in the arts of verse. He would pick up my weak thread and add more of his own. Together we stumbled through several score of poems that way, although my own contributions were very modest, consisting invariably of words my memory stole from

Bâkî, a poet of some renown whose lyrical verse I read in class, and who clearly had no such trouble with women or verse as did the prince and the page.

Jehangir copied everything into a book that he carried. He could have had a scribe do it, but he prided himself on his hand, which for all his inelegance formed clear letters. When he finished he would read them back to me. By then they were not very good, being as they were Osman gold dulled by Maltese tarnish, but they seemed to please him in any case, and he praised me as if I had done something important.

I must say his attentions did not harm me in my own life. The Chief White Eunuch was pleased that I pleased Jehangir —everyone's fortunes flower when a prince is happy—though he did not ease my schedule of studies. If the prince kept me four hours, that was simply four fewer hours for sleep that night, as I caught up with my other duties. If he kept me six hours, I had no sleep at all. Only my *lala*, Iskander, seemed disconcerted by it all. He questioned me endlessly about my sessions. He does not trust me. Of course he trusts no one completely, for that is his job, to eliminate those unfit for the Sultan's service, but I always feel from his look that I am different, that he knows I am a page of lies.

It was in the company of the prince that I spent fifteen minutes in the presence of the Sultan. Suleiman paid me little heed—very well, no heed—but was most attentive to his youngest son. The two of them walked together through the lush gardens of the fourth court as I kept far behind, trying to be no more obtrusive than a shadow, yet ready to spring forth if needed. The Sultan is well known to be melancholy of disposition, and it is forbidden even to smile in his presence. The weight of the world is terrible indeed, and there had been much of late to distract him. I saw that his shoulders seemed to stoop like those of his own deformed son. Yet I also know, as Allah is my witness, that while they strolled together in the garden, I heard the Lord of the Age laugh. It was not from the belly, but it was laughter nonetheless. I could see the salutary effect his son had upon him, while his other sons, fighting for the throne, brought him so much grief. Jehangir presented no threat. Due to his unfortunate infirmities, there was never any question that he would someday gird on the sacred sword of Osman, making him Sultan. That fact alone removed him from the venoms of intrigue and conspiracy that so poisoned the other sons.

I must confess that I sometimes wonder whether all this is a dream—that the son of Luca Borg should walk in such splendid surroundings, at the side of a son of Suleiman.

Chapter 23

Alisa.

Oh, Maria, my hand trembles as I write the word. Her beauty takes away my breath; her name is a song in my heart. When I think of her I feel in my soul the very poetry Jehangir and I cannot write.

I would never have found her but for the tunnels, and I would never have found the tunnels but for Nasrid.

I saw her first while hiding in the darkness beneath the stables, waiting for Nasrid to return with his opium.

But already I am ahead of myself. She makes that happen to me. I will explain.

The seraglio was built by Sultan Mehmet II, praise his name. The palace sprang up in an olive grove, over the ruins of the acropolis of Byzantium. Steep terraces run like giant steps from the palace to the sea, held in place by ancient retaining walls. Subterranean aqueducts built by Justinian carried fresh water to massive cisterns beneath the old city, including what are now the courtyards of the palace. Some still in use, such as the Cistern of Philoxenus, are so large as to require a thousand and one columns to support the ceilings—caverns nearly large enough to float a whole fleet of galleys. This much any schoolboy knows.

Over a millennium earthquakes reduced many of these to rubble. Others were covered over and built upon, and then forgotten—forgotten, that is, until Mehmet Ali, Suleiman's first Page of the Sword, discovered them nearly thirty years ago, when our master, the Supreme Lord of Europe and Asia, was renovating the palace. From that time, the tunnels and canals became the occasional exploration grounds of pages one might consider either brave or foolish. There are a score of ways to get into them, including at least three from within the Third Court, the Sultan's residential quarters, which include both the Enderun Kolej, where I reside, and the harem. This much I know because I learned it from Nasrid, who learned it from Abdul Matan, who learned it from Abdul Rashid, who learned it from Mehmet Ali himself.

Above the ground the serai is a maze of gardens and corridors, chambers and baths and halls, mosques and work-rooms and kitchens. It is much the same below ground—a labyrinth of tunnels, walls, chambers, and canals. Though many were blocked with rubble whenever the earth shook, others still run great distances, all the way from the Alay Meydani, the procession square where the Janissaries are paid, to the Chamber of Petitions, where foreign ambassadors are admitted into the Sultan's presence. They exist beneath the Gate of Felicity itself, and below the pavilions and hanging gardens, and beneath the menagerie and the stables. One old viaduct runs all the way down to the water. This much I know because I have been inside them.

Nasrid is my best friend, a page like myself. He is a conscript from Macedonia, the third son of an Orthodox Christian farmer. He was taken in the *devshirme,* the gathering, when the Sultan's commissars harvest the strongest and brightest sons of each village. Nasrid is certainly that and more. He is wiry and tough and fearless. When he plays the lute it is as if the angels are making song, and yet he could easily wrestle a bear to the ground. He has a fondness for opium that can be satisfied only by sneaking into Istanbul, where supplies are plentiful, arriving by camel from Cappadocia. The Janissaries take a quarter drachm a day, half a drachm when at war. It is what washes the fear from their veins. I tried some of Nasrid's but did not care for it, because it filled my head with cotton and made me sleepy.

Besides opium, Nasrid found something else in Istanbul, something not available in the seraglio: women. If there is one Ottoman custom I find disagreeable, it is that of the harem, the inviolable area. Women are never seen here, not even in ceremony. Of course I remember the *barnuza* in Malta, but I also remember seeing women on the street and in church. Here they are hidden away, guarded by black eunuchs who have had not only their balls removed but, well, their . . . *members* as well. I am sorry to be so crude.

In any event, the lack of women creates much desire in all men here, and much mischief in the *hamam,* the baths. Nasrid claimed the solution to this problem lay near the docks, in a quarter of the city with a vulgar reputation. It is quite near the palace, though for the walls it might as well be in another country. He begged me to go with him into the underground, if not into the city itself. I refused until he accused me of cowardice. I could not let that stand.

What we did would never have been possible but for the corruption of Kasib, one of the white eunuchs who watches all things here. I laugh at his name because it means "fertile." The only thing fertile about Kasib is his appetite for opium, which exceeds even that of Nasrid's. As long as a drachm or two passes his way after each trip, he turns a blind eye to our adventures, although he makes it clear that if we are ever caught, he will stand first among our accusers.

I know well what discovery would mean, and have never lost the knot in my belly that comes each time I slip from the dormitory into the *hamam* and thence to the furnace that heats the water for the baths. It is there, behind large piles of wood and stacks of bricks, that a drain allows passage into our black and forbidden world. It is quite near the fire and a neat trick to get through without being burned, but then all pages of the Enderun Kolej are good at neat tricks. We can go only once a week, on the single afternoon we are freed from our studies.

During those hours some pages sleep, others play games. Nasrid and I disappear into the dark.

We became lost the first time, for we had not the sense to bring candles. We banged around and bumped heads and were forced to return after only ten minutes. Such, thou might fairly ask, is the genius of the pages of the Enderun Kolej, the hope of the empire? The next time, with a lantern, we followed the signs that had been described to Nasrid—a collapsed pillar, the face of a statue, a peculiar succession of tiled pipes. Sometimes a ray of light would guide our way, just a tiny beam in a large chamber, streaming through a hole in a wall or kiosk. As we explored we made marks of our own, with chalk and with bits of rock that we stacked in piles. It took three visits to find the exit Nasrid sought, one that surfaced in an old water tank that had gone dry. I did not go with him into the city and took his taunts without wavering. He remained outside nearly two hours. I grew more apprehensive with each passing moment. It is dangerous to disobey in the House of Osman, where heads roll for even minor infractions. Such discipline has a salutary effect on the Sultan's order. Every man from the Grand Vizier to the lowest eunuch knows his duty, for it is imprinted upon one's mind in the same way that one's *orta,* or company insignia, is tattooed upon one's arm. Keep thy duty and keep thy head: it is easy enough to remember, as I reminded Nasrid when finally he returned. But by that time, his head already dreamy with opium, he smiled and said, "It is easy enough to forget as well."

On our next visit I did not wait for him the entire time, but decided to explore. I crawled along a broken sewer until I could smell the sea. From behind a crack in a retaining wall I saw the blue waters of the Golden Horn, nearly close enough to touch. I saw galleys ranged up and down the Galata wharf, some manned, some not. Some were the cream of the Sultan's own fleet, some the property of traders from every corner of the earth. The harbor teemed with shipping, with sturdy fishing boats and sleek canoes, and caiques skimming across the water like insects. I saw a fine beechwood vessel with a single mast and four oars and knew that with Nasrid's help I could overpower its master and sail away. I was, I admit, reluctant to approach Nasrid about it. He was the happiest and most contented page I knew, particularly when he had his opium, and I thought it unlikely he would ever wish to escape. One must be truly anxious indeed to wish to leave the agreeable surroundings of Topkapi. I knew I would have to bide my time until I had the right companions.

It was on our fifth visit that I first saw her. I was between the stables and the animal compound, beneath a battlement of the palace wall. I wriggled up between two great columns and found myself in the hollow of a stone wall, the interior of which had a staircase that guards would ascend in times of danger to assume their defensive posts. I think the base of it, beneath the ground level, was once part of a side aisle, supported by columns from the old acropolis. There were still traces of old windows and doorways, long bricked up, then covered and forgotten. One side fronted to the east, toward the interior of the palace. I found myself behind the grating of a sewer that carried away rainwater. The grate was in two parts. The first extended up the wall, while the second lay flat, along the ground. There was easily enough room for me.

It was laughter that first attracted me to the place, laughter like the tinkling of the bells of paradise. As I climbed I smelled jasmine. I peered through the grate and first saw a great negress, so ugly that I nearly cried out in fright. Her face was disfigured, and she wore no veil. Such women, I later learned, are prized as servants in the harem, in order that they may not tempt the men for whom their mistresses exist.

The negress moved away, and I saw a few of the girls, in a large garden. I could see them only obliquely, having to press my face up against the grating, as the section of wall in which I crouched faced them not directly, but away, at an angle.

It was here I most vividly felt the danger in what I was doing. For a page, the penalty for crawling around the vaults and arcades beneath the seraglio would be the light bastinado. The penalty for doing it twice would be the disgrace of banishment from the palace. But the penalty for gazing even accidentally upon the women of the harem—at least for a man still possessed of his balls—would be instant death. I did not yet know that it was not into the harem proper that I stared, and that it was not upon the concubines of the serai but only upon their servants that my eyes fell.

Even at the threat of losing my head, I could not help myself. I looked upon these women, the first I had seen since coming to the palace, and heard their gay chatter. I could hear perhaps a dozen of them, though I could see only four or five, on the opposite side of the garden from me. They were sitting on benches and seemed to be engaged in sewing or embroidery. It was only *her* face I could see clearly, and there was no question it was the most beautiful in all the realm of the Lord of Lords. She walked nearer to my hiding place, humming to herself, examining flowers, as if searching for the perfect one. She wore a small cap, cylindrical in shape, from which there hung a diaphanous veil. It covered only the left side of her face. I could see her brilliant eyes, made all the more lustrous by the contrast with her plaited black hair. She had high cheeks, a fine nose, and a perfect mouth. I watched her for long moments, scarcely daring to breathe. I cannot describe the feeling of peace and wonder, of tenderness and awe that descended upon me as I watched, fearing less the threat of execution than Allah's own wrath at the sin of gazing upon such beauty in secret.

She must have sensed my presence, for suddenly she looked toward the wall, directly at me. I shrank back in fear, not knowing if she could even see me in the shadows. Yet it was clear she could. Her hand went to her mouth, and I saw the look in her eyes—*a man!* I thought I heard her yelp a little, although that might only have been my imagination. No one else noticed. We stared at each other, our faces not ten paces apart. I saw her cheeks turn the color of henna, and then she looked back down at the flowers. She moved among them, touching peonies and hyacinths and roses. A bit closer now, she looked at me again, her eyes pools of curiosity.

I know I must have looked silly or worse—certainly like something that had been washed down the sewers. At the least my face was crisscrossed with the shadows of the bars of the grille, but she seemed not to notice. Just as I smiled at her someone clapped, a signal to depart. As she turned to leave, I felt the heavens move: I believe she smiled back at me.

We had said not a word, but I was filled with her presence.

I returned the next week at the same exact hour, hoping the timeless rhythms of the seraglio would hold true, that once again at that moment on that day she would be there.

Alas, it was beginning to rain. The garden was as empty as my heart. Sprinkles turned to downpour, forcing me to flee quickly, as the rains wished to occupy my sewer.

I myself could not come the following week. The pages were called to the sporting fields above the Golden Horn. Though many here smoke opium, it is a crime. We watched as opium dealers were tied to stakes to be executed. Many people from the city came to watch as well, eager for spectacle: sometimes bears were set on the dealers. But this day the Janissaries wished to display the astounding accuracy with which arrows could be shot from great distances. They were not mistaken. I was curious how much opium the executioners themselves had consumed before launching their arrows, but I can tell thee it was not enough to affect their aim. The display worried me—for Nasrid and his dangerous game, and even for me, and mine. But above all the worry, no thought was greater than that a second week had been lost, and I had not seen her.

I returned a week later. Allah answered my prayers. She was there! I had stolen a rose from the garden in front of the Mosque of the Aghas, and I left it on the edge of the grating. I have told thee that the *Bostanji Bashi,* the gardener, is also the chief executioner, and I do not know what his penalty would have been for my thievery, but no threat of it would have stayed my hand. The white flower was unblemished, as perfect as any in the serai. I backed away from the grille and watched. She worked her way toward my hiding place. She touched the flower and picked it up. She began to slip it into her robe but then thought better of it. The danger must have been too great. I watched her delicate wrist, and her fingers as she carefully plucked the outer petals from the flower. These alone she was able to conceal. I felt a chill all the way to my feet as I realized her efforts betrayed her determination to keep some portion of my gift. She moved away, quickly. I remained until the clap of hands. I heard whispers and giggles as the women departed. My eyes never left her, and I was rewarded. She turned and looked back at me. This time there was no doubt whatever.

I saw her smile.

The Padishah visited his summer palace at Üsküdar for a fortnight, accompanied by a mere three thousand or so of his household, the pages among them. Again I could not see her, as I took my studies in new surroundings. This did not keep me from thinking of her. I dreamed of her every night. I wondered everything about her: her name, her history, and what she ate for supper. I remembered her scent and longed to touch her. I worried that my absence might persuade her that I had lost interest. Then I worried that what I had lost was my head, in carrying on so over a woman to whom I had spoken not a word. I told Nasrid of her, and he said I should try opium instead, as the pursuit was safer.

Upon our return to the Topkapi serai I committed another crime for her. The first was cutting the rose. The second was prying a stone from the hilt of my dagger. It is not my knife but the Sultan's, as all things here are his. It was not a valuable stone, certainly not one the King of Kings would miss, but one for which his justice would have me forfeit my hand. It was simple, a blue-green turquoise, the color of her eyes. Thou wilt know the precise color by recalling the luminous waters of the grotto near Zurrieq, where as children we played together. Her eyes seemed to glow the very same way, from somewhere within.

I left the stone there, on the ledge by the grate. I saw her take it. Again I saw her smile. If they behead me for my crimes, that smile will have made it worthwhile. It was as a sunrise.

Weeks passed and I did not see her. Slipping away from the *lalas* is not easy, even with a eunuch as thy companion in deception. I worked on my studies harder than ever, so that Iskander would have no cause to fault me, and so that he himself might not appear negligent in the eyes of the Kislar Agha, who is as stern with the *lalas* as the *lalas* are with us.

The next I saw her, she came much closer to the grating. She knew I was there. I could see her looking for me—and better, I could see the delight on her face when she saw me. I chanced a whisper. "I am Asha," I told her. "A page." I would have said Nico, only no such person exists within the seraglio.

"I am Alisa." Her voice was but a murmur, yet it filled my heart like a breeze. The sound of her voice sparkled like her eyes. That was all we could say, before the awful clapping of hands sounded the end of her time in the garden. She hurried away.

For another nine weeks, that was all we knew of each other: Asha and Alisa, a page and a maiden.

It was then I began to notice the passage of time much differently than before. Minutes seemed longer, weeks an eternity. Infinite eternities intruded between our visits. I remember once placing an hourglass to my ear and hearing the soft hiss of sand marking the passage of time. Now if I did so, I am certain I would hear each grain tumbling slowly, one after another.

As I could not see her, I could only imagine. Each morning when I awoke it was to thoughts of her, even before performing my ablutions for *salat al-fajr,* the early prayer. I did not stop thinking of her until after *salat al-isha.* Of course, Maria, I did not forget the Lord's Prayer. Even then, after all the prayers, sleep would not come, for she held my dreams as well as my daylight. My mind wandered everywhere except upon the business to which it was supposed to be devoted. I nearly chopped off my own finger with a chisel while working wood one day. A physician had to sew me up. While talking to myself I fell into a fountain in the garden and blackened my eye. If I thought of her any more, I suppose it would probably kill me. But there was no helping it. I would ask myself what she might be doing right now—was she gardening? Sewing? Watching that sunset? Gazing upon that star? Was she thinking of me? Did she hear the cannon, announcing the setting of the sun? Could she hear the call of the muezzin? Was she happy? Sad? Angry?

Surely she was a princess, the daughter of Suleiman; no one so beautiful could be less. I despaired that such a wondrous woman would forever be lost to such a one as me. Then I remembered that in the glorious realm of Osman, I might someday marry even the Sultan's daughter if first I proved myself worthy. Though I felt foolish for having such thoughts, they were all I had of her. I could close my eyes and see her eyes, her face, her smile. I could put my hand to my chest, and feel her heart beating. I could listen to the larks in the second court, and hear her laughter in their song. My stomach grew unsettled; it was all I could do to eat. I will not admit to thee the thoughts I have at night, alone in my bed.

All this, from one meeting in which eight words were spoken. I know thou must think me mad.

Finally, last week, we saw each other again. This time she boldly drew near the grating. I think she must have found accomplices among her friends, for they seemed to provide some protection for her. I put my hand on the grate. To my surprise she reached for it.

Our fingers touched.

I cannot describe the moment of that touch, the grace or the fire. Even now I can bring back the sensation at will. Her skin was smoother than the silks I wear.

"You must come inside next week," I said brashly, hardly believing my own words. "I will open the grille for you."

"*What?*" The idea shocked her almost as much as it did me.

"I will have you back in half the turn of an hourglass— before the clap of hands."

"I cannot!"

"Half that long, then."

"I will not!"

"You are beautiful."

"And you are foolish. They will kill you for being here."

"Next week," I said again, not caring if she was right. I could hear that the steel in her voice of refusal was really made of clay. I knew she would come.

And now, Maria, I must put away pen and paper. The hour nears for morning prayer. This afternoon, *insha'llah,* I will see her again.

Allah's blessings upon thee. *God's,* I mean to say, of course.

Chapter 24

"Half a turn of the hourglass," she said quietly, slipping past him as he held the grate aside. He felt the air of her passage on his cheek and smelled her scent. His fingers trembled on the grate at his good fortune: *she risks everything, to see me!*

"A full turn, I thought you said."

She smiled, and it melted his heart. "I said nothing. You said half."

"Very well. We'll compromise. Half and one makes enough time. I'll have you back in a turn and a half." She giggled.

He worked the grate back into place, suddenly feeling very clumsy and self-conscious. They crouched together for a moment, watching and listening. He felt her presence at his side as if she were a fire, burning hotly. The garden was empty, save for the birds and the sound of voices at the other end.

"We are always given the same amount of time," she whispered. "Never more. My friends are helping me. Today they will throw a ball. Unless something goes wrong and they have to leave, I will not be missed."

He was less conscious of what she said than of the sound of her voice, and of his own heart beating. "Nothing will go wrong. Come now, Alisa," he said. "We will not go far—only to where we can sit straight up." He turned and led her downward into his underground haunt. He had cleared away some of the loose stones so that she wouldn't slip, but he saw she moved as nimbly as he. At the bottom of the slope a candle burned atop a marble slab, flickering beneath the vaulted ceilings. The candle illuminated colossal pillars that were easily a thousand years old. Most were broken now, and shrouded with rubble. Others still stood, supporting parts of the ceiling, their fluted tops not more than eight feet above the slab. In front of the candle was a pool, part of a canal that still carried water to cisterns and fountains. Next to the candle he had laid out a cloth for them to sit upon.

"You were so certain I would come?" she asked, regarding his preparations.

"Yes. I mean, I hoped you would." Their whispers echoed off the old stone.

She smiled again. "When I first saw you I thought you were a spirit. Even now I am not so certain. I thought only the rats crawled around in the sewers beneath the seraglio, spying upon its women. What manner of man are you?"

"A lucky one, for what I have seen," he said. "An *içoglan,* of the Enderun Kolej," he added proudly.

"The palace school!" She was clearly impressed. "A page might one day be a governor."

He accepted the adulation with a flush of pride. "This one will be *kapudan pasha,*" he boasted grandly, "or Grand Vizier. I have not yet decided." He told her briefly of the school and his studies, and life in the third court. Though their worlds existed no more than a few hundred paces apart, he might have been describing the moon. Her eyes betraying her enchantment, she hung on every word.

"But I wish to know of you," he said. "I wish to know how a princess has come to sit with me here, in my grand palace beneath the palace."

"I lived in Brindisi, in the Kingdom of Naples. I was taken by corsairs from Barbary in a shore raid. They came at night. They took nearly every man, woman, and child. They lined up all the old people and cut out their gallstones, to keep as charms. They chained the boys to the oars, violated the older women, and kept the others, the more valuable ones"—she lowered her eyes, as if in embarrassment—"and sold us in the market in Corfu. I was bought and sold three more times before I ended here."

"You will one day be the odalisque of an agha, I suppose," Nico said, unable to hide his fear at the thought.

"I would have been. Not now." Her voice was bitter. "After the third trade, we were put on a ship, bound for the Abode of Felicity. The shipmaster took drink and summoned some of the women from our quarters. He did it late at night, so that the slave master would not hear. He paraded us in front of him, without our clothes. He chose me for his night of pleasure. He was a pig, smelly and fat. I should have submitted but could not. I took a knife from his sash and tried to hurt him. I only scratched him on the leg. In return he tried to cut my throat. As luck would have it I twisted away, and he got only half his wish."

She let back the side of her veil. Starting above her ear, stretching down across her otherwise perfect cheek, and extending to her jaw and down onto her neck was a deep, angry scar, made all the more prominent by the uneven light of the candle. It looked as if it had been made not with a sharp blade but with a dull halberd or a saw. Despite himself, Nico could barely suppress a gasp.

She felt his involuntary reaction. "You see—this is what I do now to a man. He would have finished me, but my screams brought his master. For my scar he paid with his life, while I paid with my future. I would have been sold again, this time for much less, only I had the good fortune to be captured with my cousin. She was the most beautiful among us. Here she is called Durr-i Minau, the Pearl of Heaven. She convinced the slave master to let me stay with her, as her servant. She was able to pay. Now I serve her, though we are both the property of the Sultan."

Gently, impulsively, he touched the scar, even though she tried to draw away. "I think you are beautiful even so," he said earnestly.

"The room is dark," she said, tossing her head so that her veil covered the scar once more, "and you are a poor liar. I should have let him have me or kill me. Anything would have been better than this. Now I will never be wife or concubine. No man of importance will ever want me. I am a freak, as all you saw in the courtyard are freaks. It is the only reason I am able to slip away at all—the eunuchs watch the jewels, not the trinkets. And now I must leave."

"But please—you have only just arrived!"

"You know it is impossible," she said. "They will soon go indoors. I will be missed."

"Then come again next week," he pleaded.

She looked carefully at him, wary that he mocked her after seeing her face. His expression told her he did not. "If I can. If you wish it."

"I wish it. If you are delayed, then the next week, or the next. A thousand weeks, if need be. I will wait until the sun forgets to rise." She squeezed his hand. It took his breath away.

He watched her slip back into the garden and into the trees. He heard the other girls still playing, and Alisa's voice as she joined them. He sighed with relief when she was safe, and realized he was unaccustomed to worrying for someone else. The feeling made him warm.

He was enchanted by her, and troubled as well. Though he hated the man who had done this to her, he found himself somehow comforted by her story, by the familiarity of it: the anger at her treatment, the fire in her eyes as she described the corsairs. And she was not royalty, as he had expected someone who looked like her must be: she was only a slave like himself. It was her attitude about it that most troubled him. She talked plainly of herself, of her past. He knew he had not. He wondered how Maria would have reacted had she heard him talking. There was nothing of Nico—and nothing of his sister, or of Malta, or of their father the mason, or of their home, where he cleaned dung pits. He told himself he had meant nothing by it. He simply wanted to impress her—and Asha was, frankly, a more impressive figure than Nico. Still, he felt shamed at his little deception. She seemed to have none of his pretentiousness. She displayed her scars.

He crawled back into the darkness and waited for Nasrid.

❖

The young page stood before Iskander, his arms folded across his chest, his gaze downcast. "I have spoken with Asha as you required, my lord," he said.

"You did so discreetly?"

"We were at archery practice. The matter came up as if by chance, as you ordered me to arrange it. He suspected nothing."

"And what did you learn?"

"I am . . . not certain, my lord," the boy said. He was hesitant, not wishing to subject himself to the wrath of his *lala,* but neither wishing to betray a *kardesim,* a fellow page.

"Become certain, quickly," said Iskander coldly.

"As my master knows, my youth was spent in Venice, before my new life began under the Sultan, praise his name."

Of course Iskander knew this; the newly arrived page was the first from Venice since Asha, and it was for that reason Iskander had chosen him. "Proceed."

"Sire, if Asha is from Venice as he says, he surely must have spent his life in a hole. I asked him to tell me of his life in *la serenissima repubblica,* and at first he did not even know what I meant. It is the name by which all Venetians refer to their city, just as all men here know they reside in the Abode of Felicity. And he could not answer even the most simple question. He knows the waterfront and the guilds and can describe the arsenal in detail, yet apart from that he could name no quarter, describe no square or plaza. He seemed to know nothing of the Basilica di San Marco, or the doge, and his palace."

"I myself am from Pescara, not so very far from Venice, and *I* know little about the doge," said Iskander impatiently. "Why is that important?"

"The doge, sire, is liege lord of the republic. His palace is as well known as the rising sun or the stars in the sky. All who live in Venice have seen it. Yet not Asha. He could tell me nothing of it. He seemed not to know it existed. It is the same as if one asked a man here, in Kasimpasha or Galata or any other quarter of Istanbul, to name our sultan or describe the serai he inhabits. Only a very blind and weak-headed man could fail at such a task."

Iskander pondered that. Asha, of course, was neither blind nor weak in the head, and his memory was well known. Perhaps it was nothing, yet something about Asha had always made Iskander uneasy. His devotions to Allah certainly met the forms. The page could recite entire passages of the Koran at a time when other pages still had trouble reading it, and yet to Iskander something was missing. Perhaps, he knew, it was nothing in particular about Nico. All pages who came to the palace other than through the *devshirme,* the levy, were regarded with somewhat more suspicion than others. As men, after all, these pages would sit at the pinnacle of empire, discussing state secrets and holding sacred posts of power and trust. There could be no error in their elevation. It was one of Iskander's many jobs to penetrate every facet of a page, to ferret out those who were unsuitable or untrustworthy, and show them the gate of dishonor, or the executioner's fountain.

If Asha was lying about his family, or his home, then Iskander would know why.

"Very well," he said to the page. "You may return to your studies."

❖

She did not come the next week, or the week after, or the week after that. The last time he waited for her until the danger was extreme, until even Nasrid tugged urgently at his sleeve. The two pages scrambled back through the underground, knowing they were late. They slipped up behind the furnace and into the *hamam* at the precise moment Iskander came looking for them. They saw him first and quickly covered their activity with the only sort of embrace they knew Iskander would understand. He watched them for a moment, then ordered them to their room.

Nico lay on his cot, desolate.

But the next week she was there, like a beam of sunlight moving through the garden, and then she slipped inside, and he knew from her look that she had anticipated their meeting as much as he had. At once they were whispering again, excited and happy. He took her hand and together they raced downward to their pool. They sat and chattered about everything, talking in rushes, great breathless surges of excitement and shared danger and wonder at each other, talking quickly because there was so little time, and so much they wanted to say, as if they could distill two lives in less than the space of an hour. She told him of life in the harem, of the things she was learning, things her cousin taught her as she herself learned them—how to use *surmèh,* a mixture of antimony and oil that lined her eyelashes, and how to apply henna, and how to play the lute. "They do not instruct me," she said. "I am but a servant.

They teach only the Durr-i Minau, and it is she who teaches me."

He still meant to tell her of his own origins but did not. When she asked him questions he deflected them and talked instead of his training: in weapons and horsemanship, and in the science of war. He boasted of the teachers who came to the dormitory, including the Sultan's private *hoca*, his religious tutor. He talked grandly of the books that held the Sultan's justice, and wisely of Ottoman art. But he said nothing of Malta, nothing of his family there.

And just that quickly, she had to leave.

On the next visit she brought him a cup of sherbet, stolen from her mistress's table. It was made of violets, sugar, and lemon. She fed it to him. He recited some of Jehangir's poetry, telling her it was his own. He told her of the arsenal at Venice. "I will take you there someday," he said grandly.

"Very well," she replied. "And I will take you to Samos. It is the most lovely place I have seen, though I have seen but few. It is an island where we stopped for a few days in the slave ship that brought me here. There were lovely mountains, and birds. It is where I would go in the world if I had my choice of places."

"Very well," he said. "I will take you there." And they both laughed at the foolishness of the dream. For now the underground was their empire, the canal their ocean. They explored a little. They dared not go far, for fear they would be late returning. In one of the pools he held up the lantern and she saw fish, flashing in the water. He showed her the foot of a great statue, its corroded bronze toes all that remained of a forgotten god. There were the remnants of a fresco, the mouth of a dry fountain, the rubble of a bath. Leading her by the hand, he tried an unfamiliar passage. They crept along a narrow walk, smelling damp straw and an animal smell, as at the stables. They stopped dead still when they heard a low, disagreeable growl from the other side of a retaining wall. Evidently he had brought them too near the compound where the wild animals were kept. They had no idea what manner of creature made that sound and did not care to find out. They turned and fled giggling through the gloom, back to their private place. When she left that day she touched his cheek, and her lips brushed his forehead. He nearly fainted.

They never had an entire hour together, and never once met two weeks in a row. Sometimes months passed when they did not see each other, months when the demands of duty kept them apart—the needs of her mistress, or the whim of Iskander, or travel outside the palace, or weather. There always seemed to be something, when one could come but not the other. Whenever he could he left a note, just a slip of paper that said something innocuous, so that she would know he was thinking of her. Whenever she could she left a flower petal, or a shell, or even a strand of her hair tied around a bar of the grille. His heart would race at the gift, and in it he could always feel her warmth. It was never enough.

At night on his cot he realized guiltily that he was glad of her scar if it made no one else want her. She had not lost her self-consciousness over it, and it endeared her to him. It made her heartachingly vulnerable. And without it, he knew he never would have met her. Without it, he doubted she would ever have looked at him. The scar made her other perfections seem less overwhelming.

He thought of Ameerah, a woman who a lifetime ago had showed him kindness, and who had tried to awaken him to the senses of the flesh. There had been nothing to that, of course. He had been just a boy, frightened and stupid and unable to respond. But there was much more difference than simply his age in what he felt now. He did not know such feelings could exist as he held for Alisa. He wanted to hold her, to lie with her on satin sheets, free in time, free to explore. He wondered if they would ever be together that way. The thought kept a fire burning in his loins that never went out.

For the next visit he prepared a surprise. It took him much subterfuge and two trips to have everything ready. He escorted her down to their chamber and sat her with a great flourish on their marble quay. There he lit a candle and used it to light another, and then another. Her eyes went wide in delight. The candles lit three of the wooden boats he'd carved. One was a skiff, sporting a lateen sail made of cotton. Another, a galley, boasted twenty-four oars on each bank. The third, and grandest, was a three-masted galleon, complete with gunports ranged along its sides, and little wooden cannons on its deck. "The *kapudan pasha* welcomes thee," he said formally, bowing, "and salutes the fair maiden with his navy."

He set a candle on each boat and launched them one after another into the dark pool that stretched away into nothingness. They bobbed about on the water, their light flickering off the porphyry columns and tiled arches of Constantine. "To Brindisi and beyond," he said, "may the enemies of the Sultan tremble before this mighty fleet."

He turned and watched her watching, and the look of enchantment on her face did not disappoint him. The light danced off the water and danced in her eyes. He wanted desperately to kiss her. He moved subtly forward, intending to try for a quick peck on her cheek. He stopped suddenly as her hand went to her mouth, and her eyes widened once again. He saw extra light reflected in them—a great deal of light. He turned back to the water.

One of the galleon sails had caught fire, and then a second, burning quickly from the turpentine he'd used to stiffen the cotton and the varnish he'd used to coat the vessel. He rolled up his pants and quickly waded in, grimacing in pain as jagged stones beneath the water tore at his bare feet. He slipped just as he neared the ship, and went into the water up to his waist, as always acutely aware of the delightful sound of her laughter.

Grinning sheepishly, he got up and tried again for the galleon. Finally he had it. He waded back, clutching all that was left of the galleon's hull, by now not much more than a smoking cinder. "I ordered her torched," he explained. "She was infested with corsairs." By now Alisa was laughing so hard it was all she could do to sit up. In the relatively short span of his life, Nico had seen many fine sights. He knew he'd never seen a finer one than that.

❖

On her next visit he determined to kiss her. Gathering the courage took most of their time together, but finally his lips brushed on her cheek, then against the gossamer hair at the base of her neck. He smelled her perfume and the oil from her bath, and knew surely he had won an early visit to paradise. She responded eagerly. She touched his lips with her own and pressed his hand to her breast. She put her other hand to his cheek, and their eyes held each other, and there was urgency in their gaze, yet total peace, a certainty and understanding as their souls joined, a feeling even more lovely and sensual than the touch of flesh, yet it was that touch of flesh that was burning, demanding and urgent. "Come to me," she murmured, and they leaned back on the marble. His hand slipped beneath her robe, and she fumbled urgently at his pants. There was a haze after that, when everything ran together in a delicious blend of tastes and touches. He kissed her neck, and her knees, and her thighs.

He began to move on top of her, knowing instinctively, surely, what was to come next. She moaned, the sound almost covering another: somewhere above them, in a world all but forgotten, there was a muffled clapping of hands. Alisa went stiff, her eyes stricken with fright.

They'd been too long.

She straightened her robe as she raced up the slope, Nico right behind her, trying to fasten his pants. He moved the grate, and it sounded to both of them like the pealing of bells and the roar of cannon, announcing to every eunuch and executioner in Topkapi that serious work was at hand. She did not pause to say goodbye but rushed around the corner into the garden, lost to his view. He could only watch and listen, his breath rapid, his heart sick with fear. He heard nothing.

For weeks he didn't know if she'd made it all right, what she'd done to hide her crime, whether she would ever see the daylight of the garden again. He heard the women's voices at the appointed hour, but there was no trace of her—nothing on the sill, no petal or stone or shell.

At night on his cot he prayed to God to protect her, to preserve her for him. When he finished, he knew he was not finished. He got on the floor and lay on his mat, where he prayed to Allah for the same.

He hated himself for his selfishness, for having gotten lost in her, for losing track of time. His desire had jeopardized her very life. He knew if he kissed her again, the same thing would happen. Solemnly he promised himself he would never allow it, until the day he could do it freely. And that took him to the brink of despair.

Everything he dared dream of was impossible. As long as they lived as page and servant in the palace of the sultan, there would never be more time, not until he won sufficient rank to take her for his own. There was no guarantee that she would not disappear the very next day, taken by unseen hands to a destination he would never know. He might never see her again.

He felt as never before the weight of the chains that bound him to the will of other men.

It was one thing for his own eventual escape to be constantly postponed, but now there was more at stake. He wanted to free her from her captivity, to rescue her. The thought consumed him. He plotted about the galleys and imagined how he might make it happen. He would steal guns from the stores and then overpower the crew of a small vessel. He would sail with her down the Golden Horn and through the seas of Marmara into the Aegean, sail all the way to Brindisi, where he would ask her father for her hand. No. They would go to Samos, the island of her dreams. He worked it all out in his head. But for now, he didn't even know if she was all right.

He kept busy, of course. Every waking moment was filled with his duties, but no lesson or exercise ever succeeded in taking his mind off her. Late at night he wrote Maria everything, pouring out his fears. And he wrote more.

My Dear Sister,

I have sad news to relate of Jehangir, the prince who befriended me.

There came a day when the Sultan was set to march with his troops to Persia, to make war against the Peacock Throne. It was a moment of sublime majesty, as the army massed before the seraglio, preparing to depart with the Sultan. One who has not witnessed the spectacle that surrounds such an undertaking can scarcely imagine its glory. There were military bands, marching to a thunderous accompaniment of cannon fire, and Bektashi dervishes, whirling in ecstasy, stirring the troops to frenzy—and oh, what splendid troops, massed as thick on that hill as the grains of sand on a dune, troops wearing every manner of silk and armor and turban and helmet, troops whose glinting steel blades reflected the very light of heaven, troops born to give truth to what the imams were saying in every mosque, that the world has two houses—one of Islam, the other of War, and that those who cannot see the light of the first house shall feel instead the heat of the second. I will confess my own blood grew hot at the sight, as I knew that no land on earth could long withstand such power as shimmered in the sun that day before the Abode of Bliss.

As the troops streamed away the weather grew suddenly dark. The sun gave way to clouds that were roiling and black, and so low that they soon obscured the minarets of the Hagia Sophia. Lightning and thunder joined the cannon fire that still boomed over the city. A north wind from the Black Sea whipped the Bosphorus to a frenzy. I took it as an omen of the future that awaited the Shi'ite heretics of Persia, when perhaps I should have seen it as an omen of the sadness soon to settle over the House of Osman. In all it was a wretched day to travel, but nothing will stay the Ottoman sword once unsheathed.

A gold and white barge departed carrying the Sultan. He sat in the stern beneath a green silk canopy. The boat was elegantly appointed and nearly eighty feet long, powered by forty royal oarsmen, clad in white robes and blue caps. The barge was the very picture of seaworthiness, but the storm caused it to pitch on the water so violently that even those of us watching from shore felt queasy. Only the King of Kings seemed not to notice, his serene dignity untouched by the force of nature.

After the Sultan departed, Prince Jehangir stepped onto another boat, a smaller vessel with thirty-six oars. A sharp wave caught the bow. The barge had not been properly moored for the prince, who is not sure of foot. He stumbled. Three of his bodyguard managed to steady him, though two of them fell in as the barge drifted from the dock. I do not know what it is about the Turks—they live near the water, as do we Maltese, yet it seems that almost none have mastered the art of swimming. Their silks floated about them in the water as they flapped and choked and drowned.

Of greater concern to all was that Jehangir's book of poetry also went overboard. Though two men who could swim braved the depths beneath the dock, the book was not recovered. I could see it greatly distressed the prince, and that afternoon the captain of the barge paid with his head for the trouble. It was a fair price.

We watched until prince joined Sultan on the Asian shore and rode with the army to war. Anticipating his return, I devoted myself in the months that followed to rewriting the poems into a new book. It was a task for which I received parchment and reed pen from the keeper of manuscripts, and the blessings of the Chief White Eunuch. I did them, of course, from memory, and pray that Allah will forgive me that I corrected a few of Prince Jehangir's words along the way, where I thought their choice or elegance was not equal to the hand that first wrote them. I was quick to throw away any page on which my calligraphy was not perfectly executed.

All books in the serai are beautiful works of art. They consist of rich leather-covered cases bearing gilt edges and elaborate engravings. The finished parchment sheets are folded and bound together ten at a time, and placed inside the case.

I must confess I was proud of my effort. The cover I made myself, of sandalwood. I engraved the front with the *al-fatihah*, the Perfect Prayer, and the back with a verse dedicated to the Sultan: as the prince would have wished, God on one cover, His shadow on the other. It was my intent to send the book to Jehangir as a gift from a devoted page of the household. Only a small thing, of course—as small as the monkey that introduced us. When the book was completed, I sent it with one of the fast messengers who regularly carried dispatches between the seraglio and the Padishah.

The story of what happened next came to me gradually, first by the pigeon post that brings urgent news, and later by those returning from the east. There were inconsistencies in their tales, but the end was the same.

Jehangir died this winter, in Karaman.

In this palace the only thing more commonplace than jewels are rumors, and the most plentiful of those involve the Sultan's wife. She is Russian by birth, and a slave, like all here. By the foreign ambassadors she is called Roxelana. By the court she is called Khurrem, the Smiling One. By the Sultan she is called his Elixir of Paradise. I have never seen her, of course. No man but the Sultan and his eunuchs may see her face, and it is probably fortunate for my neck that I have not frequented those nether regions beneath the palace that might have carried me near her person. It is not necessary to see her to know that she captivates him. In six generations he was the first Sultan to marry. He takes no other woman in the harem, though he might have any he likes.

Khurrem is said to be as cunning as she is captivating. She covets the throne for one of her two oldest sons by Suleiman, Selim or Bayezid. If Mustapha—Suleiman's oldest son by his first concubine—took the throne, he would surely have Khurrem's sons killed. Such is the way of the Ottomans. It is not known how many times, or in how many ways, Khurrem tried to work her way against him. She once sent a gift of rich gowns to Mustapha. He was clever enough to first drape one on a slave, who died in great torment from the poison contained in the lining. There must have been other attempts. It is said he attempted to respond in kind, but without success: none but the hand of Allah or Suleiman may touch Khurrem.

Unable to prevail by her own devices, it is whispered that Khurrem then convinced the Sultan himself that Mustapha was scheming against him. It is an unhealthy occupation to be suspected of plotting against the Sultan, whether the suspicion is true or not. Suleiman's own dearest boyhood friend, the Grand Vizier Ibrahim Pasha, felt the executioner's silk when Suleiman thought him guilty of usurping too much power. There is familial love in the house of Osman, but it pales beside the love of throne: for that love have many sons and brothers died. Now Suleiman's own son was accused of plotting against him, of inciting the army to mutiny.

On campaign Suleiman invited Mustapha to his tent and listened from the other side of a linen screen as huge mutes fell upon him. Mustapha fought like seven tigers while pleading for his life, pleading his innocence of treason, but the eardrums of the mutes are pierced in order that they might not be swayed by such cries, just as their tongues are removed in order that they might never speak of their deeds. While Suleiman wept the mutes prevailed and looped a bowstring round Mustapha's neck. It is always thus that royalty is executed, for none may spill their blood.

Suleiman grieved greatly for his son, even as he ordered his body dumped in front of the tent, where the Janissaries might see what fate awaited traitors. A wise Sultan fears his Janissaries almost as much as they fear him.

Prince Jehangir was in camp that morning. He came to his father's tent, never expecting the sight that would greet him. He was as attached to his half brother Mustapha as if they had been born of the same womb on the same day. I saw them together once, in Topkapi, and they were inseparable. Jehangir, the simple one, inspired in all who knew him the same affection he inspired in his father.

Now, upon seeing his dead idol, Jehangir shrieked and moaned and fainted away. He slipped into a deep coma, from which the Sultan's finest physicians could not rouse him. For a month he lay in a stupor, and then he died. The physicians said his heart had a weakness in it. It is true: the weakness was for Mustapha. This much even I know.

When Suleiman returned to the palace, the pages assembled to greet him. We stood on a hill overlooking the royal dock. Even from that distance we could see how the light had dimmed in him. We felt it, too: no one there could ever have disliked the gentle prince. Suleiman ordered the construction of a great mosque in Jehangir's memory. For Mustapha, of course, there was nothing.

Many here whisper that Mustapha's death will also be the death of the House of Osman, for he alone had the skill to follow his father. My friend Nasrid says that his death, and Jehangir's, were unfortunate for me—that great favor would surely have come my way had Jehangir lived. My friend Shabooh says that Jehangir's death was fortunate for me—so long as I amused him, I would forever be trapped in the seraglio and never get to sea.

I will never know the truth of such things, or whether

events have been guided by a divine hand. I know only that Jehangir was a prince and I but a page, yet I felt sorry for him. I will miss him.

Chapter 25

He waited by the grate a fourth week, and a fifth, always in vain. He was ready to confess everything about himself to the Kislar Agha, who alone would be able to find out about her. Nico would do that and meet his executioner gladly, if only he could first have word of her safety.

During a Greek lesson Nico failed to respond to a question—not once but twice. By the time he rose from the fog and realized his lapse, Iskander was standing directly in front of him, his face inches away. Iskander's eyes burned with curiosity. "Do you think of your secrets, Asha?" he asked quietly. "Tell me of your secrets."

"No, sire. There are no secrets. I was only . . ." And Nico could not think of a word to say after that. His mind went blank, and he stared stupidly into the cold eyes of his *lala* and knew that his face betrayed him.

"I know a means by which we might refresh your attention span, even if it might not loosen your tongue for me," Iskander said. He made Nico climb atop a courtyard wall above the Büyük Oda and stand there for eighteen hours, without water or food. The wall was no wider than one of his own feet, and to fall would surely be to die, but Nico stood toe to heel and had no trouble staying upright, because *she* held him there. Though he could not see into that part of the seraglio where she lived, his mind saw her clearly, sitting in the garden with her friends. She looked up at him and waved gaily, and she ran to the foot of the wall. She climbed the branches of a fig tree and brought him fruit and cool water. They spoke in whispers, and then in full voice, because everyone in the courtyard below had gone away and left them alone. She stayed all day, from before sunrise, and through the heat when sweat poured from him, and past sunset into the night, when the cold air from the Bosphorus froze the sweat in his clothing and made him shiver. Only when he was back on the ground did she release him from her embrace. His quivering knees collapsed, and he slept.

And then, two weeks later, she was there—not in his mind, but *really* there. She slipped in through the grate and saw the tears of relief that welled in his eyes, and she kissed them away and held him. "My love, my Asha, I am all right. Forgive me, I could not come. The eunuch saw me that day running behind everyone else. He suspected something. He has been watching me and I could not come. I would have done so anyway, for I could not stand it any longer, but I dared not put you at risk. And then yesterday Allah smiled upon us—the eunuch fell ill of food poisoning and was taken away." Nico kept his head buried for a moment more until the lump in his throat subsided and he could control his voice and his tears. He did not want her to see a page of the Enderun Kolej so weak.

They hurried down the slope and took their place by their underground sea. Holding her hand, he immediately plunged into the subject that had consumed him. "Do you ever think of escape?"

"*Escape!*" She regarded him as if he were mad.

"Yes, Alisa, escape! I realize how impossible it must seem, but I know it could be done. I could do it! There would be the two of us, and there are other pages who would help, I know there are, pages who would gladly come." He was growing animated, excited. "We would steal a galley. . . ."

Her look doused him in cold water. "Escape to what?"

"Why, to *home*," he said.

"*Home!* Why would I want to go home? Brindisi is made of mud, which melts each spring in the rains. My father beat me every day, and there was never enough to eat. Everyone I knew in my village was taken or killed by the corsairs. But even if they hadn't been, if I returned I would have no money, no birth, no future. I would have to marry the farrier and take a pigsty for my castle. I was brought from that hell to this heaven, where even with this face I eat apples and plums, and drink honeyed water. Though I am but a servant, I

have henna for my hair and silk for my clothing. My own mistress
has tutored me in logic and Greek, and in the five sensuous offerings.
Here I know she will never be first *Khátún* to the Sultan—he sees
only Khurrem, the Bringer of Joy, and desires no other woman. But
she will please another man, certainly a lofty one, and I shall remain
at her side when she does. That man will live in a palace, and put a
place like Brindisi beneath his boot. If I were to marry—though no
man would have me—my husband would do the same." She shook
her head, to rid it of the odious notion. "Thank you, Asha, but no
man who truly cared for me would ever take me *home*."

Her reaction made him feel foolish. "*I* care for you," he said
miserably. "I only thought—"

"I know," she said. "You meant it to be kind. It was not. And if
you were to try to escape, they would kill you. They would catch
you, and—" Her reaction to Brindisi was replaced by concern for
him. "I would die myself if anything happened to you. You must
promise me you will never try."

"Very well, then," he said quickly, trying to recover his composure. "I will stay here and become Grand Vizier. You will marry
me. We shall conquer Brindisi and banish it from the face of the
earth."

She laughed and touched his sleeve. "I believe great things of
thee, Asha, Protector of Fire, yet you must find a woman who is
whole, one who is not a servant. But tell me—is your own home in
Venice such a fine place that you are so desperate to return?" She
looked at him wryly. "Or have you lied to me, Asha? Were you a
prince in Venice rather than the son of a shipwright? Do you long
to leave this palace only to return to your castle?"

Now he felt truly low and wretched. It was the first time she had
repeated his lie back to him. She still thought him someone other
than he was. And her question was unsettling beyond that, for it
raised doubt where none had existed before. There had never been
a second thought: his future held escape and return home. Everything he had done, everything he had been through, had all been for
that.

"My family is there, that's all," he said weakly. "My home."

"Your family is here as well. Is not the House of Osman your
house? Is not the Sultan your father? The other pages your brothers?

Am I not—" Now it was her turn to falter. She looked down, embarrassed.

He took her hand. "I would have you for my wife," he said solemnly, "but only when I am worthy."

She held his hand to her cheek, and now a tear fell from her eye. "I wish it were I who could decide such things," she whispered, "for I would make that so in one beat of my heart. But it is for others to write my future."

His letter that night repeated the words *I am still Nico* four times. When he finished writing he crawled from his pallet and slept on the cold stone floor, feeling guilt at the cool comfort of his cotton sheets. He pulled his coin from its hiding place, the coin Maria had given him a lifetime ago. He turned it over and over in his hands.

I am still here, Maria. I am still Nico.

Sleep would not come. He wrestled with his conscience. Things were going well in his life, he knew that to be true. The Saracen demons he had seen as a boy in the eastern sky were simply not there when he was close enough at last to touch them. Life in Topkapi was not perfect, of course. There was always an element of fear. Every man in the serai felt it: the omnipresent hand of death, the certain knowledge that the slightest disobedience or indiscipline could set in motion the cold swing of the executioner's blade. Yes, there was that steel hand of Osman, but there was another of velvet, a hand that offered learning and opportunity, a hand that pointed the way to great beauty alongside simple devotion to Allah. Even Allah had faded over time as an evil being as Nico lived so close to Him. Most lately he had prayed to Allah as well as to God to keep Alisa safe, and his prayer had been answered. Which god had answered?

He knew the passage of time was softening his resolve, and it worried him. He missed Maria, truly, but his parents hardly at all. His father was hard and his mother bitter; they were much like the land of Malta itself.

But for all that he was far from ready to abandon himself. He sought a middle ground.

Why must I be one or the other? Can I not be both?

❖

Nico counted in his mind: in the two years since he first laid eyes upon Alisa, he had been with her only eleven times. He could vividly recall each moment of each visit, each word and touch, the feel of her lips and the warmth of her breath on his cheek, the whisper of her dreams in his ear. They had never been able to fulfill their desire for each other. As difficult as it had been, he had kept his promise to himself that he would never again place her in such jeopardy. Even without that, he knew how incredibly fortunate they were to have had anything at all. Most men passed their years in the seraglio without ever seeing a woman, while he had passed two blessed years in love.

It was on the next visit, their twelfth, that their fragile world fell apart.

He set the grate in place and saw she'd been weeping. "What is it? What has happened?"

"Oh, Asha, I tell myself my fate has been written, that it is for the best." She wiped her eyes, and he saw she was trembling. He felt his heart pounding wildly in dread. They knelt together.

"Fate?" He could hardly form the word; it died in his throat. "What . . . ?"

"I am leaving the palace."

He sat weakly, the color gone from his face. He closed his eyes and fought the nausea of fear. "Please, no, not that." It was barely a whisper. "When?"

"Tomorrow, I think."

"*Tomorrow!* This cannot be. It cannot be." He threw his arms around her. They clung to each other.

She pulled back and held his face in her hands. "My mistress is one of eight from the harem selected as a gift for a *beylerbey*. A merchant is here even now. When he is finished loading his ships, he will take us back with his fleet. I cannot come again."

"I know there are traders here, more than a score of them. The Kislar Agha is having a banquet for them tonight. All the pages are required to serve. Where is he from? Alexandria?"

"Algiers."

Nico blanched. "There is no worse hole on this earth!" Instantly he regretted saying it.

"Even so, it is . . . where I must go."

"I will kill the traders. Sink their ships." His voice was thick with fear.

"You are sweet, Asha, sweet and foolish. You must leave fate to fate."

"Escape with me now. We will leave by this tunnel at this very moment. I will—"

She touched his cheek and shook her head. "You must not, and I cannot. Things are not ready. If we were caught, they would kill us both. I could not stand to lose you that way."

"Then I will follow you!"

"You know how I pray for that. But you must follow Allah's path, not mine. You must live the life that is written for you, as I must live mine." She held his hand to her face and kissed it, and he could feel the warmth of her tears. "I had allowed myself to think they were somehow written together. Oh, Asha, Asha. I love you so. I cannot bear this."

They held each other tightly. "You will never lose me."

"I must leave now. There are many preparations to be made. I was afraid I would not even have time to say farewell."

"Come back tonight, after the banquet."

"Do not ask it of me, Asha."

"*Please.* I beg you."

She considered how she might do it. She nodded. "I will enlist the help of my mistress. I will try, Asha. You know I will."

He broke his promise to himself and kissed her, deeply, longingly. "I will find you in Algiers."

When he pulled away from her his cheek was stained with tears. She kissed them away. "Yes, oh, yes, Asha. Come for me, in Algiers." They both knew how impossible that was. Wherever she went, she would be hidden away with her mistress behind a wall in a harem, a secret lost beneath a veil, inside a forbidden maze.

She turned to him as the grate slipped back into place. She put her fingers through and he kissed them, and then he brought his lips as close to hers as he could. "I will love you always," he said, and now his tears were streaming.

"And I you."

"Until tonight." She squeezed, and when she let go, he knew it was for the last time.

As she turned and disappeared into the garden, the candle behind him burned out, and all the light went from his life.

❖

The trader from Algiers nestled on deep cushions that rested on a bed of furs. He wore a white robe and the green velvet fez that signified his stature as *hadji*, a man who had made the pilgrimage. He sat in the second court of Topkapi, beneath a long portico along the length of which ranged a low feast table that stretched more than seventy meters from end to end, to accommodate more than a hundred honored guests. The court was so large that guests in one end could scarcely make out what was happening in the other. It didn't matter, for there were entertainments enough for all: acrobats and wrestlers, dwarves and clowns, musicians and dancers. Pages and servers scurried about, carrying great silver plates heaped with food and drink.

A young page knelt and washed the trader's hands in rosewater. He dried them, one finger at a time. The Algerian relished his visits to the serai, the only place on earth that made his own home seem squalid. To his regret there was no wine, but this was, after all, the sanctuary of the Shadow of God. Yet he glowed warmly, his eyes glazed with hashish, his silver cup filled with exquisite *khusháf,* a heavenly peach beverage flavored with amber and musk.

All the guests were grandees of trade, each of whom had bought or otherwise curried the favor of their host, the Kislar Agha. Aside from his duties in the Enderun Kolej and the inner court of Suleiman, the Chief White Eunuch was Head Chamberlain, one of the wealthiest and most powerful men in the empire. He owned a score of ships and traded goods from the souks of Arabia to the bazaars of Algiers.

The Algerian visited the serai each time he came to Istanbul. His ships strengthened the Sultan's fleets, his Italian brocades graced the Sultan's furnishings, and his florins lined the pockets of the Kislar Agha. He received gifts in return: around his neck was a gold chain presented to him that very evening by his host, bearing an exquisite Egyptian emerald shaped like a crescent. It was a singular gift for an honored associate.

The next morning he would sail for Algiers with four ships, carrying the usual cargo of riches. Only this time his own vessel was reserved for a most precious cargo—the fruit of the harem, beautiful women trained in the arts of love and conversation, and in household service. They were the Sultan's gift for the *beylerbey,* and it was the Algerian's honor to convey them.

His mind floated dreamlike, entranced by the hypnotic, seductive tones of the metal-stringed *kanuns;* the plaintive sighs of a *tanbur,* a long-necked lute; and the lyrical magic of a Persian reed flute—and, in particular, the boy playing it.

One of the pages caught his attention. It was vague at first, only a nagging sense of something familiar. The page was at some distance beyond the musicians, serving at the other end of the table. He wore a blue tunic, tan satin trousers, and embroidered slippers. The trader watched him. The page turned, exposing more of his face. Now the trader set down his cup and sat up. He blinked dully, trying to clear his burning eyes. He did not believe at first, could only barely comprehend. Then, as the certainty grew, he felt his pulse begin to race, felt the blood coursing in his neck, throbbing at his temples.

The page was no longer a boy but a young man. The years had filled him out, but had not changed his appearance. It was still a beautiful face, a face seared into his memory, a face his nightmares had conjured a thousand times as it peered down at the body of his beloved son lying dead in the shipyard, his skull caved in.

Yes, he knew that face as surely as he knew his own. It was a murderer's face.

He could not imagine how the boy had come to the seraglio; he was thought drowned at sea. It did not matter.

The page was from Malta. His name was Nicolo Borg.

El Hadji Farouk fought an impulse to jump up in rage and strike the boy dead then and there. Such a thing was unthinkable, of course, in the Sultan's house. Besides, there was no need for haste. The boy had not seen him and, so long as he continued serving at the far end of the court, was not likely to. Farouk sat back on his cushion again, watching, thinking, trying to clear the fog from his brain.

He could expose Nico, denouncing him as a murderer. But that course held no certainty. He knew the standing of pages in the royal household. There would be *cadis* involved, judges who might not do exactly as he wished. Perhaps, lacking proof in a matter that was under the jurisdiction of the *beylerbey* in Algiers, they would only banish Nico. That was not punishment enough for the slayer of his beloved son Yusuf.

He saw only one course open to him. He would ask his good friend the Kislar Agha to arrange a meeting with the boy that very evening. It was not an outlandish request. The Kislar Agha would think his interest carnal, and anyway he would not question Farouk. The two of them had done business together for years. The Kislar Agha owned two of the ships in Farouk's little fleet, and a third of the cargo. But just to be certain, Farouk would season the request with a purse of Venetian ducats. Farouk would have Nico brought to him in the *khan* where he was staying. There the unfortunate page would meet with a terrible accident. It would be most regrettable. Farouk himself would offer a bounty for the ruffians who had so foully disrupted the Sultan's peace by murdering a member of his household. Farouk clapped his hands and whispered to a boy, requesting an immediate audience with his host.

Half an hour later it was done. Iskander received orders to accompany his page Asha outside the palace. Iskander looked for Asha among the servers but did not see him. He asked another page. "Asha was taken ill, sire," the page said. "I believe he is in his quarters." Iskander strode to the Büyük Oda and entered the chamber where Asha slept. His pallet was empty, as was the entire dormitory. All the pages were still performing their various duties at the banquet. Iskander looked in the latrine. It was vacant. He asked Kasib, the eunuch who sat near the door. Sweating at the queries of the fearsome *lala,* the eunuch professed ignorance. "P-perhaps he is in the *gusulhane*," he stammered, "or—"

"Find him at once," Iskander snapped. "I shall await you in his quarters."

"Yes, master," Kasib squeaked. He scurried away, whimpering quiet prayers.

Iskander returned to Asha's pallet and sat down. An oil lamp burned dimly on its shelf beside the door. A spider hurried across the wall, casting a long shadow. Absently Iskander reached out with his slippered foot and crushed it. In the process he loosened a stone, one side of which slipped partway out of the wall. He nudged it with his foot to restore it, and cocked his head at the odd sound. He leaned forward and took the stone in both hands. It slid out easily. He set it on the ground and peered into the hole, where all was blackness. He took the lantern down and held it before the opening.

There, inside, he saw a bundle of papers.

❖

Bitterly discouraged, Nico crawled up behind the furnace. He'd been late, delayed by his duties at the banquet. Alisa had already been there and gone. She left him a pebble on their sill, around which she'd wrapped a strand of her hair. In the darkness he almost hadn't seen it. Now it was all he had of her, all he might ever have. In his desperation he briefly considered trying to sneak into the harem but knew it was insane—when they finished with him, she would suffer as well.

He quietly slipped the grate into place, then padded through the baths and into the corridor, where he literally ran into Kasib. The eunuch, his ashen face glistening with sweat, seemed particularly glad to see him and motioned him to hurry along. Nico rounded the next corner and stopped dead in his tracks.

There, sitting on Nico's pallet, was Iskander. His head was bowed, his brow furrowed in concentration. Nico's eyes went from his *lala* to the hole in the wall, to the stone on the floor, to the sheaf of papers in Iskander's lap.

The letters.

The shock was so great Nico nearly threw up. His instinct was to turn, to flee. But there was nowhere to run. Besides, he was dizzy, and his legs had gone to jelly. It was all he could do to remain standing.

Iskander knew he was there but did not look up. Instead he continued to read at a leisurely pace, his dark eyes moving deliberately over each word. He turned a page and then another, stacking them neatly on the bed. There were a great many—oh, so many, Nico thought, heartsick at his own prolific suicide. He watched numbly as the damning pile grew: on that page, heresy. On the next, treason. Written there, blasphemy.

There would be no simple banishment through the gate of dishonor, not for this. His life—his *lives*—false life, new life, old life: all were finished now. Before another nightfall, the salted, parboiled head with its two faces of Asha would adorn the Gate of Felicity.

At length Iskander finished. He set the last page in its place and looked up at his page. "Well, *Asha,*" he said. "As always, I must commend you on your excellent hand, which makes it so easy for me to understand whom I address. *Nico.* The son of a mason. I had thought this of you—some of it, that is, but not all of it, not even the greater part of it. I was never able to prove it one way or another and was prepared to let it pass.

"You astonish me with the depth of your duplicity, if not the quality of your deception. The Sultan shall rue the loss of a page of such singular accomplishment, such . . . virtuosity."

"I . . . I can explain, sire," Nico said stupidly. "I was only writing—"

"*Sükût!*" Iskander stood. He read the terror in Nico's eyes and wondered if he might try to fight or to run. Iskander carried no weapon here in the inner court. But he was *lala:* he needed no weapons—not with Asha, nor any page. It was a matter of no concern.

Despite the discovery he gave no thought whatever to altering the instructions he'd received from his master regarding Asha. He would follow them to the letter, of course. One deviated from the Kislar Agha's orders only at the price of one's head. Iskander would deal with this new matter in due time. He put the sheaf of letters inside his robe and took Nico by the arm. They left the dormitory and walked down the corridor past the guard, in front of the Chamber of Petitions and through the Gate of Felicity into the Second Court, the Court of Justice. The council hall lay on their right. The ruling divan met there, ministers and viziers who dispensed justice and administered the empire in the name of the Sultan, who sometimes secretly watched the proceedings from behind a latticed window. Neither subject nor vizier ever knew when, or if, he was listening. Now Nico felt the Sultan's gaze burning into his back. A breeze stirred the dark green cypress trees that towered over the court like minarets. Gazelles grazed near whispering fountains, watching his passage. It was a cool autumn night, and tressed halberdiers hurried with buckets of coals for the braziers of the harem.

They neared the gilded iron doors set below the battlements of the Orta Kapi, the middle gate. Two octagonal towers with conical roofs rose on either side of the gate, housing prisoners. Double doors in the vestibule concealed the executioner's room, where mutes awaited their orders with swords and bowstrings. Nico had long known all these things, but he had never so felt the awful terror of the place, the absolute power, the swift justice, the unyielding rules, the nearness of death. All the beauty of Topkapi had given way to dread. He stepped into the vestibule, thinking it was here and now he would meet his death. His thoughts were on Alisa and on Maria.

Alisa. Tonight, while she still slept, the eunuchs would come and hand her over to the mutes. He could have disguised her in his letters. Why had he put her at risk? And brave Nasrid, and his travels into Istanbul for opium. Even the sweet-smelling eunuch, Kasib. Because of Nico, their necks would all feel the sharp edge of the Sultan's retribution before another day was done.

To Nico's surprise Iskander pushed him along, through the gate, past the executioner's post. "Where are we going, sire?" he asked.

"Where the Kislar Agha has commanded."

They followed a winding path down the hill and through a stand of willow trees. There were a dozen guards at the wrought-iron sea gate. They stood aside as the two men passed. No one questioned their passage; their dress marked their palace rank. They walked out to the end of a covered wooden pier. Iskander summoned one of the palace caiques, a light, fast boat that would ferry them across the Golden Horn to the trading quarter of Galata.

Once outside the palace, Nico's thoughts finally turned to escape, a prospect for which there appeared little hope. He knew that Iskander, though older, could easily outrun him. A fight was hopeless. At Iskander's prodding Nico stepped into the long craft. It rocked beneath his foot. He thought briefly of waiting until they were partway across, then tipping it over and swimming to escape, but Iskander was one of the few men in all Istanbul who could swim. It seemed there was nothing this man could not do, no weakness to be exploited.

They crossed the harbor and disembarked on the Galata quay,

near the long stone wharf where a line of tall merchantmen were moored. Beyond them lay galleys of the Sultan's fleet. They passed through a gate and up rough cobbled streets, past public *hamams* and private warehouses, toward the tower that stood sentry over the quarter. They passed a *charshi,* a covered street lined with shops and kiosks, where during the day crowds thronged to purchase caftans from Damascus, tandoors from Aleppo, carpets from Persia. All the goods were laid out in long aisles, each devoted to a different type of merchandise. Now the markets were all but deserted. A guard strolled by, making his nightly rounds. Nico eyed the gleaming scimitar that hung at his side and instantly felt Iskander's grip tighten.

They passed the spice market and its mosque, and one of the many stations where huge cisterns of water stood near fire pumps. There were beggars and mules, stray dogs and drunken sailors, pious clerics and sheiks of the guilds. Along the way Nico was awash in sensation. He smelled hashish, antimony, and sandalwood, and something frying in honey. He heard the murmur of prayer, someone reciting the *al-fatihah;* he heard the rustle of silk robes and the soft padding of sandals on the cobbles. He felt the night air on the light hairs at the nape of his neck.

It was Iskander himself who had taught his pages that impending death brought such acuity of senses and clarity of mind.

Use that awareness, Iskander told them. *Take every advantage.*

Nico had no idea how to do so, and took one step after another as he walked toward his death. Iskander was right: he would never have fared well in battle.

They came to a business *mehalle,* a quarter where merchants lived and traded, and turned down a dark street. They stopped outside one of the *khans,* a two-story lodging built of wood and stone, fronted by a high wall. Traveling merchants often stayed there, in private rooms arrayed around a courtyard. Living quarters were on the second story, while beneath them were stalls and stables, shops and coffeehouses, and workrooms where raw materials were fashioned into finished products for sale in the markets.

Iskander seemed to know the place. He pushed open the gate and guided Nico through. They stepped over a wooden threshold into a large courtyard. Chickens scattered and a sheep bleated. A caretaker's shed stood vacant near the entrance. The courtyard was cloaked in shadows and gloom, filling Nico with a terrible fore-boding. His heart began to pound.

They ascended a steep wooden stairway to a landing, where their progress was blocked by an inner gate that opened onto the foyer of a large two-room apartment. Iskander clapped twice, softly. There was a rustle of curtains, and a large man appeared in the foyer. He was head and shoulders taller than Iskander, his muscular arms bare and rippling with power. From his dress he appeared to be a sailor. He opened the gate and to Iskander's inquiry inclined his head toward one of the doors and stepped aside to let them pass. Nico realized the man was mute. The thought made his mouth go dry. In Istanbul, the Abode of Happiness, mutes had but one primary occupation. He felt Iskander release his arm, which only heightened his sense of alarm. *Gather yourself!* He took a deep breath, trying to still the terror. He stepped inside, Iskander and the mute close behind him.

It took a moment for his eyes to adjust. It was a large room, dimly lit by two wall lanterns, their wicks turned low. Thick carpets covered the floor. Lavish hangings decorated paneled walls, along the top of which were latticed windows to provide ventilation. Stout beams supported a sloping lead roof. Stacked along the walls, between cabinets and shelves, were wooden trunks and leather chests, holding the merchandise of an obviously wealthy trader.

His back to his guests, El Hadji Farouk sat on a cushion at the far end of the room, staring as if hypnotized into the coals of a brazier. His turban was coiled high, topped with an aigrette nestled in a copper tube.

"Peace be upon thee, effendi," said Iskander, bowing deeply. "As the Kislar Agha ordered, I present you with the page."

Farouk did not stir. It was as if he had not heard. Iskander stepped forward, to speak again. Farouk said, still without moving, "And on you be peace, and the mercy of God and His blessings."

He turned then and stared up at Nico, on whose face the shock of recognition rose like bile. The Algerian's face was fleshier now, more dissipated with wine and soft living. It was a lifetime and hundreds of leagues—an entire world—from where he had last seen him, and that distance added to his momentary confusion. But nothing could mask that face for long. Nico felt the blood coursing at his temples as the memories roared in: Mehmet and his cudgel. The long night spent with the rats, waiting for the bastinado. Leonardus, running for the sea. And Yusuf. Of course, Yusuf. Dead on the beach, by Nico's hand.

Traders from Algiers! Nico knew he should have thought of Farouk when Alisa had told him of the ships that were to take her away. But many traders visited the palace, from Algiers and every other city in the Sultan's domains. Besides, he had long since shut Farouk out of his mind, and the thought of never seeing Alisa again had overwhelmed all else.

"So. The Kislar Agha tells me your name is Asha," Farouk said with a thin smile. "I have been expecting you, *Asha.*"

Stunned, Nico took a step back. A moment earlier he had lamented his lack of options. Now he had two: death before him, at the hand of Farouk, and death behind him, at the hand of Iskander. His eyes scanned the room, looking for a weapon.

Iskander had instantly sensed the menace emanating from Farouk. Normally Iskander would have waited outside until the business was concluded, but now he made no move to leave. No matter that Asha would forfeit his head the next day. Until then, and at any time outside the palace, the page was his responsibility.

Farouk stood. "Leave us," he said imperiously to Iskander, the palace servant. "Return to the serai. I will escort the boy myself when our business is concluded."

"For that, effendi," Iskander replied politely, "I must needs have the permission of the Kislar Agha, which, regrettably, I do not have."

"The Kislar Agha is my good friend," Farouk said darkly. "He would tell you to do as I wish."

"He is friend to many, effendi, but master to me. He has already given me instructions." The smile was correct, the refusal absolute, the hooded eyes dangerous.

Farouk was seething, though his face remained impassive. He had not expected this, but it would not be a problem. He had chosen his helper carefully, from his own ships in the harbor. Assad was a tested assassin, a silent killer who had dispatched his enemies from Antioch to Oran. Despite Farouk's thirst for vengeance and his confidence with a blade, he was not deluded about Nico, who was, after all, no longer a boy, but a man—and one trained, at that, by the best of the Sultan's warriors. While Farouk intended to kill Nico with his own hand, Assad was there to guarantee the outcome. Farouk regarded the man who brought Nico. He looked fit and dangerous, but he was a palace slave, nothing more. Farouk and Assad would simply have two men to dispatch instead of one, and the reward he would offer for the ruffians responsible would have to be doubled.

Farouk raised his hands in a gesture of gracious surrender. "Of course, I understand," he said, smiling. "The Kislar Agha is blessed indeed to have such devoted servants. Please forgive me." He looked at Assad, who read his eyes perfectly. Farouk turned toward a stand that held a porcelain carafe and serving dishes. "And now along with my apology perhaps you will accept a modest refreshment of *pekmez* and coffee." His hand never touched the service, but fell on the hilt of a richly jeweled sword that lay next to it. With murderous suddenness he turned and, with both hands gripping the hilt, swung the sword at Nico. At the same instant, Assad lashed out against Iskander with a mace, and the deadly battle was joined.

Farouk's blade sliced the air with a lethal hiss. Nico had expected something of the sort and leapt back, out of the way. Farouk recovered quickly, spun, and swung again. Nico hurled himself toward the floor, rolling, trying to catch Farouk by the legs. He caught only a handful of robe and heard the soft whump of the steel blade as it bit into the carpet next to his leg. He rolled over and was up again in a flash, crouching, looking for something to use as a weapon, or at least as a parry. Farouk swung again and again at his nimble adversary, his blade finding first more empty air, then taking a thick chunk from the paneling.

At the other end of the room, Iskander quickly disarmed his assailant, whose mace lay on the floor. Their struggle was fierce and furious as they smashed against the wall, then crashed over a stack of chests and onto the ground.

Farouk might be old and soft, but his blade was long and sharp, and he was a determined killer. He pressed Nico relentlessly. Nico tripped and fell back against one of the hanging tapestries on the wall. He ripped it from its hooks, crouched, and swung it out, catching the tip of Farouk's blade. With a mighty shove he drove Farouk into the wall. Nico closed his hand over the blade, only part of which was protected by the tapestry. The rest bit deeply into his palm. Nico's other hand worked its way down the blade toward the hilt. He turned the sword sideways, like a staff, pinning the Algerian against the wall. Farouk still had hold of the hilt, his knuckles white as he tried to wrest it from Nico's grasp, both men's arms trembling as they struggled silently for the weapon, their faces but an inch apart, their eyes locked on each other. In a contest of sheer strength, Nico had the advantage. He inched the blade up Farouk's chest, pushing robes along with it, until finally it rested against the trader's neck. He increased the pressure and Farouk began to choke.

In desperation Farouk brought his knee up and caught Nico in the groin, breaking his hold. The two of them whirled together, neither letting go of the sword. They crashed once into the wall, then into a shelf, splintering wood and scattering porcelain, and fell hard to the floor. Farouk's head hit the brazier, but his turban absorbed most of the blow.

On top, Nico pinned Farouk's legs with his own, and once more the flat edge of the sword found Farouk's neck. Nico pushed down. Farouk tried to work his fingers between the blade and his neck. His eyes never left Nico, but now the two black pools of hatred began to bulge and show fear at last. His grip began to slacken, and then he let go. His face went blue, his lips purple. He made a gurgling sound. With all his weight on the blade, still Nico pressed down, even after he felt the struggles stop.

A few feet away, Iskander stood, his head bleeding but his first battle finished. Assad's sightless eyes fixed on the ceiling, the mace buried in his brain. Iskander rushed forward and seized Nico by the collar of his kaftan, yanking him back. Nico ripped himself free and plunged forward again onto Farouk, the force compressing Farouk's neck all the way to his spine. The blow was unneeded: Farouk's eyes were grotesque and protruding. The trader from Algiers was dead.

Iskander stepped on one end of the sword to trap it and brutally clubbed his page on the side of the head. The blow sent Nico tumbling sideways toward the brazier. Iskander started for him.

Nico rolled over and grabbed the iron pot by the two front legs, the hot metal blistering his hands. He rose as he turned, and with all his strength swung the brazier up at his teacher's head, spraying coals all over the room. The pot glanced off the *lala*'s chin. Momentarily dazed, he staggered backward. Still holding the brazier, Nico struggled frantically to his feet. If Iskander recovered, even partially, the fight would be over. Iskander took an unsteady step forward.

Take advantage where you can get it, the *lala* always taught. *No quarter in war.*

Nico swung again, only this time he didn't have the strength left to swing at head level, as he intended. The brazier hit Iskander in the sternum. There was a resonant thunk, and Nico knew the brazier had broken something important inside him. Stunned, Iskander stopped and shook his head, his dark eyes determined, fearless. He sank to his knees, one hand to his chest, the other still grasping for the brazier. He would not give up. Nico prepared to hit him again, but Iskander began gasping. He fell to the floor on his side, then rolled onto his back. His eyes were open, but he couldn't move.

Winded and spent, Nico dropped the pot and sat heavily. He smelled smoke. Coals from the brazier were smoldering, and a dozen wisps of smoke rose from the carpet. Near the door he saw flames. The room was tinder-dry. The fire snaked up the wall. A shelf caught, and then a wall hanging. Flames licked at the jamb and door, then shot toward the wooden beams of the ceiling. Thick black smoke poured from wood and fiber.

Coughing, Nico got to his feet and headed for the door. His hand was on the latch when he stopped and returned to Iskander. He reached inside his *lala*'s robes, searching for the letters. Iskander weakly clutched Nico's arm, his eyes open and still hard, still full of fight. But the rest of his body seemed all but paralyzed. Nico pried his fingers away. He tucked the letters in his sash. As he rose he picked up Farouk's sword. He looked at Iskander, wondering whether to use it. The smoke and flames made his decision for him. He could remain no longer. He lurched for the door.

He burst outside and doubled over, wheezing and coughing, taking in great gulps of fresh air. He ripped open the upper gate and raced down the stairs to the courtyard. The innkeeper's shed was still empty. Nico stepped through the outer gate and into the street. He looked back up at the landing, at the door to Farouk's apartments. He worried that he hadn't finished Iskander, that somehow the extraordinary man would emerge from the doorway. If he did, Nico was ready to finish things with the sword. But the door remained closed. Smoke billowed from the latticed windows, thick and black and all but lost against the night sky. A long moment passed, and another, each easing his fear. Flames flickered through the lattices and licked at the eaves of the upper hall.

"*Yangiiiin!*" Someone on the opposite side of the courtyard saw the flames, instantly raising the alarm at the top of his lungs. Fires were a deadly reality in Istanbul. Even the Sultan would quickly be alerted to the blaze, by a girl from the harem who would appear silently before him, wearing a flame-colored shift.

People poured from doors and alleys, the crowd growing almost as quickly as the fire. Within moments there were people milling everywhere, confused, shouting, watching the blaze. A part of the lead roof melted. Flames leapt into the sky. A fire brigade was hastily organized, a long line of buckets passed down the street from a well. It was much too late to save the *khan*. They might hope only to save neighboring dwellings, or at least the quarter itself. Nico watched as the fire quickly became an inferno; he felt the heat on his face. Flames roiled and whirled outside all the windows and broke through the walls. He heard it shrieking and popping, consuming everything like the wrath of an angry God.

He watched until he knew beyond doubt that nothing—no one—could have survived. Then he turned and strode quickly away from the commotion, down the street toward the harbor, pushing through the streams of people running the other way. After a few streets he slowed and turned down an alley. He stopped and sat down. He felt light-headed and nauseous and thought he was going to vomit. He put his head between his legs and breathed deeply, waiting for the terror to subside. His brain raced, trying to absorb the horror.

He raised his head and looked out over the timeless splendor of Istanbul, lit only by a crescent sliver of moon and a blanket of stars. He could see the dark waters of the Golden Horn, and beyond it the walls of the seraglio, and the humped tin roofs of its kitchens. Behind the serai rose the glorious dome of the Hagia Sophia, and off to his right that of the unfinished Suleimaniye. To his left rose the low dark hills of the Asian shore, lights twinkling from its low walled compounds. He watched a fisherman on the Bosphorus rigging a net for goatfish. Others hung bright flares from the gunwales of their boats, seeking to attract the mackerel that swam from the cold Black Sea to the warmer waters of the strait to lay their eggs.

He thought he should get back, the more quickly the better. He started to rise, then caught himself. He sat again, thinking. Since coming to the Abode of Felicity, he had been outside the seraglio only half a dozen times, and never once without dragomen, tutors, eunuchs, or Janissaries in attendance.

Suddenly, for the first time in years, he was alone.

Suddenly he was free.

A rush of thoughts flooded in as he realized the possibilities.

He could see a French galleass at the wharf, taking on cargo. He could board her by climbing up her anchor lines and then hide in the stern. Or he could steal a boat, something small—anything would do, a caique, even a canoe. He'd planned it a thousand times. Or perhaps a horse. Yes, that was it—he could steal a horse and travel overland, into the dark, inviting mass of Europe that stretched away on his right hand. He would have twelve hours at least before he was missed. And even when he was missed, no one would imagine he was running. They would think both he and Iskander perished in the fire. No one would chase him. He could pass himself off as a *geomaler,* a pilgrim of love, traveling on his wits across Rumelia to the Adriatic. From there, Naples and Sicily.

And home.

I am free.

It was all so sudden, so unexpected, this opportunity. And so uncomfortable, thinking about it.

Free to do what? And why?

He wailed inside. *I am still a son of Malta.*

No! Malta has forsaken me! I am confusing my homeland with my destiny. Why must the one be written with the other?

He realized that his hands were shaking and that it wasn't from the fight.

I am Nico, I am Asha. I am Maltese, I am Ottoman. I am Christian, I am Muslim. I am Maria's brother, Alisa's . . . lover. I am the son of Luca, the son of Leonardus, the son of Suleiman.

He no longer knew. All he knew was that somehow his passion to escape had dimmed, or else it had never been as strong as he thought. *Alisa is right—I am someone here. And am I not already free, as free as any man of the empire? Do I not tread on a golden path?*

Alisa—

He seized on the thought of her. She was still there, in the palace. Perhaps, with Farouk dead, things would change. The trip to Algiers might never happen. Alisa's mistress might remain in the palace and be pledged to another. In five years, only five short years, he might have the hope of marrying her.

Yes, that was it. He needed no other reason. He must stay, for her.

Ten minutes later he was at the waterfront, imperiously commanding the pilot of a caique to return him to the pavilion below the iron sea gate of Topkapi.

❖

Nico remained in his quarters all the next day, pretending to study, desperate for news. He considered getting Nasrid to pass an extra drachm of opium to Kasib so that he might slip into the underground through the baths and seek her out. It was no use. Even if she was still in the harem, she wouldn't be able to come for nearly another week. He thought of making his way down to the Golden Horn, where he might see Farouk's ships and learn something of her fate. But leaving his cot was far too dangerous now. They would come for him at any moment. Worry soured his stomach, and sweat soaked his cap. He felt certain his head was destined for the salt sack and for hideous display above the gate.

It was after evening prayer when the eunuchs came for him. At double time he followed them to the gatekeeper's quarters, where he was ushered inside. The Kislar Agha sat imperiously on his low stool. To Nico's relief there were no mutes there, but the eunuch still unsettled him, as always—his voice as sexless and cold as that pallid face, hairless and waxen beneath the high white cone of his office. Dark circles rimmed tiny, deep-set eyes. Nico was glad of the protocol that required his own eyes to be averted, his hands crossed over his chest. Indeed, it was a fortunate pose for hiding cuts and burns on one's hands, and for hiding the lies in one's eyes. Nico looked submissively at the ground. "My lord?"

"You went to Galata with Iskander last night?"

"Yes, my lord. I understood it was your order."

"As it was. You saw the merchant from Algiers, El Hadji Farouk?"

"Yes, my lord, bless his name."

"What did he want?"

Nico blushed, as much from the needs of the lie itself as from the ease with which he told it. "There were two reasons, Lord. He wanted me for his . . . pleasure."

The Chief White Eunuch waved impatiently at the call of flesh. "And the second?"

"He knew my father in Venice. As is recorded in my history, he died in the shipwreck from which Lord Dragut rescued me. El Hadji Farouk recognized me serving at the banquet and wanted to give me something."

"And what was that?"

"A jeweled sword, my lord. He said it belonged to my father. He retrieved it from his ship, where he said he carried it always. Upon my return to the serai I left it with the Janissaries at the weapons storehouse."

"And why did you return alone, without Iskander?"

"It was as he ordered. He remained with El Hadji Farouk."

"Why?"

"I do not know, sire. My *lala* does not tell me his reasons for doing. He tells me only to obey."

"There was a fire in the very *khan* where he took you. Many perished." He held up a large crescent-shaped gem. The stone had lost most of its color from the heat but was clearly an emerald. "The fire was quite thorough. This was all that remained of the hadji. I gave it to him only last night." He looked carefully at the page. "Perhaps you saw the fire?"

The gash on Nico's hand burned from the salt in the sweat that soaked it. "No, sire. I saw no fire."

"Indeed. That is odd, as is the fact that Iskander has not returned. He has not been seen since he left with you. He is not a man to be absent from duty." The Kislar Agha studied the page intently, looking for any sign.

"Fortune abounds with terrible accidents, sire," Nico said blandly. "Perhaps he was among those killed, Allah forbid. But perhaps he is merely visiting one of El Hadji Farouk's ships."

"The Janissaries searched them before they sailed."

Nico's heart skipped a beat. He fought dizziness. "Sailed, lord?" His voice was more croak than question.

"Of course. There was nothing to keep them here, and much of my business to send them away. Commerce thrives, even if Farouk does not." The Kislar Agha concluded there was nothing more to be learned on the matter. "And now to a second purpose for my summons."

"Sire?" It was all he could do to concentrate now that she was gone.

"With Iskander's blessings, your name has made its way onto the list of promotion to the Privy Chamber. If it pleases the Sultan, you are to become *kaftanli*—a senior page."

Nico bowed deeply, his eyes closed tightly in disappointment. For anyone else the transition from novice to the active service of the Padishah was a glorious step on the passage to greatness. With Alisa gone, all his ambivalence returned. He had come back for *her*. Without her he had no desire to remain in the palace. In promotion he saw nothing but the death of his wish to get to sea, to become the captain of his own galley, with which he could search for her, or escape, or simply make his own way in the world. A man with a galley was a man with choices. Now he would surely die a vizier, but not without first dying a thousand other deaths along the way.

I was wrong, he thought bitterly. *I should have run.*

Chapter 26

My dear sister,

The singular events of my life have come in the guise of a treasure hunt with thee, then with a shipwright, a corsair, a servant girl—and now, most lately, a monkey. It is in the form of this monkey that I have seen the hand of Allah shaping my fate. Perhaps I should have seen the hand all along.

I was summoned to see the Padishah himself, just after the prayer of *salat al-zuhr*. My heart skipped: the Lord of the Age asked for me by name: *Asha*.

I entered his presence as humble and powerless as a leaf trembling before a mighty storm. A monarch who should have been clothed in the raiments of heaven was dressed that day as plainly as I, in a modest gown of green mohair. He wore a pearl in his ear, and a perfect ruby adorned his turban. To my astonishment I saw that there were no other pages or attendants waiting upon the person of the sovereign. We were alone.

I kissed his knee and the hem of his gown, and prostrated myself, scarcely daring to breathe until he bade me rise. Imagine my surprise as I got to my feet and saw next to him the book of poems I had written for Jehangir.

"Tell us how this book came to be," commanded the Padishah. His voice did not sound of thunder, as one might expect, but of velvet. I forgot myself and very nearly spoke out loud. One may never speak in his exalted presence, or even whisper to another. We are taught *isaret*, a sign language that is known by all in the seraglio. It is used in the royal presence by all but his most favored pages, and adds to the awe in which he is held, if such a thing were possible.

Using the signs, I began to explain—and he bade me speak! It took me a moment to recover my wits and find my voice. I told him of my visits with the prince as he wrote the poems, and of how the book was lost in the storm. As I spoke, imagine my surprise to discover that the Possessor of Men's Necks—a thousand pardons, but it is the truth—is as sentimental as a woman when it comes to the matter of his dead son's poetry. In every corridor one hears the whispers: the Sultan is suspicious and arrogant. I saw no such man. I can swear to thee I saw his eyes mist, as I know I heard his voice break in profound grief. In this, I believe, was to be found the key to my sovereign. Here was the most powerful man in all the world: in one battle, twenty thousand of his enemies perished in three hours, and he remarked only upon the weather. Faced with all the world's cares and burdens, the Padishah was reduced to tears only over the matter of his own son, Jehangir.

He beckoned me to approach his person. With his own hand he placed a handkerchief on my shoulder, a sign of great favor. I felt humbled as never before, and he spoke to me as a son. "We are reminded of Ibrahim Pasha, a good friend of our youth. He too had a quick wit, an ear for languages, and a remarkable memory. He is the only other man we know who could have done this."

"My lord is too kind," I replied modestly. I knew well Suleiman had had his best and only friend, Ibrahim Pasha, strangled. I hoped never to impress my Sultan quite so well.

"Clearly, thou art skilled with the pen, and we are told that the history of this house falls from thy lips as if written inside thy head. We shall be pleased to accept thee into our service as one of the thirty-nine pages to our person."

One of the thirty-nine! Suleiman himself made the fortieth; it was honor beyond measure, yet an honor I did not seek. I said nothing, but the Padishah was known as a shrewd judge of men, and my look must have betrayed me. "It is not thy wish to do this, we surmise."

I hung my head in shame. "No, my lord."

"Tell us, then, of thy desire," he said. "Tell us what it is thou might do in the service of the House of Osman."

And that was when I boldly seized my chance to escape the chains of court that seemed to be my destiny. It is the Ottoman custom to marry desire with ability; I had failed only in demonstrating my ability to my tutor. With my heart in my throat I took a great risk. "I wish to serve in thy galleys, my lord," I said.

"It is the judgment of thy tutors that thou art better suited for the palace."

"They are wise indeed, great lord, wise beyond measure. I wish not to prove them in error, but only to prove I can serve thee better at sea."

The Sultan, I well knew, was accustomed to giving rich gifts to those who pleased him. A magnificent palace to a vizier, the spoils of plunder to an agha, a sachet of gems to a bey. To me, a speck of dust beneath his slipper, he granted the right to serve him in the manner I chose myself. It was a great gift for me, yet a small thing for him to grant—as small as the monkey that had brought me to this audience. Is it not said that Allah makes easy the fulfilling of His desires? As easily as that, it was done.

In the morning I leave to begin my training.

❖

Nico arrived in Gallipoli to devastating news.

The fleet belonging to the Kislar Agha and the late El Hadji Farouk had been attacked by Christian corsairs off the coast of Lesbos. One of the ships was sunk, one escaped, and all the rest were taken in tow. The men aboard the vessel that escaped reported that all the officers were butchered, the crew enslaved, the Christian oarsmen freed.

The ship that sank was the largest, Farouk's own galley. A shot from the corsair's falconet detonated the powder magazine. The ship went down quickly. The fate of the women on board was not known, although it was thought doubtful any could have survived.

A pursuit by a swift fleet of galliots was hastily organized. The brigands were chased past Chios and nearly trapped in Naxos, but escaped in a storm off the shore of Candia.

To veteran seamen it was merely a routine skirmish between old enemies. "*Malish, mektoub,*" they said. *Never mind, it is written.* Their own day would come, their way lit with lamps fueled by oil from the hearts of infidels.

In living memory the pattern had not changed. The Muslims killed the Christians, and the Christians killed the Muslims. The scales tipped one way for a while, and then back the other, as each side struggled for advantage. The only thing that remained constant was the blood color of the sea.

To Nico, however, it was not so simple. His hatred knew no bounds for the man he thought responsible for the death of Alisa.

The corsair in question was the scourge of the Sultan's fleets, a ruthless cutthroat, a legendary captain called Romegas.

His ships flew the red and white cross—the colors of the Knights of St. John.

from The Histories of the Middle Sea

by Darius, called the Preserver
Court Historian to the Emperor of All God's Lands, the
Sultan Achmet

After leaving the court of Suleiman, Nicolo Borg, now called Asha, spent two years at the naval school in Gallipoli. The brilliant page was an even more brilliant seaman, a natural at the helm. After becoming captain in his own right, he spent a further two years attached to the corsair fleet of Dragut Raïs. Dragut carried the honorific title of commander of the Sultan's fleet, but in fact operated independently of that fleet except in time of war. A master tactician, Lord Dragut sailed at will in those years, sailed wherever he wished, working his way in Sicily, Naples, and Mallorca, and once sailing west past Gibraltar, where he raided shipping in the Atlantic. He outwitted his enemies, almost as sport. He taunted them; he mocked them. Monarchs fretted in their European courts, powerless to stop him. As far away as London, Queen Elizabeth received reports of his raids.

Those were eventful years in the history of the Middle Sea.

A galleon belonging to the Order of St. John called the San Giacomo *was defeated in battle by a Turkish vessel, known as the* Galleon of Rhodes, *on which Asha Raïs was temporarily posted for training in large-vessel combat. It was written that no one fought the infidel with more ferocity than he. Later that year, in Malta, the knight Jean Parisot de La Valette succeeded to the post of Grand Master of the Order, a development noted with some concern in the Sub ime Porte, where he was rightly regarded as a vigorous—and dangerous—defender of his faith. Men of prescience even then predicted the great clash to come.*

The Sultan, however, was distracted. The love of his life, Roxelana, had died suddenly, leaving him bereft and lonelier than ever. His surviving sons by Roxelana, Bayezid and Selim, fought each other in Anatolia, vying to become the next to gird on the sword of Osman. Though grieving, Suleiman was far from ready to be replaced.

The countries of France and Spain, at war for forty years, found peace.

The Emperor Charles stepped down from his throne as Holy Roman Emperor and King of Spain. He retired to a monastery, leaving his crown as king to be worn by his son, Philip. It may be said without malice that Philip was not of his father's mettle. Outmaneuvered by the Austrian Hapsburg Ferdinand in his efforts to be elected head of the Holy Roman Empire, Philip was desperate to prove himself worthy of his father. Perhaps no events were of greater moment for Philip in the year 1560 than the fate of his fleet at Djerba. He saw the opportunity to assert Spanish influence in affairs of the Middle Sea by mounting an offensive against Tripoli. That outpost had been captured from the Order a decade earlier by Dragut. Philip organized a Christian alliance. An army was raised under the command of the Viceroy of Sicily, the Duke of Mdina Coeli, and carried in the ships under the command of the Italian admiral Giovanni Doria, the grandnephew of Andrea. The fleet arrived in Malta in midwinter, already in terrible shape. Its troops were decimated by fever, which spread through the island and to other ships at anchor. Nearly five thousand men died. The Christian commanders washed their lice-infested fleet with vinegar. They sank some boats and raised them again, in hopes the seawater would cleanse the pestilence from their decks.

Philip's commanders would have been wise to read the fever as an omen of things to come, and turn tail for home. Instead they sailed for the African coast, where worse disaster awaited them in the form of Dragut Raïs and the Turkish admiral Piali Pasha. Eager for any prize, the Viceroy considered the island of Djerba, Dragut's base off the Tunisian coast, to be an easier target than Tripoli. The Grand Master agreed this was so, but argued it would be just as easy to lose again: Djerba, home to the lotus-eaters of legend, was indefensible. La Valette agreed to lend assistance, but only if the force was directed against Tripoli. The Viceroy accepted his help. After a cursory attempt at Tripoli, he broke his word to La Valette and attacked Djerba. Anticipating such a development, the Grand Master had instructed his commanders to return to Malta in the event Djerba proved to be the real target. Only his foresight saved the Order's ships and men from the disaster that followed.

The battle of Djerba was no battle at all. It was a rout, with few skirmishes of note, save one.

—From Volume IV
The Sultan's Admirals

It has been four years, dear sister, since my last letter. In that time I hope Allah has smiled upon thee, and blessed thee with great good fortune.

I have been serving aboard the Sultan's ships and galleys, most recently at Djerba, an island off the African coast where we humbled the mighty fleet of Philip, the Spanish king. I faced the encounter sitting at the helm of my own galley, from which, at long last, I could write thee freely, without fear. The irony is that after much trouble to save the letters I had already written thee, they went to the bottom of the sea, with that galley. But I am ahead of myself.

My ship—my new ship—is the tenth in the small fleet in which I sail. Ten is a lucky number, as all men know. The Sultan was born in the first year of the tenth century of the calendar of the Hijrah of the Prophet. He is the tenth Sultan in the line of Osman. He was named for Solomon, the son of King David—yes, Solomon, whom he surpasses in both wealth and wisdom. At the siege of Vienna, Suleiman challenged Charles, the Hapsburg Emperor, to manly combat. Just the two of them, to settle the matter of the city. The coward Charles refused, of course.

It is for this man that I sail.

My life since he allowed me to go to sea has been full of surprises, two of which flank my ship even now. To my port—is fate not extraordinary?—sails Raïs Ali Agha, the very man whose galley took me as a child from Malta to Algiers nearly a decade ago.

Though I went to sleep more nights than I can remember to dreams of wreaking vengeance upon him, when I first saw him it was in battle at sea, and I did not yet know his identity. By day's end I had judged him to be a good man, a good captain, and a good ally in a fight.

I met him while standing upon the deck of the man who now sails on my starboard, a man I also swore more than once to kill: Dragut Raïs. I watch him now, sitting serenely as always in the bow of his ship, reading his Koran. I have been attached to his fleet for a year, in order to learn the sea. He is a good teacher and a humble servant of the Almighty. When he kills, which is often in these times, it is because he must. It is never wanton or unmerciful. I cannot say the same for some of the others who sail with us, but of Lord Dragut it is true.

He calls me *hafeed:* grandson.

O, Maria, how my world has turned! I have often pondered what happened to my vows of vengeance. I am not certain of the answer, though I believe the truth is simple: reality overtook sentiment. What, I ask myself, had Ali Agha done to me but pluck me from a barren land and place me on the path to a better one? I do not write this to disparage the land of our birth, but Malta is thy home as well, and surely thou knowest my meaning: Birgu is no Istanbul.

And Dragut? He was a devil only in the imagination of my youth. The real man, the man of flesh and blood, has never done anything *to* me except show kindness, and—by accident or fate—pluck me from a hard sea and place me on a cushion of silk, a cushion of beauty and learning and opportunity. How can I wish him ill?

There were other realities to confront as well. Thou knowest of my dream to command a ship of the Order of St. John. How I loved their grandeur as they sailed from the harbor! How I longed to hoist their red-and-white pennons! Yet though I am talented at the helm—all right, forget that I just lost a ship—the Borg family veins run with common blood, and thus my dream was always a fool's dream. Only nobles grace the ranks of St. John. Only in Suleiman's navy could I become captain—or even, should Allah so favor me— *kapudan pasha.*

There was a final, further truth. My precious knights twice wounded me: first when they did not come for me, and second—much more grievously—when they killed my beloved Alisa. So consumed with hatred for the knights was I that for years I could not write thee, for fear the poison of that hatred would taint even thee. It was a foolish notion, but it was on my mind.

I knew a gardener once in Algiers, a simple man named Ibi. He told me something I remember well. "If you try to avenge every wrong done you in this world," he said, "your life will be spent in vengeance." Now, having thought better of my desire for vengeance against Ali Agha and Dragut, I wonder what will become of the desire for vengeance I still harbor for one man, called Romegas. It is he who took Alisa from me. I know it was only the ordinary business of the sea, but he was the one to deliver it. Four years later I still cannot pass a night in peace. I will not forget him.

It is the battle of Djerba that has made me think again of who I am, and of the nature of hatred, and revenge.

I must tell thee briefly of my command, because it is how I lost my ship. I have an excellent first officer, an Egyptian named Feroz. He was Dragut's first officer until assigned to me. "Feroz will keep you from the bottom until you learn to do so yourself," Dragut told me. I must confess it is the skill of Feroz that makes me look good. He has trained my sailors, who have no equal in the fleet, and he knows every cove and breeze almost as well as our master.

The oarsmen of my ship—yes, they are Christian slaves— row well for me. I say "for me" without hesitation. I have suffered much ridicule for it, but I treat these men better than my fellow captains treat theirs. I have two reasons. The first springs from my enduring secret, that I bear Christians no ill will. The second and more important one is that I find they perform better if they are given good rations. Where others live on hard biscuit and vinegar, my men have goat's milk and cheese, and olive oil and corn—and even fruit when I can find it. Ali Agha tells me it is my head that is stuffed with fruit.

Even with good food, there is nothing to recommend being a galley slave, and though I treat them well they all despise me—but by the beard of the Prophet, they *row* for me! I use the whip less than my compatriots, and I can think of only once in the last year when I had to order an oarsman parted from his head. The other captains laugh at my softness, but the *raïs* in me knows it is a wise course.

Along with my ship and thy letters, I also lost these oarsmen at Djerba. One in particular stands out, for he was Maltese! His name was Beraq. What a bull of a man! He was from Mgarr. He had but one eye, and though he was not yet thirty, his hair was as white as the snows that are brought from the mountains for the Sultan's sherbet. Beraq cursed me roundly—if softly—behind my back in Maltese, a language he knew a Turkish *raïs* would never understand. He knew curses that would have made Leonardus blush. I listened, amused, but could never talk to him, for to do so would reveal more about me to my crew than I cared to reveal. I was a friend to Beraq without letting him know. I never failed to treat him with special care, for he was lead oarsman and drove my men to astonishing heights of performance. In port I arranged for him to have a woman—and paid for her as well—and I always allowed him to devote his spare hours at the bench to making such items of craft as he could sell in market, and buy himself trinkets. He was with me four years, until Djerba.

Djerba! What merriment for us, what humiliation for the son of Charles!

We were a powerful fleet, with the admiral Piali Pasha at the head of the Turkish navy and Lord Dragut at the head of the corsair fleet to which I am temporarily attached. We knew Philip's forces had left Tripoli and were in the vicinity of Djerba, a sandy island of date palms and olive groves, and sturdy Berbers who are harder than the mules they drive. It is Dragut's home, though he spends little time there. We readied ourselves for the engagement, but our scout ships reported the unbelievable: the fleet was napping in the lagoon, as peacefully as if it were nestled in the harbors of Barcelona. Perhaps its men were under the spell of lotus-eaters that held the sailors of Odysseus. It is the sort of blind luck that one can only dream of in war. If luck is naught but the beneficent smile of Allah, His grin that day must have been great indeed.

Some of Philip's commanders heard of our approach, and many galleys, including one that flew the colors of the cowardly Duke of Mdina Coeli, and another belonging to the fleet's commander, Doria, managed to exit the lagoon. They turned not to fight but to flee for the open sea. Our galleys were swifter, and Lord Dragut signaled that I and certain other ships should give chase, while he and the bulk of the fleet tended to the sleeping ships in his lagoon. A score of separate battles ensued.

With two other galleys I gave chase to twelve. It was not quite the folly it might sound. Our ships were rigged and ready for war; theirs were clearly ready only for flight—all save two, which immediately made their way for my ship. Though they were not ships of the Order, I saw there were knights aboard. Their red and white *sobravestes* were like beacons to me.

I cannot adequately describe what transpires in a sea engagement, the ferocity and the speed with which death is delivered. There is a peculiar feeling that accompanies such a thing. It is as if thy veins are shot through with fire and honey at the same time—and though I admit it to no man, there is fear, Maria, though it parts quickly, like the water before my prow.

Our galleys met at the full tempo of war. I will not make a long account of it, save to say my men—sailors and slaves and the Janissaries who fought on my decks—conducted themselves superbly, with all the discipline one can hope for at such a moment. Fortune was with me, and I quickly dismasted one vessel, which one of my sister ships promptly seized.

I faced the next ship. On its deck stood a knight, staring at me as if to challenge me personally. I will never forget his broad smile, his white teeth, his black bushy beard and curly hair. A monkey sat on his shoulder—an evil-looking creature with long teeth, displaying an almost comical calm. Our ships passed within twenty yards of each other, and the battle engulfed the ships like a squall. A storm of arrows blackened the sky, and there was the steady roar of arquebus fire and the whip of chain shot. Many lives were lost on both sides. We circled to meet again.

That second pass was the last. I maneuvered more quickly than he, and my ram sheared his starboard oars at the loom, piercing his hull at midship. At the same instant a shot from his bow chaser put a great hole in my own hull at the waterline. Both ships began sinking.

The din of battle was replaced by a terrible cry that arose from the throats of the slaves on both sides. Still chained to their benches, they prepared to die. I heard prayers to God and prayers to Allah as men sought comfort for doomed souls. There was no hope of saving my ship and no point in boarding the other. The sea is the great leveler in battle: in a moment all hands would be equal in the water, except for the slaves. I called an order to Feroz and the bosun, and we set about unlocking what chains we could. We took fire from the other ship while we worked. My bosun was felled with a shot to the neck. I have taken much grief from the other captains for the folly of his death, a good man wasted unlocking Christian fetters.

Feroz and I had time enough to free only eight banks before the galley slipped beneath the water, freeing forty-eight men. The unfortunates on the other sixteen banks met their maker that day, but not because we did not try. The sea was a jumble of bodies and crates and barrels. Many men drowned quickly.

I was helping two of my deck soldiers when I came within two arms' lengths of the knight who commanded the other vessel. Neither of us could lift a weapon against the other. His monkey rode him like a hat, screeching madly, and in the flotsam and the bedlam I quickly lost sight of him.

I saw the snow-white head of Beraq, who like any good Maltese was a strong swimmer. Though choking and coughing, he managed to thank me for freeing him from his chains. "Bless you, Asha Raïs," he said, as cheerfully as if he were out for a stroll. "If I see you again, I swear I will kill you mercifully!" He kept swimming—toward the other galleys, of course, where he would be a free man at last. I was glad to see that besides him many other oarsmen made it and were pulled aboard. I must say that the other crew took no such trouble as did we. To a man, all the Muslim oarsmen on the Christian ship perished, wearing their chains to the bottom. It is the custom of the sea.

I was almost half an hour in the water, waiting while our galleys engaged the others before returning for us. In all nearly eighty of my men lived, including Feroz.

That night the officers met in Lord Dragut's castle. He was in high spirits, awed by the monumental stupidity of Philip's commanders. It had been a complete rout. Though many ships escaped, they were well bloodied, and limped rather than ran away. Most were captured—more than fifty ships and thirteen thousand men in all, enough to power the Sultan's fleets for a long while.

Lord Dragut congratulated me for having taken two ships at the cost of one. "I heard of your inglorious entry into the water," he said to me, and his impish eyes betrayed his delight in my misadventure. "You seem to have an odd preference for consorting with fish. I remember plucking you from the sea once before. While I do not share your love of the water, how I wish I had your youth, to swim so!"

He is seventy-five, but I did not exaggerate when I said, "I am certain you could outswim me, sire."

"Perhaps so. But even more, how I wish I had had your luck, to face Romegas!"

I stared at him blankly. "Sire?"

"Your opponent today. Ali Agha saw him clearly and knows him well. You held your own and sank his ship beneath him. You fought well this day, Asha Raïs, even if you let him escape."

O, Maria, I cannot tell thee how I shook at the news. I had stared into his eyes without knowing them to be the devil's own. I am certain I could have drowned him, for I was the stronger swimmer, but instead I was trying to keep other men afloat.

It is this question that plagues me now, as I ask myself if I am fit to be *raïs:* what is the price of hatred? Had I known it was he, I believe I would have acted differently. Forty-eight more slaves would have drowned than did, for I would have ignored their plight as I set out to kill one man. Forty eight lives plus one—Alisa's—for one. I would give a hundred more, including my own, and call it a bargain. Yet what of my hatred for Dragut, and for Ali Agha, that time and circumstance erased? What is hatred worth?

His hands did not hesitate as they penned the next words.

I miss thee, Maria.

But they wavered over the words that inevitably followed:

I am still Nico.

He looked at the *orta* on his arm, burned into his flesh as it was burned into his soul.

I wonder who I have become since last I saw thee.

I had a *lala*, named Iskander. He was a good and faithful servant of the Sultan. It is a pity he died exposing Nico, because Nico, like Iskander, is dead.

Only *I* remain.

Though Nico dwells within me, I am called Asha.

It is a Persian name, given me by Lord Dragut. Asha, Protector of Fire, and the Fire is the Sultan, Suleiman, Lord of the Two Horizons. He is my sun and my moon, the stars in my sky. He is the steel in my sword and the wind in my sail. He is my father, and I am his adopted son. May God make eternal his empire. I shall serve him well, as one day I shall walk seven times around the Ka'bah.

Someday fate may force me to choose between Nico and Asha. Yet on this ship there is no Nico and no Asha. There is only the *Raïs,* who laughs out loud at the pleasures of the sea. Though I have lost my urgent need to choose between worlds—the one I left still fills a warm place in my heart, while the one I now inhabit gives me great fulfillment—I have not lost my despair over Alisa's death. I have not lost my longing to make her killer pay. I pray the same thing will not happen to that desire that became of my hatred for Dragut and Ali Agha. I think it will not. It is the ships of the Order I seek, and its commanders I hope to slay.

Do not fear, Maria. The Prophet has said the bond of blood is as steel and cannot be sundered. I am still thy brother. Though I lost a ship at Djerba, I have a new one—not as fast, but worthy. I will build another and call her *Alisa.* Though I lost a crew, I have a new one, and time will make them mine.

Though I lost thy letters, I still carry them inside me. They have kept me sane through these years.

I fear thy lack of understanding about what has become of me, especially now that the other letters are gone. I wonder if they were ever meant to find their way to thee or were simply the means by which I might find and keep myself. I think it is the latter. And so I will consign this letter to join the others.

They shall live in my heart, as do thee.

He rose from his mat and stood at the rail. The sun was going down, a great golden orb descending into a copper sea. It was time for prayer.

He held the letter in his hand and set the torch to it. The pages caught fire and the wind fanned the flames. He held the pages until the flames touched his fingers, and then he scattered the ashes into the sea.

There is no God but God, and Mohammed is His Prophet.

Book five

MALTA

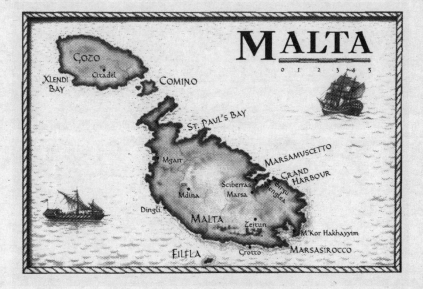

from The Histories of the Middle Sea

by Darius, called the Preserver
Court Historian to the Shadow of God on Earth, the Sultan Achmet

The convent of the Sovereign Order of the Knights of St. John of Jerusalem was scattered through Birgu, the old fishing village that lay on the small peninsula behind Fort St. Angelo, the Norman castle where the Order made its headquarters. The convent consisted of the conventual chapel of St. Lawrence; the hospital, or Holy Infirmary; the arsenal, where the Order's galleys were maintained; and the separate auberges, or dormitories, where the knights from each of the Order's eight langues, or nationalities, lived while at convent. Each langue was ruled by a pilier, or master, who in addition to his other duties often held another post within the Order. The pilier of France was usually the Grand Hospitaller, who held authority over the Order's Holy Infirmary, to which each knight, no matter his rank, devoted long hours of service. The pilier of Italy was the Grand Admiral, with authority over the Order's all-important fleet of galleys.

The Order was led by the Grand Master, elected for life by the knights. He presided over the Sacro Consiglio, the Sacred Council, the governing body composed of the Order's highest officials. There were three classes of knights. First among them were the knights of justice, those most pure of blood, whose shields bore no fewer than sixteen quarterings of hereditary nobility. Of second rank were conventual chaplains, ecclesiastical knights whose service was devoted to work in the hospital and chapel. The third rank were serving brothers, knights who were of respectable if not strictly noble birth—so long as they were not bastards—and who served as soldiers. In addition, there were magistral knights and knights of grace, honoraries appointed by the Grand Master and confirmed by the council.

Each knight was initiated in an elaborate ceremony of investiture, in which he swore oaths of poverty, chastity, obedience, and allegiance to the

Grand Master. After taking the oath, the novice would serve three seasons as an officer in the galleys, each season being termed a caravan. Afterward he would either return to the convent in Malta, to his estate on the continent, or to one of the priories or commanderies maintained by the Order in each of the countries from which the knights hailed, the income from whose crops and holdings went to support the convent. A knight's first promotion would be to commander, at which time he would be paid a salary to help defray his costs. A knight could always supplement his income by investing in a private galley, so long as its profits were shared with the Order's insatiable treasury. A knight might live in the convent or rarely visit, participating only in the General Chapters, the assemblies held every five years, or answering the emergency summons of the Grand Master.

The knights wore two sorts of crosses. The first, borne on their pennons and tunics, was a squared white cross on a scarlet field, the sight of which struck terror into the hearts of their enemies. The second was the Cross of Profession, the ritual cross with eight points embroidered on their habits or worn on a chain. Some said each point of the cross represented one of the eight langues, or tongues, of the Order. Others holding less charitable views suggested each point represented one of the seven deadly sins regularly committed by the self-righteous knights, with an extra point added for good measure: a spare sin, so to speak, for any occasion of need.

It was true that the ancient discipline of the Order had fallen into some disarray. The warrior-monks of Jerusalem had grown much more worldly as the knights of Rhodes and then Malta, their pursuits sometimes more visceral than spiritual. In theory, the convent was a united stronghold of knights, resolute in their faith and dedicated to a common purpose. In practice, the convent was an unruly nest of strong-willed nobles of eight nations, men united by vows but often divided in politics, their families prominent participants in the religious and political conflicts sweeping the continent.

It took all a Grand Master's skill to keep such men on the Order's course and from turning on each other. None took the sacred obligation more seriously than Jean Parisot de La Valette, whose primary concern upon assuming his office was to reestablish the military readiness of the Order, before the inevitable conflict with the Ottomans that already loomed large. There can be little doubt that any knight then living could have been better suited to such a task than he.

La Valette kept a lioness, so tamed by his iron will that she slept like a *lamb at the foot of his bed. He also kept a parrot, an old bird from the Malays whose vocabulary was as profane as La Valette's was virtuous. The Grand Master hunted and read poetry and wielded a mighty sword.*

He was the descendant of a noble family of Provence, a single-minded defender of his faith. He brooked no weakness, forgot no slight, overlooked no detail.

Even his enemies considered him a politician of talent, a soldier of bravery, a man of integrity. Even his enemies saw that he was, like Suleiman, not just a giant of the age but a gentleman of his time. Even his enemies saw that he was, like Dragut, not just a warrior for his faith but a simple and decent man as well.

Indeed, it is instructive to read about this man in the words of Lord Dragut:

Of all the infidels I faced at sea, none was more capable, more unbending in his faith, than that redoubtable knight La Valette. We met twice in our younger years.

The first time, he was a prisoner captured in battle by Kust-Ali, a fine seaman who managed to sink the Order's galley and put its captain in chains. La Valette spent a year at the oar. I had occasion to visit the ship and saw that he—not simply a soldier, but a knight, an honorable man, a man born to lead—was chained ignominiously to a lower bench, where because of his unfortunate location he was regularly drenched by spray from the piss of other slaves—men not of his measure, certainly, Christians of lower station than he. I took pity on his reduced dignity and managed to get him a better berth on a different bench, where he could be refreshed by the clean air of the sea while being pissed upon only by his Muslim masters. It was an act of compassion I do not regret—merely a small gesture between the best of enemies. I know he appreciated the kindness.

There is no guarding against fate. I myself was captured some years later, in the month of Shawwal in the year 946 [ed. note: May A.D. 1540] after a long chase by a superior force of infidel ships. I was taken in chains to Genoa, after which I spent four years at the oar. To this day my back bears the scars of the

Christian slave masters' whips. I bear them with pride. I bear them for my God, whose will it was that I serve Him thus. I have repaid each scar in kind many times over, though never in anger over my own misfortune.

One day in port as I sat in my chains I saw La Valette, by then long since ransomed by his brethren. He strode aboard the ship, tall, dignified, and resplendent in the colors of his Order. The former galley slave now walked with the sure mien of a monarch. He was a learned man. The first time we met he spoke Greek, Spanish, and Italian almost as well as I myself, and French much better. I now realized he had mastered Turkish and Arabic as well, doubtless from his years as a prisoner. I complimented him on his mastery, gratified that his years at the oar had served at least that purpose, that he could now trade fluent insults with me in my own language, the language of the poetry of Islam.

"I shall be delighted to insult you in whatever language you prefer, *maestro*," he said. "But given your reduced state"—he motioned at my chains—"insults are hardly appropriate. It is the way of war."

"Only a turn of luck!" I replied. "One day luck shall turn again, and I shall be free."

"A day we shall both certainly remember," he replied with good cheer.

So we two passed our time at the oar: La Valette in a Muslim fleet, me in a Christian one, both of us in chains. Three years after that last meeting, my own ransom was arranged. As La Valette has made his enemies regret his release, so each day do I strive to make him regret mine.

One can only rue such a life wasted as an infidel. What a pair we would have made had our sails been filled with one wind!

Like myself, he has spent a lifetime in service of his faith. He fought for his Order in Rhodes before Suleiman took the island from them. He was governor of Tripoli before I myself took that city from the knights. Now he makes his convent in Malta. One day the Sultan and I shall take that from him as well.

We shall meet again one day, he and I. Of this I am certain.

—Drawn from the logs of Dragut Raïs,
in the naval archives at Topkapi serai

—From Volume V, The Order of St. John,
and from Volume III, Corsairs and Beys of Barbary

Chapter 27

MALTA
1560

C hristien de Vries stood outside the surgical tent erected on the small peninsula of Senglea. Behind him the blades of a windmill turned languidly in the hot morning sun. Towering above and behind the windmill stood Fort St. Michael, one of the three forts that protected the Grand Harbor. Fort St. Angelo lorded over them all, looming at the tip of the small peninsula on which stood the village of Birgu. At the end of the largest peninsula, on which rose Mount Sciberras, the small fort of St. Elmo guarded the outer entrance to the harbor.

Christien had been in the Order for seven years. When he'd first come to Malta he'd done as all novices must, serving three tours, or caravans, in the Order's galleys, for a total of three years. He was glad to complete that part of his duty. Whether it was the smell of the galleys, the brutality and cruelty displayed by both sides in sea battle, or simply the queasiness he never quite shook while on the water, he hated the sea. He'd been ship's surgeon during those years— unofficially at first, as he possessed skill but no license. His father,

Arnaud, had heard of the arrangement and did not complain. He knew full well that no Knight of St. John, whatever his post, could long avoid picking up a sword, and so long as Christien was in the Order, the family's honor was preserved.

Christien now worked at the Holy Infirmary in Birgu and lived in the nearby auberge of the French *langue*. Most knights left Malta after their initial service, preferring to live in their homelands, where they earned money for the Order through land holdings or through ownership or service on private galleys that preyed upon infidel ships. Christien could have returned to France after completing his caravans, but in Malta he was able to sit for his surgical examinations and receive a license. Though he cared nothing for the Order's political or military goals, the knights were founded as a hospitaller order, and their infirmary in Birgu was one of the premier hospitals in the modern world. He was pleased to remain there. He practiced under the authority of the Grand Hospitaller, Gabriel Çeralta, the Order's official in charge of the Infirmary. Çeralta was also the *pilier*, or master, of the French *langue*.

Now Christien was exhausted. For two days there had been no sleep, and what he saw in the harbor promised there would be none for another day at least. A line of ships stretched out Galley Creek and into the harbor, waiting to disembark their bloodied and beaten cargo of soldiers and slaves. Several of the vessels were listing, their oars smashed, their sails in shreds. Each hour brought another one limping into the harbor after a desperate crossing from Djerba on the African coast. Between disease and Dragut, the Christian fleet had lost nearly eighteen thousand men out of the twenty-five thousand who began.

Casualties were usually offloaded in Kalkara Creek on the eastern shore of Birgu, below the Holy Infirmary. But now there were too many and the Infirmary was overwhelmed. The Grand Master ordered tents hastily erected on the empty tip of Senglea to handle the excess. The wounded were placed on lighters and ferried across the creek to the Senglean shore. There they were loaded in donkey carts for the trip up to one of the white tents, to take their turn under the surgeons' knives, or to await death from the fever that had decimated the fleet.

"My God, will it never end?" Christien said.

"Not as long as it seems the Lord is taking a hand against His own crusaders." Dr. Joseph Callus, the Maltese physician, stood next to Christien, watching the scene below. He, too, was covered in blood. "Here, drink this," he said, extending a cup of brandy. "We've half an hour before the next batch." Wearily they sat on the ground, leaning against a stack of supply cases.

Callus was a private physician who normally had little contact with the Order, but when the battered fleet returned from Djerba he hurried to offer his assistance. Christien liked the older man because although he was a physician, not a surgeon, he wasn't afraid to dirty his hands on the insides of a patient. Indeed, Callus had learned rudimentary surgery aboard the Order's own ships and was a good hand in a crisis. Further, Christien owed Callus a debt of gratitude. It was under his sponsorship that Christien had finally sat for his surgical examinations, four years after joining the Order. Though it was not the same as having received his license from the Faculté in Paris, it was enough to practice, and that was all he cared about.

Bertrand Cuvier, a look of disgust on his face, threw back the tent flap and stepped outside, carrying a chamber pot. "If I have to carry one more shit pot in the service of Jesus, I'm going to take it all the way to Constantinople and spoon-feed it to the infidel in charge." He had sailed with the initial expedition and was one of the lucky ones to return in good health. Now, in the sacred tradition of the Order, he busied himself in the field hospital, nursing patients alongside the doctors. Though the knights were warriors and noblemen, where the ill were concerned no task was too menial. Bertrand flung the contents of the pot into the latrine, wincing when some of it slopped on his boot. "Sweet Christ, I should be back at sea. Killing heathens, not healing Christians—now truly that is God's work."

"Ah, but you carry shit with such grace, and wear it with such flair." Christien smiled at his friend, who was never happier than with a sword in his hand, making work for the doctors or the burial detail. "It would be a pity to lose your talents. Here, have a drink." He filled a cup and handed it up.

Bertrand sniffed it and winced. "Keep that Dutch horse piss to yourself," he said. "I need something with more spirit." He extracted a flask from his vest and took a long draught. He wiped his mouth on his sleeve, watching the scene below with ill-disguised contempt. "Count on the Spaniards to muck it up," he grumbled. "They serve disaster in the winter and calamity in the spring. With the good King Philip in command, we'll all be dead by summer."

"It's not the Spaniards but the devil Dragut," Callus said. "He is as invincible as he is lucky."

Bertrand spat. "He buys his luck with the coin of his enemies' incompetence." He looked at the harbor. It was Philip's fleet, not the Order's, that had been humiliated at Djerba. It was Philip's commander, the Viceroy, not the Grand Master, who looked foolish before all of Europe. Yet none of that mattered. Bertrand and the other knights saw only a harbor brimming with Christian defeat.

"Well, I've more of the king's shit to carry," Bertrand said. "His men never run out." He went back inside the tent. Christien glanced at Callus, who'd closed his eyes. The sight was too much to resist. "I'll be along in a minute," he said. He was instantly asleep.

Five minutes later, a boot sharply prodded his thigh. Christien opened his eyes. Jean Parisot de La Valette stood above him, regarding him with disdain. "If you are ill, Fra de Vries, perhaps you should go inside and lie on a table, where you may be tended. Otherwise there are wounded who require your care."

"He is exhausted, Excellency," Callus said angrily. "Let him sleep half an hour. He has worked two days and nights without rest."

"If duty requires, he will work ten without, Magnificus. And while your medical help is welcome, and I thank you for it, your remarks are not." La Valette had been Grand Master three years. He was in his mid-sixties, and though it was certain he had not slept for two days himself, he showed no fatigue. He would not sleep until all the ships were in. From the time La Valette served as a rowing slave aboard a Muslim galley, the jokes had circulated. It was said a surgeon had cut the Frenchman open after a battle only to find acid in his veins, a shard of ice where his heart should have been, and a stout iron rod up his ass.

Callus fought to control his temper. He despised the Grand Master. Christien got quickly to his feet, trying to protect his friend. "The Grand Master is right, Joseph. I should be inside. I'll just wash a bit first." He leaned over a bucket of water and rinsed his arms and head. La Valette began to step past him into the tent when he saw the bottle of brandy. He picked it up and smelled it. He looked at Christien. "Did you drink of this?"

Callus stepped forward. "It is mine, Grand Master. I brought it."

"If you speak again, I'll have you whipped," La Valette said coolly. His gaze fell hard upon Christien. "Fra de Vries, did you drink of this?"

"*Oui*, my lord."

"You'll do the septaine, then, when your duties here are finished."

"*Oui*, my lord." The septaine meant seven days confined to quarters in the auberge. Seven days of fasting, broken only twice by meager portions of bread and water, followed by flogging for dessert. Seven days of endless recitations of the *Deus misereatur nostri*. Seven days of hell. Christien bristled at the punishment but was careful to show the Grand Master no outer reaction, which would only make things worse. La Valette's prohibition against drink was as unwavering as all the other rules he'd initiated since inheriting the ill-disciplined Order, and the septaine was the least of his punishments. The quarantine was forty days of the same. The Order's rules were as hard as its men. A simple breach of etiquette—arguing in chapel, for example, or berating the cook for a bad meal—might cost a knight a year in the galleys, no matter that the meal was indeed execrable and the cook deserved hanging. For more serious offenses, of which simple disobedience was one, he might find himself confined for months or years—or forever—in the *oubliette*, a tiny, windowless vault beneath the castle. There, no matter how noble his lineage, a knight might well pray to be hanged so that he wouldn't live long enough to go mad.

La Valette drew a coin from his pocket and handed it to Callus. "For the brandy," he said. Still holding the bottle, La Valette stepped past the doctor and into the tent.

"He is a pompous ass, like all of you," Callus said in a low voice.

Christien dried his face with a dirty cloth. "You're mistaken, Joseph," he said. "Some of the rest of us are just asses." His expression grew serious. "You should be more careful with what you say. He is not a man to toy with. Your meetings are not as secret as you think. If he hears of them, he'll hang you."

Callus was twice Christien's age. Born in Malta, he had nearly become a priest but abandoned that career for medicine. After completing his medical training in Sicily, he took a post as physician aboard the *Santa Anna,* the pride of the Order's navy. When the Emperor Charles granted the Maltese islands to the Knights, who had been driven from their home in Rhodes by Suleiman, Callus sailed with their fleet into Grand Harbor, with mixed feelings. His employers were now masters of his home.

He quit the fleet and was named physician to the city of Mdina. In his spare time he hunted for treasure, convinced that the Arabs and later the Jews who lived on the islands had buried their gold and silver before leaving. Christien often went out with him, more for the enjoyment of the countryside and the pleasant conversation than for any expectation of finding riches. Callus found Phoenician pottery, Punic skulls, amphoras of wine and oil, and corroded coins of forgotten ages—treasure of every sort, but never the one for which he hungered.

In the course of the hunts, Callus had run afoul of the Grand Master over a civil matter, a lawsuit brought against another man over a schooner. There were two law courts in Malta, one run by the Order, the other by the Church. Callus, wary of the Order's growing authority, filed his suit in the bishop's court. La Valette retaliated for the slight by stripping Callus of his post as physician of Mdina. It was nearly three years before Callus was able to practice again, and the hiatus made him bitter. Like most Maltese, he resented the Order's presence. Unlike most Maltese, he said something about it. In secret meetings he condemned the Order and its current Grand Master, a dictator in an order of tyrants.

Callus growled at Christien's concern. "My meetings are my business. Better to hang quickly at the end of a noose than to strangle slowly in his grip," he said.

"He gave you back your post."

"A post he had no right to take in the first place."

Christien shrugged. "He didn't need the right. He had the power."

"Ah, so power is all, then. Right matters for nothing, I suppose."

"If right mattered, it would turn the world upside down."

"Even as you incur his wrath and suffer his petty tyrannies, you seem determined to defend him."

"The septaine is not so petty, my friend, and I care nothing for defending the Grand Master—I seek only to annoy you," Christien said, grinning.

"As always, you have succeeded admirably." Callus watched La Valette moving among the cots inside the tent. "*Look* at him. He serves my brandy to the patients after punishing you for it." La Valette was talking and praying with the wounded, preparing them for their next duel with the infidel. He seemed to be the only knight in the Order who did not accept the outcome of Djerba as a defeat. He would find a way to use it as a spark, to light a fire of retribution.

"It isn't your brandy anymore, Joseph. He bought it. And his restrictions apply only to the Order."

"An Order I don't know why you joined. I continue to ask myself how a man such as you came to be here. You are no fanatical monk, like the others. Like *him*."

"You know very well why."

Callus snorted. "To know is not always to understand. You made a bargain with God. How very noble of you—but men make such bargains all the time only to break them again, once having gotten what they wanted. Just as you yourself have broken your vow of obedience by drinking forbidden spirits."

"I am an imperfect man, Joseph. I try. I fail. And my only regret with my bargain is that whenever I fail I must suffer punishment twice—first by La Valette, my master, and a second time by you, who are evidently my conscience. And now if you'll forgive me, I had better get inside and distract the Grand Master before he notices Bertrand's breath."

❖

Maria Borg stood on a wall of Fort St. Michael, watching the same stream of ships. She saw La Valette disappear into the medical tent. *Another disaster*, she thought. *The Turks must smell blood now*. The talk of the debacle was everywhere; Djerba was only a preview of what surely must soon come. The Ottomans grew bolder and more successful every year, and one day, as they had done at Rhodes, they would again try to drive the knights back into the European castles from which they'd sprung. And when they did, it would be poor Malta that would suffer.

She turned back to her work, her mind on more immediate problems. She noticed one of the *burdnara* driving his mules with a load of sand so heavy the cart creaked and trembled. He was about to dump it right in the path of the laborers. "Stop!" she called. "Put it over there, on the lee side of the wall!" He frowned, but whipped his team to comply.

She pushed her hair out of her eyes and fastened a scarf over it to tame it against the wind. She was just twenty-two and had matured into a striking woman. Her green eyes were luminescent, set against skin that was deeply browned by the sun. She still eschewed the grim Sicilian dress favored by most women, who covered themselves from head to toe in a long black *barnuża* of wool or cotton. Instead she wore a calf-length skirt and a tan oilcloth blouse, tied beneath her breasts, and over that a hip-length leather jerkin. In cool weather she wore a light woolen cloak. Her arms were often exposed, and she went barefoot most of the time, as did most peasants.

Luca Borg shuffled up. His face was as weathered as the old walls of Birgu, his features creased by deep lines. He was still a bull of a man, but he moved more slowly, his back stooping with age and the wear of his work. "You must see to the mortar," he complained. "They've fallen behind."

"We have no quicklime, Father. They ran out of brushwood to fire the lime kilns. I lent them three *manuali* to collect more. They are at the kilns now and should be back within the hour with a new batch."

"See we get paid! And the *cantuni!* This is not stone, it is rubble! Good for nothing but fill. The skin is flaking. Barbari has given us weathered surface material, as if after thirty years I won't know the difference or the price. He is a thief and has taken advantage of me through you. I suppose I must tend to everything."

"It won't matter for the inner wall. Barbari's quarry couldn't fill our order until next week, so he made me a special bargain for what we received. I bought it at third price, Father."

Luca sniffed. He took a long drink from the water skin and wiped his mouth. "See he doesn't short you for the rest."

"Of course, Father."

Luca's crew was working to extend a rampart at Fort St. Michael, the fort that stood at the base of Senglea, the sister peninsula of

Birgu. His workforce consisted of slaves, mostly Muslim, but also some Orthodox Christians and a few Jews. The slaves belonged to the Order's galleys or came from the households of the knights themselves, and were provided by the Order to civil crews such as Luca's that were working on the Order's building projects. In addition to the slaves there were two skilled masons, a carpenter, a labor foreman, and a rotating crew of able-bodied Maltese men pressed into "volunteer" service by the Order. Even with forced labor, there weren't enough hands to do it all.

The island had sprung to life under the new Grand Master. Since taking office he had embarked on an ambitious campaign to strengthen the island's defenses against the Turks and their corsair allies. At the same time he was trying to improve the Order's fleet of galleys with which to harass the enemy, he was pouring resources into the island's fortifications, which suffered from the prolonged neglect of his predecessors. Ditches were deepened, walls strengthened, gun emplacements set, and watchtowers added. Knights of the Order were arriving from Europe to take up residence in Birgu, each of them with servants and attendants in tow, all requiring housing. The Church was adding parishes. The harbor teemed with shipping and the docks crawled with activity as shipments of grain and building materials arrived almost daily from Sicily. Merchants were building new warehouses and storage sheds.

Luca Borg no longer simply performed small jobs for others. He was a builder now, with contracts and crew, and it was largely because of Maria. Neither of them ever expected such a turn of affairs, to be working together.

After the events with Father Salvago, Maria had moved into M'kor Hakhayyim, whose residents had had to rebuild their lives. Everything in the cave had to be replaced, from pots and dishes to candles and bedding. Maria caught new goats in the wild and began a new herd. Money was even scarcer than before. Elena was forced to be more circumspect in her night work, so she earned less. Fençu had to rely more on carpentering and less on thievery—at least, he said, for a while. They worked hard but lived from day to day. Whenever it seemed like they were getting a little ahead, a spell of drought or pestilence would descend upon the island and carry them back to the brink of starvation. Their days were spent hunting, fishing, and gardening. The dream Maria and Elena had shared of leaving Malta had never faded but was deferred by the necessity of making a living.

For two years Maria hadn't visited her parents. Occasionally she saw her father on the street, but they never spoke. One day word came that her mother, Isolda, had finally been granted her long-standing wish and died. Maria wasn't certain what drew her to St. Agatha's for the service. Instead of grief, she felt guilt for being so unmoved by her mother's passing. She had slipped into the rear of the church, hoping to avoid an encounter with her father, but he had seen her. In his hour of need, his anger at her had melted. He was consumed with grief, unable even to walk without assistance. She had never thought him particularly close to her mother and was surprised by the depth of his despair. She helped him home. He beseeched her to return to live with him, to care for him and their house. He cried, something that was new to her. He begged. Ashamed for him, for his weakness, she refused.

A few days later she had returned, to check on him. He was sitting in the dark. His chest hurt, he said. He hadn't been eating. He wasn't working or taking care of himself. The house was a disaster. Her anger gave way to pity and her resolve collapsed. Despite all he had done to hurt her, she had to help him. There was no one else. She promised herself it would only be until he was on his feet again. She brought fresh vegetables from the market and cooked a meal for him. She cleaned a little. At night she returned to the cave. His health improved, if not his spirits. He neither thanked her nor apologized for what had come between them before. She never expected him to do either.

Several weeks later he went back to work. He was building a storehouse for a grain merchant. Maria brought him simple meals and quickly observed that he was in trouble. During his absence he had lost two of his apprentice masons who couldn't wait for his return and had taken other jobs. Further, his mind was not yet completely on his work. He slipped from the scaffolding and twisted his knee, which swelled painfully. He could barely get around, and he was nearly out of money.

The merchant was ready to fire Luca. He had purchased a shipload of grain from Sicily that was due to arrive any day. If his storehouse wasn't completed, he would have nowhere to put it, and the fall rains might well ruin him.

Maria knew that if Luca did not work, he would not eat. She had to help him get back on his feet. She ran a few errands for him, carrying money to the quarry masters and then arranging for a delivery of quicklime. She knew little about masonry, but when she saw the pile of stone set aside for him at the quarry, she realized he couldn't use it all at once. She bought half and with what remained of the money went to Birgu and found replacements for the two masons. She lured them away from another job by offering better wages. At first they sneered at the girl, but she showed them a handful of copper piccolis, and they followed her.

Luca was furious. "You disobeyed me about the stone order, and you paid the men too much," he snapped.

"But you have enough stone to keep working, and you still have a job," she replied. Her disobedience made him almost as angry as the fact that she was right and he was wrong. He grumbled and fumed and went about his business, grateful for her help but unwilling to say so.

Each day she did a little more, stayed a little longer. She discovered she liked the smell and the color and the texture of the fresh-cut stone, and the sight of a building taking shape out of a featureless pile of stone and sand. The work was not difficult technically, although mistakes could lead to collapsed walls and lost time. She did not work the stone, of course, but quickly proved herself a genius at organization, bringing order to a process that under Luca had always been chaotic. Luca was happiest when he was laying stone. He didn't like dealing with people, didn't like the details of running a crew. It was rare that he would take a job bigger than he and another mason and a laborer or two could manage alone. On his own, he would often work until he ran out of material and only then see about getting more. If he was being paid by the piece or foot, as was customary, such delays were costly and idled his crew. It was a senseless delay but a common enough one. Maria grasped how to sequence the work, ensuring that sufficient supplies were on hand when needed.

She learned when to buy *franka*, the soft cream-colored limestone quarried near Luqa, and when to buy the harder *zonqor*, for which there was less demand, and consequently a lower price. She learned to save freight costs by combining loads with other masons. She was a shrewd negotiator, whispering to her father as he bargained with a quarry master or lime merchant. With the help of her friend Antonellus Grima, the merchant who'd bought her *The Courtier,* she made arrangements to buy certain materials directly in Messina, avoiding the middlemen who skillfully used the material shortages that plagued Malta to gouge their customers.

She was smart, good with numbers—and literate. She kept the accounts and saw to the payment of wages and materials. She borrowed a book on architecture and over time learned to read the drawings that so intimidated her father, and even to make simple ones herself. It was clear she had an eye for building, if not the skill to do it with her own hands. Many of the craftsmen would simply see the stone they were laying, without regard to the larger picture. She saw that picture and helped to make it a reality. In ordinary times she never would have gotten near a building project because of the guilds and because women were employed outside the household only for farming and whoring and weaving cotton. But she was willing and bright, and the guilds were in disarray, crippled by lack of manpower and disrupted by the Order's imperious approach and lack of respect for their prerogatives.

The more she learned, the more her father concentrated on his own work and left her to manage things. Of course he was the *mastru,* as most men did not take her seriously. Even after they saw what she could do, they would never take orders from a woman. But her influence was clear and grew steadily, until some of the workers might even grudgingly do as she said without getting confirmation from her father, so long as her request was tactfully cloaked as a suggestion rather than an order. She didn't mind so long as she got what she wanted. She knew it was a small miracle she got anywhere at all.

With Maria to organize, Luca's base of clients broadened. He received building contracts from the Università and even from the Church. When the first job was offered by the sacristan she was reluctant, but Salvago was long gone and she never saw the bishop. "The Church's money spends as well as anyone's," Elena reminded her. "You might as well get something from them." But by far their biggest client was the Order of St. John, for whom they built fortifications and other defensive works. The Order's engineer would appear frequently, sniffing and huffing as he inspected the work. His assistants took measurements and made notes in a ledger book. The engineer always ignored Maria and addressed only Luca, even though Luca turned constantly to Maria for an answer or an estimate.

La Valette himself often inspected the work, accompanied by a host of officials. He took personal interest in everything—the height of a wall, the depth of a ditch, the consistency of mortar, the cut of a stone. His concern for detail was the same whether it involved the auberge of France or a rampart on St. Elmo's. He knew building and defenses as well as any engineer or mason alive. He had learned painful lessons thirty years earlier on Rhodes, when, despite some of the most formidable fortifications on earth, the Sultan had driven out the knights. La Valette knew the range of modern artillery, knew what would stop a ball and what would not. Malta's fortifications presented great challenges. The island lacked nearly every natural resource except stone. Most materials had to be imported. There wasn't even very much dirt, useful as a shock absorber between stone walls, so constant design improvisations had to be made, in which La Valette often overruled his own engineers.

Maria had never found much reason to like foreigners, but she had to grant La Valette grudging respect. She and Elena still provided cheese for the Order's galley slaves, and though she was a peasant he always addressed her correctly, politely. Unlike most men, he was not contemptuous of having to deal with a woman—he was simply indifferent to the matter. He cared for nothing other than his objectives. If his veins ran with ice, if he governed with an iron hand, he was always honest and direct with her, which was more than she could say for some of his lieutenants. If he promised payment on a certain day, it would arrive. If she needed material from another site and he could provide it, he did. He respected ability, and one day he paid Maria a supreme compliment. She had devised a solution to support a failing curtain wall, acting without approval from the engineer. It had not taken any great engineering skill, simply a practical eye, and she considered it a minor matter. The engineer was furious, threatening to withhold payment for other work. The Grand Master heard of the matter and overruled him. "If I had a hundred *men* of your stripe who could think and improvise as you do, Signorina Borg," he said in front of the engineer, "the Turk could storm this island for a thousand years and we would not be troubled."

❖

Maria's relationship with her father never warmed. They talked only of business, never of the past. Only once did he attempt to revert to his former role, and he learned that where he had once bullied the girl, he could no longer bully the woman.

"You should live at home," he said. "Not in a filthy pit with thieves and—"

She slapped him so hard it stung her hand. His face reddened in rage, and his massive hands clenched into fists. She braced herself for the return blow. It never came. He checked himself, his mouth forming a damnation that died in his throat. In that moment she realized that he needed her more than she needed him, and he knew it.

For all his cruel and brutish ways, Luca Borg really had no spine at all.

Only once more did he try to assert his authority, over money. Luca had never offered to pay Maria for her efforts. In his mind it was sufficient that she should have enough to buy food. His offer of letting her move back home would take care of a roof over her head, and he was prepared—once every year or so—to give her a small allowance for new clothing. Surely there was little else a woman could want. Because she managed the accounts, Maria paid herself instead. She mentioned the expense when they were reviewing finances. Incensed, he forbade her to do it again.

"Very well, Father," she said firmly, closing the ledger book and rising to leave. "Pay my replacement whatever you wish. I will visit you at the Feast of the Assumption."

He surrendered instantly. After that he didn't even want to know what was in the books. He let her do as she would with them. The pile of silver carlinos growing in his money box salved his wounded pride. He had never been able to make the pile grow at all. Despite her victory Maria never kept much money, but it was far better than she made with the goats. What money she did keep she saved for one purpose. She called on every ship that berthed in the harbor, giving handwritten notices to the captains. The notices offered a reward of a hundred silver taris for information about Nicolo Borg, thought to be captive somewhere along the Barbary Coast. Without exception the captains mocked her futile search, and without exception they took her papers. A hundred silver taris was a great deal of money, of which Maria had only the smallest portion. But it was also an amount of sufficient size to guarantee interest in the shipping circles of the Mediterranean. A Spaniard might tell a Venetian, who might tell a Frenchman, who might encounter a Turk or even a Barbary corsair who might know of Nico's fate. If he was a prisoner, ransom would free him. She had to try.

Meanwhile she worried she had somehow sold her soul by helping her father as she had. She had always meant the arrangement to be temporary, but somehow one month stretched to two, and two to more, until several years had passed. She realized how much her life had changed in that time. She told herself that where she had once acted through pity for Luca, she now acted through choice, because it served her own interests. She liked what she was doing and was free to leave Luca—or Malta, for that matter—whenever she wished. Perhaps that freedom to choose was all she really needed or wanted. There would always be time to move along, and anyway there were two other matters that intruded on her dream of leaving: Elena, who was pregnant, and Jacobus, who was in love.

Elena had taken the usual precautions. When they failed her first thought was to end the pregnancy, which would interfere with her ability to earn a living. She visited Lucrezia, the witch of Rabat, who made her a poultice of snakeskin, castoreum, and pigeon dung. It didn't work. Nor did a stronger mixture, to which she added the blood of a bat. She tried potions of myrrh and pepper and opoponax, and pessaries of pennyroyal and birthwort. Elena developed rashes, and her eyes grew yellow with jaundice. Still the child grew inside her. "The baby laughs at us," Lucrezia said. "You should have it."

But Elena was resolute and steeled herself for more drastic measures. Lucrezia arranged for a midwife. On the appointed day Elena set out for Mdina with Maria at her side. Knowing well what danger awaited her, Elena's face was white with worry and she said very little. They were threading their way through the crowds near the gate when she gasped in shock, her hand clamping on Maria's.

"Elena! *X'gara? X'inqala?* What is it?"

"I . . . I don't know." Elena put her hand on her stomach and once again stiffened.

Maria steadied her and guided her to the side of the road. "Are you all right? Are you bleeding?"

"Yes . . . no. I'm all right. It's just . . . it didn't hurt. It wasn't something in a bad way. It just—" She looked at Maria, her gaze going from shock to wonder. "It *moved,* Maria."

"Do you want to rest?"

"Yes. No." She took a deep breath, and they started to walk again. Her stride, purposeful up to that point, had grown tentative, as if she no longer knew the way. She turned to Maria. "Let's go home," she said, her eyes lit with purpose. "I'm going to have a baby."

With Elli acting as midwife, a boy was born in M'kor Hakhayyim on the night of the seventh new moon, Rosh ha-Shanah. The child had a thatch of bright red hair like his father, a knight from Munich; skin the color of milk, like his mother; and a shattering cry of raw thunder, like the very voice of God.

Elli wiped him clean and wrapped him in thick wool to keep away the chill night air, as the others in the cave pressed forward to see. She handed the child to Fençu and turned her attentions to Elena. The baby wailed.

"It is fitting he is born on Yom Teruah," Fençu said, "the day of the sounding of the shofar, for with such a voice, we no longer need a ram's horn. I am certain Elohim hears this one on Mount Sinai." He lifted the child high for all in the cave to see. "And it is equally fitting he is born on the birthday of the world. He will rise to greatness, giving proof to the wonder of God's creation." He passed the child to its mother. "You should name him Ariel, the lion of God, for surely that is how he sounds."

Elena named him Moses.

There was no rabbi, so on the eighth day Fençu presided at the *brit milah,* deftly performing the circumcision with a skinning knife and a spoon. It was done neatly and quickly, pleasing everyone except Moses, who shook the walls with his mighty cry.

In honor of the birth, Fençu proclaimed a celebration to coincide with the Days of Awe. He made a special midnight visit to Mdina, returning the next day with a feast: roast mutton, a six-pigeon tart, red oranges, and a honeyed *api* for dessert. After dinner there was storytelling and dancing, and great quantities of sweet wine—not cheap *rozolin,* Fençu noted proudly, such as any commoner might drink, but muscatel, imported from Provence and fit for a king. Elli fretted over how much Fençu had stolen to pay for it all, but even she smiled as Fençu raised the *simcha* cup in a toast to Moses: "May you never know want, or fear, or plague." To those present in the cave, who had known little else, the blessing was welcome, but altogether as unlikely as the meal.

Maria stepped forward, holding a leather pouch. Worried that her efforts to end her pregnancy might have damaged the boy, Elena had sent Maria to ask Lucrezia to make a protective amulet. Lucrezia charged the outrageous sum of three scudi, because the baby was a Jew who had no soul and was therefore more difficult to protect. Maria was furious at the old witch but unwilling to disappoint Elena so she'd paid the extra herself. Now she knelt by Moses and tied the amulet around his neck. "*Tharsek mill-ghajn,*" she said, faithfully beginning the incantation Lucrezia had given her to say. When she was done she turned and threw laurel leaves on the fire.

Elena smiled broadly. Between the conjurations of Fençu and Lucrezia, all that could be done for the future of Moses had been done. "He is perfect," she said, nuzzling the child. "Perfect and pure."

Maria stepped back and let Jacobus take her hand.

❖

Jacobus Pavino was nothing if not a patient man.

Not since the corsairs had taken his family had anything so troubled him as those long dark days when Maria had suffered through some terrible and mysterious time, culminating in the raid on M'kor Hakhayyim by the *gendarmi,* who arrested him and Elena and Fençu.

For months after that he watched her from a distance, desperate to not incur her anger, which seemed to flare so quickly. He did little kindnesses for her: he left wildflowers on her ledge in the cave, and brought her fresh plover eggs instead of selling them in the market. For a long while she never seemed to really notice. Her thanks were hollow and her looks were blank. He hated whatever had happened to her, hated that he couldn't see into her troubles and help her.

Time did what he could not. Fençu had counseled patience, and Fençu, as usual, had been right. Nearly a year passed and one night Jacobus heard laughter. The cave sparkled with the sound: it was *Maria*.

Despite Maria's renewed spirit, nothing really changed for a long while, not between them. He watched her with longing, from a distance. She was not just the most remarkable woman on Malta, he knew: she was the most remarkable woman in all the world. Her talents, talents he'd never seen in a woman, had grown along with her. She was still more nimble than a goat, a better swimmer than a fish. She could outrun anyone in the cave, and her ability to read was as near to magic as anything he'd ever seen. Her beauty was more than he could bear. Sometimes when she went out he wished she would wear a *barnuza* so that other men could not see her. But she was not one for the veil, of course, and although she seemed uninterested in men, he knew they would not long remain uninterested in her. He despaired of ever bringing her around to feel the way he did. He never forgot her casual comment that had stung him so: *You remind me of my brother Nico*.

They celebrated Passover in the cave, and Purim and Hanukkah, and Passover once again. Returning from the hunt one day, he encountered her on the path from Birgu. To Jacobus's surprise Maria seemed glad to see him. She greeted him with a broad smile and fell in beside him. It was a beautiful early summer evening, peaceful and blessedly cool. The sun was low, huge and red in the sea haze, casting long shadows over brown hills. Gulls swooped and whirled beneath lazy tendrils of clouds that laced the sky, shot through with pink and purple. They walked on the path for a while as Jacobus desperately tried to think of something to say.

"Fençu says you've been working for the knights," he said at last.

She nodded. "For my father, at Fort St. Michael. A new bastion."

"It sounds important."

"Not really. It's nothing but stone piled on stone."

"Still, they don't let just anyone do that."

"There must be a hundred people working on it."

"Oh." He didn't know what else to say. Presented at last with the opportunity he had so long desired, he felt awkward and tongue-tied, all but overcome by her nearness. The having of Maria at his side was not nearly as easy as the wanting.

"Where have you been?" she asked.

"Birding. On Gozo."

"For thrushes?"

"Goatsuckers."

"How do you catch them?"

He held up a noose and stick. "With these." Reacting to her look of curiosity, he impulsively launched into a demonstration of his technique as he pretended to catch one of the birds. In the midst of his display he stopped suddenly, self-conscious, realizing how silly he must look to a woman who built things for knights. But she disarmed him with her laughter and waved him on. "You should take me sometime," she said. "I'd love to see you do that with a real bird."

"Really? Do you mean it?"

"Of course. I've never been to Gozo."

He whirled and looped and carried on, making her laugh again. They stopped to watch the sun settling into the sea, and she asked more questions about his work.

That night he could not sleep for his excitement.

The next day he asked Fençu if he could borrow his little boat.

"You use it all the time," Fençu said, puzzled. "You've never asked before."

"Well," Jacobus said, bursting with the need to tell someone, "I want it because I'm going to take Maria to Gozo."

Fençu smiled. "So. Of course." He thought for a moment. "Are you taking anything special?"

"Special? Like what?"

"A blanket to sit on, and something to eat. You have to think about these things."

The next Sunday, when Maria didn't have to work, they sailed across the channel to Gozo. Jacobus took her up to the cliffs where he'd worked as a boy. He spread a blanket. She was accustomed to sitting on the ground, but he thought she looked pleased. He served her *rozolin,* a sweet wine that he poured from a stolen crystal flask that Fençu had lent him, and he fed her roast quail that he'd caught and Elli had cooked. By the time he sliced an apple that he'd traded for a wood pigeon, she was impressed. "I think not even the Grand Master eats like this," she said.

Afterward he showed her how to catch birds on the cliffs, and he lowered himself on his ropes and soared gracefully out over the water. Each time he looked up, he saw her looking eagerly down, enthralled. "It's my turn," she called to him at last.

"What?"

"I didn't come just to watch a birdman," she said. "I came to fly!"

"But you cannot!"

"I can! I will! Come up!"

He hung there for a moment, deciding. Reluctantly he climbed the rope. He modified the sling to fit her. As she stood near the edge, his nerves nearly deserted him. It was one thing to swing from a rope himself, tempting fate high above the deadly rocks and pounding surf, and another altogether to have *her* do so. He checked every inch of the rope and double-tied the knots that secured the rope to a tree. He rigged a special loop around his waist so that he could control the rope while bracing his feet against some rocks. All the while he chattered nervous instructions. He held his breath as she backed over the edge and he lowered her slowly. "Just up and down the first time," he said. "Don't push away from the rocks. Just hang. Do you understand?"

"Yes."

He played out the rope. He raised her up and down a little, to give her the feel of it. "All right?" he yelled.

"Farther!" she called back. He let out more rope and heard her whooping and giggling. After a while he felt a familiar pull on the rope. He got into a position from which he could look, and saw she'd pushed off from the cliffs. She was doing a slow, lazy dance on the end of the rope—touching, soaring, touching again, spinning with one arm gracefully extended. "I told you not to—" he started to say.

"I don't know whether to laugh out loud or to piss," she yelled, shocking him, as she often did, with the frankness of her speech.

He knew it was useless telling Maria Borg what to do. "Do both, then," he called back, "but stay downwind."

She stayed on the rope for an hour. She startled an owl, touched a turtledove, and turned a backward somersault.

From that day, her previous reserve around him seemed broken. They walked together more frequently. He planned it carefully, getting up earlier than usual to finish his work in time so he could join her at the hour he knew she would be returning to M'kor Hakhayyim. They returned to Gozo again and again, sometimes not coming home until long after dark.

One afternoon she invited him to go swimming. They went to a lagoon where the water was warm and sparkling blue. They dove off the high rocks, seeing who could dive the deepest. Afterward they lay on the beach, warming themselves in the glorious sun. She lay on her back, eyes closed. He raised himself on one elbow and stared at her, marveling at the tenderness he felt whenever he saw her, and he grew short of breath when he regarded her wondrous figure beneath the jerkin. He resisted the impulse to move closer, to touch her, for somehow he knew it would ruin everything. He had heard of a potion made of wine and blood that could entice an unwilling lover, but he didn't want to win her that way. She would let him know when it was time. He was certain such a time would come on its own.

One day when they were sitting near the water and she was completely at ease and relaxed and happy, he could wait no more. He summoned his courage and blurted it out. "I want to be your husband, Maria."

Startled, she blushed and looked away. He was certain he had mortally offended her and that she would never speak to him again. But then she turned to him, and rather than rebuffing him she took his hand in hers. "Thank you, Jacobus. You honor me, truly you do, but I don't want a husband yet."

He nodded. That wasn't as bad as it might have been. "When you do, may I be it? Him? I mean—"

She laughed again, and he knew it was not the sort of laugh she would share with a lover or even a serious suitor. It was—still—more a laugh she might share with a little brother. "I will tell you when I know myself."

For Jacobus it was enough. At least she hadn't said no

❖

"He is good for you, you know," Elena told her the week Moses was born, when Maria and Jacobus returned from a day trip to Gozo. "I haven't seen you smile so in a long time."

Maria nodded. It was true. Jacobus was a good man. She had grown quite comfortable with him. She could talk about anything with him, except the things she would never talk about with any man. She wasn't certain what she wanted from their relationship, but she was in no particular hurry to find out. She knew that he loved her, even worshiped her. She felt great tenderness toward him, and very often the sweet things he struggled so to say touched her deeply.

She didn't know if she loved him. She wasn't at all certain what love was.

Though he had asked her to marry him, he seemed content with her response, seemed content simply to pass the time with her.

Sometimes they held hands, lightly, as they walked through the fields or stood looking out over the water. She kissed him once, on the cheek. Shyly he returned the kiss, on her forehead. He seemed to know that was enough, and stopped.

Yes, Maria thought. *He is good for me.*

from The Histories of the Middle Sea

by Darius, called the Preserver
Court Historian to the Prince and Lord of the Most Elegant Constellation,
the Sultan Achmet

Only a sorcerer could have devised a brew as potent, as pungent, as poisonous to the taste as the one created by the Emperor Charles when he granted Malta to the Knights of St. John. What a mix it was!

Though the Order, the Church, the Holy Father, and the Office of the Inquisition might seem arrows of the same quiver, each arrow made its own arc, and no arc was ever smooth or predictable. The Order was sovereign, its Grand Master a prince of the Church, his Order under the protection of the Pope. It was only natural that this would create conflicts with the formal Church hierarchy. The Order had its own clergy under the Grand Prior, who had no formal relationship with the diocese. The Order and its tenants paid no taxes to the bishopric, not only in Malta but on the continent as well. Knights were not subject to the bishop's ecclesiastical courts but were instead tried by the Order, if at all. The bishop was not without weapons in this constant test of wills; he could grant tonsure to his allies to protect them from the Order's courts. Both Church and Order ignored the Maltese Università, the civil authority whose right to govern local affairs had steadily withered since the arrival of the knights. The once-powerful nobility could appeal unpopular decisions of the Order to the Viceroy of Sicily and even to the king of Spain, but that route was as rocky and precarious as the roads of Malta. As a result, many of the noble families had simply fled the island, preferring exile in Sicily to life under the hated knights. Those who remained kept largely to themselves, shut away in their grand houses behind the walls of Mdina, harboring their resentments and clinging to their ghosts of glory past.

Ah, but this heady brew was only just beginning to ferment. Although the bishop of Malta was nominated from the ranks of the Order's own clergy, once he became bishop everything changed as he found his place and power within the hierarchy of the Church. He himself regarded the knights as ruthless politicians, impious monks who largely ignored their vows and conducted themselves as if they answered to no earthly authority, most particularly his own. Meanwhile his former brethren, the knights, regarded him as a spy for the Vatican and an agent for the Viceroy of Sicily, and through him for Philip, the king, whose interests were often at odds with those of the knights. This meant that while the bishop was automatically a Grand Cross of the Order and entitled to sit at Sacred Council, he was excluded from meetings of substance. Further, because the bishop arose from the ranks of the Order, the Vatican itself considered him tainted.

Thus it was the Pope did not trust his bishop, the bishop did not trust his knights, and the knights trusted no one at all. Did ever the intrigues of Topkapi run so deep?

The only spice that could possibly have made this mix more sour was delivered by the Holy Office of the Inquisition. As this was a period in which the tiny island of Malta was not seen to require the services of its own Inquisitor, it was deemed expedient to name the bishop pro-Inquisitor: something of an unofficial post, whose occupant could be trusted to investigate such matters of faith as might appear from time to time.

For many years the man whose fate it was to wear this heavy mantle was Bishop Cubelles, who as pro-Inquisitor had tried Father Jesuald for heresy and had seen him burned at the stake. While Cubelles was generally regarded as an honorable man, his position was quite impossible. Still, he might have remained pro-Inquisitor indefinitely but for the religious climate on the continent and for rumors that began swirling around the Order during the reign of Pope Paul IV.

Paul was despised within his own Church. His elevation to the throne of St. Peter was vetoed by Charles V, to no effect. Paul renewed the Inquisition's worst medieval terrors against heretics, squabbled with Charles, and warred with his son Philip. He ordered that the Jewish quarter of Rome be surrounded by a wall, creating a ghetto in which, he said, God wished him to impose servitude upon the Jews until they recognized the errors of their faith. He demanded that the English queen, Elizabeth, seek authority for her throne through him and repay the Holy See for properties seized by her father, Henry VIII. There were few monarchs Paul did not alienate, and his adventures did much to set a climate in which Ottoman designs might flourish. Indeed, his successor, Pius IV, noted that the very foundations of St. Peter's were under siege by heretic and Turk alike.

Calvinism was on the rise in France, where a synod met boldly in Paris. Pius funneled money to the French crown for its fight against the Huguenots, while resisting pressure to excommunicate Elizabeth, hoping to ease hostilities and induce her return to the fold of the Church. He reversed his predecessor's policy of war against Spain and made overtures to the new Holy Roman Emperor, Ferdinand.

Pius faced no more thorny issue than the persistent rumors about the Knights of St. John. A Dominican friar had been sent to Malta to investigate. His pen fairly dripped with damnation. The Order of St. John, he wrote—the very Order entrusted with protecting and defending the Faith—was itself infested by German knights carrying the Protestant plague. The stain on the Church was intolerable and could not be left uncleansed. The time had arrived, he wrote, for the appointment of a full Inquisitor.

La Valette dispatched an ambassador to beseech the Holy Father to let the Order itself try cases of suspected heresy, without interference from the Holy Office. There was no doubt, he wrote, that the Order would police itself as thoroughly as any representative of the Inquisition. He himself, Grand Master Jean Parisot de La Valette, would ensure it.

The Pope's reply came by fast galley.

—From Volume V
The Order of St. John

Chapter 28

"To our great sorrow we have been informed that the destructive poison of heresy has wormed its way into the city and island of Malta and even among members of the Holy Order of St. John. Accordingly we are authorizing the Bishop of Malta, Monsignor Cubelles, to act as Inquisitor. . . ."

The Grand Master was a man of immense dignity and composure, but before he even finished reading he slammed his fist against the table, startling the members of his Sacred Council, who sat around the long leather and oak table.

"That this should happen on *my* watch," La Valette thundered. He stood. "Is it not enough we face the menace of the Ottomans all but unaided by the very courts we protect? Now must we fight suspicion and tyranny from within the Faith itself? Now must we bend to the will of this . . . this . . . *edict!* And for all that the Holy Father does not do me the courtesy of writing me privately! He sends his message through the Holy Office! All Europe must know of this humiliation!"

La Valette threw the papers to the table and began pacing. His secretary, Sir Oliver Starkey, quickly gathered up the Pope's missive. "We could do worse than Cubelles," said Sir Oliver. "He has been both bishop and pro-Inquisitor for years without being unreasonable. He seems without guile."

"One does not fear the cub," La Valette said. "One fears the lion. As pro-Inquisitor, he had no teeth. The gulf between us is certain to widen now that his power has grown. As Inquisitor, he will surely attempt to gain a hold over us that cannot be broken."

"Perhaps an overture through King Philip, or the Emperor Ferdinand," said Degueras, the Bailiff of Negropont. "Offering support for—"

La Valette shook his head. "They will never dare."

Oliver Starkey was reading the rest of the message. "Perhaps it is not so bad as all that, Grand Master," he said hopefully. "According to this, the bishop may not act alone. You are to sit in the tribunal with him, sire, along with the Prior of St. Lawrence and the Vice Chancellor."

La Valette scowled. "Bones to a cur," he said. "The only real authority will be in the hands of Cubelles. Anyone who dares question him will himself be branded a heretic."

"Evidently not just his hands, sire," Starkey said, reading further. His broad brow knitted in confusion. "This is quite odd, as if the Holy Office does not entirely trust Cubelles himself. Perhaps his service as chaplain of the Order is too fresh in their memory. A vicar is being appointed to 'assist' him."

"A *vicar!* Appointed by the Holy Office? Who is he?"

"This does not say, Grand Master."

"A vicar, indeed," La Valette mused. "Someone to watch the watchers. Surely this will be a man to beware. If Cubelles is the snake, he will be the dragon."

❖

The baroness Angela Buqa was only occasionally unfaithful to her husband, Antonio, certainly less often than he was to her. Theirs was a marriage of convenience, arranged by her father. Love, of course, had nothing to do with it, and she saw their union very much as she saw Malta itself—a barren place, where little grew but tedium. Antonio was twice her age, soft in the belly and plain in his tastes. His chief interests were Sicilian figs and Italian grapes. He was as well born and well placed as a man could be in Malta, and yet to Angela, the greatest heights of Malta were beneath the lowest reaches of the poorest courts of Europe. She could never fathom why her father hadn't married her to a businessman of Venice or Florence, where there were suitable entertainments.

The baron did what he could to purchase diversions for her. Her wardrobe was the envy of every woman in Mdina. Her dressers held mountains of jewelry, her wardrobes scores of shoes. Antonio allowed her to furnish the house as she pleased, setting no budget to restrain her. She filled it with books he never read and tapestries he never noticed. He kept stables for her but did not ride with her, preferring a cushion on a carriage seat to the hard leather of a saddle. No matter how free the budget, the money never helped for long. "It's like burying pearls in a dunghill," she complained.

She had a few affairs but remained warily discreet, for despite his own trysts, which he hid poorly, her husband was a jealous man with a fearful temper. She never gave him any reason to be suspicious.

Until she saw Christien de Vries.

As a *jurat* of the Università, her husband was deeply involved in the affairs of Santu Spiritu, the private civilian hospital in Mdina. In the course of his duties he met occasionally with the Grand Hospitaller of the Order, to borrow or lend supplies. Most often it was to borrow, as the Order of St. John, no matter what its other obligations, took great care in provisioning its renowned hospital.

The Grand Hospitaller, Gabriel Çeralta, arrived one afternoon at the Buqa mansion to meet Antonio and Dr. Callus, the physician of Mdina. The Hospitaller was accompanied by several assistants, including a *prud'homme,* the official responsible for the hospital's provisions, and the infirmarian. But from the instant she greeted her husband's guests, Angela could not take her eyes off one of the lowly surgeons, a dark-haired knight from Paris introduced as Fra Christien de Vries. He wore the simple black mantle of the Order. He was well built but not stocky and carried himself with easy grace. His gaze was direct and friendly. He did not seem to undress her with his eyes, as other men did.

She wanted him to.

She was not invited to participate in her husband's business, so she watched from the entryway, trying to listen as the men discussed ointments of zinc oxide, plasters of beeswax, medicines of mandrake and hyosciamus, and tinctures of elettaria. She could see the surgeon in profile. He leaned forward, intent. The knights she had met—and there were not many—were generally arrogant and kept to themselves, preferring the starry reaches of their own company to that of the gentry of Malta, as if to remind them that even the most noble Maltese were not noble enough for entry to the Order. Christien seemed less aloof than his brethren. He said something that made the others laugh and nod their heads. She watched in a daze. That he was a surgeon added to her fascination: *Such a base and violent profession for such a gentle man.*

The time came to serve light refreshments. Angela found it necessary to oversee the efforts of her manservant, who had waited upon hundreds of guests in that room without her ever taking an interest. The men rose at her presence. To her surprise her husband invited her to sit with his guests. She sat next to the *prud'homme,* doing her best to ignore him as she tried to concentrate on a discussion between Christien and Dr. Callus about treasure hunting and hawking.

She watched his hands as he talked.

They were expressive, delicate, almost feminine. He peeled an orange and put a slice to his lips. She shivered, reveling in her secret thoughts. She felt that mouth on hers, felt those hands on her cheeks, on her shoulders, down her back, on her hips—she wanted them everywhere. She was clumsy with the silver and nearly spilled her own drink. She felt hot and weak. She held her cup with both hands, trying to still their trembling. She nodded absently at something the *prud'homme* said.

When the men rose to leave, much too soon, Christien smiled at her. While her husband concluded a last matter with Callus and the Hospitaller, he engaged her in a moment of polite and easy conversation. Somehow, flushing, she stammered out a response. An instant later she had no idea what she'd said. When he stepped to the door, it was all she could do not to catch his sleeve. She couldn't bear to see him go.

She thought only men felt such animal heat, yet it was her own palms that were wet, her own loins stirring. No man had ever affected her in that way, at least not without trying. But Christien seemed to notice nothing and politely bade her good day.

When they were gone she could scarcely breathe. She didn't hear her husband ask her what was wrong. She mumbled something and went to her room, not seeing his troubled look.

❖

Her first attempt was uncharacteristically awkward. She knew nothing of Christien's routine, and there was no one to ask. There was little opportunity to meet a knight unless one was a courtesan.

She couldn't very well knock on the front door of the auberge, the dormitory where he lived with the other knights of the French *langue*. She couldn't visit him at the infirmary, for women were not allowed entrance. For a woman who intended what she intended, nothing short of subterfuge would do.

Among the few things she'd heard pass between Christien and Joseph Callus was their plan for a morning of hunting. Callus was going to teach his friend the finer points of falconry. It was simple, then. She would ride out and find them. And then? She didn't know. She would have to improvise.

Ordinarily quite composed, she rode out on the wrong morning, a day early. She waited several hours before realizing her mistake. That almost made her change her mind.

He is driving me mad, and I don't even know him.

But she was there again the next day. She saw them on a bluff overlooking St. Paul's Bay. They had gone off the road. She rode toward them. They didn't notice her approach. Their eyes were on the hawk, wheeling and circling high above, playing on the air currents just heating up with the day.

When she was nearly abreast of their position, she drew up the reins, dismounted, and knelt as if to check something with one of her horse's hooves. Then she stood and jammed the heel of her boot between two rocks next to the road, intending to pretend to fall. Her boot lodged more tightly than she'd expected and she actually lost her balance. She fell hard and cried out with shock: the injury was genuine. Moments later Christien arrived, while Callus tended to the hawk. "*Barunessa!*" he said with surprise. "Are you all right?"

"*Sì*," she said, blushing, already feeling his nearness. "I ride here often. My horse took a stone. I was removing it when I tripped."

Christien helped extricate her boot. She gasped again as it came free. Her eyes watered with pain. *At least I don't have to act*, she thought.

He helped her to a sitting position. Callus arrived on his horse, leading Christien's mount behind. The hawk was hooded, riding on his forearm. He dismounted and set the bird in the shade. The two doctors got her boot off. Her ankle was swollen, the skin an angry purple.

"You'll need to have that tended to," Christien said. "A nasty sprain."

"Yes," she said. "I feel so foolish."

To her dismay the two men immediately agreed she needed the care of a physician, not a surgeon. "I'll take you to my office," Callus said, "and see you home. The baron will be quite concerned."

"I'll lend a hand," Christien said, and she brightened.

"No need," Callus said quickly, reading Angela's face. "I can manage. You take care of the hawk."

Christien helped her up onto her horse, while Callus took the reins.

"I'm sorry to have interrupted your hunt, Fra de Vries," she said, unable to conceal her disappointment.

"The pigeons send their thanks," he said, smiling. "Mind that ankle. There are those who believe Joseph a competent physician. I know better, but he's a lucky man. With that luck he'll treat you without causing further injury." She and Callus both laughed.

So it was off with Callus and not Christien that she rode, cursing herself for her own stupidity.

Must I stab myself to see him?

❖

Callus made a point of visiting Christien later that afternoon. "I saw her interest in you, my friend," he said.

"Oh? I didn't notice."

Callus looked skeptical but let it pass. "Not long ago you warned me to be careful with La Valette. I think I might pass the same advice to you about the baroness. It is obvious you are in for some trouble if you aren't careful. I have seen her wrath, which I would pit against that of the Grand Master any day."

"She seems pleasant enough to me," Christien said. "And unlike the Grand Master, she wields no noose."

"No, but her husband does."

Christien laughed. "I have done nothing, Joseph. And I intend it to remain that way."

"It is not you who concerns me," Callus said.

❖

Her ankle took two weeks to heal sufficiently that she could ride again.

Antonio was solicitous of her safety and told her to ride with the equerry. "I'll be fine, *hanini*," she said. "I'll only walk my horse. Just a short ride, toward Dingli."

She rode the other way, straight to Birgu. She left her horse at a public stable and asked directions of the groomsman. Drawing her *barnuza* tightly around her face, she entered the cramped warren of streets near the square, finding one that she knew led to his auberge. She walked slowly, examining the façades of the buildings until she saw one that bore a coat of arms over the door that heralded the combined auberges of Auvergne and Provence. She'd gone the wrong way. She backtracked and saw the escutcheon marking the auberge of France. Like the others, it was a simple two-story building. She watched for twenty minutes, but the door remained closed, and she could not see inside. Despite her *barnuza,* her nerves failed her. What if *he* opened the door and saw her?

She went around the block, passed St. Agatha's, and stared at the Holy Infirmary, the Order's massive hospital that rose three stories tall, backing onto Kalkara Creek. She watched the gallery that led to the inner cloistered courtyard. She could see orange trees in the courtyard, and someone drawing water from a well. Finally she saw a page of the Order hurrying toward the entrance. She hailed the boy and pressed a note into his hand. "Give this to Fra de Vries," she said.

Before he could reply she turned and went into St. Agatha's, her heart pounding. The church was deserted. She lit a candle and knelt before the altar.

That night at dinner Antonio asked casually about her day.

"It was all right," she said. "I went toward Luqa. The ride was boring, really. I should have gone to Dingli as I planned."

"I saw Dun Paolo today." Antonio heaped food onto his plate.

Her fork stopped in midair at the mention of St. Agatha's parish priest. "Oh?"

"*Sì.* He told me he thought he saw you in Birgu."

Angela nearly dropped her fork. "I . . . yes, I suppose he might have. I visited St. Agatha's, too," she said smoothly.

Antonio looked up at her briefly, then back at his food. "Birgu is a long way from Luqa. And your parish is here, in Mdina."

"Yes, of course. I was thinking of Giulio, that's all. I hadn't seen him in so long, I felt like visiting his old parish. I hadn't been there in years, so I went inside. It was nothing. Just a whim."

"Mmm." He washed down his food with a gulp of wine. "Dun Paolo wasn't even certain it was you."

She quickly changed the subject. Antonio didn't press her.

Despite the danger she couldn't stop herself. The next morning Antonio went off to the Università to tend to some business about grain. She rode to an isolated spot south from Birgu, near a deserted granary. She worried that he couldn't find the place or that he wouldn't come. But then he was there, his horse trotting easily down the path. He wore his black habit, which bore the small embroidered eight-pointed cross of the Order. As he drew near he nodded politely.

"Baroness, it is a pleasure to see you again. You have fully recovered?"

"Quite, thank you, Fra de Vries." She searched his eyes for some sign that he had longed for this to happen. Instead he looked a bit bemused.

"Your note said it was a matter of some importance?"

"It is," she said with an enigmatic smile. "Follow me, if you please." She turned her horse and set off at a trot to the east. Puzzled, Christien fell in behind her. Almost immediately they were out of sight of Birgu, crossing a deep *wied* and passing up onto a hill. They followed a winding path through stony terrain, picking their way through abandoned fields. Ancient cart ruts marked old roadways, now overgrown with silvery grass. Soon there were no traces of human existence. They came to the sea, and she stopped near an outcropping of rock. She dismounted and began untying a blanket rolled up behind her saddle. Christien watched with growing discomfort. "Baroness Buqa, perhaps this is not—"

"Please, I need help with this. Would you be so kind?" Reluctantly he dismounted. She smiled brightly, the ringlets of her auburn hair flashing in the sun. She handed him the blanket. "Unroll it over there, will you?" She unstrapped a leather bag tied to her saddle. She waited while he straightened the blanket, and then she sat down. She opened the bag and took out bread, cheese, a flask of brandy, and two silver goblets. She beckoned him to join her. Without waiting she poured him a large measure. "It is an excellent vintage, from your own country," she said. "I hope you'll not find it too plain."

Christien sat opposite her, keeping as much distance between them as he could while still sitting on the blanket. "What I ordinarily drink is more water than wine. The Grand Master forbids us hard spirits."

"You would never disobey the Grand Master, of course."

"It depends on the brandy," he said truthfully.

"And women? Does he forbid you them? Are your vows of chastity ironclad?"

Christien blushed, unaccustomed to such directness, and quite wary now. "Baroness, I—"

Angela leaned forward and kissed him on the lips.

He was so startled he nearly dropped his cup. He got to his knees, pushing her gently but firmly away. "I am sorry," he said. "I cannot."

"You do not find me attractive?"

"On the contrary, Baroness. You are a beautiful woman." He looked away for a moment, trying to find the right thing to say. "Your husband is a very fortunate man."

She reddened at that. "My husband does not matter."

"As you wish," Christien said. "Still, he is your husband."

"Please don't patronize me, Fra de Vries. He takes women on the side."

"How unfortunate for you. I'm sorry. It is none of my affair, of course."

She watched, disbelieving, as he rose to leave. "May I help you gather your things?" he asked.

"Don't go," she said.

A moment later she was alone, trying to collect her wits.

❖

Bertrand pronounced him a fool.

"Angela Buqa is perhaps the most luscious fruit on this God-rotted island, and you would not pluck her, even as she begs you? You are quite insane, of course. I am worried for your manhood."

"Her husband is one of the *jurati*," Christien said. "I am certain he would object to having me trample through his orchards. I have no desire to see him cleaning his guns on my account."

"Well, then, that's simple. Have her and don't tell him, as I would have done. Better still, send her to me."

Christien laughed. "She is beautiful, it is true, but I have no interest in her short of the bed. And as tempting as that might be, I have made my vows. I will honor them. Even if I were otherwise inclined, I would wish a woman somewhat less . . . married."

"Your *vows!*" Bertrand snorted. "There isn't a knight in Malta who doesn't wet his wick from time to time. The only shaft the Order really cares about is the steel one you raise against the infidel—not the stiff one between your legs."

"What other knights do is their affair," Christien said. "They must settle their own accounts with God, as I have tried to settle mine."

"You are mincing and squeamish, Fra de Vries. A disgrace to mankind. I wash my hands of you."

❖

With Vatican pennons fluttering, the galley swept majestically past the tip of Sciberras and beneath the guns of Fort St. Elmo, gliding past Gallows Point and into the Grand Harbor, her oars sweeping in perfect unison to the relentless slow beat of the tambour. Her railings were of teak, her aft woodwork panels elaborately polished and carved with scenes from the life of Christ. Four trumpeters stood in the prow, wearing broad felt caps and silk blouses that rippled in the breeze. At a signal from the captain they raised their shining instruments to herald the arrival of the galley's passenger. Their signal was but a formality. Word had already spread through the island like wildfire, passed from coastal lookout towers into every parish and home:

He is here.

Shielded by a lavender damask awning that shaded the poop deck, the Inquisitor's Vicar stood next to the captain. He was tall and bone-thin, dressed in black skullcap, black cassock, and long black robe. His face was gaunt and pale, his beard neatly trimmed, his severe features accentuated by the purplish light filtering through the awning. In one hand he held a small black leather Bible. In the other he grasped a fragrant pomander of orange skins and cloves that he held to his nose to ward off the disagreeable stench emanating from the galley slaves toiling beneath him in the merciless sun.

A gathering of church dignitaries waited at the quay, including Bishop Cubelles and his household staff, a score of parish priests, and members of the various religious orders. Nearby stood a contingent of Maltese nobility, including all the *jurati* of the Università and their families, eager to ingratiate themselves with the new arrival. Conspicuously absent were representatives of the Order of St. John.

As the galley drew near enough for individual faces to be discerned, the vicar acknowledged his bishop with a formal nod of the head. The nod was returned with a pleasant smile. The captain barked an order, and the tambour fell silent. At a call from the bosun, oars were shipped and the galley nudged the dock. Ropes were made fast and planking laid.

The vicar disembarked, stepping lightly onto the quay. He dutifully kissed the bishop's ring. "It is a great pleasure to see you again, Your Grace. The Holy Father sends his blessings, along with his edict." He beckoned to one of the priests traveling with him, who proffered the oilcloth packet. The vicar withdrew a rolled parchment. Tied with a crimson ribbon and sealed with red wax, the document contained the sacred papal brief of Pius IV, formally establishing the Inquisition in Malta and naming Cubelles as Inquisitor.

Cubelles received it gravely and handed it to the sacristan. "The Holy Office could not have made a better choice for vicar," Cubelles said. "Through them the Lord has smiled upon this poor island and His humble servant. With two of us to carry His load, the burden will seem more bearable."

"You are too kind, Eminence," the vicar replied with a thin smile.

"You must be tired after your journey. We must get you settled. I have arranged apartments for you in my palace. I fear they are more austere than your customary quarters."

"I am certain they shall be more than adequate, Your Grace. My needs are quite modest. Everything I own in the world is in that case." The vicar indicated a small black valise that stood on the dock.

They turned to the patiently waiting nobles of Mdina. He knew most of them already and greeted them politely. When he stood in front of Angela Buqa, his eyes lit with pleasure. "Angela, my dear," he said. The vicar bowed and kissed her hand. "How is it the years seem to leave no mark upon you?"

She smiled. "I have missed you, dear brother," she replied. "You must visit us immediately."

"As duty permits, of course. And now, if you'll forgive me?"

The bishop and his vicar seated themselves in the carriage for the short ride to the palace near the city wall. Neither of them saw Elena, clutching Moses to her breast. She backed away from the quay as if she'd seen a ghost.

❖

Jacobus blinked, awakening from a deep sleep. He'd been out in

Fençu's little boat until quite late, trying a technique he'd heard about that used lanterns for attracting fish. It had worked quite well, but he hadn't gotten home until near dawn. He'd slept heavily most of the morning.

He heard urgent whispers below him, and it was the clear sound of distress that brought him to the surface. Elena was weeping. He rolled over and peered down from the ledge. He could just see Maria, who must have come in while he was sleeping. She didn't know he was there. He didn't want to eavesdrop. He thought he should announce himself, or make a noise, but he hesitated, and then it was too late.

"I saw him with my own eyes," Elena said to Maria between sobs. Moses was crying, too, distressed at his mother's tears. "He . . . he was in a carriage, with the bishop."

"What are you saying?" Maria asked. "Who was it?"

"Dun . . . Dun Salvago." Elena choked it out. "They called him the Inquisitor's Vicar."

Jacobus saw Maria put her hand to the wall, to steady herself.

"I thought it was done," she said.

"You must hide!"

"*No!*" Maria's eyes flashed. "Never!"

"But Maria, when he raped you he was only a priest. Now he is more powerful than ever. He is . . . he will have to destroy you . . . he will destroy us all." She broke into tears again. The two women clung to each other.

Above them, Jacobus felt as if he'd finally fallen from one of his cliffs.

Rape!

Salvago!

He had not known the name until now, or the crime. He remembered the priest vaguely. He'd seen the man only from a distance.

He lay awake all night, drenched in sweat. The veins at his forehead pulsed and his head ached. He remembered the feeling he had had when his family was taken away in chains by the corsairs. Compared to the thought of a man—a priest—forcing himself on Maria, it was nothing.

There was no question in his mind as to what he must do.

He would avenge her.

Chapter 29

In the years since he departed from Malta, every fiber of Salvago's being had been dedicated to erasing his stain of sin. He committed no further transgression that he knew of save vainglory— he remained ambitious and proud, determined to rise in the ranks of the Church. It was a deadly sin, one he knew he would struggle with forever.

His facility with languages was quickly put to use by the Vatican. The Holy Father, Paul IV, a zealous if unpopular reformer, had been intent upon compiling a list of books and authors to be banned. It was a monumental task: the printing presses of Europe were spewing ink in a never-ending fountain of heresy. Salvago labored alongside a score of other priests, poring through mountains of books, treatises, and manuscripts. The *Index Librorum Prohibitorum* grew steadily and was published the year Paul died.

In preparation for the resumption of the Council of Trent, Salvago worked feverishly in the Palazzo Thun on the Via Lata, translating documents and assisting legates of different nationalities as they began hammering out their differences before the formal convocation of the council. Salvago's opinion was never solicited, of course, for his was but a simple black hat bobbing in a sea of red and purple. Yet he deftly performed his duties. In the course of translating and message bearing, he made the acquaintance of nearly every prince of the Church. He was viewed as sophisticated, politically astute, and sensitive to the conflicts that raged in the Church. He was particularly helpful in finding ways to overcome some of the demands of the envoys of the Catholic kings, who presented innumerable obstacles before granting authority to their bishops to attend the Council at all.

He caught the eye of Victor Lavierge, one of the six cardinals of the Congregation of the Holy Office of the Inquisition, and became

Lavierge's assistant. The cardinal's brief in Trent was to assist in spreading the doctrine and implementation of the Roman Inquisition. The Council of Trent had not yet formally opened when Cardinal Lavierge was hastily summoned to the Vatican. The Pope required assistance on a delicate matter in Malta. He had received reports of heresy among the knights. The Order was of critical importance to the Church, a bastion standing fast against the Turk. Its members represented the greatest of the noble houses of Europe, houses the Pope was desperately trying to unite against Suleiman. Yet the Pope was gravely concerned about the accusations of heresy and could not let them go unanswered.

The Bishop of Malta, Domenico Cubelles, was a man of unquestioned faith and probity, yet he was in an impossibly difficult position. He was Spanish by birth, and upon his official appointment as pro-Inquisitor he had quickly looked for guidance to Sicily, where the harsher Spanish Inquisition still flourished. A natural enough instinct, perhaps, but the Holy Father could not afford this on the island of the knights. Neither was he prepared to accede to the Grand Master's suggestion that the Order act as its own Inquisitor. The knights were already too independent. A delicate balance needed to be struck between the Order and Cubelles, with the Vatican holding the scales.

So it was, Pius explained to the cardinal, that the good bishop needed a wise shepherd to assist him in walking a difficult path. He would need to be a learned man, one who understood the emerging nature of the Church. He would need to be a clever man, who understood the vain and proud knights. He would need to be a tactful man, of great virtue and iron disposition, strong enough to challenge heresy where he found it, yet diplomatic enough to avoid overzealousness at a time when the Turks presented as grave a threat to the Church as did heresy.

Even if such a shepherd could be found, his task would be complicated by the fact that while gently guiding Cubelles, he would officially be subordinate to him.

It seemed impossible, Pius lamented, that such a man should exist.

Cardinal Lavierge had no such doubt. "Holy Father, I know just such a shepherd."

Salvago spent two hours in private audience with Pius, overcome with humility at the great task being thrust upon his shoulders. Here was his chance to redeem himself, to serve his Father in heaven, to atone for his sins by rooting out those of others.

Far from resenting Salvago's presence, Bishop Cubelles was glad to have a foil, someone to raise disagreeable issues with difficult people while leaving him free to pursue a higher pastoral road. When Salvago arrived, Cubelles made it clear that he wished the vicar to be quite active in his pursuit of heresy and fearless in his challenges to the Order, and to trouble him with details only if absolutely necessary. The arrangement suited both men perfectly.

Only hours after arriving and settling into his apartments, after first praying in the chapel, Salvago went to work. He was unable to actively begin his investigations just yet, for he had arrived on the island on the eve of Carnival, when no official business would be conducted. He would begin in earnest when the celebrations were complete. For now there were files to review. Working by the light of a single candle, he began poring over the reports.

In a fit of anger, the Carmelite sister Margherita shattered a statue of the Madonna. . . .

Consalvo Xeberras denounces his neighbor, the butcher Allesandro Zammit, for bigamy. . . .

Case after case. So much evil, so many foul and forbidden things. The files were endless.

The merchant Johanes Dimech is accused of usury, charging interest of three chickens for the loan of only forty-eight scudis. . . .

His mind kept wandering, to *her*. What had become of Maria Borg? Would he see her? He felt weak at the thought, felt himself tremble, felt the sickness rising inside. He wanted to close his eyes to that part of his life. But whenever he closed his eyes, he saw her.

The German knight Fra Abelard Altbusser, heard to utter Lutheran heresy. . . . Eight entries in all for the knights of St. John, all Germans. There would be no end to the obstacles they would place in his path, no end to their clever schemes to conceal, to obscure. . . .

He wanted *not* to see her, and yet her beauty came to him unbidden. Even in Rome, when months would pass without lustful thoughts, his base urges would surface despite his will otherwise, and he would awaken to visions of her, and he would be drenched in sweat, consumed with self-loathing, but hard. . . .

Don Matteo Pisano, keeping a concubine in Mdina and a wife in Birgu . . .

He would not go near her. He would not allow her to corrupt him again. He would not, would not. . . .

Georgio de Caxaro had denounced himself for eating eggs and cheese during Lenten abstinence . . .

The quill pen he was holding snapped in two.

❖

If the knights brought much with them to Malta—including more food and a measure of security, more work and a measure of culture—none of these changes brought more pleasure to the inhabitants of the islands than Carnival.

It was the highlight of the year, a splash of exuberance and color eagerly anticipated by all, whether peasant, noble, or knight. At Fort St. Angelo, a heavy stone was suspended from the beam where the harsh punishment of *strappado* was ordinarily administered, to show that even justice would take a three-day holiday. There were games of every sort, from draughts to cards, dice to cockfights. Boats raced in the Grand Harbor and horses along the heights of Santa Margherita. The knights held jousting contests. The sport had long since fallen into disuse in Europe, but the Maltese crowds loved it. Rations of wine and food were distributed to the poor. There were balls and receptions, illuminations and Masses, and every manner of debauchery.

La Valette tolerated it all, though only just. For all the grim authority he wielded, for all the discipline he sought to instill, he never forgot the difficult circumstances under which his hot-blooded and emotional knights served their Order. Consequently, during festivals he busied himself otherwise, hunting and inspecting coastal defense towers, so that he would not have to observe behavior that on another day would earn its perpetrator hard penance.

Just three days before the celebrations, Gabriel Çeralta, the *pilier* of the French *langue,* called Bertrand into his study. "You are to produce a brief performance," he told the surprised knight. "A skit. Nothing too political. Something lighthearted for the French *langues*. The Italian, German, and Spanish *langues* are doing the same, as usual. I expect you to outshine them, of course."

"Outshine them, sire?"

"But of course. For the Germans, that should require only a measure of sobriety on your part, Cuvier. For the Italians, the slimmest of wits. For the Spaniards, a heartbeat alone should suffice. On occasion you are thinly endowed with all three, although about sobriety I am not always so certain."

Bertrand suppressed a groan. "At your order, *molto illustrissimo*." He turned to leave, then hesitated. "Excuse me, sire, I had always thought to serve with a sword, with which I am blessed with some small skill, rather than a pen, with which I am not. There are others in the *langue* far better qualified. Why me?"

Çeralta barely glanced up from his papers. "Because a moment ago you passed by my door and I saw you. Bad luck."

"Indeed, sire. If you please, I shall need help."

The *pilier* waved dismissively, anxious to move on to other business. "Choose whomever you will and tell him I command it."

Christien complained that he had more entertaining work at hand, such as abscesses and amputations, but Bertrand would not let him shirk his duty. That night while Christien was at the Infirmary, Bertrand began the skit. There were no rules to guide him. The content of such skits was always unpredictable and often risqué.

Most of Christien's books were devoted to medicine and surgery, but Bertrand found a few more popular works, ranging from Sir Thomas More's *Utopia* to Dante's *Divine Comedy*. "Deadly and dull," he muttered, leafing through them. "We need something with more flair." Finally he found two volumes that suited him better—one by Rabelais, the French doctor turned satirist whom Christien's mother had known in Paris, and the other by Erasmus, the Dutch satirist trained as an Augustinian priest and schooled in Paris. Borrowing heavily from their pages, he worked through the night, reed pen scratching furiously on paper.

"I call it *In Light of Lunacy*," Bertrand said proudly when Christien returned from the infirmary.

"Well, you have the title right," Christien agreed after reading it, "but I think the rest may be a little extreme for our audience. This is not exactly the sort of fare one sets on the Grand Master's table."

"He won't be there. Nearly all the other high lords have agreed to attend the Germans' performance, in the name of unity and politics. It is their loss, of course—they shall suffer indigestion at the hand of the Bavarians, while our audience digests a fine Rabelais. Our play shall be savored only by the lesser gods of the *langues* of France and Provence, and by a few mere mortals of Malta, on whose empty heads such savage wit shall be lost entirely."

"I hope you're right," Christien said. He read through it again. "What the devil," he said. "If we're going to get in trouble, we might as well not do so over a line as pathetic as this." Boldly he scratched through a few words, replacing them with his own. Other words fell, and then whole paragraphs. When the sun came up they were still at it, amidst a pile of papers, laughter, and a half-demolished bottle of brandy.

They needed actors. They considered recruiting other knights but settled instead on eight hapless pages, who, despite having read the skit, lacked sufficient rank to refuse their invitation. The boys were set to manufacturing props and costumes and mastering their lines.

❖

The next morning there was a public reception at the bishop's palace. Domenico Cubelles and Giulio Salvago stood before a table of crimson damask, greeting an endless stream of visitors. The line stretched through the hall and down the stairs, winding through the beautiful cloistered garden, past dark doorways leading to subterranean cells that no one cared to imagine, and all the way to the outer gate. Suppliants and well-wishers of high and low birth alike awaited their turn to greet the Inquisitor's Vicar, many bearing small gifts of eggs, packets of grain, or loaves of bread.

There were coughs and prayers, gossip and nervous chuckles, as men wondered if other men—*that man,* more precisely—could see into their troubled souls and perhaps guess their secrets. Whatever the truth of it, the line gave proof to the notion that it was better to see and be seen by him than to hide and leave him to wonder.

When at last they stood before the vicar, some were unctuous, others sweaty with fear. From a few came vague whispers of scandal or murmured rumors about friends. Salvago listened carefully and forgot nothing, occasionally turning to say something to an aide, who disappeared to scribble a note in a book whose pages were devoted to tales of blasphemy and apostasy, sorcery and whoring and pandering. There was nothing formal, of course, for this was a festive occasion. Salvago would take up these matters in good time.

Jacobus shuffled forward with the rest of them, patiently awaiting his turn.

He felt the knife beneath his tunic, the cold steel of the long blade pressing against his upper thigh. He hadn't slept the previous night. Instead he had sat in pitch darkness, listening to the soft hiss of his blade against the whetstone. He'd worked the steel until its edge would separate a hare from its skin without alerting the hare.

What he longed to do was cut away the priest's robes, slice off his balls, and stuff them into his screaming mouth. Jacobus wondered what would kill him first, the choking or the loss of blood. But there were guards in the palace, leaving no time for such sweet study.

Instead he would kneel before the vicar and kiss his ring, and look him in the eye so that he would know his killer. He would rise, drawing his knife, so that for at least one instant Salvago would know the cold flush of fear.

Then he would simply gut the man, all the while keeping his lips to the priest's ear, whispering as he twisted the blade in his belly, so that Salvago might know the reason why his life blood was pouring onto the ground.

"*Maria,*" Jacobus would say to him. "*This is for Maria.*"

Jacobus would strike down anyone who tried to interfere, unless it was the bishop. Cubelles was a man of God, and Jacobus would not raise a hand against him. After it was done, he would run away and hide in the caves of Gozo, where no man could ever find him.

If only Maria were his wife, he could kill Salvago without fear of punishment. It was a man's sacred right to uphold the honor of his wife, mother, or sister. But she was not his wife. If they caught him, he was prepared to die in the dungeons beneath the palace. They would use their wheels and ropes, their curved tools and hot irons, and he would die secure in the knowledge that for Maria he had delivered Salvago to his Maker's gate for final judgment.

Now there were only five people in front of him. He could see the vicar's gaunt face, his slender features beneath his robes. He would be an easy kill.

He stepped forward. Now there were only four. The vicar's crucifix flashed on his chest. Jacobus rested his hand on the hilt of his knife.

A man moved on. Another step forward. Only moments now.

Jacobus found himself quite calm.

Suddenly a bell sounded from the tower. Cubelles said something to Salvago, who nodded. Cubelles smiled apologetically to the people in the line. "Dear brethren, duty summons us, I fear. May the Lord bless and keep you all." At that the two men departed through a door at the rear of the hall.

"Come again," a guard said, lifting his arms to turn the crowd away. "The reception is concluded."

"*Imma sinjur,*" Jacobus said, pleading. "I have waited hours for a blessing."

"*Jiddispjacini.* It is most unfortunate. Perhaps you can see them again tonight. There will be a procession from St. Agatha's to St. Lawrence for a midnight Mass."

❖

Christien spent the afternoon tending his patients and serving them veal, cheese, and wine. Along with Christmas, Easter, and Pentecost, Carnival was the only time a man might consider himself lucky to be an inmate at the Order's infirmary: his leg might be rotting or his brain burning with fever, but his stomach would spend the day in paradise, feasting on a meal served by the noble hand of a Hospitaller Knight of St. John.

As he was leaving he encountered Angela Buqa at the front gate. She was arguing with the guard. Behind her stood two footmen bearing heavy baskets of food. She saw Christien, and her expression made it clear it was he she had hoped to see. She called to him. "Fra de Vries! Kindly tell this man I am not a Saracen horde here to invade these serene quarters. I have a modest contribution of food, that's all, and he will not permit me to enter the courtyard."

"My apologies, *Barunessa*. He labors under orders." Christien snapped at the guard, who relieved her footmen of their burden.

"This is very kind of you," Christien said. "Our supplies are sorely lacking." He nodded good day and turned to leave, but she walked with him, leaving her footmen behind.

"You are on your way to the jousting?" she teased.

Christien smiled. "I'm afraid not. I think my great-grandfather was the last in our family to try. There is a portrait of him made some years later, with one eye missing. I think I would be lucky to fare even that well. I do better with smaller blades. For now I must help my friend Bertrand with his chores at the pen."

"I have heard of your skit. The *pilier* was good enough to grant me special admittance this evening."

"I fear the performance will leave you in need of my services as a surgeon."

"I shall be delighted to require your attentions, Fra de Vries."

Christien looked steadily at her. "Your husband, of course, is welcome as well."

Her face clouded. "He is otherwise occupied."

❖

At that moment Bertrand was receiving unsettling news from the *pilier*.

Each year one of the *langues* produced its skit for the public, in the square. This year it was to have been Italy's turn, but that morning word had come that one of their supply galleys had suffered damage when a powder packet exploded, and was in danger of foundering off the coast of Gozo. Two of the Italians dispatched to deal with the situation were the same knights producing the skit, so the Italian *pilier* had begged off.

"There must be a performance in the square, of course," Çeralta said to Bertrand. "The Maltese expect it. Therefore the duty falls to us."

"But sire, our skit was written to be performed in our auberge, for a French audience—of knights, at that. Others might not find it so . . . so . . ."

"Don't bother me with this, Cuvier. The Maltese won't understand anyway."

Chapter 30

Though he spent most of the day shadowing Salvago, Jacobus never got close to him. The vicar attended a service in the cathedral at Mdina, but rode in a carriage, accompanied by horsemen. There was an afternoon reception, but it was closed to the public. Jacobus watched a stream of tonsured Benedictines, barefooted Carmelites, friars of the Hermits of St. Augustine, and parish priests parading in and out of the bishop's gate. When he tried to join them, guards barred his way.

He wanted to kill Salvago at close range, eye to eye. But there was no telling how long it might be before the vicar again appeared in a place where Jacobus might get near him. It might be weeks or even months. Waiting was out of the question. His insides were twisted with rage. Her honor could not go unavenged another day. He would have to do it another way.

He went to the town plaza, through which the midnight procession would pass. The large cobblestone square was the center of village life, where heretics were burned, stories told, and announcements made by criers. On one side was St. Agatha's, where the midnight procession would begin. The opposite side was dominated by the old Norman-style clock tower. On another side, near a row of shops, a low stage was being erected for a performance.

The clock tower was five stories tall, with windows at each story. At the top was a balcony, enclosed by a wooden rail supported on large corbels. He saw a watchman but knew the man would stay at his post only during daylight hours, when he could see shipping and approaching squalls. From dusk till dawn the tower would be empty. Jacobus could hide there unseen, with a commanding view of the square. It was perfect: at the stroke of midnight, he would give the crowds another entertainment.

The hour was growing late, and he raced back to M'kor

Hakhayyim, where he took a crossbow and a handful of bolts from the cache of weapons. As he emerged he encountered Maria. She was bringing food, and he thought she would likely spend the evening there. She was certainly not of a mood to go to Carnival. Though she smiled, the strain on her face was obvious, and only hardened his resolve. She glanced at the crossbow. "You are going hunting?"

"Yes," he replied.

He caught a ride to Birgu in a peasant's cart. He realized he had brought nothing to hide the weapon, and stole a sackcloth from the cart to cover it. It was well past dark when he arrived in the crowded square. Throngs of people milled about. He could just make out the form of the guard in the tower. The man was leaning on the balcony rail, watching the square. Jacobus wandered through the crowd. He wasn't hungry but forced himself to eat a piece of bread, knowing he would need his strength. He washed it down with weak wine.

He moved toward the stage, where the play was about to begin. An audience of several hundred people ranged around the platform, which was brightly lit by torches. At the rear of the stage a curtain was stretched over a frame, to hide the actors.

The night was oppressively hot. People cooled themselves with paper fans and chattered gaily, waiting for the performance to begin, and for the grand party that would follow. At ten o'clock the bell sounded in the tower. The crowd parted to make way for several high officials of the Order, who took their places on armchairs of blue velvet. A page appeared on the stage and blew a trumpet.

Jacobus glanced up again. The guard was still there. *Be patient. Still plenty of time.*

❖

"I thought you said no one of rank would be here," Christien hissed. He peered past the makeshift stage curtain into the crowded square. As he expected, Christien saw French and Spanish knights in the audience, along with a great many Maltese. But there were also several high lords of the Order. Besides Çeralta, who was *pilier* of the French *langue* and Grand Hospitaller of the Order, there was the Grand Chancellor and a general of the galleys. Of more concern to Christien was Oliver Starkey, the secretary to the Grand Master. "*Merde,*" Christien said. "Even Sir Oliver is here."

Bertrand was struggling into his costume. "Look at the bright side," he said. "We should be honored that an Englishman prefers our drivel to that of the Germans."

As the page blew his trumpet, Bertrand took a deep breath. Dressed as the Queen of Lunacy, he stepped through the curtain, curtsying to the laughter that greeted his broad skirts and frilly blouse. With a flourish he produced a scroll. "Illustrious Fools and Distinguished Drunkards," he read, "take heed, for herein lies my tale, the tale of Lunacy, and how I covered a whole country with my mouth, and what treasures I swallowed."

To loud hisses, the Sultan Suleiman burst onto the stage, attired in dirty robes and turban, atop which stood a crown fashioned from a bird's nest, from which sprouted a lone weed. He spied a peasant, sitting next to an island-table covered with a glittering pile of jewels. The Sultan threw his cloak over the island, muttered a few hasty incantations, and then withdrew it. Bertrand's finest stage magic, accomplished by a page hiding beneath the draped table, had transformed the jewels into a pile of rusting iron pots. The peasant approached humbly. "O Benevolent Majesty, a bauble from thy box?" The Sultan knocked him to the floor.

Standing at the fringe of the crowd, Jacobus watched absently, his mind elsewhere. This time when he looked up, he saw the guard was no longer in the tower. He decided to wait a few more moments and then take his position.

Wearing the ears of a jackass, Christien de Vries stepped onto the stage. A crude sign on his chest identified him as AVLA, a thinly disguise reference to the Duke of Alva, a Spaniard in the court of Philip. Some of the French knights jeered at the sight of the man they detested. The bumbling Avla crossed swords with the Sultan, who escaped easily with the jewels. The duke's eyes grew wide with avarice as he spotted the pots. He spread his own cloak, crossed himself, and pulled away the cloak. The collection of rusty pots had now become a pile of dung. The crowd loved it. The peasant rose to greet his new master, palms upraised. "O Beneficent Lord, a crumb from thy granary?" Avla knocked the wretched man to the ground.

Jacobus walked down a narrow lane to the iron gate that gave way to a tiny courtyard behind the tower, that faced away from the square. Glancing up repeatedly, he saw no sign of the watchman. The platform was empty. The gate was kept closed by a loose loop of chain. There was no lock. Sweat beginning to pour from his brow, he unwound the chain as quietly as he could. The street was dark, nearly everyone in the square. He raced across the courtyard, opened the heavy wood door to the tower, and closed it behind him. He climbed the stairs, pausing at each landing to listen. He heard laughter from the crowd. On the top floor he cautiously stepped into the tower room.

❖

Changing backstage, Christien could hear Maltese chatter, which he could not understand, and laughter and hoots and howls, which he could. The Maltese didn't understand the French or the politics or anything but the silliness and the visual effects, and for them that was enough. He had no idea how the play was going over among the Order's officials, whose expressions betrayed nothing. It was far too late to worry.

He returned to the stage wearing a soldier's uniform, an oversized codpiece, and golden spurs. A few years earlier the late Pope, the unpopular Paul IV, had created an army called the Golden Spurs. The Spanish knights hated Paul because he'd used that army to attack Spain. The French knights hated him because his ill-fated effort had reignited a long war between France and Spain.

The soldier strutted grandly, set fire to a village, and blessed it with the sign of the cross. He took a drink from a flask and stopped at a brothel to fondle a wench. He spotted the pile of dung and the peasant nearby, who was just rising from the floor. "O mighty lord, a morsel of thy favor?" The soldier drew a short sword from his belt, slew the peasant, and turned his attention to the pile, which he set on fire. The crowd gasped in delight as the dung—having been sprinkled with a dash of saltpeter—flared with a roar.

Jacobus took a few steps into the tower room without venturing onto the outer platform. He could see it was as he anticipated: a perfect perch, with an unobstructed view of St. Agatha's. He drew the crossbow from its sack, and reached for the bolts.

"What—what are you—?"

Jacobus whirled. The watchman was sitting in the shadows on the floor, a bottle in his hands. He slurred the words as he struggled to his feet. "No one comes in here without—"

Jacobus swung at him. The guard fended off the blow and grabbed Jacobus by the arm. Even drunk, the man was hellishly strong. Jacobus swung the crossbow with his free arm and struck the guard a glancing blow to his temple. The guard staggered. He caught hold of Jacobus's shirt and pulled him along. They crashed into a wall and then to the floor.

In the square below, no one heard their struggles. "Fear not Lunacy's drought," Bertrand cried, "for there is piss enough left in her cup to offend all and spare none."

As Jacobus pummeled the guard with his fists, a wild free-for-all erupted on the stage, which besides Avla now included a queen dressed as a harpy, a king clad as a clown, and warriors in ancient armor and helmets, all of whom danced at the end of Lunacy's strings. Swords waving, they circled around the table under which lay the dead peasant, and fought madly over the smoking pile of dung.

Five stories above them, the watchman sagged under repeated blows and ceased struggling. Chest heaving, Jacobus dragged him by the ankles to one corner of the room. He heard the sound of wood clashing on metal, helmets tumbling to the stage, and raucous laughter. He tore strips from the sackcloth and tightly bound the guard's hands and feet. He gagged him, and as a precaution added a blindfold as well. He didn't think the guard could have seen his face clearly—he himself had fought little more than a shadow in the blackness—but if the man awakened he didn't want to take any chances.

Jacobus felt terrible for having injured an innocent man. There was only one person he meant to harm. He knelt over his victim, leaning close to make certain he was breathing. The guard's breath stank of alcohol. He was alive but out cold.

Onstage only the Duke of Avla remained standing. The victorious Spaniard poured water over the smoking dung, then covered the table one last time with his cloak. When it was lifted, even the dung had been stolen.

Jacobus sank from his knees to a sitting position, catching his breath as Lunacy's lament rose from the stage. "And thus were all offended and none saved, as light gave way to darkness. With Reason perished and Faith fallen, only I remain untouched, devoted mistress of all mankind."

Jacobus turned and slid on his belly out onto the platform. Lunacy bowed deeply, to cheers and huge applause. As the cast appeared to take a bow, Jacobus examined his crossbow, fearing it had been damaged in the struggle. He lifted the weapon and sighted down the shaft. It seemed all right. It was heavy steel, a windlass-drawn crossbow. Like most of the small arsenal at M'kor Hakhayyim, it was both old and outdated, and at distance inaccurate. Yet at close range it was quite as murderous as any weapon on earth. He was less than fifty yards from where his target would appear. His first shot would have to be perfect, for there would be no time to reload.

He sighted on a woman in the audience, and then on a street vendor selling brochettes near the door to St. Agatha's, and finally on the forehead of the duke of Avla.

Jacobus smiled.

One shot would be enough for the priest. He would put it through his eye.

❖

Sweating profusely in their costumes, Christien and Bertrand watched uneasily as the dignitaries of the Order approached. The opinion that concerned them most was that of Sir Oliver Starkey, who, because of his closeness to the Grand Master, was the most powerful man there. He was the last of the English *langue* in Malta, most of his brethren having been beheaded by King Henry VIII. It was common knowledge that Sir Oliver was a friend of Cardinal Pole, the archbishop of Canterbury who had been persecuted by the very Pope the play had just finished roasting. On that basis they hoped he would like it, but his first words did not put them at ease.

"If the Grand Master had seen that display of sacrilege," Sir Oliver said sternly, "he would order you both defrocked and bastinadoed. Pray he never hears of it, though I don't know a man foolhardy enough to tell him." His face crinkled with a smile. "Certainly I shall not, for he'd put the wood to my soles as well for my pleasure in it. Well done, lads, well done."

He turned to Çeralta and shook his hand vigorously. "In all the Order I suspect only the French *langue* could have produced such a dazzling display of wit supported solely on a foundation of excrement, *Pilier*. The Italians would have just mucked it up with taste and refinement, and would have shirked from the task of offending the Inquisitor's Vicar as well. How very original of you, Fra Çeralta. Vastly entertaining. Vastly." Chuckling heartily, he wandered off.

As Çeralta turned to his two knights, his smile turned to icy fury. The Hospitaller was a pious man. He excoriated their judgment, their taste, and their timing, given the vicar's recent arrival. "To swallow that much waste I thought one needed to suck dry the entire hold of an Arab galley. The only thing keeping you from the whip is the fact that I myself asked you to do this. I assumed you would display a modicum of dignity and taste. Get out of my sight before I find a weapon."

The two playwrights needed no further prompting, especially since Christien had glimpsed Angela Buqa standing nearby. He led Bertrand the other way, and the two melted quickly into the crowds. It was quite easy. There were parties in the taverns and dancing in the streets. Acrobats turned somersaults over pigs, while drunken men threw knives at targets mounted on doors. Courtesans lured knights and bakers sang with sailors.

There were costumes and masks of every conceivable description, made from fish netting or straw, from sackcloth or silk. There were dragons and dimwits, pirates and crowned royalty, grim Spaniards and gay Venetians, elegant Florentines and foppish French, wily corsairs and wicked Saracens, pompous captains of the sea and long-toothed fish that ate them. Some masks were simple, held over the eyes with a stick, while others were more elaborate, festooned with feathers and lace.

Christien and Bertrand joined a rowdy and drunken band of Rhodiots. They tossed darts and sang off-key to a fiddle. They raced two mules down an alleyway big enough for only one, and both men ended on their backsides. Bertrand seemed to have an endless supply of excellent brandy, which he produced at regular intervals.

At eleven-forty, seeing activity near the door of St. Agatha's, Jacobus attached the crossbow's tackle to the cord and stepped into the foot stirrup. He turned the crank a dozen times, the tackle drawing the cord tightly up the shaft. He locked the cord into place. He looked behind him, into the tower room. The guard had not stirred.

Bertrand encountered a courtesan he knew. Waving a happy farewell to Christien, he disappeared with her down a darkened street. Christien allowed himself to be carried along in a crowd of revelers. Some held candles, others danced and sang as they poured into the square, where a dozen different celebrations were underway. Near St. Agatha's a reasonably orderly crowd was growing, waiting to join the midnight procession to St. Lawrence.

At eleven-forty-five the bells of St. Agatha's rang, announcing the end of the first service. Jacobus set the bolt in the trough, the notch in its haft fitting into the cord, and again sighted down the shaft. This time his aim took in the breast of a courtesan, the ear of a mule. It seemed to be growing even more hot and humid, despite the lateness of the hour. He wiped a trickle of salty sweat from his eyes.

A woman in flowing skirts caught Christien by the elbow and pulled him into the shadows near the clock tower. She was masked with the face of a cat. Christien assumed it was another prostitute. She threw her arms around him and laid her head on his chest. He smiled, closed his eyes, and began to sway with her to the music. It was not a dance but a sexual movement, her body pressing against his. Christien felt himself stirring and decided Bertrand had the right idea after all. He opened his eyes and pushed back her mask.

He stopped cold. It was Angela Buqa.

Christien blinked through his brandied haze. "*You*—"

"*Me*," she whispered, and her mouth hungrily sought his. She put her hands on his chest, and then around his back.

"*Barunessa*, please." He began to push her away, but she clung to him. His resolve softened. They were simply two revelers among hundreds, lost in the noise and the color, the music and the darkness. She was beautiful and it was late. She stretched up on her toes, and now her hands slipped inside his tunic. She ran her fingers over his chest and lightly caressed his nipples. Her hand slipped down, to his groin. He gasped and pressed against her.

Jacobus tensed as the doors of St. Agatha's opened. A stream of acolytes emerged from within. An altar boy followed, holding a brass cross on a tall wooden pole. Behind him came a line of chanting, ghostly figures, their faces illuminated by their candles and by torchlight from the square. They would pass along one side of the square and down the hill toward the church of St. Lawrence. The holy procession moved in solemn contrast to the revelers nearest the tower, where the festivities continued without interruption. The square was an eerie blend of hymns and prayers mixed with laughter and drink and forbidden delights. *God at one end of the square, the devil at the other,* Jacobus thought. *Which end am I?* He licked dry lips and waited for his shot, every muscle taut.

Standing in one of the shadows near the tower, his face obscured behind the mask of a dragon, another man was watching a different scene. Baron Antonio Buqa thought his heart was failing. It was difficult to breathe. He fought tears of rage and pain. He had been following his wife all evening, as he had been following her for days. Only now, having finally seen what he dreaded he would see, did he regret his suspicions. He desperately wished he could turn back and unlearn the awful thing.

At first when Angela swept the man into the shadows, Buqa hadn't seen his face. But then he saw it was the Order's surgeon, de Vries. *He has been to my house.*

Blind with agony, the baron tore at his collar and threw down his mask. He staggered away, down a street that led from the square.

Jacobus sighted on the brass cross, borne by the young altar boy. The crimson-robed Cubelles walked behind him, his hands clasped in prayer.

And there, just behind the bishop, came the gaunt, black-robed figure of the vicar, walking next to the Captain of the Holy Office, the official responsible for the administration of corporal punishments ordered by the Inquisition.

Jacobus cocked the trigger and sighted on Salvago's head, just beneath the line of his cap.

The tower clock tolled midnight. Jacobus fired. As the bolt flew, the crossbow's old cord snapped under the immense pressure. He yelped in pain as the broken end of the cord whipped around the front of the crossbow and lashed him on the arm. The *thwang* reverberated through the square, the noise all but lost amid the commotion. Bishop Cubelles heard the noise and looked up at the tower.

The broken cord minutely altered the flight of the bolt. It missed Salvago's eye and passed through his shoulder, breaking the right collarbone and exiting just below his shoulder blade. The bolt buried itself in the hard earth between cobblestones.

The procession behind the vicar stopped in confusion around the fallen man. At first people thought he'd only tripped, but cries of horror arose at the sight of his face and the pool of blood growing beneath him. Shock telegraphed itself through the crowd. Cubelles turned, took in the scene, and knelt beside Salvago, cradling his head. Salvago's eyes were open, but his face was white with shock. Blood trickled from the corner of his mouth. The bishop motioned to the Captain of the Rod and pointed at the tower. "*Hemm fuq,*" he said. "I heard something. Look there, quickly." The captain barked an order. Two guards began pushing swiftly through the crowd.

Jacobus staggered to his feet in shock and pain. He heard screams, and his heart surged when he saw that his target was down—and then he saw the guards coming. He snatched up the weapon, jumped over the inert form of the guard, ripped open the inner door, and flew down the steps, taking them two and three at a time. Over the noise of his flight he heard more screams. Surely the devil was dead.

At the third-floor landing he glanced out the window. The guards were already at the fence. They tore off the chain, wrenched open the gate, and raced into the courtyard. As he reached the next landing he heard the tower door bang open.

The only exit was blocked.

He crawled through a window overlooking the courtyard and knelt on the narrow ledge. He was still two stories above the ground. Stone pillars supported the iron fence that surrounded the courtyard. He heard heavy steps behind him. There was no time to think, and only one thing to do. Crossbow in hand, the birdman leaped from the window, intending to land atop one of the pillars, and from that continue his fall the rest of the way to the ground. He landed awkwardly, unable to catch and steady himself. His momentum propelled him onward, toward the wicked iron spikes rushing up like spears to impale him. He twisted, trying to avoid them. He almost succeeded, but one caught him at the breast, breaking his ribs and tearing into his chest. His agility saved him from death. Rotating as he hit, he rolled off the spike and fell the rest of the way to the ground. The crossbow clattered away.

Gaping at the apparition that had tumbled from the sky into their midst, several drunken onlookers stepped back.

Jacobus struggled to his feet. Gasping, trying to hold closed a great flap of torn skin on his chest, he pushed past them and staggered into the night, leaving a trail of blood behind.

❖

Christien had just touched Angela's lips with his own when he heard the resounding twang of the broken cord. The screams that followed shocked him to his senses. He broke away from her and ran toward the noise.

One of the parish priests saw him. "Fra de Vries! Thank heaven you are here! Quickly, this way!"

The victim was conscious, his eyes dark but alert. Bishop Cubelles had removed the white silk stole from around his neck and pressed it against the exit wound, which was bleeding heavily.

"Your Grace," Christien said, acknowledging the bishop. He knelt beside the wounded man. "Let me have a look." He pulled away the cloth, its stain of dark crimson growing. He probed with his fingers, gauging the wound. He glanced at the captain, who was scraping between cobblestones with his knife. "What was it?" he asked.

The captain had exposed the notched end of the missile. The rest of the shaft remained buried between stones, but it was enough. "A bolt, from a crossbow."

The priest groaned. Christien packed a corner of the stole into the wound to stanch the bleeding, then turned his attention to the entry wound. As he probed near the shattered collarbone, Salvago stiffened and cried out.

"I'm sorry, Father. I'll need to get the bits of bone out, but it's a good clean wound. It should heal well."

"God willing," Salvago gasped, grimacing as Christien covered the wound. "A Knight of the Order, tending the vicar," he said weakly. "Surely the Grand Master will have your head."

The light of recognition dawned on Christien's face. Every knight had this man's name on his tongue. "You are Father Salvago, then."

"*Sì.*"

"I cannot presume to speak for the Grand Master, Father, but I think it safe to say he would order you treated." *And declare the bolt was from heaven,* he did not add.

At Christien's direction, six men, three on each side, gently lifted the vicar and carried him the short distance to the Infirmary.

Chapter 31

Fençu arrived back at the cave quite late, having spent the evening hours selecting silver from the mansions of Mdina while the owners were out enjoying the festival. He had made his best haul in years.

He slipped in quietly, trying not to awaken anyone, and set down his heavy bag near the fireplace. He cocked his head. The sound was barely audible, almost a lowing sound, coming from the rear of the cave. He took up a candle in one hand and a sword in the other, and crept carefully forward, thinking a wounded animal had somehow gotten inside. He saw the sleeping form of Elli, and, in their niches, some of the other inhabitants of the cave. The lowing grew louder, coming from a mound of straw in the dark recesses at the back of the cave. He stepped closer, holding the candle before him.

"*Jacobus!* What in—" Fençu knelt. Writhing in pain, Jacobus was deathly pale, his shirt soaked in blood. "Elli!" he yelled. "Come quickly!"

Blinking away sleep, Elli appeared a moment later. At the sight of Jacobus her hand flew to her mouth. "I'll get bandages," she said, racing off.

Fençu bent over the birdman and gently lifted away the cloth. "What happened?" he asked. "Did someone shoot you?"

"Yes . . . no. Dun Salvago . . . killed him. Shot . . . dead. I . . ."

"Jacobus! Wake up! Did they see you? Do they know who you are?" Jacobus muttered something and shook his head. He drifted.

Fençu cursed. "Elli, quickly! He's bleeding to death!" He looked over his shoulder and saw Maria standing there, her eyes wide with the shock of what she'd heard. She rushed to his side and took Jacobus's head in her lap. "Jacobus, Jacobus, no, no . . ."

Fençu exposed the wound and grimaced at the bloody field of yawning flesh. Jacobus was breathing with difficulty, the sound of air coming from his chest. "May Elohim help him," Fençu said quietly. "I cannot tend this."

"Dr. Callus," Maria said.

"If we take him to Mdina, they'll arrest him." *And all the rest of us,* Fençu thought. "We must ask the doctor to come here."

"There's no time. I won't let him die. And they didn't see him. Didn't you hear? We'll make a story."

"We don't know that."

"If you won't come along, just help me get him into the cart."

Fençu sighed. Maria was like Elli that way. When her mind was made up he might as well argue with a rock. Elli arrived with bandages, and Fençu bound the wound as best he could.

The trip to Mdina was excruciatingly slow, every jolt and bounce telegraphed through the wooden wheels of the cart. Maria rode in back with Jacobus while Fençu drove. "You're going to kill him if you aren't careful," she said as they jolted and bounced, but there was nothing Fençu could do.

In Mdina she pounded on Callus's door. To her surprise he was not sleeping. She thought she heard other voices inside. He appeared to be having a meeting of some sort. He greeted her warily, closing the door behind him. "Maria! What in heaven's name?"

"Please, Doctor, it is Jacobus. He needs your help."

Callus disappeared inside and returned with a lamp. Jacobus was unconscious. Callus examined his chest and shoulder. "What happened?"

Fençu glanced at Maria. "He is a birdman. He was hunting on the cliffs. He fell onto the rocks," he said.

"In the middle of the night?"

"We only just found him."

"This is not something I can treat properly here."

"Please," Maria said. "You must help him."

"Of course, but it is a serious chest wound. He needs more than I can give him at Santu Spiritu. There is a man at the Hospitallers' clinic. A surgeon, a Frenchman of the Order."

"A *knight?*" In a panic, Maria shook her head. She wanted nothing to do with them. Surely a knight would betray Jacobus. "Please, Dr. Callus. You do it. No doctor is better than you."

"Maria, don't be foolish. He is a close friend. I would trust my own life to him. He is this man's best chance for living. His only chance."

❖

Christien had just finished treating Salvago, who was now asleep in one of the wards, when Joseph Callus hurried into the infirmary. Christien followed him outside. With barely a glance at the kneeling woman, he examined the injured man, whose breathing was labored and shallow. He pulled back the bandage to see a light red froth bubbling from the wound. He probed a bit and then felt the man's pulse. "He's all but gone, Joseph," he said in a low voice. "An injury like this almost always goes bad. He'll be dead before the day is out."

"I thought you said he was good," said the woman to Callus, speaking Italian. "The arrogant lord of the Order gives up as easily as a child. No—not even a child would quit before he'd begun."

"Maria!" Callus snapped. "Hold your tongue!"

"I will not! I will not let Jacobus die! The Italian *langue* has a clinic. Let us carry him there and see whether we can find a *surgeon*."

"I have hardly given up, madam," Christien said testily. He did not wish to engage in debate with a woman, but something in her voice made him lift the lamp.

By the warm yellow light of the lantern, softened by the rose-colored light of dawn just beginning to streak through high clouds, he saw her face. He thought perhaps his reaction was due to the brandy, of which he'd had far too much in recent days, or to sleep, of which he'd had far too little. Or perhaps it was the hour, or simply the purity of the morning light. Whatever the cause, looking at her was like looking into the folds of heaven itself. A flood of warmth and confusion washed over him. She wore the dress of a commoner but had the bearing of an aristocrat. Her eyes were vital and expressive and alive, her face as rich in character as it was soft and lovely. She was quite the most wonderful and astonishing woman he'd ever seen. Despite the unmistakable hostility he saw in her eyes, he felt himself go weak inside, as if from hunger. He froze in a moment of wondrous shock.

He felt as if he'd known her forever, as if every nuance of her expression was as familiar to him as his own. Her eyes told him he was not alone in his instant of awe. She was as motionless as he. Her initial look of antagonism melted into wary mystification. She'd been ready to blister him with shame, but the words died in her throat.

Callus cleared his voice. "Christien! We'd better get him inside, don't you think?"

Christien realized he was crouching there stupidly, just staring at her. For reasons he did not fully understand, saving this man suddenly became terribly important.

"*Certo,*" he said, his voice thick.

❖

With Callus at his side, Christien worked feverishly on Jacobus. The patient's heartbeat was fluttery and weak. He remained unconscious, allowing Christien to probe delicately and almost at leisure for the bits of rib nearest the lung.

He packed the innermost wound with a length of linen he soaked in a mixture of egg yolk, turpentine, and oil of roses. He attached a string to the linen so that it could be pulled back if the movement of Jacobus's lungs should draw it into his chest cavity. While Callus held the string out of the way he packed it as best he could, trying to create a protective barrier above the lung. He clipped away dead skin and shredded muscle of the birdman's chest and shoulder, washing everything with wine.

He went through six lengths of catgut for all the stitches, stopping twice to ease his cramping fingers. Finally he covered the wound with a large bandage plastered with gypsum, which he wound round the chest and back to prevent excessive movement, leaving only the strings to the linens accessible in case he needed to pull them.

When Christien finished he was quite pleased with the result. He'd spent a great deal of time tending the patient—more than he would have ordinarily, he admitted to himself, given the likely mortality of such a wound.

"Nothing to do now but wait," he said. He rinsed his hands and face in a washbasin on a wall stand. Despite the early hour it was already scorching outside, and the water felt blessedly cool. He knew he needed sleep. As he was drying himself he glanced out the window. The woman—Joseph had called her Maria—was sitting on the step of the building opposite, reading from a slim leather volume. She glanced up every so often to look at the gate. He felt the same surge of wonder, as taken with her from a distance as he had been up close.

Callus stood next to him, drying his own face. "I see Maria is still here," he said absently. "I'll talk to her on my way out."

"No," Christien said, too quickly. He felt himself reddening at Callus's knowing smile. "I . . . was going out anyway. I'll do it." Christien hurried down the stairs, through the courtyard, and into the street. She stood to meet him.

"I didn't realize you were waiting, *signorina,*" Christien lied.

"I asked for you at the gate a while ago, but they sent me away. They said I might see you when you left."

"I regret that you cannot come in. The rules are quite inflexible."

"I don't mind," she said. "How is he?"

"Alive, if only just. A rib punctured his lung. Joseph and I put him back together as best we could."

"Will he die?"

"I don't know. Sometimes such injuries heal by themselves, sometimes not. It is a good sign that he is not coughing up blood. And he is merely warm with fever, not hot. If that changes for the worse, he will surely die, as he will if . . ." He stopped. He was telling her more than necessary. He saw there was great strength in her, but he saw, too, the tears welling in the corner of her eyes, and her struggle to control them. He wished desperately to wipe them away. "I'm sorry, *signorina*. There is never a time I feel more helpless than when I have done all I know to do, and have given such an injury to God. I wish I could do more. But he is strong."

She nodded. "Thank you for what you are doing." Maria was usually certain of herself and confident in what she said, but now she struggled awkwardly for words.

"*Per favore*, Fra de Vries," she said. "If anyone asks . . . well, Jacobus hunts birds in the cliffs. He fell on some rocks. I didn't know if Dr. Callus had told you that."

"Really." He studied her face, his heart beating quickly. "I wouldn't have guessed that from the wound."

"I cannot explain just now. I beg you. Please," she said. "He fell on some rocks."

He knew she was lying. He thought he knew why. He cared nothing about a dispute between a birdman and a priest. He cleaned up after such things all the time. Unless it involved the Order, it simply didn't matter. Now her eyes held his, and he was swept before her gaze, as powerless as a leaf before a gale. "*Signorina*, it will be some days before we know whether he will recover. I wish I could invite you to wait in the courtyard, out of the heat."

"It's all right. If I may, I'll come back tonight."

He felt a flush of pleasure at the thought. "Certainly." His eyes did not leave her until she had disappeared into the square.

❖

The *gendarm* of Birgu mounted an intensive search for the would-be assassin. His men followed the trail of blood from the tower to where it disappeared near the throat of the harbor. From the blood and bits of flesh on the tops of the iron spikes, it was clear the man was badly wounded. The tower watchman had still been drunk when they'd untied him, and couldn't remember anything of use. If anyone else had seen something, they were either still too hung over to talk or too fearful of becoming involved. Even the fool guards at the city gate had seen nothing. The crossbow was discovered in some bushes at the base of the clock tower, but it might have belonged to anyone.

The broken drawstring explained why the shot had missed. In fact, both the *gendarm* and the bishop believed the real target had been the bishop and not his vicar, Salvago, who after all had only recently arrived in Malta—hardly long enough to have made such a determined enemy.

In the search for the wounded man, the *gendarm* visited the Santu Spiritu hospital in Mdina and the clinic of the Italian *langue* near the slave prison, without success. Finally he visited the Order's Infirmary. Despite the *gendarm*'s complete lack of jurisdiction and authority within the Order's walls, the infirmarian cooperated fully with his inquiry.

After exchanging pleasantries with the *gendarm*, the infirmarian summoned Christien de Vries, who had treated Salvago. "I just left the vicar," Christien said. "His wound is painful but not life-threatening unless infection sets in. He is sleeping a great deal. If all goes well, he will be here only another day or two, after which he can safely be moved to the bishop's palace."

"Thank God," the *gendarm* said, crossing himself. "And now I must ask if you have treated anyone here with severe wounds of the flesh."

Christien looked to the infirmarian, who nodded his approval. There were five, Christien said. Two knights, one German, the other Italian, both suffering deep knife wounds administered to one another in a brawl. A dockhand with a compound fracture of the leg, suffered when a knot failed and the corner of a crate struck him. A farrier, all but gutted when a horse he was shoeing went wild. Lastly there was a birdman of the parish of Zurrieq. Christien looked directly at the *gendarm*. "He fell from his ropes while hunting and landed on the rocks."

"I wish to see the farrier and the birdman, *honorabile*," the *gendarm* said.

Christien smiled, more politely than he needed to, for the *gendarm* had no right to see anything. "It would be without purpose, sir. The farrier is dead. The birdman is unconscious, but he cannot be the one you seek." Christien felt it odd that the lie came so easily to his lips. "I removed bits of rock when I patched him up, along with half a *rotolo* of seaweed. He would make better mule fodder than a murderer."

The *gendarm* laughed. "Very well, sire," he said. "As there was no seaweed on our fence, I suppose you're right. No doubt our man is lying dead in some field, anyway. We'll find his bones soon enough."

"God willing," Christien said.

"God willing," replied the *gendarm*.

❖

It was midafternoon before he could slip briefly away. He desperately needed more sleep, but there had been no time for even a nap. Instead, he went outdoors, as he often did to refresh himself. He entered the street behind the Infirmary and went to the wall overlooking Kalkara Creek. A fresh northerly breeze ruffled his hair, and he breathed deeply of the salt air. He could see Fort St. Elmo at the tip of Sciberras. He leaned on the wall, his mind racing.

He didn't hear the approach of the woman who slipped out of the shadows and stood beside him, her face all but covered by a veil. "I waited by the gate and still almost didn't see you leaving," she said. "I'm glad you came this way."

Startled, Christien emerged from his reverie. He'd known he would see her again, but had not thought it would be so soon. He looked up and down the street. There was little foot traffic along this side of the Infirmary, and certainly no one near enough to hear their conversation. "I regret what happened last night, *Barunessa*," he said. "It was wrong of me."

"There is nothing to regret. As I recall, precious little happened before you rudely ran away." Her voice was teasing.

"I intended no rudeness. Surely you know what happened."

"Of course, and you have my gratitude for treating my brother." Christien raised his eyebrows. "The vicar is your brother?"

"*Sì*, and in his hour of need I could not have wished him to be in better hands." She smiled coyly. "But now I myself need your attentions. I thought perhaps you might join me where we met the other day, near the coast. Tomorrow morning."

"I cannot."

"Of course, I understand. Your hours of duty must already be set. The afternoon, then, or the next morning, when you have your leisure."

"No."

"Surely you can find a moment—"

"*Barunessa*. Forgive me, but even if I could, I would not. I cannot see you again under any circumstances."

"A matter of your vows?"

He grew impatient. "Perhaps you should concern yourself with your own vows, *Barunessa,* and leave me to mine."

She did not get angry, as he expected. Instead she smiled. "I find your rudeness attractive, Fra de Vries. I felt the resolve of your vows last night when we kissed. I shall not give up so easily as that."

"Then you will waste your time. *Addio*."

He strode back to the Infirmary, knowing her eyes were still upon him. He realized that she hadn't even inquired about her brother's condition.

Pushing aside his fatigue, he went back to work. As evening approached he found himself passing frequently by the window near the basin, glancing outside each time. Before long he was looking almost constantly.

The woman he'd hoped to see was there at dusk, and again at dawn the next morning. Each time he hurried out to meet her. Each time he felt a little foolish, but a moment with her erased it. Each time, no sooner had she gone, than he found himself impatiently looking out the window once again.

❖

Baron Antonio Buqa received a report from the houseman he sent to follow her that his wife had seen the knight once again, outside the auberge. He had hoped somehow it was all a hallucination, a terrible dream, but now the truth of it could not be denied. He paced, his fury growing with each step. He shattered a mirror and pulled down a heavy cupboard of dishes, smashing them all. He would kill her. No, he would never do that. He loved her. He thought of her in that man's embrace and he felt his chest constrict and his vision begin to blur. He would lock her up. She would never again leave the mansion. That, too, was foolish. She was too strong-willed for that. She would never stand for it. He didn't know what to do about her.

What of the knight? He could inform the Grand Master, pitiless and hard when it came to breaches of discipline and vows. Yes, that was it. De Vries would be drummed from the Order altogether, or imprisoned. But there would be no satisfaction in letting another man handle it. Worse, all the world would know the cuckold. No. He could not let the Grand Master tend to his business.

Antonio Buqa had not fought anyone in years, and then only in a brawl with knives, when highwaymen in Sicily had overtaken his carriage. He and his coachman had bested them in a bloody fight, leaving two of the blackguards dead and two others running for their lives. If the years had softened him since then, he was still a big man, strong and capable. He knew just the man to help him tilt the balance, a savage Greek who'd served as a mercenary aboard a Venetian war galley. He worked in Mdina now, in the stables of the Baron La Recona.

He sent the houseman to fetch him.

❖

Maria felt a fever of confusion. She was mortified Jacobus knew about Salvago, but his reaction was completely logical. He'd only done what she thought her father should have done years before. She wished the attempt had been successful. Now, apart from her worry, she was furious with him for failing, for opening the old wounds again, in a manner over which she had no control.

Before he acted she hadn't decided what to do about Salvago. She didn't want him to feel safe, or to feel that she had forgotten or forgiven. She would never run from him, but she didn't know if she would confront him, either. It was a decision that did not need to be made quickly. Now Jacobus had taken everything out of her hands. No, that was nonsense, of course, to think that such things were ever in her hands in the first place.

She talked with Elena, Fençu, and Elli, trying to decide what to do. If Salvago discovered what had happened—and how could he not?—then everyone living in the cave could easily guess the terror that awaited them. The hot wind of his wrath years earlier as *kappillan* would be nothing against the fiery typhoon of the vicar. He held powers now that none of them even understood.

They could not agree on what to do. Elena, fearful for Moses, wanted to run. Fençu was adamantly opposed, arguing that the only refuge from Salvago would be found in Sicily or beyond, where they could not hope to travel. Maria didn't express an opinion, fearing that whatever she said might be wrong and that they would suffer for it.

In the end they agreed to remain in M'kor Hakhayyim. Their continued safety would depend largely on the Knight de Vries—whether he would realize the truth, and what he would do with it.

De Vries.

Maria neither understood nor trusted the feeling she had when she was near him. He was a foreigner, a knight of the French *langue,* whose members were by far the most haughty of a thoroughly arrogant lot. Perhaps he was not as bad as the others, but he was a knight nevertheless. She'd hated them most of her life, hated them since they'd abandoned Nico. They acted in their own interest and cared nothing for anyone else. They even hated Malta, fortifying it only because they were afraid of the Turks rather than from any desire to protect the Maltese, whom they openly despised.

Despite all that, she found herself drifting back to the street in front of the Infirmary, to sit with her book and wait. Was she waiting for word of Jacobus, or waiting for the man who brought the word? She didn't want to confront the truth about that. Every time she sensed movement near the Infirmary gate, she glanced up without moving her head, hoping to see the black habit and its small embroidered cross as he emerged.

She had always been careless of her looks, running her fingers through her hair and rarely glancing into Elena's looking glass. Somehow it never seemed important. But this morning she'd not only looked but then borrowed Elena's brush. After that she'd carefully tended her clothing. She suddenly regretted having no shoes. She wondered whether all women in France wore them, or only the rich ones. Despite his vows of poverty, Christien de Vries undoubtedly came from a wealthy and noble family, as all the knights did. He had probably never seen a woman without shoes, until Malta.

Angrily she pushed the thoughts away. Jacobus lay near death, for her. How could she think of shoes?

She didn't even know Christien de Vries. How could he hold such power over her? She always saw things with crystal certitude, but he'd turned it all to mud. She'd seen him only five times now, and each time it got worse.

She saw him coming. She remained absorbed in her book, seeing not one word of it, and then feigned surprise when he stood before her. She saw him brighten visibly at the very sight of her. She was intensely conscious of him, and also of her own every movement, and of every breath, of being so near him. It took all her concentration to follow what he said.

He told her of the patient's condition, which remained tenuous. She thanked him for his care. Then something he said about Jacobus triggered her anger at herself once again. He mentioned a shipment of supplies he was awaiting. It included Venice turpentine, which Jacobus needed for his dressings. "With fortune the galley will arrive soon," he said.

"I don't know why your Order needs galleys when all its knights think they can walk on water." She regretted it the moment she said it, but he seemed not to miss a beat.

"I sink every time I try it, especially when I'm wearing armor," he admitted ruefully. "But all the rest can do it."

Similar exchanges had occurred several times over the past few days, when her attitude shifted as suddenly as the spring winds. *He must think me a crackbrain.* Now it took all her will to hide her smile. She was furious with herself for letting him penetrate her hostility.

❖

Callus stopped by to inquire after the patient, and Christien took the opportunity to ask him, as casually as he could, about Maria Borg.

"I met her some years ago, when I was caring for her mother. Maria was just a wisp of a girl. She knew I hunted treasure. Who doesn't make fun of me for it? All the children talked of it, including Maria. I told her stories. She begged to come along, wanting to help, but her father refused permission. Her mother is dead, but her father is still alive. He's a builder. She works for him, or should I say he works for her—it is a matter of some note here. I believe the Order employs him from time to time. I've seen her off and on over the years. I've watched her grow into an extraordinary woman—should your interest surpass medicine." Callus's eyes sparkled; Christien ignored it.

Christien asked the Order's engineer about the builder Borg. An hour later he stood as inconspicuously as possible in a crowded street, watching her. He had seen this particular building site only from a distance, never really noticing it, and certainly not her. It was one of many projects constantly under way, as the Grand Master sought to strengthen the island's defenses, still so weak in many places that a determined assault by even a ragged band of corsairs might breach them. This was not a large project, but it was a busy one. The crew was fortifying a section of the eastern wall of Birgu and adding a bastion. Mules driven by slaves from the Order's prisons hauled carts containing dirt from Senglea and limestone from the quarries. Masons dressed the blocks on the ground, while others set them atop the walls.

He did not see her at first. He became fascinated watching a simple pivoting crane with which individual blocks of stone were raised to the level of the wall. The remarkable thing was that it was powered by a slave walking inside a treadmill, from which the hoist line passed through a series of pulleys and ended in a claw. A single slave walking inside the treadmill could lift a stone many times his own weight, while the pivot allowed it to be swung easily into position well above his head. He'd never seen anything like it.

He spotted her at last, standing atop the thick wall. She was with a mason and was using a bob on a string to check the plumb of the structure on which he'd been working. Christien watched, amused, as the man's expression changed. While she leaned over the wall and dangled the line, his face was hard and angry. The instant she turned to him it softened. He nodded at something she said, and rejoined his crew. She moved into a spirited discussion with a cartwright, and after that called out orders to laborers pushing barrows and hefting shoulder boards sagging under heavy loads of mortar and quicklime. She spoke frequently with a thickset man he guessed to be her father, and regularly consulted a large sheet of paper held in place by rocks on each corner, to keep it from blowing away. Undoubtedly it was the plan of the Order's engineer.

He was captivated. Not only could she read a book and a plan and understand whether a wall was in plumb, but somehow she managed to find a way to tell tradesmen what to do, in a way they would listen. He would have thought only a woman armed with an arquebus could have done such a thing, yet her only weapon was her bearing. She seemed enormously excited by what she was doing, and completely absorbed in her purpose. The sun glowed in her hair. He could have watched all afternoon, but knew he needed to get back to the Infirmary. Just as he was about to turn away, she glanced up and saw him. A look of terrible alarm crossed her face. She dropped her papers and raced along the wall, all but flying down a wooden ladder onto a low scaffolding, then onto another ladder to the ground. She ran toward him, her bare feet stirring up dust. All the color had gone from her face. "Fra de Vries! Is there anything wrong? Is he all right?"

Christien felt terrible. He hadn't even meant for her to see him. "No, it's nothing. I'm sorry to have frightened you. Jacobus is all right. He is not awake, but his breathing seems easier."

"That's wonderful. But then . . ." She gave him a quizzical look.

"I was just . . . walking. I was near, and . . ." It was a weak lie. There was no street there that led to a city gate, no structure nearby that belonged to the Order.

There was no reason on earth for him to be there other than to see her, and they both knew it.

He felt himself blushing. "I asked Joseph about you," he admitted. "I just wanted to see for myself. He said you worked as a builder, that on the walls you looked like the master of pyramids for the pharaoh. I thought that as improbable as it was interesting."

She smiled. "And do I?"

"I believe the master of pyramids needed a whip. You seem to do as well without."

She shrugged. "They listen not because they want to. They listen because I keep the money box."

She saw his interest in the pivoting crane and gave him a closer look. "It's really quite simple," she said. "A very old design, all but forgotten. An engineer lent me a book about the building of a cathedral in France. There was a simple description in it of a machine like this. I made a drawing. One of Father's carpenters built it from bits of an old galley the Order captured. The hull was worm-eaten, but I found parts that were still usable. I traded the Order for it—the galley and the wood in it for work on a rampart in Fort St. Angelo. The Order's engineer says it works much better than scaffolding. We can take it apart in two hours and move the whole thing on carts. It doesn't work everywhere, but where it does my father can do twice the work in half the time."

"A prospect his men find a mixed blessing, no doubt. And all from a drawing you made from a book you read!"

"Is that so odd?"

"Well . . . yes. Of course it is."

"Odd that a woman could understand it, Fra de Vries, or that a man could invent it in the first place?"

He laughed. "I will certainly not argue the point with the pharaoh's builder. And now I must let you get back to your pyramids." He nodded and turned to leave.

"Fra de Vries," she called.

He turned. "*Signorina?*"

"May I visit again this afternoon? To see about Jacobus?"

His look was all the answer she needed.

Chapter 32

The bishop's carriage left the Infirmary courtyard and turned into the narrow street. Salvago sat stiffly on the cushion, his shoulder bound in a sling. Guards sent by the Captain of the Rod walked in front of the carriage, forcing people to press themselves into doorways to let Salvago pass on the short journey to the bishop's palace. There the prelate's physicians would see to whatever care he needed. The Order's surgeon, de Vries, had seen him off. It was nearly the dinner hour. There had been no fanfare, no one else from the Order to wish him well as he left. A nest of cobras, he knew, was always glad to be rid of a mongoose.

Salvago returned the muted greetings of people who watched him pass. The carriage was partway through the crowded square when the driver stopped. "I am sorry, Dun Salvago," he said, "but the harness bolt is loose. I won't be a moment." He climbed down and set to work.

Salvago tried to will away the throbbing in his shoulder. He would be glad to be done with his short, disagreeable journey, glad for the tranquility of the palace. The air in the square was sweltering. It stank of humanity and rang of crass commerce. Scanning the crowded plaza, he noticed Fra de Vries, who had apparently left the Infirmary at the same time he had. He was talking with someone. The knight was blocking Salvago's view, so he couldn't see who it was. Then de Vries moved to make way for a vendor pushing a cart.

Salvago sat bolt upright, almost tearing open his sutures.

She saw him at the same instant, her eyes drawn past Christien to the carriage. Their eyes locked.

The sight of her tore at him, stirring demons he had long sought to bury. She was more stunning than ever.

In the instant he saw more in her eyes than mere hatred, more than anger. It was but a fleeting look, a brief shadow that clouded her eyes, but it was enough. It was a look the vicar saw often now and knew well.

It was the look of fear. Unmistakable, visceral fear.

It puzzled him deeply. *Why does she show fear?*

Perhaps, of course, it was something quite simple. After what had transpired between them, perhaps she feared he would strike out at her again. Or perhaps the answer was that deep inside, all men and women feared the vicar.

But he knew Maria Borg. She was as hard and unyielding as the rock of Malta itself. Even as a girl she had not given way to terror. He would never forget the sight of her standing above the road to Mdina as she calmly tried to kill him. Her shot had not missed by much, he remembered, absently touching the spot where a small scar remained, hidden by his cap. Then, when her gun was no longer of use, she'd picked up rocks to have her way, and thrown those. She'd stood defiantly, challenging him. Had he chased her then, she would have used her fingernails.

Yes, even as a mere girl Maria Borg had been a formidable adversary. It had taken all his skill to break her, and even then, she gave up only when her friends were at risk. The woman would certainly be no softer than the girl.

And then it came to him.

It was the key to Maria Borg, her only vulnerability. She would never show fear for herself. She would show it only for someone else.

Of course.

She was behind all this, still working her vengeance. She had not fired the crossbow herself—but she knew who had.

Yes. For this and this alone would she betray her fear.

The Captain of the Rod had said the assassin was seriously injured, and now the commoner Maria Borg was talking with a surgeon of the Order, the Chevalier de Vries. As she was no whore, the very scene was as extraordinarily unlikely as to see a dog conversing with a king.

It was not coincidence, of course. There was no such thing in Salvago's world.

Perhaps even now the assassin was in the Infirmary, or was himself a member of the Order. There were endless possibilities, which might involve more than mere vengeance.

A conspiracy against the Church and her servants, perhaps.

Or heresy.

The driver finished his work on the wheel and climbed back into the carriage. "We'll be there in a moment, Your Grace," he said apologetically.

Salvago didn't hear him, his mind racing with the tasks at hand.

There were men to set watching, as there were men to summon at midnight, men to invite into the dark rooms beneath the bishop's palace, where they would whisper in fear, trading secrets for salvation.

❧

The next morning when she came Christien appeared almost immediately to greet her. He had a bright linen in which he'd wrapped food. He took her behind the Infirmary, and they perched on the wall overlooking the creek. There was fruit, and a cheese that far surpassed the quality of any she'd ever delivered to the Order.

"The Order's reputation for feeding its patients the best food is apparently well deserved," she said. "I hope you didn't steal this from a patient."

"He was asleep," Christien said, smiling, "and weighs twenty stone already. He won't miss it."

The news about Jacobus was excellent. The fever they dreaded had not materialized. The chest dressings had held. "He is awake more often now," Christien said. "He asks for you." Even in semi-consciousness, Jacobus had been mumbling her name since the night he'd been brought in.

"How I wish I could see him. Please send him my—please tell him I said hello."

"I will." He fought the impulse to ask who Jacobus was to her. He knew almost nothing about either one of them, and then he had lied for her. He had a right to know more than he did. "Why did Jacobus do it?" he asked quietly.

"Do what?"

"I saw the fence where he fell, near the tower. I still don't know how he lived after that."

"I don't know what you mean." She looked panicked. "I told you what happened."

"It's all right. The *gendarm* was here already."

"Did you . . ."

"Tell him about the rocks? Yes."

Relief flooded her features. "Thank you." She ate in silence. "If you knew, why did you do as I asked? Why did you lie for me?"

"A fair question, to which I confess I have no ready answer. Why did you *ask* me to lie?"

"Because it is a demon, not a priest, who wears the vicar's robes. Jacobus only tried to kill evil. He should not suffer for it."

"I suppose there are many in the Order who would share that view of the vicar, but few who would shoot him for the opinion."

"They don't know him as I do. I wish I could explain. I can only pray you will continue to protect Jacobus, and that you will believe me when I tell you that you are doing an honorable thing."

"That is a great deal to take on faith."

"Yes—and far more than I have a right to ask of you. I am in your debt, Fra de Vries."

"Considering I might end in the Inquisitor's dungeons for you, do you think it too forward of me to ask you to call me Christien?"

She smiled. "No. Thank you, Christien de Vries."

After she left he sat alone for a while. He instinctively believed her. He knew little about Salvago or his history and guessed that the vicar had persecuted someone close to Jacobus—perhaps in Sicily or Italy, before coming to Malta. He still did not know who Jacobus was to her, although he dreaded that the injured man was her lover.

He worried about the ease with which he had lied for her, and about what that said of his attraction to her. He had no wish to test his vows. His life was full and rich, and whether with baroness or commoner, he was not looking to complicate it. He wondered if he ought to go to the chapel.

Instead he found himself wanting only to grant her wish, to make her happy. He wished he could collect her inside the Infirmary. Such a thing was quite inconceivable. The only people allowed in the wards were those who were ill, and those who tended their bodies and spirits and—

Of course!

The idea was worthy of Bertrand. It would mean breaking every rule of the Infirmary and the Order, a breach that, if discovered, would earn him far worse than the septaine. It didn't matter, and he knew that despite the danger to Maria herself, she would do it. He was just beginning to collect an idea of the measure of this woman.

He stopped at the *linciere*'s storeroom, where the linens were kept, to get what he needed. He returned to the ward, where he set to work with knife, needle, and sutures. Sewing skin was far easier than sewing fabric, he decided, but he was pleased with the result.

That evening she looked mystified at the bundle in his hands.

"Do you still wish to see him?" he asked.

"Of course! I thought it was impossible."

"There is some risk to my method," he admitted, "but it is the only way. Put this on and meet me right here just before midnight."

The tower clock was just tolling the hour when the Carmelite nun followed Christien into the loggia and through the gate. The guard barely looked up. They walked through the *cortile grande,* where there was a large rainwater pool, filling a reservoir created when the stone used to build the Infirmary had been quarried. There were fragrant orange trees in the courtyard and small vegetable gardens near the water. They passed between vine-covered pillars and through the refectory, past the laundry and storerooms, and then silently up two flights of stairs, to one of the wards in the rear of the building.

It was a large room. Long rows of beds were arranged along both walls, beneath a high quadripartite ceiling that kept the room cool. There was a chapel at one end. The ward was quiet save for snores and occasional low moans. The wall lanterns burned low. Maria passed between the rows of beds and stopped next to Jacobus. His chest and shoulder were heavily bandaged. She took his hand. He stirred but did not awaken. She leaned over and whispered something to him. She kissed him on the forehead. One of the *barberotti,* a surgical student who worked the wards at night, saw it and gave Christien a puzzled look.

"She knew his parents," Christien whispered, as if that explained something. The student nodded uncertainly and moved on about his business.

Christien busied himself at the other end of the room, trying to leave her in privacy. He kept glancing at her, distinctly uneasy as she displayed her obvious feeling for the birdman. He felt a terrible pang when she kissed him, unable to tell whether it was a kiss for a brother, a lover, or a husband. He had not been able to bring himself to ask Callus about it. To ask such a question at all would be to admit more about the way he was feeling than he was prepared to admit, even to himself.

Maria was on her knees praying when Jacobus awakened. He looked around the darkened room, then at the nun holding his hand. He blinked and then stirred suddenly as he recognized her. He tried to sit up but quickly collapsed. "Maria? Is it you? Or have I gone to heaven?"

"You are in the Infirmary. You are alive." She squeezed his hand and brushed back the hair from his forehead. "Oh, Jacobus, you should not have done it."

Jacobus spoke in a whisper, his throat dry and thick. "Is he dead?"

"No."

"*Ḥaqq ix-xjafek!*" Jacobus winced. "Damn the devil! Then I failed you. I will not miss a second time."

"There can be no second time. You must leave it alone."

"Never. He wronged you."

"A long time ago. It is not your battle."

"It *is* my battle." He took a deep breath. "I want to marry you, Maria. I want you to be my wife."

Her face flooded with emotion. "You are feverish," she said, her lip trembling.

"I know what I'm saying."

"There is time to talk of this later."

"I want to talk now. Do you love me at all?"

"Of course, Jacobus. You know I do."

"As a brother? Or as a man?"

She squeezed his hand. "I don't know what I want," she said. "Except that I want you out of here. I want you safe. Then we can talk."

His eyes clouded when he saw Christien hovering behind her, just out of earshot. "Is he going to arrest me when he's healed me? Do others wait outside with the noose?"

"No, they do not. And he is a friend."

"A knight, a friend? How can that be?"

"He saved your life, Jacobus. He knows what you did."

"Then I am a dead man."

"No. He lied for you already. You must trust him." She told him what he must say when asked how he was hurt. He nodded in thankful disbelief. He was growing weak again.

"Sleep now, dear Jacobus." She rose, tenderly squeezed his hand, and kissed him again on the forehead. She turned and nodded at Christien, who saw her eyes welling with tears. He walked her outside and down the stairs. Outside the gate they moved into the shadows.

"Thank you for that, Christien. For everything you have done."

It gave him an unexpected rush of pleasure to hear her say his name. He could only look at her.

They stood in awkward silence.

"I must be getting home, I suppose," she said.

"It's late. I will accompany you."

"I will be fine alone." It sounded more defiant than she intended.

"I assure you, you have nothing to fear from me."

"I do not fear you," Maria said truthfully. *It is me I fear,* she thought.

"As you wish, then. If you would rather be alone, I understand. It's just that my mother would never forgive me for failing to see a nun safely home."

She laughed. She'd almost forgotten. She slipped the habit over her head and gave it back to him. She shook her head to straighten her hair. "It's not that. It's just that it's quite far." She hoped this time her resistance sounded more feeble.

"It would be my pleasure."

They walked through the silent streets of Birgu, deserted now but for cats stalking their prey. The sound of his boots echoed off the high walls. They heard a ship's bell from the harbor. They walked in silence until they left the city gate, neither of them aware of anything but the other's presence.

Outside the city they began talking, quietly at first, but then more animatedly as they felt the freedom of the open fields. He told her of Paris, and of his ancestral home outside that city, the Château de Vries. He regaled her with tales of Bertrand and life in the Order. He talked about surgery and poked fun at himself. She asked endless questions and laughed at his answers. He was surprised at the things she triggered in his memory, things he hadn't thought about in years—of the two-headed snake and the king, and of floating on a wooden raft in the Seine, and of the glorious Bois de Boulogne, where by dispensation of the Valois kings the de Vries family hunted game.

Maria said little about herself at first but opened up gradually. She told him about Nico and talked about her books. She owned eleven of them now and knew them by heart. He asked how she'd learned to read. In her only evasion of the night she simply said, "A priest taught me."

Much too quickly they arrived at the carob tree that marked the hidden entrance to the cave. Neither of them was ready to part. By unspoken agreement they kept walking slowly. They ran out of path and had to make their way carefully. The moon was a pale sliver, providing so little light that she felt it necessary to take his arm in hers and guide him lightly. She led him down the slopes of a dry *wied* that ran to a small sandy beach. Christien spread the nun's habit on the ground and they sat with their backs to the cliff. They listened to the waves against the rocks and gazed up at the grand amphitheater of stars, watching as they slowly gave way to the dove-gray light of dawn. The sea air was perfect and fresh. It was a magical, enchanted night in which everything was perfect and there was nothing but each other—neither hunger nor thirst, nor heat nor cold, nor anything but the wonderful rush of words and shared laughter.

The sun was already well above the horizon when they realized the hour. "You were most gracious to walk me home," she said. "But I'm afraid you've made me late for work. I now require you to accompany me back to Birgu, Fra de Vries. My father will be expecting me."

She never stopped at M'kor Hakhayyim. They walked even more slowly than they had the previous night—they were both certain of it—yet by some sleight of celestial magic the trip seemed much faster. They lingered outside the city walls, prolonging the moment of parting. He wanted to take her in his arms, to hold her. He knew from her look that she wanted it, too. It took all his will to resist the impulse and walk her through the gate. He walked her the short distance to the wall where her father's crew was working. She turned to face him. "I'd better say good night here," she said reluctantly.

"Or good morning."

She hurried to the ladder, where her father saw her. He snapped at her and shot Christien a suspicious, hostile glance.

Christien watched until she stood atop the wall, where workers immediately descended upon her, peppering her with questions and problems. She ignored them, instead fixing her gaze upon him. They held each other that way for a long, lovely moment.

Christien returned to the Infirmary in a daze.

This time there was no hesitation. He went directly to the chapel and got to his knees.

Father, forgive me, for I have sinned. I beseech Thee to preserve me from the evil of temptation, to keep my covenant with Thee. I joined the Order of

my free will, given in full faith. To break the vows of that Order is to break
my oath to Thee.

I have lied, Father, by word and deception.

Help me find my strength, which is Thy strength. Help me to see Thy
way and Thy light. Help me to keep my sacred oath.

Help me . . . help me . . .

❖

For those who labored in the nether reaches of the bishop's palace,
it had not been difficult to discover that the name of Jacobus Pavino
was among those recently admitted to the Holy Infirmary.

Nor was it difficult to discover that he lived in M'kor
Hakhayyim.

Salvago remembered the cave, of course. He knew that Maria
lived there, too. It was more than enough. The *gendarm* had already
interviewed Fra de Vries, the Order's surgeon, and been persuaded
by his story. The bumbling civil authorities would proceed no
further. As for the Order, he did not doubt its enmity. Its officials
would do nothing to hunt down a man who had tried to kill him—
or, more precisely, the Inquisitor's Vicar. This was a matter only the
Church could resolve.

He considered having Maria brought to him, here in this
windowless room where the door was so low she would have to
bow to enter. Here, or in the darker rooms below, she would
eventually tell him whatever he wished to know, no matter how
strong she was.

Yet that was not his wish for her. Yes, he wanted to summon her
so that he could see her once again. Not to torment her. Not to hurt
her. Though he knew she would never believe it, Maria Borg had
nothing more to fear from him. He longed for her to see the pain
that remained in his soul after his sin against her. He wanted her
forgiveness.

He knew she would never give it.

After all these years, she still held a terrible power over him. She
brought pain to his heart and a stirring to his loins that he could deny
to anyone save himself and the Almighty. He dug his nails into the
flesh of his palms until he bled. He closed his eyes and cursed his old

weakness, that until the sight of her in the square he thought he had successfully slain.

No. He would not bring her here. Not now. He could not trust himself to do that, could not cross that line of temptation. His sin against her had led to years of exemplary behavior. Because of his horror at that sin, he had begun to ascend the long ladder of redemption.

The priest, the man, would leave Maria in peace.

But there was a matter of the vicar. A matter of duty. Though he bore her no ill will, he was not willing to allow himself to become a target for her assassins. A crime against his person, or that of the bishop, was a crime against the Holy Office itself. He must deal harshly with Jacobus Pavino. In so doing he would send her a clear message, to retreat before others dear to her paid in blood for her unwillingness to leave the past in the past.

He was prepared for what Pavino would say. The birdman would talk—oh, yes, he would talk. If not freely, then most assuredly after the blandishments of hook and wheel. He would claim to his interrogators that he was defending the honor of Maria Borg for what he believed Salvago had done to her years earlier. Even if Pavino survived long enough to explain all that to the bishop himself, Salvago knew, it mattered nothing: Maria herself had recanted in the presence of Cubelles.

The unpleasantness could be dealt with neatly and quickly, leaving him to tend to more important matters. After that he would be able to sleep. His brush with death left his insides jellied with fear. He thought of that bolt flying through the air, striking him down like a rabbit in the hunt, and his insides still quivered. He was not a man to suffer violence. It was one thing to see torment visited upon the deserving. It was another matter altogether to suffer it oneself, delivered by a common thug.

He summoned his secretary. "Send me the Captain of the Rod."

❖

On his rounds Christien stopped first at the bed of Jacobus, who was again awake. His color was good, his breathing strong. Christien fought his impulse to ask questions, though there was no way to even begin. The birdman spoke only Maltese, a Moorish-sounding muck of which Christien knew nothing. Even if they could talk together, he knew the birdman would never speak freely, never answer his questions.

Christien tried to imagine what might have driven the man to such a desperate act. If not persecution, then a dispute over money, perhaps, or land, or some other family matter. He'd heard the Maltese were hotheaded and quick to violence. Whatever the reason, he knew that what really tore at his heart was the thought that they were lovers. Maria was merely using Christien to protect him, and he was willing to let her do it. He had never acted so recklessly in his life, and never with so little reason.

She is his lover, not mine. Why should I protect them?

He knew he shouldn't. He knew he would.

He completed his rounds and left the infirmary for the auberge. At the door he encountered Bartholomew, his page. Bartholomew was fifteen, the eager and somewhat hapless son of a minor nobleman of Gascony. He hoped one day to wear the Order's colors—not the scarlet *sobraveste* of a full knight, for his lineage was inadequate, but at least that of a serving brother, a military knight-at-arms. The lad ran errands for him and was helpful in many ways, although Christien had no idea how he would ever become a Hospitaller. The boy fainted dead away at the sight of blood.

"Ah, *bon,* sire, there you are," the page said. "I was just coming to find you. I was beginning to worry you'd be late for arms." He was struggling to balance a heavy load of armor and weapons.

With a groan Christien remembered. It was the afternoon for weekly training, from which no knight was excused. The Grand Master insisted his men remain at the very peak of their fighting abilities. From the time a novice arrived in Malta, his training included lectures on the art and science of war, on fortifications and artillery, on armaments and munitions. Practical instruction included training in marksmanship, wrestling, and close combat with a sawtooth dagger. The theory of tactical warfare at sea was taught on land and then honed during the caravans, the long stints at sea each knight served aboard the Order's galleys as they raided and harassed enemy shipping.

Due to his work in the Infirmary, Christien received deferments from service in the galleys after his first caravan, but he had no such luck with routine training. This week's rotation was by far the least agreeable, a three-hour skirmish in full body armor. They would shed most of that armor in actual combat, for in the age of the arquebus it was of little value. But for one afternoon, hinges would close and straps would be cinched on armor emblazoned with dragons and saints and venerable coats of arms. Visors would be lowered and gauntlets raised in salute to the *piliers*. Then the centuries would melt away and the bailey of the fort would ring in a medieval melee of steel against steel as the men of iron practiced their ancient trade.

With Bartholomew's help Christien donned his armor and joined his compatriots in the bailey. He was a natural swordsman but took no pleasure in it, felt none of the thrill of danger that made his brethren so fearsome and deadly. He looked at the circle of combatants and knew the afternoon would not go easy. There were knights from both the French and Castilian *langues*. Though their respective nations had spent most of the last forty years at war, the members of the two *langues* generally shared a friendly rivalry, although tempers could flash hot. There was Alain Bremont, the Count of Limoges, robust and red-bearded, his shaking big belly belying his speed with a blade. Gilbert, the Baron de Bergerac, was a cold and ruthless killer and a renowned womanizer. The Mallorquin Antonio d'Anconia had been wounded in three campaigns and was now one-armed, but still as deadly as any man with two. Beside him stood Fra La Motte, a pious and belligerent monk, the very epitome of the Order's traditions. He lived simply, faithfully tending his duties in hospital and chapel, regularly sharpening his sword on the necks of his Order's enemies. And of course there was Bertrand Cuvier, the hard-drinking, hard-fisted, hard-fornicating champion of Christ. All were accomplished warriors, and no doubt all of them had slept more of late than he.

Christien got through the afternoon on adrenaline, swinging his weapon fiercely but mechanically, without finesse, his mind on other things. The skirmishes dragged on, the heat sapping his strength. He faced four knights and three times managed to land on his back, requiring the help of pages to get to his feet.

In the last exercise he found himself paired against Bertrand, who was perhaps the best swordsman of them all. He carried a long blade in one hand, a blunted mace in the other. After their first brief but ferocious encounter Bertrand looked at him oddly. "You seem distracted. Is something wrong?"

"No," Christien huffed, swinging wide. "Why do you ask?" Bertrand drove him to the wall and nearly pinned him, but Christien sidestepped and escaped with a clumsy pirouette.

"I don't mean something wrong, like a fever. I mean something wrong, like for what reason you should look so sly and contented, as if you've been rummaging through my stores of brandy." He grinned broadly through his visor, his face red from heat and exertion.

"I haven't any idea what you're talking about." Christien swung his sword mightily, intending to give his friend a new seam on his head plate. Bertrand easily avoided the blow, moving with an agility and grace that Christien would have thought impossible in armor. A moment later they were close together again, struggling for position.

"I have it now! I'd know that look anywhere. I've worn it myself often enough. You've a *woman!*"

Christien's hesitation lasted no more than a heartbeat, but it was enough for Bertrand, who clubbed him cleanly on the helmet with his mace. Christien crashed to his back in a clatter of metal.

"There, you see?" Bertrand stood over him, gloating. "You aren't paying attention at all. A woman it is, and she's got your brain in the clouds. If I'd been the devil Turk just now, I'd be wearing your balls for a bracelet and your tongue for a tie." He removed his helmet and extended a hand. Pages raced to help. Christien caught Bertrand's hand and struggled to his feet. His knees wobbled and his head still rang.

"A woman!" Bertrand chortled. "By God, the monk is a man!"

❖

As if in divine answer to Christien's prayers, and certainly in direct response to the excesses of Carnival, Grand Master La Valette announced the imposition of *collachio,* the cloistered existence of the knights that until Malta had always been characteristic of the Order. In Rhodes, a wall had existed to keep the knights separated from the pleasures of the city. No such physical barrier was possible in Birgu, where the auberges of the eight *langues* had been built where space permitted. Knights mingled freely with temptation. Therefore, ordered the Grand Master, "the walls of *collachio* must exist in your minds and hearts, and in your rededication to your holy vows."

The knights of the *langue* of France heard the news as they ate dinner at the long table in the great hall. After the *pilier* departed there was quiet grumbling as the young and randy men reassured each other it was only temporary madness on the part of the Grand Master. His attentions would soon return to where they rightly belonged, from crotch to cross, from temptation to Turk. Until then, no one would dare test his will.

Christien remained pensive while the others commiserated. Absently he pushed his food around on the plate. The sense of relief he hoped to receive from the orders did not materialize.

He knew what was in his heart. It made him afraid.

❖

The Baron Buqa had Christien followed so that he would know where the knight was when he wished to strike. He practiced twice a day with his tutor, the Greek mercenary, who pronounced himself pleased with the baron's progress with a blade. Antonio was not as soft and out of practice as he'd thought. What skill he might be lacking would be more than overcome by the shock of surprise and the energy of rage.

❖

"By authority of the Holy Office, I have come for the inmate Jacobus Pavino."

The Captain of the Rod stood at the Infirmary gate. He carried a shield bearing the coat of arms of Bishop Cubelles, four crowned lions on a field of red and white. An ivory likeness of the Pope hung from a gold chain around his neck. A page stood next to him, carrying the captain's rod of office. Behind him stood four *familiares,* part of the Inquisitor's bodyguard. They were armed, though their swords were sheathed.

The vicar had sent the captain for Pavino rather than the courier who generally handled such chores. Although only the gate of the Infirmary was guarded, its grounds were still the property of the Order. Pavino needed to be extracted quickly, before anyone in authority could be summoned. The vicar had told him the hour to come, when the Hospitaller and Infirmarian would be absent. "Bully your way past the rabble at the gate and fetch the man here," he'd ordered. Once Pavino was in the bishop's palace the Order would be impotent.

The Infirmary guard was a simple Maltese civilian, armed with a sword he'd never used in anger. He eyed the symbols of the captain's authority uneasily. "You'll have to wait until—"

"I'll wait for nothing." The captain pushed past him, his men close behind. The guard yelled for them to stop. They ignored him, moving swiftly in the darkness across the courtyard to the stairs. They started up.

"What do you want?" Christien de Vries was just descending the stairs. He looked past the captain to his *familiares,* their forms barely discernible in the poor light of the wall lantern. He saw the glint of a sword. "How dare you bring arms into the Holy Infirmary?"

The captain recognized de Vries and hesitated, cursing the incompetence of his spies, who had reported de Vries had left the Infirmary an hour earlier. Evidently they'd missed his return. There was nothing for it but to press on. "I have come for the inmate Pavino."

"By what right?"

"By the right of the Holy Office of the Inquisition. By the right of the Inquisitor General himself. This is the order, with his seal. It demands the release of Pavino, who tried to kill the vicar."

Christien merely glanced at it. He tossed it back at the captain. "Your brief is worthless here. You may not enter this hospital. None may enter without authority of the Hospitaller."

"I represent a higher authority than the Grand Hospitaller."

"Within these walls, sir, there is no such thing."

"You say this at the peril of your immortal soul."

"My soul is not in the hands of the Holy Office, Captain, nor shall Pavino be."

The captain's hand tensed on the hilt of his sword. "I will not accept the authority of a *cutter*. I will have him, and now. Move out of my way." His guards drew their swords.

Behind Christien, several unarmed hospital aides had descended the stairs, watching. Sensing violence, they edged quietly back up.

Armed only with his black habit and its eight-pointed cross, Christien towered above the captain and his men, the wall lantern behind him casting his long shadow down the stairwell. "Do as you will, Captain. A *cutter* is now all that stands between you and hell."

Though prepared if necessary to use force against a simple guard, the Captain of the Rod was not ready to raise his sword against a Knight of the Order. The vicar had made it clear he wanted no bloodshed, counting instead on swiftness and stealth. The captain clenched his teeth. "You will regret this, Fra de Vries," he said. "We will have Pavino one way or another." He turned and led his men back through the courtyard and out the gate.

Christien watched their retreat with a sense of dread. He had won this round, but the terrible path upon which he had almost casually embarked was quickly growing steeper, and vastly more treacherous.

❖

The next afternoon Christien was summoned to Fort St. Angelo, where he was ushered into a formal meeting of the Sacred Council. As he entered the chamber, a dozen pairs of imperious eyes rested upon him, Grand Crosses and *piliers* and commanders. He was not invited to sit.

"Fra de Vries," the Grand Master began without preamble, "the bishop is demanding to see me. Before I do, I wish to know what it is that has him breathing fire—other than your skit at Carnival, of course, which I'm told you are fortunate I missed. The Hospitaller tells me the Infirmary—or *you,* to be more precise—turned away the Captain of the Rod this morning when he came for a patient. Who is this man, this Pavino?"

"A birdman, my lord. A simple hunter, nothing more. He has been in my care since being admitted to the Infirmary after a fall. I made a full report to the Hospitaller."

"What do they want with him?"

"They believe it is he who attempted to kill the bishop or his vicar, sire."

"A pity he missed," mumbled Chevalier Gil d'Andrada.

"*Silence!*" La Valette thundered. "No such sentiments will be expressed around this table, or anywhere in the Order!" He stared at Christien. "Well, de Vries, what is the truth of it?" Now all their eyes were upon him as he stood alone at the end of the great table.

A haze of unreality descended over Christien, as if it were someone else speaking to the lords of the Order. "He could not have been the man, sire," Christien said. "I treated him. I cleaned his wound." He repeated the story about seaweed, hoping no one could hear the catch in his throat or the pounding in his chest. "The *gendarm* himself was satisfied he could not be the man." *God forgive me.*

"Sir Oliver?" La Valette looked at his secretary. "Your thoughts?"

"We should grant him asylum, sire."

"*Asylum!*" Fra Giovanni Gonzaga, the Prior of Barletta, nearly choked. His fist hammered the heavy oak table.

"Of course. As a matter of both law and practice, the right is absolute and well established, protecting him from the persecution of the civil authorities or the bishop, or anyone else outside the Order. We have granted asylum many times, just as the bishop himself has used it against the civil authorities—and against us. Has he not granted tonsure to a score of his cronies to protect them from the Grand Master's justice? Only last week another one—and tonsure differs little from asylum, except that it lasts for a lifetime."

Gonzaga sat forward. "Yes, but what is our interest in granting even temporary asylum? Why should we needlessly antagonize the Holy Office? We must select our battles with more care. Guilty or no, let the Church have him. He is but a birdman. A peasant. Of what possible consequence is he to us?"

"It is a matter of larger principle, my lords," Sir Oliver Starkey said. "The appointment of the bishop as Inquisitor was merely the first step. The arrival of his vicar was the second. Already eight of our number have been summoned to give witness in this hunt for heresy. Where will it stop? They probe for any weakness, plotting to attack us on every front—our piety, our devotion, and now our very independence. If they find a breach in our defenses, let it not be in our will. The bishop's arrogance in trying to spirit away a patient in such a manner is indication of their determination. It is a direct challenge. He must not prevail."

Starkey glanced sternly at Christien. "If I were to fault you for what happened last night, Fra de Vries, it would only be for allowing the captain to leave the Infirmary with his head still on his shoulders. You should have removed it for his insolence in breaching the gate." Starkey's eyes twinkled. "In fact, considering your unique skills, you should have done so surgically. You could have reattached it to his hindquarters and returned him to the vicar properly arranged at last." There was great laughter at that; even La Valette could not suppress a smile. Starkey's expression turned serious once again. "On every front, in every way, gentlemen, we must resist the Inquisitor as if he were the Grand Turk himself."

There were murmurs of agreement, but Gonzaga wanted none of it. "He will take the matter to the Holy See, sire, and claim it is a direct affront to the Holy Father himself. They will say we are hiding an assassin for the purpose of thwarting his wishes."

Starkey waved impatiently. "As no doubt they will suggest we ordered the attempt itself," he said. "Let them say what they will."

Gonzaga started to reply, but the Grand Master cut him short. He'd heard enough. "I have no fear of engaging them on this or any front, but I have no wish to do so if it means harboring an assassin. Fra de Vries, I must ask again. You are content this man is innocent?"

Christien's head pounded. Only this one instant remained to make it right. He could even hedge the answer, say he was not certain. But he saw her face then, as clearly as he saw La Valette's, whose gaze he returned evenly.

"Yes, Grand Master. He is innocent."

"Very well. Asylum is granted. A small shot across the bishop's bow. Fra Çeralta, post the appropriate order under my name. I shall inform Monsignor Cubelles. That is all, Fra de Vries. You may return to your post."

"Sires." Christien bowed and left the room. He was torn by the unexpected turn of events—happy that she would have what she wanted, but disgusted at his own hand in it. Suddenly a simple birdman was a pawn in a chess game between the Order and the

Holy Office, moved by a knight whose own hand was guided by forces he could control but would not. Each move was another falsehood in a growing deception, a clear violation of his oaths to the Order.

He found himself in St. Anne's, a simple chapel that stood in the courtyard of the magisterial palace, on the promontory of Fort St. Angelo.

Inside, he got to his knees. This time when he tried to find words of contrition he could not. His deceit was too calculated. He could not fully explain his own actions to himself, much less confess them to God.

Yes, Maria had asked him to lie. He didn't have to do it. She did not force him in any way. She had only looked at him and asked. Given nothing, promised nothing. He had done it without knowing anything but the complete surrender he felt before her. Had she asked him to jump from the cliffs, he believed he would have done so as well.

Sick at heart, he stood without praying. He would not sin further by pretending to God that it wouldn't happen again. He was already anticipating her next visit to the Infirmary.

A realization hit him like a thunderbolt.

She doesn't know they came for Jacobus.

What if the Captain of the Rod sought her out next? The Holy Office would easily learn she was somehow linked with the birdman. They would find her.

He cursed himself for his failure to think. It was midafternoon. Already twelve hours had passed. He had to warn her.

He hurried from the courtyard of the inner castrum, down the stairs beneath the blunt towers of the barbican, ignoring the greetings of other knights. His stride was normal at first, but each step brought more fear to his heart. By the time he reached the main gate he took the steps two at a time. By the time he reached the outer wooden drawbridge he was running. He raced down the main street through the square, past the Infirmary, and along the road overlooking Kalkara Creek. He pushed people out of his way, growing ever more frantic as his fear heightened.

He was too late. The building site was deserted. All the workmen had gone home for the day. He knew she wouldn't return to the

Infirmary until later that evening. That was too long to wait. Every moment increased his certainty that she was in danger.

He ran to the public stables just outside the city gate and commandeered a horse from the bewildered stable master, promising him money when he returned. He leapt into the saddle and started south. The roads were too bad to canter. He drove his horse as fast as he dared. Peasants pushing carts loaded with grain stood aside to let him pass. With each stride of his mount he felt unreasoning terror constricting his throat. If Salvago wanted Jacobus badly enough to try to take him from the Order's property, the danger to Maria was even greater.

The Holy Office would stop at nothing.

And then he saw her. She was walking toward the cave, alone, her bare feet stirring up dust along the path. She turned at his approach. He saw her lovely face, her emerald eyes, her skin the color of burnt gold, her soft hair radiant in the afternoon light. Her eyes widened with apprehension and pleasure when she saw him. He stopped beside her and slipped from the saddle.

"I'm glad I found you," he said. "They came for Jacobus last night. He's safe. They didn't take him."

"What? Why not? How—?"

"He has been granted asylum by the Order, at least for the moment."

"Asylum! Why would they do that? Why would they care to protect him?"

"It has nothing to do with him, really. It is a larger matter, between the Order and the bishop."

Her mind turned to the meaning of it. "But that means Salvago *knows*."

"Yes. But he can prove nothing, do nothing, so long as Jacobus remains in the Infirmary. He cannot act on mere suspicion."

She shook her head. "I know him. He will not stop. He will try again. He will come after Fençu, after Elena, after everyone. He will come after *you*." Her own terror was growing now. She glanced in the direction of the cave. "Maybe already—please, take me there."

He remounted his horse, then reached down and caught her by the arm. She swung up behind him and put her arms around his waist. He left the winding path, setting out straight across the fields toward the coast. The horse stepped gingerly, picking its way through rocks and ruts and cactus.

They rode in silence. The sun was low in the sky, and he knew the warmth he felt was not the sun's but hers. Presently they saw the carob tree, and near it the *sukkah*, the stone hut they used for the fall holiday. There were no carts, no horses, no officials standing above the cliffs. From the distance they saw a woman sitting outside with her small child, playing a game. "That's Elena," Maria said, "with Moses. Everyone must be all right. He hasn't been there." He heard the relief in her voice. She rested her head against his back. She spoke quietly. "Before we go in there, there is something I must tell you. I have put you at risk, Christien, asked you to violate every oath I know has meaning for you, and you don't even know for what." He turned partway in the saddle to look at her, but she clutched him more tightly. "Please," she said. "Don't look or I won't be able to do this."

"All right." He turned forward again and loosened the reins so his horse could graze.

She stumbled and stuttered at first, hesitant as she tried to find the words. Then the story came in a rush, pouring out with her tears, as she told him what had happened so many years ago. She clung to him tightly, trying to hide her face on his back.

A moment later they were both standing on the ground. He didn't know how they'd gotten down. He held her, his arms around her. He kissed her forehead. His lips brushed her cheek, and he tasted the salt of her tears. He looked past her to the sea, holding her, afraid to look at her again, for the certainty he would kiss her if he did. He held her until her storms passed. "*Va bene*," he whispered, stroking her hair. "*Va bene*."

Of all the reasons he had imagined for her deception, the truth had never occurred to him. He felt guilt for ever doubting her word that protecting Jacobus could somehow be an honorable thing.

At least it was an honorable thing for Jacobus, he thought grimly. *I am no less a liar who has betrayed his oath.*

❖

The residents of M'kor Hakhayyim regarded Christien with

suspicion but listened as Maria translated what he said. The Holy Office would not leave them in peace, he said. No friend or relative of Jacobus was safe. They must all find somewhere else to live, at least for a while.

"You mean hide," Fençu said angrily. "You mean let them drive us from our home."

"*Yes,*" said Elena, clutching Moses.

"*Yes,*" said Elli, Fençu's wife, remembering.

"*Yes,*" said Cawl, the silversmith, and Villano, the water seller. Their wives nodded, too.

Fençu sighed. "*Tajjeb wisq,*" he said, dispirited and beaten. "I know another cave. There are others closer, but this one is more isolated. If we are going to hide, we might as well do it right. There is no spring. We'll have to carry water."

Maria told Christien what they'd said.

"Tell them they'd better leave now, tonight, under cover of darkness," Christien said.

Fençu, who spoke some Italian, bristled at the suggestion. "I don't need a foreigner to tell me how to hide from foreigners," he said testily.

They packed their belongings, loading some in the cart, some on their backs. Maria and Fençu argued in Maltese about something. She turned to Christien. "He says with your horse he can get everything in one trip. By your leave, he will return it tomorrow, wherever you say."

"Of course. I can walk back." Christien was confused. He realized she wasn't going with the others. "Why haven't you packed anything?"

"I'm not going anywhere—at least not with them."

"You're not?"

"Of course not. It would only put them in danger."

Christien couldn't dispute the logic of that, although he didn't like it. "Perhaps you're right, but you can't remain here, and you must stay away from your work. You'll have to tell your father."

She bristled at the orders. "Whatever makes you think I would stop living my life?"

"Surely you're not serious. Salvago will find you."

"There is nothing more he can do to me. The only way he can

hurt me is through them." She nodded at the others. "That is why they must leave."

"There is a *great* deal more he can do to you, Maria, and I may not be able to help you."

"I will not hide," she said. "And you need not worry about helping me. I can take care of myself."

"You are foolish," he said angrily. "An extraordinarily stubborn woman."

She nodded thoughtfully. "I will accept that as a compliment."

❖

Christien waited by the carob tree while she quickly bade the others goodbye. She lingered longest with Elena, who kept looking over Maria's shoulder at the Frenchman.

"You are in love with him," Elena said.

"I am not."

"You should stay away from the knights. They're all the same."

"He's different," Maria said angrily. Then, hastily, she added: "But it doesn't matter that he is. There is nothing between us, I tell you."

Elena laughed gently. "If only I were deaf and blind and didn't know you at all, I might believe that."

"Well, you're wrong, that's all."

Elena hugged Maria. "You are my best and only friend in the world," she said. "I don't want to see you hurt. You must remember Jacobus. He has given everything for you."

Maria flinched. "I didn't ask him to."

"And he did it anyway. He loves you, Maria. Stay away from the Order."

"The Order brought you Moses."

"Yes, and he is the light of my life," Elena said. "But I am a whore. His father might as easily have been a baker or a sailor. It is not the same for you. You can choose. You must choose well. You will never do better than Jacobus."

"Enough of this. Go now. I will see you soon."

It was deep dusk when the little band of refugees set out over the rocky road, their way lit by a sliver of moon. Pots and pans and

Fençu's stolen silver clanged in the cart, while children, goats, and dogs trotted and trailed behind.

Maria stood watching until they were swallowed by the night. When there was only silence she was almost afraid to turn, to face him. He was still standing by the carob tree, watching her.

She walked to him. There was awkwardness now, not the easy comfort of before.

"I worry for you," he said. "You should at least find another cave."

"Yes, I intend to."

"May I help you?"

"I'll be fine."

"I should leave, then," he said.

"Please, not yet. Walk with me."

She did not take him to the cave, but led him along the cliffs until they were able to descend to the shore, the moon giving off just enough light to enable them to see.

"Will you be in trouble for being so late?"

He laughed. "Beyond trouble. The Hospitaller will probably order me to remove a piece of myself. It doesn't matter. I'll tell him something or other. I've gotten to be quite a liar of late."

"I'm sorry. You've done so much, and I've been so rude."

"I don't mind."

"Do you love the Order?"

"The Order, not at all. Surgery, a great deal. There is no better hospital in the world. I am fortunate to be there."

She turned to him. "I want to know everything about you, Christien de Vries," she said. "About every—" She never finished.

He took her in his arms again and kissed her. She responded eagerly, hungrily. Christien took the pack off his shoulder. He spread his cloak on the rocks. They made a pillow of his pack and never felt the rocks.

He unlaced her jerkin, his fingers trembling. He felt her tension. "Am I hurting you?"

"No. It's only that I am . . . afraid. I have not known a man since . . ."

He brushed her hair and kissed her neck. "I am afraid as well."

"I did not want this," she whispered, and there were tears in her eyes.

"Nor did I," he said, his voice husky. "I'm sorry. I should leave." He began to sit up.

She pulled him back to her and kissed him. "No. Please. Never leave me."

"Never."

The world outside faded as they lost themselves in the pounding of the waves and the passage of the stars overhead and the soft, secret places of each other.

Chapter 33

Christien entered Birgu in a heavenly fog of afterlove. He pushed away the thoughts that deviled him, pushed them to a place where he could deal with them later. For now he would enjoy the glow of peace, a happiness and fullness and longing such as he had never experienced. He wanted nothing to interfere with his thoughts of her. The town of Birgu was lovely, the island of Malta sublime, the colors of the sky brighter, the look on people's faces friendlier. His senses were alive as never before. He walked near the wall above Kalkara Creek, watching the shipping in the harbor. He whistled, his step light. He hadn't whistled since he was a boy.

Baron Antonio Buqa stepped from between buildings. He held a sword in one hand, and thrust another at Christien.

Christien stepped back. "This is foolish, Baron," he said. "It is not necessary, I assure you."

"Ah, but it is," Buqa said. He tossed the sword. Christien caught it but held it to his side.

"It is time for you to pay for what you have done to my wife."

"I have done nothing."

Buqa lunged. Christien stepped easily aside. "I will not fight you," he said.

"Damn you! I will kill you whether you fight or not." He swung again. Christien raised his blade to meet the blow and parried it easily.

"I will not fight you," Christien said again.

Buqa began swinging with both hands, back and forth, vicious and determined. If there was no artfulness in his swordsmanship, there was fury. Christien twirled and ducked and backed away again. Buqa's sword rang against the low wall, taking a chunk from the limestone. His face reddened with his impotence. He went for the knight's knees, then spun around and whacked at his chest, and saw he'd missed again. He howled in frustration that his hands could not deliver the murder in his heart.

The next time he lunged he ended on his back, Christien atop him. Buqa wheezed and coughed, his eyes red with rage. Christien had him pinned to the ground, his forearm at the baron's throat.

"I did not touch your wife," Christien said.

"You lying French pig. I saw you, in the square."

"What you saw was nothing but an embrace during a celebration. There was nothing more, Baron. There never will be. For that I give you my word."

"Your *word!* You saw her again the next day, in front of this very building!" He struggled to free himself.

"Yes, we talked. That was all."

Christien pressed down on the baron's windpipe until his face went purple. Beaten, he nodded. Cautiously, Christien let him up. The baron struggled heavily to his feet, his eyes haunted with humiliation, with utter defeat. There was dust on his cheek, and he'd drooled into his beard. Christien held out the swords. Buqa did not take them. Shoulders sagging, he turned and pushed his way through the small crowd that had gathered.

Later that morning Christien was summoned to see the Grand Master in his residence just outside Birgu. Christien had expected it. Very little involving his knights escaped La Valette's attention for long.

He was with the Order's engineer, reviewing plans for the

defensive walls. He dismissed the engineer, who hurried past Christien with a sheaf of papers.

La Valette motioned Christien to step forward.

"Sire?"

"I have heard of the altercation between you and Baron Buqa," La Valette said.

"A misunderstanding, sire, nothing more. It is finished."

"*Nothing,* indeed. I am told it involved swordplay. I am told it involved his wife. I will permit neither activity to disrupt the convent."

"There was precious little swordplay, sire. No one was hurt. The baron thought I had been with her. He was mistaken. I told him so. He took me at my word."

The Grand Master's gaze was hard. "And your word is good?"

Christien took a moment to respond. "I never touched her, sire. She kissed me in the square. I have rebuffed her. That is the truth."

La Valette looked at him carefully. "Need I remind you of your vows, Fra de Vries?"

Christien swallowed. "No, sire. You need not."

"Very well. Let that be the end of it."

❖

The Captain of the Rod and his *familiares* did come to M'kor Hakhayyim. They left empty-handed. There was nothing even to burn.

On the bastion near Kalkara Creek, Maria waited for them to come for her. She worked every day as usual, looking up whenever anyone appeared on the streets below the wall. They did not come.

At night she slipped away to meet Christien, making certain no one followed.

Each time he saw her the relief in his eyes was evident. "Stay away for a while," he asked her again. "Surely your father can manage without you."

"I will not," she said. Her tone put an end to it.

To get away from Birgu Christien lied to the Hospitaller about visiting Santu Spiritu in Mdina, saying Joseph Callus had asked for his help on a medical case. It had happened before, so Çeralta was not suspicious.

They returned to the shore and hid themselves again in the rocks where the cliffs were high. They found a grotto where the water was crystal. They watched the sun set and watched it come up again, watched the colors in the water changing from gold to black to indigo to blue under the perfect sky. They swam naked and made love in the sand and on the rocks and in the water, never tiring of exploring each other. They cooked over an open fire and slept under the stars.

He brought her a leather packet of books from his library. She held them like gold. They read to each other. He brought the skit he and Bertrand wrote for Carnival. He read it to her and acted some of the parts in the nude. She collapsed in laughter. He told her to keep the packet and the books, so she might read on the nights when he couldn't be with her. "I never want time to read," she said. "You must always be with me." They slept little and loved much.

Jacobus grew stronger each day. He paced the courtyard restlessly, knowing he could not leave the grounds. Every time Christien told her of the birdman's progress, he could see the pain in her eyes.

"I haven't been to see him since that night," she said guiltily.

"It can be forgiven," he said. "I will be certain he understands. Few visitors can be expected to sneak in wearing the robes of a Carmelite."

"It isn't that. I feel I've betrayed him."

That made him quiet. Finally he asked, "Have you?"

"No. Maybe. I don't know. I know nothing except that I love you, Christien de Vries. *Inhobbok.*"

"*Inhobbok,*" he repeated. "It has a nice sound. *Te amo.*" He picked her up and whirled her around. "*Je t'aime,*" he shouted. "*Amo te! Te quieros muchos!*" and they ended on the ground in a warm tangle of lips and hands, and endearments whispered in six languages.

After they made love she fell asleep. She awakened to see him sitting up, staring out to sea. She put her arm around his waist and leaned against him. Looking up at him she saw pain in his eyes, and the glistening of tears. "What is it?"

"I am disgusted with myself. I feel I am descending into hell, and I am powerless to stop it."

"Oh, my darling," she said. She brushed her fingers against his cheek. "I did not mean for this to be. I'm so sorry I—"

"No." He took her hand in his own and kissed it. "I am frightened for my soul, yet I am happy, deliriously happy. I am weak of character and completely, madly in love with you. I have dishonored my family name. I must resign from the Order, or I must leave you. I cannot resign from the Order because I made a vow, and I cannot leave you because . . . I cannot."

She was too frightened to say anything. She leaned her head on his shoulder, and they sat listening to the waves.

❖

In the morning they heard someone coming, hiking down from the cliffs above. Too late, they scrambled for cover. Joseph Callus stepped into the clearing, a shovel over one shoulder, a bag with small tools slung over the other.

He saw them and fairly jumped in surprise. He took one look at the two of them, saw what was in their eyes, saw the blanket and the food, and understood immediately. "My God, Christien," he said. "I expected to find Punic bones here, not yours. The rocks must be excruciating. I will be away for three nights, in Gozo. You may use my home. It has a decent bed, at least, and the sand fleas will leave you in peace."

Maria was mortified at being discovered, but Dr. Callus laughed easily and seemed genuinely happy for them. Her embarrassment faded. They shared a cup of *rozolin* together and passed a pleasant hour until Callus saw the longing glances they traded with each other. "Well, you've kept me long enough," he said, draining his cup. "I must be off before someone steals my treasure."

That night Christien did not attend the obligatory dinner in the auberge, or assembly the night after that. He'd already told Joseph Callus about using him as an alibi, and now he asked Bertrand to lie for him as well. He'd told him everything.

"You need to be more careful," Bertrand said.

"Why? There's no more creative liar than you in all Malta,"

Christien said more lightly than he felt. What if Bertrand got in trouble for the lie? Was he willing to sacrifice even his friends in order to betray his oath?

"You know I'll lie for you, but now is not a good time to be trying the patience of the Grand Master."

"When is it ever?"

"*Oui,* but even I have set aside such pleasures for a while. Wait six months or a year. It will be easier then."

"I cannot, Bertrand."

"Very well, then. I'll tell the *pilier* you're pregnant."

❖

The home of Joseph Callus was small but very comfortable. The tables and shelves were filled with bits and pieces from his hunts— arrowheads and pots and sherds and odds and ends of corroded brass and copper. Maria touched the furnishings gingerly. She sat in every chair and ran her fingers along the polished wood of the dining table. She stared long at the bed and prodded it tentatively.

"What is it?" Christien said, coming into the room with brandy. "Is there something in it?"

"It's just that . . ." She hesitated. "I've never been in a real bed before. I've never slept on anything but straw. I didn't know anything could be so soft." She looked uncertainly at him, sorry she'd told him, and suddenly acutely conscious of her background. "The nobleman must think the lady terribly simple," she said. "I have no fine clothes or jewelry. How you must long for someone of culture and means and birth." The words came tumbling out in a rush. "How you must long for someone with shoes."

He set the brandy down and took her in his arms. He kissed her. "The nobleman thinks only how very lovely the lady is," he whispered. "Just now if you had shoes and fine clothes, I'd only have to rip them off you." He held her close. "The nobleman thinks only how he wishes he'd spent every night of his life with the lady, whether on straw or silk or rocks," he said. He looked at the bed. "But let us not waste this while we have it."

Later, she awakened from a light sleep and listened to him breathing. She raised herself on one elbow and watched him, overwhelmed with love. She played with the curls on his chest and thought again about her bare feet. No matter what he said, it was the hardest part of loving him, knowing that he could never settle for a woman such as she—even if his vows were not in the way.

His *vows*. She knew how fragile their time was together. She kissed him on the cheek, and on the ear, and on his nipples. He smiled and stirred lazily. She kissed him more, farther down, until he was no longer lazy. They made love again.

Afterward he realized she was weeping. He looked into her eyes and saw that the tears were not of sorrow. "I never dreamed anything could be so lovely," she whispered as he kissed them away.

❧

The Baron and Baroness Buqa had quarreled bitterly. He confronted her about Christien, then struck her indignantly when she challenged him about his own affairs. He ordered her to stay indoors, then stormed off to take one of his own galleys to Sicily, supposedly to tend to his business interests there. She knew he only needed to hide like an injured dog, to lick the wounds of his humiliation. He would be back in a month or two, and they would find a way to pretend it had never happened.

He could not keep her indoors while he was in Sicily, and she had bribed the houseman to ignore his orders to follow her. One afternoon she went out to purchase a strand of pearls for her hair and was returning home when, nearing the Università, she halted suddenly. His back was to her, but she immediately recognized the familiar black habit, the purposeful stride, the thick black hair. Christien de Vries was walking toward her house! Could it be?

She hurried after him. But then he turned early, near the market, and walked two blocks more through the tight streets. He stopped at the doorway of Joseph Callus's house. Other than the pang of desire and disappointment, she thought little of it. She hid in a doorway, watching as he let himself in, and she immediately began plotting a pretense for visiting Callus.

A woman appeared, coming from the far end of the street.

Angela thought she looked vaguely familiar. She was quite beautiful, dressed in jerkin and skirt. A peasant. She went to Callus's door and knocked lightly. Angela watched, riveted, as Christien let her in. He glanced both ways, then took the woman's hand as she stepped over the threshold. The door closed behind them. Angela had a clear view of his face as he let her in. There was no mistaking his expression at the sight of his guest. It was the look Angela desperately wanted from him. This was no patient visiting the home of Dr. Callus.

It had been years, but there was something about the peasant woman's face that stayed in her memory. It took a moment for the name to come back, and then she had it.

Maria Borg. Angela flushed in anger and humiliation. *Giulio's little wench, the parishioner who smelled of goats?*

She looked for any sign of Dr. Callus, hoping he might be there, that the visit was strictly professional. But Callus never appeared, and no patients came or went. She asked at the apothecary's. The doctor, he said, was in Gozo.

Night fell, and she watched. She saw a lamp in the window. It was never lit. She seethed in jealousy.

It was not long after dawn the next morning when Maria stepped through the doorway and hurried down the street toward the gate. A few moments later the door opened again and Christien emerged. Angela was walking by at that very instant. She brightened in surprise at the sight of him. "Fra de Vries! How wonderful to see you in Mdina!"

"*Barunessa.*" His look made it clear he was not pleased to see her.

"I have heard, of course, of your quarrel with my husband. I must beg your forgiveness for his boorish behavior." Her eyes sparkled. "However, I must say I am flattered."

Christien had had enough. "Don't be," he said. "It is true the baron attacked me, but I assure you, *Barunessa,* it was not over you. It was only *he* who thought it was."

The force of his dismissal and the ice of his insult shocked her. At that instant she knew it was hopeless, and her own anger flashed. "You would sleep with that common little whore who just left here, and not with me?"

He slapped her so hard it hurt them both. A vendor approaching on the street watched in horror as a knight struck a baroness. He turned and hurried the other way.

❖

Angela Buqa sat in her drawing room, nursing her ego and her cheek. The hours passed, and her anger grew with her disbelief.

Maria Borg was an unwashed goat girl who could neither use a fork nor plait her hair with anything but brambles. A tasty enough morsel for some, perhaps, but surely not a meal for a knight.

She thought of the look she'd seen on his face. He'd glared at her with . . . with *contempt*. No one had ever looked at her that way. No man had ever looked at her with anything but desire.

As the hours passed the bruises to her ego turned to scars, the scars to fury, and the fury to a plan.

She knew what to do to a man who would cultivate weeds rather than flowers.

She went to her bureau and sat down with paper and quill pen. She wrote a note that she did not sign. She folded the paper and put it into an envelope. On the front she wrote *La Valette*. She gave it to her houseman and told him to deliver it at once to Fort St. Angelo.

After that she drew a quantity of silver coins from the box in her bedroom. She knew the price of a man's soul. She started with her equerry. She paid him to pay a man to pay other men, until there were layers no one, however determined, could ever penetrate.

She didn't know whether it would long fool Giulio. Surely a false denunciation would eventually fall apart of its own dubious weight. Or would it? In the end, it didn't matter. All that mattered was that along the way, the goat girl would feel a measure of hell she would not soon forget.

An hour after the equerry left, Angela was at the bishop's palace, sitting with her brother in the chancellery.

❖

The next day the Hospitaller himself intercepted Christien at the Infirmary gate. From the look on his face Christien knew it was not good news.

"You have been excused from the morning's duty," Çeralta said icily.

"Excused, sire?" Such a thing had never happened.

"You will report to the Grand Master at once."

Christien walked to La Valette's palace, in the former Jewish ghetto of Birgu. It was his third summons in short order, he thought grimly. That was more times than he'd seen him outside services or assembly since the day he'd become Grand Master, when Christien knelt to give his personal oath to the man.

He was shown immediately into the Grand Master's study. La Valette had just come from Mass and still wore his formal attire, his ermine-lined cape and his *berettone*. He was occupied with a page who held a tray of dispatches. His cold glance commanded Christien to silent attention.

La Valette scribbled something on a paper and gave the page instructions. He took off his robe and hat and handed them to the boy. He loosened the silk sash that held his *scarsella,* the leather purse that signified his role as patron of the poor, and added them to the pile. The page bowed and closed the door softly behind him.

La Valette stood at his desk, empty save for an inkstand and a piece of paper. He pushed the paper across his desk and beckoned his knight to draw near. Christien stared at the paper. He picked it up. He didn't recognize the hand.

By the second sentence, his stomach had a pit in it. He swallowed hard.

By the third, he knew the Grand Master could see his color rising.

By the last, he knew his world would never be the same. He set the paper back on the desk and stared straight ahead.

La Valette paced the room, letting the silence work itself on his knight. Finally he stopped and turned. "Need I remind you of your vows, Fra de Vries?" he said in a scathing mimicry of his own voice, just days earlier.

"No, sire."

"Well, then. Is this note true, or is it a lie?"

"Sire, I—"

"Is it true, de Vries?" His voice thundered like the cannon it commanded.

"Oui, my lord."

"Is it that your vows mean so little, or do you break them merely to defy me?"

"Neither, my lord."

"I am not a fool, de Vries. Play me for one at your peril."

"Of course not, Grand Master. It is that I love her."

"*Love!* It is Christ you must love! Are you so frail you cannot control your primal urges? Your weakness is despicable, Fra de Vries, as contemptible as your sense of duty to God and the Order, and as barren as your oath to me."

La Valette turned to the window, his hands clasped behind his back. "Give yourself over to the master-at-arms," he said.

❖

They came for her at the bastion.

There were five of them for one woman: the Captain of the Rod, his page, and three *familiares*. They called her down from the walls. Work at the site came to an abrupt halt as every member of the crew stopped and watched in fearful disbelief as the *maestra* was taken away. Luca Borg stood at the base of the wall, paralyzed. His big hands clenched his stone cleaver as his daughter passed within a foot of him. He averted his eyes and made no move to challenge her captors.

It was a very short trip past the armory to the bishop's palace. They took her through the gate and courtyard and down a long, narrow set of dark stairs. She was shown to a small, damp room without windows. There was a chair and table and clean straw on the stone bench that served for a cot. It was not as unpleasant as she had expected. The captain closed the door behind her. She waited. A woman brought food and water but would not answer her questions.

Upstairs, Salvago went about his other business. Until now he had had no intention of doing anything about Maria. He had not changed his mind and did not trust himself to bring her into the palace, to be alone with her. He wanted to keep his distance. But then his sister had come to see him with an extraordinary story. Her equerry, she said, had approached her about something he'd heard from a friend in Birgu. A woman named Maria Borg was guilty of

Lutheran thought. The equerry had been deeply troubled and wasn't certain what to do.

Salvago tried to hide his astonishment at the name and did not believe her story for an instant. Oh, how he wondered what devious web she spun! What on earth could it be? Why Maria Borg, and why Angela? He had heard, of course, of Antonio's confrontation with de Vries, but he didn't see any relevance to that. As he thought of it he remembered that he'd seen Maria Borg with de Vries the day he'd been released from the Infirmary. But that would have been nothing more than her concern for Jacobus Pavino. Or perhaps it was something more. Perhaps Antonio had been sleeping with Maria Borg. He thought not, and his mind raced with possibilities, but they all led nowhere. It bothered him that he did not see through Angela as easily as he saw through most people. The only thing of which he was reasonably certain was that his sister was using him as Inquisitor for her own purposes.

"Forgive me, Angela, but I cannot help but wonder what scheme you cook," he had said when she finished her tale.

She was taken aback, genuinely shocked. "Why, nothing at all, brother dear. It is simply that she is evil. I thought it my Christian duty to report it."

Salvago only nodded, and decided right then to ignore her report. But then—she was thorough in her work—three people denounced Maria, their condemnations delivered formally but anonymously through the Captain of the Rod. Their recitations were specific: times and places and phrases.

Was his sister remembering his fascination with Maria? She knew, of course, that Maria had once accused him of rape and then recanted. After all that, did she think he would not act? Whatever the case, now his hand was forced. He had to bring Maria to the palace, but his interviews with her did not need to be conducted in front of anyone. He let Maria stew in the cellar and did not go near her. After two days he had her brought to him in his study. He dismissed the guard.

She stood defiantly, waiting, holding his gaze.

"Your assassin is fortunate to be in the Order's care. He will remain there until he dies, or until the Vatican Secretary of State orders him to leave, at which point he shall find himself in my care.

For your sake, I hope he remains in the Infirmary. Indeed, it would be to his advantage were he to die there of his wounds. I wish that for him. I wish it for you, if you care for him."

"He is not my 'assassin,' as you put it. If it was he who shot at you, I am sorry he missed. But I doubt he did it. There must be many men you must suspect—men you've injured, men of honor who would have enjoyed the shot."

Salvago let it pass. "I brought you here to tell you I will leave you in peace, Maria, if you will leave me in peace. I have no wish to harm you."

"Further, you mean? Harm me further?"

"Quibble with words as you will. I have no wish to harm you."

"I will make no such promise."

"I did not expect you to. I only wanted you to know that your safety—and that of your friends, of course—is in your own hands."

"Better robes have not changed the man, I see," she said.

"I wish you well, Maria Borg."

She laughed. "When you recant to the bishop, as you made me do, then I will know you wish me well."

"You would be wise not to press me too far," he said. He called the guard. "There is no cause to hold her. Release her."

Christien did not meet her that night, or the next. She waited for him outside the Infirmary, her anxiety growing. When he didn't appear she asked the guard at the gate, who told her nothing. She went to Joseph Callus, who gave her the news.

❖

Jacobus Pavino spent hours in the garden of the Infirmary, sitting beneath an orange tree. Though he was much improved, his shoulder was still nearly useless, hampered by the loss of muscle in his chest. He could not yet move his arm, and any deep breath brought pain. What brought greater pain, however, was the knowledge that Salvago's heart still beat.

His first reaction upon being told he'd been granted asylum was relief. But as the days passed and his head cleared, the sweet relief turned sour.

He had failed Maria. Asylum would never heal that. Only one thing could.

Even though the Order allowed it, he could not hide. There was no honor in that.

The thought ate at him until he could take no more of it.

He rose from his bench, drew his bandage more tightly around him, and walked on slightly unsteady legs out of the gate, into Birgu.

✤

"The birdman has flown his sanctuary," Cubelles told Salvago the next day at breakfast.

"Pardon, Your Grace?"

"I spoke with the Grand Master this morning on another matter. He informed me our dispute over Pavino need go no further. The man left the Infirmary of his own accord. I suppose we had better increase my bodyguard."

"Of course, Monsignor. I'll see to it at once."

"Is something the matter? You don't look well. Your face has lost its color."

"Just a chill, Your Grace. I'll be all right." Salvago went to his quarters and latched the door. He vomited into his chamber pot. From the day he had been beaten nearly to death in Rome, the day he'd taken his first step on the road to Christ, physical violence had had that effect on him.

He tried to go about his business as usual. It was impossible. He had to accompany the bishop to a service in Mdina. Along the way he saw shadows behind every rock, death atop every wall. A bell rang, and he jumped. In the Mdina cathedral he pleaded fatigue, and the bishop carried on without him. Salvago hid in the sacristy and peered out through a grate, looking for a killer he didn't know. He searched men's eyes, looking for a hint of menace, a glimmer of danger. It was in vain. The man could be anywhere, death launched from any direction.

In his nightmares he felt the bolt of the crossbow again, only this time it passed through his eye. In the morning his pillow was soaked with sweat. He developed a nervous tic in his cheek, just below his eye. It twitched incessantly. He fingered his rosary and mumbled endless prayers. At Mass his hands shook so that he spilled the wine on his chasuble. He could not eat. His eyes would not focus on the words in his files. He could not remember the names and charges that penitents whispered in his ear.

He did not want to die. Not this way.

Finally he could stand it no longer. He summoned the Captain of the Rod. "Bring Maria Borg," he said.

❖

She stood before him early the next morning. "Call him in," he said without preamble.

She looked at him blankly.

"Your birdman. Tell him to give himself up to the Captain of the Rod."

"He has the Order's protection. Why should he ever come out?"

"He fled the Infirmary, although I'm certain you knew this already."

Her look of surprise was genuine. "No."

"You will speak with your family, with your friends in the cave. Tell them to find him, to convince him to surrender himself."

"Never."

"Then you will remain here, as my guest, until he does. If I am harmed, it is you who will pay a heavy price."

The faintest hint of satisfaction grew in her eyes. "You are afraid," she said. "A coward, hiding behind a woman."

Salvago absently put his hand to his cheek, trying to still the tic. "Call him in," he said again. "Make him give himself up."

"Go find him yourself. I'm sure you'll find him in a cave somewhere. He'll be glad to meet you, face-to-face."

"There is great peril to you if you hide a murderer."

"Not yet, Dun Salvago," she said, enjoying his obvious discomfiture. "He is not a murderer *yet*." Her defiance rose. "You must release me. You have no reason to hold me."

"You have been denounced."

"Whatever the denunciations, they are false and you know it."

"We shall see," he said. "Sometimes such things take a great deal of time to investigate."

"Hold me forever if you will. But you will not have *him*."

"We shall see how time softens your resolve." Salvago nodded to the guard. "See her to a cell." The man took her by the arm and picked up her leather packet.

"What is that?" asked Salvago.

"She had it with her this morning, Your Grace."

"Open it."

A moment later the books were spread out on the table. Salvago turned them over one by one. "Boccaccio's *Decameron*. I enjoyed it greatly. Rabelais, *Gargantua and Pantagruel*—a delight. And Erasmus! What hours of pleasure he has given me! My, how your mind has advanced."

"Enough to know what evil is. I didn't need to learn it from books, either. I learned it from you."

He ignored the comment. "So these books are yours?"

Maria did not sense the danger that was coming. "Yes." She said it proudly.

He went to the shelf and drew a small ledger from it. "This is the *Index Librorum Prohibitorum*," he said. "Is your Latin polished enough to know what that is?"

Maria stared at his ledger.

"I need not look to tell you that your books are in the *Index*," he said. "I placed two of them there myself. The possession of these works is a sin."

"Then I will join you in hell, Dun Salvago."

"And this? What is this?" He thumbed through the pages. "*In Light of Lunacy*. A skit, it seems." He found a passage about the Golden Spurs and read it aloud. "If this is not blasphemy, I fear I do not know what is." He looked up at her with triumph in his eyes. He was on very solid ground. "Call him in," he said.

"Never."

❖

The *oubliette*. The forgotten place.

It was called the gagga, the birdcage.

It was a small bell-shaped chamber cut from the living rock below Fort St. Angelo. Situated just outside the door of the Nativity Chapel, it was ten feet below the ground, accessible through a hatchway and ladder. Once the hatch closed, there was only blackness inside, blackness and loneliness and endless time to contemplate the sins of one's existence.

Christien paced in the darkness. *One, two, three, four.* His nose grazed the wall, so close he could feel his own warm breath reflected back at his face. He turned and took four again, stopping precisely in time. The scab on his forehead had taught him the limits of the place, the length of the pace. Now he could do it with his eyes closed—no great achievement, he thought grimly, for eyes open, eyes closed, it was always the same, except for the moment every third day when they brought his food. A guard would open the hatch and toss down food and a skin of water, and snatch up the empty skin he was to leave on the upper ledge. If he failed to leave it, he wouldn't get new water.

He explored every inch of the chamber with his fingers. He found old coats of arms, carved into the rock by prisoners from decades past. He knew little of the history of the pit—only that birth meant nothing there, rank meant nothing there. In the darkness, all knights were equal as they awaited the harsh justice of their Order. Dukes and counts and viscounts, the sons of the noble houses of Europe, knights all: abandoned here until the Grand Master decided their fate, or forgot them altogether.

Most men who entered the *oubliette* left it only to die. Some were hanged, their bodies dumped in the streets until the dogs had done with them. Others were pitched into the Grand Harbor after the humiliation of the defrocking ceremony, in which they were declared *putridium et fetidium.*

Christien expected no mercy. When a lowly knight himself, La Valette had once been sentenced to the galleys for two years, and then to two years in Tripoli. Knights who'd served in that north African town said it was one of the few places on earth worse than the galleys. All that for simple disobedience. La Valette would not have forgotten that, of course. It was what had put the iron rod up that noble ass of his. Christien's crime was more than simple disobedience. La Valette would not suffer his lies gladly.

He prayed a great deal. There were moments when he hoped he would be left with a choice by the Grand Master so that he could redeem himself. Then, as he contemplated that choice, he shunned it in terror.

There were moments when he hoped La Valette would make the choice for him. The best would be if La Valette took his habit and expelled him from the Order in shame. It would mean he could have her. But that would be an even greater perversion of his oath, to so dishonor it for the expediency of having a woman he wanted. Should he let the one sin—the many, now—drive him to even greater sin? Or should he give her up and rededicate himself to his vows?

He doubted La Valette would have ordered him to the *oubliette* if he intended simply to expel him. Yes, there would be punishment. The Grand Master was lord of all who served him. He could order men put to death on a whim, order them imprisoned without trial or evidence. In theory he answered to both God and the Pope. In fact he answered to none but God.

And in this case, Christien knew, God and La Valette were certainly allies.

He knew he was there because of Angela Buqa. No, not really. He was there because he was weak, because he sinned.

He deserved no mercy.

Surely the dogs would have him for dinner.

❖

Despite the urgent instructions of the vicar, the Captain of the Rod could find no one who had lived in M'kor Hakhayyim. The cave was still deserted.

He visited Luca Borg at his work site. "Tell the man Jacobus Pavino that the day he surrenders at the gate of the bishop's palace, your daughter will be released."

"O-of course, Excellency," Luca stammered.

Luca hurried to the vacant cave. He waited for a night and a day, to see if anyone might come. He sat alone in the dark, despairing. *This is how she lives,* he thought. *This is what she prefers to me. This is what has brought her to ruin.*

He knew two names from her life: Elena and Fençu. He'd met Elena, of course, years earlier. Now he wandered the streets of

Mdina, his dignity in shambles, asking discreetly if anyone knew of the prostitute. No one had seen or heard of her. If she was working, it was no longer in those streets.

He went to the arsenal, where he knew Fençu sometimes worked as a carpenter on the Order's galleys. He found him on the second day.

Fençu began to tell Luca where he should look for Jacobus on the south coast, while Fençu himself looked farther north. Luca held up his hands and shook his head. "I want nothing more of her shame," he said. "I have my work."

Fençu recruited Elena, who left Moses with Elli and walked the fields where she knew Jacobus hunted, and the springs where he drew water.

Fençu looked in every cave near M'kor Hakhayyim, calling out in each one, only to hear his voice echoing emptily back. He took his boat to Gozo, where Jacobus had lived as a boy. He walked the cliffs, looking for signs that the birdman might be hunting there once again.

Nothing.

"If he's hiding," Fençu told Elena, "he's too good at it for the likes of us. We won't find him until he wants to be found. Maybe he's dead."

"I don't believe that," Elena said. "But if we can't find him, we must try to rescue her. Maybe we could hire sailors, or—"

"You are mad!"

"She would do it for us. You know it."

"Yes, and she is mad as well." Fençu was no coward, but in this he knew the reality. "Maria is somewhere inside that palace. We don't even know where. It is as strong and well guarded as any fort. There is nothing we can do for her there. Not now. Not without Jacobus."

Elena knew he was right.

❖

The hatch opened. Christien cringed. Even that little light was too much.

The small loaf thumped on his back and dropped to the floor. He scrambled for it. His fingers tore at the bread and he stuffed it in his mouth. He smelled something else, a fragrance he'd all but forgotten. An orange! He scrambled around on his hands and knees, until he found it just next to his latrine. Round and rough and wonderful, and he lay on his back and ate it, skin and seeds and all, the sweet juice running into his beard.

Who?

He took a long drink from the water skin and felt something else unusual. He almost missed it. It was tied to the neck of the water skin. He explored it with his fingers. It was a piece of paper. Someone had sent him a message.

Next time send a candle as well, if you please.

Three days later when the guard came, he was ready. As the hatch opened Christien didn't look up, but stared at the paper in his hands. The reflected light was so bright he had to blink. He squinted and cursed. He had it upside down. He flipped it over, his fingers fumbling in their haste.

The food thumped behind him. The old water skin went up, while a new one came down.

Christien, the note began.

He recognized Bertrand's hand immediately.

Enjoy the orange. It cost you your best pair of boots. We are doing what we can to affect your . . .

The hatch closed. He groaned. It would be three days before more bread came, and he could finish the sentence. "Please don't be long-winded or flowery, my friend," Christien mumbled, "or it will take me a month to read your note."

It touched him deeply that Bertrand risked his own safety to send him food and a message, even though he knew Bertrand always had the sort of luck that permitted him to break every rule of the Order and never get caught.

Three days passed. The hatch opened.

. . . fate, it said. *The Hospitaller has defended you in council. You have many friends in the Order, but the Grand Master is making an example of you. Be strong of heart. I shall not rest until you are freed. Regret Maria Borg . . .*

The gregale was howling outside, and a gust flipped the hatch back with a bang before he could finish. He pounded on the wall, trying to make them think he was dying or going mad. *I am going mad,* he thought. He howled like the gregale and screamed and shrieked. Anything, he thought, to make them open it—for just a moment, just to give him ten seconds of light to see the words that followed.

Regret, Bertrand had written. Bad news, then.

Maria Borg . . . dead?

Maria Borg . . . exiled? What would the Grand Master do to her? Was his own torture not enough, that La Valette had to punish him through her?

What else could it be? Perhaps she'd fallen from a cliff, or—

Salvago. Yes, of course. It wasn't La Valette after all. It was the Inquisitor's Vicar, the devil himself.

He was mad with fear. He cursed Bertrand for telling him anything at all, hated him for leaving him hanging that way.

"La Valette, you bastard, let me out! Let me *see!* I will do anything you ask!"

He pounded until his fists bled, scratched the limestone until his nails cracked and broke, his fury muffled in the solid rock. If they heard his feverish pounding, they ignored it. Two more days he passed in madness. No two days of his life ever spanned such an eternity.

He passed the time reliving every moment they'd spent together. There hadn't been many. He dreamed of her touch, her softness. He cried to her, and cried to God. He didn't know what he wanted. In his despair he kept coming closer to what he knew was the truth, that he'd stepped from the path of honor, the path he'd promised God for the life of his mother, whose words as she lay near death he had not forgotten: *Above all things, a man must do his duty.*

He could not betray the Lord.

There could be no Maria Borg, ever. He had to give her up.

No!

He started to bargain again, for her life. Just as quickly he stopped. *I will not give her up! I will not! Take her from me if you must. Take me if you will—oh, please, take me instead. But I will not make another promise to you I cannot keep.*

The third day he held the paper at the ready. He'd folded a corner of it, so he'd be holding it properly when his precious seconds of lightness came. He waited, staring at it in the pitch-blackness, imagining the words that were to follow.

He heard the noises, the shuffling, the footsteps, the grunting as the hatch went up. As he'd feared, the light brought the darkness:

. . . *taken by Captain of the Rod to the bishop's palace. Will do all possible to help. Bertrand.*

The hatch closed. He crumpled the note and curled into a ball, holding his knees to his chest.

Chapter 34

I n another subterranean prison at the landward end of Birgu, Maria sat in her cell beneath the bishop's palace. She had no cot now, no chair. The room was barren save for a handful of straw, a chamber pot, and a niche in the wall into which a limestone crucifix had been propped. There was a heavy ironwood door with a small hole in it. She stood on her tiptoes to look out. She saw other doors, other holes. She was alone in the room but not in the cellar. She could hear that others were imprisoned there, some of them together. She heard quarrels, and voices that pleaded and threatened and cried. Once she heard a peal of laughter, gay and uninhibited, laughter as misplaced and welcome in that hall as a ray of sunshine.

There was more food than she expected: thin soup and stale bread, and always a jug of brackish water, replenished each morning. *I've had less at home,* she thought. *He must be fattening me up for the slaughter.*

She minded nothing so much as the noises that came when the shadowy men who worked the cellars reverted to methods that were thought to have been ended with the medieval Inquisition. They did not come often, but when they did there was no way to shut them out. Days would pass without a sound, and then she would jump at a sudden groan or shriek. Some noises were softer and came from below her cell. She could almost feel them through the stone: the creak of ropes straining against wood, muffled screams as the efficient machines of the Holy Office did their work. A woman sobbing, softly. The cry of a child—a cry of loss, perhaps, rather than pain. She thought of Moses. There was chanting, and a bell, and the forlorn murmur of a desperate prayer.

Someone approached her door. She heard the soft shuffle of sandals on stone, the rustle of robes. Then silence. Her pulse raced. She stared at the hole, waiting, trying to still her trembling hands. Whoever it was did not look in. She tiptoed to the wall near the door and listened. She held her breath. She knew they were still there, just on the other side, listening to her. She could hear her own heart, its strong beat pounding in her ears. When she could hold her breath no more, she exhaled softly. She waited like that ten minutes, twenty, thirty. Finally, as if she were listening to the flutter of a butterfly's wings, she heard the person on the other side go away.

She waited. Days passed. She prayed and slept and thought of Christien. Callus hadn't told her so, but she knew his arrest must have had something to do with her. She would gladly give her life if they would only let him go. She remembered being a small girl, standing on the ramp near the castle, watching as a knight was hanged for some infraction of the Order's rules. At the time she'd agreed with the older Maltese standing there, who thought it was good riddance and grand entertainment: the island of Malta was lighter by a knight. Soon it might be lighter by one more, because of her.

She tried not to think of Salvago, of what he might do.

She wondered what sort of noises she would make when he finally did it.

❖

When he summoned her, it was to a room one level below hers, the room from which she'd heard the worst of the sounds. There were two guards, *familiares* who led her down the hall toward the stairwell. "God keep you," called a faceless voice from behind one of the ironwood doors. She looked for the source of the voice, but all the grates were empty.

As she descended the cold stone stairs, she thought briefly of trying to run. Her hands were not bound, and surely her captors would never expect such a thing from a woman. But there was no opportunity. One walked close in front, the other just behind.

Her lips moved in silent prayer. *Let it be quick, O Lord.*

Despite her outer calm, her heart was pounding wildly by the bottom step. She stepped into a short corridor that had four doors. They took her to the last one. The door groaned open on heavy iron hinges. There was no one inside. The air was acrid with smoke from two oil lanterns that dimly illuminated the room from opposite walls. There was a long bench in the middle of the room, and a table and chair to one side, where the scribe would sit to make transcripts of confessions. A large box holding leather and iron implements stood on one wall, near iron rings embedded in stone that was grimy with age. Ropes were suspended from the ceiling, supported by heavy beams. Coals burned in a brazier, their ash glowing red and white at the faint breeze of their entry.

The door closed behind her. The room smelled of sweat and urine and fear and blood and burned flesh.

"Unbutton your jerkin," a guard said.

"No."

He drew a knife from his belt. Light glinted dully off its curving blade. "Unbutton your jerkin," he said again, "or I will do it for you."

Her fingers trembled at the buttons. The jerkin parted, exposing a strip of flesh down her front. She wore nothing beneath it. She blushed but stared straight ahead, determined not to cry, or cry out.

"On your back," one of the men said, indicating the long table. Now she shook her head. She backed away from the table, but they caught her roughly by the arms and forced her down. She struggled wildly, scratching and kicking. They lifted her bodily onto the table. One of them held her while the other tied straps to her wrists, securing them to wooden rods near the floor. He did it with practiced moves, as quickly as he might truss a hog for slaughter. He did the same to her ankles, so that she lay spread-eagled on her back, staring at the low ceiling. She was sobbing softly, her breath ragged now, as fear gripped her more tightly. As the man finished, one side of her jerkin fell free, exposing one of her breasts.

In vain she tried to wriggle in a way that would lessen her exposure.

The *familiares* stood near the foot of the table for what seemed an eternity. She felt their eyes on her. She closed her eyes, trying to shut everything out, but the blackness was worse. She opened them again and stared at a hook protruding from one of the heavy ceiling beams. The room was suffocatingly hot. Beads of sweat trickled down her temples, as waves of horror washed over her and through her. She willed herself to remain strong. *Our Father, who art in heaven . . .*

She heard the door open. The guards stood a little straighter. She turned her head, straining to see, but she couldn't. She gave up. She didn't need to see. She knew who it was. He stood silently for long minutes. Her breathing went through its cycles: steady, then more rapid, then ragged, more sob than gasp, then steady again. She knew it was the only sound in the room. She couldn't make it stop.

"Leave us."

The guard looked puzzled. "Your Grace?"

"I will summon the scribe should I need him. Leave us."

Casting a last appreciative and disappointed glance at the woman on the table, the *familiares* hurried from the room.

The door closed on worn, heavy hinges. Salvago stood for a long while without moving, without speaking. Now she could hear him breathing. She felt his presence, as she had felt it on the other side of her door.

"Let me go," she whispered. "By all that is holy, Dun Salvago, do not do this."

He walked around to her side. She saw he carried a birch rod, the end of it shredded and stained. He looked at her, his eyes moving slowly from her head to her foot, his gaze lingering on every curve, every swell. She bit her lip until it bled.

With the tip of the rod, he lightly traced a line along her flesh from the base of her throat to her navel. She recoiled at the touch. She strained at her ropes and let out a muffled sob.

He walked around her, pausing just at her head. He leaned to watch her, to look into her eyes. She stared back at him, her eyes wild now with undisguised fear and hatred. Her chest was heaving, as much as she tried to still it. She felt her nakedness and her vulnerability, felt the touch of his gaze the same as if his hands were upon her.

"Your eyes are remarkably steady," he said, "for someone in your position. Perhaps not as fearless as you would like them to be, I suspect."

He straightened up and looked at her chest. Slowly, deliberately, he started to reach for her jerkin.

"*Please,*" she whispered.

His hand stopped, poised just above her nipple. "I did not ask them to do this, Maria. You must believe that." Then, with a delicate motion, he took the loose edge of the jerkin and covered her. He set the rod down next to her on the table. Slowly, deliberately, he began to button the jerkin, his long fingers working carefully, starting at the bottom and working his way up. Twice she felt his flesh as a finger brushed against her.

Again she let out a muffled sob.

Salvago finished the last button. His face was close to hers.

"When last we spoke you mocked me for feeling fear, Maria. Perhaps now you understand something more of that feeling." His voice was soft, soothing. "I assure you, the fear is nothing compared to the reality of what might still happen to you here in this room." His finger lightly traced the notch at the base of her neck and lingered there. Then, noticing a strand of hair out of place, he carefully brushed it from her forehead, and gently smoothed it back. "Do you believe that, Maria?"

Almost imperceptibly she nodded.

She felt the warmth of his breath on her face. His lips were at her ear.

"I wish you no harm, Maria Borg. I will send your father to see you. Perhaps you will persuade him to work a little harder on your behalf—or the next time I meet you in this room, I fear the restraint for which I've prayed today might fail me altogether."

"I will not."

"Oh, but you will. I reread something you had when you came here—a skit penned by the Knight de Vries."

He saw from her eyes that his guess was right. He had brooded for the longest time over Angela's scheme, and then finally, when he heard that de Vries had been imprisoned for a dalliance with a commoner, he had put it together, ashamed at his own slowness of thought. His sister had acted from jealousy, because Christien de

Vries was sleeping with Maria Borg, and Angela wanted Christien. People were so simple, their sins so predictable. Lust or avarice: when did men—or women—act for any other reason? For his purposes there was nothing earth-shattering in such a base revelation. It was merely another arrow he might pull from the Lord's quiver, another weapon to force Maria to help him bring an assassin to justice.

He leaned near her, to whisper the lie. "The play is blasphemous, of course. Your lover was released from the Order's prison, and now I have arrested him."

Her eyes went wide in horror. "That is not possible! He is a Knight of the Order! You have no authority over him!"

"Perhaps so. The Grand Master himself has made that argument to the bishop. Only the Holy Father himself can decide now. I'm sure he will . . . in good time. For now your lover is down the hall from us. Perhaps you heard him last night. You must hear such horrid sounds."

She struggled against her bonds. "You are the devil himself," she whispered.

"It will all go away, Maria. The knight can be freed. All you need do is call Jacobus in." As if he had timed it that way, they heard a muffled scream. A man's.

He smiled tenderly and brushed a tear from her cheek with the back of his hand. "Call the birdman in, Maria," he whispered. "Call him in."

With that he left the room.

❖

When Luca came he stood outside the door, looking through the little window. He was shocked at her appearance. "They told me you would say where I could find Jacobus," he said. "They said you would know how to reach him, and what I should say to him."

"I don't know. I don't know. Have you any word of Christien— of the knight Fra de Vries, Father? Did they tell you anything? Is he alive?"

"I know nothing of any such man. What has he to do with this? What have you become involved in? How can you have done such wrong?"

She pushed back against the wall, her knees drawn up to her chest. "If I knew where Jacobus was, I would tell you," she said, weeping.

And then she shook her head. "I would never tell you. Tell him I would die first before I would choose. Tell him he must kill me."

✤

He counted the days. It was one hundred and twelve now—or one hundred and thirteen. He couldn't be certain what time it was outside, whether it was night or day, raining or boiling, whether the gregale was howling or the doldrums stilled the harbor.

His beard was long. Every third or fourth feeding brought a surprise from Bertrand, a piece of meat or fruit or a nougat, but it was never enough. His belly rumbled always, shrinking at the same time the pile of excrement in the corner pit was growing: both changing, in awful little bits.

He began to think he would die here, in the birdcage.

He found a spot of wall that had no carving. He drew her face, using a pebble to scratch against the stone, to make the lines. He checked it constantly with his fingers, to be certain she was still there, to be certain he had not imagined her. Every day she returned, faithfully there each time, to greet him. She was but a wisp in the rock, as lightly drawn as a cloud, but he could feel her, feel the contours of her neck, the sweep of her hair, the touch of her cheek, the lovely eyes. He kissed her lips, kissed her neck. He whispered to her, and dreamed with her, and made plans with her.

I don't want to die. I must live long enough to see you again.

He exercised, determined not to let himself wither. His muscles cooperated for increasingly short periods of time, when they would cramp, or quiver uncontrollably, or refuse his commands to move. He found insects in his hair and ate them.

His prayers to God were said aloud, as he said most things aloud. His voice was jarring in the confined space, but it was the only way he could be certain he was still alive. If he closed his eyes and fell silent, he would be dead. He knew it.

Somehow Bertrand managed to get him a water skin filled with brandy. *Happy Carnival,* the note said. Christien drank it like the water. He sang and danced and had a one-man parade. He recited lines he remembered from *Lunacy* and laughed out loud until he cried. He nursed a hangover for two days.

He shivered most of the time, a shiver that ran hot and then cold and then hot again, a shiver of sweat and tears. There was precious little air circulation. He found a spot where fresh air seemed to come into the birdcage, but like the food, it was never enough. He all but used it up, just before they came to feed him. When he felt he could hardly draw another breath, the hatch would open. A bit of air would circulate, while another morsel was thrown to the dog and the hatch closed again.

The dog howled.

❖

Fençu never found Jacobus. Jacobus found him, when he was ready. He appeared one Sabbath morning at the cave where they were living, scaring Moses and Elena half out of their wits. He moved stiffly, and his right arm hung limply at his side.

Upon leaving the Infirmary, he told them, he'd hidden in the fields, afraid to come to M'kor Hakhayyim for fear they'd be looking for him. The injury had become infected. He'd fallen into a fever and nearly died. Some men had taken him in to a cave at Ghar il-Kbir, near Rabat, and nursed him back to health. Now the muscles in his chest and shoulders were shriveled, his right arm all but useless. "I'll never swing from the ropes over the cliffs again," he told Fençu, "but it doesn't matter. I've only come to beg the use of a weapon. I won't fail a second time."

Fençu glanced at Elena. "They have Maria," he said.

All the color left his face. "What?"

"She's been in the bishop's dungeons for months. Her father came to see me again only last week, pleading that I find you." He looked away. "Maria begged him not to come, but the Captain of the Rod threatened him with her life."

Jacobus struggled for control. "What are they asking?"

"They want you. Otherwise they say they will never release her. She'll die there, Jacobus."

Jacobus walked to the entrance of the cave and stood looking out at the sea. He knew it was over. Salvago had won. There would be no revenge. And then the noise that rose from his throat sounded more like a wounded bull than a man, and in the cave they heard it and tended to their business and tried to close it out. It was another hour before he came back. "I must give him what he wants," he said.

"There *must* be another way," Elena said.

"Yes, I think so, too," said Fençu, without much conviction. "Come, eat with us now. We'll think of something together."

Elli served them stewed turtle. They sat drinking *rozolin* until late that night, talking and plotting. Jacobus suggested kidnapping Salvago. They could demand Maria's release in exchange for him. They would steal a boat, and once she was free they would cross to Sicily and make a new life.

"The bishop will never allow such a thing to succeed," Fençu said. "Everyone with a brother or wife in the dungeons would be making off with his priests."

"How can he stop it? His vicar will be returned to him without a head," Jacobus said hotly.

"He'll get a new vicar," Fençu said, shrugging. "They can't be that hard to come by."

"And Maria?" Elena asked. "What do you think would become of her if we did that?"

Jacobus had no answer for that. He nursed his drink.

Elena suggested a direct assault. "We can do it late at night. Capture a guard and make him tell us where she is. We could have her away before they knew we were there." Jacobus brightened.

"Two of us cannot do it," said Fençu.

"Three of us," Elena said. "*I* will help you."

"*Three* of us cannot do it," said Fençu.

Jacobus sat up, his interest aroused. "I'm certain I can find men in Ghar il-Kbir who will help. They're all Jews, scoundrels and night men." He caught himself and flushed. "I'm sorry. I didn't mean—"

Fençu waved it off. "I know what you mean. What about them?"

"They've been persecuted for years. They despise the Church," he said, his enthusiasm growing. "If only we could pay, I could get a dozen such men."

"We can." Elena hurried to her niche and took her money box from its hiding place. "Maria has more, but I don't know where. I'm sure if we look we'll find it." She tipped the box. There was a glittering pile of fourteen golden ducats and a score of smaller coins. It was everything she had in the world. Her eyes shone like the money.

"If we can raise just a few more men," Fençu said, looking at the pile, "we can do it."

Jacobus set off at dawn with a bulging money purse on his belt. Fençu busied himself with his arsenal, which consisted of three old muskets, two crossbows, a halberd, and an assortment of knives and swords. Elena and Elli helped him clean and sharpen the weapons. "We'll have her out by tomorrow night," she said confidently.

When Jacobus returned his face told the story before he opened his mouth. "They are cowards," he spat. "They wanted no part of it." He put Elena's money on the table. "They said they'd rather face the Turk than the Church."

"There are others," Fençu said. Near dusk the other men of the cave returned—Cawl, the silversmith; Villano, the water seller; and Cataldo, the boot maker. All of them loved Maria and listened carefully as Fençu outlined his plan.

"It would be insurrection," said Villano.

"I'm too old," said Cataldo.

"I have a family," said Cawl.

"You're all spineless," Fençu snapped. "Even Elena is not afraid. Will you not stand behind her skirts with a weapon?" He heaped shame upon dishonor and dished it to them for an hour, but to no avail. They moped around the cave and found excuses to leave.

For a long while no one said anything. Elena busied herself with Elli, tending to the stew pot. Fençu wrapped and stored his weapons. Jacobus slumped on the floor near the fire. He rested his head on his knees and was silent. When he looked up his eyes were red. "There is no other way," he said. "It must be done."

Elena began to cry. Fençu only nodded. Jacobus went outside and found himself a niche in the rocks, where he watched the sun come up. He gave his fishing line, hooks, and two knives to Fençu. He removed his shoes and gave them to Elena. "They're for Moses," he said, "when his feet get big enough."

Later that morning he presented himself at the bishop's palace gate.

At the explicit instructions of the vicar, the guards led him through the corridor that contained her cell. They stopped and pushed him to the door, his face at the grille. He looked inside, trying to adjust to the dim light. "*Maria!*" he whispered when he saw her.

"Jacobus!" She flew to the door, but he was already gone. She pressed her face to the opening. All she could see was empty corridor. "Jacobus! Jacobus!" She pounded on the door. There was no response.

She heard the noises again that night. This time she knew the throat that made them. She wrapped her arms around her head, trying to shut them out.

It was nearly two days before they stopped.

❖

They came for Christien in early April.

He'd been in the *oubliette* nearly nine months. Two men stood ready to support him by the elbows, but he stepped from the hole and stood alone, a bit wobbly but upright. The hardest thing was adjusting to the bright Maltese sun. His eyes watered and ran and his head ached from it, but he relished the sight of things long unseen: the chapel, and the ramp that led down alongside the wharf, and the galleys and the fishing boats in the harbor, and the gulls overhead, and the walls and streets of Birgu, filled with noisy people and dogs and pigs and garbage. He blinked at it all in wonder and awe, thankful to be alive.

He looked for her face in the crowds. Of course she wouldn't know he was there, any more than he could know whether she was still alive.

They took him to the auberge. "You've the morning to clean yourself and rest," the master-at-arms told him. "We are to present you to the Grand Master this afternoon."

It was not a good sign, he thought, that they did not simply tell him to present himself as an act of honor. They must think he would run, fearing the sentence to be pronounced. He had given long thought to what he was going to do. If La Valette gave him a choice, he was prepared to make it, and he was not going to run.

Bartholomew, his page, greeted him eagerly. "Sire, forgive me, I didn't know you were coming. I would have prepared. I'll get water for a bath and a barber for your hair."

"Never mind all that now," Christien said. "Just find Fra Cuvier for me, quickly." He was desperate for news.

Christien got the cook to heat water and sent another page for a barber. He took a lukewarm bath, trying to rinse the stench of confinement from his pores. By the time the barber finished, Christien felt a new man.

It was late morning when Bertrand burst in and lifted him off his feet. They embraced warmly. "There's nothing left of you," Bertrand said. "I'm sorry I couldn't send more food."

Christien started to say something in thanks, but Bertrand waved him off with a grin, immediately producing brandy and two cups. He filled Christien's and handed it to him. He knew exactly where to start with his news. "They let her out, Christien," he said, "two months ago. She's alive. I met her when she came out. I offered her my help, but she insisted she was all right and would accept nothing from me. She asked only of you. I must say I was taken with her. She seems an extraordinary woman."

Christien couldn't say anything. He nodded, his eyes brimming. He took a long drink and felt the brandy burning inside as wonderfully as the news. He walked to the window of the auberge and looked out to the street below.

"I have other news," Bertrand said, his voice different. Christien turned, knowing from his tone that it was not good. "It's about Joseph."

"Callus? What is it? Is he all right?"

"He's dead, Christien. The Grand Master had him hanged."

Stunned, Christien sat. "The Grand Master! What—" He stopped. He could guess.

"He wrote a letter to the king, complaining about the Order's authoritarian tactics and petitioning for greater autonomy for the Università, or some such foolishness. The letter was intercepted before it ever left the island. It was sedition, Christien. The Grand Master could not let it pass. *Je suis désolé.*"

Christien threw his cup to the wall, splattering brandy all over the room. The cup clattered to the floor. "I always told him his politics

would get him hanged," he said. "May God *damn* his stubborn soul."
Christien kicked the cup. "God, how I hate politics," he said. "God,
how I hate this bloody place."

"Let us hope you fare better with La Valette," Bertrand said. "They
took a vote in full council yesterday, so there must have been some
disagreement about your case. I haven't been able to get word of their
decision."

"You've always been a betting man, my friend," Christien said.
"Where is your money on this?"

Bertrand paced. "In truth, I think the Grand Master wants your
head. The rumors of Turkish mischief are growing. While La Valette
can always use a good surgeon, as a commander what he needs more
is absolute order in the Order. My guess is that he'll . . ." His voice
trailed off. He drained his cup. "*Merde,* my friend. My guess is that
he'll make you an example."

"Please, find Maria for me," Christien said.

"After all that has happened? Are you truly so stupid? What if I'm
wrong? If La Valette intends a pardon, this would change his mind.
He would knot your noose himself and you'd be swinging by
nightfall. Besides, you're confined to the auberge, and I'd never get
her in."

"If they hang me this afternoon, I want to see her one last time.
If they don't—if he gives me a choice—I still need to see her,
Bertrand. One last time."

"So you have made your choice."

Christien nodded. "Although I must confess my heart is not in it,
particularly after hearing of Joseph. He was one of the few truly good
men I ever met. I wonder how far a man can go to defend this bloody
Order."

"As I wonder how far you will go to honor that oath," Bertrand
said. "I think you are a fool, my friend. But if that is your decision,
you are even more foolish to see her."

"Bertrand, I don't want to argue this with you. Just find her for
me."

Bertrand sighed. "Tell me where to look. If it can be done, I will
do it."

❖

La Valette was in his library, writing a letter. He looked up at Christien as casually as if his knight had been gone barely an hour. His expression was as imperious and unreadable as ever. He did not set down his pen. The tip of the quill scratched busily on paper as he talked.

"I trust you have had time to reflect upon your sacred oaths?"

"I have, sire."

"I expect you would like me to make it easy for you, to give you a choice of leaving the Order or honoring your vows."

"I expect nothing, sire, in a decision that is rightly yours. If you give me a choice, I will make it."

"There is no choice. A man does not reinvent his vows as matters suit him, and you shall not do so today. I will ask a different question, then. What would you do with you were you Grand Master?"

"In honesty, sire, I would have me hanged."

La Valette kept writing. "And it was my first thought to do that as well. Fortunately for your neck, cooler heads have prevailed. Chevalier Romegas departs on the morrow for the season's campaigns. You will serve three caravans with him."

Three caravans. Three years in the galleys.

❖

Bertrand missed her at the ramparts, at the quarry, and again at the kilns. It was after dark when he appeared at M'kor Hakhayyim, only to discover she'd gone to Mdina with Elena, whose son, Moses, had taken ill. In Mdina he asked at a dozen houses before he found the one that belonged to the witch Lucrezia, who told him they'd already gone. He returned to the cave. She still had not returned, so he left word with Fençu, telling him that Christien was being sent away in the morning with the fleet. Dejected, Bertrand returned to the auberge. Christien could do nothing but write her a note.

Maria got word late that night from Fençu, too late to do anything. She was waiting at the wharf at dawn. There were already crowds there, watching from vantage points all around Birgu Creek as the Order's galleys were readied for departure. She found a perch atop a wall near the Church of St. Lawrence. She desperately wanted to get closer to the flagship, so that if she saw him she could call to him, but then she worried she might further endanger him, so she stayed where she was.

There were five galleys, their sterns to the quay. Provisions and oars were being loaded at a feverish pace. It was a scene being repeated in every port from Istanbul to Algiers, from Marseilles to Venice, from Djerba to Valencia, as galleys were readied to prey upon enemy coasts and shipping. It was the deadly sport of the age, and among the great seamen, the Arabs and Turks, the Moors and renegade Christians, no one but Dragut was better at it than the knights making this caravan. Their robust commander, Romegas, went cheerfully about his ship in white blouse and leather doublet, personally testing shrouds, checking canvas, shouting orders, making certain all was ready aboard his freshly scrubbed galley. A pet monkey followed close behind, leaping from post to tiller to oar, chattering its own commands.

"Maria!" She turned and saw Bertrand, pushing his way through the crowd. He handed her a folded paper. "He'll have no chance to see you now. He asked me to give you this." She took the letter gratefully, and he hurried off. She sat on the wall and opened the paper, the hubbub around her lost in his words.

My darling Maria,

I scribble this in haste. It is nearly dawn, and there is little time before we sail. How I wish I could hold you.

You must know that I love you as I have never loved before. Through these long months, only thoughts of you kept me sane.

I thought long about what I would do if the Grand Master gave me a choice—whether I would kneel before him and renew my vows, or kneel before you and renounce them. Part of me wishes I had had that choice, and that I would have felt the freedom to follow my heart. Part of me is glad I did not, knowing that I could not.

Through my sentence at sea, the Grand Master simply reminds me of that which I already knew, that I have given my oath to God and to him. How I wish it were not so.

My heart will always be with you.

Inhobbok. I love you.

Christien

She looked up again, tears streaming down her face. Hundreds of bronze-skinned slaves marched to the dock, naked and double file, their fetters scraping over the cobbles as they trudged from their winter prison on land to their summer prison at sea. They streamed onto the ships, to be chained three abreast to the sheepskin-draped pine benches where they would row and sleep and eat and relieve themselves until the end of the caravan, or until death released them.

The slaves had just finished boarding when she saw him. He was walking in the midst of other knights, and she had to strain to see him. His hair was thick and black but his face was wan, his step a bit unsteady. She put her hand to her mouth, watching as he walked along the quay and stepped onto the planking to the flagship. She saw him looking in the crowd for her.

Look this way, my love, she breathed. *Look this way.* But his back was to her. He stepped onto the ship and she lost sight of him among the arquebusiers and swordsmen and archers, taking their places upon the crowded decks. Porters stocked hen coops and animal pens, and loaded the last of the stores, food and barrels of wine and boxes of ammunition.

Soldiers secured deck guns against their chocks. On the corsia that ran between banks of slaves, the overseer tested his whip against the mast, its tip snapping like a gunshot. A bell pealed in St. Anne's Chapel. From the ramparts of Fort St. Angelo, the Grand Master watched, his silver hair lit white by the sun.

Romegas stood behind his pilot on the poop deck, issuing his instructions. Shouted orders echoed quickly through the fleet, carried out with military precision. The last of the porters stepped ashore, and the gangplanks were withdrawn. The bosun's silver pipe shrilled once. The slaves took up their oars, waiting. The pipe shrilled twice.

Thrum. The tambour drummed. The oarsmen heaved backward on their benches, their backs arching and arms straining as they threw their weight into the looms of their oars. The galley shuddered and began to move.

Thrum. The other galleys followed suit. There were scattered shouts from shore as Rhodiots and Greeks and Maltese wished their fleet well.

"Christien," she whispered, desperately seeking his face on the deck. He was nowhere to be seen. Pennons fluttering, the flagship nosed out of the deep creek toward the main channel.

There! He emerged onto the upper deck at last, moving to the rail. She ran barefoot along the street and onto the quay, hair streaming as she tried to keep up, tried to stay with him.

"Christien!" Her shout was lost in the noise.

The galley turned out of the creek and into the harbor. She lost him again as the galley disappeared behind the promontory of St. Angelo.

Thrum. She ran across the narrow neck of Birgu to the opposite side of the peninsula, pushing her way past vendors and old women and pigs. She could go no farther than the curtain wall behind the Infirmary. After a moment she saw the iron-tipped ram of the galley pulsing into view again as it passed the fort, long oars gracefully skimming the smooth water of the harbor, the morning sun glinting from droplets thrown with each sweep. Water poured from the cutwater of the prow in a thin curl that shimmered in a rainbow of colors.

Thrum. The faces at the rail were growing too small to make out. Two other galleys stroked into view, and two more, their decks spotted red with the *sobravestes* of knights making this caravan.

She fell to her knees, watching in despair as, for the second time in her life, a galley carried away someone she loved. One had belonged to the enemy, the other to the Order. There seemed little difference.

Thrum. The ships passed Gallows Point and into the open sea. Puffs of white smoke appeared as the guns of St. Elmo thundered farewell and Godspeed. The sails of the flagship were unfurled and hoisted, whipping and bucking as the winds filled them.

Thrum. She began to cry. "Christien," she whispered. "Christien, Christien. I love you."

As one, the galleys turned toward Africa.

Thrum. And then he was gone.

Book Six

THE SIEGE

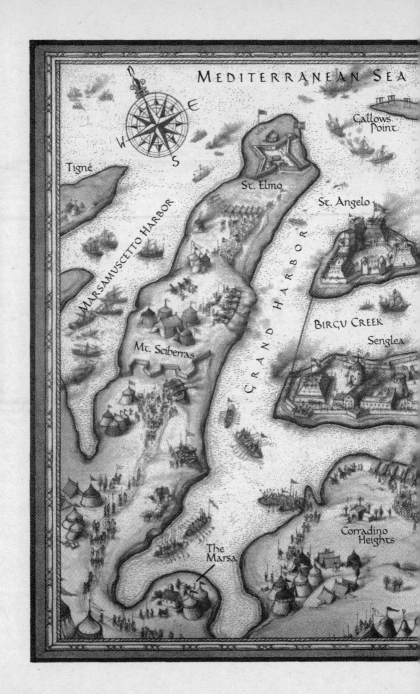

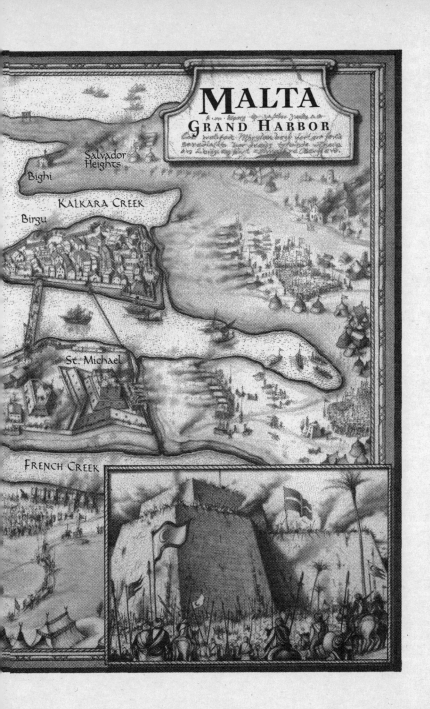

MALTA
GRAND HARBOR

Salvador Heights

Bighi

KALKARA CREEK

Birgu

St. Michael

FRENCH CREEK

from *The Histories of the Middle Sea*

by Darius, called the Preserver
Court Historian to the People's Sun, the Sultan Achmet

It is well recorded that in the third year of his reign, Suleiman had driven the Order from their fortress of Rhodes. The young Sultan was greatly moved by the gallantry of the knights who so bravely defended their island. Rather than executing those who survived, as was his right, he showed them mercy, allowing them to sail away in exile. He did so after the Grand Master, L'Isle Adam, gave his solemn oath that the Order of St. John would never again raise arms against the Ottomans.

The oath was broken as quickly as it was made. Even now the knights interfered with the holy pilgrimage of the faithful to Mecca, and their raids grew bolder with time. In recent years the Order had taken nearly fifty Muslim ships. Most lately Romegas had captured the Sultana, *a ship owned collectively by the Chief White Eunuch, the women of the seraglio, and the Sultan's own daughter, Mirahmar. Her favorite nurse, an old woman, was taken captive along with the governor of Alexandria, and of course the ship's holds were brimming with precious cargo. In the great ebb and flow of events of empire, it was but a minor thorn in Suleiman's side, yet it inspired the mullahs to soaring rhetoric in their calls for jihad against the godless knights. It was one thing to plunder, the mullahs said, but the Order's interference with the pilgrimage was an affront to Allah.*

To capture the island of the knights would right an old wrong and give the Ottomans command of a strategic jewel, permitting the Sultan to marshal his forces there should he decide to move against Sicily and Italy. Time was critical, Suleiman's viziers counseled him, for the Christian allies remained weak after their great defeat at Djerba. It was important to strike before they could regain their strength.

A further advantage lay in the disarray of the European courts and the diplomatic isolation of the knights. It did not require an astute observer to see that there would be precious little help to the island from the Christian princes of Europe. The German emperor was occupied with his own borders, which the Ottomans were harrying at every opportunity. The French King Charles was a mere boy of fourteen, and firmly under the thumb of his mother, Catherine de Médicis. Mother was leading son on a tour of France, which was preoccupied by the religious conflicts that would so consume it in years to come. Why journey a fortnight to kill a Turk when there were so many Huguenots near at hand? Besides, the king had treaties with the Porte to honor, treaties of commerce and prosperity. While Charles would give no aid to Suleiman, the many French knights among the Order would simply have to fend for themselves, with the good wishes of a grateful king.

The English queen would sit upon her Protestant throne and lament the loss of a Christian citadel, but her hand was too weak to be raised in defense of a nest of troublesome Catholic knights, particularly if in so doing she might lend aid to the Spanish. The Pope had few troops, and what little money he had was dedicated to exterminating the Calvinists and Lutherans seething like serpents at his door.

Only Philip, the Spanish king, was in a position to do anything at all. If Malta fell, it was his own soft Sicilian belly that would next feel the sting of the Ottoman scorpion. Yet his resources were spread thin, and his long-standing enmity with other European rulers only added to his difficulties.

Finally, Suleiman believed that the Maltese themselves so hated the foreign knights who ruled them that they would do little to help them in a fight.

It was time to strike.

—From Volume VII
The Great Campaigns: Malta

Chapter 35

Asha stood atop a wall overlooking a garden of Topkapi, gazing out over the Golden Horn. He was twenty-three now, his features boyish, but hardened and bronzed by his years at sea. He wore a light silk robe, and a turban adorned by a small yet perfect emerald, an exquisite gift from a grateful Sultan.

As always when he stood in that spot, he felt the majesty and beauty and grace of the Abode of Felicity, while behind him he felt the serenity of the Abode of Bliss, the palace where the wind whispered through silks and cypress, and gazelles paused to drink from cool bubbling fountains, all at the very center of the universe.

Truly, he thought, in all the world there was no more magnificent sight than the hills of Istanbul, sparkling with golden domes of the mosques, their minarets pointing toward heaven, and the empire's ships plying the Bosphorus, where Asia and Europe met.

Truly, nothing could be so stirring as the sight of Suleiman's forces preparing for war, on those hills and the arsenal and docks below them, now teeming with the Sultan's new resolve.

Truly, nothing could be so troubling as the knowledge that the hammer of God was poised to strike, and that the anvil was Malta, the land of his birth.

The five years since the great victory at Djerba had been good to him. He'd towed three ships laden with slaves and rich cargo back to Istanbul. It was then the Sultan had given him the emerald. After that he'd cruised the coasts of Crete and the Morea, learning every inlet and current and cove. He'd sailed a season with Piali Pasha, the admiral, and most lately had his own squadron of four galleys, with which he raided the coasts of Dalmatia.

In one off-season he'd overseen the construction of his own galley, remembering well the lessons of Leonardus—the lessons, he thought wryly, that would *not* send a ship to the bottom. He knew the result would have pleased the shipwright. The galley was sleek and fast and built of fig wood, like the Sultan's own, and was the envy of every captain in the fleet. He could see her now in her berth as his crew prepared her for the voyage. Most Turkish captains chose Italian names for their vessels, and he followed suit: his was called *Alisa*. He lovingly carved the name himself, in a piece of sandalwood that graced the deck. He still dreamed of encountering Romegas once more. How sweet it would be to send him to his grave with a shot fired from the *Alisa!* Alas, the sea was big and he'd never seen the man again, but perhaps now he would have his chance after all. The whole of his last year had been taken up with preparations for war, a war that might somehow bring him once again face-to-face with the demon himself.

Allah moved in mysterious ways.

In the week since Asha had arrived at the Sublime Porte, he had prayed with the Sultan, who had extended this great honor to select *aghas* and captains. In the private mosque near the Has Odasi, Suleiman knelt with his men before their common master. Asha was humbled that the Lord of the Age remembered him, calling him by name. Suleiman's court still embodied all the magnificence of the empire, and yet, Asha saw, the Shadow of God had truly become a shadow himself. Granted, he was seventy, but somehow it seemed a violation of Allah's covenant that His Deputy on Earth should be touched by time.

Suleiman seemed more melancholy than before. He was certainly paler, his face stricken with the pains of age. He had gout and was swollen with some malady the court physicians could not cure. As Asha's lips touched the hem of his robe, he worried for his master's health. He knew well the tragedies that had befallen him. All the empire whispered of them. His wife, Roxelana, whom he worshiped with poetry and flowers, had died suddenly. Not long after, he had had another of his sons, the prince Bayezid, strangled with a bowstring, the unfortunate result of family politics. There were other troubles in the empire, it was true. Suleiman's shoulders stooped now, with the cares of his office and the burdens of his lonely grief.

Yet for all the ordinary troubles of empire, none could long doubt that he was still the Sultan of the Two Continents and the Emperor of the Two Seas. Proof of it now lay in the Golden Horn, its waters boiling with the fever of war. His forces were gathering from every corner of the empire—forces beyond measure, all to be directed at the Knights of St. John and their home of Malta.

The reasons for the decision to invade Malta were manifest and just. No citizen of the empire doubted it. So the preparations were ordered, to be mounted against an enemy whose weaknesses were readily apparent. Asha saw with his own eyes the clay relief models, fashioned by spies of the Porte who had disguised themselves as fishermen and spent the previous winter in Malta, measuring her fortifications. Their work showed that the island had changed little since his youth, when his father was working on the new fort, St. Elmo. Now St. Elmo lorded over the entrance to Grand Harbor, while St. Michael protected Senglea and St. Angelo protected Birgu—but they were hardly invincible. Birgu had built a wall protecting its landward end. Mdina, the inland city of the nobles, and the *castello* on the island of Gozo were still isolated citadels. The spies' work seemed thorough enough, and the older commanders looked at the knights' lair with satisfaction. "It is but a shadow of their defenses at Rhodes," Mustapha Pasha said. The old general had served Suleiman in Hungary, and was to be the land commander of the invasion. He had fought at Rhodes, where the knights had spent two hundred years erecting the most formidable defenses known to man—defenses the Ottomans had broken. Despite the efforts the Grand Master had obviously put into strengthening Malta, her walls and forts would be but stalks of wheat before the scythe of Suleiman.

Yes, all the historical, political, and military signs were auspicious. The soothsayers and the astrologers read their leaves and consulted the heavens, and they agreed: there was no better time to strike. Everyone knew the island was full of men who would die well and hard in her defense. Malta would not fall easily, but she would fall. Men had predicted it for years, and now, as if to put the seal of God on the prophecy, Suleiman's *firman* decreed it should be so.

The preparations were enormous, even by Ottoman standards. As Asha looked down upon the Golden Horn, it was hard to find a patch of open water. It was a magnificent fleet of nearly two hundred ships—galleys and galliots and the great galleasses called mahonnas; and bigger still the roundships, huge merchantmen that swallowed war matériel like ravenous dragons.

Over the winter and spring the foundries of Istanbul had roared white-hot as artillery was forged and cast for battle. No one on earth had mastered artillery like the Turks, and some of the new pieces were so large that they had to be transported in pieces on special carriages built just for them. They had iron axles and wheels that stood as tall as a horse. They could fire massive iron balls, of which countless tens of thousands rolled from the armament sheds. One such basilisk was so large it required its own galley. Shields and armor stood in great piles, beside thousands of cases of shot for the smaller arms. There were endless barrels of powder to feed all the guns— forty thousand quintals in all. "Surely the whole island of Malta itself," the armorers said, "does not weigh forty thousand quintals."

Troops who had trained endlessly over the winter now streamed toward the waiting ships, some in the Golden Horn, others near Izmit. There would be nearly forty thousand fighting men when all loaded, plus those men needed to support them. From all over Anatolia, from Karesi and Konya and Teke, Sipahis poured in, the cavalrymen sent by their *sanjak beys* in answer to the Sultan's call. There were the Iayalars, the fanatics who would hurl themselves into the mouths of Christian guns, praying for death in the holy cause. There were mercenaries—renegade Christians, Greeks, and Levantines with their own ships and men, eager to buy favor with the Porte. And of course the fleet would be joined by the Sultan's Barbary allies, ships carrying fierce Arabs and Berbers and Moors, all thirsting for Christian blood. The cream of all these forces were the Janissaries. More than six thousand of them would carry the Sultan's holy fire to his enemies and set them alight with it.

The quays sagged under all the freight required to sustain the force during the siege, for their target was a barren rock that would neither feed nor clothe nor shelter them. Donkeys brayed as they struggled with supply wagons, carrying leagues of cables and ropes, and a city of tents, and sheets of canvas for sails and for making screens to hide troop movements on an island where there were few places to hide. There were bales of cotton and extra clothing and blankets and medical supplies. There were picks and shovels and pry bars for the sappers, the men who dug mines under defensive fortifications. Horses were loaded onto the merchantmen in special holds. A few would be used for reconnaissance and light patrols by the cavalry, while others would help drag the heavy cannons up from the beaches to their positions.

Asha himself had spent six months on the Black Sea where the forests were thick, helping oversee the construction of twenty new galleys to add to the fleet. Then, with other captains, he'd conducted lightning raids on the coasts of the Aegean, enslaving oarsmen from Anatolia to Greece to the Morea, oarsmen needed to propel the massive armada.

Now Asha trembled at the might arrayed against his boyhood home. The din was enormous as the army boarded its ships. Men shouted and bands played and dervishes whirled among the troops, whipping them to battle frenzy. Greater invasions had been mounted by the Ottomans, but always by land, never by sea. Surely the little island could not long stand against such power as he saw arrayed around the Golden Horn.

It was still his secret, of course, that he was Maltese. The deception born long ago on the advice of Leonardus, to say his home was Venice, had nearly gotten him killed at the hand of Iskander. Now that lie would mean he would see service against his former homeland—a conflict those who oversaw the *devshirme* were always careful to avoid.

It had first hit home when he sat quietly in the seraglio, as the commanders spoke with Suleiman. Mustapha Pasha was there, along with Piali Pasha, with whom Dragut and Asha had shared the victory at Djerba. Piali was still a young man, married to the daughter of Selim, the Sultan's sole surviving son and heir apparent. He would command the precious fleet of ships that would carry the invasion forces. There was also Dragut, who had no official role—save the blessing of his Sultan, who would not be leading the invasion. "Mustapha, look upon Piali as thy son," he said. "Piali, reverence Mustapha as thy father. And both of you shall listen to Dragut as if his voice were the Sultan's own."

These were men of legend, men Asha revered. He listened, oddly detached, as they calmly discussed the annihilation of his birthplace.

It was driven home again two nights later, when he'd had a wonderful reunion with his fellow pages. Nasrid, the mad Macedonian with whom Asha had explored the netherworld beneath the seraglio, was now the lieutenant *agha* of a corps of Janissaries. He wore a leopard-skin cap and had a brass quill driven through a pinch of skin above his eyebrow. His mustache looked as sharply pointed and neatly sharpened as his sword. His eyes still smoldered with opium fires. He was a man whose look itself struck terror into the hearts of his enemies, yet to his old comrades he was as playful as ever.

Shabooh, the scrawny Bulgarian, held the same rank in the Janissaries. He looked somewhat less fierce than Nasrid, having lost half an ear in a skirmish—a fact he tried unsuccessfully to conceal from his old friends with a clever turn of his turban, quickly uncovered by Asha. They'd shared a drink together and laughed over old times. Asha listened quietly as Shabooh and Nasrid both talked, almost gleefully, of the Maltese lives they would take in the upcoming campaign, when the barren island would at last become another lush garden of the Sultan's, planted with the flower of Islam and watered with the blood of its infidel defenders.

Asha's color drained at that. Of course Malta was not his anymore. Certainly he would gladly kill any knight he met, and the Maltese themselves would be better off, he knew, under the protection of the enlightened empire of Suleiman.

Yet he also knew what a tempest was about to ravage the little island, a maelstrom of iron and fire such as the world had never seen. He thought of his father and mother caught in that storm, and of course Maria, precious Maria. Perhaps Luca and Isolda had died since he'd last seen them, but he knew Maria had not. He carried a note that he'd read a thousand times in the last year. He'd gotten it from the captain of a Corsican galley, who'd taken it from a dead Dalmatian corsair. It was written in Italian, offering a hundred silver taris as ransom for a boy taken captive years earlier. Asha had seen a hundred notes like it; ransoms were the currency of slavery. This one had been folded, creased, drenched with sweat and seawater: it had the look of a thousand leagues about it. And it was signed by Maria Borg.

He had seen much in his life, but little had affected him so deeply as that note. Was it her own hand that had written it? He thought not, as the women of Malta were not taught writing. Even so, it was her heart behind the words, and when he read them, the grown Asha had to wipe tears from his eyes for the lost life of the child Nico.

Might Maria have lived all this time, and sought her younger brother thus, only to die at his hand?

In the years since he had risen to command, he had never really had to confront his identity. The blood of Malta coursed through his veins, but his heart beat with the Sultan's drum—and it had never really mattered. Perhaps he still did not have to confront it, knowing that Allah had chosen his path, a path on which each step was foreordained.

If he was to meet his death there, *malish, mektoub*. He was content.

If, *insha'llah,* he was to enter the streets of Birgu among the conquerors, then he was content.

But it was not that simple, and he knew it. How would he feel when ordered to fire upon Birgu, knowing he would kill Maltese along with knights? He remembered his countrymen as ignorant, superstitious, and dirt-poor, but theirs were not the faces of the enemy. Theirs were the kindred faces of his ancestors. He could not knowingly fire upon them. What if he struck a member of his own family with a shot? How would it feel to raise a sword in combat, realizing too late that the neck it was about to sever was his father's? How would it feel if after Malta fell he saw the corpse of his own sister, raped and murdered by troops intent upon taking the flesh and plunder that was due them? It was not so far-fetched. Such, he knew too well, were the awful fortunes of war, delivered in equal measure by Muslim and Christian alike.

Maria, Maria, may God protect you from harm. He could still see her face perfectly. It hadn't aged, of course, not a day. It was still fresh, dirty, mischievous, and thirteen, as perfectly preserved in his mind as every detail of his home and of the coast where they had hunted treasure. He still had the coin she'd given him that day. It was as shiny now as the day it was minted, only the image on it had been worn smooth by his restless fingers.

Maria, Maria, may God protect you from . . . me?

He knew it was pointless to torture himself with such thoughts. Better to take shelter in the safe harbor of his faith: his path had been chosen by Allah, who alone saw its end. Now it was only left for him to walk it.

MALTA
April 9

The Chevalier Bertrand Cuvier stood and wiped his brow and took a long drink of watered wine. "Nothing but cursed rock, this place, and somehow every bit of it is in the wrong spot. Couldn't God have simply laid down some neat walls here and there? Dropped a ravelin up there, where we need it, or cut a ditch down here?" He wiped his mouth and handed the water to Christien, then, muscles rippling, he leaned and heaved another shovelful of rock and dirt into the barrow.

Christien was just glad to be back on solid ground. After three caravans, even manual labor was a pleasant relief, so long as it was on land. He still got queasy on the water, but far worse were the long periods of boredom, interrupted by the brief and bloody sea battles led by Romegas, captain of the little fleet. True, the man was a genius at the helm. The grand prize of their last voyage, a magnificent carrack that belonged to influential officials at the Sublime Porte, was now safely anchored in Birgu Creek. They'd brought it back complete with notable hostages and priceless cargo.

Perhaps, Christien thought, the problem was that Romegas enjoyed his work so much. With another thousand like him, surely the Order would rule the world. They'd encountered a galliot under the command of a well-known corsair, a renegade Calabrian named Conciny. There was a fierce engagement in which all the knights, including Christien, took up swords and leapt onto the galliot's deck to engage the enemy. It was a fair battle, hard fought.

When it was over, the victorious Romegas stood by as the slave crew dealt with the corsair captain. Wounded, Conciny fell from the corsia into the ranks of his still-chained and long-suffering slaves, who quickly and literally took matters into their own hands. The first slave, lacking any weapon save those given him by nature, tore at Conciny's flesh with his teeth, biting deeply into his shoulder. At the other end of the corsair, the slave's bench mate did the same to Conciny's calf. Screaming for mercy, the man was battered and bounced along on the laps and shoulders of the men at oars, up one row and down the other, one bench at a time, each slave taking another bit of revenge. By the last bench there was little left of Conciny, whose screams had gone silent somewhere near the middle. Romegas stood on the deck above, loath to interfere in the justice of the sea. Indeed, Christien observed, the expression on his face made it clear he regretted not being invited to join in.

That night at dinner Romegas was ebullient. "The desserts of war," he joked.

Such incidents served only to remind Christien that he would never be suited for life at sea. Most troubling was the paradox that he himself had joined Romegas with his sword and then spent two days sewing up the damage to friend and foe alike.

❖

Christien had come back twice during his three years at sea, spending the winters in Birgu when the weather was unsuited for corsairing. His work at the Infirmary consumed him. He ordered every book and pamphlet published on the continent about medicine and surgery. He devoured them all, working late by the light of an oil lamp. Resurrecting a practice of his youth at the château, he began filling pages of notebooks, making detailed illustrations of wounds and notes about treatments he'd tried, keeping track of what succeeded and—more often—what did not. He had an endless supply of wounds to treat, and the Hospitaller allowed him to purchase every conceivable instrument. It was, in all, the perfect place for a surgeon to practice his trade. Despite the fulfillment of work, however, he longed for something more.

No, not *something,* of course. He longed for her.

The yawning chasm he'd felt inside for three years was slowly being filled by the demands of his life in the Order, but not nearly quickly enough. For the first year he never slept more than an hour or two at a time. Now he could sleep in longer stretches, but it always took painfully long to drift off, hours when he knew each time he closed his eyes visions of her would haunt him. The ache never seemed to leave him. He tried to push it away with will and prayer and work. In three years it had gotten marginally easier. In another ten, he thought, perhaps he would sleep a whole night through. He could not dispute Bertrand's complaints that he'd gone all serious, that he didn't laugh as often or as deep.

Every morning he longed to walk the shore near the caves or along the defenses of the city, hoping he'd see her. He never took the first step, knowing it would be impossibly difficult to turn back. He wondered and worried. With Joseph Callus dead, there was no one to ask about her.

The first winter he had seen Salvago. The vicar passed in a carriage, acknowledging the knight with a correct nod. Christien stood immobile, trying to decide whether to finish what Jacobus had begun. The question had plagued him during his first season at sea, and while vengeance was not in his nature, he knew that, unlike Jacobus, he would not fail.

A few days later he had seen Elena, leading her small son by the hand through the streets. He called after her.

"Fra de Vries," she said brightly.

"It's Christien," he replied. "Hello," he said to Moses. The boy peered shyly up at the tall knight from behind his mother's skirts but said nothing.

"Are you all well?" Christien asked.

Moses came a little farther out, his eyes riveted on a shiny chain and small golden cross that hung around Christien's neck.

"Yes, we are, thank you." She understood his real question. "Maria is also. She still works with her father and lives with us."

Christien, watching Moses, undid the chain and removed the cross. He looked at Elena for permission. "Is it all right?"

"Of course, but really, you don't need to."

"I'd like him to have it. I can get another." He held the chain out to the boy.

Moses flashed a bright grin and hung the chain around his neck. He immediately disappeared again behind his shield of skirts. "What do you say, Moses?" his mother asked.

Moses peered out. "Do you kill people?"

"*Moses!*" Elena said crossly.

Christien laughed. "Only when I'm trying to save them," he said.

They walked together for a while. Moses wandered behind, throwing stones into puddles and chasing cats. Christien was bursting with questions, for when he'd left the island so suddenly Bertrand had had little information other than that Maria was safe. Now Elena told him about Salvago, that Maria's release from the dungeons had come at the price of Jacobus's life. She did not tell him that Salvago had doubled Maria's torment by making her believe that Christien was a prisoner and that Maria could free him if only she betrayed Jacobus. She had spent months thinking that was the case, and it had nearly driven her mad. To tell Christien that now would accomplish nothing but to incite revenge, the very thing Elena hoped to avoid. What she had told him, however, was more than enough to darken Christien's expression. "You are wondering what to do, I think," she said.

"Yes."

"I would cut off his balls if I could," Elena said unabashedly. "Yet I know what Maria would say."

"What?"

"To do nothing. In fact, she would beg you. When it first happened she tried to get back at him. We both did. They took everything we had and burned what they didn't want. Fençu and Jacobus ended up in prison, and they hung me in a net. And then Jacobus died for it. She would not see you die for it as well. If you harm Salvago now, somehow I think it is Maria who will end up paying the price. She and Salvago must live in peace on this island. If that is not what she would prefer, it is what she knows they both must have. Do nothing, Fra de Vries. Leave him alone. The price of honor is too high."

"I wonder that very thing every day," Christien said, looking at her with new appreciation. "I'm glad she has you for a friend. Please, tell her I . . ." His voice trailed off.

"What?"

"Never mind. It's better if you say nothing."

As Elena watched him go, she wanted to tell him the rest of it, but she had seen what was in his eyes, and couldn't. It would only cause him further pain. Maria had heard the signal from the watchtower that the Order's galleys were returning. She'd raced the miles from M'kor Hakhayyim to the wharf at Birgu, beating his ship by minutes.

She'd hidden behind a wall and watched him descending the plank to the quay. Seeing he was safe, she'd turned away. She knew that he needed to keep his vows, just as she knew that she could never come near him again without placing him in terrible danger.

She'd wept for a week.

❖

Christien's back glistened with sweat from the hot spring sun as he labored beside Bertrand. He threw all his weight into every swing of the pick. Other knights were scattered around the massive works, doing their part. They weren't alone, of course. Every slave and prisoner, every page and cook, every galley soldier and butcher, every woman and child was laboring on the defenses.

There was an urgent pitch to the work, growing more intense each day. Spring was the beginning of the campaign season, the season when fleets would sail. Reports poured in from spies all over the Mediterranean, especially those in the Porte: the massive Turkish fleet was nearly ready. If there was disagreement in other places about where the Turks would strike—Sardinia, as some thought, or La Goleta, the Spanish-held presidio in North Africa—there was no such confusion here. From the Grand Master down, all believed that when the Ottoman lance flew, Malta would be its target.

It seemed all but hopeless. There was so much to do, so many weaknesses to correct. Walls were strengthened and heightened, watchtowers added, cannons ordered from the continent. Ditches were deepened at the landward ends of Birgu and Senglea. These two peninsulas, jutting like fingers out into the Grand Harbor, would form the core of the island's last defenses. It did not take a practiced eye to see how very weak and exposed they were. They were surrounded on all sides by high ground, from which enemy artillery could pour destruction like rain. To the north was Sciberras, to the west Corradino Heights, to the south the heights of Santa Margherita, and to the east the heights of Salvador. Every military engineer who had studied the harbor area since the knights came to Malta had warned of the vulnerability.

For reasons of politics, finance, and timing, however, the Order had never built its citadel and city on the heights of Sciberras, the peninsula that formed the opposite shore of the Grand Harbor from Birgu and Senglea, and which would have been easier to defend. The only defense work on Sciberras was Fort St. Elmo, standing at its very tip. The fort guarded the entrances to Grand Harbor, to its south, and to Marsamuscetto, the harbor to its north. Even St. Elmo itself was exposed, occupying low ground, not high.

No one needed to be told how precarious the defenses were. Instead the inhabitants of Malta labored on, doing what they could to improve them. A wall was hastily thrown up along the western shore of the Senglea peninsula facing the heights of Corradino, so that now at least the whole of Senglea was surrounded by a wall. The ravelins and cavaliers of St. Michael, on Senglea, and St. Elmo were strengthened, while other defensive works were added. Only the village of Bormla was left unimproved. It had sprung up when there were too many people for Birgu. When the Turks came it would be abandoned.

The manpower situation was even grimmer than the defenses. Knights of the Order arrived every week, answering the Grand Master's call, yet there were still fewer than five hundred of them on the island. There were Spanish and Italian troops, a few Greeks and Sicilians, the soldiers and slaves of the galleys, the household servants of the knights, and perhaps three thousand Maltese militia. In all, eight thousand men, more than half of them poorly trained, were available to defend the island against five times their number, all of them seasoned troops. A flurry of letters flew from the Grand Master's desk to every European monarch, pleading for immediate help. He received flowery declarations of moral support from some, and either silence or promises from others. Only the Spanish offered any real hope at all, and there was no sign their help would be forthcoming soon.

Bertrand spent his evenings training militia how to shoot. Men who had never handled an arquebus had to be taught how to load, to prime, to fire. The sound of their practice punctuated the dusk. Each man could take three shots and no more, for powder was at a premium. After that they could only sight down the barrel, imagine the enemy, and pretend to shoot. It was tragic, Bertrand complained each night. "Only a highly trained Italian could fail to shoot as well as a completely untrained Maltese," he said.

"Don't worry," Christien said, having spent the day working on the physical defenses. "They won't have to aim. The Turks will be so close they'll be eating shot straight out of the ends of their barrels."

"By God, let them come, then," Bertrand said, relishing that idea. "We'll see they have a hearty meal."

After the day's labors, Christien tended to affairs at the Infirmary. There were rounds to make, although the most critically ill of the patients had already been shipped to Sicily, to keep from draining precious resources. Extra beds were brought in and the courtyard cleared out for the expected crush of casualties. Drawing upon his experience at Metz, Christien ordered every conceivable supply, including medicines and ointments, bandages and splints, surgical tools and tinctures. There were braziers for cautery and catgut for ligature, all the boxes stored in underground chambers.

After such details were attended to and his rounds complete, when every fiber of his being pleaded for sleep, Christien would crawl into his bed, knowing sleep would not come, not for hours. In the morning he would return to the ramparts and dig, in a race against time.

As he filled yet another wicker basket, a signal sounded from a coastal tower. Nearly thirty Spanish galleys had been sighted off the coast. Rumors flew immediately: surely the ships brought much-needed reinforcements, sent at last in succor by King Philip.

Men whooped and cheered, but not for long. The Viceroy of Sicily was rowed in to meet La Valette. The message he brought, repeated that night in every auberge, caused Christien to do what for three years he had promised himself he would not.

He went to find Maria.

❖

Moses scampered down the tunnel. He was five now, scrawny and bronze and as tough as the brambles in which he played. His thatch of red hair was thick, his eyes the very picture of his mother's. His lashes were long and curled, his laugh quick and infectious. "Water, Mama," he called. Elena paused in her work and took the skin. She wiped the dirt from her eyes and brought him onto her lap. She took a drink and passed the bag to Maria. Beyond her, in the cramped darkness, Fençu grunted as he chipped away at the soft limestone.

They were digging a new tunnel. They'd worked on it every day for two months. Maria devoted every spare moment to the effort, coming to the cave to help every evening as soon as she finished work with her father's crews in Birgu.

M'kor Hakhayyim was already a formidable lair, naturally suited for defense against corsairs and improved over the centuries by successive occupants. There were three entrances. Two emerged into a winding ravine that cut along the back side of the hill above the cave, while the main entrance was situated above the water at the base of a path that led from the carob tree on the hillside above. The new entrance, being added at Fençu's insistence, would exit much closer to the water, hidden from the view of the main entrance by a spine of rock. No matter where the enemy stood, there would be a way out of the cave without being seen or trapped inside.

All visible signs of the cave had been hidden. The main entrance was masked by natural rock formations, although a well-worn path led to it. They hauled rocks and dumped them on the path, then scattered dirt to mask its hard-packed surface. The other entrances were elaborately concealed with stone and brush, so that a man could pass within inches and never realize it. Just inside each opening, within easy reach, were niches that held weapons—the swords, knives, crossbows, and guns that Fençu had collected over the years.

Other defenses were added. Heavy netting had been strung over the main entrance and now strained with the weight of hundreds of rocks, lifted one by one into place. Restraining ropes held the netting up, each secured with an iron pin embedded in the rock. If the stays were cut, the net would fall, dumping the rocks onto the entrance.

The cave itself, of course, offered a thousand natural hiding places. Passages fed off the central chamber, leading to smaller galleries. Some of those were connected to others with natural passageways, others with tunnels dug by man, while still others went nowhere. Over the centuries steps and handholds had been carved in strategic places, permitting anyone familiar with the cave to move about quickly. Where the cave narrowed in the rear, stalactites and stalagmites grew together, creating a forest of limestone pillars. In all, it was a fortress.

Fençu thought the Turks were unlikely to be anywhere near the cave, isolated as it was from the fortresses of Grand Harbor, where the coming Ottoman storm would certainly rage most fiercely. But if they did come near, Fençu and the others were confident they were as safe as they could be anywhere on the island. Even Maria, by now something of an expert at defensive preparations, was comforted by its well-planned design. Once the new tunnel was finished, there would be no hiding place in Malta more secure.

Elena gave the water bag back to Moses. "I'm going outside, Mama," he said.

"Stay close."

He sighed at her oft-repeated caution and scurried off. A moment later he was back. "I saw a man coming," he said in a loud whisper. "He didn't see me."

Fençu cursed, dismayed that Cawl had allowed a visitor to approach undetected. He reached to the arms ledge and took up a crossbow, left cocked for just such an occasion. "Stay here," he said to the others. Quickly he worked his way up, weapon at the ready.

Sunlight streamed through one of the holes in the seaward wall, and lit the visitor's face as he stepped into the chamber. Fençu lowered his crossbow. "Hello, Fra de Vries," he said. He nodded at Cawl, who had seen the intruder too late, and now moved with his own weapon back into the shadows.

"Hello, Fençu."

Maria emerged from the new tunnel and stood motionless, her face flushed as she saw Christien. Fençu glanced at Elli, who had been at the oven, and cleared his throat. He nodded toward the back of the cave. "I'm hungry," he said, and he followed her to the communal kitchen. Elena and Moses crawled out of the tunnel. Elena greeted Christien, while Moses grinned shyly, remembering the knight whose necklace he still wore. "Come along, Moses," Elena said. "I'll play outside with you."

Alone, Christien and Maria looked at each other for a long moment. "You look well," he said, breaking the awkward silence.

"As do you." She put her hand on the rock, to steady herself.

"I have missed you."

She nodded, her eyes glistening. She sat down on the ledge next to the spring, trying to find her voice. "I saw Spanish ships off the coast today. My father thought help might have come."

He sat next to her. "I'm afraid not. The Viceroy promises aid before the month of May is out, but mainly he came to say he could leave no men."

"He brought so many ships to say that?"

Christien smiled at the salt in the remark. "Apparently, and to advise the Grand Master to build a ravelin at St. Elmo. But his ships are why I came. They're leaving tomorrow for Sicily. They're being loaded with civilians, to carry them out of harm's way. There is a place for you, Maria. For everyone here in the cave."

"The ships are for people who are too old or ill to help. I can help. I'm not going. This is my home."

"The Turkish fleet has already sailed. Our spies say it is quite large."

"No one even knows for sure if they're coming to Malta."

"They are. And when they come, this will be a terrible place to be. I could not . . ." His voice caught. "I could not bear it if anything were to happen to you."

"Fençu and Elli are here, and Elena and Moses and Cawl and the others. They're not leaving. I won't, either. You know me better than to ask."

"Surely you're not intending to stay in the cave. The Turks would not go easy on *conversos*. They might even think you one."

She flashed at that. "The *Turks!* Who treats Jews worse than Christians?"

"I only meant—"

"I know what you meant. I just don't know yet. I haven't decided. I can be of some use in Birgu, I think. But the others will stay here, and probably be safer than anywhere else. There's grain enough for six months, and the cave has a spring. Fençu says the cave is stronger than the forts, anyway. He says all the Turkish guns will be pointed at the—" Her face went white at the thought. "At the knights. He doesn't think it will come to that. He remembers when the Turks came before. They saw the defenses and went away to Gozo. The island is even stronger now. He thinks they will turn away again."

"Not this time. This time they'll come to win. They'll stay until they're all dead, or until we are. There will be Turks all over the island, Maria. If they find anyone here—I don't have to tell you what will happen."

"And what will happen to anyone they find inside Birgu? Will that be any better?"

"No. The only thing that will be better is if you're away in Sicily, where they can't touch you at all." His eyes betrayed his pain. "Oh, Maria. You have been taken from me once already. I cannot bear to lose you again."

"I wasn't taken from you. You chose a different life." She caught herself. "I'm sorry. I didn't mean it that way."

"I know you must be very angry with me."

She looked into his eyes, and shook her head. "How could I be angry with you after what you have been through because of me? I am angry at God for taking you from me. I am angry at the Order, and I despise the Grand Master for his cruelty. I'm angry at your mother for losing her leg, and I'm angriest of all at myself for hating that you'd ever made that oath. But in three years, Christien, I have never spent one moment angry at you. I would have come to tell you that in the winters when you were home from sea, but it would have been too dangerous for you, and too painful for me. Seeing you now only opens the awful pit I feel here." She put her hand to her stomach. "I want it to go away, and it won't."

He reached to touch her on the cheek. She turned away. "Please don't," she whispered. "I don't think I could bear it." The tears were building, and she fought them, trembling.

He lowered his hand. "I'm sorry." His own eyes were watering. "I suppose . . . I had better go, then."

She nodded. "Yes, please."

"If there is anything you need, any supplies, anything I can do . . ."

She nodded again.

"God be with you, Maria."

"And with you."

❖

The next day a supply cart arrived at the cave, driven by

Bartholomew, Christien's page. There was oil and butter and honey and grain. Fençu threw back the cover below the food and found something even more precious: a small cache of weapons. There were three new arquebuses, a quantity of powder and lead shot, a coil of slow match, and twenty earthenware incendiary pots, complete with fuses. "Tell Fra de Vries we are grateful," Fençu said to Bartholomew when they'd finished unloading.

"The Chevalier de Vries said to tell you he knows nothing of it," Bartholomew replied earnestly.

At the wharf in Birgu, Angela and Antonio Buqa joined a score of other noble families who were making their way onto the Viceroy's flagship, families who had no intention of participating in a fight they viewed as the Order's. Angela's housemen carted crates of her possessions into the hold, reflecting her hope that the Turks would prevent her from ever returning to the hellhole of Malta. Late that morning, his ships laden with the old, the infirm, and a host of nobles who were neither, the Viceroy's fleet departed the island.

The Order's engineer came to inspect the walls where Luca's crew worked. He knew Maria lived outside Birgu and asked if she was going to remain inside the walls when the Turks came. "There will be thousands of civilians inside Birgu and Senglea," he said. "The Grand Master needs people who can help keep things organized." *Even women*, she read in his expression. "He specifically mentioned you, Signorina Borg." Maria wondered if Christien was behind this, too, although it didn't really matter. She had already decided as much. It was not in her nature to hide in a cave. In Birgu she could do something to help. She would live in her father's house.

Every few days, rumors that the Turkish fleet had been sighted whipped through Birgu like wildfire, each one bringing a heightened sense of urgency as preparations continued at a feverish pace. A labyrinth of subterranean storerooms had been cut from the rock beneath Birgu and Senglea, and a human supply chain now stocked them with supplies for a long siege: forty thousand casks of fresh water and wine, ten thousand bushels of wheat and barley, and huge quantities of cheese, dried tunny, salted meat, olive oil, and butter. Crews toiled around the clock, making gunpowder in the magazines beneath the forts.

Despite all the efforts to lay in stores, there were still critical shortages. Ships passing anywhere within reach of the Order's galleys were boarded, their captains cordially invited at gunpoint to sell to the Order whatever useful supplies they carried.

Three of the Order's galleys were secured in the moat between Fort St. Angelo and Birgu. Two more were berthed at the quay, while others were sent to Messina. A massive chain was stretched two hundred yards from the tip of Senglea to the tongue of rock beneath St. Angelo, sealing the entrance to Birgu Creek. Stretched into position and supported on pontoons and boats, the chain was secured at one end by the anchor of the Order's old flagship, and at the other by a giant capstan, which turned to lower the chain to allow ships to pass.

By mid-May nothing more could be brought in from the outside, for the rumors were rumors no longer.

The Turkish fleet had been sighted off Sicily.

Chapter 36

18 MAY 1565

Fençu heard the rumble of cannon fire from St. Angelo.

Three blasts.

He scrambled to the entrance of the cave and slipped outside. A moment later he stood atop the hill by the carob tree, from where he had a grand view. Although he had been expecting the sight for months, the scale of it stunned him.

"May Elohim preserve us." His voice was but a whisper.

Elli clambered up from below and stood next to him. Huffing from the exertion, she took her husband's hand in her own. A moment later Elena and Moses joined them, and then Cawl, Villano, and Cataldo and their families. They stood in silence, trying to absorb the enormity of it. Even Moses stopped his play and straddled his mother's hip, staring in silent awe.

The sun was just rising, burning away the predawn mists to reveal an Ottoman sea. The horizon was a forest of masts and sails, above a solid field of ships of every description. Still some distance away, the fleet sailed in the form of an arrowhead, moving inevitably, almost casually, toward the island. At the point of the arrow were the galleys, their oars waving and dipping, their goose-winged lateen sails stretched before them. Behind them were the larger galliots, and behind those the roundships, merchantmen of two thousand tons or more, very high fore and aft, their decks a woodland of pikes and halberds, the turbans and helmets and blades of the soldiers providing bright splashes of color and flashes of light. There were flags and banners and pennons of every description, heralding the identities of the pashas and *aghas* and their proud regiments. Every deck bulged with guns and stores and men.

Fençu led the others back inside. It was, he reminded them, the eighth day of the month of Sivan, in the year 5325 of the Hebrew calendar. His voice echoed off the rock walls as he led them in prayer.

"Hear, O Israel, the Lord our God, the Lord is One.

"In this time of Shavu'ot, a time when the Torah was given on Mount Sinai, a time when the first fruits were brought to the Temple, let us remember that death is not a tragedy, but a beginning. In this, thy temple of M'kor Hakhayyim that is the source of life, O God, let thine enemies who breach its spaces know the might of thy sword . . ."

When his prayer was finished they drank goat's milk sweetened with honey. Elena and Cawl ran outside to bring in all the chickens and their three remaining goats. Maria had taken the rest with her to Birgu. The cook fire was put out for fear the smoke might be seen. Fençu cut the throat of one of the goats and butchered it. The other goats would follow sooner or later, depending on when the Turks might come close enough to hear them bleating.

The Jews of M'kor Hakhayyim took up their posts, to watch and wait.

In Birgu, in the conventual chapel of St. Lawrence, where it was the eighteenth day of May, Anno Domini 1565, the Grand Master solemnly addressed his knights. Behind him, resting in its jeweled silver case on a stand of velvet, was the most sacred of the Order's relics, the severed hand of John the Baptist. "A swarm of barbarians are rushing upon our island. It is the great battle of the Cross and the

Crescent which is now to be fought," La Valette said, in his voice of iron. "We are the chosen soldiers of Christ. The hope of all Christendom rests upon our efforts. If Heaven requires the sacrifice of our lives, there can be no better occasion than this." His knights shared the body and blood of Christ, took up their armor and weapons, and streamed from the church, racing for their assigned stations.

Aboard the galley *Alisa* it was the Sabbath, the seventeenth day of the month of Shawwal, in the year 972 of the Hijrah of the Prophet. Beneath a fluttering green banner of Mohammed emblazoned with the red crescent of the Ottomans, Asha Raïs finished his ablutions and knelt on his prayer mat. He faced the rising sun, pressing his forehead to the mat. He listened to the fervent prayer of the *mokkadem* on the flagship, whose voices floated like the morning mists over the water and through the fleet.

"And those who disbelieve will be gathered unto hell, that Allah may separate the wicked from the good.

"The wicked he will place piece upon piece, and heap them all together, and consign them unto hell. Such verily are the losers.

"And Allah said, 'I will throw fear into the hearts of those who disbelieve, then smite the necks and smite of them each finger. . . .' "

In the parish church of St. Agatha's in Birgu, Monsignor Domenico Cubelles celebrated Mass, assisted by his vicar, Giulio Salvago. The bishop called upon the Angel of Death to strike down the Lord's enemies.

"In the name of the Father, the Son, and the Holy Spirit, Amen. O loving and mysterious Father, preserve Thy soldiers who fight darkness in Christ's name. We remember the words of Jesus, who said, 'All power is given unto me in heaven and in earth. Go ye therefore, and teach all nations, baptizing them in the name of the Father, and of the Son, and of the Holy Ghost. . . .' "

Women crossed themselves and clutched their children and wept. Men crossed themselves and clutched their weapons and set off to their posts.

Across the piazza, the bell chimed in the watchtower. From the quay beneath Fort St. Angelo, a fast galley set out for Sicily, carrying the Grand Master's urgent message to Europe.

The battle for Malta had begun.

❖

The ancient fishing village of Birgu occupied a small triangular spit of land that jutted into Grand Harbor. At its tip, which was only a hundred paces across, a deep sea ditch spanned by a drawbridge separated Birgu from the promontory on which stood Fort St. Angelo. Birgu's landward end—the triangle's base, six hundred yards long—was protected by a strong wall with bastions and a dry ditch. From base to tip, the triangle was no more than another six hundred yards. One side of the little peninsula faced Kalkara Creek and the deserted hills of Mount Salvador beyond. The other side faced Birgu Creek, across which stood Birgu's sister peninsula of Senglea. At Senglea's landward end stood Fort St. Michael. Only a few windmills and houses and the Grand Master's stables were scattered beyond the fort in the open space of Senglea peninsula. Each one of the eight *langues* of the Order of St. John was responsible for one of the bastions or other defensive posts.

Birgu and Senglea were in chaos that morning, a tumult of noise and dust as refugees streamed in from the countryside seeking shelter. They came through the main gate near the Post of Aragon, leading their animals and carrying what possessions they could on their backs. Their carts groaned under heavy loads of grain and vegetables. Men shouted, donkeys bawled, and horses whinnied, the din increased by the sounds still coming from the arsenals and arms sheds, where workmen were hammering out chain mail and helmets. The forges still roared red-hot, spewing new weapons and shot.

Maria settled six families, twelve sheep, eleven goats, and a score of chickens into her father's small home. Wide-eyed children stared down at her from beneath the rafters where she'd slept as a little girl. Some of the older ones played tag, giggling and swinging from the ladders, while their mothers cooked and brushed away chicken feathers that drifted down from makeshift roosts. His bed filled with strangers, Luca left for work that morning grumbling that he might as well sleep in the ditches with the cattle. When the house could not hold another soul, Maria helped fill others. She helped husbands find wives and children find mothers. When Birgu itself could not hold another soul, the Grand Master ordered the gate closed, sending new arrivals to the shelter of Fort St. Michael, or to the walled town of Mdina in the central part of the island.

In the afternoon Maria helped demolish houses in Bormla, the new village just outside the walls of Birgu. Her father's crews had built many of the houses, hastily erected to provide shelter for the workers who came to support the Order. Now there was danger those houses would provide shelter to the Turks instead. Roof beams were stripped, every piece of timber salvaged. Donkeys strained against creaking ropes. Walls crashed down, churning up great clouds of dust. Every stone and shovel of dirt was loaded on backs or into wicker baskets and carried inside Birgu by the legions of women and children, slaves and soldiers, horses and mules. Inside the walls it was all heaped in strategic locations for later use in making repairs.

At the first sight of the fleet knights raced to the Marsa, the lowland at the throat of the Grand Harbor where the principal freshwater wells and springs of the island were located. They poisoned the water with a potent mixture of arsenic, flax, hemp, and manure. The same was done to every other water source on the island outside the defended areas. The fields were barren, having been harvested early to deprive the Turk of a single grain or vegetable.

Despite the Grand Master's orders, not everyone sought shelter. As at M'kor Hakhayyim, there were still peasants in the countryside and coastal caves who believed the Ottoman storm would pass quickly. The few noble families of Mdina who had not fled for Sicily now could only pray that their poorly garrisoned inland town would not become a target of the invaders. They closed their gates and shut themselves into their great mansions, determined to let the knights reap the harvest of death they'd sown with their endless arrogance.

Shadowed on land by a cavalry detachment and on sea by four of the Order's galleys, the Turkish fleet sailed unopposed around the southern end of Malta and up the west coast, where it anchored overnight. The next morning it returned to Marsasirocco, the large bay at the southern end of the island. From there it was several miles to where the Turks intended to place their main camp, in the Marsa at the throat of Grand Harbor. Artillery and supplies would have to be hauled overland. Troops began disembarking from their ships.

❖

Fençu and Cawl lay hidden together in the ravine by the cave, which was within a quarter mile of the landing site. Each holding a crossbow and scarcely daring to breathe, they watched as the fleet disgorged men and supplies into a huge staging area. Mountains of sacks, boxes, and water skins waited to be loaded onto pack animals and carts for the overland journey to the main Turkish camp. Whips cracked and galley slaves groaned along with beasts of burden as man and animal began pushing and pulling giant artillery pieces up the embankment from the harbor. Both men felt the ground rumble beneath their bellies and heard the eerie creak of wood and iron wheels as the great war machine began snaking its way inland.

"Which are the Janissaries?" Cawl whispered nervously as they watched the troops massing into their regiments. "I heard they're the worst."

"I don't know," Fençu said. "All the godless bastards look the same to me." The landing area was a swirl of color as men in bright tunics and satin trousers, flowing robes and dazzling embroidered uniforms mingled together. There were turbans and bonnets of every shape and color: tall brown cones and thick white loaves, red fezzes and white onions, puffy golden globes and tightly twisted yellow ropes of cotton and silk, all beneath a waving profusion of egret feathers and golden tassels and broad battle standards.

Not many horses arrived with the fleet, but the few that did were as magnificent and proud as the troops. They pranced down sturdy planks laid from ship to shore, and after a long confinement at sea were just as restless as the men for the battle to begin. "Look at that saddle," Fençu, breathed in awe when he saw the mount of an *agha*. "There are enough jewels on it for a man to live ten years."

"*Hàqq it-torok!*" Cawl whispered urgently, pointing. "They're coming our way." Since the first landing, numerous mounted and foot patrols had fanned out over the southern tip of the island. Now twenty men filed up the slope toward their position, carrying packs, swords, bows, and rifles. The man in front, tall and leonine, wore a helmet shaped like the dome of a mosque. A boar's-tooth necklace dangled at his throat. He wore a green silk surcoat over light chest armor. A battle axe gleamed in his sash, and his hands rested on a long scimitar draped casually over his shoulders. A brass quill was driven through a pinch of skin at his forehead, just above and between brooding dark eyes. His gaze was everywhere as he scouted the brushy hillside. He seemed to look directly at them.

Fençu and Cawl crawled back on their hands and knees. They quickly slithered through the narrow opening to the cave, pulling rocks and brush in behind them. At the base of the tunnel, the others looked up anxiously at their entry. Cawl motioned for them to be still and to douse all the lamps. They huddled in the darkness, sweating, listening, their children on their laps. Soon they heard bits of muffled Turkish conversation and laughter. The noise grew louder until they could make out individual words clearly, although no one could understand what they meant.

The Turkish patrol stopped literally on top of the cave, beneath the carob tree. Its lieutenant *agha* scanned the surrounding landscape. The position had a commanding view from which he could see any approaching enemy troops that might attempt to threaten the fleet disembarking below. On the opposite side of the harbor, other patrols were taking up similar positions. On a rise just visible in the distance, a larger temporary camp was being established for stores and munitions.

"This is perfect," said Nasrid to his Janissaries. "We'll make camp here."

Twenty feet below his boots, Moses stirred restlessly in Elena's lap. His foot knocked some pebbles loose from the ledge where they sat. They showered down to the floor of the cave, in what sounded to everyone there like a rumbling waterfall. Elena quickly wrapped him in her arms and buried his face against her chest, her eyes on the blackness of the tunnel above them. The stream of Turkish continued unbroken.

Twenty feet further down in the cave, blood still dripped from the necks of the last two goats. Elli had slaughtered them along with the chickens, concerned about noise as the fleet anchored unexpectedly at their doorstep. The goat meat could be salted, but there would be no more milk or eggs until after the siege.

❖

The *Alisa* made her way to her station off the Grand Harbor, where with other galleys she was to maintain a blockade. As she swept along the coast, a flood of memories washed over her captain, who stood on the poop deck. Asha recognized landmarks, saw cliffs where he'd played and caves he'd explored. He saw the mouth of the cove where he'd been kidnapped years before. The actual place, he noted with some satisfaction, matched his memory in every detail.

Off Gallows Point he gave a signal, and the bosun's tambour fell silent. All oars were shipped. He stared into the mouth of the Grand Harbor, at the proud Fort St. Angelo, and at what he could see of Birgu, nestled behind the fort. Other than new defensive works, little appeared to have changed.

He felt none of the surging war lust that sometimes swept through his veins before a battle. Instead he was seized by sadness at the spectacle unfolding before him, and by an urge to strip off his turban, step into a dinghy, and row to the quay below Birgu. He would walk up the street, greet his fellow Maltese, and tell them to lay down their arms and embrace the world of Suleiman—a world far better than the one the pompous Knights of St. John would ever give them.

His foolish reverie was interrupted as one of the cannons on the walls of St. Elmo's roared. The shot fell off his bow, well short of his position, making a fountain of whitewater. The people of Malta were quite content to defend their lot.

✤

La Valette inspected the defenses near the bastion of Castile, one of the prominent defensive projections in the walls, near the throat of Kalkara Creek. He was unsatisfied. He ordered the demolition of houses just inside the wall all the way along the creek as far as the Infirmary. He directed that a new section of inner wall be constructed where they'd stood, in case the outer defenses fell. It was a huge amount of work to be done in cramped quarters. The Order's engineer barked instructions from his post in the town square, where the Grand Master had established his headquarters.

Luca's crews were assigned a section of the work. Maria helped her father organize the brigades of militia and women and children who comprised their work detail. While her father supervised unskilled workers, Maria kept a steady stream of stone and soil moving to supply the masons.

She heard an odd sound and cocked her head, listening. The laborers' shovels stopped. Picks fell silent and men on the walls hushed each other as everyone paused to make sense of the shrill, discordant sound coming from outside the walls.

"Bagpipes," a slave said. After that there were clarinets and trumpets and drums, and above those there rose men's voices, a thousand of them, then five, then ten thousand, all singing in unison, voices deep and confident and sonorous, rising in a frightful rhythm of war that drifted over the walls of Birgu and settled there like the plague.

Maria's palms went cold. Ever since the fleet had been sighted, there'd been only isolated noises—a shot here, a cannon there, but mostly an eerie silence suggesting that perhaps the Turks had been an illusion after all. Now they stood massed in the thousands on the heights around the monastery of Santa Margherita, up the hill from the landward end of Birgu, taunting the defenders below them. She wanted to climb up to see for herself, but the walls she'd helped build and where she'd stood so often now bristled with knights and soldiers. She was content to let them have it. Women fell to the ground, crying in fear. Dogs barked and howled.

The Grand Master ordered flags and banners unfurled. Drummers within the gates sent up their own booming reply to the resonant Turkish music. Eager troops pressed shoulder to shoulder, massed just inside the gate. At a signal the gate opened. A force of cavalry and arquebusiers sallied forth in a furious attack, every man screaming at the top of his lungs. Maria pressed against the wall as they streamed by, their faces hot for battle. She looked for Christien. She assumed he was at the Infirmary, but she had no way to know. She closed her eyes and willed him to be safe.

The clash lasted several hours, entirely hidden from her view. Maria rarely touched a tool; usually all her time was devoted to organizing others. Now as the fighting raged she took up a shovel, working furiously until her hands were blistered, more in an attempt to shut out what was happening on the other side of the wall than to accomplish much on this side of it. The noise was awful. There were volleys of gunfire and some artillery. She didn't know whose any of it was. Was that a Turkish gun firing? A Maltese peasant screaming, or a Spanish knight? Was that a horse dying, or a mule, or a man? And still there was the music, that awful music, and bits of prayer, and then more gunfire and screeching.

She was helping to move a heavy rock when a large explosion shook the ground beneath her feet. Bits of iron and stone showered down upon her, blown from somewhere clear over the wall by the force of the blast. She worked faster, issuing orders to keep the women busy, to keep them from crying as she felt like doing. Her father stood nearby, his ashen face streaked with sweat. At each new sound he looked up. She wanted to run to him, to bury herself in his massive arms. Instead she put her head down and kept working.

In the afternoon, not wishing to risk any more of his troops against the superior enemy force, the Grand Master ordered an end to the engagement. At a blast of the trumpet they began streaming back inside, their blood up and their spirits high. There were wounded, some dragged by their fellows into the gates, others limping along under their own strength. The dead were carried solemnly inside. Maria saw the face of one. It was young and peaceful, almost serene, his eyes closed beneath a gaping hole in his forehead. Maria had no experience with such things. Her hands began to shake. She turned and bent once again over her shovel, gripping it to still her nerves, determined to show no one her fear, determined that the wall would be strong and straight and perfect, and at least twice as thick as ordered.

Near dusk there was a new commotion atop the wall. A dozen Turkish heads appeared on spikes, hoisted triumphantly by hooting soldiers who planted the poles in the masonry at odd angles. Some of the heads still bore turbans, some helmets that glinted gold or silver in the setting sun. The sightless Turkish regiment stared out at its former comrades in their camps on the heights. A captured banner was unfurled beneath them, to mock and flutter from the outer wall. In Fort St. Michael men laughed and cheered at the sight.

Maria ran to the trench and threw up.

Later that night the defenders of Birgu learned that two knights, including one who'd served as page to La Valette, had been captured the previous evening by Turkish troops. Undoubtedly the two men had been tortured. The fact that the Turks then moved against the most heavily fortified section of wall meant that the two men had lied to their tormentors about the weakest points of defense and been believed.

In that first engagement, the Turks lost several hundred men, the defenders only twenty-one—or twenty-three, assuming the two captured knights had now paid the price for their deception. "Ten for one," men boasted that night on the walls and in darkened streets and shops. They were jubilant, emboldened by the sweet taste of first blood. At that rate, they assured each other, the thirty or forty thousand devils gathered outside the gates had no hope of prevailing. None at all.

The Turks, they chortled, hadn't brought nearly enough men to the party.

Maria spent the night on her knees, praying for strength.

❖

That night Asha and six other squadron captains were ferried ashore with orders to join Piali Pasha at the war council. The council was convened in a large silk tent in the Marsa. Lord Dragut had not yet arrived in Malta; he was en route from Tripoli, bringing more ships and men. Mustapha Pasha and Admiral Piali were debating strategy for taking the island. Asha sat in the rear among the lesser *aghas* and captains, listening as the two pashas and their lieutenants argued tactics.

Mustapha, the old land general, wanted to take the island of Gozo first and then the citadel of Mdina, to seal off the island from the north. Then, he said, Birgu, St. Angelo, and St. Michael would fall, one after the other. Turkish blood need not be spilled taking St. Elmo. The fort was isolated at the tip of Sciberras and would wither of its own accord.

Piali, the young admiral, was concerned above all for the safety of the Sultan's fleet. He disagreed vehemently with Mustapha. St. Elmo must be taken first, so that the fleet would have a safe berth in Marsamuscetto, the harbor that lay on the opposite side of Sciberras from Grand Harbor. St. Elmo's guns protected the entrance to both harbors and they had to be silenced. This would protect the fleet both from the winds of the gregale and from the guns of St. Angelo. Ships, he argued, were harder to replace than men and had to be preserved.

St. Elmo's very isolation, Piali reasoned, was its fatal weakness. It would fall quickly, after which the fleet would be in an ideal location to support the Sultan's troops and artillery as they moved against Senglea and Birgu. Then Mustapha's objectives could be swiftly and efficiently undertaken. It was merely a difference of days, Piali argued, and the advantage to the fleet was incalculable.

The military engineers agreed with Piali's assessment of the fort. "St. Elmo is poorly constructed," one said confidently. "It will fall in five days, six at the most."

Mustapha Pasha argued that to waste even a single shot or man against St. Elmo was foolish, but in the end he had to relent. His troops and supplies were captives of the fleet. Without Piali's help he could do nothing, so the admiral carried the argument.

St. Elmo would be attacked forthwith.

Asha left the tent unsettled at the disagreement. He had no experience in siege warfare and both arguments sounded wise to him, although in his memory the gregale, the wind that so worried Piali, did not blow at this time of year. He wished Dragut were there. Above all else, he wanted the siege over with quickly.

Despite the disagreement, spirits among the *aghas* and captains were high. Clearly the siege would not last more than a few weeks at best. St. Elmo, St. Angelo, St. Michael, it made no difference: all the Christian forts would fall before Allah.

❖

Shabooh made camp with his Janissaries on the lee side of Mount Sciberras. The gun carriages still rumbled and chucked along the long rocky route around the Marsa and up the ridge behind him. Wheels creaked and wood groaned as slaves and oxen and Maltese peasants who'd been captured in the countryside fought to coax the massive loads along the awful roads that were strewn with rocks and crisscrossed with ruts. Wheels broke, and even some of the oxen dropped in their tracks. But nothing could stop the flow.

Sciberras teemed with slaves. They dug trenches and breastworks to shield the troops and gun emplacements from the cannons of St. Elmo, at the foot of the peninsula, and of St. Angelo, directly across the water. Despite its name, Mount. Sciberras was no mountain. Its crown rose no more than two hundred feet above the water, but it was the loftiest ground near the Grand Harbor. From its heights the big guns would have a commanding position. Shabooh saw that the gunners would be shooting downhill at St. Elmo, whose walls now crawled with defiant infidels, waving their banners and shouting their challenges. It reminded him of the hunting preserves near Topkapi, where the game was so plentiful one could bring down three animals with a single shot, without stirring from the comfort of one's seat. St. Elmo's was no different. *Penned lambs, awaiting slaughter.*

La Valette was surprised but pleased when he realized that St. Elmo was to be the first target. Though he knew St. Elmo could not last very long, the move would give him more time to improve his core defenses in Birgu and Senglea, and would give the monarchs of Europe more time to organize a relief. He moved quickly to reinforce the little fort. A Provençal knight, Colonel Mas, was sent with two hundred soldiers and more than sixty knights, all of whom had volunteered to serve with the garrison already inside the fort. They were joined by freed galley slaves, not Muslims but Christian convicts released with the promise of pardon for their good efforts. The men and supplies were ferried across the harbor from St. Angelo in a stream of *dghajjes* and barges, under cover of the Order's cannons that laid protective fire on the Turkish troops on Sciberras, forcing them to keep to the far slopes. Despite that, Turkish sharpshooters occasionally would find their mark, and someone in one of the boats would topple into the water.

Civilians and cattle had initially taken shelter in the deep defensive ditches around the fort. Now the women and children among them huddled in the boats, making the return trip to Birgu, while the men remained behind to fight and the cattle were brought inside the fort.

Shabooh and his men watched impatiently, anxious to engage the enemy, but their *aghas* held them back. For the moment their role was defensive; the fort would be reduced by artillery before men were sent to storm the walls. Yet they must remain vigilant. Already some of the knights had engaged in a brief and bloody sortie, only to be quickly beaten back by Shabooh's men. Shabooh doubted they would try again. So he waited while the race between artillery emplacement and fort reinforcement went on.

Christian galley slaves dug furiously alongside Turkish engineers and troops, while others hauled soil by the basketful to heap on protective works. The Maltese rock was solid, yet in just two days their trenches already extended nearly to the ditch surrounding St. Elmo. The fort's defenders could not see their approach because of the slope of the hillside. Sniper positions were carved from the rock and camouflaged with wood and brush. Above Shabooh, near the crest of the hill, some of the biggest guns were nearly ready, including the great basilisk that was so large it had to be moved in pieces and assembled in place.

Just six days after the initial landing, the first of the guns were ready, including the basilisk, two big culverins, ten eighty-pounders, and a host of smaller cannons. Mustapha Pasha himself appeared, inspecting trenches and emplacements, verifying targets, encouraging the artillerymen, and testing the wind on his own battle-seasoned face.

"Cover your ears," Shabooh shouted to his men. They wadded bits of cotton or balls of mud and used them as plugs. Those nearest the basilisk clenched bits of wood between their teeth to keep them from breaking.

Mustapha Pasha nodded once.

The immense guns opened fire. When the great basilisk roared, rings of water rippled out from the shores of Sciberras, disturbing the glassy stretches of harbor on either side. To the occupants of M'kor Hakhayyim, sitting miles away in dead silence, it was an awesome and terrifying noise, such as none of them had ever heard. Behind Christien de Vries, suturing a wound in the infirmary, a jar of spirits of turpentine crashed to the floor. The dogs of Birgu set up a great howl, and horses in the public stables went wild, kicking and bucking against their restraints.

from **The Histories of the Middle Sea**

by Darius, called the Preserver
Court Historian to the Prince of Mecca and Aleppo, the
Sultan Achmet

The Grand Master received a message from Sicily, carried by one of the small, fast boats that by night managed to sneak through Piali's naval patrols. Only weeks earlier the Viceroy, Don García, had vowed to send help before the month of May was done. Now he lamented the grave difficulties he faced mustering a force of sufficient strength to stand against the Turks. It was folly to send insufficient reinforcements, he reasoned, for their ships would never slip through the Ottoman noose around the island. Better to wait until the force was adequate to ensure victory. "Endure in patience and faith," he wrote La Valette. "Feel confident that I am doing all that can be done. I have few ships at my disposal and request you send the Order's galleys to Messina."

La Valette remained coolly diplomatic at the request that he, the besieged, devote the thousand men it would require to man the galleys, which in any event were trapped within Grand Harbor. He merely replied that he could not possibly do so. Morale was high, he wrote. "The defenders will hold to the last man." The boat returned to Sicily with a flurry of new letters to the Pope and the Christian monarchs of Europe, beseeching their help.

—From Volume VII
The Great Campaigns: Malta

As La Valette had foreseen, the Turkish decision to take St. Elmo first gave the defenders of Birgu and Senglea precious time to improve the defenses, a task at which all able-bodied persons labored until they slumped from exhaustion.

The Grand Master reacted quickly to developments. New Turkish guns were being placed in positions to fire on St. Angelo and the tip of Senglea. La Valette ordered two of the Order's galleys that were exposed to fire to be sunk in shallow water, from which they could be raised again. He cleared the ramparts of St. Angelo and raised a ravelin that would support a gun platform high enough to reach some of the Turkish positions. He emptied the dungeons beneath St. Angelo of their remaining prisoners, freeing everyone but the Muslim slaves, promising liberal rewards to any man who defended Christianity.

❖

The bishop, Domenico Cubelles, formally suspended the Inquisition for the duration of the siege. He oversaw the conversion of his palace into a refuge for civilians and their animals. His gardens became a grazing ground for goats, while his kitchens produced great vats of soup. He ordered that all the silver dishes and candelabra that had been brought to the palace from every parish be melted, and he gave the proceeds to the Grand Master for the defense.

Without files or tribunals to tend to, Giulio Salvago became once again Dun Salvago, *Father* Salvago, *kappillan* of the new parish assigned him by Cubelles—the cellars and catacombs beneath the palace. He had stood on the battlements the day the Turks arrived, and had felt the old fear, the nausea that came from physical violence directed at *him*. He stared at the Turkish fleet and prayed God to grant him strength against this great enemy of his Church and all Christendom. He descended to his new parish. He was stiff and uncomfortable in the role. People viewed him differently than they had in his days at St. Agatha's. They were unsure whether to treat him as *kappillan* or as vicar.

For most of the first week he devoted his time to the solitary pursuits of prayer and reading. It took a mild rebuke from the bishop to bring him from his chamber. The dungeons were crammed with sweating, crying, unwashed humanity huddled in fear. "It is good to help them with prayer, Dun Salvago," Cubelles said. "But I think you'll need to dirty your hands as well."

After that Salvago threw himself into the task. He comforted the sick, prayed with the terrified, and helped nourish the poor. He emptied chamber pots and served food cooked on braziers that in other days had heated the Inquisition's iron implements of torture. In one morning he baptized a baby and gave last rites to its mother. The more he did of his old work, the more comfortable he felt. It was good, he reflected, to bend his back once again for a parish. The stench of the cellars and the needs of those in them succeeded in removing most of the vicar's patina.

There was food to be distributed, and children to quiet, and livestock to . . . well, he didn't know quite what to do with the livestock. Pigs, goats, and Christians roamed freely in the dark corridors. Only the dogs had been evicted earlier that day, to comply with the Grand Master's order. La Valette said to kill them all, even his own prized hunting animals, lest they disturb the sentries at night or consume food and water needed by people. Salvago coaxed the animals away from the children and took them up to the courtyard, where one of the *familiares* of the Captain of the Rod carried out the order.

Even deep underground one could not escape the awful rumble of the guns. Cannonballs shattered in the streets near the square. One ball bounced off the bastion of Provence and hit the bishop's palace, still having sufficient force to knock down part of a wall. The falling stone killed two women and a goat. Terrifying as those shots were, they were nothing like what was being directed at St. Elmo. Salvago trembled like everyone else, trembled like the earth itself, whenever a shot came too near. At those times the dungeons swelled with hymns and prayer as men and women tried to drown out the sound.

Chapter 37

The cannons of Sciberras rained stone upon St. Elmo. The thunder rumbled night and day without respite, making sleep impossible. During the hot, windless days the yellow dust was so thick men often could not see all the way across the fort. The Turkish gunners hammered at specific spots in the walls, expertly alternating ordnance between iron and marble and stone, each of which had a different effect on the masonry. Within hours of the beginning of the bombardment, the walls were already beginning to crack.

Any defender showing his head on the landward side of the fort was quickly shot dead by snipers, who were shielded from return fire by protective screens and by the high guns behind them. Consequently the sentries could not fire upon the slaves sweating in the trenches, bringing death ever nearer the defenders, one shovelful at a time. The gunners inside St. Elmo fired their own cannons, but their targets were uphill and difficult to hit.

Undaunted by covering fire from St. Angelo across the harbor, the Turkish engineers atop Sciberras finished constructing a sturdy parapet of heavy timber and earth from which their artillery had a clear shot at St. Elmo and the men within its walls. The fort had been built cheaply and quickly with limestone blocks of poor quality that crumbled easily. A problem that proved even more lethal for its defenders was that the fort lacked the traditional subterranean passages and inner protective walls that would allow them to move safely about inside wherever they were needed. Casualties were heavy from granite balls that crashed down inside the fort, shattering into razor-sharp splinters that ripped flesh from bone.

Each time a breach appeared in the outer wall, the men inside worked feverishly to repair it or to construct new defenses just inside. The damage came more quickly than the repairs. It appeared the predictions of the Turkish engineers were overly pessimistic: after only two days of bombardment, the walls of St. Elmo were already crumbling. Great jagged chunks of masonry toppled under the steady fire. Additional Turkish guns were brought into service every hour as troops and supplies were moved into place. Each night dozens of gravely wounded men were rowed across the harbor to Birgu, to be treated in the Infirmary.

There could be little doubt that the Turks would soon be mounting an assault. The commander of St. Elmo, Luigi Broglia, believed that despite the damage to the fort, St. Elmo could hold for a long while, if it had nightly reinforcements. He dispatched a Spanish knight, Don Juan de la Cerda, to convey that message to the Grand Master.

De la Cerda appeared before the council in near physical ruin. He'd had no sleep in days. His eyes darted around the room. The incessant Turkish barrage still seemed to shake him from within: he stumbled and stammered, unsure. His fear prompted him to go further than his brief from Broglia. "The fort's position, sires," he said, "is hopeless. It is a slaughterhouse whose walls are dust. The men inside have been reduced by the Turkish guns to little more than ghosts. They are brave men, but they die in vain, without inflicting damage on the enemy." The effect of his words on the men in the room was palpable. "We can hold out," he said, "for no more than eight days."

La Valette knew that Malta's chances hinged largely upon how long St. Elmo could resist. Each day it survived was another day to reinforce Birgu and Senglea. Each day it survived was another day closer to the relief promised by the Viceroy. Even though the fort was certainly doomed, it must hold out to the last moment, to the last man. The traditions of the Order demanded no less, and the Grand Master had no intention of allowing despair to settle on the defenders so early in the siege. If de la Cerda's views were shared by the other men inside St. Elmo, La Valette would replace them all.

"If the fire of the cannons is too frightening for you to bear," La Valette said frostily, "I myself will lead reinforcements to St. Elmo tonight. If we cannot at any rate cure your fear, we will at least make sure that the fortress does not fall into the hands of the enemy!"

La Valette instantly had more volunteers than he could manage, although his council persuaded him not to lead them. With de la Cerda humiliated, fifty knights and two hundred soldiers made their way across the harbor under cover of darkness. All knew that their Grand Master would never yield.

❖

"*Bis 'mallah. Ar-Rahman. Ar-Rahim.*"

Shabooh was commencing his morning prayers when he was interrupted by the sound of gunfire. His men massed quickly, weapons bristling. He went forward for a better view. The Christians had burst forth from St. Elmo and were pouring through the trenches where the labor forces were working. A pitched battle was under way. Panicked workers were fleeing with their picks and shovels, their screams all but lost in the gunfire.

Mustapha Pasha appeared in the predawn light, his massive turban signaling his presence. He quickly gave the order for which Shabooh's men had been hoping.

"Janissaries, forward."

Shabooh led a howling, swirling horde of white-robed warriors into the fray, swarming over the crest of the hill and pushing the knights back with terrifying speed and force, overwhelming them with superior numbers. The Janissaries quickly recaptured the trench, hacking and clawing their way forward. Within moments the knights and their soldiers were back inside their lair, dragging their dead and wounded behind them. Marksmen within the fort were firing into the ranks of pursuing Janissaries, but then those gunners had to take cover as the sharpshooters behind Shabooh opened fire.

Shabooh's men did not stop. To the beat of the great war drums and the clash of cymbals they surged forward, swords glistening red, their throats raw with the savage cry of battle. When the dust cleared, the Janissaries not only had retaken all their previous positions, but their flag flew atop the outer defense works of the fort. They were stronger than ever. Shabooh himself planted the flag. He realized he'd been wounded on his arm. The muscle was laid bare, a crimson streak staining his sleeve. He felt nothing but the exhilaration of the morning's glory. He knelt to finish his interrupted prayers. Afterward he raised his head and saw the sun rising blood red above the horizon, its rays lighting the crescent fluttering beside him.

❖

A new fleet appeared from the southeast. There were thirteen galleys, two galliots, and twenty-five other ships belonging to allied corsairs. The guns of the Turkish fleet boomed in salute while Turkish troops cheered. It was not the arrival of twenty-five hundred seasoned men or the additional siege guns or provisions that caused such elation among the Ottoman forces, but the identity of the man who sat in the flagship.

Dragut Raïs, the Drawn Sword of Islam, had arrived from Africa.

The Admiral Piali Pasha led nearly half the fleet out to meet the corsair. Asha had the honor of sailing at his right flank. They escorted Dragut to St. Julian's Bay, just to the north of the Marsa. Dragut disembarked, impatient to meet with the commanders. He walked past a line of pashas and *aghas,* assembled on the shore to welcome him. Dragut greeted them in turn. He stopped in front of Asha, who bowed deeply. "Peace be upon you, Grandfather," Asha said.

Dragut rested a hand on Asha's shoulder. "And on you be peace, my *hafeed* Asha Raïs, and the mercy of God and His blessings." Though he was eighty, Dragut's eyes had lost none of their fire, his step none of its quickness, and his temper none of its edge. It flared almost the instant he entered the command tent.

"You should have awaited my arrival!" he thundered. "To have attacked St. Elmo is a fool's errand, good powder spent on a worthless cause. You might as well piss on them. Our force is diverted. Gozo and Mdina could have been taken easily. The rest would have fallen to our guns. St. Elmo's could have remained isolated until every man inside its walls died of the French disease that rots them all. A thousand pities you have chosen this path—a thousand times a thousand."

Pleased that Dragut's assessment agreed with his own, Mustapha suggested they change course immediately. "It is too late," Dragut said. "We must finish what we have begun. To abandon our course against St. Elmo now would make us appear indecisive. Morale would suffer, and the Christians would think us weak."

Dragut then outlined the weaknesses in the attack on St. Elmo. Most commanders had thought the siege was progressing quite well, but Dragut was not so easily pleased. He pointed out that the fort was being bombarded from only one direction. "The walls must be reduced from every point of the compass," he said. He ordered that the big guns on his ships be carried to Tigné, a point of land on the far side of Marsamuscetto harbor. From there they could batter the north side of the fort. Other guns were to be placed at Gallows Point on the south side of the harbor entrance so that a cross fire could be established. In all fifty guns were to be added to the cannons of Sciberras.

Despite his grasp of strategy, the force of his arguments, and the trust of his Sultan, Dragut was not the supreme commander. For reasons known only to himself, Suleiman had split that authority. Dragut still had to contend with Piali Pasha. The admiral—married to the Sultan's granddaughter—was adamant about the overriding need to preserve the Sultan's ships. He refused to offload the cannons at Gallows Point, pointing out it would needlessly expose his ships to hostile fire. "Take St. Elmo first," he insisted. "When I have my harbor, you shall have your guns."

Dragut was not a man to waste time arguing. Further dispute could only harm morale. "I shall place the guns with my own ships," he said acidly. "You shall have your harbor." Dragut's men succeeded, without the loss of a single ship.

The intensity of the Turkish attack on St. Elmo quickly rose to new heights. The walls and bastions were reduced by the hour from every direction. There still weren't enough guns to stop the nightly flow of boats between St. Angelo and St. Elmo, but the men on both sides knew that was only a matter of time.

Asha resumed his station blockading the harbor mouth. It was boring and undistinguished duty, but he took comfort in Dragut's energy and wisdom, knowing that, Allah willing, the old corsair would soon have the knights on their knees, with the damage to the Maltese people contained.

❖

Bertrand Cuvier strode into the Infirmary, where he knew Christien would still be working. An entire ward had been converted into an operating theater. Two surgeons and four barber-surgeons worked feverishly alongside physicians, the atmosphere in the room one of controlled pandemonium. The ward was lit with lanterns mounted every few feet along the walls or by candles flickering in candelabra mounted on the headboards of the beds. The room smelled of blood and smoke and sweat. Patients were carried in and out on litters. The apothecary checked supplies, sending his assistant to the pharmacy for more. Pages stocked shelves with bandages and splints and cleaned surgical tools whenever they became too encrusted to use. They filled buckets with seawater to wash wounds, and brought food to patients and to the doctors, who ate standing when they ate at all. The crush of patients grew worse each day, with the worst coming on the nightly boats from St. Elmo. There were scores of patients awaiting treatment.

Christien looked up. "Ah, my friend, you've come to help. Soak this for me, will you?" He handed Bertrand a piece of tow and indicated a bowl near the table.

Bertrand put the tow into a mixture of egg whites and wine and stirred it with his fingers. He sucked them when he was done. "The eggs are underdone and the wine is terrible," he said, wincing. "It'll kill him for sure."

Christien rapidly finished suturing the flap of skin. He plucked the tow from the bowl and packed it around the wound. "We've plenty of shit to haul if all you're going to do is complain about the menu," he said.

"*Merci,* but I see the shit is in good hands already. I came to tell you I'm going to St. Elmo. I leave later tonight."

Christien's fingers hesitated briefly. "Go upstairs," he said quietly. "I'll be along when I can."

Bertrand passed through corridors crowded with groaning men. He stepped through a back window onto a terrace that overlooked Kalkara Creek. From there he climbed a ladder to the roof, the private retreat where he and Christien often sat together. Half an hour later Christien joined him. Exhausted, he sat beside Bertrand on a box near the parapet wall, from which they could see the expanse of the harbor. They could see St. Elmo but not the main Turkish guns on Sciberras, hidden from view by the bulk of Fort St. Angelo. Behind St. Angelo the night sky flickered as the guns fired. From St. Elmo there were brief flashes from the muzzles of the sentries' guns, as they tried to pick off slaves working in the trenches. From the fort's bastions and cavaliers, cannons belched orange flame in answer to the greater Turkish fire rolling down upon them.

"An eerie scene," Bertrand remarked. He passed his flask to Christien. "That it should be so calm here while the fires of hell burn around St. Elmo."

"The fire will be here soon enough." Christien took a drink and wiped his mouth. "I've heard there are plenty of volunteers for St. Elmo," he said, trying to keep a light tone to his voice. He looked at Bertrand, whose face was briefly lit by a flash. "Go later, when they'll really need you. Just now they'll only throw you out when they find you've come with no brandy and they're stuck with a sober Frenchman." His voice thickened. He coughed.

"Who said I'll be without brandy? And I might not be able to get in later. Surely some dolt among the Turkish command will finally think to shut off the passage of boats relieving the fort every night. . They're the only reason it's holding out."

"But when they do . . . no one will get out, either."

"*Non.* I suppose not."

"Go later," Christien said again.

Bertrand shrugged. "It is the battle I have wanted all these years. I was born for this. And I won't concede St. Elmo, no matter the odds. The relief could arrive any day."

Christien spat. "My mother's last letter said everyone in Paris is more concerned with killing Huguenots than Turks. Apparently even my brother, Yves, is consumed with it." Arnaud de Vries had died three years earlier, making Christien's brother the new count.

"What a pity your father died. He would have raised an army and come himself," Bertrand said. "The only thing he hated worse than Spaniards were Turks."

Christien smiled. "I remember when he caught us with that corpse. Had it been a Turk instead of just a Protestant, I might not be here today. I'd be a stuffy member of the Faculté, teaching students to dissect Lutherans."

"You should leave the Order, you know. You have no business here. If you get out of this alive, you should consider your oath honorably discharged. God could ask no more of a man, even if La Valette could. Take Maria and leave. You should be cleaning out the pockets of rich patients in Paris, not cleaning out the guts of poor knights in Birgu." It was the hundredth time since Christien returned from caravan that Bertrand had expressed that opinion.

"By God, but you beat a thing to death, if you can't stab it."

"I try my best." Bertrand rose. "Well, my friend. I must find a chaplain to hear a rather lengthy and overdue confession, and then get my things together before they leave without me."

They faced each other, their faces somber. "God be with you," Christien said.

"And with you." Bertrand gave him a great hug. "I will not say *au revoir,* my friend. Just now it might be bad luck."

Christien remained on the roof, looking down at the street. He saw the glint of Bertrand's cuirass as he emerged from the gate and strode away, his step as sure and jaunty as always. He almost seemed to strut. He turned, looked up, and waved. Christien waved back and watched until he was gone.

❖

Nasrid chafed at his inactivity. He and his men were camped above the bulk of the fleet anchored in the bay below, watching as the smoke rose during the day and the fires spewed at night over the battles to the north. It was like watching a volcano erupt, only he was not born to be a spectator. He wanted to feel the volcano's heat on his own face, and to add his own fuel to its raging fires.

His impatience was soothed by the knowledge that so far only artillery was doing its work against the enemy. The moment of pitched battle was still to come, and it was for that moment he and his men lived and breathed. But until the fleet was safely anchored in Marsamuscetto, they would have to remain at their station. There were reports of lightning sorties by the cavalry based inside Mdina. The infidel had already struck at Turkish supply lines and isolated camps. Nasrid kept two squads of four men on constant patrol, for besides cavalry he was wary of the *widien,* the gullies that scarred the island and offered infinite hiding places to the enemy. There was no telling when a Maltese peasant might take a shot at one of his men. But the danger was small, he thought, as most of the Christians were trapped behind their walls, awaiting death.

Nasrid and his men prayed five times daily and cooked rabbit stew in their brass pot over an open fire, which they kept burning with brambles gathered from the surrounding countryside. To pass the time they held archery contests, using a knot on the carob tree as a target. They sharpened their scimitars and oiled their guns and practiced throwing their axes. One of his men was a master of the cane flute, another of the fiddle. At night they danced and whirled above the water, singing and clapping. There was little else to do but smoke hashish. Nasrid rationed it carefully, wishing to keep an edge on his men.

Beneath the Janissaries, the Jews of M'kor Hakhayyim crouched in terror. The cave was secure in many ways, but they had never anticipated that someone might camp right on top of it. In the rare moments when the low rumble of cannon fire did not fill the air, they could hear the men on the hill above them, chattering and laughing and playing their instruments. Now they feared that their slightest noise—a cough or a slip on the rocks—would be amplified in the narrow tunnels that emerged onto the hillside. Fençu had never thought to test such a thing. He never knew when the guns might fall silent for even a second, so he permitted no noise even while the guns were firing.

It was worst for the children. Villano had two sons, ages six and eight, Cataldo a daughter who was seven, and there was Moses. There were no games to play, nothing to amuse them that wouldn't put them in danger. They squirmed through hour after hour of forced inactivity. Day and night they all sat, eyes fixed on the black tunnels, fearful they would hear a rush of robes or see a sudden silhouette, followed by the glowing match of an Ottoman arquebus or the glint of Damascus steel.

After many days Fençu tried crawling with the children into a remote gallery that had once been the bed of an underground stream. It was as far removed from the hillside as he could take them. The gallery was cramped and pitch-black. There he whispered a story. Cataldo's daughter giggled, and he hushed her, worried anew that perhaps some hidden vent might betray them even there. That ended the stories. There was nothing to do but wait and sleep.

There was plenty of grain, but cooking in the pot and baking in the rock oven were out of the question. They ate salted fish and goat meat, and crunched on hard biscuits. They held each other and prayed.

Two days passed when they did not hear the soldiers because the low rumble of the guns didn't stop at all. In the middle of the night Fençu sneaked up one of the tunnels, moving an inch at a time. At the top he set aside the rocks and slithered out of the hole, letting long moments pass between movements, every sense alert as he tried to assess the situation. He saw a blanket of stars and only a few low clouds, which reflected a steady flicker of light from the north. Silhouetted against the stars, he saw the sweep of a turban and the tip of a weapon. The man was propped against a rock and didn't move. Fençu couldn't tell whether he was awake or asleep, or even which way he might be looking. He carefully slipped backward into the hole, replacing the rock.

"They're still there," he whispered to Elli and Elena, huddled together in the darkness. "I'll check the lower tunnel." He disappeared down the narrow hole of the newest tunnel. At the opening he cautiously inched out until only his head and shoulders were exposed. He twisted and looked upward, scanning the rocks above. He saw no one. The surf ground against the rocks just beneath him. He was glad of his foresight in adding the new tunnel. The whole Turkish army might camp above them, but this would still be a way out. Erosion had carved a steep basin from the rocks, open on one side to the sea. Unlike the main entrance to the cave, this entrance was hidden from the view of anyone on the open water by the shape of the little cove's rock walls. He'd sunk his little boat in the shallow water and weighted it down with rocks. In an emergency the boat could be easily refloated, although he reflected grimly that not everyone in the cave could fit in it, and there was of course the small matter of the Turkish fleet anchored a stone's throw away, in the bay.

In all it was a terrible place to be, he thought, but not nearly as terrible as with the poor souls caught beneath the Turkish artillery. He couldn't imagine how many guns there must be to make such light, to make such noise, to make the very earth rumble beneath his belly. Surely they could be heard all the way to Jerusalem. He was confident his decision was right. Better to live whispering in M'kor Hakhayyim than to die screaming in Birgu.

He went back inside and told the others what he'd seen. "We must be patient," he said for the hundredth time. Elena turned over and tried to sleep, her arms draped over Moses. She slept almost on top of him, afraid he would have a nightmare and cry out.

She had a constant ache in her stomach. She wondered how long she could bear it.

❖

There are many paths by which a man may reach his destiny, the Koran teaches, but all of them are paved by Allah.

And so it seemed to Asha that his step was directed by the unseen hand of God.

Like Nasrid, Asha chafed at his inactivity, though not out of desire to carry a weapon into battle. While he was relieved not to be an active participant, he was agitated to simply stand by. There was little for the fleet to do. Some of the bigger ships laid fire on St. Elmo with their deck guns. Others patrolled the coasts, trying to maintain a blockade. Others ferried water from wells in the north, as it appeared from sickness growing among some of the troops that the water near the Marsa had been poisoned.

The *Alisa* and her consorts continued to stand off the entrance to Grand Harbor. During the day Asha paced the deck and watched the firestorm over St. Elmo, listening as the sounds of battle raged in its trenches when weapons clashed and men screamed and died, and yet the fort still stood. At night he often visited the command tent, where he could hear firsthand about the progress of the siege.

Dragut's gun emplacements were savaging the fort, battering its walls from every direction. The nightly flow of supplies and men to the fort had been greatly reduced. In a great stroke of luck, a key ravelin had fallen to the Janissaries. The *ravelin* was one of the detached defense works outside the walls, just beyond the northwest corner of the fort. Combat engineers surveying the trench works discovered that the *ravelin's* exhausted defenders were napping. Minutes later the Janissaries stormed in. There was a quick and bloody rout. The few survivors struggled across a bridge of wooden planks that spanned the ditch, shouting at the men inside the fort to raise the portcullis and let them in. The Janissaries very nearly got inside along with them. Had the defenders not managed to close the gate at the last second, the battle for St. Elmo would have been over. The gate closed, but the unexpected battle raged on. From his position in the water Asha could see the tops of the Janissaries' scaling ladders being placed against the fort itself. Around him his men cheered the assault.

Waves of troops stormed the fort from opposite sides, first swarming near the ravelin, then attacking the entire landward side from the slopes of Sciberras, their efforts accompanied by the roar of arquebus fire as sharpshooters tried to clear the walls of defenders.

Troops seethed at the bases of the walls, and every ladder sagged with climbing men. Just when it appeared they would succeed, the men of St. Elmo launched a firestorm. Fire grenades sailed over the walls, their fuses leaving long, lazy trails of smoke. They exploded amidst the Turkish troops. Flaming hoops were hurled into their ranks, setting robes and turbans and flesh on fire. Flame-throwing trumps poked through the battlements, belching a fiery mix of oil and turpentine, spewing streams of fire as if from the mouth of a dragon. The Ottomans wore silk and cotton in battle, and their clothing ignited an inferno.

The cheers around Asha died. By the time the retreat was sounded, the trenches near St. Elmo were filled with smoldering dead. The day was calm, with no wind to carry away the stench of burnt flesh and hair that wafted over the harbor. The screams of burned and dying men could be heard in Birgu. Even before proper aim had been reestablished, a few Turkish gunners opened fire, just to drown out the awful sound.

That night in the command tent Asha learned that nearly two thousand men had lost their lives in the attack. Mustapha Pasha considered it a cheap price to secure the ravelin. He ordered his engineers to begin constructing a great mound of earth behind it, a cavalier that would soon be taller than the fort itself. After it was complete, whenever the men inside St. Elmo looked to their God in Heaven, they would see instead the cannons of Islam, ready to carry them at point-blank range to hell.

At the same time, slaves worked to fill the ditch between the ravelin and the fort. They were shot dead by the hundreds as they worked, succeeding in death at their task by virtue of tumbling into the trenches themselves. Soon their skulls might be used as stepping-stones to the walls.

Each night the Ottoman commanders agreed that the end of St. Elmo was surely in sight. From every angle the star-shaped fort seemed a complete ruin. No matter how hard the knights and their men labored to repair shattered defenses, they could not keep up, particularly not when faced with relentless bombardment and sniper fire. Already the cannonade had lasted nearly three weeks. Each day the intensity increased, until great sections of wall gave way and crashed into the sea. Inside the fort there was a never-ending hailstorm of marble and granite balls. More general assaults were mounted, each more furious than the last.

Yet somehow the fort held, day after day. In the command tent, excuses flew as thick as flies as *aghas* and engineers sought to explain why the world's most seasoned troops and experienced artillerymen could not crush the resistance of the little fort. The problem, said the commanders, was that the infidels inside the fort fought like demons possessed.

This stubborn refusal of St. Elmo to die was what most troubled Asha. Birgu and Senglea were more heavily fortified than St. Elmo. There were more defenders, with better supplies. If they fought with the same tenacity, the siege could last months or even years. The blood cost would be incalculable.

One evening Dragut and Mustapha were planning where the artillery should be placed after the fall of St. Elmo. Dragut set different-colored pebbles on the maps of the harbor area to indicate his choices. "It is a pity we do not know the exact disposition of forces and stores within Birgu and Senglea," he said. "It would ease our task to know what La Valette has been up to."

The words made Asha's heart race. Surely this was the path Allah had chosen for him. He could be of use in a very real way: he could enter Birgu and learn the location of powder magazines, troop placements, and stores. He could assess the strengths and weaknesses of the fortifications. He could reconnoiter subterranean passages and learn of emergency plans and tactics. Armed with such knowledge, the old corsair Dragut and the brilliant general Mustapha would surely find the quickest route to victory—and that would save both Turkish and Maltese lives. It was a way Asha could help without taking up arms, a way to bridge his two lives. It was perfect.

He could not explain to Dragut, of course, or to Piali or anyone else. He didn't know what they might do to him if they learned the truth, even after his long and faithful service. Dragut was particularly unpredictable: he might well chuckle at the clever deception, or he might order Asha's head lopped off, or both. So he would have to do it alone, surreptitiously. If his identity was discovered, when he returned with this priceless information, so be it. Any penalty for a lifetime of lies would be mitigated by the lives his information could save. He was certain he could get it, too. He knew the island, knew every ravine and well and place name. He knew her language, her customs, and her people.

I can do it.

He lay awake for hours, thinking and planning. He decided to act the following night.

The very next day the unthinkable happened. Lord Dragut had pointed out many times that the only reason the knights still held St. Elmo was that they were able to ferry supplies and reinforcements to the fort each night under cover of darkness. He devised a plan to dig a trench down the slope of Sciberras facing Fort St. Angelo. The trench would be covered with a screen of brush and stone, shielding his men from the fire of St. Angelo's cannons. From a protected position near the Grand Harbor, the long and deadly guns of the Janissaries would at last be able to close off St. Elmo's lifeline.

Dragut was in the trenches inspecting the work when a Turkish gunner atop Sciberras fired an errant shot. The ball landed in the midst of the officers. One, the *agha* of Janissaries, was killed instantly. A long splinter of granite pierced Dragut's skull, just above his ear. He fell to the ground, bleeding from ears and mouth, saved from instant death only by the thick coils of the turban he wore.

That night Asha came to see him. The doctors had done all they could, which was little. Dragut's fate was in the hands of Allah, they said, and it was clear Allah would soon bring his servant home. He lay on his back on a cot. His features were serene, but his face had a terrible pallor and his breath was labored. He drifted in and out of the ether, restless but always unconscious. Sometimes he mumbled, and once he laughed. Asha knelt beside his cot and tried to make him more comfortable, fighting the lump in his throat. More than any other man, perhaps, Dragut Raïs had helped shape his life.

He thought of the day Dragut fished him from the sea. Dragut could have enslaved or sold or killed him. Instead the old pirate had seen something in him, and the many blessings of his life had followed from that. He thought of Dragut's premonition that he would one day die in these very islands. The brash child Nicolo Borg, still dripping wet, had thought Dragut the spawn of Satan and had promised to the old man's face that he himself would deliver that death and hang his enemy's head from the ram of a galley of the Order of St. John. How different the life ordained by Allah than the life Nico foresaw! Now he hovered close to the man he had sworn to kill, wishing only that he knew a way to keep him alive.

"*May-ya.*" It was barely a whisper, as light as the breeze that rippled the sides of the tent. *Water.* Asha filled a cup and tilted it to Dragut's mouth. Dragut licked at it, wetting his lips and tongue. He did not awaken.

He leaned over and kissed his mentor's forehead. He squeezed Dragut's hand. "Good night, Grandfather," he whispered. "The Prophet will be much blessed with you at his side."

Asha rose and left the tent, pushing aside his sorrow as he hurried to his galley, his mind churning. Dragut's loss would be a devastating blow to the Sultan's forces. More than ever, Mustapha and Piali would need the information Asha was going to get from Birgu. The riskiest part, he knew, was his own galleys. He had command over four of them, and he could not afford having a senior officer of the fleet inquire as to his whereabouts, or to have his own crew report him missing.

On the poop deck of the *Alisa* he spoke to Feroz, his first officer. He explained he had been given the honor of spending several days in the trenches with Mustapha Pasha, to observe the art of siege warfare. Asha told Feroz to take his galleys on patrol in the channel between Gozo and Malta and to return for him in exactly five days. He was to leave at first light. Asha's instructions were within Piali Pasha's general battle orders and so raised no question in Feroz. "I am honored in your trust, Asha Raïs," the officer said gravely.

Asha had himself ferried back to shore aboard a dinghy. God willing, he would be back aboard his galley before anyone else knew he was gone. He walked to the slave compound near the Marsa, where reed torches burned at intervals around the perimeter. The men chained inside the compound included galley slaves and a great many Maltese peasants who'd been captured in the countryside. They worked twenty hours a day, and now they lay exhausted, huddled together under the watchful eyes of the guards, waiting for the call that would take them back to the trenches. Asha scanned their ranks. He selected a man whose height and weight were close to his own. He summoned the guard, a massive Anatolian. "I require a slave," Asha said, pointing imperiously. "Bring me that dog."

"At once, effendi."

The slave was a lean, middle-aged peasant. His expression as he was brought before the Turkish officer betrayed his certainty that he was about to meet his Maker. A moment later, hands bound, he was following Asha out of camp. They walked past the latrines and straight into the darkness toward the village of Msida, as if heading for Dragut's anchorage in St. Julian's bay. The perimeter guards watched their passage without interest.

They came to a *wied* and Asha left the path, turning inland. The peasant hesitated. Asha prodded him along with the blunt edge of his saber.

Ten minutes later, well away from curious eyes, Asha stopped and cut the man's ropes. "*Inza hwejgek,*" he said in Maltese. "Take off your clothes."

The peasant was stunned. "Master?" he said. "My clothes?"

"*Haffef,*" Asha said. "Quickly, or I'll cut them from your dead body."

The man stripped, dropping his clothing at his feet.

"Where is your home?"

"Near Mgarr, master." It was a village on the west coast. Asha was relieved. Had the man said Birgu, he would have had little choice but to kill him.

"Go there, now."

"Master?" He seemed dumbfounded.

"Are you deaf? You are freed. Go quickly, before I change my mind. Take care this time you don't get caught by the Turks." Overwhelmed at his good fortune, the man started to babble and bow. Asha impatiently waved his saber, and the man shot off into the darkness, disbelieving, naked, and free.

Asha knelt. He unwound his turban and took off his silk robes. He donned the man's baggy knee-length trousers. The shirt was loose-fitting, the long sleeves perfect for concealing his *orta,* the tattoo on his arm. In the manner of a peasant he tucked the shirt in, cinching the cloth belt in place. The clothing smelled faintly of excrement and garlic. He laced on the sandals, which were nothing more than leather soles secured to his feet with strips of leather. He shook out the farmer's *biritta,* a long stocking cap, hoping it wasn't lice-infested. He realized his beard was too well groomed for a peasant's. He sawed at it with his knife until it felt properly ragged.

He smudged dirt on his face and neck and donned the *biritta*.

Despite the cap he felt naked without his turban. He kept only the emerald from his turban and the coin he always carried. He concealed everything else—clothing, weapons, and amulets—beneath a rock, hoping he'd be able to find them again.

Asha scanned the countryside nearby, wary of patrols. He would have to move with extreme care. He was now a man between worlds. If caught by the Turks, he would be accused of desertion. If caught by the knights and exposed as a Turk, he would be accused of spying. Neither prospect boded well for a man's neck. He knew the forces on both sides would be distracted. A major assault was being launched against St. Elmo at dawn.

In a crouch Nicolo Borg hurried across the fields toward the walled village of his birth, his way lit by the flickering night fire over Sciberras.

❖

7 June 1565

"St. Elmo can hold no longer."

Sent by the commanders Broglia, Miranda, and Degueras, the Chevalier de Medran stood before the Grand Council. There were burns on his face and blood on his tunic, but no hint in his eyes of the battle nerves that had so unsettled the earlier messenger, de la Cerda. DeMedran was calm and realistic in his appraisal. "The walls are breached and in ruins," he said. "It is the recommendation of the fort's commanders that we blow up St. Elmo and its remaining stores and bring our men out of that defenseless hell to join the defenses of Birgu and St. Michael."

There was considerable sentiment in the council to grant the request, but La Valette was resolute. "No death in the defense of St. Elmo is wasted," he told the council. "I have received a new letter from the Viceroy. He has promised relief by the twentieth of June, but the Viceroy does not care to put his ships and men at risk for a lost cause. He will send aid only if St. Elmo holds. There can be no surrender." He walked among them, stopping to look at each of them. "Every post, every position, every piece of rubble will be defended to the last man. If I myself must row to the defense of St. Elmo, I will do so."

Though they knew it was certain death, fifteen more knights and fifty soldiers volunteered to return to St. Elmo with de Medran.

After another day of fierce fighting, fifty-three of the younger knights inside St. Elmo, unhappy with de Medran's message that they simply await slaughter, signed a letter to the Grand Master.

Most Illustrious and Very Reverend Monsignor:
When the Turks landed here, Your Highness ordered all of us Knights here present to come and defend this fortress. This we did with the greatest of good heart, and up to now all that we could do has been done. Your Highness knows this, and that we have never spared ourselves fatigue or danger. But now, the enemy has reduced us to such a state that we can neither make any effect on them nor can we defend ourselves (since they hold the ravelin and the ditch). They have also made a bridge and steps up to our ramparts, and they have mined under the wall so that hourly we expect to be blown up. The ravelin itself they have enlarged so much that one cannot stand at one's post without being killed. One cannot place sentries to keep an eye on the enemy since—within minutes of being posted—they are shot dead by snipers. We are in such straits that we can no longer use the open space in the center of the fort. Several of our men have already been killed there, and we have no shelter except the chapel itself. Our troops are down at heart, and even their officers cannot make them anymore take up their stations on the walls. Convinced that the fort is sure to fall, they are preparing to save themselves by swimming for safety. Since we can no longer efficiently carry out the duties of our Order, we are determined—if Your Highness does not send us boats tonight so that we can withdraw—to sally forth and die as Knights should. Do not send further reinforcements, since they are no more than dead men. This is the most determined resolution of all those whose signature Your Most Illustrious Highness can read below. We further inform Your Highness that Turkish galliots have been active off the end of the point. And so, with this our intention, we kiss your hands.

Dated from St. Elmo, the eighth of June, 1565

La Valette dispatched three knights to assess the situation. They reported chaos in the fort. Two thought St. Elmo could hold a few more days at best. A third, Costantino Castriota, said that with fresh troops he could hold out longer. He quickly found six hundred volunteers among the knights and soldiers in Birgu and reported to La Valette he was ready to cross Grand Harbor at their head.

The Grand Master was furious that any of the knights inside St. Elmo should question their orders at all, even though it was a minority of them. "If knights begin deciding how and when they wish to die, then from that moment our cause is lost," he said in council. "It is the duty of a knight to obey his orders. It is the duty of a knight to die not when it seems convenient but when he is *ordered* to die."

He decided to try something else before sending Castriota. He wrote a reply to the letter, saying that a volunteer force had been raised to defend St. Elmo. "Your petition to leave St. Elmo for the safety of Birgu is now granted. Return, my brethren, to the convent and to Birgu, where you will be in more security. For my part, I shall feel more confident when I know that the fort—upon which the safety of the island so greatly depends—is held by men I can trust implicitly."

Shamed, the rebellious knights implored the Grand Master not to replace them. They would follow his orders to the death.

There was a night battle, the first of the siege. All day the Turkish guns had fired without cooling between rounds, fired until they were in danger of melting. When they stopped, an eerie silence enveloped Grand Harbor. Everyone knew what it meant.

Christien climbed to the Infirmary roof to watch the awful scene unfold. Around him on the walls of Birgu, St. Angelo, and St. Michael, other men and women did the same.

A rumble of drums and trumpets rose up in place of the guns, and a great mass of screaming Turks rushed down the hill toward St. Elmo, some carrying torches that made the slopes of Sciberras glow as if smothered in a flow of molten lava. From the walls of the fort, pots and hoops and flame-throwing trumps rained fire upon them, turning night into day as their silk and cotton robes burst into flame. Into certain death the Iayalars and Janissaries came, surging forward, the men in front pushed by the men behind, all of them yelling, climbing, surging fearlessly toward the weak points in the walls.

Some of the men whose robes were blazing broke away from the walls and raced farther down the hill. Christien saw them leaping from a promontory below the fort, robes streaming behind them, flaming like meteors until they were snuffed into darkness by the cold black waters of the harbor. Flares soared high over the fort, adding light to the battle. Men clashed atop the walls. Arquebus fire roared steadily, the muzzles flashing orange and yellow and red. Christien watched, transfixed, mesmerized by the horrible beauty of the Ottoman sea of fire lapping at the shores of St. Elmo. He prayed that Bertrand, trapped somewhere inside that inferno, would die quickly.

The battle raged all night. At dawn, though it seemed impossible that anyone inside the fort could have survived, the flag of the Order still fluttered over the smoldering ruins.

❖

16 June 1565

Bertrand Cuvier lay in a torpor in the shelter of a mound of earth, just behind the inner cavalier. Clouds of flies competed with the rats for the rotting flesh that filled the trenches around the fort. Many of the dead could not be carried away and were left to decompose in the blistering sun. Languidly he watched a rat scurry from beneath the swollen corpse of a Janissary, its whiskers glistening red as it darted for the shelter of a crater. Beyond it, over the remnants of the wall, he could see the slopes of Sciberras crisscrossed with enemy trenches. Turkish flags sprouted here and there, marking the zigzag course the slaves had dug, bringing death ever closer to the walls.

A Maltese soldier crawled to Bertrand's position, bringing a sponge soaked in wine. Bertrand held it to his parched tongue and sucked it as if it were his precious brandy, which had long since run out. His lips were cracked and bleeding. He baked inside his armor. The heat of mid-June turned the suit into an oven. He envied the Turks their cool silks—at least until he saw the firepots turning them into living torches. His armor had saved him from that. His own arms were badly burned, blackened during the night attack six days earlier. One of the Turkish incendiaries had stuck to his armor and exploded, spraying him with fiery jelly. He would have roasted but for the big vat of water nearby, one of many placed around the perimeter for just that purpose. He had jumped in, dousing the flames, and then, in a moment that later left him weak with laughter, nearly hadn't been able to get out again for the weight of his armor and his extreme fatigue.

Imagine drowning in a firestorm, he thought.

His arms looked as if they'd been left on a spit over a brazier and forgotten overnight. The skin was blackened and charred, the joints at his elbows raw, cracked and oozing. He could barely move them, and what worried him was that he would not be able to use his sword effectively. He clenched his teeth and forced himself to bend his arms, knowing that otherwise they would stiffen. He heard his skin pop and crack and tear. He cried out and did it again.

He'd lived through ten days of it. He knew he could live through ten more if he could only get some rest. He was punchy with fatigue, his brain in fog. During the day the cannons went on without end, hurling huge granite balls that bounced and crashed around inside the walls of the fort, breaking into lethal splinters that killed men where they crouched. Most nights the cannons fell silent, but there was little rest then, either. There were dead to be buried and wounded to be tended or put on the boats bound for St. Angelo. Night raids had to be guarded against. After all that, every remaining ounce of strength was devoted to putting one stone on top of another, to raising the defenses once again, so they could be destroyed once again the following day.

Each dawn he scanned the horizon over walls that were lower than the day before, certain that at any moment he would see the Viceroy's relief fleet sweeping into view. Despite Christien's pessimism on the subject, Bertrand didn't believe for one moment the Christian monarchs of Europe would forsake them, for if they did, it was their own necks that would next feel the scimitar. Surely they saw this was the time and place to eradicate the godless bastards from this end of the sea. From his state of near delirium he lectured King Philip and scolded the boy King Charles, and bloodied his hands heaping stone upon stone.

As he surveyed the devastation around him, he was as amazed as anyone that St. Elmo still held. Almost to a man its defenders were wounded. The bakery was destroyed, so there was little to eat except when the Grand Master managed to send fresh supplies by boat, a task that was possible only at night now, and then quite uncertain. The smell was worse than the noise: vomit and burnt hair and fat, and above that the stench of rotting flesh from corpses bursting in the broiling sun.

By God, he thought, it had been a fight. He'd faced Janissaries at sea, in battle among galleys, but never on land. Even when they came in the hundreds, they were human. They died like any other man, just a little harder. It was the other ones who were unnerving, the Iayalars. They came first sometimes, waves of them. Unlike the Janissaries, who were clever in combat and did not waste themselves in futile attack, the Iayalars were fanatics who wished to smother their enemies with their bodies, praying for the sweet release of death and entry into Paradise. They smoked their hashish and were beyond fear. They reminded Bertrand of moths swirling around a candle, dancing and fluttering until they were sucked into a fiery death.

When he stood in battle Bertrand felt a similar purity of spirit, a closeness to God that he rarely felt at other times in his busy life, times when he only partly adhered to the Order's vows. In St. Elmo he was at peace, certain of the rightness of the Order's cause, and ready to die for it. That was why he knew he would not. He would not die in this siege—unless, that is, he had to talk with any more Italian or Spanish or German knights, hardly the sort of company one wished to keep in difficult times. He longed for Christien's companionship. He found himself talking to his friend often, joking and laughing as if he were there while Bertrand polished his blades, cleaned his arquebus, wiped the sweat from his brow, worked his burnt joints, and waited for the next attack.

One night he had heard a Turk calling from the ditch between the captured ravelin and the fort. "Knights of St. John," the man cried in Italian. "Soldiers of Spain and Genoa! Brave men of Malta! The Lord Mustapha Pasha sends his greetings to the defenders of St. Elmo. You have fought honorably and well, but your cause is lost! On the graves of his ancestors, and by the beard of the Prophet, Mustapha swears that any man who leaves the fort this night shall be granted safe passage, as Suleiman mercifully granted the same at Rhodes." He began to repeat the offer. Bertrand made a lucky shot, and the voice of surrender fell silent.

The following day had brought sporadic attacks, mixed with a bombardment more intense than ever. The guns on Tigné placed by the Turks after Dragut's arrival had been destroyed in a furious cavalry raid from Mdina under the command of Marshal Copier. But the Turks quickly had new guns in place; their cannons seemed as plentiful as their Iayalars. The iron and granite balls would hit again and again, churning great clouds of yellow dust into the air until whole sections of wall toppled, crushing the men beneath them.

Each night the defenders took advantage of the respite from sniper fire to prepare for the coming dawn. Siege warfare had changed little over the centuries, although some of the weapons were more sophisticated. Arquebuses were loaded and laid on the ground next to boxes of powder. Cannons were filled with grapeshot or chain, and pointed at the breaches where the greatest numbers of attackers were expected. Every knight had his mace, his battle axe, his sword, and his shield, but so far in the siege it was fire that had done most of the work.

Pots of pitch were set to boiling along what remained of the walls. Stacks of fire hoops stood ready for use. They were a new invention, and so far had proved one of the most effective weapons of all. They were rings of wood soaked in oil and tightly wrapped with strips of cotton and wool dipped in a mixture of black powder, saltpeter, and tallow. Then—in a step not lost on Bertrand, of course—they were soaked in brandy. The steps were repeated multiple times, until each hoop was as thick as a man's neck and would burn long and white-hot. Once lit they were hurled with large tongs into the advancing silken hordes.

Next to these were the flame-throwing trumps, and beside those great stacks of wildfire pots, each a grenade filled with a sticky, flammable mixture that could be lit with a slow fuse and thrown. The pot broke when it hit, spraying fire everywhere, the mixture clinging like jelly to anything it touched. Slow matches, which were simply long fuses, burned at regular intervals near the incendiaries, ready to set them alight. On the battlefield, the Turks were as frightening and deadly as any force on earth, but here they were forced to attack in ways that made them highly vulnerable to such weapons. One man could kill scores of the enemy with them. The problem in St. Elmo, Bertrand knew, was that each day there were fewer and fewer men to do so.

All night long troops massed outside the walls, their weapons reflecting the light of their camp fires. Somewhere on Sciberras a man's voice rose in a half chant, half song, singing a few verses in Turkish. All the army below him answered in unison, their voices carrying clearly in the night. The lone voice chanted again, and was answered again. There were drums and lutes and trumpets. Men prayed loudly on the hillside and quietly inside the fort.

Near dawn there were a few quick raids, nothing more than probes searching for weaknesses and dead sentries. Each was repulsed. The knights sallied out and set fire to a section of bridge the attackers had partly laid in place across the ditch from the ravelin.

Under cover of darkness, much of the Turkish fleet had positioned itself around the tip of Sciberras, unloading thousands of troops ready to join the assault. Arquebusiers knelt among them, at the ready.

The sun peeked over the horizon. A trumpet blew, and the assault began.

The arquebusiers began a withering fire, kneeling to reload as the ships of the fleet opened fire with their deck guns, joined by the larger cannons on Sciberras, Tigné, and Gallows Point. Bertrand crossed himself and put on his helmet, closing the visor. The cannons fell silent, and with a great throaty roar the Iayalars stormed forward. Bertrand stood at the southwestern wall, flanked on either side by knights and soldiers. He fired his arquebus, then picked up another and fired again as the world seemed to explode around him. Round after round of shot decimated the screaming attackers, who were immediately replaced by other men storming over their bodies, and others storming over theirs. There seemed no end to them. Scaling ladders hit the walls. Men swarmed up them only to topple back again, screaming as the boiling pitch did its work. Makeshift scaling platforms constructed of bits of wood scavenged from the fleet were dragged into the fray. Defenders rushed to overturn them or hack them to pieces as quickly as they touched the walls.

Bertrand never felt his burned arms. When his guns were empty he used the pots, lighting and throwing them one after another with devastating effect. Across the piazza, the smaller cannons fired chain shot, two balls joined by a length of chain, cutting a bloody swath through the masses of Turks. Fire hoops bounded off walls and rolled down hills and into the ditches, igniting one man after another, sometimes entrapping two or three men together, joined at shoulder or waist until the flames consumed them.

First dervishes—howling and praying, to help drive the invaders to religious frenzy—and then Janissaries began surging through and over the ranks of the fallen Iayalars. Bertrand had no more room to use incendiaries, and at last he was in his element. Taking up sword and shield, he stood at the wall and swung and stabbed and hacked at the men pushing up. His heavy armor saved him repeatedly as halberds and sabers and pikes vainly sought his flesh. He felt himself wounded in the thigh, and again in his side, but fought on madly as men around him fell. He lost his sword and ripped his battle axe from his belt, swinging it with deadly efficiency. As the battle wore on he struggled to remain upright, his footing unsure. The ground around him was covered with bodies, making it difficult to move without falling. To fall was to die. Sometimes the smoke was so thick he couldn't see beyond the man he was facing. New enemies would appear suddenly out of the mists, like phantoms. Somehow the line held, and the Turks never breached the walls.

There was a terrible stench of blood and powder and sweat and death, and a discordant chorus of men's voices as they lay bleeding, their bones and bodies shattered, the air filled with prayers in six languages. A blast inside the fort shook the ground. The main store of incendiaries caught fire and exploded, killing nearby defenders.

Above the battle, Mustapha Pasha stood on the ravelin, shouting orders as he directed the attack, ignoring the danger to himself. Across the harbor, the cannons of St. Angelo fired again and again, the balls crashing through the ranks of the attackers massed on the slopes outside the walls of the fort. A group of Janissaries began scaling the post just to the west of Bertrand. The gunners in St. Angelo tried to knock them from the wall, but their aim was off, and eight defenders died instead. The next shot was better, shearing the attackers from the fortifications like wool from a sheep.

The battle raged all day. Troops withdrew, regrouped, and attacked again. The Chevalier de Medran was killed by arquebus fire. Captain Miranda, one of the fort's three commanders, was severely wounded. As the sun went down the trumpet sounded, halting the attack. Had just one more wave been launched, the fort would have fallen. A thousand Turks littered the slopes and trenches and courtyards, their bodies steaming as the temperature dropped and dusk turned to night. A hundred and fifty knights and soldiers lay dead within the fort. The defenders slumped where they'd fought, shaking and spent.

Both sides were stunned. St. Elmo, the old-fashioned and cheaply built fortress that no one on either side believed could hold out more than five or six days, had already survived three times that long, still held by a ragged and bleeding group of defenders.

All night the Turks dragged away their dead while the knights sent boatloads of casualties to Birgu. In the chapel where the wounded were waiting to be evacuated, Bertrand managed to pen a note for Christien.

Waste no more volunteers, he wrote, his hand shaky, the ink smeared with his blood. *Require only one barrel of brandy. For the hoops, of course.*

He folded the note and stuffed it in the sash of a Spaniard with a belly wound. He had a second thought, took the note out again, and added a sentence.

Two would be better.

At dawn the bombardment began once more.

Chapter 38

Asha crouched in the darkness, studying the walls on the landward end of Birgu. They were massive and heavily defended. He could see the standards of the different auberges at the bastions along the walls: the post of Castile, closest to Kalkara, and then those of Provence and France, each emblazoned with the banners of the knights who stood there. He memorized every detail.

He considered various ways to enter the village. Clearly there was no way to slip in undetected. A thousand eyes watched every inch of ground. His first thought was to swim in, entering Kalkara Creek and coming ashore somewhere between St. Angelo and the Post of Castile, perhaps near the sally port outside the old Holy Infirmary. He could claim he'd escaped from the Turks and swum across Grand Harbor. The advantage to the route was that it was not yet under the gun—he wouldn't have to worry about being shot by his own troops while trying to talk his way in. He crawled through the ruins of Bormla, a village that hadn't existed when he was a child. The village had been all but demolished now, clearing a no-man's-land between the walls of Birgu and the Turkish camps on the highlands.

It took him two hours to make the distance, crawling through deserted streets, working his way toward the ditch that would take him to Kalkara. He stopped and cursed. A Turkish encampment blocked his way.

There was only one other choice. He would go through the front door, then. He crawled back, toward the main gate, as it was farthest from Turkish lines.

His heart began pounding as he closed the distance. *I am Maltese,* he reminded himself. *I have nothing to fear.*

When he could crawl no further he stood up and ran directly toward the wall, waving his arms. *"Hallini nidhol!"* he yelled in Maltese. "Let me in! I've escaped from the Turks!"

Cautious guards at the battlements waved him to the gate. They peered out into the darkness beyond him, suspecting a trick.

"Quickly!" he shouted, looking over his shoulder in panic. "Before they have me! *Jekk joghgbok,* you fools!"

Still fearing treachery, the guards threw down a rope. Asha climbed up quickly, acutely aware of what an inviting target his back would make for a Turkish sharpshooter. Strong arms pulled him over the top. He stood on the wall near St. John's bastion, out of breath. Half a dozen men surrounded him.

"Who are you?" a knight of the *langue* of Provence asked him in Italian. He wore a plumed helmet, his armor exquisite silver and brass.

Asha shook his head as if he didn't understand. *"Grazzi hafna,"* he said in Maltese. "Thank you, thank you. I thought I was a dead man." Like a buffoon, he tried to kiss the knight's hand. The man impatiently summoned a Maltese guard to translate.

"*Int min inti?*" the guard asked. "What is your name?"

Asha had given careful consideration to his answer. "Nicolo Borg," he said. "From the village of Zejtun. The Turks captured me when they landed. I was trying to bring in my cattle from Bir id-Diheb, but I wasn't quick enough. They put me in their camp near the Marsa. The bastards forced me to push their guns up Sciberras. I'd rather push them up their ass. If you'll give me a pike and let me stand beside you on the walls, that's exactly what I'll do." He used all the right words, knew the local place names, and knew that other Maltese had escaped the Turks in similar fashion. Some of the Maltese laughed.

The guard translated to the knight. He seemed satisfied and issued instructions. The guard turned to Asha. "By God, you're a lucky one, all right," he said. "Take shelter here. Get something to eat. They'll feed you in the bishop's palace. The Order will assign you to a post."

Asha bowed and clutched the man's hand in gratitude, then turned to the knight to do the same. The knight had already walked off. Asha hurried for a ladder.

A moment later his feet were on the ground.

Birgu.

The long-awaited reality was dizzying. From that instant Asha's attention was fixed on the present, on armaments and fortifications and manpower, while Nico was gazing into the past, looking for the affirmation of memory and for the faces he longed to see. He was immediately pushed aside by an imperious soldier who was guiding a cart laden with cannonballs. "Out of the way, fool!" Asha nearly hit the man, but Nico stilled the instinct. *I am a stupid peasant.*

People hurried in every direction, carrying themselves as people did who knew where they were going and what they were doing. Even most of the children seemed purposeful and well organized, he thought; no hands idle during a siege. He realized at once there were many more people inside Birgu than he'd thought. They'd make a formidable force.

He walked along the landward wall, his eyes scanning battlements, curtain walls, and mighty bastions. Pennons told him which *langue* of the Order was defending which area. At the strongest point, near Kalkara Creek, were the Castilians. Next to them were the Italians, the Germans, and the knights of Auvergne and France. Beyond, in Senglea, the Aragonese held the wall of St. Michael. He counted troops and noted where they were concentrated. He observed where fixed ladders rose to the walls, calculated the width of catwalks, and studied how men moved from one area to another.

He saw that new walls had gone up near the perimeter, while old houses had come down. La Valette was a clever adversary indeed. There was a sure trap for the Turks should they storm the wall near the post of Castile. The Grand Master had created an inner compound of walls behind the walls, where troops storming through a breach would be trapped like cattle in a pen, awaiting slaughter. The information would save hundreds, perhaps thousands of Turkish lives.

Nico saw a place where he'd once pushed a twine ball down the street, running to catch it before it bounded into the water of Birgu Creek. Now Asha saw a dozen troops there, talking. Above their heads was a demi-culverin, and beyond that three versos, hidden to view from outside the walls. Just there, below that point, a mine would bring down an entire stretch of wall.

He made his way toward the square, pushing his way through busy crowds and livestock. The village that was neatly laid out in Nico's memory was now quite different under Asha's studied gaze, more compact and crowded. Only a few buildings had not changed at all: the auberges and the Infirmary, and the knights' Church of St. Lawrence near Birgu Creek. St. Agatha's had a new campanile. Nico had played just where it stood. Asha walked inside, stepping over sleeping peasants and their meager bundles of possessions. He stopped before the altar, still a simple affair of cloth and cross, with a tapestry on the wall behind. Crates of swords and arquebuses were stacked next to the altar, awaiting distribution in the hour of need. He counted them, but his eyes kept returning to the cross. He felt an uneasy tingling at the nape of his neck. He had not stood in a Christian church since . . . since he'd stood in this very church. Despite his comfort in Islam, he could not dismiss the feeling that the God of his fathers was watching him now. He went back outside.

The square was clearly the command center of the siege. He

counted *sobravestes* to estimate how many knights were commanding the troops. He had already considered what he would do if he saw La Valette. Although the information Asha was gathering was crucial and would help bring a swift end to the siege, La Valette was no ordinary commander. By all accounts he was an extraordinary man. The loss of his leadership would undoubtedly help the Turkish cause more than mere information about a storehouse full of powder or a trap inside the walls. La Valette had to die. Asha would get past his bodyguard and strike him down, forfeiting his life. Romegas was more troublesome. It would take every bit of Asha's will to put aside revenge and leave the man in peace, but that was what he knew he must do. If fate smiled upon him, he would meet the man in the final battle for Birgu.

Asha lingered for nearly an hour in the crowds around the perimeter of the square, watching, waiting, but neither the Grand Master nor Romegas appeared. He knew it might be hours or days before he saw either of them, if ever.

He made his way toward the street where he'd lived. Nearby he saw a low stone building, and it evoked a particularly strong memory. He could still smell the aroma of hot bread that wafted from that door every morning, sometimes awakening him in his own bed three streets away, setting his stomach to rumbling. Luca couldn't afford fresh bread, and they usually had to wait until it was gray with mold or as hard and cheap as limestone. One glorious morning Maria had found a coin in the street. They knew just what to do with it. They'd quietly dipped some honey from the clay pot in Isolda's kitchen and raced to stand in line—just there, where Asha saw a pallet on which stood a pile of canvas-wrapped grape-shot. Maria handed her money to the baker, who sliced off half a loaf. Still fresh from the oven, it steamed in the cool morning air. They'd taken it to a bench in front of St. Agatha's, where they'd smothered it with the honey and eaten the prize, their faces grinning and gooey as they licked their fingers and fought off the flies. Now Asha counted loaves being brought out on carts, and from that made a rough estimate of how many people they might feed.

Maria. Where are you?

He walked on, studying, memorizing. Twenty men, thirty, forty-two . . . a detachment of Greeks, a gathering of Rhodiots. A man looked at him looking, stared at him as if he were different. Asha lowered his head and hurried on down the street. Self-consciously he touched his *biritta*. No, it was only his imagination. He didn't simply look like a Maltese, he reminded himself. He *was* Maltese. Yet he wondered how much the lie must show. Perhaps he carried himself differently than a true Maltese, to whom a lifetime of poverty and subjugation to the hated knights must surely affect even their posture, must surely give them a demeanor that marked them as Maltese as surely as the *orta* on his arm marked him as . . . as something else. He could not know anything for certain save one thing: he was a changed man in a village of strangers.

He came to the street where his house had been. There were new dwellings around it, but he recognized the door, and the window where his mother shared gossip of an afternoon with the old hag Agnete, the tyrant who one day had broken one of his knuckles with a piece of oak when he helped himself to a sweetmeat from her sill.

In his mind he could see the dark pit of dung beneath that house, the pit so tied to the day that had changed his life. He watched everyone who entered or left the place. There was no way to know if the Borg family still lived there at all. Evidently a score of people were crammed into the place. In only twenty minutes eleven people entered or left. He saw two women who might be his sister—each as pretty as his memory of her, and about the right age. One had children. Did Maria? So much he didn't know about her life. Surely she was married now, would have married at fourteen or fifteen. Her oldest child—his nephew or his niece!—would be eleven or twelve. Perhaps that man there was her husband, his own brother-in-law. And his mother? He saw several women who might be Isolda, but for their veils he could not tell. Of his father he saw no trace. Luca, he was certain, would still look like Luca. He would know his father by his hands, if nothing else.

Asha fought with Nico against the urge to run to the house, to announce himself at the door and demand answers to his ten thousand questions. Asha was the stronger and forced the thought away. Questions would only draw attention to himself and raise suspicions. He must do what he came to do. Reluctantly he turned away. Near the bishop's palace he saw a ramp leading to a cellar beneath a house where they were making ammunition. He watched powder kegs rolling in and saw boxes of Greek firepots being hauled out. The Turkish gunners would make short work of the place.

He saw the first familiar face: the old boot maker, a man as ornery as a hornet. He stared. He shouldn't have; a soldier saw him lingering, the sure mark of a man who needed something to do. "You there! Come here!" he called in Italian, and Asha turned away as if he didn't understand, but the soldier caught up with him and pushed him toward a ramp that disappeared beneath the foundations of a house. A moment later Asha was crawling into a candlelit room with a low ceiling. There was a spring there, from which clay water jugs were being filled. It hadn't been there when he was a boy. Sometimes Nico had had to go all the way to the Marsa to draw water. Now Asha realized the spring meant Birgu could hold out all that much longer: another target for the gunners. He labored to get the jugs outside, where they were loaded onto a heavy cart with old, cracked wooden wheels. When the cart would hold no more, men and donkeys and even a priest began straining at the ropes. They were all exhausted. One of them said it was their fourth trip of the day. As Asha leaned into the work with them, he looked carefully at the priest. Time had made him thinner and more severe-looking, but there was no mistaking the man's identity: it was Dun Salvago. It took all of Nico's willpower to restrain himself. *How often I have heard your words inside my head. How often I repeated your prayers!* The priest didn't know him, of course, and anyway his attention was focused on the need to balance the water jugs. "Mind the side there," Salvago called to one of the men, "that it doesn't—" It was too late. One of the bottles rolled over the rail and fell to the ground. The heavy vessel did not break. Nico bent to retrieve it. Straining, he lifted it back onto the cart.

"Your help is welcome," the priest said, wiping perspiration from his brow. "Thank you."

"It is nothing, Dun Salvago."

Salvago looked at him. "Do I know you?"

"No, Father. I am from the country. I know who you are, that's all. Everyone does."

They managed to get the cart through a maze of streets and inside the palace gate. The courtyard gardens had been denuded by goats, who trotted forward at their approach. He saw the bishop—Cubelles was his name, Nico recalled—in the doorway of the chancery, helping serve soup from a large cauldron to a line of the hungry. Asha estimated stores piled on the wall as he struggled with heavy water jugs during several trips up and down the steps to the dungeons. He'd heard of these rooms, once said to be filled with horrid instruments of torture. Now he counted noses, mostly old people and children who were crowded into the dark spaces. Each of them seemed to have a request of Salvago, who listened patiently to all. "An extra ration for my grandmother? She is weak today." "A sweet, Dun Salvago?" "Is there medicine for my mother?"

Salvago was a good man, Asha thought, watching.

This was a place for the gunners to leave alone.

It was nearly dusk, and he began to think of how to get back out of the village. After it was dark he would find somewhere to slip over the wall, and brave a swim in Kalkara Creek. He walked that way, to reconnoiter.

Partway there he stopped. He could not do it. No matter Asha's sense of discipline and purpose, Nico could not have spent most of a lifetime dreaming about this place, about his family, only to leave without trying to find them, whatever the risks. The sight of Father Salvago had made it very real: the people of his memory *were* real. He had to find them.

He worked his way back toward the square. He caught a man by the shoulder. "Do you know Luca Borg?" he asked. The man shook his head. "Luca Borg, the mason? Maria Borg? Isolda Borg?" He stopped another man, and another. "Luca Borg! You there. Do you know—"

"You! *Durak!*"

He spun without thinking at the Turkish command, and caught his breath in shock. A burly Maltese was staring at him, wearing burgonet and chain mail. Beneath the man's helmet was a full, thick head of white hair—*as white as the snows that are brought from the mountains for the Sultan's sherbet*, he'd written in a letter to Maria. It was Beraq, the Maltese slave Nico had freed from his chains as his galley was sinking at Djerba. Beraq, staring with his one good eye at the hated figure of the Turkish *raïs* on whose ship he'd labored for four years.

"*Merhaba,* Asha Raïs," Beraq said.

"I don't know what you mean," Asha retorted in Maltese. "I am no *raïs.*"

Beraq stepped forward. "I'm only missing one eye, not two," he said. He clasped Asha by the arm. "I would not forget you in a thousand lifetimes." Men nearby began to take interest.

"Let me go," Asha said in a low voice. "I freed you. I could have let you go to the bottom."

"As you should have. But you did not. It was God's will that I should live for this very moment."

Asha pushed, and Beraq stumbled. Asha began to run.

"Stop him! He is a Turk! A Turkish spy!" Asha nearly made it through the cluster of men, but strong arms caught him, and held him to face his accuser.

"He is an infidel!" Beraq said. "A Turkish captain, called Asha Raïs! I was enslaved on his ship! I would know him anywhere!"

"He lies! He's mad, I tell you! Seeing Turks in his dreams, I'll wager!"

"Pull down his pants," Beraq said to another soldier. "You'll see."

Asha fought furiously, protesting the indignity, but he was quickly overwhelmed. His pants were yanked down around his knees. "I am a *converso!*" he said ferociously. "I was *born* Jewish. My family converted when I was a boy."

Beraq stood in triumph. "I have no idea how you come to speak Maltese so fluently," he said, "but only Muslim pigs and Jewish dogs have no skin there—and you are no Jew." He looked to the others. "He is a Turkish *raïs,* I tell you." He kicked his captive in the groin. Asha doubled over.

"*Che cosa?*" Men stepped back to the voice of authority. A knight stood before them. Beraq hurriedly explained.

The knight took Asha by the wrist and lifted his arm, exposing the tattoo. His eyes rose slowly, to meet Asha's. "This is an *orta,*" he said.

Asha stared defiantly, saying nothing.

"Hang him," said the knight indifferently.

Beraq grabbed Asha roughly. His hands were tied behind his back, and he was dragged to a wooden frame supporting a parapet walkway. A man threw a rope around one of the beams that protruded from the wall, while another fetched a wooden crate for the condemned man to stand on.

A flood of thoughts roared through Asha's brain. He was disgusted with himself for having gone to find Maria. He should have done what he set out to do, and then gone. To have been caught so, by a mere slave, after he'd fooled so many so well!

The rope looped around his neck, the hemp burning his skin as they cinched it tight. They forced him up onto the crate. Beraq stood before him. He reached out with his boot for the honor of kicking away the crate. "Strangle slowly, Turkish pig," he said.

Asha was not afraid to die, but he was not prepared to do so just yet. "Wait!" His voice croaked; the rope was strangling him. Blood pounded in his temples. "I am not Turkish. My name is Nicolo Borg. My father is Luca Borg, a mason. My mother is Isolda. My sister is Maria. I was born here in Birgu."

"I know Luca Borg," a man said, "and his daughter. I worked for them on this very wall."

"Get them, then," Asha said. "They'll tell you. I'm as Maltese as any man here."

The knight nodded, satisfied. He'd had no intention of hanging the suspect until the Grand Master had seen him. A noose had a way of loosening a man's tongue.

"Take him to the prison," he ordered. "Then see if you can find his father. We'll know soon enough who he is."

Chapter 39

The guns over St. Elmo stopped. A rare quiet descended over the island, the sudden silence almost as unsettling as the artillery itself.

On the hill above M'kor Hakhayyim the Janissary Abu stared up at the thick carpet of stars. He lifted his robe and heard the splash of his piss on the rocks. The others were in their tents or sitting at a small fire by the carob tree, playing a game of cards.

As he finished and turned to take up his post, he tripped and with a grunt went down hard. He fell into a hole, all the way to midthigh. He pulled himself up, rubbing his leg, and heard an unexpected sound. He'd knocked loose some rocks, and heard them tumbling down a hill—a hill that wasn't there.

He moved some of the rocks and cleared away some brush, thinking that perhaps it was one of the caves that riddled the island. They'd already explored one on the coast, not far away. Seeing there was an opening, he crawled down a little, stopping again to listen. There was only silence. Returning to the fire, he took up a torch.

"What is it?" Nasrid asked.

"I may have found a cave, sire."

"Kareef, go with him," Nasrid ordered. Another of the Janissaries jumped up and followed.

Abu poked the torch in the hole. "You see? A tunnel." He and Kareef pushed away a few more of the rocks at the entry. Holding the torch in one hand, saber in the other, Abu slithered in, Kareef close behind.

Fençu was closest to them, crouching behind a stalagmite near the base of the tunnel. At the first sound of the rock fall, everyone inside the cave had crawled to their posts and taken up their weapons, as they'd been drilled to do. They hid in absolute silence, prey awaiting the predator. Fençu rested his finger on the trigger of the crossbow. The bolt was in the notch, the bow taut.

Abu came fast down the slope, scooting along on his backside. The tunnel opened onto a narrow ledge that descended steeply into the cave. He stopped near the bottom and held up his torch. It was a large cave, with no sign of life. It looked like an excellent place to make camp. He scrambled down the last bit of incline, to flat ground. The roof of the cave soared away above him, lost in the darkness beyond the light of his torch.

Kareef stepped down beside him, barely making a noise. "By the bones of our fathers," he breathed in awe as they both looked around the huge cave. Abu stepped cautiously forward, his sword at the ready. He saw the fireplace and a cook pot. Obviously the cave had been occupied at some point. He knelt by the fireplace and put his hand into the ashes. "Old and cold," he said. "They probably ran when they saw the fleet."

"They left grain," said Kareef. He'd found some wicker baskets and earthenware jars.

Abu was wary. "Let's see what else they left." He raised his torch and turned, illuminating one section of the cave after another, his eyes darting in the long shadows. There was a ladder, and the opening of a niche. Stepping up onto the rung, he peered inside and found himself looking into the wide eyes of Elena, crouching there with Moses. The boy squeaked in fear. Startled, Abu stepped back, his sword rising. "Ka—" he started to say. The bolt of Fençu's crossbow struck him in the temple. He fell without uttering another sound. His sword clattered to the ground and his torch fell with him.

Kareef's yell of surprise was cut short by a blow that felled him from behind. Cawl stood above the dead man, holding a double-edged great sword.

Moses began to whimper. "Be quiet!" Elena hissed. She held him close, burying his face against her chest.

"Get the weapons from the other tunnel!" Fençu whispered. "Be ready to run." Villano and Cataldo hurried up the second tunnel in the rear, quickly reappearing with guns and swords. They heard shouting on top of the hill. The Turks had heard.

Nasrid and his men were on their feet instantly at the sounds, at full alert. They snatched up torches from the fire and fanned out over the hill, calling for their missing friends.

Fençu lit two more slow matches from the torch, giving one to Cawl and one to Villano. The pungent smoke made Villano sneeze. Fençu put the stock of the crossbow on the ground and held it steady with his foot while he turned the crank. When the cord was locked into place he put in another bolt. He handed it to Elli, who was as accurate with the fearsome weapon as any man alive. "Shoot the next one down," he said. She knelt and waited. Cataldo knelt on the other side, his arquebus ready. Fençu tossed the reed torch to the side of the cave so that its fire would backlight the men coming down.

"They were over here," a Janissary called from the ravine. A moment later he found the opening. "Here it is!" He went in, feetfirst. Two men quickly crawled in behind him, and a moment later two more. "Look for other entrances," Nasrid said, and his men combed the hillside as they called out for their missing friends.

Inside the cave the first Janissary reached the floor, his sword at the ready. He fell instantly to Elli's crossbow. The man behind him heard the distinctive noise and yelled up to warn the others. An arquebus flashed, and its roar filled the cave. The Janissary slid to the bottom, dead. Above him others swarmed into the hole, yelling.

Cataldo threw down his arquebus, ignoring the one that lay ready beside it. He raced for the second of the rear tunnels, to join his wife and the children in their hiding place in one of the small upper galleries. They would wait there until it was safe to leave, whether their opportunity came in a minute or a week. By earlier agreement, they'd all decided that if they were discovered, they'd try to leave by different exits, to improve everyone's chances of getting away.

Fençu knelt by the pile of incendiaries, his slow match ready. He heard more men coming down the front of the cliffs toward the main entrance, knocking rocks loose as they scrambled down the old path. "Villano!" he called. "The nets!"

Villano ran to one of the ropes that restrained the nets holding the rocks. He used his sword and whacked wildly, too frightened to take his time. He missed, and missed again. On the third swing he caught it cleanly. The rope parted and the net gave way as three Janissaries were coming in. The rocks crashed down with a roar, kicking up choking dust. A Janissary screamed, his legs crushed beneath the cascading rocks. The men behind him jumped back in time. Villano cut another rope. More rocks tumbled with a roar, piling on the first. He cut the last stay and the final load dropped. The Janissary's screams stopped. The entrance was blocked. On the other side of the pile of rocks there was more yelling.

"Go!" Fençu yelled to Elli and Elena. "Use the lower entrance! Get to the water!" They scampered for the second waterside entrance just as a Janissary hit the floor of the cave by the rear tunnel. Moses was first down the tunnel, his mother just behind him. The Janissary heard rather than saw the motion and threw his axe. It struck Elli. She fell without crying out; Elena didn't hear. Cawl rushed the Janissary from the rear, swinging his sword. The Janissary ducked and whirled, whipping his knife from his belt. He lashed out. Cawl jumped back behind a stalagmite, and the Janissary's blade rang against the rock. Cawl snatched up his arquebus and set the slow match to the powder pan. The boom was deafening in the confined space. The Janissary crumpled. Cawl snatched up the last arquebus, left there by Cataldo, and set the match again. Another Janissary fell.

Other Janissaries were partway down now, and more were coming behind them. Fençu touched his slow match to the fuse of a firepot and hurled it. A sheet of flames engulfed the men nearest the bottom. Fençu threw another, and another, throwing them high so they struck the wall above the incline. Flames showered down upon the turbans and robes of the next three men. They writhed and cried and burned, blocking the way of those behind. It would only be a few moments before they were pushed out of the way and the others followed.

Fençu ran for the lower tunnel, leaping over the body of a Janissary. He tripped over Elli and fell hard. He turned and in the flickering light he saw the axe and realized whom it was he'd tripped over. "Elli!" He pulled the axe out and turned her over. "Elli! Elli!" He shook her. She didn't respond. He crawled around in front of her and started dragging her into the tunnel by the arms, having to work from his belly when the tunnel got too narrow. Cawl came up behind her. "Help me!" Fençu said, gasping. "It's Elli." Cawl pushed while Fençu pulled, and together they slid her along. Behind them they heard children crying, and Villano yelling. They heard another gunshot, and another. Villano had no gun.

They arrived at the outer ledge. They were six feet above the water. Elena was already in the water with Moses, who was paddling, treading water. Elena dove again and again, pulling the rocks out of the bottom of Fençu's boat. She had to do it by feel, as it was almost as dark outside as it was in the cave.

"I've got to get Elli down, Cawl," Fençu said. "There are two more crossbows here. Use them when they come. Block the tunnel with their bodies."

"Elli is dead, Fençu. Leave her."

Fençu wasn't listening. He slid her to the edge and pushed her over. She made a great splash in the water. Fençu leapt in after her, nearly landing on Moses, who took a mouthful of water and started coughing.

Cawl got out onto the ledge and turned around, so that he faced up the tunnel. He waited, trying to still his breath so he could hear. He heard one of them coming, heard his grunts as the man slithered through the narrow space. When he could just see the dark smudge that was either a face or a turban, just an arm's length away, Cawl fired the crossbow. Almost immediately he heard another man behind the first, grunting as he tugged at the dead man's robes. *My God, they're fanatic,* Cawl thought. He reached for the second crossbow and lifted it up near the ceiling of the tunnel so that the bolt would clear the dead man's body. He felt the man being pulled backward. Cawl fired. He heard a grunt, and then nothing. Cawl left the crossbow where it was. He scooted back until his legs hung free, and dropped to the water. It was cold and black and took his breath away.

They were in Fençu's little cove, sheltered from the view of those above. With luck, Cawl thought, it would be dawn before the Turks realized where they'd gone. But luck had already departed them this night. They had to go.

He heard Elena calling. "Cawl! Help me with the boat! I've got most of the rocks out!" Cawl paddled over to her. On the way he passed Fençu, who was trying to keep Elli's head above the water. She was floating on her back, completely limp. She kept slipping under, but each time Fençu managed to get her up again. "Elli!" he kept saying to his wife between gasps for breath. "Elli, we have to leave. Wake up, Elli. Wake up."

Cawl took a breath and dove. He could see nothing. The water stung his eyes. He came to the surface, sputtering. He drew another breath, then went down again. This time his hands found the front of the boat. He got the last of the rocks out, and as he tugged it began to rise. They got it to the surface and turned it over, so that it trapped air. Elena immediately grabbed hold of the side, clinging to the thole pins that supported the oars on the boat's gunwale. Exhausted from her efforts, Elena was coughing and sputtering, her breath coming in great ragged gasps. Moses clung to her dress and then got an arm around her neck. They floated with the boat, resting.

"Fençu, come on!" Cawl hissed. "I need your help!"

Fençu, oblivious, was still treading water. "*Elli!*" he said. "Wake up. You've got to swim. Elli!"

"Fençu! Quickly! They'll be coming soon!" Cawl was getting desperate.

Elena took Moses's hand and guided it to the thole pin. "Can you hold on?"

"Yes, Mama," he gasped.

Elena paddled over to Fençu, barely making him out. "Fençu, please. We need you." She realized Elli was floating face down. "There's nothing you can do," Elena said, choking now herself. "She's gone."

"No," Fençu said. He kicked furiously, trying to keep them both up. He couldn't do it any longer, and she slipped below the surface. He dove for her and caught her by her blouse. With superhuman effort he got back to the surface, but her head was underwater. He cried in frustration, kicking and struggling, but she was too large and she wasn't helping and he couldn't get her nose and mouth to the air. Finally even he knew it was over.

"We need you," Elena said again.

She heard a great wrenching sob. "I've got to bury her," Fençu said.

"You can't. We'll all die. Leave her to the sea." She tugged at him. "Please, Fençu."

Elena heard him moan, then choke as he took in water. At last Fençu let go of his wife. She sank immediately. Somehow Fençu gathered himself after that and followed Elena, paddling until they reached the boat. Together they towed it into shallower water, where the men could support themselves on some rocks. There was no gentle shore in the cove, only rock walls. They got the boat turned over. They put Moses in first, and then Elena, and the two bailed water with cupped hands until enough of the boat was above water that the men could get in.

They heard muffled shouts from the hillside above, but still no one had spotted them. There were no paddles. They used their hands, Cawl and Fençu in front, Elena and Moses behind, furiously making their way out of the shelter of the little cove and into the bay. Much of the fleet was gone, but a few galleys remained.

Above them Nasrid was furious at his losses. These were not soldiers but civilians who had killed so many of his men. There were four enemy dead—a man, a woman, and two children, who'd taken three of his own men with them when their hiding place had been discovered. There were five prisoners: a man, a woman, and three children, captured when smoke choking the tunnels made one of the children start coughing. Nasrid tried to interrogate them, but he couldn't understand the gibberish of their Maltese. He sent them under guard to the slave camps of the Marsa.

His men were still exploring the galleries and swallow holes and gorges inside the cave, working with torches, looking for others. Nasrid expected they'd all fled. Surely, like rabbits, they had more than one way out of their warren. It was nearly two hours before his men confirmed that fact. When they pulled the last two Janissary bodies out of the lower tunnel it was nearly dawn. The tunnel fell away to the sea, his men reported. There was a body in the water, a woman, but no one else.

Nasrid separated his men into patrols, and they raced along the nearby shores, looking for the others.

❖

The little boat hugged the shoreline. It passed beneath the very bow of a galley, so close they could hear men snoring on the deck. They paddled silently, unseen. Fençu guided them mechanically, his face still wet with tears. They worked their way out of the bay and up the east coast, toward the Grand Harbor. Before dawn they found shelter in another cove near St. Thomas Bay, where they were able to slip the boat just beneath a flat rock that overhung the water.

Stunned and exhausted from the previous night's horror, they lay all day in the little boat, listening to the water lapping on the rocks behind them. The relentless summer sun beat on the water, reflecting its light into their hiding place, baking them like game in an oven. Moses cried for water. Elena held him close. "Soon," she whispered. "We'll have water soon." Turkish galleys passed up and down the coast within a hundred yards of their position, oblivious to their presence. They heard men somewhere on shore, but the voices remained distant. The hours passed wretchedly slowly.

When it was dark again they set out. They paddled for hours without stopping. They rubbed their arms raw on the gunwales, collecting splinters and blisters. Their skin chafed from the seawater and their heads ached from dehydration.

Sometime after midnight they were able to make out the shape of a large rock formation that rose above them in the darkness. "I think that's Sala rock," Fençu said dully. "We'll never get closer on the water. They're sure to have galleys everywhere near the mouth of the harbor. We'll have to go overland from here."

Fençu and Cawl sank the boat and filled it with rocks again, in case they might need it. They started inland, making their way cautiously over the open, rolling countryside in the direction of the Grand Harbor. They held on to each other in the darkness—Fençu in front, then Elena and Moses, and Cawl in the rear. Weak from hunger and thirst, they had to stop often to rest. Every noise frightened them. They saw only one campfire and gave it a wide berth. They kept to the *wieden* and went well out of their way in order to keep what little shelter the landscape offered them, still fearing that at any moment they would stumble onto a Turkish camp. A patrol passed nearby, coming so close they could hear the rustle of robes and the shuffle of feet, but they never saw anyone. The Turks were moving silently toward Bighi Bay, not muttering or even coughing. Fençu kept them down for nearly an hour, long after the patrol was gone.

It was getting light when they arrived on Bighi, the spur of land to the northeast of Birgu. The spur rose to a barren height in the middle called Mount Salvador. Most of Bighi was deserted, although the outlines of tents were visible in the Turkish camps to the south, near the throat of Kalkara Creek. To the north, across the Grand Harbor, fires burned near St. Elmo. To the west, across Kalkara, they saw the looming shadow of St. Angelo, and to its left the great dark hulk of the Holy Infirmary. Farther along the shore, the massive bastion of the Post of Castile marked the landward end of the defenses. Beyond Castile, on the heights of Santa Margherita, the Turks seemed to have established a city.

Quietly they debated whether to try for St. Angelo or for a point somewhere along the walls of Birgu. Fençu seemed indecisive, and Cawl knew little about Birgu. It was Elena who decided. "We'll swim for the sally port below the Infirmary," she said. It was two hundred yards across the creek, a distance in which they would be completely exposed. Elena looked anxiously at Moses. He was a good swimmer, but now he seemed so small and frail, and his eyes lacked their usual luster. He was parched and tired. But he smiled gamely when she asked if he could make the distance. "I bet I can beat you," he said.

It was nearly dawn. "We should wait through the day," Cawl said. "They'll see us by the time we're partway there."

"If we wait here, they'll see us for sure," Elena said. "We'll never last another day without water, and there's no good place to hide. We've got to go. *Now.*"

They crawled the last hundred yards on their bellies and slipped into the water. Four abreast, they started swimming across the creek. Despite his bravado, Moses was exhausted. He quickly began to falter. Elena helped him but she struggled, too, her own reserves of energy all but gone. Cawl crossed over. He caught Moses by the trousers and propelled him along, then swam alone for a moment and did it again.

By the time they were at the halfway point, they could see the sun glinting on the cannon barrels of Sciberras. The siege guns suddenly opened fire on St. Elmo, startling them with their intensity. As they neared Birgu they were seen by a guard on the walls. "Men in the water!" he yelled. Behind them, a Turkish guard also saw them. Several Turkish sharpshooters hurried up Mount Salvador and began firing. Their bores were longer than those of the defenders' guns, their range and accuracy greater. They could hit without being hit, although they were still too far for a good shot. As they fired they laughed and made wagers. These were not soldiers in the water. This was not battle but target practice. Their arquebus balls hit the creek and sent up small geysers near the swimmers. Elena heard one plink nearby and realized what it was. "Moses!" Frantically she started toward him. Cawl yelled for her to keep going. "I've got him!" he said. "Get ashore!"

She reached the shore just behind Fençu, who was already up on the dock. He turned and hauled her up. A ball struck the dock next to him. Splinters struck his foot and he went down with a cry. Elena yanked at his arm and got him up and going again. She could see Cawl arriving at the dock. Above them on the walls, the soldiers were laying down a covering fire. It had little effect on the out-of-range Turkish arquebusiers. Soldiers raced down the stairs of the sally port to help.

Cawl literally hurled Moses up onto land and clambered up after him. He picked the boy up and started running across the narrow wharf where boats disembarked patients for the Infirmary. He carried Moses out in front of him, both arms wrapped around the boy. It was awkward but the only way to protect him. More rock splinters flew nearby. Cawl stumbled and recovered his footing just as a shot caught him in the back. He fell without a sound, landing hard on top of Moses, who yelped in pain.

Elena saw them go down. She screamed. She let go of Fençu and turned back. "No!" Fençu tried to hold her. "They'll kill you for sure!" Elena ripped free of his grasp and raced back toward the water. A pool of blood spread around Cawl. "Mama!" Moses cried, trapped beneath him.

Cawl was heavy, and she couldn't move his dead weight off her son. She caught Moses by the arm and yanked at him, while Moses tried to squirm out from under. Elena heard the boots of soldiers crossing the dock to help. Moses popped free. Elena swept him up into her arms and raced for the sally port, covering his body with her own. More shots rang out. The soldiers took Cawl by the arms and started dragging him behind. Fençu hobbled for the sally port, his foot bleeding.

The distance was only twenty yards, but to Elena it was miles. She seemed to be running in slow motion. Her soaking-wet dress made movement difficult. Her muscles were cramping and her lungs were burning. She saw Fençu swallowed into the shade of the sally port. Something tugged at her skirt. She tripped and fell. Moses hit his head on the dock and started bellowing, his cries all but lost in the bedlam. On the walls men yelled encouragement and fired at the distant Turks. Smoke from their guns curled across the dock, and she heard the discordant cry of a gull. Across the harbor the cannons roared. Elena got back to her feet. She lifted Moses once again and kept running.

An instant later she reached the sally port and raced inside, not stopping until she was halfway up the stairs, well within the safety of the thick walls. The terror and the exhaustion caught up to her and she collapsed, not certain whether the wailing in her ears was coming from Moses or from her own throat.

Chapter 40

A t the slave prison they gave Luca a lantern and let him into the cell.

He took one step in and stopped, trying to see past the ring of light cast by the lantern. He let his eyes adjust to the gloom. The room was small, its stone walls stained with time, its floor lined with filthy straw. The other prisoners who would have been here were out in labor crews. He saw just one man, standing against the far wall. He was naked, his wrists held to the stone with iron bracelets. Luca couldn't see his features clearly. He stepped forward. The lantern lit his own face perfectly, and it was the other man who spoke first.

"Father? Luca Borg? Is that you?"

Luca moved forward carefully, as if it were a lion awaiting him in the gloom. When he drew near enough and could see he peered carefully into his son's eyes. "Nico?" It was almost a whisper. "Nicolo? Can it be? Is it truly you?"

Nico nodded, his eyes welling, too overwhelmed to speak.

"They told me they had you," Luca said. "I could not believe it. I was certain you were dead."

"The corsairs took me away, that's all. I've been to Algiers and then . . . but there is time for that later. What of Maria, and Mother? Tell me. Are they all right?"

"Your mother is dead, God keep her. Maria is well."

"Dead? When?"

Luca seemed not to hear. His face was deeply creased. "Outside they told me you'd become a . . . they told me you were circumcised. I told them they were fools. I hit one of them. I shouldn't have. My temper still gets the best of me sometimes. I told them it could not be."

Nico said nothing to that. Luca swallowed hard. He lowered the lamp and looked at his son's groin. His whole body went still. All the color drained from his face. He looked up into Nico's eyes, waiting for an explanation.

"I have lived in Istanbul, Father. Constantinople," Nico said. "I am the captain of a galley. I lived in—"

"Are you Muslim?"

"Yes, but please listen, Father. I know what it must seem to you, but it isn't what you might think. I can explain to you, show you the beauty I have found. I am still Nico. I am still your son. I—"

Luca quivered, fighting for control. He drew himself up to his full height, his old body still as hard as steel, and stared for a long moment at Nico. And then he spat in his son's face. All the hardness seemed to go from him then, and his shoulders sagged. He turned and shuffled to the door.

"Father, wait! Please, come back! Father!"

Luca emerged from the cell and handed the guard his lantern. "I knew there was a mistake," he said. "Tell the Grand Master that man is not my son. My son Nico is dead."

❖

Christien worked furiously. During the siege of Metz the bodies had come steadily, all day. Here they came in a nightly flood, carried on the boats from St. Elmo. Last night there were sixty. None had minor wounds, because men with those simply stayed at their posts or were treated in the chapel at St. Elmo. Christien treated only the most seriously injured, men whose flesh was mangled by shrapnel and lead ball, men with eyes pierced by splinters, men with gross powder burns or compound fractures, men with puncture wounds from pikes or the deep, clean cuts left by scimitars. He gave first priority to anyone who could return quickly to his post, leaving the more gravely injured for later. In all there were four barber-surgeons and two surgeons working in the ward, among smoking braziers and blood-spattered buckets and piles of limbs and an endless sea of moaning men. The hallways and courtyard were overflowing. The Infirmary already held more than two hundred patients. The Grand Master had ordered the auberges to make room for more.

Bartholomew hurried into the ward, his face smudged with powder and dirt. He spent part of his time at the Post of France and the rest at the Infirmary. Between the two assignments, the page had finally learned not to faint at the sight of blood. "Sire," he said, "there is someone to see you at the gate."

"I haven't time," Christien snapped, tying off a suture.

"I told her that, sire, but she's quite pigheaded and wouldn't leave. She said it's urgent. She said to tell you her name is Maria Borg."

❖

He saw the strain on her face, and her relief when she saw him. "Maria! Are you all right? I'm sorry I couldn't come sooner."

"Yes, I'm all right. I would never have come, but it's Nico," she said. "He's a prisoner."

"Nico? Your brother? Here?"

"Yes. He was taken at the wall. They say he's a Turk, Christien. A spy. They've locked him in the slave prison. I've heard they're going to hang him. My father saw him but wouldn't tell me anything. I tried to get in myself, but the guards wouldn't let me." She fought her tears. "Please, Christien. I don't know what to do. I need your help."

The slave prison housed galley slaves and was only a short distance from the Infirmary. The guard was a Greek. He glared at Maria, who'd already given him so much trouble, but of course yielded instantly to the Chevalier de Vries. He opened the cell door. The room was empty but for the one prisoner. Maria stepped inside, Christien beside her. Christien waited by the door as she moved forward into the gloom.

"Nico?" It was almost a whisper, as she tried to make out his face. "Is that you, Nico?" She walked forward until she stood before him. His wrists were still clasped in the iron rings, and he couldn't move his arms. His face was bloody, one eye swollen nearly shut, his cheek laid open to the bone. His chest and stomach were bruised, his groin a bloody mess. He looked up and managed a grin. "I knew I'd see you again. I knew it." A pink tear rolled down his cheek.

She threw her arms around him. He buried his face in her shoulder, unable to hold her for his chains.

"Maria, dear Maria," he said, his voice breaking. "I saw the note you wrote to ransom me. And I had my coin, all these years. Until today, that is. They took it."

"Coin?" She gave him a blank look.

"You found it the day they took me. You gave it to me. I've had it ever since."

"Yes, yes, I remember," she said, her eyes welling with tears. She touched his cheek. "Oh, Nico, Nico, what have they done to you?"

"They were making sport with me, to see what I might tell them of the fleet."

"The fleet? What do you mean? How dare they? You are Nicolo Borg! What do you know of the fleet?"

He steeled himself for what he had to say. "I am more than Nico now. I am called Asha. I live in the house of Allah, Maria. My home is Istanbul—Constantinople."

Maria had already heard the guard call the prisoner a pig of Islam, but to have Nico himself admit it stunned her. She knew what such an admission meant for his prospects. "Nico, no! This cannot be! You were a boy when they took you. Say you're sorry! Say they made you!"

"No one made me do anything, Maria. What I am, I am of my own will."

"*No!* You must lie. You must deny everything. You cannot have returned to me only to die. You must live, Nico. For me. For Father."

Nico's eyes went hard. "My father has no son."

"He is proud, you know that. It will take time, but it—" She stopped herself without saying it. She'd almost said *it will pass*. They both knew that for Luca Borg such a thing would never pass.

There was no time to say more. A serving brother of the Order entered the room. He nodded deferentially to Christien. "I am ordered, sire," he said, "to fetch the prisoner to the Grand Master."

The Greek guard unchained Nico from the wall and shackled him again with wrist chains. He pushed him roughly out the door. Still naked, Nico walked toward the main square, an object of great curiosity as he passed through crowds who parted to let the little procession pass. As Christien and Maria followed they exchanged glances. She saw the sadness in his eyes, the grim set of his mouth. She knew what he was thinking: Nico was a dead man. She gritted her teeth, already forming her arguments.

La Valette kept his headquarters in a merchant's shop. He was standing at a large map table, surrounded by aides and giving orders to a knight whose black hair was dusty from battle. There were two pages, one holding the Grand Master's helmet and shield, the other his pike. Behind La Valette the Bailiff of the Eagle was conferring with the Order's Conservator, La Motta, and other knights. The men in the room barely noticed Nico's arrival, save one. Nico recognized him immediately. It was Fra Mathurin d'Aux de Lescout. *Romegas.*

The chevalier came forward. He nodded at Christien and regarded the prisoner. "Well! I'd heard we had a Turkish *raïs*. So this is the fearsome one." He walked slowly around Nico, examining him. Nico stared at him with undisguised hatred. Romegas returned the gaze, but with curiosity rather than malice. He was simply trying to recall. His own memory was legendary, and the community of sea captains in the Mediterranean was not large. Even from opposite sides, captains often knew each other. "The unhappy state of your face makes it difficult to be certain," he said, "but I have seen you before. I do not recall where."

"Strike these chains from my wrists and give me a knife, and while I'm cutting your throat I'll remind you."

Romegas laughed. "By God, the prisoner has fire. Asha Raïs. Now I recall. Djerba! We swam together!"

The approach of La Valette cut short their exchange. "Fra de Vries," he said to Christien, "I assume there is an explanation for your presence."

"Signorina Borg asked my help in seeing the prisoner, sire," Christien replied. "This is her brother."

"Your *brother!* Is this so, *signorina?*" La Valette asked.

"It is, Grand Master."

"I was told your father said otherwise."

"My father was mistaken, Excellency."

"Indeed? In the matter of his own blood?" La Valette looked at Nico. "Well, what is the truth of it? Are you Maltese or Turk?"

"By birth I am Maltese."

"It is not the skin you wore as a child that is of interest to me. It is the skin you wear today. Answer my question."

"I am not Turk but Ottoman."

La Valette examined Nico's arm, staring at the familiar *orta*. "And an officer in the Sultan's fleet, it would appear."

"*Sì.*"

Maria shook her head, her eyes betraying her fear. "Nico! Tell him—"

The Grand Master waved her off. "Be silent." He looked at Nico. "What were you doing in civilian clothing in Birgu?"

"I sought to learn your preparations, to bring a swift end to a siege whose outcome is already ordained. It was my wish to keep the loss of Maltese life to a minimum. That and nothing more. That is the truth of it."

"Maltese life, you say. What of the Order?"

"When the Order of St. John is erased from the earth it will not grieve me."

La Valette seemed amused. "A risky statement for a man whose neck is so near the noose," he said dryly. "You have an opportunity at this moment to save yourself, to do what is right for the land of your birth. Tell me the intentions of your commanders. Tell me the plan of battle."

"I will not betray my fleet, Grand Master, any more than I will raise arms against my own flesh and blood."

"Yet you *spy* on your own flesh and blood. In the end you are more Ottoman than Maltese."

"I am not ashamed of what I am."

"I do not expect you to be ashamed of it," the Grand Master said. "I expect you to hang for it." He beckoned to the guard. The interview was over.

"Wait!" Maria stepped forward. "Grand Master, please, you cannot! This is your doing as much as anyone's! You should feel shame for this!"

"Maria Borg, if I did not regard you with a measure of respect, I would have you whipped. Explain yourself."

"You don't remember? I came to you the day the corsairs took him. You had a galley but would not give chase. Whatever my brother is today, he is because he was failed by the Knights of St. John."

"Of course I remember the incident. You were but a girl then, though your tongue was no less tart than today. You accused me of . . . *cowardice*, I believe."

"A comment I have come to regret, Grand Master. But Nico was only a child. He was not even *ten*. He had no choice but to convert. Could any child resist? Had you—had the Order—done your duty that day, my brother would stand here now as an officer in your own ranks. He would be piloting one of your galleys."

Nico could not restrain himself. "I am Maltese," he said. "The Order does not admit even *noble* Maltese to its hallowed ranks. Perhaps I could have cleaned his bilge." La Valette nodded at the Greek guard, who savagely lashed Nico across the face. Nico stumbled but did not fall. He licked the blood trickling at his lips, his eyes defiant.

"I will not credit your argument," La Valette said. "It is not the Order that took him that day, nor the Order that suggested he change his religion."

"The Order promised King Charles to protect these islands, and the Order did not. Grand Master, I beg you: do not punish the man for the weakness of the child. You told me that day that God would protect Nico, and now with your own lips you would order his death?" She drew a deep breath, knowing the danger in what she was about to suggest. "The Order should not pass judgment on a man the Order itself consigned to apostasy as a child. Let him be judged by the Church."

Christien watched Maria in awe. Few *men* dared address the Grand Master in such a frank manner, yet her very boldness gave him the first glimmer of hope for her brother. La Valette was a fair man who responded to reason, a man who could change his mind when circumstances warranted. Now he paced, weighing what she said.

"You ignore a notable fact," the Grand Master said. "Whatever the circumstances of his youth, he stands before us not only an unrepentant Muslim but a spy as well. For that alone, his death is warranted."

"Grand Master, if I may be so bold." It was Romegas, who had been listening with an amused expression. "Perhaps I have a solution." He drew La Valette aside and whispered to him. Presently La Valette nodded.

"The Chevalier reminds me of that which I am painfully aware," he said to Nico. "I am short of manpower and have no room for idle hands. You stand before us neither fully Turkish nor fully Maltese. As you seem to be a man of both skins, you may reap the reward of mixed loyalties, and work between the two. You will join the slaves at the walls. If you survive, then I will leave it to the Inquisition to decide your fate."

Nico didn't know the significance of the walls, but Maria did. Nico would never survive long enough to be judged by Cubelles and Salvago, and La Valette knew it. "But Grand Master," she said, "the walls are a death sentence! The only difference between them and hanging is a matter of time."

"If it is God's will that he survive long enough to burn in the Inquisitor's fires, then he will survive. A man can ask no more than such a chance, Signorina Borg, and neither can you. Now be silent. My patience with you is at an end."

❖

23 JUNE
Bertrand groaned, mortified. He realized he had shit where he lay, and for a long while hadn't even noticed. He fumbled for his flask and took a blessed drink. It was a gift that came a few days earlier, with the last man in the last relief boat from St. Angelo. A Maltese soldier crawled through the rubble to bring it to him, reverently handing it to the knight as if it contained the Holy Grail. It was a powder box secured with leather straps, marked under the Grand Master's seal for the Chevalier Cuvier. Puzzled, Bertrand fumbled at the straps and opened the box. There was a flask inside, and a note.

Sorry there was no room for a whole barrel, Christien wrote. *Enjoy what there is. It cost you your best pair of boots.* Bertrand laughed out loud and wondered how Christien had managed the seal. He took a long swig of the blessed liquid and saved the rest.

St. Elmo was completely surrounded. The Turks had managed to get a bridge across the ditch at enormous cost of life. Now their guns were placed so the defenders could not remove the bridge. The Turks were entrenched everywhere, hidden behind the screening walls, safe from the covering fire of St. Angelo. A Maltese swimmer carried a note to the Grand Master from Miranda, who wrote that virtually every man was wounded. They were all but out of wildfire and powder. The fort would fall at any hour.

That night the men in St. Elmo watched as yet another small force of volunteers tried to cross Grand Harbor to reinforce them, with no less a seaman than Romegas himself at the helm of the lead boat. Turkish fire raked them from every direction. They were forced to turn back.

From that moment St. Elmo was alone.

The battle raged all the next day. Much of the combat was hand-to-hand, the men of both armies fighting with unmatched bravery and ferocity. Losses were heavier than ever—more than two thousand on the Turkish side and more than two hundred within St. Elmo.

Somehow St. Elmo held.

That night Bertrand went to chapel. He had to crawl there, to avoid Turkish fire. He made his confession and received the Holy Sacrament. Afterward he and some other knights helped the chaplains dig up part of the floor. They hid the crucifix and relics beneath the stones. Things that would burn—tapestries and vestments and furniture and even Bibles—were dragged outside and tossed into a bonfire, the men determined that nothing might remain that could be defiled. After they finished they rang the chapel bell and raised a great cheer, to let their friends in St. Angelo know they were still there, still fighting.

Bertrand crawled back to his post, stopping every time a flare burst overhead. The Turks were trying to illuminate night targets for their snipers, who could now fire into the fort from nearly every direction. Bertrand didn't freeze quickly enough, or else his armor reflected the light, or else someone just made a lucky shot. He took an arquebus ball in his thigh. Alone, he cried out.

He lay still for a few moments, sweat pouring from his brow. There was no point crawling backward for help. There was no one to give it. He waited until the next flare died and in the darkness slithered to his post, leaving a trail of blood. He settled himself against a pile of stone. Gasping, he loosened his breastplate and ripped off a piece of his shirt. He wrapped it around his thigh to stanch the blood oozing from the wound. He grimaced in pain but knew he was lucky—the ball had missed the artery. He fumbled at the knot. His fingers were barely cooperating with his brain. They seemed to have a life of their own. Finally he had it. With great effort he got his armor cinched tightly once again. Every movement was an effort. Besides his new wound, he had half a dozen others, crusted with blood. The joints of his burnt arms had caked with serum until they were as stiff as timber. Three of his teeth had broken when a piece of wood thrown up by a ball hit him in the jaw. He was burning with fever now, and always desperately thirsty no matter how much he drank. He no longer wanted to eat. In the twilight before dawn a soldier brought him bread soaked in wine, but it wouldn't go down and he wasn't hungry anyway. Bertrand spat it out and waved him away.

At dawn he savored the last drink of brandy in his flask, raising a silent toast to Christien in Birgu. As always he scanned the horizon, still confident he would see the Viceroy's relief force, sailing into view. By God, the sun proved him right. He saw ships off the tip of Sciberras. Lots of them. He wiped his eyes and shook his head.

Merde. Wrong fleet.

Piali's ships thronged offshore, disgorging men and opening fire with their bow guns. He heard distant strains of music, horns and drums, and a great cry of war rising from the throats of countless thousands of men.

The entire Turkish army joined this attack. Bertrand saw them pouring down the hill of Sciberras and over the ditches, saw their green shields and golden bonnets, saw them flowing up the ladders, hurling themselves at the remaining ranks of defenders, who could not possibly possess the strength or numbers or weapons to push them back. Like the others, Bertrand somehow found the strength to lift his weapons one more time. Somehow in the next hour the defenders managed to push the attackers back—once, and then again. Bertrand fought feverishly, realizing with growing elation and surprise that he was going to live to see another sunrise. The Viceroy had promised help by the twentieth of June, but only if St. Elmo held. It was the twenty-third, he knew, and St. Elmo, by the grace of God, still did.

The Turkish command, however, knew victory was at hand. Their troops regrouped and surged forward again.

This time there was no stopping them.

The commanders Degueras and Miranda were so severely wounded they could no longer stand. They ordered chairs brought up. They sat in them, swords ready, defending the breach from their backsides. The circle of defenders had grown smaller, pressed back on every side toward the chapel. Bertrand dragged himself from a moment of rest to his knees, and then to his feet, and watched the latest surge. He had only six firepots left. He lit the fuses and hurled them one after another. He didn't have to aim or throw far to hit the enemy, now only twenty feet away, no longer slowed by a wall. Men burst into flames through which others ran, scimitars flashing as hot as the fire. There were *Sipahis* and Iayalars and Janissaries and dervishes, all coming at once, swarming, fighting, firing, screaming. He took another ball in his shoulder. The ball pierced his armor and the impact nearly knocked him from his feet. He tried to raise his sword but his arm wouldn't work. He dropped it. Holding his battle axe in his other hand he waded forward into the Turkish troops. He fought without pain and without fear, everything seeming to take place in slow motion, the sound lost, a light fog over his eyes. He felt something hack at his leg. His knee gave way and he sank, weighted under his armor, his axe still lashing out, hacking and cutting flesh until the blade tangled in silk and iron mesh and bone and he could no longer move it. He let go his axe and found his knife and used it then, stabbing and clawing. He took another blow, and another. The dust and the smoke and the Janissaries swirled around him and he fell, and Bertrand Cuvier felt no more.

❖

Barely conscious, Dragut Raïs lay on a cot in his tent in the Marsa. A messenger raced in with word from Mustapha Pasha. He leaned over the old corsair and fairly shouted the words. "St. Elmo has fallen, my lord. Our day of victory is near."

Dragut opened his eyes and looked upward. His lips formed a prayer. He took a deep breath and died.

Piali Pasha ordered his ships into the harbor of Marsamuscetto, sheltered at last.

In the ruin of St. Elmo, Mustapha Pasha wandered among the dead, stepping on the standards of St. John that were laid before him like carpet. At last the Sultan's banners fluttered over the fort. The many men who even now lay on their bellies in prayer, lamenting the passing of Dragut, could not fail to be cheered by the achievement of his goal.

Yet Mustapha was troubled in victory. He stopped at the southern wall and looked across Grand Harbor, its waters sparkling and peaceful in the late afternoon sun. St. Angelo stood on the headland guarding Birgu. Beyond it lay St. Michael, guarding Senglea. Each fort was surely ten times more formidable than St. Elmo, whose rubble he had just purchased with the lives of eight thousand men. "Allah," he said, "if so small a son has cost us so dear, what price shall we have to pay for so large a father?"

Mustapha Pasha was furious with the defenders of St. Elmo. Not because they had fought bravely; he expected that. But once the outcome was no longer in doubt, they had ignored their time-honored duty to surrender. They would have been spared— ransomed at best, put to the oar at worst. It was thus in nearly every siege, in every battle, on both sides. It was the rule of war. By holding out they had caused needless death. Now, enraged beyond measure, his men slaughtered the last of the wounded.

Mustapha knew it was important to send a clear message to La Valette—or, more importantly, to those trapped with him behind the walls of the remaining fortresses. He must make them understand that his resolve was stiffer than ever, that the Sultan's losses to date were nothing. For every warrior who'd fallen there were four more to take his place. Mustapha remembered that at Rhodes, forty years earlier, it was in large part the failure of the populace to support the knights that helped to defeat them. Now it was time for every man, woman, and child of Malta to know what would happen to them should they fail to surrender.

Every commander knew how to send such messages.

First the heads of St. Elmo's officers were planted atop pikes on the ruined walls, their armor nailed beneath them to make their identity clear. The bodies of other knights were dragged forward.

The heads were stricken from some, the hearts from others. Crosses were carved into their flesh. Their bodies were fixed to crude crosses fashioned from bits of masts and spars and shoring timber. They were dragged down to the water and tossed in. The sun was setting as the current began to carry them across Grand Harbor to Birgu.

The word spread quickly the next morning, as the bells rang Angelus. Christien was at the Infirmary, where he'd worked all night. He was one of the first to respond, arriving just before the Grand Master himself. Christien took the covered steps of the sally port two at a time and emerged onto the dock. He looked across at the smoking ruins of St. Elmo, at the Sultan's flags now flying from its ramparts. Only a few Maltese swimmers had managed to escape. They reported nine knights taken alive, though no one knew what had become of them.

His eyes scanned the bodies floating on Kalkara Creek.

Dear God, let him be one of the nine.

But then he saw him, certain only because of an old shoulder scar he immediately recognized, a red scar on white skin that was visible even from a distance. Christien waded out, and when it was too deep to walk he swam, ignoring the shouts from shore that he wait until fishing boats could be sent.

Christien caught hold of the wooden cross and towed it back toward land. Men waded into the shallows, trying to fish other bodies from the water. Christien didn't see or hear any of them. He got the wood up onto the dock, pushing away those who tried to help him. Gently he removed the knots binding the hands and feet. One wouldn't come loose and he had to cut it. His hand was trembling, and he accidentally nicked Bertrand's ankle. He cursed his clumsiness and wiped at his eyes with his sleeve, but they kept blurring anyway. His hands automatically touched Bertrand's many burns and wounds of battle, cleansed now and bleached by the sea. He smoothed them in his practiced way, as if to heal them.

Christien removed his robe and gently wrapped it around his friend. He picked him up, surprised at how light he was. He carried him through the sally port and up the stairs, and then through the streets of Birgu, making his way through crowds of respectful and silent Maltese who had gathered near the walls to see.

He crossed the drawbridge to Fort St. Angelo. The guard opened the main gate for the knight. Christien mounted more stairs, climbing to the little cemetery where the Order's dead were being buried. There was no time for ordinary services. If Bertrand was to be buried at all, it had to be without delay.

Christien sent a workman for one of the chaplains. While he was waiting he took a shovel from one of the slaves working at the deep pit in which bodies were being buried together. He climbed down into the pit and made a place away from the others, digging until his shovel clanged against the rock. He set the shovel aside and picked up the shroud, carefully lowering it into the grave.

Father Roberto came and said the prayers. By then there were many bodies and he spoke quickly, mumbling over each. He had hardly finished when a worker appeared pushing a barrow from which he scattered lime, preparing for the next layer. The priest made his apologies to Christien for his haste and departed for the Church of St. Lawrence. It was the Feast of St. John, the patron saint of the Order.

Christien climbed to the battlements of St. Angelo and stared out at St. Elmo. A light north wind ruffled his hair, carrying with it a stench of death. On the slopes of Sciberras, Turkish slaves were already dismantling some of the gun emplacements, preparing to reposition them so their fire could be turned against Birgu and Senglea.

At the conclusion of services in St. Lawrence, Jean de La Valette emerged, resolute after prayer. "We shall teach the Muslim a lesson in humanity," he said. He gave the order for some of the Turkish prisoners to be brought to the yard of St. Angelo, near the chapel of St. Anne. Christien passed them on the drawbridge as they trudged in, heads down, chains clanking.

The prisoners filed into the yard, where they were forced to kneel. As the Grand Master watched they were beheaded, one after another. Their bodies were tossed into the sea. La Valette ordered his gunners to their posts on the cavalier. Charges were set and the cannons began to roar, firing at the Turkish troops still picking through the rubble of St. Elmo. The balls bounced through them and caused no damage, for they were not granite or iron, but Turkish heads.

The cannons kept roaring until they were too hot to touch.

Chapter 41

The night St. Elmo fell, five weeks after the siege had begun, a small relief force arrived from Sicily. Four galleys carried seven hundred men. They made anchor in Piedra Negra, a remote spot off the northwest shore of the island. Firelight glowed from the mouth of a cave, set there to guide the ships.

The naval commander, Don Juan de Cardona, had express orders from the Viceroy in Sicily not to disembark the troops if St. Elmo was in the hands of the enemy. He dispatched a French knight, the Chevalier Quincy, to assess the situation. "St. Elmo has fallen," the Maltese waiting in the cave told him.

Quincy was aware of Cardona's orders. "You are mistaken," he told them. "If anyone asks you, the fort still holds."

"St. Elmo," he reported to Cardona, back on the ship, "remains in our hands." Cardona gave his permission for the force to disembark. A Maltese scout named Toni Bajjada, a former slave of the Turks who knew the island intimately and often carried messages between Birgu and Mdina, led the force to Birgu, using a route that was not yet occupied by the Turks. Passing within earshot of scattered Ottoman camps, the men marched through the night in absolute silence, their presence concealed by darkness and by a heavy mist that blew in with the scirocco, unusual for that time of year. They gathered on the shore of Bighi, near the spot where the survivors of M'kor Hakhayyim had set out swimming. Small boats ferried them across Kalkara, and by dawn they were inside Birgu. Not a shot had been fired.

The Viceroy had promised thousands of reinforcements and sent only hundreds, yet their appearance was greeted with jubilation by the defenders. Viewing the banners of the new arrivals fluttering from the walls of Birgu, Mustapha Pasha reversed his earlier stance and decided once more to offer terms of surrender: honorable departure from the island, with full protection of the Sultan's fleet. An old Greek slave, a member of Mustapha's own household, was dispatched with his offer. He was received by La Valette, who threatened to hang him until the slave pointed out he was merely acting as a messenger. The Greek was blindfolded and led outside the gates, to a spot between the bastions of Auvergne and Provence. His blindfold was removed. He was shown the walls towering above him, protecting the landward side of Birgu, and the deep ditch that ran beneath them. "Tell your master that this is the only territory I will grant him," La Valette said, indicating the ditch. "He may have it for his own, so long as he first fills it with the bodies of his Janissaries."

Mustapha was enraged. In a score of campaigns he'd waged from Hungary to Persia, he had never seen such callous and rude disregard for the obvious: the defenders were in a hopeless position, and yet they spurned his mercy. He would not make such an offer again.

Mustapha set into motion the plan he and Dragut had devised before the latter's death. The knights had protected the sea end of Grand Harbor with the guns of St. Elmo and St. Angelo. No one had ever anticipated that boats might be launched from the landward end of the harbor, at the Marsa—but then, no one had ever reckoned on the determination of Mustapha Pasha. Like Hannibal over the Alps, he set out to do the impossible. The masts, rowing benches, and cabins of eighty galleys harbored in Marsamuscetto were removed to make them lighter. Their hulls were dragged up onto the beach with capstans and heavy ropes, and set atop masts laid out like rollers. Oxen, horses, and slaves began pulling and pushing the boats up and over the gentle slopes of Sciberras. On the far side, nearly a mile distant, they would be floated again in the Grand Harbor, near the Marsa. When the fleet was reassembled, an assault would be launched against the unprotected southwestern shore of Senglea. At the same time, the bulk of the army would storm the small peninsula from its landward end, protected only by the weak fort of St. Michael.

The battle would be preceded by an intense artillery barrage. Thousands of men began toiling to move artillery into new positions on the heights of Corradino, across French Creek from Senglea on the opposite side from Birgu. Others were placed along the heights near the monastery of Santa Margherita. As at St. Elmo, the guns would all be higher than the defenses. Their massive barrage would soon reduce Birgu and Senglea to the same oblivion that had swallowed St. Elmo.

It was, Mustapha knew, a master stroke.

❖

Shabooh's guts were on fire. He lay on a cot in the shade of a tree in the Marsa, where the army had established its main field hospital. There were too many sick and wounded to fit in the medical tents, so hundreds of men lay in the open. More were suffering from dysentery and disease than from the wounds of battle. Some said the army had already lost a fourth of its men; others said even more. Of the twenty Janissaries in Shabooh's command, fourteen were out of commission, none from wounds.

Someone had finally realized the knights had done something to the water. It was an artful, subtle poison they had used. The wells were being decontaminated, but too late for many. Some of the worst cases were being carried away in galleys to Tripoli. A doctor included Shabooh in their number, but he refused evacuation. He crawled back to his cot on all fours. He had already missed St. Elmo and could not bear to miss Birgu. Despite his determination, however, he was not recovering. After weeks of it he was still sick from both ends, not knowing whether he needed most to squat or to kneel. His head pounded and his tongue wouldn't move. He had never been so ill. He drifted in and out of delirium. In his lucid moments he worried that if he died, Allah would not consider the death to have been earned in jihad against the infidel. Surely, he thought, after a lifetime spent in preparation for war, it could not be Allah's will that he die from the inglorious shits.

❖

One of the small bones on the top of Fençu's foot had been shattered on the dock by the arquebus ball. The wound was painful but not serious. It was the Janissary's axe in the cave that had done the real damage. Fençu despised himself for the choice he'd made prior to the siege. He'd deluded himself into believing he could avoid the fight between the Order and the Turks, thinking he could let them kill each other while he hid in a hole. He'd been a fool, and it had cost Elli's life and, he assumed, those of Villano and Cataldo and their families as well. Though he had no love for the knights, there was no question about what he would do now.

He found shelter in Luca Borg's house, along with Elena, Moses, and nearly forty others. At first he lay on the floor beneath the kitchen table, nursing his foot and brooding, his only companion a sheep awaiting its inevitable appointment with the stew pot. Everyone else had gone to help with the defenses, even Moses. The Grand Master had ordered more houses demolished outside the landward walls of Birgu and Senglea. Every woman and child who could carry a stone was doing so, lugging them inside the walls where they were broken into pieces that could be thrown upon the enemy when that day came.

The first night four fewer people came home to Luca Borg's, killed by the incessant bombardment that was not yet a tenth part of what it would be when all the Turkish guns were in place. Already there were twenty-four guns and two great basilisks pounding the village walls. Luca's house was out of range, although that would change as soon as the Turks completed their gun platforms on the heights of Salvador, across Kalkara Creek from the Infirmary. Even so, the walls shook all day and dust streamed from the rafters.

The screaming Fençu heard in the streets was relieved only by the frightened bleating of the sheep, and he knew he would go mad if he stayed indoors another day. He wrapped his foot tightly and tried it out. He gasped in pain and thought he'd better wait another day or two. But then he saw the tortured faces of the women and children who came home that night, and knew his waiting was over. He couldn't carry rocks, but there was plenty of other work. He fabricated fire hoops. He helped sew the cloaks and clothing of the dead into sacks that would be filled with earth and crushed stone and placed in piles where they could be used to make fast repairs to breached defenses. At the arsenal he helped break apart some of the larger fishing boats moored in Birgu Creek. Every nail was saved for use in explosives, every piece of wood salvaged for use in retaining walls. He worked twenty hours a day.

A Turkish soldier named Lascaris, a man of the old Byzantine nobility who'd been kidnapped by the Turks years before, had defected to the knights. He revealed to La Valette Mustapha's plans for the seaborne assault. The Grand Master had already guessed the general outline, having seen the streams of laborers toiling with the boats, but Lascaris added valuable details. La Valette decided to build a palisade along the unprotected shore of Senglea. The palisade, a row of sharpened stakes set close together, would angle out toward the water, a first line of defense against attacking ships.

A call went out for expert swimmers. Fençu volunteered, knowing the water work was something he could do well, even with an injured foot. He and the other swimmers, mostly Maltese fishermen and sailors, dove repeatedly into the water off Senglea, driving massive stakes into the deep sand, or wedging them between rocks. Where depth or hardness prevented that, they bound together ships' masts in an elaborate underwater web, bridging the distance between stakes, then fixing shorter stakes to the framework below the waterline. The tips were capped with iron hoops, through which chains were passed to hold them in line, creating a formidable barrier to men and boats alike. All the work had to be done at night because of the Turkish snipers ranged along the hillsides above French Creek. Between dawn and dusk the Turks commanded the area. Between dusk and dawn, the waters off Senglea churned with swimmers.

Every morning all eyes turned to the head of the harbor, to see how many more Turkish ships were now in place. When there were eighty, Lascaris said, the attack would commence. On the fourth morning, there were fifty-three. The fifth morning, there were sixty-two. Troops could be seen massing in camps on the Corradino heights above St. Michael, the weakest point in the defenses. Meanwhile, the Turkish artillery never ceased firing. More than seventy cannons now pounded walls and houses, with more being brought in all the time. At the end of the first week in July, a new fleet of galleys appeared off Gallows Point and sailed into Marsamuscetto, flying the pennants of Hassem, the Viceroy of Algiers and son-in-law of Dragut. He'd brought well-armed ships and twenty-five hundred Moors to join the fight.

The defenders' labors rose to a fevered pitch. La Valette ordered a bridge of boats laid between Birgu and Senglea to allow reinforcements to pass between the two peninsulas as they were needed. The great chain already lay in place between the tips of the two peninsulas, protecting Birgu Creek against a seaborne assault. A second chain was laid across the water and supported on pontoons to protect the creek's inner basin. On the opposite side of Birgu, facing Kalkara Creek, workers filled barges with stones and sank them along the shore, and strung more chain between them. Ammunition was laid into a secret gun battery beneath St. Angelo, near the water.

❖

> Prayer is better than sleep!
> Prayer is better than sleep!
> Allah is great, great is Allah.
> There is no God but God,
> and Mohammed is His Prophet!

The reedy call rose from the corner of the dark cell, chanted by an Algerian who lay beneath the high tiny window through which they could hear the morning bells of Angelus ringing in the Church of St. Lawrence.

Asha turned over. He groaned, his voice lost in the chorus of misery coming from the other slaves in the room. He dragged himself to his knees. He'd thought himself in superb shape, but every muscle ached. Every movement brought a fresh pain, a new searing somewhere. His arms and legs were ragged, blistered, and torn. His head ached. His tongue was swollen from incessant thirst, and his ears rang like the guns. The night before it had been almost impossible to sleep as men cried and moaned. It seemed he'd only just closed his eyes, and already it was time for another day of it.

He did his best to perform his ablutions, using a handful of filthy straw to cleanse his face and hands, then falling into the comforting ritual of the salah.

Praise be to Allah, Lord of the Worlds, the Beneficent, the Merciful, owner of the day of Judgment. . . .

The words kept him sane, although he had moments when he scarcely cared if he died. He knew it must be near. La Valette had been as good as his word, having devised a torment that was worse in some ways than hanging. Asha could scarcely believe that a mere two weeks could have taken so much from him. Beside the horror of life on the walls, food and water were scarce. Each day he grew weaker. He'd heard that Dragut had died. Although he'd known it was inevitable, confirmation brought a deep depression. He felt the loss of the man as deeply as he knew the Sultan's forces would feel the loss of their coordinating genius. Without him it would not be long before the arguments of Mustapha and Piali would drown out the thunder of the cannons. The siege might last forever.

His own position was worsened by the defection of Lascaris, whose assistance contrasted so sharply with his own refusal to cooperate. Word spread quickly in the dungeons and along the walls. All the guards knew of Asha Raïs. They did their best to add to his special hell, using their whips more quickly on him than on the others. They put him in the worst positions on the walls. They spit in his face and pissed in his meager rations, which were shorted anyway. They taunted him mercilessly, hoping he'd show a flicker of defiance so they could deliver his death. He was determined not to give them the satisfaction. He would do what he had to do to stay alive.

There was more danger still from the civilians of Birgu, whose sufferings through years of depredations by the Turks and their allies Asha understood as well as anyone alive. With St. Elmo fresh in their memory, roaming gangs snatched prisoners from the walls, stoning them or ripping them apart, then dragging them through the streets, with children playing in the bloody trails. The Order encouraged the activity. If Asha's Maltese birth made a difference, it was only evident in that the guards kept such bands from killing him, determined instead to subject him to the more exquisite terrors of the walls.

The door clanked open. "Mohammedan swine to the slop!" snarled the guard. Men struggled to their feet and straggled to the yard, where they received a cup of thin soup, a scrap of bread, and a drink of water. It was barely enough for the morning, much less the whole day. Asha stood, but the man he was chained to, an Algerian named Mahmoud, only groaned. "I've had enough of this madness," he said. "I'm not going."

"There is no choice," Asha said.

"There is the choice of death. I will choose it gladly."

"And you shall have it if you don't come along. Get up now, or we'll have no food." Mahmoud crossed his arms and closed his eyes. Asha pulled. He was stronger than the Algerian, but Mahmoud was little more than dead weight. Asha began dragging him.

A guard noticed. "Stand up, pig," he said. Mahmoud shook his head defiantly. The guard lashed him savagely with his whip. "Stand up, pig," he repeated.

Still Mahmoud refused. The guard's knife flashed, slicing off most of his ear. Mahmoud shrieked and got to his feet, covering the bloody mess with his hand. Someone tossed him a strip of cotton to wrap his head. Mahmoud whimpered and blubbered and cursed, but he joined the line of living ghosts making its way to the walls.

The sun was just rising into a perfect sky in what promised to be another blistering day. The slaves walked along the defenses above Kalkara Creek. At every street Asha looked for Maria, knowing she'd be there somewhere. Sure enough, she appeared near the armory. She watched the guards and timed it perfectly, emerging from the street and walking against the line of prisoners, their chains rattling. Her hand moved swiftly and he deftly caught the bread, still warm from her touch. He longed to talk to her but had to content himself with the silent smiles they traded, when the years melted away and their spirits joined again for the briefest of instants. She was gone a moment later. Sometimes while he worked on the walls he saw her in the streets below, watching him. He wished she would retire to the safety of some shelter, but he knew if there was any such place, it wouldn't exist for long. He thought she looked gaunt, a little more tired and haggard each day.

He took comfort in knowing the next heavy blow would fall on Senglea and not Birgu. But then he also knew that when Senglea fell, Birgu would not be far behind. Its walls were high and thick, but they would not stand for long against the relentless pounding of the firepower arrayed against them. All along, his worst nightmare had been that he would see her dead in these streets. He knew now that might well come to pass, and that he would not be able to help her.

He and Mahmoud arrived at their post and began the day's labor repairing damage to the walls. Still chained together, they wrestled bags filled with earth and stone up the steep scree of debris that had been created as Turkish artillery reduced the masonry and earthen defenses to rubble. They dragged the bags up one at a time, each man taking an end, each man struggling to find sure footing. Inevitably they would get a few steps up, then one would slip, slide backward, and fall. Each time they went down, they lost a little more skin to the overseer, who stood at the bottom, encouraging them with his whip. They worked this way until they'd gotten twenty bags near the top. Then they faced five minutes of sheer terror, exposing themselves to Turkish fire while lifting the bags the rest of the way up, onto the top of the damaged portions of wall.

Asha had always heard that the Turkish gunners were the best in the world. Now he saw proof of it firsthand. There were errant shots, of course, and the danger from those was extreme, but most were dead-on accurate. The gunners would select a particular spot on the wall and put a shot there with a basilisk, the largest of which could put a ball through twenty feet of earth. A moment later another shot would follow, this time from a culverin mounted farther down the line, each gun working the spot from a slightly different angle, each blow beginning to tell in the spot where it would make the most difference. The same process was repeating itself at selected points all along the defenses. While the walls were being thus methodically pulverized, other cannons fired into the towns and forts, sowing random terror and death. Hour after hour, day after day it went on, softening the defenses for the storm troops to follow.

Asha and the other slaves stood exposed to it all, performing work that had no end. Almost as quickly as the bags were placed, a new shot would take them down again. There was no safety in the fact they were obviously prisoners of war. The gunners were ordered to prevent the repair of walls, and shot anything that moved. Their granite cannon balls made a peculiar whistling sound that gave the slaves a little warning. When they heard it they would drop to their bellies and try to wriggle beneath the rubble as the ball burst into deadly shards. The polished marble balls were more fearsome. They came silently, carrying away legs and heads and whole men without warning.

The Turkish trenches were still some distance away. As they

snaked closer and the arquebusiers got within range, death would come more quickly to the slaves on the walls. Asha had trained with the very Janissaries who would be sighting him with weapons whose accuracy had no equal in the world.

❖

In the Turkish command tent, Mustapha and his aghas reviewed plans for the coming day's assault. Every fighting man had an assignment, save a thousand Janissaries who would be held in reserve to exploit any weakness that might appear in the defenses.

Hassem, the Viceroy from Algiers, listened patiently to Mustapha's plan. "It is quite thorough," he acknowledged, "but unless it is delivered with more passion than was brought to bear on St. Elmo, it can only fail. I cannot imagine how it took so long to take that modest fort, or fathom how victory was bought at such a cost." He looked boldly into the suddenly wintry eyes of the old general. "If you will permit me the honor, sire, my Moors will show your troops how men of true will can fight."

Mustapha Pasha smiled thinly. "A brilliant idea. We will put your men in the forefront of the land assault, over which I grant you command. Your lieutenant, Candelissa, will lead the seaborne assault. Pray inform him his boats are ready in the Marsa. I look forward to your easy victory."

That night, as before every engagement, the sound of prayer enveloped the Grand Harbor like a fog.

❖

15 JULY

Fençu swirled under water, desperate for air. His lungs were searing and he knew he could not fight the impulse to take another breath much longer. His face was only inches away from the Turk's, whose hair and long beard waved in the underwater eddies. The Turkish diver swung at him with his axe, but his upper body was entangled in the webbing around one of the stakes in the palisades, the force of his blow diluted by the water. The side of the axe glanced off Fençu's shoulder, with no effect.

Fençu twisted away and used the mesh to push himself downward. He'd lost his knife during their initial encounter. Now he was on the other side of the mesh from the Turk, pulling the man down by one arm, in a desperate tug of war to see who would drown first.

The Turk got one shoulder through the webbing. With a better range of motion he swung again, bubbles streaming from his mouth. This time a corner of the weapon bit into Fençu's shoulder. A cloud of blood billowed around them. Fençu felt the blow but no pain. Lungs tormented, Fençu yanked down on the Turk's arm at the same time as he brought his knees up to his chest. He kicked out, pulling the Turk toward him. His feet connected below the mesh, hitting his opponent squarely in the chest. Bubbles burst from the Turk's mouth and his eyes bulged in panic. Fençu felt him weakening.

Fençu kicked again. There were more bubbles, and the Turk let go of the axe. It floated downward, disappearing into the murk. He'd stopped struggling, his arms and legs hanging free, his body relaxed. Fençu shot for the surface. He burst through, gasping for air, his muscles burning like his lungs.

The first Turks had come before dawn. They sent their best swimmers to cross the four hundred feet of French Creek to Senglea, carrying their weapons and tools in their teeth or strapped to their backs. They'd begun a furious effort to demolish what they could of the palisades, to clear the way for the seaborne assault. They were hacking at the ropes and tugging at the stakes when the first wave of Maltese fell upon them. Fençu was among them, hobbling across the beach on his bad foot. A Spanish soldier who couldn't swim thrust a knife into his hands, and Fençu plunged screaming into the water, eager for battle. Now he'd slain his first Turk. He wanted to kill more.

All up and down the waterfront the bloodstained water roiled with men grappling for advantage. Some fought below the surface, while others thrashed on top. A few hung from the stakes, swinging their weapons with their free hands while men swam around them, their blades flashing up out of the water, clashing in the air. On land, marksmen from both sides held their fire, afraid to strike their own men.

In the midst of battle the Turks managed to maneuver a few small boats next to the palisades. They carried grappling hooks and coils of thick hawser, rope used for towing galleys. Their crews hurled the hooks into the water, catching the framework beneath the surface. While men battled around them they rowed furiously back to the far shore, playing out the thick hawsers behind them. On the shore beneath Corradino, slaves toiled at capstans to pull the hawsers tight, trying to yank the palisades out of place. Although the Turkish swimmers were no match for the Maltese, Fençu saw their effort was partially succeeding. Some parts of the palisades were weakened, others sagging or completely down.

Fençu dove twice and found the Turk's axe on its bed of sand. He swam to the nearest hawser and started hacking at it. The rope was as thick as his wrist. Even with the razor-sharp axe, the work was nearly impossible underwater. He sawed and slashed, coming up three times for air. Finally, just as the hawser was being pulled taut by the capstans, the last strands parted and fell away free.

Gasping for air, he started for the next one. At that moment he saw the Turkish fleet bearing down on him, countless galleys approaching from the Marsa at the full pace of war. A forest of oars worked the water, waving and dipping, propelling an armada bristling with scarlet robes and white turbans and jewels, men heavily armed with bows and muskets, axes and halberds, sabers and pikes. An *imam* stood bravely in the lead boat, reading to the troops from the Koran.

Fençu turned toward land and swam for his life. He heard men on the walls shouting warnings to the other swimmers to clear the water. Those who failed to flee were quickly swallowed up in the approaching storm.

The Turkish galleys spread out as they entered French Creek, intending to storm the entire Senglean foreshore. In most places the palisades held, but in others they collapsed and partially sank, allowing boats to get past.

Candelissa, the Algerian commander, found his own boat stalled. Undaunted, he leapt into the water, sinking up to his shoulders, his robes floating about him. His men poured out of their boats, plunging in behind him. Some went in over their heads and emerged sputtering, their gunpowder weapons and incendiaries ruined, while others got tangled in the palisades and drowned. Most found the shallows and managed to keep their precious weapons above their heads. They waded ashore, some dragging scaling ladders as they crouched behind their shields and advanced into the withering fire now pouring from the walls.

Once on shore, Fençu had collapsed with his back to a wall, doubled over with nausea. He coughed up seawater, retching violently. His left shoulder burned from the salt. The axe had laid open his muscle. Like his foot, the wound was more painful than serious. As long as they kept taking such little bits out of him, he thought, he could keep going.

He took off his loincloth, the only material available, and another swimmer helped him bind his shoulder. He drank deeply from a cistern, then gathered his strength and stood up, fighting the wave of dizziness that came over him. He rushed toward the tip of Senglea, where the bulk of the fleet was attacking.

At the same instant that the sea assault commenced, the land attack began. Algerian and Turkish troops led by Hassem swarmed down from the heights toward St. Michael, oblivious to the cannon fire ripping through their ranks. They threw themselves at the walls, the living climbing over the dead. There were thousands upon thousands of them, every man screaming.

The western and southern fronts of Senglea were engulfed in the Ottoman storm.

❖

Christien was dressing a deep wound in a soldier's back when he heard the trumpet through the window above the sounds of the attack. It was the emergency signal for all floating reserves to report to the square. It was his first call to battle. Except in extreme emergencies he was to stay at his post in the Infirmary, patching up men who could return to arms. He dropped his instruments and raced off, calling to one of the civilian barber-surgeons to finish the job.

His weapons were in the cloistered courtyard, at the ready. His hands still slippery with blood, he needed the help of a page to don his armor. Though the sweltering suit weighed more than a hundred pounds, it was well tailored and barely hindered his movements. On the way to the square he joined Romegas and three other knights who were racing from the Hub, their post near the slave prison. Any position not under direct attack was sending whatever men could be spared.

Moments later they were making their way into the tumult, across the pontoon bridge that crossed Birgu Creek to the center of the Senglea peninsula. Most of the reinforcements ran to the left to join the battle raging near St. Michael, where eight thousand Algerian and Turkish troops swarmed upon the fort from the landward side. Christien ran to the right, toward the spur of the peninsula where the brunt of the sea attack was taking place. Three thousand men had already poured off the boats; more were coming. At both ends of Senglea, parts of the wall had been breached.

A powder magazine exploded near the windmills and knocked Christien off his feet. He struggled up, shaken, and ran past men who lay burnt, dazed, or dying from the blast. Turkish standards were appearing on the walls. He reached the wall and looked down onto the shore seething with assault troops struggling to get more ladders into position.

Fençu stood naked among a group of knights and soldiers, all of whom had thrown down their arquebuses and were hurling stones down at the troops. Women and children from the village gathered around the pots of water boiling on fires placed every few yards along the battlements. Together they lifted them and turned them over onto the men ascending the ladders or surging at the base of the walls. The Turks were massed tightly together, making such primitive defenses deadly effective. Pots of wildfire flew through the air but did less damage than usual, as the robes of the attackers were still dripping with seawater.

Christien faced a Janissary just reaching the top of a scaling ladder. The man raised his sword to strike. Christien shoved the ladder with his foot and sent him tumbling backward. Others rose to take his place. Much of the fighting was hand-to-hand. Men clutched together in death grips and toppled as one. Smoke eddied back and forth along the walls in an uncertain wind. Cannonballs crashed through the lines, killing Muslim and Christian alike. The din was otherworldly.

Hour after hour Father Roberto, sword in one hand and crucifix in the other, made his way from post to post, shouting encouragement to the soldiers, inspiring them to ever greater effort. "Blessed are they who die in His name," he shouted. "For it is written that at the name of Jesus every knee should bow, in heaven and on earth and under the earth."

Mustapha Pasha watched the course of battle from his post in Corradino. He saw that the line of defenders was now stretched perilously thin as it tried to hold both the south and west walls of Senglea against overwhelming numbers. Piali Pasha was pressing his own attack against Birgu, to prevent further reinforcements from reaching Senglea. Victory, Mustapha saw, was finally within his grasp. It was time for his reserve, the Janissaries he'd kept waiting for just such a moment, when the tide of battle might be turned. He nodded to a messenger, and a trumpet sounded. Ten galleys carrying a hundred Janissaries each set off for the tip of Senglea, intending to land near the anchor point of the chain that stretched across Birgu Creek to St. Angelo. There were not enough defenders to stop them.

Hidden with his troops near the waterline beneath Fort St. Angelo, in a position that had never been observed by the Turks, the Chevalier Francisco de Guiral saw the boats coming directly toward him. He ordered his cannons loaded with sacks of stones, iron bars, bits of chain, and spiked iron balls. The guns were swung into position. Oblivious, the galleys swept forward.

When the galleys were only two hundred yards away, de Guiral gave the order to fire. A massive salvo roared from the battery. Chain shot ripped open keels and shredded the men inside. A second round was quickly loaded and fired.

Nine of the boats sank quickly. The tenth swung round in a rapid turn and sped toward the shore of Sciberras. When the smoke cleared, the water was a bloody froth. A carpet of colorful turbans and robes floated on top, marking where nine hundred Janissaries had perished. Except for those in the tenth boat, not a single man survived.

At Fort St. Michael, Hassem's eager Algerians surged forward again and again, unable to gain a permanent foothold as the guns on the walls shredded their ranks. The hours of slaughter finally took sufficient toll, and they began to retreat in disarray.

On the spur where Christien was still fighting, the attackers saw the retreat from St. Michael. They sought to withdraw as well, but were trapped on the shore, stranded by the fleet and completely exposed. Under fire from the cannons of St. Angelo and the batteries beneath the windmills, many of the boats were milling offshore just out of range, unable to help.

Seeing the tide turning, troops inside the walls sallied forth and began a slaughter. Christien emerged with them through the gate. Maltese, Spanish, and Greek troops poured past him with unrestrained fury. Fençu was among them, having armed himself with an axe and a scimitar he'd gotten from the body of a Janissary. Shouting "St. Elmo's pay," the defenders overwhelmed the Turks, taking heads and no prisoners.

Exhausted and nearly overcome with heat, Christien sagged to his seat, stunned at the butchery, which he watched numbly. In the harbor swimmers began a systematic harvest. They towed some of the debris to shore, while others dived repeatedly beneath the surface. The sunken boats held plentiful supplies, including butter and honey and raisins, food intended to sustain the attackers once they'd captured the spur of the peninsula. Fishermen pulled up the bodies of dead Janissaries and stripped them of jewels, money, and weapons. Bodies sank and bodies floated in a grisly flotsam of war.

The battle was over by noon. Three thousand Turks and Algerians lay dead along the foreshore and ditches of Senglea. Inside the walls two hundred and fifty defenders were dead, among them the son of the Viceroy of Sicily. There were countless hundreds of wounded.

Christien closed his eyes to the sight of the dead strewn everywhere over the rocks. He smelled the smoke and the blood and listened to the cries of the wounded. He tried to get up to help them, but collapsed again. His lips were parched but he lacked the strength to crawl the twenty feet he needed to go for water.

He realized his side was sticky with blood. He unbuckled his cuirass and saw the white tip of bone near his hip. He had no idea when it happened. It still didn't hurt. The bleeding had almost stopped. He looked at it in a detached manner, as if it belonged to someone else. It was nothing. Every man and woman he'd seen in the last few hours had a wound at least as serious. Absently he packed it with a sweat-soaked cloth.

A shadow fell over him. He looked up to see Father Roberto, his face caked with blood from a wound he'd sustained on his scalp. As a priest, he was not to have taken up arms at all, but his sword glistened with the stains of his day's labors. "Illustrissimo de Vries," he said, his eyes glowing with victory. "We have done God's work this day."

Christien looked up at him with dull eyes. "Have we, Father?"

"You may take comfort in it. Come now. Let me help the doctor, so he can help the others." Father Roberto took Christien's hand and helped him to his feet. The priest was almost as weak as Christien. With supreme effort they supported each other, and together they tottered back toward Birgu.

❖

Mustapha Pasha was troubled by his losses but resolute. Siege warfare was a slow, bloody, and difficult business, typically requiring at least five attackers to overcome a single defender. If there had been error in the attack on Senglea—aside from Hassem's blithe indifference to the determination and courage of the knights—it was that the little peninsula had been insufficiently reduced by artillery beforehand. He rejected the idea of another sea assault. His men could be used more effectively on land.

Mustapha decided to bide his time, to let the guns do their slow but certain work. When sufficient breaches appeared in the walls, when enough houses inside were reduced to dust, when those inside had nowhere left to hide except beneath a pile of the dead, another mass assault would be launched against both Birgu and Senglea. Candelissa, who had led the seaborne assault with bravery if not success, was given overall command of the vessels maintaining the blockade, while the admiral Piali Pasha, without a naval battle to lead, was placed in charge of the land forces preparing to attack Birgu.

Slaves began the task of hauling the fleet back over Sciberras to the Marsamuscetto harbor, while engineers toiled to complete the remaining gun emplacements. Trenches were dug from the heights of Salvador down to the waterfront of Kalkara Creek, directly across from Birgu, giving snipers cover from which to work. New gun positions were completed on the heights above them. The guns of Sciberras, including those in the ruins of St. Elmo, were repositioned to more effectively attack St. Angelo and Birgu. On Gallows Point, there were guns already placed by Dragut, while on Corradino and Santa Margherita, the landward heights behind the two peninsulas, new cannons arrived daily.

Mustapha's iron garrote tightened relentlessly, fed by an endless supply of ordnance. His guns began the most intense bombardment of the siege, and the heavens roared with Turkish thunder. The two small peninsulas with their forts and villages were cut off from the outside, their walls and houses pounded from virtually every direction.

The rear walls of the Infirmary were breached. The surgeries were moved forward in the building, to the opposite side from the creek. The building shook as Christien worked. Dust fell onto and into his patients, while men died beneath collapsing walls. There were many places inside the Infirmary where he could look up and see the sky. Every time he did, he thought of Maria, of what it must be like for her outside.

A hailstorm of granite and marble and iron showered the roofs and houses of Birgu. The balls tore great holes in stone walls and roofs, bouncing and crashing down narrow streets. They brought death without warning. There was no longer any safe place on the streets. People raced from shelter to shelter, trying to hide from the unseen terror falling from the skies.

The landward defenses took the greatest punishment. The gunners concentrated the most intense fire against the Post of Castile, at the southern end of Birgu, and on St. Michael, the fort at the foot of Senglea. The dust from the shattered fortifications hung over the Grand Harbor like a suffocating blanket, beneath which the defenders tried desperately to repair the damage.

❖

Asha shuffled toward the Post of England, where he was to spend the day working with his new chain companion, a skinny Anatolian named Abdullah. Mahmoud had fallen to an arquebus ball. Each of Asha's five chain partners had complained worse than the last, and Abdullah was no exception.

As the guard called them to a halt, he heard the booming voice of Romegas. "Ah, the great Asha Raïs, come to grace our humble lines." Romegas jumped down from where he'd been inspecting a wall. He was grinning broadly. He not only appeared unfazed by the artillery fire, he seemed almost to relish it, to draw energy from the fury of the Turks. Normal men took shelter when cannonballs crashed nearby. Romegas stood as if in a light summer rain.

He yelled instructions to the overseer, who began separating the slaves into work details, some to carry blocks, others sacks, still others to work the picks and shovels. The work of reinforcing the outer walls had gotten too hazardous for the civilian population. La Valette decreed that only slaves be used for the purpose now. In two short weeks hundreds had already died.

Romegas had to raise his voice to make himself heard. His mind was evidently not on the business at hand, but on the sea, and he addressed Asha as a captain. "Tell me, Asha Raïs—is the trim of your ship as good as the last? Who built her? I was thinking of plucking her from your fleet when I chase the others out of here. I must confess I was impressed with your speed and turn when last we met. My own does as well, but of course it's because of the cleverness of her captain, not the cut of her keel."

Asha turned to face him, Abdullah glowering and silent beside him as they confronted one of the great enemies of Islam. "Better even than you think. I will be on her deck when you try to take her, and that turn of hers will show you the bottom, as I nearly did last time."

Romegas laughed. "Such pretty bluster from a man in chains! I see your Ottoman guns are now only three hundred feet away. I hope I have the great pleasure of seeing you perish at the hands of your own gunners. Perhaps your executioner will be from your own ship."

"They will not succeed," Asha said. "Not until I have had the opportunity to kill you. I owe you a death, and it will be your own. Take these chains from me now and give me a sword, and we need wait no longer."

Romegas's eyes gleamed with merriment. "Under normal circumstances I would be delighted to take your measure with a blade, but just now I have more than enough to reckon with outside these walls," he said. "But come, we are gentlemen of the sea, you and I. Your hatred of me seems to have no bounds, and I am such a kindhearted man. You owe me a death, you say. Is this because I am a better seaman than you, or because I am better-looking?" His laughter boomed like the cannons.

Asha did not smile. "You caused the death of someone close to me. A woman."

Romegas's eyebrows arched at that. "I do not make a habit of killing women," he said earnestly. "What woman was this?"

"She was a slave in a ship that belonged to the Kislar Agha and El Hadji Farouk, bound from Istanbul to Algiers. A galliot. You took her off Lesbos."

"Of course, I remember it well. Five ships, a good haul. One sank—a shot to the magazine. Hardly what I'd planned, as you can appreciate. The hold was full of silk. I rued its loss as much as any man."

"She was aboard. It was said you let everyone drown rather than stir yourself to save them."

"It was said wrong, then. The blast killed many, but we fished a few from the water. There were soldiers, of course, that we put to the oar. But there were women as well, and even a fat old eunuch or two. Perhaps your woman was among them. If not, it was not I who ended her life—it was the will of God that took the ship."

Asha lifted his chained wrists. With his finger he traced a line from his temple to his jaw. "She had a scar, like so," he said.

Romegas nodded. "I remember her. But for that scar, she was quite striking. She was not dead then, Asha Raïs. Nor was she dead when I left her in Zante. Honestly," he said melodramatically, "I am grieved that your opinion of me should be so low. Why would I leave such a one to die?"

Stunned, Asha hardly knew what to say. "You sold her, then?"

"Of course not. She was Christian. I left her and the others at the next port, when we took on water. They were all free to go, and it was their wish. Only a barbarian such as yourself would have done less." He pointed to a spot on the walls. "For now, alas, there is your helm for the day, Asha Raïs. Keep a steady tiller. Watch for squalls, and take all the prisoners you like." His laughter boomed again and he hurried off.

Dumbly Asha watched him go, ignoring Abdullah's lament that he had not struck out at their captor. Only when he felt the guard's whip did he begin to move. He was in a fog. Was Romegas lying?

There was no reason. Romegas thought him a dead man anyway, and Asha believed from his expression that he'd told the truth. It was all he could do to keep from falling to his knees in prayer.

Allah be praised, she is alive!

Asha moved along, his mind churning furiously. He and Abdullah lugged a sack of stone, and another. A ball smashed into the base of the wall just outside his position. It was a three-hundred-pounder, fired by one of the big culverins. The ground shook when it hit. Asha and the others standing nearby fell to the ground. A cloud of dust rose twenty feet in either direction, mushrooming into the air. Asha picked himself up, struggling to his knees. He spit out grit and part of a tooth. Abdullah nursed a bruised shoulder and issued a stream of obscenities.

Asha realized that suddenly the crash of cannonballs was more terrifying than it had been just an hour or two earlier. He wanted very much to live. He didn't believe that Allah had brought him here simply to die on the walls, but each close call tested the strength of that belief, and he fervently prayed that Allah was paying careful attention to his case.

She's gone home, to Brindisi. No, not Brindisi. She would never go there. She told me once where she would go if she were free. And she is free! Alisa is alive! I know it!

Maria found him in midafternoon, having searched for him all along the walls when he didn't report to the Post of Castile, where his crew had worked the last few weeks. Now she couldn't get near him because of the guard. She stood in the shelter of a doorway beneath a heavy stone arch, waiting until she might have a chance to come closer. Asha saw her and shook his head for her to leave. It was no longer safe for her to come, but of course Maria was concerned only about getting his ration of bread to him.

Though standing chained on that wall, linked to another man and exposed to almost certain death, in that instant Asha felt nothing but exuberance. "She's alive!" he yelled on an impulse. The guard looked up at him, and then toward where he was yelling.

Maria looked at him blankly. "Who?" she yelled back.

Asha laughed out loud. Of course he'd told her everything about Alisa—in letters he'd burned years ago. "Alisa!" he said. "I'll explain someday. Get out of here, will you?" The guard made a threatening gesture. Maria waved and disappeared. He wished she would not try again, but he knew she would.

Asha passed the rest of the afternoon quickly, almost cheerfully, as he pondered the new dimensions of the world. He still noticed every shot, however, fearing the next one might be the last.

In fact, when it came, he never heard the ball at all.

It hit the wall at an oblique angle, glanced upward into a corner of a rampart, and shattered into three pieces. One struck Abdullah. Asha's chain was wrenched violently from beneath him by the force of it. He was jerked from his feet and flew backward through the air, landing near the inner wall, face down and stunned. It took a moment before he stirred. He got to his knees, coughing in the choking yellow dust. There was nothing left of Abdullah but his right leg, still attached at the ankle to the chain, and a very small part of his torso. All the rest of the Anatolian was gone, carried away by the ball.

Asha heard the groans of the men nearby. A few of the slaves were getting up. Others lay broken, crying or dead. A few stood watching in their midst, completely untouched. The guard was down, not dead but on his back, groaning, his hand at his forehead. The instant Asha saw him he realized his moment had come. He got to his feet and scrambled awkwardly through the rubble, dragging what was left of Abdullah behind him. He made straight for the damaged section of wall. He would get up and over it, run across the narrow docks and plunge into Kalkara Creek. Once the Turkish gunners on Salvador saw him escaping he knew they would provide a covering fire. It was not a good chance, perhaps, but it was his only one.

He tripped and fell hard. Abdullah's leg was caught among the stones. Asha picked up the remains of his companion, tucked them under his arm, and ran for his life up the hill. He expected cries of rage from behind, the shot of an arquebus, the burn of a ball in his back. Instead he heard only the eager shouts of a few prisoners, cheering him on.

He chanced a look around. The guard was still down, now

struggling to get to one elbow. Asha was going to be over the wall before the man's head cleared.

He was going to make it.

He was almost to the top when the basilisk boomed again. The gunners knew their business and hit the wall exactly where they intended, just where it was already collapsing. The massive ball threw up a new shower of debris. A piece struck him square in the temple and knocked him senseless.

That night, bruised and bloody but very much alive, Asha awakened in the slave prison, chained to a new partner.

❖

"We should abandon Malta, Excellency," said Don Alfredo, one of the Viceroy's counselors in Messina. "The Turkish force is too large. It is not worth the risk."

"The risk! That is contemptible!" said Gian Andrea Doria. "We have given our solemn oath to come to their aid."

The argument raged over lunch as the Viceroy and his two guests dined on veal and roast pheasant. The Viceroy himself was in no particular hurry to do anything, hoping that somehow the situation in Malta would resolve itself without his having to jeopardize his monarch's ships and men. He intended to proceed—for after all, his own son was in Malta—but only when he had a large enough force to guarantee victory. He was making slow but steady progress at assembling that force, despite endless obstacles. The fleet had been decimated at Djerba. The arsenals of Barcelona and Malaga were working at full capacity, and requests for help had been dispatched to every possible quarter, but still he had only half as many galleys as he wanted.

In the meanwhile, sentiment was strong that nothing be done at all, that Malta be allowed to wither on the vine of neglect. "Who came to their aid in Rhodes?" asked Don Alfredo, pressing that point. "No Christian country. Did it matter, in the end? Will it matter now? The Knights of St. John are an arrogant order, despised in every court of Europe. They swear no fealty to Philip or any other monarch. Why should we squander lives and ships in their aid?"

Doria pounded the table and knocked over a goblet. "Because

their cause is our cause. You are only incensed that your own son was refused entry into the Order."

"I am insulted by your insinuation, sir," Don Alfredo replied hotly. "The only thing that matters to me is that La Valette and his Order set their own table. Let them accept the terms of surrender of the Turk or dine on the consequences."

Doria stood. "Excellency, I myself will take three galleys at my own expense. Give me troops and Christian oarsmen, with the promise of freedom if they fight well. *I* will go to the aid of La Valette."

Don García considered the generous offer but decided he could not spare the Italian admiral. Instead he decided to send three other ships, two of which belonged to the Order, manning them with troops sent by the Pope. A small force, perhaps, but it was something. Meanwhile, the Viceroy said, Doria could continue marshaling other men and ships.

The three galleys could not penetrate the Turkish blockade and returned to Sicily. The Viceroy wrote another letter, which he sent by small boat to Malta.

Be patient, he wrote once again. *Everything possible is being done.*

Chapter 42

I AUGUST

The Turks had arrived in May, and already it was August. For Fençu, Maria, Elena, Moses, and the other civilians trapped inside the walls of Birgu and Senglea, the only respite from incessant terror was through backbreaking labor. Even while the artillery was reducing their surroundings to dust, the women and children often began work before dawn.

During the day they repaired inner walls. After dusk they labored in cramped subterranean rooms, manufacturing incendiaries.

Nothing had proved more effective against the Turks than fire. Besides the firepots and hoops and flame-throwing trumps, they made fire bags, pitch-coated sacks whose insides were stuffed with a long-burning mixture of cotton and gunpowder. Even arquebus balls were coated with lard. The balls retained their heat when fired, igniting clothing and hair and even skin. It was all hot, smelly, dangerous work, performed at various locations around the two villages. No one was too young or too old to help.

Moses, age five, was one of the runners who carried the finished product to the walls. Elena scarcely breathed from the time he left until he returned, but knew his duty was better than filling firepots, which sometimes went off in the hands of those who made them. He scoffed at her worry. "I am a *man*, Mother," he said. "I can run faster than they can shoot."

After the work came the long, awful hours of night, when there was nothing to do but huddle together in the darkness and try to sleep or pray, and listen to the sound of the balls crashing against masonry, waiting for one to find them. The pounding and the heat and the fear made sleep all but impossible.

Nothing could prepare a person for such a bombardment as, hour by hour, day and night, the great guns ate away the masonry defenses of Birgu and Senglea. A fine yellow powder all but blotted out the sun. People hacked and coughed. The dust colored their bread and caked their tongues and irritated their eyes. It lay in a film on the water, giving it a sour and metallic taste. The ground shook constantly. They had all witnessed the slow, agonizing death of St. Elmo. Now they could only wait as the Turks ground down the walls around them, too. The relentlessness of it, the very patience and persistence of the gunners, added to the fear and to the sense that the outcome was inevitable. Even civilians began to be able to tell some of the guns apart, a culverin from a basilisk from a double verso. They learned to hear the inexorable rhythms in the fire, and to feel their guts twist in knots whenever a silence lasted more than a moment, perhaps signaling another savage rush of frenzied men.

Maria saw Christien sometimes, usually from a distance and during an attack, when he left the Infirmary. They always seemed to be rushing in different directions, with no time to stop, no time to touch except with their eyes, a touch they held for long precious seconds. She saw Nico more often, in his hell on the walls where he could not even defend himself. Worrying about them was more agonizing for her than enduring the Turkish artillery. Sometimes she wished for the quick release of death, so that she would not have to die piece by piece over the two of them.

Late one evening Fençu slipped from the street into Luca's house. He rarely came there now, spending most of his time on the ramparts. The night probes of the Turks were coming with greater frequency as they sought to find weak points in the defenses.

Moses peered out from under the table. He was grimy from head to toe. "Uncle Fençu!" he cried. Fençu hoisted him high in the air and turned him upside down. He set him down, reached behind the boy's ear, and magically produced an *api*.

Moses snatched it from his hand and wolfed it down. "I know that trick," Moses bragged, smacking gooey lips.

"Then do it," Fençu said. He leaned over, waiting.

"I can't." Moses grinned. "I have no more *api*."

Fençu tousled his hair and opened the sack. "But I have more food," he said. It was a treasure trove. There were eight radishes, shriveled with age but quite edible; a hefty chunk of Gozo cheese; a cloth filled with almonds; and six boiled eggs. Sick of biscuits, the others eyed the bounty in wonder, knowing better than to ask where he'd gotten it. Fençu was a man of extraordinary talents. A cannonball landed nearby, shaking dust from the ceilings. They paid little attention.

There were still other families in the house, but Maria had curtained off a small area in the kitchen near the front door, draping it with long pieces of cloth to provide a bit of privacy. They had the heavy kitchen table for shelter. Now she drew the curtains and they sat on the floor to eat.

Fençu shared news of the wall, and it was not good. "We can see the Turks' preparations," he said. "Their ditches are close now, and tonight they were gathering on the heights. They say there will be a general assault tomorrow." Elena and Maria looked at each other. It would be the first such assault on Birgu. "They'll need you on the walls," he added.

After dinner Elena took out her new reed flute. The dulcimer she played so beautifully had been abandoned in the cave. She'd found the flute when it slipped from the pocket of a Genoese soldier she was helping drag to the burial pit. The instrument was simply made, and Elena mastered it quickly, blowing only an occasional sour note. Fençu and Maria held Moses between them off the ground, swirling and twirling to the bright notes. Moses shrieked in delight, and even Fençu managed a smile.

Afterward Fençu and Moses sat under the kitchen table and made up games with stones, the only plentiful material at hand. The wonderful sound of the boy's laughter filled the room.

"It's good to see him laugh," Elena said, watching. "I worry he'll forget how."

"He'd laugh if the Turks would go away. You'd see a smile on his face in no time. Maybe we can pay Lucrezia to make them disappear."

Elena giggled. "I wonder what's become of her. Hiding in Mdina, I suppose, casting spells." She blew a short, plaintive melody on the flute. "I wonder if we could get Moses there."

"To Mdina?"

"It's not under fire. He'd be safer."

"Not for long," Maria said absently. She regretted it immediately. She tried never to sound discouraged, though it was getting harder each day.

Elena put her lips to the instrument but made no sound. She was crying. Lately she was that way a lot: giggling one moment, crying the next. They both were. Maria put her arm around Elena's shoulder, and they listened as Fençu told a story to Moses, who fell asleep in his lap.

They awakened the following morning to the most intensive bombardment of the siege. Such heights of fury could not long be sustained, a sign that the assault was indeed coming. Elena told Moses to stay inside that day.

"I have to help with the hoops," he whined.

"*Stay here*," she said, and she and Maria raced off to work the walls near the Post of Castile. From every part of Birgu, women and many of the older children were doing the same.

Near noon the cannons fell silent.

Maria looked up from her work to a sight that took her breath away. Like a great carpet spread over the hills above Birgu, thousands of Turks in their colorful robes were massed in attack, pressing forward to the walls, their voices raised in battle song. To her right she saw the same thing happening at Senglea, where an even greater concentration of Turks rolled down upon the defenders. It was a horrible spectacle of sound and silk, of smoke and savage fury. Soldiers on the wall poured a murderous sheet of fire onto their attackers, using incendiaries and cannons filled with grapeshot, cutting bloody swaths into the advancing ranks. It reminded her of lying on the beach, trying to stop the surf with one hand. Like the surf, the Turks still flowed over and around the wounded and dead, filling in every gap with fresh men.

Maria ran wood and brush to the fires where iron cauldrons boiled with water and oil, while Elena carried smaller buckets of steaming oil to replenish the pots. She dumped them in and ran back to the ladder where a bucket brigade passed up more from larger pots below.

"Help me here!" a Spaniard cried, struggling with a heavy pot. Using their skirts for pads, Maria and Elena helped him tip it over the battlements. Maria burned her hands. She didn't see what became of the scalding cascade but heard its effect, as men screamed on the ladders below. The stench of burnt flesh filled her nostrils.

Some soldiers lit incendiaries and threw them, while others laid down a hail of arquebus fire into the massed attackers. The wall spouted smoke and fire like a volcano, while arrows soared back and forth. Trying to shut out the noise and the smoke and the smell, Maria ran in a crouch behind the soldiers, trying to do her job and stay out of the way.

Not all the women were so timid. Some stood on tiptoe at the battlements, heavyset women in black robes and *barnuži,* braving death as they hurled stones down onto turbans and upturned faces, all the while shouting curses and prayers. One was shot dead in front of Elena. She and Maria dragged her out of the way by her ankles. They slumped together over her body, gathering their strength and wits for the next effort. If they had ever tried to imagine hell, they could not have concocted such a scene as the one in which they spent that afternoon.

Knights directed the troops on the walls, yelling orders into the bedlam. Signals were passed with trumpets, whose meaning only the soldiers understood. A Janissary leaped over the wall directly in front of Maria, and another came behind. They were shot dead immediately, while behind them she saw the tops of ladders and the tips of pikes, and heard the clash of scimitars and screams in Turkish and Arabic.

Maria was carrying three loaded crossbows from a rearming station to a ladder when she stopped still. The street was crowded with civilians and soldiers rushing back and forth on a thousand errands. Giulio Salvago was pushing a barrow loaded with heavy sacks. She followed him, watching, keeping in the shadows beneath the platform of the wall. Near the street that led to the palace, the barrow tipped over and spilled the sacks onto the street.

Salvago's brow glistened with sweat as he struggled to right the heavy load. He got the barrow up and heaved one sack inside, and then the next, steadying the load with his hands as he prepared to lift it once again.

The sounds of battle receded into the background of her consciousness. She watched him, her head pounding. She knew she could kill him right then and there, do it in front of a hundred people, and no one would ever know. People were running, occupied, oblivious to all but their own concerns. She put two of the weapons down. Steadying herself against a post, she sighted on his back and then raised her aim a bit, to his head. Only a slight pressure would be needed to let the bolt fly. He would fall in the street, another body among dozens, unnoticed, unmourned. She thought of Jacobus, holding a similar weapon years earlier. She thought of the dungeon, and of his screams, which still filled her nightmares. She thought of all the horror over the years that this man had brought her. And she thought of another outrage that might yet come, one day after the siege when Salvago might yet stand in judgment of Nico. Her hands trembled, and she breathed deeply and closed her eyes.

For Jacobus, she thought. *For Nico. For me.*

With a sob of frustration and anguish she lowered the weapon. She couldn't do it.

Salvago pushed off with his load. He turned down the next street and disappeared from view. Drained, she let out her breath and returned to the walls.

The assault lasted two more hours after that, six in all. As fierce as the attack was against Birgu, it was St. Michael that took the brunt of it. By dusk the ditches in front of both were filled with the dead. Inside the walls dying men were dragged to the Infirmary, past mounds of the already dead.

Maria was furious with herself. It was a day in which thousands of strangers had killed each other, done it in front of her, and she had not been able to bring herself to kill the only man among them whose death she knew was justified, a man whose death she wished above all things. It was not nobility or morality that had stopped her. She didn't know what had.

❖

The medical situation in the Infirmary was dire. There were insufficient supplies of ointments, bandages, and drugs. Many of the stores had been destroyed in the bombardments. It was almost impossible to walk through the hallways. Every spot not filled with debris had a patient in it, and patients were periodically killed when new balls crashed through the wall nearest Kalkara Creek, facing the heights of Salvador. The auberges were filled to overflowing, and even private houses had been requisitioned to make more room for the wounded.

Christien worked past exhaustion, worked until his vision blurred. Despite the heat and humidity in the ward he generally wore his breastplate so that he wouldn't have to take time to put it on during a call to the walls. Such calls were coming more often now.

Nearly every person in Birgu and Senglea had an injury of one sort or another. Christien saw only the most serious. He amputated limbs and set compound fractures. He removed stone splinters from eyeballs and arrows from every part of the body. The instant one patient was carried away, another took his place. Battle turned him from a fast surgeon into a blur. His hands flew through the carnage. The hardest part was working on patients who were awake. Most often he had two assistants to help hold them down, but sometimes they had to run to their battle stations, leaving him alone. He learned a new technique in which he applied pressure to the carotid artery.

Syncope followed, a state of faintness resulting from lack of blood to the brain. If he did it right, the effect might last five or six minutes, by which time either he was finished or the patient was.

Most often the wounded endured their treatments fully conscious. Christien had long since gotten used to the awful noise that resulted, knowing that it was when a man didn't scream that his chances seemed to dim. Yet the sounds that came from surgery in those months of the siege were often more disturbing and very nearly as loud as the Turkish artillery, haunting even the most battle-hardened soldiers.

He treated Bartholomew, his own page. The boy had been assigned full-time to the walls. He'd deflected a scimitar. Two fingers were cleanly severed, the third and fourth hanging by bits of bone and sinew. The whole time Christien worked, the page did his best to joke and laugh. He talked of hunting with hawks, asking questions to keep his mind off what Christien was doing to his hand. "I'd like to learn, sire, if you'll teach me."

"It would be my pleasure, but you'll have to be more careful handling swords," Christien said, smiling gently as the page slid off the table. "The hawks need somewhere to land."

Bartholomew grinned sheepishly, his brow glistening with sweat. "The blade was heading for my neck, sire," he said cheerfully. "In the end it was his neck that was lost. A good trade any day."

The next night he was back with a deep chunk of his thigh muscle gone, taken by a cluster of errant grapeshot fired by his own side. Christien cut away tissue and probed for the pellets. He cleaned and packed the wound and sewed him up. This time Bartholomew was not making jokes. His face was chalky with pain, and he swallowed a gasp every now and again. He held his rosary in his good hand and quietly mumbled his prayers.

This injury was serious enough that Christien ordered him to the ward. If the wound didn't fester and kill him first, he knew the leg would be gimpy. But Bartholomew would have none of it. He had seen other men with even more serious wounds return to their posts. He would do no less. "I have Turks to kill, sire," he said with chilling good cheer, "and I can still hold a sword." Christien scrounged a piece of wood for a crutch, and Bartholomew hobbled back to his station at the French Curtain, his left hand and right leg useless.

Three nights later he was back again. They carried him in on a narrow plank. This time Bartholomew had a sucking chest wound Christien could not repair. He died on the table, still clutching his rosary in his one good hand.

Christien's assistants stacked him in the hall, atop the others.

❖

3 AUGUST

Mustapha was beginning to feel the profound unease of a man whose goals, despite his best efforts, were slipping away from him. He ordered the bombardment intensified, telling the gunners not to let their weapons cool so long between shots. No one inside Birgu or Senglea could ever have believed the fire could become heavier, but it did. The cannons belched fire and smoke around the clock for five days.

Near midnight of the third day the guns stopped. Stretched out on the floor on either side of Moses, both Maria and Elena tensed, fearing the silence meant a night attack. The sudden quiet woke Moses. "Mama? What is it?" Elena shushed him back to sleep.

In the trenches outside the walls, voices called out to the men and women huddled in the ruins. "Throw out your masters," they shouted. "The Knights of St. John are your oppressors. Arabs, not the knights, are your brothers. Join us!"

One of the Maltese yelled back, "We would rather be the slaves of St. John than the companions of the Grand Turk!" He followed that with a roar from his arquebus.

The cannons started up again.

❖

The bells of Angelus combined with the guns of the Turks to awaken Fençu at dawn. Maria got up at the same time. She went to the far wall of the kitchen, stepping carefully over the sleeping forms of some of the twenty people who were still living in the house. The guns had taken their toll; only a few weeks earlier there had been forty. Maria took an onion from a sack hanging from the cupboard and gave it to Fençu, who waved goodbye and stepped outside.

There were only two onions left, half a loaf of bread, and a dozen biscuits. She decided to go to one of the storerooms near the square, where daily rations were dispensed. If she went early there would be no line. Afterward she would go to the walls.

Beneath the kitchen table where the sheep used to sleep, Moses stirred against his mother. "I have to go piss, Mama," he murmured sleepily.

"All right." Elena lifted her arm. Moses wriggled out from under the table. Elena turned over and tried to go back to sleep.

Maria smiled at Moses and gave him a pat on the head as he walked by her on his way to the pit, that was located farther inside the house. He barely noticed her touch; he was almost sleepwalking. Maria picked up a water jug and stepped into the street.

At that moment a ball from one of the culverins hit the top of Luca Borg's house. It slammed through a masonry parapet, blew a hole in the roof and smashed into the back wall of the house, which was cut from the stone of the island. The ball shattered, each piece crashing downward through the structure. One fragment bounced off the stone floor and plowed obliquely into the front wall, tearing out a great section. The other blasted through an outside corner, bringing down a side wall. The entire front wall of the house collapsed. Without the support of the first-floor walls, tons of stone dropped from the second floor. Heavy timbers fell from the loft and roof, followed by more masonry.

Maria had been knocked from her feet. She got up and raced back to the house. When the ball first hit she'd heard people screaming from inside, but now their voices had fallen silent. The dust was thick, and she could see very little. Behind her, more balls struck other houses in the same block. The noise was deafening. The whole world was crumbling.

She crawled over a beam and pushed her way forward, grabbing stones and heaving them aside. She worked her way under one of the timbers, where there was a short space to crawl. The back side was blocked.

"Elena! Moses!" Grunting, gasping, she worked madly. A moment later Fençu was at her side, digging, his strong arms and hands making quick work of the rubble. They worked furiously at the pile, cringing every time another ball crashed outside.

Suddenly they stopped. Fençu caught her by the arm, for silence. "What is it?"

"Listen." The cannons had stopped, giving way to an ominous quiet. From somewhere beyond the walls they heard the awful chorus of musical instruments, and the throaty roar of troops beginning the attack.

"I don't care," Maria said. She leaned forward and kept digging.

"I must go," he said. Her cry of protest was lost in the dust and rubble. He was gone. Outside, other men and women raced past in the street, sprinting for the walls. She cried out for help. If anyone heard, they ignored her.

The Turks were coming.

She was alone. She dug more furiously than ever. The pieces were heavy, many of them sharp, and they savaged her hands. She tore at them without feeling. "Elena! Hold on! I'm coming! I'm here!" It was only four or five feet to the table, but it still took her nearly an hour.

She found Elena's arm first, extending from beneath the rubble. It was caked with dust, the fingers curled. She grabbed the hand and tugged. Already the heat of life had gone from it. "Elena! No!" She started to cry again, digging harder still, pounding at the stone as if it would yield to her fury.

She kept digging well after she knew it was too late. Whenever she got some of the stone loose more would fall, sliding down the pile. Once she thought a whole section of wall was going to come down and she jumped back in a panic. The wall held.

She pounded and cried and clawed at the stones, her fists flailing against the unyielding pile. She ran into the street, desperately seeking aid. Everywhere it was the same. Much of the block was devastated. There was no one to help. There were only bodies, and people staggering out of their own ruins, too stunned themselves to respond to her cries. She heard the screech and roar of battle from the walls, and knew no help was coming. She ran back into the ruins.

Near the Post of Castile, the Turks succeeded in breaching the outer wall. Masses of them poured forward into the breach. The defenders let them come for a moment. Certain they were winning the day, the Turks suddenly found themselves confronted with one of the inner walls that created blind corridors, the trap that the Grand Master had ordered constructed, a trap of walls built with the hands of women and children.

Then, when the crush threatened to break down the inner walls, the defenders opened fire from the ramparts above. Trapped in the maze, the Turks were slaughtered in the hundreds. The troops still outside the outer wall pressed against the backs of the men in front, all surging forward eagerly in a frenzied rush to join the imminent victory, pushing their own troops further into the meat grinder. Only when the awful panic managed to telegraph itself back outside the walls did the pressure cease, allowing the few survivors to retreat.

The battle raged unabated on either side of the breach.

Luca Borg had slept at his post for weeks. Now he stood with other militiamen near the breach, firing an arquebus into the ranks of attackers. He loaded and fired repeatedly, his big hands working slowly but methodically, taking care that every shot counted. He was pouring powder into the flashpan when a Turkish arrow pierced his throat. He toppled from the wall into a sea of Turkish silk.

At Senglea across Birgu Creek, the battle was much tighter. Again and again the ladders fell against the wall as men rose to certain death, only to be replaced by others. Finally the overwhelming numbers of the attackers began to tell. La Valette watched with mounting dismay. He could send no further reinforcements to aid St. Michael's, lest he leave Birgu undefended. Janissaries poured through multiple breaches, their banners planted atop the masonry piles marking what had once been the walls. They surged forward, victory at hand.

From the walls of the citadel of Mdina, the Chevalier Don Mesquita watched the distant battle. From the smoke and the noise he could tell it was a general assault. He summoned the Chevalier de Lugny, one of his knights. "Take every available man," he said. "Attack the Turkish camp in the Marsa. It will be poorly defended." Moments later, every knight and soldier inside Mdina roared through the city gate.

Christien fought hand-to-hand at St. Michael's, standing in a ring with other knights. All along the wall pots of Greek fire detonated. Trumps roared and swords flashed. He fought mechanically, madly, sweat soaking him inside his armor, fought long past the time when he thought they could possibly hold, long past the time when he thought he could raise his sword again. Men fell beside him and behind him. The battle moved back and forth like current in the sea—surging here, faltering there, shifting one way and then back the other. He could see only a small piece of the whole, but it looked as if things were going badly all along the wall, as ferocity met savagery and men died by the scores, and then by the hundreds, and still more came.

We're losing, he thought.

❖

Frantic and alone, oblivious to the battle, Maria kept digging, working her way toward where she'd last seen Moses. The collapse of the walls had left the rubble piled at such a steep slope that she had to drag stones out into the street to make enough room to work. She didn't know how she managed to lift some of the pieces, so large and heavy she'd never have tried but for her desperation. She had nothing with which to break them. So she dragged them, falling and crying and cursing and praying all the while.

It was nearly noon when she first heard his weak cry, and an hour later before she could get the rest of the way to the latrine pit. She pulled away the last of the stones and looked through the little hole.

He'd fallen in along with a great deal of debris, but the rim of the pit sheltered him. She lay on her stomach, reached down and pulled him out. His little body heaved with sobs as he clung to her. Numbly, she sat with him in the ruins, rocking him, their tears mingling. After a while she gently pulled him away, checking him for injuries. He had nothing more serious than cuts and bruises. She carried him to get water from one of the clay cisterns near the square. He sucked it down desperately, the water running over his chin and onto his chest. She tried to clean him of the filth of the pit, all the while whispering, comforting. He asked about his mother and all she could think to tell him was that she was gone now. She brushed his hair back and kissed his forehead, her tears falling onto his cheeks.

In the distance, it sounded as if the world were coming to an end.

❖

Mustapha Pasha himself was in the thick of battle, smelling triumph once again. He yelled orders and shouted encouragement to his men, who were surging through the ranks of defenders. Senglea was within his grasp. A horseman appeared through the smoke and madness. "Lord! The base camp at the Marsa! A large force of Christians has attacked! It must be the relief from Sicily!"

Mustapha saw smoke rising from the site of the camp. He roared in frustration. "Damn Piali's fleet of incompetents! They must have gotten through the patrols!" He turned to his signalman. "Sound the retreat!"

"Sire!?" The signalman was shocked at the order. Even he could taste victory.

"Now!" Mustapha roared. "We'll be trapped from behind! The whole army will be destroyed!"

The strident call of the trumpet rose over the battle, stunning the Janissaries who had finally succeeded in breaching the defenses at such great cost. Other trumpets picked up the signal and repeated it, urgently and unmistakably sounding the general retreat.

The knights and their soldiers watched in disbelief as the Turkish troops broke away from the fighting and fled back over the walls. Turkish detachments raced up the heights of Corradino toward the Marsa.

The tents in the Marsa were a smoking ruin, every man dead. There was no Christian relief force at all. Don Mesquita's horsemen from Mdina had swept through the camp in a whirlwind of death. It was mostly a hospital and as the knight had correctly guessed, there were few guards. Almost everyone was too ill or wounded to fight.

Shabooh was among them. Still wracked with fever and dysentery, he died where he lay, on his cot, unable to lift a weapon. Hundreds of others met the same fate. Stores were torched, animals hamstrung or shot, tents ripped down and set ablaze. There were no survivors. Far worse, for Mustapha, was that the false alarm had cost him the battle. As he pondered the magnitude of it all, Mustapha swore to leave only one man alive in Malta: the Grand Master, Jean de La Valette. He would be led in chains to Istanbul, where the Sultan alone would decide what fate should befall him.

On the ramparts of Birgu and Senglea, men embraced each other and cheered. Surely it was a miracle, God's verdict on the Turks. In the streets there was an eerie silence: the gunners had not expected the sudden end of battle, and their cannons had not yet started up again.

Maria carried Moses through the streets of Birgu, looking for new shelter for him. St. Agatha's was a ruin. The belfry her father had built had collapsed and slid into the street. The auberges were being used only for injured soldiers. Everywhere she looked, another familiar building or house was gone or partially destroyed. She was too numb to cry. There was a quarter near St. Lawrence where many of the houses were still intact. She inquired at one after another, only to be turned away. Every room, every nook and cranny, already had someone huddled inside, taking shelter.

She found herself at the bishop's palace. It was the only place she knew where there might still be room and where he would be safe. At the gate she asked them to take Moses. The guard was sympathetic, but he refused. "I cannot help," he said. "We've a hundred more than we can handle already. Besides, he's too old. He should be helping on the walls."

Maria felt her rage growing and her voice rose as she argued. The walls were thick and the palace was huge, she said. There was always room for one more. He could sleep in the courtyard, and for the love of God, the boy was only five. She fought to control her tears. She would not be denied.

The guard called the sacristan. He was clearly overwhelmed with his duties and did not care to listen. "Kindly get out," he said.

"I will not!" And she pushed against the gate even as the guard sought to shut it.

Someone approached from the courtyard, out of her view. "What is it, Joseph?"

The sacristan sighed. "Another one wanting in, Dun Salvago. There's no room, of course."

Salvago appeared in the doorway. His cassock was smeared gray with dust, his cheek grimy with blood and grit. He stood just two feet from her.

Maria sought to find her voice. "Not for me," she said quickly. "Only for Moses." Even as she said it she stepped back, as if suddenly uncertain. She clutched Moses more tightly, her face stricken with indecision. Of course she'd known Salvago was there, but now, seeing him so close, she changed her mind. "Never mind," she said. "I'm sorry to trouble you. I'll find something else."

"Maria, wait," Salvago said. "Of course we'll find a place for him."

"But Dun—" The sacristan started to protest. Salvago waved him to silence. "This is the best place for him," Salvago said to Maria, knowing what was in her mind.

The awful sounds coming from the village began to register upon her then, and she knew he was right. She held Moses close. "Go with Dun Salvago," she whispered. "You'll be safe downstairs. I'll come back for you, I promise."

Moses nodded unhappily. He was used to taking orders, used to obeying without question, but when Maria started to hand him over to the priest he clung to her, weeping uncontrollably, his fists tight little balls clutching at her jerkin, refusing to let go. He was strong, and Salvago had to pry him away. It was a wrenching battle, and Maria was crying herself by the time Moses let go.

Salvago turned and disappeared into the cloistered courtyard, taking Moses to the dungeons where the balls could not reach. Maria stood in the doorway, weeping. The gate closed. She sank to the ground, spent.

After a while she went to the walls near the Hub, trying to find Nico. Dead slaves lay everywhere. He was not among them. Already those who'd survived were back at work, repairing the breaches before the next attack. She asked a guard at the prison gate. He scowled and told her nothing.

She wandered back down the street. Some areas of the village were almost intact, others destroyed completely. There were animals dead in the rubble along with people. Only the rats seemed unfazed by it all, scurrying through the ruins. Small fires burned here and there. No one bothered to put them out. In some places there was nothing left to burn. She helped a woman looking for her daughter in the same sort of pile Maria had been working at. They didn't find her.

Aimlessly, Maria walked back toward her father's house. She realized she hadn't even seen Luca for a week. She didn't know whether he was alive or dead.

Her street was no longer as tall as it had once been. Four houses were down completely, and the top stories of several others had collapsed. It was eerie; houses she'd known since she was a child no longer existed. All that remained of the baker's house was a second-story balcony, balanced precariously on pillars while all the rest of the wall had fallen away.

As she picked her way through the mounds in the street she stopped suddenly. A knight in full armor stood with his back to her, looking at the ruin of her father's house. Trembling, she took a deep breath and walked forward.

He heard her and turned. He was dirty and bloody, his breastplate dented in three places where he'd been hit with arquebus balls, his armor blackened with soot where a firebomb had glanced off him. His face flooded with relief when he saw her. He let his shield and helmet slip to the ground.

Around them more people were beginning to appear from their shelters, running to help where they could. Others were straggling back from the walls. Maria and Christien saw none of them. She ran the last few steps. He dropped his sword and she was in his arms, hardly feeling the hot steel of his armor. They stood that way for long moments, holding each other amid the smoke curling up from the ruins. He stroked her hair and lifted her gently off her feet.

For a long while neither of them could say anything. Finally he whispered to her. "I had only one prayer today," he said, his voice choking. "God has just answered it." He kissed her tenderly on the forehead.

She told him about Elena then, and about digging out Moses, and she collapsed against him, crying like a baby, all her terror and sadness and grief pouring out in a torrent of tears that she had not been able to release until then. She had no strength left, not a shred of it, and he held her. "I never knew anything could be so awful," she sobbed. "I'm so tired of it, Christien. I can't stand the noise anymore and everybody's dead, or dying. I wish the ball had taken me instead."

"Never say that. *Never.*"

"What does it matter? I've lost Elena, and I've lost you, and maybe Nico, too. And now Elena's buried in there all alone and I couldn't even get her out. I couldn't help her, Christien, I couldn't do anything. All of them in that house, they're all dead but me, because I went to get some bread and they didn't."

There was nothing he knew to do but hold her until it passed. "Moses made it because of you," he said. "You saved him." She nodded at that, and seemed to take strength from it. "Where is he now?" he asked.

"The bishop's palace," she said.

"There's no safer place except the dungeons of St. Angelo. He'll be all right there."

He took off his cuirass and his other armor and threw it into a pile. She saw there were ugly wounds on his arms and back, but they seemed not to trouble him. He led her back into Luca's house and began to dig. She knew he should be at the Infirmary, for there were many living who needed him, but when she mentioned it he simply dug harder. She knelt beside him and together, working as carefully as they would have had she still been alive, they uncovered Elena.

Tenderly, Maria wiped Elena's face with her dress and brushed the hair from her forehead. She tried to smooth her clothing and clean away some of the debris from the folds of her dress. She found the flute, broken in two pieces. She put them in Elena's pocket.

"They bury everyone in the pits," she said. "I don't want to put her in a pit."

"We'll do it here, then," he said. They built a little crypt of stone, just two rows high, nestled against the ruins of the back wall.

Gently Christien picked Elena up and set her inside. There was nothing for a shroud. He removed the quilted pad he wore over his shirt and covered her face with it.

"I know some of their prayers, but I don't know the one to use now," she said. "Fençu would know." She had a troubling thought. "Do you think if I say the wrong one it will keep her from heaven? I don't know how Jewish souls work."

"No," he said. "I think any prayer will be good."

"There's one I've heard a thousand times in the cave. Fençu says it." She looked at him, her eyes brimming with tears. "After all those times, I don't know what it means. It's Hebrew, I guess. I never asked what it meant." She looked forlorn and she began to cry. "I never asked, because it was Jewish." Christien squeezed her hand.

The tears ran down her cheeks and when she could go on, her voice broke in sobs as she recited the words she'd heard so often, but never said aloud. "*Yit-gadal v'yit-kadash sh'mey rab-ba, b'alma di v'ra hirutey. . . ."* Christien bowed his head and said his own prayer. Afterward they covered Elena with dirt and another layer of stone. When it was done they knelt for a time in silence.

After a while Christien got up. He picked up a skin of watered wine that he had discarded with his armor, and they sat back in their amphitheater of rubble. It was already dark. The moon rose above them, looking huge and golden through all the dust that was just beginning to settle.

It was at that moment that Mustapha's rage transmitted itself to his gunners. One cannon boomed and then another, and then five more, and then whole batteries opened fire simultaneously and built to a crescendo as nearly eighty guns resumed their slow and deadly work.

Christien and Maria didn't move from their shelter in the remnants of the wall. Oblivious to the balls and to the crumbling masonry and to the occasional cries they heard from within Birgu, he put his arm around her and talked to her about Paris. He told her about the forest surrounding his home where he and Bertrand ran as boys, about the great lazy river that flowed through the heart of the city and past his country home, and how in the spring and summer the ground was crawling with bugs, and how they'd catch them and put them in jars and he'd draw pictures of them and take them apart. She sniffled and even laughed at times through her tears. A ball smashed through the street nearby, but she didn't even notice, didn't cringe, just nestled in the crook of his arm and listened and let all the rest of the world slip away.

They watched the moon climb higher in the sky, lost sometimes in the clouds of smoke that rose from the guns, and they saw the awful crimson beauty of the cannon fire reflected off all the smoke, like a great dry lightning storm of summer.

Hours passed, and here and there around them in Birgu more walls fell down and more people died beneath them, and they whispered about things, unimportant things, trivial things, about swimming and birds and hawks, about goats and boats and fishing and cheese, and every so often Bertrand or Elena would come up and their voices would get thick and their eyes would water and they'd laugh at some memory, and then move on.

It was well after midnight. Her head rested on his shoulder. He dreaded breaking the spell, but knew he could avoid it no longer. "I must go," he whispered.

"I know."

"Where will you stay now?"

She shook her head. "I don't know yet."

"I will try to find you," he said. "Leave word at the Infirmary gate if you can. I can do this better if I know you're safe."

He looked at her in the bright light of the moon and saw it reflected in her eyes. "You must know that I love you forever, Maria Borg."

Tears welled in her eyes. "As I love you forever, Christien de Vries. *Inhobbok*. Thank you for this night. Go with God." She leaned forward and kissed him on the cheek.

Christien pulled her closer and kissed her mouth. He brushed her cheek with his fingers, desperate not to let go. But then he rose, collected his armor, and dashed through the perilous streets to the Infirmary.

❖

12 AUGUST

The garrisons inside Birgu and Senglea knew a message had been received from Sicily. As always, there was great expectation that the message contained blessed news of the relief, promised so often. Already the siege had lasted nearly three months. The Sacred Council met until late. The word was spread by men who quoted the Grand Master's words to small groups of troops, who spread them again, until every man and woman had heard.

"We stand alone," La Valette had said to the council. "There is no hope except in the succor of Almighty God, the only true help. He who has up to now looked after us will not forsake us, nor will He deliver us into the hands of the enemies of the Holy Faith.

"My brothers, we are all servants of our Lord, and I know well that if I and all those in command should fall, you will still fight on for liberty, for the honor of our Order, and for our Holy Church. We are soldiers, and we shall die fighting. And if by any evil chance the enemy should prevail, we can expect no better treatment than our brethren who were in St. Elmo."

In fact the Viceroy had promised a relief force of fourteen thousand men by the end of August, a promise that rang as hollow to La Valette as all the earlier ones. He did not wish to raise the hopes of anyone inside the walls. They must depend only upon each other and their faith and prepare themselves to die. In this, La Valette was able to share good tidings from the Pope. Pius IV, he told them, had granted an extraordinary plenary indulgence to all those who lost their lives in this momentous battle against Islam. Those Christians who died in the siege would be considered to have died for their faith, and all their sins forgiven. The news removed the fear of death without absolution and was a tremendous boost to morale. It was the very same promise of heaven that motivated the Muslims on the other side of the wall. The ground between gods had been leveled.

Christien heard the finality in the speech, and it brought him to a firm resolve. If he was still alive when the Turks finally broke through, he would leave his post and kill Maria himself before he would let her fall into their hands.

Chapter 43

from The Histories of the Middle Sea

by Darius, called the Preserver
Court Historian to the Possessor of Jerusalem, the Sultan Achmet

The siege guns could be heard in the salons of southern Sicily. In Syracuse observers recorded that the populace went outside at night to listen, wondering if anyone could survive under such a wrath of arms. Only Etna in full eruption was known to make such thunder.

In Messina, the Viceroy Don García de Toledo suffered visit after visit from impatient knights, who were arriving in Sicily in growing numbers from their estates throughout Europe. La Valette's letters detailing the heroic defense of Malta were stirring great passions among even those who did not care for the knights. The Viceroy's leisurely pace in assembling a relief force began to bear the distinctive odor of scandal. It was clear the defenders of Malta would never make terms with the Ottomans. Further delay could only be seen as outrageous. Even the Protestant queen of England, Elizabeth, sensed the import of the hour. "If the Turks should prevail against the island of Malta," she said, "it is uncertain what further peril might follow to the rest of Christendom."

Goaded by the impatient knights, the Viceroy promised to quicken his pace.

—From Volume VII
The Great Campaigns: Malta

16 AUGUST

Nasrid and his men had moved their camp to Salvador hill, where their tents were pitched across Kalkara Creek from Birgu. Morale was sagging. Janissaries were never slow to grumble, and they were grumbling now. Piali Pasha was commanding the siege of Birgu. Piali was as incompetent a general as he was an admiral, they muttered, and every piece of ill fortune that could befall the Ottoman forces seemed to have done so. Uncounted thousands were dead, and with their lives Piali and Mustapha had purchased only the ruins of Fort St. Elmo. The campaign was ill conceived. The Marsa was full of disease and the bleak island was costing too much blood. Even the ranks of their own platoon had been thinned by a simple band of savage peasants, hiding in a cave. It was a humiliation none cared to discuss. Nasrid's men were proud and brave, and as skilled in warfare as anyone on earth. The lives of their brother Janissaries had been squandered for naught.

"It is not the will of Allah that we should prevail," one said.

Nasrid struck him to the ground, his eyes flashing with fury. "We are the flower of the empire," he snarled, "the sons of Allah. Never do I wish to hear defeat in your voice. We have nearly succeeded once. We remain strong. We shall prevail once again. When the great mine is finished under the walls of Birgu, so will the knights be. Ready yourself for that. If I hear such thoughts again, it is the edge of my sword you will feel." He stormed away. The instant he did, the grumbling began again.

❖

Tap, tap, dink dink.

Asha lay at a steep angle on the village side of the wall. His ears rang from the noise of the guns, but in the rare seconds when some cannon or other was not firing he could lay his head against the earth and hear the sappers digging their mines somewhere in the limestone below the wall.

Tap, tap, dink dink.

He felt it in his bones. They were mostly Egyptians, he knew, the finest sappers in the world, their lithe bodies small enough to fit in the tunnels. Their picks and shovels and pry bars never stopped, chipping away at the limestone somewhere beneath what was left of the walls, digging until they arrived below key defensive positions. It was a superhuman task, almost beyond comprehension. They had to dig beneath the outer ditch and then to the walls, working in hellish conditions. They measured the distances with knotted lengths of string. When they estimated they'd at last gone far enough they would drag massive charges inside, to be detonated at the moment of attack. Such sappers had won sieges for the Sultan all over the world—even at Rhodes, against these very knights.

Tap, tap, dink dink. Tap, tap.

He wondered where they were now. Directly below him, or a hundred yards away? The stone masked their location. It didn't much matter. There seemed precious little left to blow up, and Allah knew he wouldn't require nearly so much powder himself when the time came.

He was amazed to be able to contemplate the sappers' progress at all. Along with the artillery, the arquebusiers had started taking their deadly toll. He was now on his ninth partner in chains. The Order would soon run out of slaves. There were only so many to send to certain death on the walls and in the streets. Once again he'd felt the hand of Allah on his shoulder, protecting him. What else could explain it? Even the overseers were dying, and the engineers who came to plan the work. Each morning he awakened expecting death. Each night he returned to the slave prison, to give thanks for another day.

He'd been wounded six times by bits of rock. His arms and legs were shredded, his hands a gruesome mess. He had only a loincloth to wear, and his skin was raw and blistered from the sun. At midday it grew so hot he thought surely even the Grand Harbor must boil. One of his chain mates had died from that sun; he had no idea how the knights could survive in the ovens of their armor. Only twice a day was he given water. It seemed to disappear even before it reached his throat. His tongue was thick and when he tried to talk he could only croak.

Each day it became harder to do the same work, more difficult to lift a stone. He was glad of one thing: that Maria no longer could bring him food. He missed the bread, but knew she was safer behind the new barricades that had been erected within the walls, to protect people from snipers who were now close enough to pick off their targets almost at will. He knew she was still alive because just that morning he'd seen her dragging a sack of something for the walls. She'd seen him, too, and waved.

Tap, tap, thunk. Tap, tap, thunk.

He knew they would blow it soon. The moment he no longer heard the sappers, the explosion could not be far behind. He saw some of the soldiers listening, too, removing their helmets and putting their ears to the ground. He knew the knights had their own sappers down there, driving their own countertunnels forward, trying to find the little Egyptians and destroy them before the explosives could be set. As dangerous as it was aboveground, he was glad they did not make him work down there, down in that underground hell where battles were fought with picks and shovels, and men died without seeing the sky.

❖

18 AUGUST

The countersappers did not succeed.

On a hot August morning the artillery abruptly ceased. Everyone braced for the attack. At Senglea, Mustapha threw his forces against St. Michael, now reduced to very nearly the same state as St. Elmo in its final hours. Iayalars led Janissaries toward the walls. The hills swarmed with silk and swords and screaming men, who knew the critical battle was at hand.

Nasrid stood with his men among the twelve thousand troops quietly massed on the heights of Santa Margherita, all watching for the signal to spring Mustapha's trap.

Mustapha hoped that La Valette, seeing that only St. Michael was under attack, would drain away precious reinforcements from Birgu, leaving that city's walls poorly defended. Mustapha waited in vain. Despite the ferocity of the assault against St. Michael, the pontoon bridge linking the two peninsulas remained empty. La Valette was as cunning as ever, but to Mustapha, it didn't really matter. He had the mine.

Mustapha nodded. A fire was lit on Corradino. An engineer, seeing the signal, handed the slow match to the little sapper, who slithered into the tunnel to light the fuse. Nasrid held up his sword, readying his men. Up and down the lines, other commanders did the same.

Three minutes passed, then five.

The sapper flew out of the tunnel as if he'd been shot from the mouth of a cannon. He fled over the open ground toward the camps. He wasn't fast enough. The blast tossed him into the air. A massive quantity of powder blew beneath the equally massive Post of Castile. Earth and rock were hurled high into the sky, as if Etna itself had erupted. Defenders flew from the walls, their bodies broken. Their comrades were dazed from the force of the explosion, so powerful that even the combatants on the walls of St. Michael paused for an instant to look. The concussion killed many just inside the walls, and left others stunned and bleeding from the ears. When the dust began to settle all could see the large breach in the wall that was already critically weakened by the endless cannonades of the past two months.

Screaming, Nasrid led his men over the hill and into the breach. They followed the Iayalars. Fire poured down from the walls, lighting the fanatic warriors like candles. Hoops bounced down, spitting flame and tripping up the attackers. Nasrid saw the most exposed point and raced directly for it. A wildfire pot crashed in front of him, spewing liquid fire. Some got to his beard and eyebrows. He raced through the flames and somehow kept his robes from the fire. He slowed long enough to smother the jelly with one arm, crushing the flames. He started forward again, his eyebrows smoldering, his turban blackened. A Spanish soldier appeared in the breach, in the midst of the Iayalars. Nasrid cut him down, and then another behind him. His men crowded around him, the fighting hand-to-hand. Nasrid fought with a great grin on his face as he waded into the storm, in his element at last. There was no higher calling.

❖

The bells pealed in St. Lawrence, the dread signal that the Turks had breached the walls of Birgu. Christien raced through the streets to his station at the French Curtain.

The alarm brought virtually everyone else who could walk to help. From the Infirmary and auberges many of the wounded dragged themselves to their feet, holding their bandages and calling for weapons, determined to die fighting rather than be slaughtered in their beds.

Beneath the bishop's palace the blast caused part of a floor to cave in, partly burying some of the people who huddled there, only old women and young children now. Confusion reigned as Salvago and others dug them out. Goats ran up and down the dark halls, bleating in panic. Adults screamed and children cried.

Moses was one of the oldest children, and he helped guide the littlest ones out of the dust and across the hall to a safer place. He saw an old woman sitting against the wall. Her head was back, her eyes open as she gazed toward the heavens. She was quite dead, of age or stroke or fear. She'd been caring for an infant, an orphan now bawling on her lap. Moses snatched up the baby and ran across the hall. He gave the child to a four-year-old girl. "Here," he said. "You be the mother now." The girl nodded gravely and sat down with the child.

The bishop ran down the stairs, his hat askew, his hands shaking, his dignified demeanor completely shattered. "The end is at hand," he shouted to Salvago. "We must go to the streets, all of us. Leave only the smallest children. Everyone else outside. We must help the soldiers."

Crossing himself, Giulio Salvago followed the prelate back up the stairs, Moses on his heels. "Stay here, Moses," Salvago said.

"I heard the bishop, Dun Salvago," Moses said. "I'm a runner, and I'm *not* the smallest." And he darted into the courtyard and through the gate. He knew where the hoops were stored, and knew that was what he should be doing. He'd done it before, though never during battle.

Salvago couldn't keep up with him. When he entered the courtyard Moses was long gone. The air was choking with dust. The noise of battle was very close, and it sounded to Salvago as if the Turks were breaching the walls of the palace itself. Coughing, he ran out into the street. He found the bishop near the arsenal, and together they began dragging some of the wounded back toward the courtyard of the palace. Most were soldiers who'd been hurled from St. James' Bastion by the force of the blast. Salvago saw men atop the walls, firing down on their attackers. His heart chilled when he saw the huge breach at the end of the wall near the Post of Castile. He saw turbans and scimitars and a flag that bore the crescent. The infidels were inside. He and the bishop dragged faster. The noise was terrible.

Maria had been on the walls since before dawn. The Grand Master had ordered all the cauldrons set to full boil, knowing the attack must come at any moment. She made several trips up and down the ladders for brush, and was on the ground when the mine went up. The blast knocked her down, but she was up in an instant, climbing back up the ladder to her station near the arsenal, not more than forty yards from the breach. Turks swarmed in the streets below, and she saw they had stormed the cavalier on the Post of Castile.

The women worked the cauldrons. They filled smaller pots with oil and water and heaved the scalding contents onto the Turks below. They snatched heavy stones from the piles and lifted them high overhead, hurling them down onto the attackers.

With a start Maria saw Moses, carrying fire hoops down the street with three other children. Not one of them was older than six. She could do nothing to protect him now. There was no woman or child who was not helping.

Fençu knelt atop the wall with a crossbow and a pile of bolts. From the shelter of the battlement near the bastion of St. James, he methodically fired, loaded, then fired again. He never missed, never once, and he hardly had to aim. It was like shooting into a bucket of flesh. Even when men raised their shields against him, the bolts went through and did their work. Arquebus balls smashed near him, shattering masonry and rock. He kept his head down, frantically rewound the string, straightened up and fired, then ducked again to reload. Knights were positioned at key points on the wall, their armor flashing in the sun, their voices all but lost in the din. Soldiers used pole-mounted arquebuses to fire down into the attackers without exposing themselves, using the lard-covered bullets that set clothing on fire.

When the blast came, the Grand Master was at his command post in the square with some of the reserves. He was watching the situation in Senglea, expecting that Mustapha was still intending to spring some trick. The bells rang and a messenger brought news of the breach. There were no reserves. La Valette grabbed his helmet from one of his pages and his pike from another. "Sire!" one yelled. "You must not expose yourself to fire!" La Valette raced for the breach.

Asha shook his head, trying to clear it. The shape of the inner walls had directed part of the blast toward him and had shorn him from the wall he was working to repair. He lay in the street. His ankle ached, where it had been jerked by the body of his companion, who lay unconscious. He was near the Post of Germany, on Kalkara Creek. A dozen slaves lay dead; others were wounded and groaning. His guard was dead. Birgu was in pandemonium. Knights and soldiers and women and children rushed past him, racing to the breach where the Turks were pouring through.

He dragged his companion over to the fallen guard and fumbled for the ring that held the simple iron key. He ripped it off the belt and worked at his lock. It was jammed with dirt and the key wouldn't go in. He kicked down, smashing the lock against the ground, and tried the key again. The lock sprang open.

He snatched up the guard's halberd, a combination of spear and battle axe mounted on a pole, and sprinted for the walls near the Post of Castile. The sappers had opened the breach, and he intended to use the confusion to get out. He wore only his loincloth. The Turks would know he was a slave and would have no reason to strike him. The same was not true of the knights and soldiers of the Order, of course, but there was nothing he could do but run past them and hope they'd only worry about killing the men trying to kill them. He had no intention of killing anyone—he intended only to run. He neared the breach and stopped in his tracks.

Maria!

He saw her past Turks flooding into the streets, and the knights and soldiers there to meet them, in a great tangle and clash of silk and steel. It was the very nightmare that had plagued him since leaving Istanbul. Maria was there among the other women, carrying brush and hoops and weapons, and suddenly the battle was beginning to swirl around them: knights and Maltese, Iayalars and Janissaries, swords and scimitars flashing and cutting. The women tried to stay back, to get out of the way, but their way was blocked by the buildings behind them. The women and children of Malta had been ready combatants, heaping death upon the Turks from the walls. There would be no prisoners, no quarter. Ottoman warriors swarmed toward the knights, tightening the circle. One woman fell to a sword, and then another.

Nico raced toward Maria, his halberd up. He had not intended to raise arms against the Maltese, and now found himself in the opposite dilemma: it was Turks he must kill. He never hesitated. He plunged into the melee, swinging his weapon. He beheaded one Iayalar and lifted another off his feet on the tip of his blade. He had it out of the man and was swinging again even as his last victim hit the ground. He fought with all the fury and skill his masters had taught him. He faced a Janissary, glad only that he didn't know him, and the Janissary died. He worked his way toward Maria, who was scrambling for a crossbow that had clattered to the ground.

She saw him. "Nico!"

He stood with his back to her, trying to keep the others away. The Turks were concentrating not on the women but on the men with weapons.

"Get away!" he yelled. She scooted backward, snatched up the crossbow, and got to her feet. She backed away from battle, toward the relative safety of the armory. A Knight of St. John, posted to the Hub with Romegas, turned and recognized Asha. Maria screamed a warning, and her brother's halberd swung at the knight's neck at the same instant Maria fired the crossbow. The bolt went through the knight and struck down a Turk behind him. The knight died with his sword poised to strike.

At that moment La Valette himself appeared at the head of a group of knights and Maltese. He rushed into the melee, heedless of the danger. His seventy-two years seemed irrelevant; he was Grand Master. Bodyguard at his side, he joined the battle. A cry went up, rallying the troops. "The Grand Master! The Grand Master!" Maltese swarmed around him, swelling the ranks of those protecting him, and together they pressed forward with renewed fury. An explosion near La Valette ripped his leg open. He fell but immediately struggled to his feet, supported by his men. He pushed them away and resumed the fight, undaunted.

Maria saw the tide changing. "Nico, run! Get out while you still can!"

Asha's eyes were on the Grand Master's exposed neck, which would part easily to his blade. Fewer than twenty feet separated him from the master of the Knights of St. John, and he knew he could close the distance and kill the man. He held the fate of the siege in his hands, in a halberd that already dripped with blood.

"Go!" Maria screamed. He looked at her and was bowled over by a Maltese rushing a Janissary. His halberd was knocked away. He got to his feet. The Grand Master had taken a few steps in the other direction, soldiers at his flank. Nico looked for Maria again but lost her to sight, behind more soldiers streaming into the area.

The moment was lost.

He leaped over bodies and raced forward into the breach, past Turks and Maltese and knights. A Janissary saw him coming and raised his sword. "I'm Turkish! A slave, you fool!" Asha shouted. The Janissary turned his attention to a Spaniard. Asha easily deflected a blow from a Maltese soldier, but then felt a jolt on his back from a pike intended for another man. He never slowed, racing over ground slippery with blood and oil, making his way through carnage that was as thick as the rubble on which he'd worked. The bolt of a crossbow felled a man immediately in front of him. He hurdled the man's body and kept running. Another Maltese turned and faced him, raising his weapon. "I'm Maltese, you dolt!" Nico yelled in faultless Maltese, and he flashed past the man, unharmed.

The Grand Master's arrival at the breach began to turn the tide of battle near the Post of Castile. The defenders gradually turned the invaders back as the men atop the walls rained fire down upon the Turks caught in the low ground.

As Asha crossed the ditch outside the walls he was hit on the back with boiling water. He screamed, staggered and fell, and picked himself up again. He kept running, cleared the ditch, and scrambled up the far slope. The fierce battle raged unabated all up and down the landward front before Birgu and Senglea. Like a violent storm at sea, the furious Turks crashed like breakers against the rock-solid Maltese shore, churning up a tumultuous spray of terror and blood and death.

Finally, after hours more, Piali's trumpets sounded retreat. The rocks had held, and turned back the sea.

❖

Maria saw half a dozen children being shepherded back into the palace by Salvago. "Moses!" She ran through the streets to him and swept him from his feet, crying and hugging him. Her relief was tempered by the look of him. His clothes were torn, his face grimy and grave. Like all the others with him, Moses was not a child anymore. But he was alive. He returned her hug, and fought back tears. "It will be over soon," she said, stroking his hair. "I promise."

The others were waiting. "I must go with Dun Salvago now," he said. She set him down. She looked at Salvago, whose face was without expression. He gave her the briefest of nods, then turned and led his charges toward the palace.

She returned to the arsenal to look through the bodies near the wall. Numb to all the death, she turned many over, looking beneath them, for others. Nico wasn't there. Christien wasn't there. Her father wasn't there. There were more, many more at the breaches, but she couldn't go near because the cannons had begun again. She climbed a ladder. The view was better. She didn't see any of the bodies she feared seeing, but there were too many, heaped in the trenches and beached on the shores: a whole red sea of death.

❖

Christien put one foot in front of the other, trying to get back to the Infirmary. He was covered in blood, none of it his own. The rest of the day passed in a fog. He treated the Grand Master's leg, which La Valette permitted only after seeing the last Turkish banner stricken from the walls. Even as Christien worked on him, La Valette was issuing orders to his commanders, making troop dispositions and asking questions. Christien cleaned and sewed his flesh, and the Grand Master never flinched. "Every slave to the breach for repairs," he ordered, "and keep the pots boiling. The infidel will give us no respite. They will seek to exploit our weakness. They will attack again tonight."

In the hours that remained before darkness Christien worked in the Infirmary. Once again the contrast between what he'd done that morning, when he joined in the slaughter, and that afternoon, when he tried to repair it, haunted him. He saw no end to it, and no alternative. He wanted only to leave, to find Maria, to know that she was safe.

A Maltese soldier was set in front of him with a long Turkish arrow protruding from his chest. Behind him there were a score of others, waiting their turn. There were only two surgeons left. The others were dead. Christien lifted his knife. A wave of emotion and fatigue welled up inside him and he felt himself beginning to weep. He hid his face, wiping it on his sleeve. His hands were shaking too much to work. He set his knife down on the soldier's belly. He went to a bucket of seawater, where he rinsed his face and gathered himself.

I'm just tired, that's all, he told himself. *It will pass.* The tremors calmed, his pulse slowed, and he got control of himself once more.

He finished extracting the arrow. He did it neatly and perfectly and the soldier died anyway.

That night the trumpets sounded, and he raced out again and took his place on the walls. The battle was fought by the light of soaring flares and Greek fire and the long, dreadful tongues of the trumps. Orange and red flame spat from the tubes, licking at flesh and clothing, consuming everything it touched.

❖

In the Turkish camp Asha learned the *Alisa* was stationed off the neck of Gallows Point. He had himself rowed out to her by the light of the flares bursting over the night battle of Birgu.

Feroz, his first officer, welcomed him ecstatically. Asha Raïs told him he'd been captured and held prisoner. He lay on his stomach and watched the firestorm over Birgu. He was consumed with guilt. The only deaths he had caused were Turkish. He had helped Maria only for a single instant. She was still in mortal danger, and there was nothing he could do for her. He had missed his chance with La Valette. He did not wish to report to Piali Pasha or Mustapha; he had little to tell them anyway. Events had outstripped the early intelligence he had gathered.

The fleet surgeon gave the *raïs* a strong opium tea and worked on his wounds and his burns. He applied an ointment of aloe, salt, and onions to reduce the blistering. The tea eased the pain of his flesh but not that of his soul.

His freedom had not bought him the elation he expected.

He was a disgrace to the Sultan, a disgrace to his father, and, most important, a disgrace to himself. He was not a man, only a repulsive serpent who crawled among men.

That day he'd killed a Janissary.

That day he'd killed a knight—or had Maria?

I am not Turkish but Ottoman, he'd told La Valette.

I am Turkish, he'd yelled during his flight.

I am Maltese, he'd yelled a moment later.

His was a life of lies. He'd lied to Dragut, lied to Iskander, lied to his gods about lying to his gods.

Yes, I am all those things. And that means I am nothing.

I am the son of many fathers, whose son has failed them all.

As the fires died down in Birgu they grew in his own mind, feverish from the opium and the burns and the torment of his soul.

Alisa!

Maria!

God help me! Allah help me!

from *The Histories of the Middle Sea*

by Darius, called the Preserver
Court Historian to the Lord of the White Sea and the Black
Sea, the Sultan Achmet

For both sides it was the lowest moment of the siege, when any minor incident could turn the battle either way.

Both sides were aware that the relief force might arrive at any moment, and aware that it might not arrive at all.

Both sides were desperate, stretched beyond human endurance.

Yet both sides found the strength to carry on.

—From Volume VII
The Great Campaigns: Malta

Chapter 44

19 AUGUST

Mustapha's engineers completed a siege tower, a mammoth wooden structure that towered over the high landward wall of Birgu. The base was wrapped in leather doused in water, to keep it from being set on fire by the defenders. Janissaries climbed up its framework, shielded by wooden planks. From the high platform they were able to fire down onto the walls and streets of Birgu, clearing the way for other troops to pour across a bridge that would be lowered from the tower to the walls. It was an ancient but effective method of siege warfare. Two of the knights, including

La Valette's nephew Henri, rushed out in an effort to destroy the tower. They were shot dead, and after more fighting raged around their bodies, they were brought back inside the walls.

Christien was with the Grand Master when he viewed their bodies. Always so resolute, so strong and sure-minded, the Grand Master allowed himself a moment of gloom. "These two young men have only gone before the rest of us by but a few days," he said. "For if the relief from Sicily does not come, we must all die. To the very last man—we must bury ourselves beneath the ruins."

La Valette set about destroying the tower. He ordered workmen to make a hole in the wall near ground level, only yards from the base of the siege tower, stopping just short of breaking through all the way. A large cannon was brought forward and loaded with chain shot. The last stones were broken out. The cannon roared. The balls and chains tore through the supports, toppling the tower.

The Turkish engineers designed a special powder keg, so large it took a dozen men to carry it. It was the largest single explosive device the engineers had ever devised, filled with explosives and shrapnel of chains, nails, and grapeshot. While the defenders of Birgu were occupied with the tower and the defenders of St. Michael's were beating back an attack, a slow match was lit on the keg. Troops hauled it to the top of a section of ruined wall in St. Michael and rolled it down into the midst of a group of defenders.

The long fuse was still burning. The defenders threw down their weapons and furiously dragged the keg back up to the ramparts. They rolled it back down the other side, directly into the mass of Turks waiting for the devastating explosion to begin their assault. It blew up in their faces. The knights led their troops outside the fort, carrying the attack to the attackers. The engagement was brief but a rout.

From a military standpoint these were but minor setbacks for the Turks, though other, more serious problems were mounting for the high command. The siege was to have lasted no more than a month. Food was running short, as was powder for the guns. Supply ships sent to Tripoli were not returning. Mustapha correctly guessed that they were being captured by Christian ships lying off the African shore. Some of the cannons were failing from overuse. Nasrid and other commanders reported increasing unrest among their troops, who were growing disheartened by the campaign's failures. If victory was the will of Allah, why were so many stumbling blocks placed in the path? Each failure made it harder to order their men to the next attack. There were no braver fighting men alive, but they had no desire to die in vain, and the mounds of rotting dead spread disease along with disheartenment.

It was nearing the end of August. Mustapha began considering the necessity that his troops winter in Malta. Piali argued with him, saying the fleet could not stand such a thing. The harbor they'd won at such expense was inadequate for wintering. It was out of the question, Piali said. Either they would capture the island by mid-September, or he would set sail for Istanbul. "When the first gregale begins to blow," he said, "the Sultan's fleet shall sail—with the army or without it."

Beset by such difficulties, Mustapha remained resolute. His family was descended from none other than Ben Welid, who had carried the standard for the Prophet Mohammed himself. Mustapha had led difficult campaigns for Suleiman from Persia to Hungary, and he had always found a way to prevail. It was true the Knights of St. John were made of stern stuff, but they were mortal and few in number. He had beaten them at Rhodes, and he would beat them again. He had no intention of standing before Suleiman with news of failure.

However grim his situation might be, he knew that surely it could be nothing compared to that faced by those inside the walls.

❖

If Mustapha erred in his assessment of conditions inside Birgu and Senglea, it was only in underestimating the desperate straits of its defenders.

For the first time since the beginning of the siege, Christien spent virtually no time in surgery. There were not enough soldiers to man the walls. He and the rest of the Infirmary staff remained on the ramparts as the Turks bombarded, then attacked, then bombarded again. Women took over care of the wounded, who died by the score without surgical treatment of any kind.

Because Christien's post was now at the French Curtain instead of in Senglea, he saw Maria nearly every day. Ordinarily it was just a glance, only enough for each of them to know the other was well. She tried to work near his post, and once, between attacks, she managed to bring bread to the men. She moved along the row of knights and soldiers slumped at their posts, dipping the bits of bread in watered wine and giving it to them along with murmured words of encouragement. She stopped before Christien and knelt. His eyes were closed. He was asleep sitting up. She dipped the bread and put it to his lips. His eyes opened. It seemed to take him a moment to realize where he was and what he was looking at. He stirred, but she stilled him.

"You are a blessed sight for tired eyes," he whispered.

"As are you for mine." While he ate she tore a bit of cloth from her sleeve and dipped it in water. She wiped his forehead, and his cheek, and his lips. His eyes never left hers.

"Is Moses well?"

She nodded. "I saw him just this morning. He and some other boys were rolling a fire hoop with a stick, like a toy."

He grinned. "Good for them." The guns began, and they heard the roar that signaled another attack. She picked up her basket to go to the next man.

He squeezed her hand. "Do you need anything?"

"Only an end to it. And only for you to stay alive."

"And you." He watched her leave, and turned to face the advancing Turks.

❖

23 AUGUST

"Birgu is doomed."

The Chevalier Gilbert, the Baron de Bergerac, addressed the Sacred Council. He had just finished his rounds of inspection, and his report was one of uninterrupted gloom.

"The damage caused by the explosion of the mine beneath the Post of Castile cannot be adequately repaired because we haven't enough manpower. We need every hand for the walls—and even then there are not enough men to guard the full perimeter.

"The Turks are driving new mines. The whole ground near the ruined walls is honeycombed with them. They will be ready within days, perhaps hours. The Turks hold the landward ditch. It will take precious little for them to break through now." His report went on, detailing the deficiencies of their position and of their stores.

"We must abandon Birgu, sires," he said in summary. "We must withdraw into the safety of Fort St. Angelo. It is the most heavily fortified position in Malta. From there we can hold out and make a final stand."

He sat to silence, as the men in the room absorbed his words.

"I agree," said Alain Bremont, the Count of Limoges. "Abandon Birgu."

The Bailiff of Negropont nodded his assent. "Withdraw to the fort."

Around the table it went, every assessment from the seasoned warriors the same. "Let us make our final stand in St. Angelo," the Grand Hospitaller said.

La Valette listened to them all. Finally he looked to Sir Oliver Starkey, his secretary. "The baron is right," Starkey said. "The time has come to abandon Birgu."

The Sacred Council was unanimous, save for one man.

La Valette rose. "I respect your advice, my brethren," he said. "But I shall not take it. If we abandon Birgu, we lose Senglea, for the garrison there cannot hold out on its own. The fortress of St. Angelo is too small to hold all the population as well as ourselves and our men, and I have no intention of abandoning the loyal Maltese, their wives, and their children to the enemy. Even supposing that we could get all the people within its walls, St. Angelo's water supply would not be adequate. With the Turks masters of Senglea, and occupying the ruins of Birgu, it would only be a matter of time before even the strong walls of St. Angelo would fall before their concentrated fire. At the moment they are forced to divert their energies and firepower. Such would not be the case if we and all our brothers were locked within St. Angelo."

He stood erect, hands behind his back, his eyes lit with conviction as his gaze fell on each of his fellow knights. "No, my brothers, this, and only this is the place where we must stand and fight. Here we must all perish together or finally, with the help of God, succeed in driving off our enemy."

For a moment no one spoke. The Bailiff of Negropont broke the silence. "Very well, Excellency. Then let us at least move the archives and sacred relics of the Order into St. Angelo," he said. "We have the hand of St. John the Baptist to preserve for the ages, and the whole written history of the Order. All could be secreted beneath the dungeons, safe from the desecration of the infidel."

"Such a move would only seem desperate. Morale would suffer greatly. In any event, it will matter little. If we do not prevail," La Valette said, "there will be no Order of St. John. The hand of the Baptist, gentlemen, shall remain in Birgu, as shall we all."

That afternoon, to make certain that retreat would never be considered, the Grand Master ordered most of St. Angelo's garrison into Birgu, along with powder and other stores. He left only a small contingent in St. Angelo, to man the cannons. The drawbridge between St. Angelo and Birgu was destroyed.

There was no longer any choice.

They would meet victory in Birgu, or death.

from **The Histories of the Middle Sea**

by Darius, called the Preserver
Court Historian to the Lord of Both Halves of the World, the
Sultan Achmet

The Gran Soccorso, *the long-promised relief of Malta, departed Messina on the 21ˢᵗ of August, but not for Malta. The fleet was bound for Syracuse, where it was to join other forces. The very day Don García sailed, yet another general assault was launched against Birgu and Senglea.*

Two days later, a relief force of nearly ten thousand men gathered on the gentle hill above the harbor of Syracuse, waiting for the last of the transport ships to arrive. Among them were Knights of the Order, Spanish troops, and soldiers of fortune from Italy, France, and Germany. Don García fretted to anyone who would listen that still he did not have enough men to ensure victory. No one present knew how many Turkish troops remained to fight, or what condition they were in. If the rescue failed, if the fleet was lost or the troops defeated, Spain herself would be endangered, King Philip would be enraged, and Suleiman would be unstoppable.

Mutterings of his spinelessness rippled through the ranks of the impatient knights, who were powerless to make the Viceroy move more quickly.

It rained.

—From Volume VII
The Great Campaigns: Malta

24 AUGUST

On his knees in the palace chapel, Salvago heard the guns outside gaining power. They sounded louder than before, because the walls that once helped muffle their sound were all but gone. It was rumored another attack would come that afternoon, that it would be the worst of all, that the Turks were desperate and would not stop this time.

Give me the strength to carry on, O Lord.

The prayers always helped, but only so long as he remained on his knees. Once he left the sanctuary, his strength and serenity evaporated. Other men did not appear to be as fearful as he felt. Even the bishop seemed to go fearlessly wherever he was needed, placing himself in harm's way, while Salvago's own guts were jelly. He took every opportunity to find something to do in the dungeons when the real work was outside, near the walls. But he could not help his fear. Men were blown to shreds right next to him, or burned to death, or shot. Whether his eyes were open or shut, the nightmares were endless. He could not sleep. During the day he could not stop shaking. He had to force himself outside, force himself to carry on, and it never got any easier.

Some of the knights asked if he would join God's fight and carry a weapon like Father Roberto. It was out of the question. Even in the last gasp of this fight between the Crescent and the Cross, he knew he could never confront a screaming fanatic swinging a sword. "I am a priest," he told them, "not a soldier." Yet he knew that was not it. *The truth is I am not a soldier because I am a coward. Even the children seem braver than I.* The boy Moses lit fire hoops for the troops. Six-year-old girls poured boiling oil from the walls. Women broke Turkish heads with bricks. He would never do any of those things.

Violence made him ill.

As he prayed the guns fell silent. He heard the dread instruments blaring and the war cry rising in Turkish throats as they swarmed down the hills. His own throat tightened in dread. They were coming again.

Salvago crossed himself, took a deep breath, and ran outside. He was to carry ammunition, but at the bastion a knight yelled at him over the rising noise of battle. "Go to the Infirmary, Father," he shouted. "The Grand Master has called for all the wounded. We need every last man."

Salvago ran through Birgu. There were too many dead in the streets to pick up any more. There were dead women beside their children, dead cats beside dead rats. The poor souls who ran among them knew that if the Turks didn't kill what was left of the living, pestilence or plague soon would. A stench hung in the air, permeating everything; it was almost viscous. Never breaking stride, he crossed himself and prayed for their souls and tried not to gag.

The Infirmary courtyard was milling with wounded men waiting to be helped to the walls. Besides Salvago, only women and children remained to help move them.

A Spanish arquebusier took up a staff in one arm and draped his other over Salvago's shoulder. With his free arm Salvago carried the man's gun as they limped toward the Post of Castile. The Spaniard looked up at the men on the walls, where the battle had not yet reached its full fury. Some men were slumped over, others firing down the other side. Smoke billowed from the trenches. "Hear my confession, Father," he said. And they bowed their heads and hobbled the last few yards, praying.

Salvago blessed him and helped him onto the ladder. He forced himself to follow. He got the soldier propped in place. The Spaniard took up his arquebus and set his sword on the ground. Shots whistled by, shattering bits of parapet. Salvago peered over the wall and nearly vomited with fear. He turned and flew back down the ladder, cringing at the bedlam.

On his way back he helped return a young soldier to the Infirmary. The man had no armor and was skinny enough that Salvago was able to drape him over his shoulder. By the time they got to the Infirmary, the man was dead. It was just as well, Salvago thought. At the Infirmary he would lay untended anyway. Salvago's mumbled last rites were finished by the time he'd set the man down.

A huge knight bellowed to get to the battle. He was Alain Bremont, the big-bellied Count of Limoges. He looked frightful, his fiery red beard singed nearly off, his face blistered and raw from burns. An iron ball had taken both his feet the day before, killing the man beside him. Bremont was feverish and weak but determined to do battle. He was too large for one man to carry. "Find me a chair, by God," he yelled, and a sturdy oak chair was located in the Hospitaller's office. They set him in it. Salvago and a big woman tried to lift him, but the knight was too heavy and the chair too awkward. It nearly tipped over. "By God, you're going to kill me before the Turks do!" Bremont cried.

Two other women rushed forward, each taking a leg of the chair. Salvago lifted his corner and faltered a little. One of the new women was Maria Borg. She met his gaze. If she felt anything, she was too tired to show it. He looked away. They carried the count in silence, struggling and stumbling. They couldn't get him up a ladder, so they left him near one of the breaches, roaring at the top of his lungs for the godless Turks to come and get him.

Bremont was the last of the wounded able to come from the Infirmary. Salvago ran toward the French Curtain to carry ammunition, while Maria ran the other way, toward the Post of Castile.

❖

Christien was on his knees at the wall, watching the Turks massing yet again for attack. He was not certain he would be able to rise to meet them. At the signal the Turks swarmed down the hill, over the ditch, and up toward the walls once more. In some places they didn't need ladders at all. They clambered up hills of rubble, directly into the fire pouring from the top. Christien was puzzled—troops facing his position were holding back, while up and down the line the battle was fully joined. He saw a sapper scramble out of a tunnel, jump to his feet, and run.

Too late, he realized what it meant. "Mines!" he yelled. He pushed himself to his feet and scrambled backward, as the other men nearby did the same.

There were two separate blasts, the first directly beneath where he'd been kneeling. It threw him into the air and off the wall. As he hit the ground a second explosion ripped through a section of wall ten yards to his left. The sappers had done their work superbly. A large section of wall collapsed, much of it toppling toward him in a torrent of limestone, reinforcing timbers, and earth.

He felt a stabbing pain in his leg, and it helped him cling to consciousness. He shook his head and raised himself to his elbows. He was lying on his back in the street, half buried. Two men lay dead beside him. Beyond the pile, men were rushing for the new breach—the Turks from the outside, knights and soldiers from nearby positions to meet them in battle. Already men were locked in hand-to-hand combat. Through his dizziness and with all the dust it seemed to be a battle fought in the clouds, a surreal clash of swirling robes and flashing swords and thundering guns and exploding pots of Greek fire.

The battle was surging in his direction.

He struggled to free himself and gasped in pain. He could feel his leg was horribly broken. He tried to pull back, but it was pinned. He cried out again. Sweat poured from his forehead.

He could only partially sit up because of the angle at which he lay in the rubble. He started clearing away stones. For each one he moved, two more slid down. A large piece of timber lay squarely across his shin, its ends buried beneath tons of rubble.

The fighting grew ever closer. A Maltese fell near him, shot dead. His morion clattered to the ground. Another man toppled off the portion of the wall at whose base Christien lay, as more of it gave way. People streamed by, some running in panic for shelter, others to reinforce the weakened positions, still others carrying supplies. No one paid attention to the wounded, or, in his case, to the trapped. If he couldn't get loose quickly, the Turks would kill him where he lay.

Firepots exploded atop the pile of rubble near the breach. Another mine exploded, showering debris everywhere. A piece struck him, and blood streamed from a gash in his cheek. He struggled again to free his leg. It was impossible. He lay back, gasping and exhausted. Staring at the sky, certain he was about to die, he cried for help. Someone stopped and knelt near his head. It was

Father Salvago. Christien saw his lips moving, but couldn't hear what he said over the noise of battle.

Salvago got behind Christien and grabbed hold of him beneath his arms. He pulled, straining. Christien screamed and shook his head. Salvago tore at the rubble himself, then at the beam pinning Christien. He ran around and tried to get hold of it, but it wouldn't budge. He tried to throw off more of the debris, but there was far too much.

Salvago turned and yelled at a soldier to help. The man dashed by, hurdling over Christien's head as he raced headlong for the breach. The fighting was less than thirty feet away now, a hundred men locked in a death struggle.

"The halberd, Father!" Christien yelled to Salvago. "Get the halberd!"

Salvago saw the weapon on the ground near a fallen soldier. While he scrambled for it Christien tied the cloth he used to wipe his face around his leg just above the knee. He gasped again, each movement bringing searing pain. He unbuckled the straps of his jambeau, the flap of armor guarding his shin, and managed to pull it partway up his leg.

Salvago knelt by him with the heavy weapon. He ducked as another piece of wall tumbled nearby, enveloping them in a rolling cloud of dust. Coughing, he took the end of the halberd and tried to jam it beneath the beam, to use it as a pry bar.

Christien tugged at his cassock. "No, Father," he yelled. "It's for me. You've got to take it there." He showed him the spot on his leg, six inches below the knee.

Salvago's face went white. "*What?*"

"Use the halberd! Take my leg! Quickly, Father! There is no time!"

Salvago shook his head. "I cannot do it!"

"Then I will die," Christien shouted. "Please, Father. It is the only way." The battle was closer than ever.

They heard a commotion at the end of the street. Reinforcements were arriving from within Birgu, summoned from the Hub. Romegas led them. Salvago pointed hopefully. "They'll be here in a moment!"

"They'll be too late for me," Christien said. He gripped Salvago's arm tightly. "Do it, Father. *Now.* Take it as close to the beam as you can." He lay back and closed his eyes.

Giulio Salvago rose on unsteady legs. The long handle was heavy, hewn from golden oak. The head weighed nearly twenty pounds, its blade dulled from combat. He hefted the weapon high, his lips moving in prayer as he beseeched the Almighty for a reprieve of some sort, hoping the knight on the ground would change his mind and call him off. He faltered and felt himself swaying. Fear pounded at his temples.

But there was no reprieve, only the turmoil of battle and the surging of Turks. Gunfire roared nearby and the terror rose in his throat and he could wait no more.

Guide my hand, Father.

With all his might he brought the halberd down. It glanced off the beam and did not hit the leg cleanly. He closed his ears to the scream. He raised it again and struck a second time. Still the leg did not part. A final blow cut through to the ground and the awful thing was done.

Drained by the effort, he threw down the halberd and caught Christien behind the shoulders, dragging him away from the approaching melee. De Vries was unconscious, and Salvago saw he was leaving a trail of blood. He stopped to tighten the tourniquet, praying God to stop the trembling in his fingers long enough to let him do it. Then he pulled him into the shelter of a doorway. He fell to his knees, his chest heaving. He was shaking all over, sick to his stomach with fear and horror. He wanted nothing more than to drag Christien all the way to the Infirmary, away from the carnage behind him. Surely he'd done enough for one day.

But he heard the soldiers yelling for ammunition and help, heard the screams of children, and he forced himself to get to his feet, to go back to the walls. Two women emerged from the gate of the palace, carrying a basket of wine-soaked bread for the men on the walls. "Get him to the Infirmary if you can," Salvago yelled to them, pointing at Christien.

He ran back into the street near the French Curtain. At the breach he was almost relieved to see the battle had moved even farther inside the wall, to the very spot where he'd just been. De Vries had been right. He'd done the right thing after all. The Turks seemed to have gotten as far as they were going to, however. They were being driven back in a furious counterassault, their line faltering before the onslaught of Romegas and his men.

Salvago moved away from the breach. He carried a sack of Greek firepots to the next ladder and hauled them up to a French knight, who was throwing them with deadly precision into the breach. The priest climbed back down for more, but all they had ready at the arsenal was a trump, one of the flame-throwing tubes. It was almost too heavy to carry, but he got it back up to the walls. The knight grinned at the sight of him. "Just in time, Father," he said. "You'll have to help me deliver this hellfire to His enemies."

"I cannot!" Salvago yelled back, but he saw the Turks had half a dozen ladders nearby, the men engaged everywhere on the walls. A trump took two men, and there was no one else to help. Salvago got to his knees and lifted one end of the tube. The knight touched his slow match to the end of the trump, dripping with fuel.

The pipe exploded in their hands, spraying hot metal and jellied fire in every direction. Shrapnel ripped through the knight's armor, killing him instantly. The Turks nearby toppled backward, their robes alight. The fiery mix showered down on Salvago, engulfing him in flames. The jelly stuck to his face, searing his mouth, his nose, his eyes. He tried to beat the fire away, but the jelly smeared, and his flailing only spread it more. Screaming, he staggered toward the water barrel. "God help me!" he cried. More Maltese soldiers rushed past him to the post, to battle the Turks mounting the ladders.

Salvago crashed into the barrel. It was empty. He fell to the ground and rolled over and over, frantically trying to extinguish the blaze. The jelly would not be smothered. As soon as it touched air, it burst into flames again. Shrieking, tormented, he got to his knees, then to his feet, tearing at the burning flesh of his face. He staggered forward and blindly toppled from the wall, straight onto a Turk ascending his ladder. Together they crashed downward, bouncing off the ladder and landing at the bottom in a flaming, tangled heap. Still Salvago did not die. It was another ten minutes before his writhing and screeching stopped.

The battle lasted two more hours. Nowhere was it fought with more fury and rage than near the exploded trump, where so many had seen Father Salvago die so bravely for his faith.

Chapter 45

from The Histories of the Middle Sea

by Darius, called the Preserver
Court Historian to the Majestic Caesar, the Sultan Achmet

The relief force of twenty-eight ships carrying ten thousand men left Syracuse. The force immediately encountered a violent storm, which battered and very nearly sank the fleet. Supplies were lost, rigging destroyed. The troops aboard were seasick and in no condition to fight. The fleet limped for cover to an island off the west coast of Sicily, to regroup.

Sometime in the night, a thousand troops deserted.

—From Volume VII
The Great Campaigns: Malta

25 AUGUST

Asha sat stiffly on the *Alisa*'s deck. His burns made movement painful, but he got around all right and his injuries were the furthest thing from his mind. He and his ships were stationed off Gallows Point, maintaining the blockade. He was glad to have the unimportant duty—glad not to have to confront his choices and his failures.

The news from the lines of battle around Grand Harbor was bitter for Asha, sweet for Nico. Desperate for a victory, Mustapha had ordered his men to pull away from Birgu and Senglea and to march on Mdina, thinking he could conquer the weak-walled city and use it for a winter post, or at the very least present it to the Sultan as a partial victory.

His army found the walls of the citadel swarming with defenders, who fired their muskets and cannons at the approaching army in a prodigious and wasteful display of firepower long before the Turks were even in range. This had to mean they had uncounted quintals of powder and shot inside the walls and that their troops were fresh and eager for battle. Concluding the fortress was impregnable, the Turkish army turned back without firing a shot.

The assault on Senglea and Birgu was renewed, but morale suffered greatly from the failure at Mdina, and from the desperation the attempt itself had revealed. Mustapha and Piali were constantly at loggerheads, their arguments loud and sometimes violent. There were rumors that there was grain enough only for a few more weeks at best. Still more ships had failed to return from the African coast with provisions, and winter was fast approaching. There had been no end to the ravages of fever and pestilence felling the Sultan's troops, and while the ditches of Malta were filled with Turkish dead, the decks of half the fleet in Marsamuscetto were filled with sick and wounded. In all of the campaigns fought by the Ottomans in the last forty years, none had met a resistance stiffer or more cleverly managed than that of the knights and people of Malta. There were whispers about troops refusing to fight. *Janissaries*, refusing to join the battle. If this was so, then surely the end could not be far off.

In all the depressing news, Asha took heart in only one thing: in his wildest imaginings, he had never expected that the little island might somehow withstand the force arrayed against it. Yet so far it had. Its defenders simply refused to yield. His sister was alive when last he saw her. Although Mustapha was a determined and resourceful general and might still find a way to prevail, Maria at least had a chance. That was more than he'd given her before.

He contemplated his own role in what was to come and found himself hoping there would be none. He could think of nothing better than to end the siege sitting there on his galley, and then to sail away, even in defeat. The thought took root and blossomed in his mind, and as the days passed and nothing changed he actually believed it might happen. Once returned to Istanbul, he would set about finding Alisa. There would be life after the siege.

It was not to be. A messenger from the command tent dashed his hopes.

"By order of the pasha," he said, "you and your men are to report to the Marsa at first light. You will join the morning's general assault on Birgu."

So they were stripping men and officers from the fleet. It was an act of desperation, but no matter. He had his orders.

He stood alone in the prow of his ship. The moment of commitment could no longer be delayed, and his position was no less impossible than it had been in the beginning. His resolve had not softened: he would not raise arms against Maltese. But to refuse his orders meant he could not return with his ship to Istanbul, either.

He prayed and paced the deck and wondered how he had lost his honor so completely. He wasn't even certain when he'd lost it. Was it the day he disobeyed his father and went treasure hunting with Maria instead of cleaning out the dung pit? The day he lied to Dragut? The day he killed Iskander? Was it when he denied his Christian self, or his Muslim one? Was it when he claimed to be Ottoman? Turkish? Maltese?

In his heart, he knew there was only one truly honorable course open to him. He must present himself to Mustapha and Piali, confess his past, and respectfully refuse to obey their order. The lies would be at an end, an end that would almost surely be delivered with the edge of a scimitar. Yes, perhaps that was the end of Allah's long path after all.

When the hour was late and he could delay no longer, he summoned Feroz. "I am going to see Mustapha Pasha," he said. "If I am not back at first light, you will lead our men to the Marsa."

"At your order, Asha Raïs."

He took a last long and melancholy look at the *Alisa*. He stepped into the ship's caique and had himself rowed into the harbor.

❖

The next day brought a downpour of rain, carried on a frigid north wind.

Nasrid stood in the mud among his men, his silks as sodden as their spirits, the noise of the storm drowning out the sounds of battle they were about to join. His men were not of a fighting mood this day. He struck one down with his sword, but he knew that was not the way. He closed his eyes then and summoned a vision of Iskander, his fearsome and mighty *lala,* sitting astride his massive Turkoman in the ruins of the Hippodrome in Constantinople. Iskander, the perfect Ottoman warrior, prancing back and forth on that noble horse, stirring his pages to battle, teaching them in those glorious days at Topkapi how to live and die for their Sultan, for their faith. *War is brutal,* Iskander said. *War destroys. Yet there is an ecstasy to it that the rest of life cannot match.*

And now Nasrid found Iskander's voice, found his spirit, and with scimitar flashing inspired his men to do battle once more.

"*God is great!*" he thundered.

The rain poured down and lightning flickered in a charcoal sky beyond the walls, and he could see the forms of the infidels atop the battlements, where the Grand Master had ordered them armed this day with crossbows, because fire would not work in such a rain, but the Grand Master was wrong—fire *would* work this day, so long as it was fire of the belly, fire of the spirit, fire for the love of God, a holy inferno of fire that could consume even crossbows: fire for the Sultan, fire for the Prophet, yes, fire such as men had not seen on the face of the earth.

When you die on the field of battle, when you know you are about to perish for the glory of Allah, you will dance in your own blood, secure in the knowledge that you shall sit in Paradise at the side of the Prophet. . . .

Nasrid's men surged forward, their lust growing at last, lust driven by that fire in his voice, a voice that rose above the storm, the very voice of God, moving men toward His glory.

"*Allah Hu Akbar!*" they roared as one, roared like the pages had roared in the Hippodrome, Iskander's own passion pulsing through their veins as they stormed the walls once more.

They slipped and slid that cold morning through the mud and the blood and the dead, screaming, surging forward through the rain, carrying their holy fire into a river of bolts launched from a bristling forest of steel crossbows.

And thus it was that Nasrid took a bolt in the chest for the glory of Allah, and got his fervent wish, to sit at the hand of His Prophet.

❖

Maria dragged herself along, working the walls by day and then the auberges or the Infirmary at night. She was functioning on adrenaline alone, weeks past exhaustion.

She had not seen Christien for two days, since the mine blew beneath the French Curtain. Desperately she'd gone from post to post, asking if anyone had seen him. No one had. She'd stood on the rubble and refused to believe he was buried beneath it, where men died so anonymously. It simply wasn't possible. She searched the Infirmary and the auberges. She went to the ruins of her father's house, thinking he might be there, waiting for her.

He was not there.

Her father was not there.

She walked every foot of wall along Kalkara, braving the fire of the snipers from the slopes of Salvador. She looked in the Italian auberge, where there was a small clinic that was now completely unmanned. The dead lay in heaps, the dying in long rows. He was not among them.

She lived on hope. Maybe he'd been called to Senglea. No one could say for sure, could they? Maybe he'd gotten ill and was resting somewhere. Maybe, maybe . . .

It was nearly midnight as she moved down the darkened halls of the once-great Infirmary. She carried a lantern in one hand, a water bucket in another. The wounded filled every inch of floor space. There were two and even three men to a cot. There were knights among common soldiers, neither asking for nor receiving special treatment. She stopped at each cot, where she knelt and put a ladle to the patient's lips. Some were dead, others unconscious. There were no doctors left to tend any of them.

Every so often she would run across a patient eager to hear gossip or to share it. The Turks, one told her, had been fooled by a great deception inside Mdina, where the governor had dressed women as soldiers to make the Turks think the garrison was heavily manned. They'd shot off the last of their stores of powder on wasteful shots, to make the Turks believe they had powder to spare. The Turks, he chortled, had swallowed the deception whole. "If we can only get a few more days," he whispered. "That's all we need. A few more days, and the relief will come." He clutched her hand, and died with that hope on his lips.

She knelt at another cot and held the patient's head up so he could drink. He was a Genoese whose clothing was bloody all over. She couldn't tell where he'd been hurt, or even if the blood was his. He sipped a little. "His Holiness was right," he said, looking at her in the flickering light. "I have died and gone to heaven at last, and am seeing the angels." She smiled and helped him to more. As he drank she looked beyond him, toward the collapsed wall that had once been part of a corridor leading to the rear ward. There were still more patients there. Surely, she thought, they could not fit another man into the Infirmary. She had to crawl beneath a cot to get to them.

The first two were dead. She knelt by a Spaniard, who moaned weakly. She gave him water and moved on. A Maltese, a Portuguese, and then . . . "*Christien!*" Her bucket crashed to the floor. He was unconscious and hot with fever. She held the lantern higher and gasped at the sight of his leg. She crossed herself and tried to still her nerves and to think what to do. She knew nothing about such things. She pulled back the ragged cloth of his pant leg and saw the wound had not been dressed. It was ugly around the cut, dark and unhealthy-looking, and there was a ragged, dirty edge of bone. "Help me God," she whispered. "What should I do?"

She saw the cloth was still tied tightly, to stop the flow of blood. The skin near the cloth looked too dark, and she loosened it a little. The blood oozed dark red past raw scabs. She loosened it a little more, and it flowed a little more. She tightened it again, then ran to one of the cisterns where seawater was kept for cleansing wounds. She used it to clean him. He groaned but did not awaken.

She soaked a cloth with water and put it to his lips. He licked them, getting just a trickle. She used another cloth to drape his forehead, trying to cool the fever. She knew she was not really helping. She held his hand for a moment, thinking. She had to find someone to help. Reluctantly she left him and raced to the walls, to the Post of Provence, where some days earlier she'd seen one of the barber-surgeons. The walls were quiet. Men were slumped at their posts, trying to sleep among sentries who paced back and forth. She asked one of them, and then another, and a third. Each shook his head. At last she found the man she sought. He was snoring. He was difficult to awaken and at first refused to move at all. "I am weak and wounded myself," he snapped.

But Maria Borg would not be denied.

They worked for an hour in the Infirmary, in the cramped dark hallway. She held the lantern for him. He was distressed to find there weren't any cauldrons going so that he could cauterize the wound. Grumbling, he had no alternative but to suture the vessels and sew up the leg. "It'll kill him for sure," he said.

❖

4 SEPTEMBER

After recovering on an island off the coast of Sicily, the storm-ravaged relief force regrouped on another island nearer Malta, called Linosa. From there the fleet set sail in two detachments. For a second time bad weather pounded the seas. The main part of the fleet once again found itself at anchor off the coast of Sicily, while the smaller advance force sailed for Gozo.

The *Alisa* was now under command of Feroz Raïs. Asha had not returned, which could only mean he was dead. The general assault had been mounted, but Feroz and his men had been pulled back as they were preparing to disembark for that assault. They waited all day in the harbor, listening to the sounds of battle, but with no orders. The next morning they were ordered to join the galleys patrolling the north. Feroz knew he and his men had escaped almost certain death. He regretted the loss of Asha. The *Alisa* was a fine ship, and he vowed to do honor to her late captain.

He worked the channel between Gozo and Malta, looking for signs of Christian ships. The storm pressed in from the north, roiling the channel and battering his galley, nearly swamping her. Feroz stayed out as long as he dared, but visibility was dropping and galleys were not made for rough seas. He ordered her brought about, and returned swiftly to the calm of Marsamuscetto. At the moment he turned, less than a mile from his position, parts of the advance force made it to safety on Gozo, undetected at the critical moment when they could have been crushed.

Commanding the main body of ships now anchored off Sicily, Don García found a new reason to hesitate. Fearing that any reduction in the relief's strength might place the entire expedition in jeopardy, he wanted word of the safety of the balance of his fleet before he gave the order to sail. He addressed a gathering of knights in his cabin.

"His Majesty has made it quite clear he is not prepared to sacrifice his fleet, which may be needed should Malta fall and the Ottomans knock next at his door. I have orders to proceed only if assured of victory. I have no such assurance," he said. "The bulk of the fleet will wait until I do."

A knight from Provence rose. "I tire of tact," he said, "and diplomacy gives me boils. All of Christendom looks to this force to succor the beleaguered Knights of St. John and the people of Malta who are dying for the Faith. You give no sign of eagerness to join the battle, Don García. If you fail to commit yourself and this force now, at this instant, your name will be associated with the dogs of cowardice through all history. Already you have disgraced the memory of those who have died so bravely."

White-faced with fury, the Viceroy stood, as if to strike the man. But he did not.

❖

Inside Birgu, the alarm bells rang again and again, and Maria had no choice but to return to the walls. In the next three days she fought alongside the men, using crossbow, Greek fire, and stones against the Turks. She returned to Christien's side whenever she could. He remained critically ill. Delirious, he didn't know her. Each night she took what food she could find to the bishop's palace, where Moses slept in the rubble in the cellar. There were a dozen other children there, all smaller than he. "You are the man here," she told him. "You must keep them all here. Keep them safe, do you hear? It's a big job, Moses. A man's job. We'll manage on the walls without you."

"All right."

The next day she saw him running firepots through the smoking ruins near the Post of Castile. She could do nothing to stop him.

❖

7 SEPTEMBER

Nearly four months after it had been promised, the relief force arrived in Mellieha Bay, in the north of the island of Malta. A runner brought the news to La Valette's headquarters in the square of Birgu. "The force is nine thousand strong, sire," the man said.

While those around him erupted in joy, La Valette was dismayed. The force was far smaller than promised—perhaps too small to turn the tide. Mustapha Pasha still had many more thousands to throw into battle. "If he finds out how few have come to our aid," La Valette said quietly to his commanders, "he may not give up."

"Perhaps a ruse is in order, sire," said Sir Oliver. "Surely the relief force is far larger than reported."

La Valette smiled and turned to Romegas. "See that a galley slave is allowed to escape from your dungeons," he said. "But first see that he overhears your men talking." The Grand Master told him precisely what was to be overheard.

The slave escaped in a hail of gunfire. A succession of Turkish officers heard his report. He soon found himself standing before Mustapha and Piali. "Lords, lords," he said, trembling to bear such news to such men, "the world is ended! The relief force has landed at Mellieha. It is sixteen thousand strong. The infidels are dancing and shouting that the siege is all but finished. I saw them mustering their soldiers, preparing to sally forth, to mount a frontal attack!" He groveled before them, fearing a messenger's fate.

Mustapha Pasha whirled on Piali. "This is *your* doing! Your failure to stop the relief from landing is indefensible. From the first you have worried over nothing save the safety of your precious fleet, and then you fail to use it to effect! You have failed your Sultan, your men, your God! By the beard of the Prophet, your incompetence will earn you the edge of the Sultan's sword!"

Piali sneered at the old general. "Even with forty thousand men, your ineptitude is such that you cannot master a fifth their number. You have had four months to take an island that should have fallen in one, and have nothing to show the Padishah but a mountain of dead and the rubble of St. Elmo. Your troops are near mutiny. Their heart is gone and they fight like women—and it is you who the Sultan may thank! If his sword passes through my neck, it will be on the way to take yours!"

Mustapha stormed from the tent. "Sound the signal!" he yelled at his *aghas*. "Prepare to evacuate! Put to the torch what cannot be carried!" In a flurry of robes he strode through the camp, issuing orders. From the medical tents, sick men dragged themselves from their cots. Slaves were rousted and put to the work of hauling supplies to the ships. The camp was in an uproar.

Part of Don García's fleet sailed around the entrance to Grand Harbor, each of its cannons firing three times in salute. The galleys had disembarked the relief force in the north of the island, and now some of the empty ships were returning to Sicily, to take on more troops. Maria saw them from the walls and began weeping. All around the harbor the Turkish guns fell into an eerie silence.

Maria ran for the bishop's palace, but the children were not there. She hunted for them in the streets but knew they could be anywhere. She ran to the Infirmary.

Late into the night, from her place by Christien's cot, Maria could see flares bursting. At times they were so intense they lit the inside of the Infirmary as if it were day. The flares were no longer for assault, but for retreat. There was only sporadic gunfire. She listened to Christien's ragged breathing and said her hundredth prayer of the night. She asked the barber-surgeon if Christien would live. "If it is God's will," he said. When her eyes would stay open no longer she laid her head on his chest and fell asleep to the sound of his heartbeat. She awakened at dawn. His condition had not changed. She went out to see what had happened during the night.

The sun lit Corradino Heights, and they were free of Turkish tents. The top of Sciberras was barren. Gun platforms were empty and smoldering, having been torched. She could not see a Turkish flag anywhere. She could stand on the wall, erect, without fear. From Birgu and Senglea she heard scattered shouts of joy, of disbelief, of thanksgiving.

The relief force had camped near the village of Naxxar for the night, on good high ground where they could not be easily attacked. At dawn patrols advanced toward the Grand Harbor. They encountered the extraordinary sight of Turkish camps being stricken.

The Grand Master ordered the gates of Birgu and Senglea thrown open, as the bells of St. Lawrence signaled not battle but thanksgiving. Townspeople streamed through the gates and made quickly for the trenches, where they began stripping corpses of valuables and weapons. From the Inquisitor's dungeons beneath the bishop's palace, Moses led six small children from the ruins in the courtyard and scrounged in the kitchens for food. The cook laughed and sang and tossed them biscuits and dried beef. From hollows beneath toppled walls and crevices surrounded by rubble, women rose from the ruins and clapped their hands in joy.

Gilbert, the Baron de Bergerac, led a contingent of knights and soldiers to Sciberras. They raced up the long slope, from which Marsamuscetto harbor on the far side could be seen. Gilbert's severe features retreated before his smile as he took in the view. "For the love of Christ, lads, look at that." Just two weeks earlier, the baron had recommended to the Grand Master that Birgu be abandoned. Now, all around the Marsamuscetto, it was the Turks who were abandoning their posts. Mules struggled up boat planks with heavy loads. Sailors worked in the water, clearing the heavy seaweed from around the hulls, where it had grown during the summer. Troops were packed tightly onto the decks of galleys.

"Cannons!" Gilbert roared to a courier. "Get to Birgu and bring me light cannons!" Half an hour later six Portuguese versos were set up near St. Elmo, from which the baron directed their fire down into the embarking fleet. "By God, it feels good to have the high ground!" he gloated as his men rained shots on the Turks, who returned only sporadic and ineffective fire. More soldiers arrived from Birgu with arquebuses and crossbows. A knight dispatched by La Valette brought a flag of the Order, which soon fluttered above the remains of St. Elmo.

Just then La Valette's ruse unraveled.

Mustapha Pasha received two reports, one from a mounted scout, the other from a captain in the fleet, that the number of ships and men in the relief force was much smaller than initially reported. He paced the deck of his ship.

"We must leave now," Piali said. "The ships are under fire."

"To the devil with your ships!" Mustapha thundered. "They've tricked us! Too much blood has been shed to give up now. It is *not* too late! We will prevail! *Aghas!* Order the men disembarked!" The Ottoman discipline held, and a mad scramble ensued to unload the men.

Piali could not countermand the order, but once the ships were emptied of troops he gave the signal for his captains to withdraw toward the open sea, out of the range of the small guns. He ordered them moved a few miles up the coast, toward St. Paul's Bay. Meanwhile, more than nine thousand of Mustapha's troops massed near the village of Msida. They began marching inland toward Mdina. At the first sign of their intention, the Baron de Bergerac sent word to La Valette: Mustapha is not finished. The Grand Master dispatched a messenger to alert the commander of the relief. Inside Birgu and Senglea, euphoria turned suddenly to shock: incredibly, victory was not yet secure.

On the eastern hills of Malta, the two armies took the other's measure. Mustapha's force was still the stronger of the two. The commanders of the relief were under strict orders from the king himself not to engage the enemy but to endeavor to drive him off with a show of force. Yet neither King Philip nor his Viceroy, Don García, nor anyone else reckoned with the passion that had built up among the men of the relief, led by the Knights of St. John, who had waited for weeks and months in Sicily to come to the aid of their fellow knights. Now, in sight of the enemy, they would not suffer restraint. "Hold lines!" shouted the commander as horses reared and formations rippled and swelled and nearly broke.

"Hold!" he shouted again, but the knights were off, some mounted, some on foot. With a whoop and a cry, the troops behind them surged forward, and suddenly the entire army was charging down the long gentle hill.

The sight of that rush broke what was left of the will of the Turkish army. Panicked, many broke ranks and fled toward St. Paul's Bay. Amid the retreat bloody skirmishes erupted between the *sipahis,* the Turkish cavalry, and the mounted Knights of St. John. There were other brief clashes among infantry units for unimportant bits of advantage, but to the officers watching from both sides, the picture was clear.

The Turks were running.

Seeing that his hopes of quick victory were in vain, Mustapha's attention turned to providing cover for his troops as they fled for Piali's ships. He saw a weak point in the advancing Christian troops, and personally led a charge of Janissaries against the tide in order to sow confusion. Meanwhile riflemen from Piali's fleet took up stations near the bay and began laying down covering fire for their army, the bulk of which was now dashing in total disarray for the safety of the water. The Turks splashed out toward the little rowboats waiting to ferry them out to deeper water where the Sultan's galleys waited. Men trampled others in their dash, many drowning in less than two feet of water.

The advancing army was spread out, the mounted knights in front, foot soldiers lagging behind. While Piali watched from his ship, Mustapha Pasha remained in the thick of battle. His horse was shot from under him. He mounted another; it died, too. He mounted again and was nearly overrun by knights. Some of his Janissaries turned back the danger, while Piali's arquebusiers, arrayed on high ground around the bay, managed with ripping fire to disrupt the advance, giving their comrades more time. While much of the Turkish army made it onto the ships, many did not, caught in the water by their pursuers.

The last battle of the siege was fought hand-to-hand in the water of St. Paul's Bay, turning the sea into a churning maelstrom of death, as the last of the Turks sought to escape their fresh and vengeful pursuers. As night fell, so did the Turks. The last galley in the fleet limped past the islet of Selmunett, where St. Paul had been shipwrecked. Behind the galley, the waters of his bay were fouled with the dead.

It was the last slaughter in a long summer of killing, in the charnel house that was Malta.

from *The Histories of the Middle Sea*

by Darius, called the Preserver
Court Historian to the King of Believers and Unbelievers, the Sultan Achmet

In all, the Ottomans lost nearly thirty thousand dead out of the forty thousand who began, while the Order and its allies lost seven thousand, including two hundred and seventy knights, out of the original garrison force of nine thousand. On the day the relief force arrived, the Grand Master had only five hundred men still able to bear arms, and they were nearly out of powder and shot. Mustapha Pasha had been within weeks, if not days, of mastering Malta.

Piali Pasha had the sense to send a galley ahead with the news so that the Sultan's fires might dim before they faced him. In his long life Suleiman had tasted little of defeat. Only the great walls of Vienna had stopped his armies, thirty-five years earlier.

The Sultan ordered the fleet to wait until darkness to enter the Golden Horn, so that its humiliation might be cloaked by night.

The Possessor of Men's Necks pardoned Mustapha and Piali. "It is only in my own hands," he said, "that the sword of the Ottomans is invincible." He vowed to personally lead an expedition the following year to take the island.

—From Volume VII
The Great Campaigns: Malta

Chapter 46

Christien lay on his cot, enjoying the warm autumn sunshine. A letter was open on his lap. It was from his mother, Simone. The religious wars simmering in France had come to a boil at the Château de Vries. His brother, Yves, the count, had been assassinated by a Huguenot.

So much death, in God's name. And this one makes me the new count.

Simone begged him to come home, to tend to the affairs of the estate.

He struggled with his duty as he struggled to adapt to life without a leg. It had been the loss of a leg that had gotten him into the Order. He wished the loss of his own would be enough to get him out, but nearly every surviving knight had severe injuries. La Valette would never release him for that.

You are no fanatical monk like the others, Joseph Callus had scolded him.

You have no business in this Order, Bertrand had said.

He knew they were right.

Yet he could not forget his oath to God, delivered in good faith on his knees. *If Thou wilt save her, I will join the Order of St. John, in Thy service.*

God had done His part. And now was his own word so empty? *Above all things*, his own mother had once told him, *a man must do his duty*.

He prayed for guidance. It did not come. Whenever he could he went outdoors, to practice with his crutch on the dock beside Kalkara Creek. Maria knew the hours he would come. She walked beside him, and each time as they parted he despaired, knowing he would soon have to withdraw from her life once again, into the *collachio* of his vows.

The Grand Master summoned him. La Valette had reestablished his headquarters in Fort St. Angelo and kept him waiting nearly an hour. Christien clumped into the room to find the savior of Malta surrounded by important papers and dutiful pages. He was working through a deep pile of correspondence and looked up at Christien's entry. "Ah, de Vries. My condolences on the death of your brother."

"I was not aware you knew, sire."

"Your mother wrote me." His pen scratched on paper. "In fact, she asked me to release you from your vows. She wrote that the affairs of your family require your devotion now, as the new count."

Christien was surprised. His mother hadn't mentioned writing the Grand Master. He waited, thinking perhaps it was going to be simple after all. La Valette studied his face, his gaze as severe as ever. "What do you say for yourself? Is that your wish as well?"

Christien returned his gaze as he gathered himself. "My wish, sire, is that I could be more worthy of this Order. I confess that I am weak in my faith. I have come to realize that I don't love God enough to kill for Him. So my answer is yes, sire. I wish to be released. I wish to leave the Order." A flood of relief and guilt washed through him when he said it.

"I grant that you have given superb service," La Valette said, "save the unfortunate events of three years ago. During our struggle against the infidel you gave a leg for this Order, and helped God heal men who otherwise surely would have died." He continued writing. Christien allowed himself to believe it was going to happen.

The Grand Master set down his pen and stood up. "In all that, there is nothing extraordinary, nothing more than is required of any Knight of St. John. Your vows are not a matter of convenience, Fra de Vries, though you seem to believe so. Your father was a man of substance, a man of nobility and honor. I should think he would have instilled in you a deeper appreciation of such principles. Or perhaps he did, and you failed at your lessons. In any event, it is clear you are not of his mettle.

"I understand weakness of faith. It is something that afflicts most men from time to time, even the most devout. It is something to overcome, not something to make a man turn tail and run.

"If you wish to leave the Order, Fra de Vries, you shall do so without its blessing. You shall do so knowing the full disgrace and humiliation this will bring upon your name and the name de Vries for generations unborn. There is only one honorable course open to you," La Valette said. "You must honor your vows until the day of your death. This is what you swore. This is what you must do. And that is my final word."

The Grand Master turned back to his correspondence, the interview concluded.

Christien turned and slowly hobbled from the room.

❖

Fençu returned to M'kor Hakhayyim. He built another sukkah, a hut made of stones and brambles that stood on top of the hill by the carob tree. He carved a *shiviti,* a plaque that marked the direction of Jerusalem, and guessed as best he could from the stars and from stories he'd heard where that might be.

He prayed and danced alone now beneath those stars, without Elli, and without the music of Elena's dulcimer. He danced with ghosts to the music of the sea.

Alone, he celebrated Purim, the triumph of good over evil. To make certain he would not forget—for the time when he hoped the laughter of children would once again ring in the cave—he acted out the story of the Persian king Ahasueros and Haman, the villainous Grand Vizier. Now there were only crows to watch the mad Jew dancing on the hill, crows who skittered off at the raucous sound of his grogger.

He met a Jewish armorer newly arrived from Sorrento, whose family of six was crowded into the ruins of Bormla. Even without asking, Fençu knew the man was a *marrano,* a fraud like himself. Suddenly he was alone no more.

Fençu fished and trapped game and pulled crabs from the sea, to sell at market. There would be plenty of work coming, of course, because the Knights of St. John were building a new city, an impregnable fortress on Sciberras. To make such a big place, he knew, they'd even need Jews.

Best of all, that autumn the nobles of Mdina began returning from their temporary exile in Sicily. It was none too soon, he thought. He was completely out of silver.

Chapter 47

Moses scampered around the deck, swinging from the shrouds, testing the force of his piss off the prow, and balancing himself on the capstan of the weather deck. He'd never seen such a big ship. She carried her own complement of soldiers and gunners, fierce men in leather and armor guarding a rich cargo of olive oil, cumin, and cotton. She had four masts, her sails stretched taut in the quartering breeze. After leaving Messina she called at Sardinia, and then at the Genoese island of Corsica. Off the coast she encountered three North African galleys. The corsairs trailed along off the stern for nearly a day, deciding whether to try to take her, but the big deck cannons boomed at their approach and settled the matter quickly. The corsairs retired, seeking easier prey.

Maria stood near the beak head, watching the gulls wheeling and playing on the wind. Each day at sea pushed the horrors and sadness further into the shadows of her mind. The coast of Europe loomed in the distance.

Europe! After all the years and dreams, it stood before her.

There were sails of ships entering and leaving a harbor. They were still just specks of white, dappling a gray sea. Just beyond them she could see the trees and coastal hills of Provence.

She heard the clomp of a crutch on the wooden deck behind her. She smiled and felt the familiar tingle as he drew near. "You'll never be able to sneak up on me, you know," she said without turning, drawing his arms around her waist.

"I have no intention of sneaking. I intend for you to hear, so that you can prepare to be ravished full on." He kissed her ear and nuzzled her neck with his chin. She laced his fingers with hers and they looked out at the coast and felt the breeze in their faces. "That is Marseilles," he said. "From there we shall be three weeks to Paris, rogues and God willing."

She brought his hands to her lips and kissed them. "I pray you have done the right thing in this," she said. She knew the awful price he was paying and would continue to pay.

La Valette had been cold to the end, ever firm in his resolve to humiliate his errant knight. He was planning a new city, a mighty fortress of a city to be built on the Sciberras peninsula, so that no invader might ever again place cannons above the defenses. It would be called Valetta, after him, and he had been consumed in its planning. All Europe adored him and celebrated his victory. The Pope offered him the hat of a cardinal. La Valette refused it—not from modesty, but from fear that accepting the red hat might require him to bow before the Pope. La Valette no longer knew how to bow before anyone but God.

He had not been too busy, however, to deal with the matter of Christien de Vries. The *pilier* of France evicted Christien from the auberge and stripped him of his habit. The coat of arms of the House de Vries was ripped from among those that had somehow withstood the siege and still hung on the wall. His name was stricken from the registers of the Order. He was refused passage out of Malta on the *Saint Gabriel,* the Order's galley that had been scuttled in the Grand

Harbor during the siege and then refloated for a voyage to Messina. Instead he'd had to wait until he could book passage on a merchant ship. Some of the more senior knights shunned him. He had no idea what form further retribution or disgrace might take, for the Order's members came from powerful families, and he would certainly cross paths with many of them in the years to come.

The idea that he had broken his vows to the Order concerned him a good deal less than whether he'd broken his vow to God. He knew Bertrand would make a powerful argument that he had not, but then Bertrand was always clever at that sort of thing. His own mind was torn on the matter. It would be years before that changed, if it ever did.

Without Maria, his decision might have been different. Now, holding her, he felt a contentment that nothing else in his life had given him, along with a growing certainty that somehow he would make his peace with God.

"I have done what I had to do," he said. He turned her around to face him. "And you, madam, will make a beautiful countess."

Maria felt her tears coming again. She kissed him and thought of Salvago, as she had so often of late. She would always hate him and the devil inside him. Yet at the same time she was glad for his life, for what he had done for Christien. Without Salvago she never would have met Christien in the first place. Without Salvago she would not have him now.

In the hyperbole that often followed events as dramatic as those of the siege, there had been talk that Cubelles would lead an effort to beatify the priest, who after all had perished in flames while defending the Faith. She didn't care anymore. She was glad he'd died exactly as he had. She hoped he'd suffered horribly and she didn't care if they made him a saint.

It had taken her weeks to find someone who knew what had become of her father, that he had fallen to the shot of an archer. If he was buried at all, it was in one of the anonymous, bottomless pits of the dead.

She had no idea what had become of Nico. The last she'd seen him he was running for the breach. She would always believe that he made it. She thought of the day he'd been taken from her, when as children they were hunting for treasure. She'd boasted to him that one day she would live in a castle and that she'd have servants and fields of lupine. One night while she and Christien lay together in their cramped quarters behind the captain's cabin, she revealed that dream, laughing as she recalled that Angela Buqa had informed her that lupine was only a weed.

"I'll admit the château is not exactly a castle," Christien said, "but there are servants, and lupine is more than just a weed. We keep cattle near Paris, and we feed them lupine."

Maria could scarcely believe it.

Even in that, her dream had come true.

❧

Battered by heavy weather but still afloat, the Maltese fishing boat arrived in Peskaria, the port of Cephalonia, a mountainous island in the Ionian Sea that Homer had called Samos. Over the ages it had been ruled by the Romans and the Normans, by the Turks and most lately the Venetians. Barbarossa and Dragut had hidden in its lovely coves and harbors. On the hills above the port there were olive groves and vineyards, and beyond those lush forests of cypress and pine. Meadows of wildflowers dotted the slopes of Mount Aenos, whose summit was veiled beneath a soft mantle of clouds.

The captain lowered the sail, and the hull of his boat gently nudged the dock.

He had no money, no country, no home. He had only this boat, stolen one dawn from its berth in the Marsamuscetto.

"There comes a time in a man's life," Leonardus had once told him, "when he has to choose between what is right and what might keep him alive. They are not always the same."

He knew that perhaps the choice he had made was not right—but it *had* kept him alive.

That night in Malta when he'd intended to see Mustapha Pasha, to formally refuse to obey his orders, he walked for a long while along the shore, listening to the surf. As badly as he suffered for his failings, in his heart he knew he was neither disloyal nor a coward. He was not ready to die, at least not in this battle—not for either side.

There was only one thing left to do.

He'd walked past Mustapha's command tent to the quartermaster's, where he'd roused the man from his mat. He'd requisitioned a keg of water and four cases of hard biscuit and salted meat. From there he'd gone to the far side of the Marsamuscetto, where the captured Maltese fishing vessels were moored. He found one that suited his needs, a small but sturdy vessel with a single mast. The sail was old but in good repair. No one noticed his departure.

The journey had been treacherous. Twice he had nearly foundered in heavy seas. But he'd made it.

Am I Asha, or am I Nico?

He'd spent most of his lifetime so far trying to find out. He had never found it difficult to know what was honorable and what was right—except in the matter of his own identity. In that, right and wrong were as blurred as the lines between Nico and Asha. Now, for the first time, it didn't matter, didn't matter at all. The wharf was teeming with merchants and seamen, the quay piled high with sacks of raisins and olives. In the harbor, fishermen threw their nets into azure waters, hauling in rich catches of mullet and tunny. He heard the exquisite strains of a lute and smelled the aroma of fresh bread. The hills were green, the sky deep blue, the world full of promise. He felt completely free. He wanted to laugh out loud.

He knew that every step on his long path had been a step on the way to this place.

He knew this because he knew that Alisa was here. She had once told him, as they sat in their secret seraglio beneath Topkapi, that this was where she would go if ever she were free. She'd seen it during one of the stops of the slaver's ship on which she was captive.

Now he saw it was as perfect as she'd described it.

She was here, and he was going to find her.

When he did, he would build another ship. A galley, he thought, with twenty-four banks of oars, a sleek and fast craft that would make even Leonardus proud. He would take his place at her helm. Alisa would sit beside him, and together they would make their way in the world.

from *The Histories of the Middle Sea*

Endnote

Suleiman died the next year in a tent pitched on a muddy plain of Hungary as his army lay siege to Szigeth, the last bastion of the Hapsburgs that remained in that country. He died the night before the fortress fell. His death was hidden from his troops, so that his successor might prepare himself. Suleiman was embalmed, his body dressed in imperial silks and propped up inside his royal litter for the journey home. He was buried behind the Suleimaniye mosque, next to his beloved Khurrem. The empire fell into a period of mourning such as the world had never seen.

Alas, the next Sultan to gird on the sword of Osman was not of Suleiman's measure—but then how could any mortal be? Suleiman himself had killed off the best of his offspring. It was the last and least capable of his sons, Selim, called the Sot, who rose to the throne. Selim was a corpulent and ugly man with no discernible talent for statecraft. He died of his fondness for the grape. His son Murad carried endless wars to Persia and Austria, while at home social and economic troubles multiplied. During his reign the women of the harem grew increasingly in importance, as later did the aghas of the Janissaries and the eunuchs, until it was not clear in whose hands lay the fate of empire.

The Grand Master of the Order of St. John, Jean Parisot de La Valette, outlived his contemporary Dragut by three years, and Suleiman by two. Not long after the cornerstone had been laid for his new city, he died while hunting, of heatstroke. His body was entombed in the chapel of Our Lady of Victory.

Dragut himself had been laid to rest in Tripoli, where his grave remains a shrine for pilgrims who journey from all over the empire.

Six years after the events of Malta, the great fleet of the Ottomans was defeated at Lepanto, in the greatest sea battle of the age. Even in defeat the Ottomans were resolute. Their fleet was quickly rebuilt, to carry forward the endless struggle between Cross and Crescent.

Christien, the twentieth Count de Vries, had four children with his wife, Maria, in addition to Moses. His life after the siege was consumed with his practice of surgery. He made several notable discoveries about the human body, though his work, like that of Paré before him, was considered unorthodox and was largely rejected by his peers. His career was interrupted by the religious wars in France that had taken the life of his elder brother, Yves, and by a call to service from his king.

I know certain of these histories because I have been fortunate to have access to the archives of Topkapi, by grace of the Sultan Achmet. I know certain other of these things because I have been told them by my mother, Alisa, and my father, Asha Raïs, who witnessed many of these events with their own eyes. Even in old age, my father's memory remained undimmed.

My presence in the palace schools was arranged by my father, who knew well how to accomplish such a thing. In all the world, he said when he sent me away, there is no finer place for a man to learn to make his way than in the palace schools of Topkapi. In this he was correct, yet for all the enlightenment of those schools and the court they mirror, I shall hide these histories, which shall not be published until after my death. I have tried to write in them a balanced truth—as balanced as the blood of East and West that runs in my veins. But even an enlightened monarch such as Achmet would part me from my head for such balance. I am grown fond of that head and would regret its loss.

The extraordinary events of my parents' lives after the siege of Malta are well known to every informed student of modern affairs, and would fill another book of history altogether. O, that I had space to tell of it now.

But theirs is a tale for another day.

—The Histories of the Middle Sea
by Darius, the Preserver;
called by his family Marco Borg

Completed at Istanbul in
the Year 1017 of the Hijrah of the Prophet
(A.D. 1610)

Afterword

Though *The Sword and the Scimitar* is a work of fiction, I have tried to remain as faithful to the history and cultures of the novel as research and personal observation would permit. As is often the case, there are scores of conflicting accounts of the events and real characters depicted in these pages. For example, there is disagreement about the place and manner of Dragut's death. Some contemporary observers placed him in the trenches of Sciberras, a victim of friendly fire. Others said he died across the water at Tigné, cut down by a Christian cannon. In all such cases, I have used what I thought to be the most plausible version of events. While I consulted a large number of works on the lives and times of this story, one of the most masterful and compelling accounts of the events of the summer of 1565 was written by the late Ernle Bradford, upon whose *The Great Siege* I have relied heavily, particularly for direct quotations of historical figures.

With apologies to purists, I have taken liberties with certain place names and phrases. The city made famous by Constantine has worn almost as many names as it has cultures and religions. Byzantium was the first of those names, after the Greek fisherman Byzas, followed by New Rome and Constantinople. In Suleiman's time the name Konstantiniyye was used by the Ottomans on official papers and coins, but to Arabs and Turks it was already Stamboul, or Istanbul, a derivation of the Greek *Eis ten polin*, or Istinpolin, which meant 'in the City.' I used Senglea for the peninsula in the Grand Harbor of Malta rather than Isola or l-Isla, which is the term most often used by the Maltese, and in various other ways have tried to soften some of the difficulties of the Maltese, Turkish, and Arabic languages.

As a writer I continue to be amazed and thankful for the role editors play in bringing a novel from inception to bookshelf. Tracy Devine is proof that there are still editors of classic distinction who represent the best of an old—some say dying—tradition. She spent countless hours with the manuscript, showing the good sense to restrain me when I needed it, the ability to inspire me to reach higher when I needed that, and—best of all, perhaps, for this is the true gift of an editor—to share and help articulate the vision for the novel I myself sometimes had trouble seeing. To whatever extent *The Sword and the Scimitar* has succeeded, I am deeply indebted to her. To the extent it has not, it is not for want of an attentive, devoted, and talented friend and critic, whose dedication made the exquisite torture of writing this book one of my life's great pleasures. Assistant editor Micahlyn Whitt made excellent suggestions for improving key scenes, in addition to handling the myriad details of manuscript, artwork, maps, calligraphy, and revisions. I am also grateful for the many and tireless efforts of Nita Taublib, deputy publisher at Bantam, and of Clare Smith at Random House UK.

Jean Naggar has built a literary agency that is marvelous to work with. Jean and her colleagues Jennifer Weltz, Alice Tasman, Jamie Ehrlich, Rosemary Walls, and Lillian Lent all manage to suffer the agency's clients with poise and grace.

I am particularly indebted to the incomparable Vanessa Borg, my researcher in Malta who spent hours combing through dusty archives to find answers to my endless questions. She helped with translations, wrote research papers on selected topics, and twice read the manuscript in a search for errors. The many that were corrected are thanks to her, while the ones that remain are my own. Others who have helped in ways great and small include Professor Godfrey Goodwin, Bekir Kemal Ataman, Professor Victor Mallia-Milanes, and Dr. Simon Mercieca. Many people read and made comments upon the manuscript, including Carol Rasmussen, Rabbi Jack Gabriel, Thom Barnard, Barbara Burton, Laura Uhls, Linzie Burton, Erin McIntire, and Martha Rasmussen. There was something almost mystical about a Bat Mitzvah to which Nili and Graham Feingold invited me, during which I closed my eyes and was transported back in time to discover the cave and inhabitants of M'kor Hakhayyim. Many thanks also to Nancy Leibig, Jane Maxsom, Mike and Terri Lischer, Denise and Chuck Elliott, Mike and Joanie Graber, Nawab Saleem, Joseph Rossa McGrail, Dr. Jeff Pickard, James Kirtland, Robert Kawano, and King Harris.

Last, but always first, my thanks and love to my wife Melinda and children Ben and Li, who usually did a masterful job of hiding their impatience as they endured my research trips and writing. With them at my side, completing a book is difficult. Without them, it would be impossible.

Valetta—Istanbul—Paris—Wondervu
February 1997–November 2002